James M. Ratcliffe
50

EUROPA
IN
LIMBO

EUROPA
IN
LIMBO

ROBERT BRIFFAULT

NEW YORK
CHARLES SCRIBNER'S SONS
1937

TO

HERMA

EUROPA

IN

LIMBO

In EUROPA, *Laurence Foster, a journalist, the son of a manu-
facturer in the Midlands, recounted the career and mental development of his college friend, Julian Bern, from his childhood
in his father's home, in Rome, to the outbreak of the World
War. Julian had, in his Cambridge days, taken up the study of
biology and undertaken a work on the subject in collaboration
with his teacher, Sir Anthony Fisher. Later, he learns to perceive that human beings are as much the product of social conditions as of biological laws, and eagerly follows contemporary
social and political thought, till his hopes are shattered by the
betrayal of German social democracy on the eve of war. The
awakening of Julian's emotional life is marked by a love affair
with Zena, the daughter of his father's friend, Prince Gregorie
Nevidof. After Zena's marriage to Prince Hruzof, several
women cross his life-path: Sylvia Chantrey, an artist-journalist,
the Honorable Eleanor Astley, whose emotions are turned into
the channel of social reform, Lady Irene Sexborough, a cousin
of Julian's friend, the Honorable Everard Pallier, afterwards
Earl of Bar. Julian meets Zena again on the French Riviera, and
the first love is rekindled to flaming passion. They withdraw
from the world in Princess Hruzof's German estate of Reizenfels, where they propose to spend their lives. But the outbreak
of war dispels the dream of happiness; Julian and Zena have to
leave Germany hurriedly.*

The story is taken up at this point by the narrator, in EUROPA
IN LIMBO.

I

SOME children were playing on the wasteland, where the fortifications had been demolished to make way for the new road to Wommelghem and Viersel. Shouting and laughing, they slid down the grass bank that sloped to the greenish, rush-bordered water of the moat. From the hummock, covered with bushes and outcrops of rubble, the maze of the old fortifications could be seen, to right and left—terrespleins with barred portcullis gates leading to covered caponiers; wide glacis sloping from the star-shaped bastions, with advanced escarpments bordered by an outer moat as wide as a small river. The masterpiece of military engineering of the last century stood abandoned and unmanned. Only a few of the redoubts were used as ammunition dumps. A sentry in a quaint glazed black hat, like an old-world postilion's, stood by the barbed wire across the Wommelghem road. He shouted across and made signs to the children, pointing to the notice on a post: *Verkeer verboden.* They had no business there, but laughed back at the sentry, who had to remain at his post on the other side of the road.

There were some six boys and girls. The eldest girl had a shock of flaxen hair tied up with blue ribbon. She was dressed far too young, obviously, for her age. Her bosom bulged beneath her check blouse, and her skirts were almost indecently short. When she came sliding down the bank, she displayed legs like a grown woman's.

Near the railway bank a woman stood with arms akimbo by the two pails she had been filling at the street tap, and called across to the girl in shrill tones.

"Keetje! You indecent, good-for-nothing baggage! A fine hussy you are to let your mother do all the fetching and carrying. And Heinje waiting for the water to wash!"

Keetje looked over, bored.

"*Aanstonds, moederken. Ik kom aanstonds terug!* —I'll be coming directly," she shouted back in the Flemish patois. But she made no move to come, and as one of the boys came tumbling down on top of her, she started running up the bank again, laughing.

Her mother turned, shrugging her shoulders, to two other women who were drawing water from the street-tap.

"Did you ever see the like of that hoyden of mine? "she said. "There's no doing anything with her. Not a stroke of work will she put her hand to! And with all the water now having to be carried. Heinje, Kris's sister's son, has just come on a twenty-four hours' leave, as dirty as a scavenger. It will take two whole buckets to get some of the grime and mud off the lad. And that girl spends her time romping round with all the gutter-snipes in Borgerhout parish!"

"Eh, let the children be enjoying the holiday, Vrouw Dools," said the younger of the two women.

"And let me tell you, my Jantje and Naatje are not gutter-snipes," said the other.

"No offence, Vrouw Finek. I had not noticed your kids were there," replied Vrouw Dools.

"Not such kids, neither!" said Vrouw Finek. "Jantje is fifteen. He wanted to go when Pierke was called up, and he wouldn't have been the youngest with the colors. Pierke is up near Termont. He says we're beating back the Germans all right. They tried to cross the bridge the other day, carrying mattresses before them as shields. Our lads kept mum till the Boches were right in the middle of the bridge, and then let go. The mattresses went up in flames. Great fun it was, Pierke said, to see the Germans squirm on the blazing bridge and to hear them yell."

"Ah! It'll take more than that to stop them, Vrouw Finek," said Vrouw Dools, "with their big guns shooting from eight miles away. All these weeks that Heinje's been in the trenches and seen dozens of our lads killed, he's never yet set eyes on a German. The Germans will have their way all right. And, after all, what does it matter? I ask you, what difference will it make to you and me, Vrouw Finek, whether the government are Germans or a lot of Frenchified rascals of politicians who don't even speak our language?"

"Maybe, maybe you're right, Vrouw Dools," admitted Vrouw Finek, wagging her head. "I've always said I don't see any sense in their taking our boys to fight for the French and English. Haven't noticed that the French or the English ever did much for us."

"Do for us? Let our men ask for higher wages, and you'll see what they'll do to us, whether they're English, French, Walloons, or Germans," said Vrouw Dools.

Before they picked up the splashing buckets, Vrouw Dools shouted once more across the road to Keetje, berating her in voluble Flemish. Then the three women waddled away, passing under the railway arch, and disappeared in the winding streets, where the outskirts of the town ended abruptly in an irregular conglomeration of houses.

Only the din of the children's shrill voices now broke the stillness of the autumn afternoon. But presently, as the children sat down a while among the bushes, another sound became audible. It was a deep rumble, as of breakers booming and dashing against a distant cliff. The children were used to it. It had been going on for days. But it was louder that afternoon than usual. It was becoming louder and louder and sounded nearer.

"They're having a battle over there," said Jantje, who had sat down by Keetje. "Do you think the Germans will come?"

Keetje shrugged her shoulders. "Maybe they will," she said.

She sat hugging her knees, dreaming. There had been two Germans that used to come to Aunt Lena's café in the Schoytestraat, when Keetje helped there. It was great fun helping in the café. Often she had played truant from school to go to Aunt Lena's. Anyhow her father, who was a socialist, disapproved of her going to school at the Sisters'. Her mother used to send her there without telling her father, because it was better, she said, than the State school. When he found out, there was a great row, and he had come to the school to take Keetje away. There were lots of people at Aunt Lena's and it was very jolly. The men told dirty stories. It was more amusing than the silly lessons about the Virgin Mary, St. Joseph, and the ass, or the quarrels that went on at home. The people in the café gave Keetje lots of sous, with which she bought sticks of barley-sugar and peppermint balls. Aunt Lena was always very nice to her. She was handsome and had plenty of money too. Uncle Marcus was rich. He was always going over to Holland, and came back with diamonds which he sold to people. Great bargains, he said. He had always something to sell as a great bargain. When it wasn't diamonds, it was a car, or a dog, or a house, or some company shares. So that Aunt Lena had lots of fine clothes, and when she went out all dressed up you would have taken her for a lady. She had lovers, Aunt Lena; Keetje knew it all right. Uncle Marcus got frightfully jealous, and there were great scenes, and Uncle Marcus would go off to commit suicide. But everything turned out all right in the end. Uncle Marcus was good-natured, and he and Aunt Lena made it up. She was always smiling and good-tempered, except when she was very much in love with a man and wanted to run away with him. The two Germans who used to come to the café joked with Keetje when she brought them their beer, and one of them pinched her legs. They were not bad fellows. They used to give Keetje sous. Yes, the Germans were not so terrible as people made out.

"They say the English are coming too," said Jantje.

"Oh, the English!" Keetje said with a pout. "There were two here yesterday, you remember! A lady and a gentleman—English, because I heard them talk. The lady smiled at me as she passed, very grand. And she left a trail of expensive smell behind her." Keetje wrinkled up her nose disdainfully. "Ha!" she said. "There they are again! See, they are looking over from the bridge, the same lady and the nice-looking man. Spies, of course. Else why should they want to be prowling round here?"

The young woman was beautiful and elegantly dressed. Jantje looked at her with an admiration which did not escape Keetje.

"I could look beautiful too, if I had expensive clothes like that," she said. "Her shoes are difficult to walk in, and her skirt is so narrow at the hem that she has to take little steps. Bulges out at the hips like the trousers the clowns wear at the circus. 'Drones and parasites,' that's what my father calls such fine ladies!" Keetje hated fine ladies. The young man was also, presumably, a drone and a parasite; but, somehow, Keetje did not mind him so much. He looked nice, with clean, clear-cut features, rather tall, in his light English tweeds and soft gray hat.

Boo-oom! Boo-oom!

It was much louder, certainly, and nearer than it had ever been before, the noise of the guns. The sentry on the Wommelghem road was shouting and gesticulating at the children. And there was another man now, a fat corporal or sergeant, who looked very angry and was coming over towards them!

Keetje rose, laughing, and putting her thumb to her nose cocked a snoop at the fat irate warrior. All the children started scampering down, and ran over the causeway that crossed the old moat.

"Let's go up to the railway bank," Keetje proposed. "We can see quite a long way over from there."

Near the signal box a flight of narrow steps led up to the embankment. The line was not used now. Numerous trains stood shunted, which had come from all over the country when the army had retired. There was no one about except the man and the woman on the bridge. The children clambered on to the platform of a first-class carriage. The man and woman turned round a moment to look at them, then continued to watch, leaning over the iron rail of the bridge.

Through the gap in the fortifications the view stretched over the flat "campina," level as a billiard table to the horizon. Farmhouses had been demolished and trees cut down to clear the sight for the guns. To the right, between Lierre and Duffel, a line of brown smoke was to be seen, where the little river Nethe ran. Coppery clouds rose and drifted. Three strangely shaped yellow balloons, like sausages, hung above a copse of trees. All else was still and seemed deserted. Not a human being in sight. Under the autumn sunlight, the distant line of smoke was but a detail in the drowsy landscape; the rumble of gunfire but as the droning voice of an unseen sea.

The man pointed overhead. High up were white balls of smoke, appearing suddenly, remaining for a while unchanged.

"There, a little to the left," he said to his companion, "do you see the black speck, like a tiny cross? A German plane, a 'Taube.'"

"I can't see it," the young woman said. Then with a little cry, "Oh yes, I've got it!"

The speck moved in the direction of the city, and was presently lost to sight behind a gadding wisp of cloud.

The man and the woman continued to watch in silence.

Much nearer now, exploding shells tossed up the brown earth in the neighboring fields, bursting with a dull echoing thud.

"They are going for the second line of forts and the main communication roads," said the man.

The young woman drew off her white glove and placed her hand in his.

"Fools that we are!" she said. "We should have kept away."

"Are you afraid?" he asked, smiling.

"Oh no. Not at all," she said brightly. Then, after a while, "I know it would be strange, wherever one went, whatever one did. Only unreal things are happening . . . as in a dream, when one knows that it is but a dream, and it does not much matter what one does. Who would have thought three months ago . . .?"

"Perhaps that was the dream," he said.

How remote it now seemed, that dream-world that had seemed to obliterate all else! To recapture it was not possible, were one to flee to the ends of the earth. Perhaps, for ever impossible. It was a world that was being blasted, and for twenty years and more the souls of untold generations might be without abode.

Shells were now exploding by the Viersel road and round the abandoned fort of the Three Kings. Great spouts of brown earth shot up like geysers, tossing strands of barbed wire and stakes into the air. All along the Malines road, to the right, partly hidden by the gas works and the Porte Leopold, the shelling was going on.

"Shall we go back, Zena?" he asked.

"No, no, it is rather exciting," she said. "I can quite understand people getting excited. To blast and pound something, after so much pretence. . . . That one was quite near!"

A shell had dropped among the demolished houses, throwing up a dark cloud, and, for several seconds, things came dropping to the ground.

"Not so near as it seems. It is a good distance away," he said.

"Julian, look at those children. Whoever allows them . . .?"

Another explosion, nearer still, drowned her voice.

"The Germans will not shell the town. Not without warning," Julian said. "Some of the Naval Division are already in the trenches. It will make a difference. Another contingent is expected at any moment. You heard what Winston Churchill said at the hotel?"

"Oh, that man!" Zena laughed. "I could never put much trust in a man with a face like that—like a bottom. It was comic melodrama. 'Monsieur le bourguemestre, Anvers est sauvé, Anvers est sauvé!'"

She waved her arms in a grand gesture. "One of the American newspaper men remarked that a boy scout would have known better."

There was a rending hiss and a tremendous crash. A shell had dropped on the tramrails of the Viersel road, just beyond the barbed wire. Flying debris filled the air, fragments were heard whining like sleepy tops, and some pinged against the railway bank.

Zena clutched Julian's arm. There were screams and cries. The children ran down the steps, scattering across the road. Keetje was bending over a little boy, who lay screaming. There was blood on his leg.

Zena and Julian came up, hurrying.

"Is he hit?" Zena asked, bending over the child.

It was nothing. In scrambling down from the railway carriage, the child had fallen and barked his leg on the sharp ballast. He was more frightened than hurt, but screamed lustily. Keetje alternately soothed him and smacked his face, telling him to be quiet.

Vrouw Dools came running up, waving her arms.

"God in Heaven! Is Franke wounded? They told me he was killed!"

Zena and Julian reassured the woman, and after binding a handkerchief round his leg, they carried the child across the road. Vrouw Dools led the way to a tenement house near by. As they came up to the arched entrance, she asked Zena and Julian if they would come in a moment. Zena said she would be glad enough to sit down.

In the brick-floored room opening on the court, the father was sitting with the soldier cousin in discolored uniform, his tasselled cap over his ear, drinking wine from earthenware jugs. They rose awkwardly at the entrance of the unexpected visitors, and offered them chairs. Talking volubly the while, Vrouw Dools heated water in a kettle and she and Zena washed the child's leg. It was but a graze. Kris Dools shrugged his shoulders after satisfying himself that Franke was not badly hurt.

"So they're firing on the city, now," he said, turning to Julian.

Julian said he scarcely thought they intended to do so. They were shelling the roads and the forts.

"There's not much left of the forts," said Heinje. "At Lierre, Waelhem, and Wavre, they are pounded to rubbish heaps. They can waste their ammunition on the forts, and on the roads too, for that matter. We are not such fools as to use them!"

"How did you come up? By train?" Kris asked.

"Yes, by train. In queer company, it was. With three hundred mad women!"

"Women?" Zena said.

"Yes, ma'am. There's a big asylum at Duffel. They had female lunatics there in charge of Sisters. The place was getting pretty warm. Kettlefuls of shrapnel landing in the garden, and one corner of a ward knocked out. Twenty of our fellows were detailed as escort, while they got the women away, to the line where a train was waiting. It's a pretty nasty stretch, nearly a mile, in the open. And the Germans were furious because our guns had prevented them from getting over to the station at Wavre St. Catherine. They were crumping two a minute. The whole place is pocked with shells. Not the sort of promenade you would take for pleasure. Had we been alone, we should have skipped over it pretty smartly. But those damned lunatic women couldn't be got to move on. They would sit down and sing and jabber, and stood clapping their hands and laughing when a shell came over. And the poor Sisters kept running from one to the other, talking to them quietly to get them to move. We started pushing the creatures along with the butts of our rifles and prodding them on with our bayonets. There's no fun in getting laid out for a pack of lunatics, is there? Better if they had shot the lot, as they did with the lions and tigers at the Zoo here. One bitch— beggin' your pardon, ma'am—kept leering at me and using filthy language, lifting her clothes. I kicked her off. But a Sister came and took her by the shoulders, talking to her ever so gently. You know what I think of the silly women, Kris. But there's no denying they were damned plucky. And no sooner had we got the crazy creatures to move a few steps, we had to get them down because of a crump. How we got over to the railway-line is a miracle. And no one touched except one fellow who got a small splinter in his arm. And so I came over on an asylum on wheels, the damned women shouting and singing all the way."

Julian had a bitter chuckle: "An asylum on wheels! The sort of conveyance on which we are all travelling. How long will the wheels keep turning?"

Kris Dools' eyes brightened responsively.

"Do you hear, Heinje? Those women from Duffel are not the only lunatics you're risking your skin for. And it's the lunatics who'll be the last to be shot. Why couldn't our boob of a king let the Germans through quietly, as they proposed? They were bound to get through anyhow, so why get our country and our people blown up to smithereens while they did? You're English, monsieur, aren't you?" he said to Julian. "No doubt your people think it's very grand and heroic. It may be heroic for you; it isn't for us."

Vrouw Dools gave a snort.

"Shouldn't be surprised if we have more trouble in getting rid of the English than of the Germans. They have a way of sticking in a place once they get a foot in it," said Kris.

Vrouw Dools gave Kris an admonishing smack on the shoulder as she passed.

Zena rose to leave, bending to press a coin into Franke's hand. "For being brave," she said. She hesitated a moment beside Keetje, wishing to give her something too. But Keetje's sullen gaze was a definite refusal. The two men rose with awkward civility. Vrouw Dools followed Julian and Zena to the street, friendly and voluble.

After passing through the deserted streets of the outskirts, Zena and Julian reached the Turnhoutshebaan, the long street that led to the town and the station square. The trams were not running and the shops, except for those selling food, were closed. But the street was crowded. The population had been almost doubled with refugees from Malines and the surrounding country. There were peasants, men and women, looking strange and awkward in the city. Some dragged about their belongings on handcarts, others carried bundles on their heads. Women stared at the windows of the closed shops. A photographer's show-case was filled with pictured bridal couples. There was a large shop of plaster virgins and saints, highly colored, mingled with other statuary products, dainty little ladies in scanty bathing costumes, and female versions of the Brussells Manneken, which, with realistic Flemish humor, were fitted with rubber tubes and squirts. Pious peasant women in quaint headdresses knelt for a moment and crossed themselves before the saints and the little bathing ladies.

Soldiers in highly colored uniforms were everywhere. Staff cars, dispatch riders on motor bicycles, hurried importantly. The cafés were full. Officers and civilians laid down strategical theories.

At the Avenue de Keyser there was a general commotion. The word was going round that the English had arrived. Crowds rushed out of the cafés and hurried towards the Place de Meyre. Julian and Zena, walking on past their hotel, followed the crowd. People waited about some time, but there was no sign of the English. Presently, however, three strange red vehicles, filled with green canvas packages and boxes, came rumbling along. On them were advertisements of Pear's Soap and Bovril. They were marked: Hammersmith, King's Road, Piccadilly, Strand, Liverpool Street. They were London buses.

Julian and Zena strolled back to the hotel. One of the managers said that the English contingent had come over from Ostend and detrained in the Western quarters. Zena felt deadly tired. She went to her room, while Julian once more joined the crowd that was now pouring down the rue de l'Hôpital in the direction of the Place Leopold.

"The English! The English!" people shouted.

They were coming. In the distance, singing could be heard.

> "It's a long way to Tipperary,
> It's a long way to go. . . ."

The sound grew in volume—

> "It's a long way to Tipperary,
> To the sweetest girl I know. . . ."

Julian caught sight of Keetje with some of the children who had been playing near the fortifications.

"Here they come!" they shouted.

The British army, as represented by odd detachments of the Naval Division, just recruited from the streets, did not present a very imposing military appearance. The men in dark blue were, many of them, long-haired and bearded. They kept step badly on the unaccustomed cobbles. They were imperfectly equipped. Some had no scabbards, and had their side arms tucked into their puttees, which gave them the look of stage pirates. Some had brown-paper parcels tied to their equipment. One man carried a Gladstone bag. Julian noticed another wearing town boots.

These were probably English eccentricities, he heard people round him remark. The English did funny things, but they generally managed to muddle through. Besides, this was only an advanced detachment. The main body of the British army was landing at Ostend. They were bringing big guns, too. The Germans were going to get a terrible licking. Antwerp was now saved. *"Vive l'Angleterre!"*

"It's a long way to Tipperary! . . ."

The children danced and skipped in front of the British army that had come to save Belgium.

The hotel presented a pretentious air of festivity. The large hall was full of people, newspaper correspondents, Belgian officials and innumerable officers in bright uniforms, lounging importantly, smoking cigars and ordering liqueurs from obsequious waiters. The place was bedizened with the Ally flags. A gala dinner followed by a dance was to be given to celebrate the arrival of the British. Women rustled in in evening gowns or, with seasonable coquetry, in prim nurses' uniforms decorated with red crosses.

Zena was unexpectedly greeted by an old acquaintance, the Vicomtesse de Houthem.

"Fancy meeting you here, Princess Hruzof!" the Vicomtesse exclaimed, agitating her ostrich-feather fan and her twitching ocular muscles. "Is the dear Duchess of Friedland with you, and Grand Duchess Isidore?"

"My mother and sister are in Petrograd," said Zena, and presented Julian.

"Why, we have met before! At Saxford House, was it not?" said the Vicomtesse with a cheerful spasm of her right eye. *"Ah, cette guerre! Cette terrible guerre!* But it is only right that we should try to keep up our spirits, our morale."

Mr. Baffles, the correspondent of a large English daily, was holding forth on the situation amid a large audience. The English view is so important.

"Of course, our troops are not at the moment sufficiently numerous to influence the military situation," he said. "It's the psychological effect that matters."

It was at Mr. Baffles's suggestion that Julian and Zena had come over from The Hague, where they had spent most of the time since the morning when they had been set down in Holland after their exodus from Berlin. Mr. Baffles had blown in one afternoon at the small hotel where they had been, most of the time, the only guests. It was just after the long silence, during which no news of what was taking place was heard, had been broken by the announcement in the Dutch papers of the sweeping German victory. Mr. Baffles had been at Amiens during the foregoing weeks. He had come, he said, to rest for a few days, his nerves being, he admitted, a little rattled.

"Amiens looked rather gay in those first days," he said, while smoking a big Dutch cigar and sipping Holland gin. "Filled with French and English troops, fraternising for the first time in history. The cafés were crowded with people of every nationality. Then suddenly, the crowds left and it was a sleepy town again. Only hospital units, ambulances, Red Cross men, looking rather absurd in their military uniforms, remained. And for a time the absence of news was as complete as elsewhere and even more oppressive. The first we knew was when, one afternoon, train after train arrived, packed with a miscellaneous mob of British soldiers of all units—guards, Highlanders, gunners, cavalrymen, sappers, in complete confusion. All that was left of England's regular army. 'The Germans are coming! The British army is wiped out,' the men announced. They thought only of making their way to the Channel ports to board the boats.

"I got talking with a Royal Fusilier sergeant, when he had got a bit refreshed after the looting of the station buffet. Asked him where was his battalion. 'There ain't no blooming battalion no more, sir,' the man said. 'Far as I know, I'm the only fellow left. Wiped out. No, I ain't running away. Can't rejoin a unit that ain't no more, can I?' The fellow looked pretty jumpy. Muttered something about a Lancashire witch that had cast a curse on the battalion. 'Look 'ere, sir,' he said. 'You know this 'ere ribbon? Sudan medal. Yes, sir, I was at Omdurman, I was. Well, it was something like Omdurman, was this show. Only it was us fellows who were the blooming dervishes. We was supposed to have two machine-guns per battalion. Never noticed them much myself. But the Germans had whole rows of them facing us. And them big howitzers. We was the silly dervishes coming on with spears and shields.'

"Of course, the good people in England have not been told," said Mr. Baffles, puffing nervously at his cigar. "They probably never will be told. They don't want to; they don't like to hear things like that in England. The British public has been provided instead with some story about 'the angels of Mons.'"

Though he had come to Holland avowedly to rest his nerves, Mr. Baffles managed to find some copy, nosing round. He announced one evening, after he had been talking with some Germans, that the conquest of Europe, which would not occupy much time, would be followed immediately by the extension of German culture to other continents. The ground had been carefully prepared for the annexation of Mexico, whence the United States would be dominated by German power.

Then, as every one was waiting to get the first official announcement of the Germans' entry into Paris, came instead the astonishing news that the whole German army was in full retreat, with the French in pursuit!

Baffles had rushed into the hotel lounge, all his four limbs waving, in great excitement. The war was to all intents over! The English were about to land a new army at Antwerp to help in the final strangling of the German hordes! With arms outstretched, pincer-like, Baffles had demonstrated the strategy. He was off to Antwerp to witness the final act, he was going "to be in at the death!"

"You should come too," he had said to Julian and Zena, "instead of sticking in this sleepy hole. It's only a stone's throw from here, and there is one of the best hotels in Europe."

Though he had told himself that it was unreasonable, Julian felt a morbid curiosity to see something of the unbelievable events that were changing the world. There was no great harm in the excursion. They could always come back.

Now, in the festive Antwerp hotel, while the orchestra was playing tangos, Baffles was again demonstrating the pincer strategy that was to encircle the German hordes.

"Our troops, though perhaps insufficient to influence the military situation," he declaimed, "will nevertheless afford an invaluable stiffening to the Belgian defence. A crisis has been reached. The morale of the German troops is at its lowest. What little optimism remains to them cannot survive this final blow."

The Comtesse de Merode came and whispered something in Madame de Houthem's ear. There was a general agitation throughout the rooms. People spoke in whispers. Many were leaving, hurriedly.

"What is it?" asked Mr. Baffles of the Vicomtesse.

"The King and Queen are leaving . . . and the Government," she said.

The music had stopped. In a few minutes the crowded rooms emptied, and the place was deserted.

The next morning, Julian and Zena could not, for some time, obtain an answer to the service bell. An old porter in a green baize apron eventually appeared.

"De l'eau chaude? Ah, mais il n'y a plus d'eau. Enfin, on verra," the man said.

He came back presently with a minute jug of warm water.

"C'est la guerre, Madame. A la guerre comme à la guerre," he said, in reply to Zena's rueful exclamation. He was unable to offer definite hopes of breakfast. *"Il faudrait s'informer à l'office."*

That scoundrel, Baffles!

When Julian went down, scouting, he found the place practically abandoned, save for a few departing guests. The hall was stacked with luggage, servants were hurrying about in a preoccupied way. It was difficult to secure the attention of any one.

In the street, a long line of troops, field-guns, ammunition wagons, lorries with dismantled airplanes, were clattering along in the direction of the quai St. Michel and the pontoon bridge to Waeland.

As Julian stood at the door of the hotel, he caught a glimpse of Mr. Baffles with some other journalists crowding into a car. Baffles called out to him in an embarrassed way.

"Frightfully sorry, Bern," he said. "But, as you see, we are full up. I doubt whether you can find another car in the town. But there will be plenty of boats. Ask that chap over there in the bowler. He's the agent. Hi! Mr. Brehm!" he called to the man. "Here's a gentleman wants a berth. A friend of mine. See if you can fix him up! Awfully sorry, don't you know, that I can't arrange a lift. Good-bye and good luck!" And Baffles slammed the door as the car moved off.

Mr. Brehm, a fat little Jew who spoke with a strong German accent, was solicitous and obliging. There were plenty of boats at Ostend, he said. But they were going to bring some up to Antwerp. Most would be going from Flushing to Folkestone. But Mr. Brehm was expecting a boat direct to Harwich. He advised Julian to wait for it, directed him to his office on the quai Van Dyck, and took down his name. He would have places reserved. If the lady and gentleman would be at the quay towards evening, he would see that they got a passage.

In the hotel, Julian managed to obtain a jug of coffee, some rolls, and two hard-boiled eggs. He took them up with him.

He found Zena engaged in performing, as best she might, her ablutions, standing in a basin placed on the floor.

"*Nettoyage à sec!*" she laughed.

Julian told her his news. She slipped on a dressing gown and they sat drinking the coffee and eating the hard-boiled eggs.

"We shall have to try to pack into two suitcases," Julian said.

Zena bit down reflectingly into her dry roll. Then she cast a humorous look round at the disordered hotel room, with bed unmade, soiled towels, an unemptied bucket of slop water.

"Looks like the collapse of civilization, doesn't it?" she said.

She rose and bent over trunks, sorting clothes. She tossed one garment after another in a heap on the floor.

"Remember this dress?" She held up a dove-grey gown adorned with lace.

Julian had a dry feeling in his throat. The room seemed unbearably stuffy and dingy. He wanted to breathe more freely.

"Better keep these," Zena said, holding up her jewel case, toying with the ropes of pearls, the chains of gold. "Might want to pawn them."

Zena placed the things she wanted to keep on the bed. The rest lay in a pile by the washstand. She drew herself up, stretching her arms, revealing her white body.

"*Voilà!* Princess Zenaida Ivanovna Hruzova Nevidof! Naked came I out of my mother's womb . . ."

"Don't be morbid!" Julian cried, a tension of despondency within him seeking vent. "Why are women such pessimists? We'll be in London tomorrow or the day after. Your wardrobe will be demoded, anyhow. You'll amuse yourself replenishing it."

Zena looked at him in silence. The forced laughter in her eyes threatened to change to tears. He regretted the impatience with which he had spoken. He went to her, encircled her in his arms, and his lips sought the fresh roses of her breasts, which stood out from her gaping gown.

Her face crisped. "No. Not in this squalor," she said, repelling him.

In the streets, small groups with dazed expressions on their faces were reading the notices warning that the city was about to be bombarded. From the petrol tanks at Hoboken, which had been set on fire, black clouds of smoke were drifting as from a volcano. Shops were shuttered. Loaded carts, horse cabs, miscellaneous vehicles, groups of people carrying bundles, were on their way to Putte, across the Dutch border. Over the road leading there flowed a motley stream of vehicles and humanity. On the quays surged a human sea, boarding the boats to Flanders Head, to Flushing.

Vrouw Dools and Keetje had worked all morning tying pots and pans together, making up bundles of clothes, sheets and blankets. Keetje made a parcel of her hair-ribbons, her best stockings, and some colored postcards. Kris Dools had spent the day out in the town searching for some vehicle or other upon which to load their goods. The children played about the floor, delighted with the confusion. It was like a picnic. Vrouw Dools had been unable to find any food in the market save a loaf of bread. So they had cleaned out the larder, eating up all that was left in the house. They were going over to Zuylen, in Zeeland, where their grandmother lived. The children thought it all great fun.

The Loowers, next door, had gone long ago in a big cart. So had the Fineks. The street for a time was full of people pushing handcarts, carrying packages. Then silence. The street was deserted.

Darkness had come, Kris had not returned, and Frankie had begun to fret. The town was ominously silent. There had been no firing for twenty-four hours. Vrouw Dools sat on a bundle of clothes, her knotted hands folded over her stomach. She strained her ears for the sound of Kris's footsteps. Now and then she called out sharply to the whimpering child. At last Kris came, pushing a rickety handcart of battens.

"Pete Veisch's," he said. "They've already gone. They left it."

The cart was not large enough to hold all the things. Vrouw Dools sorted out what could be left behind.

It was a long way to the river. There were no street lights; there had been none since the Zeppelin raid. But there were red reflections in the sky against the black clouds of smoke. Keetje helped push the cart, and they walked along in silence. Their footsteps echoed in the deserted streets. Now and then they met another group of people pushing a barrow. When they met some one they knew they called out greetings briefly, in subdued voices.

The houses were shuttered. They had an unfamiliar look.

Suddenly there was an explosion. Then the whining of shells overhead was heard at regular intervals. Kris Dools counted the seconds. "Every half minute," he said. The dull boom of explosions was mostly in the direction of Berchem. Others, presently, sounded nearer. Then, with a crash of masonry and the rattle of broken glass, a shell burst not far away. Little Franke started to cry. They put him on the top of the bundles and gave him the coffee-mill to hold.

They hurried on. Now and then a cellar door opened and a light from the cellar showed where people were sheltering. There were sandbags at the entrances. Then the door would close and on they would go in the darkness.

There was now an almost continuous whining of shells, several at a time, and explosions, some far, some near. There was a smell of kerosene in the air. The tawny reflections in the sky grew redder, casting a weird light.

As they were about to turn into a street that made a short cut to the St. Jacob market, a sudden cyclone and a tremendous explosion brought them up short. For a moment a cloud of dust hid everything. Cries were heard amid the noise of falling debris. Then, again, silence.

When they could see again, they were aware of a big hole in the middle of the street before them, which was strewn with plaster and broken glass. A heavy dray lay tipped over and shattered. The horse was lying on its side, in a dark pool, its four legs stretched out stiffly. Keetje could see the feet of the driver sticking out from under the dray.

Frankie, who had jumped off the cart, was clinging to Vrouw Dools's voluminous skirts.

Keetje was shaking, and felt a strange inclination to laugh.

"Look," she said, pointing to a window in one of the houses.

A man was hanging over the railing of a balcony, his arms and bald head dangling down. He did look funny—like a puppet in the Punch and Judy show. His brown smoking cap was lying in the street.

A cellar door nearby opened, showing a slit of light.

"Here, you fools," called a voice. "This is no time to be taking the family for a walk. Come here, will you!"

A fat man was beckoning to them.

"Leave the cart where it is!" he called.

They followed him down into the cellar.

The place felt warm and cosy, coming from outside. It smelt strongly of leather. The man was a shoemaker. There were four men and three women sitting about, their faces half in shadow. Two candles were stuck in brass candlesticks, three others were thrust into the necks of bottles. The men sat in silence, their hands hanging heavily down between their knees, their faces averted. One of the women was telling her beads and moaning spasmodically, "O Mother of God! O Mother of God!" A fat, good-natured woman, who seemed to be in charge, made a place for the Dools, perching little Frankie on a pile of leather hides.

"Heat up some coffee, mother," the fat man said to her.

There was a little stove in the corner. The woman fanned up the fire, then handed cups and glasses. She gave the children some bread and dripping.

The noise of explosions outside was now continuous and furious. The whole place shook at times. But the children were tired and, having eaten, soon fell asleep. Keetje herself felt sleepy, but struggled as long as she could against the inclination to close her eyes. One felt safe here, and it was warm. The men began to play cards. Kris joined them. In the pauses of the explosions could be heard the shuffling of the cards and the muffled voices of the men, the mumble of the woman with the beads. The cobbler brought out some beer. He passed it round, but Keetje declined. Her hands felt heavy. She knew she would not be able to lift the glass. She was very sleepy. The booming outside rocked her to sleep, at last, like a stormy sea on board a ship.

The grey morning light was filtering down from the entrance of the cellar when she woke. Shells were still dropping at intervals, but not so frequently. About eight o'clock they stopped altogether.

The cobbler's wife served coffee and bread and cheese.

"The Germans are having their breakfast," said the cobbler. "They'll be starting again after they have eaten and had a smoke." They must hurry while the bombardment had stopped.

The handcart was where it had been left. The dray and the dead horse, and the man whose feet projected from under the dray were still there, too. But the man on the balcony had been removed.

The streets leading towards the quays were full of hurrying people carrying packages of all kinds. As the riverside was approached, there were more and more people. They carried suitcases, baskets, old-fashioned carpet-bags, things tied in handkerchiefs and wrapped in paper. A little girl who clung to the coat of an old man held a doll and a picture-book. A woman was carrying a cat, another had a cage with a canary. One tall youth was carefully carrying a large brass-mounted barometer. The crowd grew denser. They kept close to the houses.

The pavement was littered with broken glass and flakes of plaster. Several houses had gaping holes in their walls. In front of a café, the street was blocked with debris, twisted iron tables, fragments of ornamented plaster. Through the demolished front the inside walls painted with dancing women could be seen. In the Place Verte two houses were ripped open. Smoke rose from piles of brick and plaster and fallen beams. One house had its front sheered off, and the rooms stood open to view with their furniture, as in a doll's house. A bed dangled over the side of the sagging floor of a room with pink wallpaper. There was a dressing table with brushes and bottles on it, and across a chair a woman's stockings and underclothes.

In the Suikerrui the press was so great that the handcart had to be abandoned. Each had to carry as many of the packages as possible. The throng on the quai Van Dyck was holding up those who were trying to reach the waterside. People pushed. Women shouted. Children screamed.

Shells began to drop once more in the southern quarters. And at each explosion a moan went up from the crowd, which surged wildly forward like a drove of frightened cattle.

Step by step, Keetje and her people reached the quay. The scene there was even wilder. Only a fraction of the mass of humanity that poured from the adjoining streets could hope to board the boats. Every available floating craft was packed with black bunches of human beings. The river was crowded with boats: ferry-steamers, trawlers, fishing-smacks, rowing boats, canal barges, launches, mercantile vessels, private yachts, improvised rafts lay in the stream, weighted down with men, women and children, occupying every inch of room, sitting on the gunwales, hanging to the rigging. A barge which had been carrying straw was filled with sleeping people, who had been there all night, half-buried for the sake of warmth, under the straw. The silk-sheathed ankle of a woman protruded beside the muddied boots of a workman in the steamy promiscuity of the human dunghill.

As soon as a boat, having ferried over its load, returned and came alongside, a frantic rush took place, and in a moment the deck would be again filled as by a swarm of rats. People fought and trampled one another, with elemental egoism. Some were pushed into the water. There were no police. The boatmen kept off with oars and poles the people who clung to the rail, seeking to board the overcrowded craft. In a few seconds all available room was occupied, and the boat would push off once more into the stream.

Two large steamers and a smaller one, bound for Flushing, were just moving off, loaded, as Keetje's family arrived at the waterside. The congestion on the quay was considerably relieved. But thousands had been unable to get on board, and the crowd which surged towards the waterfront was constantly increasing. Among those left behind were many who had spent the night there. Piles of packages, household goods, bedding tied up with rope, stood in the middle of the cobbled pavement. Sitting and lying about on sacks, bundles, boxes, the homeless people waited resignedly, interminably. Peasant women were suckling their babies. Among them sat women in expensive furs. Young girls and children looked after tottering old men and women. Nuns sat reading their breviaries. One old woman lay on a stretcher, shivering with fever.

A man was selling small loaves and sandwiches. Those who had made provision produced food from their bundles and proceeded to eat. An elegantly dressed woman in a flounced silk skirt, carrying a crocodile-leather suitcase with a coronet on it, went up to the man and asked for a sandwich.

"Ten francs," said the man.

"I have no money," the woman said.

A bare-headed young woman who was sitting with four others beside a group of nuns drew some money from under her skirt, bought a sandwich, and gave it to the woman with the suitcase.

"It is a terrible thing," she said, "a great lady without money." She spoke to her companions. They were whores from the municipal brothel. They made room for the lady, who sat down, eating ravenously.

"I may be able to repay your kindness some day," she said. "My name is Vicomtesse de Houthem."

Some hooligans were looting a warehouse opposite. They were smashing open cases of oranges. The golden fruit rolled over the cobbles, and was picked up by the hungry crowd. Keetje gathered up an armful. A wineshop nearby had been broken into and some youths were drinking brandy and Chartreuse from bottles. There was the sound of splintering wood and breaking glass, and one of the youths sang a ribald song.

Two men from the British Naval Division, mud-covered and without equipment, stood awkward and bewildered, having lost their way.

"You dirty English swine, it is you who have betrayed us!" shouted a woman, pointing a finger at them.

The hooligans joined in the abuse and began pelting the men with oranges, potatoes, tomatoes. One of them, the youth who had been singing, approached, brandishing a bottle and proclaiming vociferously his intention of breaking it on their heads. The crowd urged him on. He raised the bottle high in the air.

But as he was about to bring the bottle crashing down, his arm was clutched from behind. Julian, who happened to be passing, pulled him back and sent him staggering over. The crowd, changing its temper, cheered.

"Where are you fellows going?" Julian asked the two Naval Division men.

"We've lost our unit, sir," said one of them. "Gone over to Holland, we believe. But we don't know our way about this place, and you're the first person we've met who could speak English."

Keetje came up.

"The *militaires*," she said, "have crossed over by the pontoon bridge."

The girl showed the way, and they walked, with Julian, over to the southern quays.

"You'll be interned, you know, if you go over to Holland," Julian said.

"That's where our unit has gone, sir," said the man who had spoken first, "so I expect there's nothing to do but follow. We'd rather get back to England, of course. Don't know what they sent us here for, I'm sure! It was all over with the Belgians when we got here, and what could we do without heavies?"

The place where the pontoon bridge had been was a wreck. It had been blown up after the last retreating units had passed. The Naval Division men swore softly.

A raft, constructed of barrels and odd timber, was pushing off from the water's edge. It was manned by Belgian stragglers. Keetje called to them in Flemish to wait. Would they take the two Englishmen across? At first they stood out. The raft was already overcrowded, they said. But with the aid of a few coins, Julian was able to persuade them, and the raft at last drew away with the muddied Naval Division men aboard.

Julian walked back with Keetje.

"Are you always to be found at points of danger?" he asked her, teasingly.

She looked at him.

"And where are you going?" he pursued.

"Nederlands," she replied, abruptly. Then, kicking out her legs, she ran ahead.

"It was kind of you to show the way," Julian called after her. "Good-bye."

She dived into the crowd and was lost from sight.

Julian rejoined Zena at Mr. Brehm's office, where they had spent the night, wrapped in blankets, she on the horsehair couch, he on two chairs.

A sailor from one of the boats' galleys was brewing some coffee and cooking potatoes in the cinders of the open fire.

"It is almost worth all this to have an appetite such as mine!" said Zena, as she drank the coffee.

Her eyes were dark with excitement, and she was looking miraculously fresh. During Julian's absence she had managed, thanks to Mr. Brehm, to make herself immaculate. He had sent in fresh towels, soap, and hot water. Mr. Brehm, impressed by Zena, had been extremely attentive. The office had been placed at their disposal. "I am flattered to be able to assist you," he kept repeating in his heavy Germanic English. "The Chermans vill not bombard the waterfront," he said, "they vill have need of it themselves."

The boats for England did not arrive until late in the afternoon, when several boats came alongside at the same time. In the growing darkness the rush and confusion were worse than they had been in the morning. The bombardment was being renewed, and the light of bursting shells joined, spasmodically, the other reflections in the dark water. Above the sounds of the explosions could be heard the shrieks of the fighting crowd, the cries of frightened children.

Without the aid of Mr. Brehm and two stout English sailors to shoulder a way through the throng, Julian and Zena could never have got past. Even so, they were beaten back many times before they reached the gangway.

As Julian stepped upon it, he felt a tug at his coat. It was Keetje.

"What's the matter?" he asked.

"*Mijn ouders verloren,*" she replied.

"Lost your people? Well, jump aboard. We'll find them later," he said.

"Be quick, sir," a ship's officer called. "Is the young lady with you?"

"Yes," Julian said.

They had but reached the deck when the gangway was shipped and the boat pushed off. It lay in midstream, waiting for the tide.

The river was thronged with craft, shadowy in the failing light. Near Saint Michel quai, a three-master was on fire, burning quietly. In various parts of the city, smoke and sparks were also rising from burning houses. A red glare flickered on the black blanket of smoke that lay low across the sky, gashed by the scarlet gleam of a dull, hidden sunset. The tower of the cathedral glowed, as though red-hot, in the reflection of conflagrations. A lurid light was mirrored in the black water. Laden with humanity, the countless boats looked fantastic, as though ferrying ghosts across an infernal river, or bearing a migrating people, in the twilight of an epoch, towards new worlds.

I I

JULIAN was not a little surprised when, at Liverpool Street station, he was met by his sister, Viola. She had only a few days before arrived from India. Harry was in France. His Gurkha regiment had, shortly after the outbreak of war, been ordered to the western front, and had landed, when Viola had last heard, at Marseilles. She had sailed alone for England. Julian had sent a telegram from Harwich to his mother. Viola had come to the station, their mother being slightly indisposed.

In a few words, Julian explained Zena. Viola's undemonstrative manner gave little indication of her feelings, but her way of meeting situations without outward surprise or emotion was always adequate. Despite her upbringing abroad, Viola had become thoroughly, and even superlatively, English. It was a grey, rainy morning, and in her navy-blue mackintosh, she looked somewhat dowdy, which, in England, imparted to her a certain style.

There was no difficulty in disposing of the little Belgian girl. The station platform was thronged with women expressly intent upon procuring Belgian refugees. It was at the moment considered indispensable to the self-respect of an English household to own a Belgian refugee. There were a considerable number on the train. They were immediately set upon by determined women who seized them almost forcibly, tearing them away from their relatives, snatching them from one another, and hastening away in triumph with their prey. Julian himself had been accosted by one eager virago with the question: "Are you a Belgian refugee?" He had managed to protect Keetje from their assaults. Viola said that she would be glad to have her. She proposed going down shortly to Bognor, and would need an extra servant. The girl could, meanwhile, help in the Brompton flat.

Julian would go with Zena to an hotel. Viola would make the appropriate explanations till he should visit their mother.

Zena's spirits which, despite a brave show, had been getting increasingly depressed, recovered somewhat in the civilised surroundings of Claridge's. The ghastly North Sea crossing in the reeking, overcrowded boat, to the sound and smell of puking, had been a nightmare. Except for a short stay in London, some years before, on a visit to Grand Duke Michael and Countess Torby, Zena did not know England. On the present occasion, her introduction to the country had been in the dismal greyness of a drizzling dawn, on a wet, creaking wooden wharf. On landing, she and Julian had been herded with a mass of miserable and malodorous humanity in a corrugated-iron shed, where they had been subjected to the inquisitorial enquiries of suspicious officials, as though under a charge of vagrancy. Zena, who had her passport, had cleared her character with less difficulty than Julian, whose statement that he had been born in Rome created difficulties. "Rome? That's in Rumania," the inquisitor objected.

After the run through the flat, featureless Essex country, wreathed in trailing mist, Zena had been introduced to the imperial metropolis by way of Ilford, East Ham, and Stepney, through the unspeakable squalor of avenues of backyards and long perspectives of wooden privies, and had at last been deposited in the grimy, ramshackle station. She had hesitated to enter the evil-smelling London taxicab, with ripped cushions. England did not expend itself on providing favorable first impressions.

When the tension had been released, Zena felt thoroughly exhausted from accumulated fatigue, two sleepless nights, and strenuous days. After a blessed bath, she went to bed, begging not to be disturbed till the Greek Calends.

Julian went over to Brompton. He had not remembered the little flat which his mother occupied as being so dingy. There was a musty smell about, which caused Julian to ask Viola whether they kept cats. They didn't. Relics of the old home in Rome, a worm-eaten inlaid Italian cabinet, a bust of Lucius Verus, much too large for the tiny room, some of the Piranesi prints and other objects of more sentimental than decorative value, gave a junk-shop appearance to the drawing room.

Mrs. Bern looked startlingly aged. Her face had assumed a wax-like tinge, her large eyes burning in deep sockets. Although Julian had not seen his mother for over a year—and so much had occurred since then that it seemed much longer—she was, he thought, singularly detached and incurious in her reception of him.

"How did you manage to get away from those horrible Huns?" she asked.

It was almost the only personal question which she addressed to him. "This dreadful war, this dreadful war," she kept murmuring. Mrs. Bern had a great deal to say about her own war activities, the socks and cholera-belts which she and Mrs. O'Gorman had been knitting for the soldiers, and about Father Clare's fund for providing every Catholic recruit in the New Armies with a medal of Our Lady of Loretto. Many soldiers had already had their lives saved by the image, she told Julian. Over the chair where she sat were an ivory crucifix and a rosary.

Julian found the visit trying and depressing. He chided himself inwardly for his involuntary revulsion. He spoke gently, affectionately to his mother, and his tenderness was sincere. But how utterly impossible was the slenderest communion of feeling, the slightest communication or contact! His mother did little to help to put him at his ease. She now lived almost exclusively entrenched in her voodoo world, her mind benevolently, peacefully comatose with narcotic consolations and resignations.

How baffling were the emotional problems of kinship, of the bonds of tender obligation to persons who were more strangely remote than most strangers!

Scarcely easier was it to establish any free, spontaneous contact with his sister. Julian noticed—as he should have done before, even through the concealment of the mackintosh, had he been more observant—that Viola was expecting a baby.

"It was very brave of you, Vie, to come over like that alone," he said to her. But Viola did not care to dwell on her feelings.

"I saw Laurence Foster for a few moments before he went over to France," she informed Julian. "Lord Bar also is at the front."

That was to be expected, but Julian felt, nevertheless, a disappointment. He had hoped to see Everard, had tacitly counted on his counsel.

"You know, of course, that he is married?" Viola said.

Julian winced. "What? You don't mean that he has married that woman . . .?"

"Laurie mentioned the name, but I have forgotten."

"Vera Sherman."

"Yes, I think that's the name," Viola said.

"My God!" Julian exclaimed.

"Why? Is she quite impossible? I have not met her, of course."

"Oh, I suppose one has not the right to judge. She may be quite a nice girl. One can never tell; she may make Everard quite happy."

"What are you going to do?" Viola asked, a little later. "I am afraid that Zena will find it very dull just now in London. Everybody is so busy. There is little time for entertaining. And all the men are in khaki." There was a slight tone of questioning reproach in the manner in which she said the last words, with a look at Julian, as though she thought he should be joining. He did not attempt to justify himself or explain.

"You might perhaps take a house in the country," Viola said.

"Possibly. There has hardly been time to think of any plans yet, has there? We are merely refugees." He enquired about Keetje.

Viola would be going at the first opportunity to the Belgian Committee to register the girl, she said. They had a very efficient organisation for tracing relatives, she understood. The girl seemed quite content, curious of the novel, strange country.

Julian was relieved when he stepped out into the street. He breathed deeply, as though in need of fresh air.

He strolled back along Knightsbridge and Piccadilly, working off his uneasiness, curious also to revisit the familiar streets. The face of London had changed. It was a changed England to which he had come back. Under all the prescriptive solemnity and gravity, the commonplace formulas about "this dreadful war," "the horrors of Armageddon," under all the portentous phrases and beseeming seriousness, there was, much more conspicuous and real, a universal excitement, an unwonted vivacity and almost joyful exhilaration, which was a novel note in the English scene. The streets were animated. People moved with sprightly, springing steps. The men in khaki, who were everywhere, bubbled over with animal spirits, with extolled self-consciousness. The elderly men, whom one had been used to see dawdling, stiff with gout or rheumatism, to their clubs, were now hurrying along in amazing uniforms or with badges on their lapels, upon urgent business, rejuvenated and puffed up with self-importance. The women had forgotten all about votes.

They fussed around on their way to committee meetings, to offices, canteens, hospitals. They paraded in uniforms, in nurses' caps and capes. Everybody, the young men, the old men, the young women, the old women, appeared to be having the time of his life. War-time London seemed *en fête*.

The deadly, leaden weight of boredom was lifted. It was an unimagined release. Life had, or seemed, or was thought to have, an aim, an immediate task and purpose. Even the hand of actual tragedy lifted it out of the intolerable slough in which it had been bogged. The women whom one saw in deep mourning, who had had a son, a husband, or a lover killed, were uplifted by the consecration of their sorrow. They were as conscious of the eyes turned upon them as were the swaggering warriors on whom the young women smiled. The horrors of war! Why, it was a godsend, this jolly war.

A democratic fellowship was noticeable in the general consciousness of the new-found zest in life, which broke down the barriers of snobbery. Even the shopkeeper and the waiter exchanged an understanding smile with the customer, which came from the exuberance of general flushed well-being, and seemed to say: "Are we not all having a jolly time?" There was a freemasonry, a Christmas spirit of brotherhood in the delightful joy of release. Little suburban ladies hobnobbed with duchesses and found them quite human. The super-exclusive club of the army was now being submerged in a flood of "temporary gentlemen"; and although the enormity could not but arouse a first shudder of protest on the part of the "pucka" gentlemen, yet their very tradition required them to remain good fellows and to be "decent," without distinction, towards all who joined them in the great common cause of England.

From every wall glanced the slogans, the recruiting posters: "Business as usual"; "Keep on smiling"; "He is happy, are you?" "This place is for you." *Punch's* cartoon representing the King of the Belgians heroically defying the German Kaiser was enlarged as an inspiring, melodramatic poster.

In order not to disturb Zena's rest, Julian spent the day idling about at the Monico, in the lounge of Claridge's, reading the papers. He had been prepared for the outbreak of war mendacity. Had the public pronouncements of official opinion, in England especially, ever consisted

of anything but lies? He remembered something of the improbable
feats at the time of the Boer War. But he was nevertheless staggered
by the unshamed blatancy, the naïve childishness of the headlines, the
propaganda, the press communiqués. They were an affront to intelligence. He had imagined that at the present date, official and popular
patriotic blatancy would at least show a little more subtlety. The general
public of the second decade of the twentieth century had, after all, the
whole nineteenth century behind it, all the straining endeavors of modern thought. Yet it was treated, serenely and securely, as though it consisted of babes and imbeciles. This sort of thing had been exposed to a
good deal of exploding criticism, denunciation, and derision in the years
since the Boer War, and by some of the very men who were now in the
government. Yet there it was all over again, and a hundred times more
blatant, more defiant of ordinary sanity, of mere common sense than
ever before. The people responsible for the propaganda knew doubtless
their business best. They appraised the intelligence of the British public more accurately than he himself would have done when they treated
the "heir of all the ages" as a moron and mental defective. In that
revelatory release of the war, the mentality of the masses of the people
exhibited itself more plainly in its true light. The inconceivably naïve
chauvinistic blather which filled the public press probably represented
the actual value of that mentality more truly, more sincerely than the
pretentious judicial objectivity, the spurious detachment and profundity
of the pre-war years. It had been but a sham and a pretence, that
ostensible reasonablenes. In the excitement of the moment it showed
itself for what it was—an amazing stupidity and will to untruth. There
was a cliché phrase among some people that the world had gone mad.
That was not true. It had been mad all along. A lunatic may go un-
detected until the particular occasion which reveals his delusions and
discovers him a raving maniac. The world had probably been just as
stupid these many years as it was when it had allowed itself to be blown
up in chaos by half-a-dozen certifiable idiots entrusted with human
destinies. The stupidity had merely been disguised, camouflaged, as the
new war jargon had it, as judicial wisdom, profound insight, mature
conclusions. The war had not made the world mad; it had merely made
the madness visible.

Zena, when Julian visited her for a moment in the evening, was only beginning, she said, to feel a little rested. He did not disturb her more than to say good night before retiring to the separate apartment which, in deference to English susceptibilities, he had engaged.

After nearly twenty-four hours' repose she was, next morning, sufficently restored to view the world with her customary fortitude. Not that the outlook was encouraging. It was a brown, dark London morning, a genuine "pea-souper." The lights, both indoors and in the street, were on as though it were night. But the glowing coal fires with flickering blue flames, the smooth perfection of thickly carpeted and upholstered English comfort, and English service, dispelled to some extent the chill impressions. She and Julian came down to breakfast.

In the lounge and breakfast room, the hotel crowd, which was unusually cosmopolitan, appeared subdued and preoccupied. Women in Red Cross uniforms were in the company of heavily jewelled dowagers who read the paper through their lorgnettes, and had Pekingese dogs on their laps. There were angelic-looking boys wearing the white band of the O.T.C., with their proud parents up from the country. Some French officers were called from their breakfast and led away by a young red-tabbed staff-captain speaking very British French. A sallow-faced Serbian general in a shabby green uniform had difficulty in making his wants understood by the waiters. He examined with curiosity the table silver and toast dish, wondering as to the purposes of the various utensils.

"Poor devil! I feel almost as *depaysée* as he does," Zena remarked with her bright laugh.

"Wait a while. I am going at once to look up Lady Irene Sexborough. You know the sentimental interest she takes in you. She will be overjoyed, and will soon make you feel at home in England," Julian said.

Zena was above all anxious to call at the Russian embassy, where she hoped to obtain news of her mother and sister. She would, however, have to wait until she had procured some clothes. It was almost impossible for her to go out; she was practically naked, she pointed out to Julian.

Julian took a taxi to Saxford House. It had been turned into a hospital for officers. There was an ambulance under the porch when he drove up. The pillared hall was encumbered with surgical trollies and wheeled chairs; orderlies in white overalls, nurses, hurried up and down

the famous monumental staircase. The place smelt of ether and car-
bolic.

In an office filled with files of case-sheets, temperature charts, and
clicking typewriters—a dismantled morning room of the duchess's—
Julian found the assistant matron who, after many enquiries and a
long wait, produced an aged man-servant who was acting as caretaker.

Her ladyship, the man informed Julian, was in France. He had no
idea where; letters were addressed: "Sexborough Hospital, B.E.F.,
France." His Grace was, he believed, at the Admiralty, but he was not
sure. Her Grace was in Devonshire, at Tanbren Hall.

Julian, a good deal disappointed, walked round to Half-Moon Street.
An enormous calico placard over the porch of his Aunt Aurora's house
informed whom it might concern that it was the headquarters of the
W.W.W.C.C. By the aid of some notices posted on a board by the
front door, Julian was able to decode the cipher, which had at first suggested to him some triple brand of public convenience, but turned out to
have reference to the "Women War Workers' Central Coordination
Committee." The door was answered by Hopkins. Her ladyship was
at the moment at Penwood, but might be coming up to town at any
time. She went back and forth a good deal; she had the use of a war-
office car. The general was in town and would be either at the War
Office or at the United Services, where he was putting up. "The general" was, of course, Sir Horace, who now occupied an important appointment on the General Staff. Would Master Julian like to speak to
the general secretary of the Committee, who was in her office? She
might be able to tell him more precisely when her ladyship might be
expected. Julian suffered himself to be introduced to the lady, who was
installed in the transformed smoking room, and turned out to be no
other than Mrs. Montague-Douglas.

She greeted him with a friendly nod, while engaged in shouting down
a telephone, as though they had met an hour before. People were always
turning up again. When, after disposing of half-a-dozen inevitable interruptions, she could spare a few moments, Mrs. Douglas scarcely listened to Julian's replies to her casual questions. She was not interested
in the bombardment of Antwerp.

"Antwerp? Oh, yes, Antwerp. Do you know that General Ballyagh—
he's a lieutenant-general now—has got a D.S.O.?"

The rebel Ulster army had placed itself at the disposal of the King. F. E. Smith, Carson's first lieutenant, was appointed head of the Government Press Bureau. General Ballyagh had highly distinguished himself by a large capture of prisoners and a German field-kitchen.

Julian noticed, both then and subsequently, that the people in England were very slightly interested in the war. They were so engrossed in their own war activities that they had little attention to spare ,for military operations, unless they happened to have reference to some relative or acquaintance. They were, in general, amazingly ignorant of the general military situation, of geography. Although people spoke a great deal about "the Front" and "the trenches," they were bored by any account of them and showed little curiosity.

Mrs. Douglas barely found time, amid telephone interruptions and clerical reports, to mention to Julian some of her many activities. Besides being responsible for the co-ordination of numerous feminine warlike units, she had founded a Women's Agricultural Battalion intended to release more men for the Front. Sylvia Chantrey had designed a very becoming uniform for them. Mrs. Koe-Billings and Marion Prince were running a dairy.

While Julian had been out, Viola had looked up Zena. They had gone shopping together. Julian was amused, when they returned, at the notion of Viola, in her blue mackintosh, piloting Zena through the London shops. Their combined instincts had, however, proved adequate, and the shop-people, impressed by Viola's mackintosh, which suggested the possibility of her being a duchess, had been attentive. Zena, who had wished for the simplest things only, was quite satisfied with her purchases at Jay's and Redfern's. But Viola had indicated a slight measure of disapproval when Zena ordered one or two somewhat brighter frivolities at Worth's. To Julian's surprise, however, Zena got on remarkably well with his sister. Viola's level-headed directness appealed to her.

When Zena called at Chesham House, Count Benckendorf, whom she had met in St. Petersburg, was all solicitude. She was above all anxious to obtain news of Nadia and of her mother as quickly as possible. She had had none, except one letter received in Holland. Daria had had the palace on the Nevski fitted up as a hospital for the wives and children of soldiers at the front. Nadia was assisting. Zena had written several times, but, as she had been unable to give a permanent address, it might be long before replies could reach her. Communication with Russia was difficult and Count Benckendorf promised that he would take every possible step so that she might communicate more quickly. He would notify the Foreign Minister in Petrograd, and have Princess Hruzof's correspondence sent by the diplomatic valise.

There was also the question of money. Zena needed some at once. It was almost impossible to effect transfers. The ambassador, to whom Zena gave her letter of credit, said that he would take up the matter with Baron Rubinstein. Eventually he was able to obtain a payment, but, in the circumstances, two thousand pounds was all that could be procured at the moment.

Julian found himself also in a difficult position financially. No remittance from Russia had come since several months before the outbreak of war. The minute revenue derived from Belgian investments had, of course, likewise stopped. He thus found himself practically penniless. There were but a few hundred pounds in the bank. For the sake of economy, he gave up his apartment at the Claridge, and put up at his old quarters in Arundel Street, where they allowed him special terms. The delicate sensitiveness of English conventions also made the change advisable. Viola had dropped a word to him on the subject.

"Of course I have no prejudices in the matter," she said. "But some people might find it difficult to call on Zena while you are staying at the same hotel, and it would make it all the more difficult and unpleasant for her."

Viola's sense of English proprieties received immediate confirmation. Lady Penmore, who had given no sign of her existence since Julian's return, arrived to call on Zena the very day after he had moved to Arundel Street. She blew in like a whirlwind, breathless from the pressure of engagements. She had just heard of Princess Hruzof from Mrs. Douglas, she said effusively, and had at once hurried over, as soon as she had been able to get away from a committee meeting.

"How extremely fortunate that dear Julian was able to rescue you from those awful Huns, Princess," she said. "They are absolute savages. Do you know that they have not paid one penny on all the money which I invested in their Essen factories, believing as I did in Germany's honor and goodwill towards England, which has been so good to them? And they have actually confiscated, that is, stolen, the personal property which I had in Germany! People who act like that, to say nothing of their cutting off the hands of all the children in Belgium, cannot be regarded as civilised, can they?"

Princess Hruzof had doubtless, Lady Penmore presumed, met her son Welby at the British embassy in Petrograd. She was anxious that Zena should meet some of the workers in her organisations.

"You may know the honorary colonel of our Women's Volunteer Reserve, Madame Tchaykovsky. They are perfectly trained and now ready to go in the trenches," she informed Zena. "I want you, Princess, to join our Russian committee. You must take the chair at our next meeting. We are working so hard for those brave, dear Russians. We are arranging to send over a large consignment of peppermint drops for the Russian army. Sir Haakon Wrung says that they are an infallible preventive against typhus."

Zena was afforded little opportunity to signify either assent or reserve in regard to Lady Penmore's suggestions, so overwhelming was the stream of words under which she was submerged.

"You heard, of course, about the Russian troops which passed through from Scotland to go over to France? Naturally it had to be denied. But I hear that they are driving the Germans back over the Rhine. Isn't it splendid? I am so anxious that the Russians should soon get to Berlin, because after that dreadful trap which the Germans, who have no idea of clean fighting, laid for them in East Prussia, the Russians have not paid any interest at all on their bonds. I am quite sure that the dear Tzar will see that the payments are resumed, will he not? You don't know the sacrifices I have made for Russia! And, while I think of it, Princess, you must really speak to the Russian ambassador. I have been told by a member of the government that the whole of the correspondence from the embassy is being sent in duplicate to Berlin. Isn't it dreadful? The government have protested again and again to Count Benckendorf. They have made enquiries about every one in the personnel of the embassy. But they cannot find any trace of the spy. Those Huns are so clever. It is perfectly fiendish the spying that is going on. I am always very careful myself as to what I say.

They put machines into the walls of the houses, so that one is really never safe in saying anything. I am positively afraid to open my mouth."

Lady Penmore sought to establish possessive claims over Zena, in much the same manner as the suburban ladies over their Belgian refugees. She spoke to her friends about "my Russian princess," as Mrs. Douglas, whose slatternly little maid had had to leave on account of advanced pregnancy, and who had reduced to slavery a big Flemish peasant woman, spoke of "my Belgian refugee." Zena, who, out of civility and consideration for Julian, consented to attend once or twice his aunt's meetings, resisted, however, her attempts at enslavement. She declined various invitations to sell flags in the street, and excused herself from acceding to Mrs. Douglas's suggestion that she should run a chicken farm.

Zena declined, indeed, most of the invitations which were pressed upon her by the various ladies whom she met at Lady Penmore's. One of the most insistent was Mrs. Turldey, the wife of the Bishop of Shoredich, who was a particularly influential member of the war-committees. An added dignity was imparted to her high position by the fact that she had herself lost a son who had been killed in France. Although Bertie's untimely end had preceded by some months the outbreak of war, his bereaved mother overlooked the slight chronological discrepancy when alluding to her loss, and had become so accustomed to the implication that he had fallen fighting for King and country that she at last came to believe in the version of Bertie's demise. Some time later a stained-glass window was set up in Shoredich cathedral in commemoration of the hero, the fund for the memorial being raised by voluntary subscriptions throughout the diocese. The commemorative window was consecrated with great solemnity by the Archbishop of Canterbury, who on the occasion preached a moving sermon on the "Supreme Sacrifice."

Zena strove bravely to make the best of the strange surroundings, the peculiar company in which she found herself, so different from any to which she had been accustomed. But her efforts could not altogether conceal her discomfort, and her attempt to do so, for Julian's sake, created an even more painful sense of constraint between them. They seemed now to stand on the ruins of dreams which had, not long since, appeared so real that there could be no reason to doubt their everlastingness. The atmosphere of gloom, the depression of spirits which had attended their coming to England, far from becoming dispelled, became, as the weeks drifted by, more unendurable.

As Julian pointed out, their present arrangements were merely provisional and transient. They had come to London as to the nearest refuge. They could now consider more permanent plans. A house could be taken in a secluded part of the country. There were plenty to be had now. The English country had its undeniable charm. But would not the obvious thing to do be to return to Cannes? The Riviera was not likely ever to become a theatre of war. It was now no longer the vulgar playground of the pleasure crowd they had known. There was the clearly indicated refuge, ready, awaiting them.

Zena admitted the argument, but she must await news from Russia before taking any decision, making any plans. Unsatisfactory as it was, they decided to wait, for the present.

There was in London at the time little of the social life, the deliberate gaiety, which later developed during the war years. The newly found delightful game of supremely important activities was, for the present, sufficiently engrossing. An atmosphere of austerity, which was to give place a little later to a different mood, was still accounted befitting to the solemnity of the times. For those who, like Zena and Julian, did not take part in those activities, the situation almost amounted to a stoppage of life, a marking of time, which seemed at a standstill. The mere civilian who had not even a seat on some committee, the badge of some society on his lapel, was made distinctly conscious of his position as an outsider. Julian felt at times, in the street or in a restaurant, as unpleasantly embarrassed in his serge suit as though he had been clad in the rags of a tramp and manifestly unfit for human society. When he or Zena, in the course of a casual meeting or conversation, returned vaguely negative replies to the question: "What are you doing?" which signified: "On what war-work are you engaged?" they received blank looks that were full of moral disapproval.

Lady Penmore asked Zena down to Penwood. She did not include Julian in the invitation. He advised Zena to excuse herself.

"You will find it deadly," he said.

Zena gave a shrug. It was all pretty deadly; a little more or less, what did it matter?

But the visit turned out even more trying than anything she had imagined, and even her sense of humor did not entirely avail to palliate the ordeal. Her fellow guests were old Lady Cope and her daughter, Claudine, Mrs. Hope-Pinker, the Dean of Walchester, who was in khaki, having been appointed chaplain to a camp in the Eastern Command, and a member of Parliament, Sir Hugh Hinchpin, a retired upholsterer and pillar of the Church of England.

Lady Penmore was practising economies, from patriotic motives, she said. Outward retrenchment was an obligatory part of good form. Although it was freezing, a small coal fire only was lit in the drawing-room after dinner.

"I think it only proper to save coal," said Lady Penmore. "So much is needed for the navy. Besides, we have no right to indulge in creature-comforts while the men are enduring such hardships in the trenches, have we?"

The ladies, purple with cold, wrapped knitted shawls over the goose-flesh of the skeletal anatomies they denuded for dinner. The fare was abstemious, "to save the national stock of food." A dish of lentils, served with all the pomp of a silver dish cover, appeared one evening at the table as the *pièce de résistance*. There was no wine. The King had set the example by dispensing, according to official communiqués, with his whiskey and sealing the cellars at the Palace. Hopkins ceremoniously filled the guests' glasses with water. But Lady Cope was indulged in a glass of brandy, which was necessary for her digestion. To add insult to injury, the Dean offered a lengthy grace before every meal. Zena made special excursions into Basingstoke to lay in a secret stock of meat-pies and port wine, which she consumed surreptitiously in her bedroom to stave off inanition.

To please Claudine Cope, who conceived a great admiration for her, Zena played a little music despite her frozen fingers. Lady Penmore decided that she must give concerts in the hospitals, completely waved aside and ignored Zena's firm refusal, and drew up a list and time-table. It almost came to an open outburst.

Zena returned fuming. "I cannot stand those old women and this confounded country any longer," she raged.

She broke down and burst into tears. The pent-up irritation, the secret misery, which had been accumulating, found vent at last in the storm. It was a blessed release. She sought comfort in Julian's arms.

"Oh, drujok, drujok, shall we ever again be happy? Is it no longer possible, any joy?" she cried.

He held her trembling form, soothing, pacifying her. She was as a little child now, as a weak, helpless child. His own secret bitterness, the unspoken constraint that had been between them, found release in her crisis.

"Dearest, let us go. No matter where, let us go," he murmured, holding her. "I had forgotten, I had not sufficiently remembered England. No contact, no pinpoint of a contact with any reality is permitted or possible in a world of shams, a world in which emotions even are a sham. No reality of joy even. I had forgotten. Let us go, dear. Let us go to Cannes."

She looked into his eyes, smiling through her tears.

"Forgive me," she said. "I'm afraid I'm behaving badly. But I have been overwrought. Of course we must not go away. Not yet, not until I have some news from Russia. Forgive me!"

In the community of misery they found a joy now such as they had not known for some time, and it was almost a happiness which came to them in the crisis of release.

Viola had gone to Bognor. She asked Zena and Julian down. They were glad enough of the change.

The neat little house, standing in its own grounds, somewhat beyond the Western Parade, overlooked the sea, and was pleasantly furnished. It was bright and clear, after the gloom of London, and remarkably warm. Although it was December, one could at times sit on the lawn for tea.

Zena, making the most of the gentler, more soothed mood that was now upon her, sought to bring out Viola's reticent, self-contained nature. She was curious of her stolid, almost fierce attachment to Harry. Viola yielded a little of her reserve, glad enough to be made, almost by force, to confide something of her feelings and her anxiety, her consuming anxiety.

"I could not do otherwise," she said in reply to Zena's renewed admiration for her courage. "I had to be near Harry for when he should come on leave."

But it was terrible, the unremitting strain, the anxiety. She had, since leaving India, received but one letter, in a green field envelope, bright and cheerful, saying scarcely more than that Harry was well. He had, it appeared, written twice to India before he knew that she had come over. It would be a long time before the letters would reach her.

There was a bond of sympathy between the two women in that anguish over the unsurmountable delays of communication.

Viola again suggested that Julian and Zena should take some place in the country. There were some available quite near, and Viola knew a good agent. But Zena smiled at the simple notion of her becoming, even temporarily, an English country lady.

"The vicar's wife would call on me!" she said, bursting into laughter.

The quick walks which she and Julian took along the sea front were invigorating, in the keen Channel breeze. But the people they casually came upon, the twittering, dowdily genteel women, the eccentric gentlemen whom one turned round to look at, doubting if they should be at large, the smiling smugness of the nursemaids and governesses of good family, the tradesmen who twittered about the weather—were they alive? Was the whole somnolently genteel, twittering place really alive? Could any human being really live there?

Viola did not quite understand Zena's foreign, un-understanding imperviousness to the charm of England, the spell of the English country.

Keetje seemed to have become quite adapted to her novel surroundings. She looked decidedly pretty, though rather comical, in her English maid's black dress and apron. With remarkable rapidity she had already acquired an adequate, and even colloquial English. Her parents had been traced without difficulty. They had at first gone to Zuylen, in Holland, but had now migrated over to England and were living at Walthamstow. Kris Dools had found employment in a munition factory. Katie went over once a week to visit them in London.

"She is rather fond of going out," Viola mentioned in a tone of disapproval. But on the whole, the girl was satisfactory.

It was a pleasant change, the visit to Bognor. Viola pressed Julian and Zena to stay on. But Zena thought it better not to. The baby might be expected at any time, and they would be in the way. Viola was not sure of her dates. They would return. They would come back, if they were still in England and all were well, for Christmas.

Only a day or two before they had intended to return to London, the news came. All three were sitting on the lawn, looking at the sunset over the Channel. A Canadian troopship accompanied by two torpedoboat destroyers was gliding over the gleam of the steely surface. As was the case on still evenings, one could, if one listened hard, hear the distant, but distinct, rumble, like far-away thunder, of the guns in Flanders. Viola was particularly bright.

"You must come down in any case for Christmas. Quite possibly Harry may be given home leave by then," she was saying.

Keetje appeared, running excitedly across the lawn towards them. "A telegram, M'am," she said.

Viola smiled quietly as she rose to take it, but she had already turned pale.

"Excuse me," she said, as she tore open the envelope. Her hand was shaking violently.

She stood for a moment stony still, her eyes closed. Then she swayed a little. Julian caught her in his arms, and they took her, half carrying her, to her bedroom.

Zena sat up all night with her. Viola did not move or speak.

It was not until some days later, when Viola received letters from the Colonel of Harry's battalion and from some of the officers she had known, that particulars were available. The Gurkhas had been ordered to attack a machine-gun position. The ground was covered with snow, and the dark uniforms offered an easy target. All knew beforehand that they were going to their death. It was an insane order. Scarcely any survived. Harry had fallen almost at the moment that he stepped over the parapet. It was the first day he had been in the line.

Zena offered to stay with Viola until her time should come.

"I think, if you don't mind, I would rather be alone," Viola said. They did not see her cry. She kept very quiet, "for the sake of the child," she said.

III

ONE morning Julian came upon Eleanor Astley in Oxford Street. She was boarding an east-bound bus, but turned joyfully to greet him. In English surroundings and in an attire better fitting her Greek goddess figure she looked more like her former self than when he had last seen her in Berlin. He congratulated her on having got away from Germany.

"Did you have much trouble?" he asked. Often he had wondered what had become of her, and reproached himself for not having, in the hustle of the last moments, done something to assist her.

"Let us go into some place where we can talk a moment," Eleanor said.

They went into an A. B. C., fortunately empty at that hour. There was only one man, nodding behind the outspread pages of the *Daily Mail*. They sat in a corner over cups of watery coffee.

Eleanor's experience had been, she admitted, distressing. She had narrowly escaped being confined in an internment camp. Only thanks to the exertions of Berlmuth and other Reichstag members on her behalf, had she been permitted to leave the country.

"The worst of it was that the very people I had worked for and befriended turned against me," she said. "It was almost impossible for me to appear in the street without being greeted with cries of 'Engländerin.'"

Eventually she had been granted a passage to Holland. The officials and authorities had been, in general, courteous and considerate. But her most trying experience had been at the military station-master's office before she was permitted to entrain. Eleanor flushed scarlet. Not only had her scanty luggage been minutely searched, but she had been required to undress.

Eleanor hastily enquired concerning Julian's own doings.

"So you stayed . . .," she said with a bright flash in her eyes.

"Till the great betrayal," he said with sardonic bitterness. "I did not flee from war, but from the ignominy of surrender."

"It is even more sickening here, the ignominy," she said. "Norman Angell, Green, of the Peace and Arbitration Society, Hyndman, that Tory who had been masquerading as a socialist, H. G. Wells—all turned into jingo war-mongers. Even Bernard Shaw. You have read his pamphlet?" Eleanor had her handbag stuffed with pamphlets and newspaper cuttings. She drew some of them out. "Fine scathing words worthy of the honor of being suppressed in England," she said, turning over the pages. "And then this for a conclusion: 'We are supporting the War as a war on war. . . . It stirs the blood and stiffens the back. . . . We must have the best army in Europe. . . . We in England are fighting to show the Prussians they shall not trample on us.' "

" 'We!' Which 'We'? The England of profiteers or the England of driven sheep? As though only the Prussians threatened to trample upon them!" Julian fumed.

"I had believed in Bernard Shaw," Eleanor said sadly, dropping the paper.

"As you had believed in the German social-democrats, with their one hundred deputies and millions of adherents."

Eleanor picked up another pamphlet. "And in the Webbs. And this is what Sidney Webb says: 'Great Britain in 1936 will be a finer country to live in than it would have been had not the sharp prick of war aroused us.' "

"A land fit for heroes, in fact," said Julian.

"Beatrice Webb is doing war-work," Eleanor said, with eyes upturned. Then: "What time is it?" she asked. "I am due at my office."

"So, you too are doing war-work?" Julian scoffed.

"The other war. For the defence of English homes and English women and children against the defenders of England, home, and beauty," Eleanor retorted. "I have engaged the services of a couple of friendly lawyers to help provide some small measure of protection to some of the victims of unscrupulous pauperisation and exploitation." The distress, she said, was appalling. Hundreds of thousands of families had been suddenly left without breadwinners. The derisive separation allowances of one shilling and a penny a day were not paid, were left for months unpaid, were withheld and denied on all manner of pretexts. The Prince of Wales' Fund established with a great blare of patriotic press trumpets had been appropriated, all but about a quarter of it, by the War Office. The remainder was administered with the usual eleemosynary parsimony by the old Boards of Poor Law guardians under the presidency of Arthur Balfour, who answered indignant questions in Parliament by bland lying. The gifts sent by the Dominions to alleviate hunger and distress had been likewise appropriated by the army. The potatoes sent by Canada had been sold in the open market. Despite the moratorium proclaimed on the declaration of war, soldiers' wives were being illegally evicted. Queen Mary's Workshops, commonly known as Queen Mary's Sweatshops, set up to relieve female unemployment, paid a maximum of ten shillings a week. Girls of sixteen and eighteen were paid twopence an hour with a maximum of five shillings a week. Most women earned from three to six shillings a week. It was worse than the old Jewish sweatshops. While the men were told by patriotic employers to "Enlist or go," the women engaged to take their places were paid half the former wages of the men. Profitable patriotism! In the clothing trade, the sweating was unbelievable. Two shillings and threepence was paid for making army greatcoats which were sold to the Government at twenty-eight shillings. Soldiers' shirts were given out at two shillings and a penny per dozen, less a deduction for the cotton. Military jackets were paid tenpence three farthings a dozen, and sold to the Government at twelve shillings and sixpence each. Contracts were sublet four and five times, colossal profits being drawn by each contractor. The cost of living had already risen all round by 25 per cent; bread was 75 per cent more than its prewar price, and the population of India was perishing of famine to keep up the price. Coal, which cost less at the pit mouth than before the war, owing to the loss of foreign markets, was being sold in London at thirteen shillings and sixpence a ton.

The wholesale starvation and unemployment of the first few months of war, which had driven the men into the army and the women into the sweatshops, was now gradually eliminated by enrollment in the munition works, where women were paid half the rate of male unskilled labor, worked ninety-five hours a week, and earned wages of eight to sixteen shillings. And the press circulated stories, which rich and patriotic dames repeated, about the prosperous "munitionettes" buying fur coats and pianos. Every protection formerly afforded by the Factory Acts was now ignored. Infant labor was reintroduced as in the worst days of the industrial revolution. Men had been killed by the collapse of jerry-built walls; women and girls had died from the effects of fumes and dope. Legal protection was almost unobtainable. Recently a girl of sixteen, after working continuously for over twenty-five hours, had been caught in the machinery and maimed for life. The case brought up against the contractor was dismissed by the magistrate with the remark that "the only important thing was to have munitions." On the other hand, workers were fined at every turn, on every pretext, for being five minutes late or for not working on Sundays. The orgy of profiteering and exploitation went on with the connivance of the Government, which shielded it behind a smoke-screen of control regulations that remained dead letters. It was the same in every trade, in the canning industry, the breweries. Boots had been known to be sold to the Government three times over, after having been condemned. The shipping companies were making fabulous profits. On many lines the charges were increased by 400 per cent. American wheat transport charges had risen from fifteen shillings to fifty-five. Yet the Government took 80 per cent of the war risks, and the maximum rate charged by underwriters was 5 per cent.

Julian felt nauseated. He had not realized the full enormity of the ruthless infamy which no hyperbolic exposure could measure, much less exaggerate, and which used moral edification, patriotism and religion as the outward vestures of its unscrupulous and homicidal rapacity. He should have known by now that a world which has always been based and built upon that unchecked and relentless greed for individual profit could not but seize the opportunity offered by barbaric war to wallow in shamelessness and crime. It was all, in truth, no different from what had always gone on, magnified and dramatised by the spectacular occasion, that was all. "Business as usual." Callous wading to plunder through blood, as usual; legal and governmental support of robbery and homicide, as usual; fulsome masquerading of the whole cesspool of infamy in the soiled lap of edifying moral sentiments, liberal grandiloquence, religion, patriotism—as usual. Patriotism! Whiteheads were manufacturing torpedoes in their Austrian factory at Fiume to blow up British ships; Vickers were paying Germany the patents on shell-fuses and submarines. A wave of angry impatienec surged within him.

"And you are fighting the other war with two attorneys! Where are the armies of the war of liberation? Where is the recruiting office?"

"In Russia, perhaps," Eleanor said. "I met one of their men at Clara Zetkin's when I was overwhelmed with hopelessness. They will not compromise. They are fighting compromise and betrayal. You should go to Russia."

"Perhaps I shall," Julian said.

Since the tragedy at Bognor, Zena had relapsed into the gloom from which, for a moment, she had seemed to be lifted. There were still no letters from Russia. The minister at the embassy sought to reassure her. Every step had been taken. The delay was nothing unusual. Communications with Russia were extremely slow. There had scarcely been time yet for a reply. One would come, without doubt, very shortly now. She must have patience.

Zena's nervous uneasiness reacted upon Julian. To add to the depressing influences which weighed upon him, the unlucky book to which, in collaboration with Sir Anthony Fisher, he had devoted his energies for years had come out in the autumn. It attracted, as was to be expected, little general attention, although a little book written by a doctor, which showed in scientific language that the German nation was biologically analogous to a pack of wolves, whereas the British might aptly be compared to a hive of bees, was enjoying an enormous popularity and receiving much praise in scientific circles as an important contribution to biological philosophy. A short notice of Sir Anthony's and Julian's book appeared in the *Times Literary Supplement's* "graveyard." It was a fine example of studiously distilled venom. "The authors of this prolix and pretentious work," wrote the anonymous reviewer, "have set themselves deliberately to antagonize the competent scientific authorities before whom their book naturally comes for judgment. . . . Their style is turgid and windy, and their book verges for the most part on the unreadable. They constitute themselves the champions of scientific thought, and shout shrill defiance at all Weismannists and Neo-Darwinians. . . . A little more scientific thought and less talk about it would have made a better book." Despite the discrete silence which surrounded in general the publication, references to it appeared here and there in the scientific press, showing by the unacademic violence of their lan-

guage the ire to which it moved "the competent scientific authorities."
The scope and theme of the work were misrepresented, and it was described as a revival of "the long exploded theories of Lamarck," to
whose work the authors insufficiently acknowledged their indebtedness.
The *Journal of the Royal Biological Society* had a paragraph of contemptuous and particularly scurrilous abuse. Old Haverstock Wallace,
the authority on depravity, who had himself suffered formerly from
English covert censorship, went out of his way to review the book
with much condescension in a sheet devoted to the advertisement of
rubber goods, and deplored the "predilection for the paradoxical which
handicapped the authors' literary temperament." Professor Bronislawski, who had obtained much honor in England by proving the accuracy
of the story of Noah's Ark, and had been appointed in consequence
to the chair of Natural History in the University of Aldwych, was
particularly combatant. The book, he said, was dangerous to public
welfare, sapping as it did the foundations of national patriotism in
racial heredity and the family. He approached the Home Secretary
and the Archbishop of York with a view to having the work suppressed on grounds of immorality. The *New Statement* stated that
"Professor Bronislawski has once and for all disposed of Sir Anthony
Fisher's and Mr. Bern's puerilities." Sir Anthony was, shortly after,
dismissed from his lectureship at Cambridge and his post at the Marine
Biological Station.

The uncritical abuse did not hurt Julian. Only critical truth, or at
least plausible approach to it, can hurt. The animus of the reviewers
was so patently unintelligent and unjust that it was deprived of all
sting. He laughed heartily over the concentrated bile of the poor anonymous curate of the *Times Literary Supplement,* a clerical and reactionary sheet in which it were a humiliation and condemnation to be praised.
He shrugged his shoulders over the excited combativity of the Ruritan-
ian charlatan.

It was not through his vanity that he was hurt—he would have been
equally indifferent to praise. But the sense of intellectual isolation was
added to his loneliness. A great loneliness weighed on him. He felt
appallingly alone, not only in his intellectual world, but in his life, almost
physically. To this London, which he had been in the habit of looking
upon as, after all, his local habitation, his home city in so far as he

could be said to have one, which he had loved in a way from habit and familiarity, he now felt himself almost as much a stranger as did Zena. He had thought of himself as possessing a considerable circle of friends and acquaintances there. And now there seemed in truth scarcely any one, man or woman, to whom he could turn with pleasure. They were all either away in France or so absorbed in their various activities that the casual social intercouse which had formerly been the main business of their lives had lost its importance. Julian, being neither in uniform nor engaged in any of the many spurious war activities, found himself in a sort of limbo separated from the environing world. He was made to feel as though he were almost a pariah. When, occasionally, he came upon an acquaintance, he was confronted with the invariable question: "And what work are you doing?" When he answered "None," he was met with an absent, disinterested look. There could obviously be no longer any common ground of interest between his interlocutor and himself.

If he could speak to Everard.

Coming out of a tube-station, one morning, after a somewhat un-satisfactory interview with the manager of his bank, Julian was amused at the aspect of a group of women who were in front of him. One, in khaki uniform, with pleated skirt, high laced boots, a rough-rider hat turned up at one side, lanyards, whistle and leather pouches, had the crown and star of a colonel on the shoulder-straps of her tunic. She carried a swagger stick which she switched about somewhat to the peril of those who happened to be near. The feminine colonel was talking to three young women in navy-blue V.A.D. uniform, so loud that she might have been heard half-way across the street. Her conversation, cheerily interspersed with much giggling, consisted largely of such alphabetical expressions, as G.H.Q., C.O., Q.M.S., F.D., as were current in khaki language. So entertained was Julian by the appearance and manner of the feminine warriors that he walked a little way behind them, inwardly chuckling, though nobody else appeared to be taking much notice. At the corner of Southampton Row, the "colonel" and the three V.A.D.'s parted company, the latter clicking their heels at attention and saluting, while the "colonel" took the salute with the non-chalance befitting her rank and called out: "Well, cheerio chin chin, girls!" Julian had then an opportunity of clearly seeing the feminine officer's face, and recognised Miss Thorpe, who at the same time caught sight of him and hailed him with a comradely: "Hello, Bern!"

Julian would have gladly dispensed with the meeting which he had inadvertently brought about, but it was too late to evade it. He congratulated Colonel Thorpe on her military promotion, with an unapparent irony which she did not detect. Hermione Thorpe said that she owed the honor largely to the interest taken in her by Lady Bar, whose praises she sang, and who was very active in promoting war service for women. Miss Thorpe recited, in her newly acquired alphabetical vocabulary, the vital services which her amazon troops were rendering in the defence of the country. They were now most efficiently trained in both trench and open warfare and excelled in musketry. The work was, of course, very exacting and entailed heavy responsibilities. Hermione Thorpe was answerable for the morals of her troops.

"Have you heard whether Lord Bar is expected on leave?" Julian hastily put in during a pause for breath.

"I believe he is expected at any time," Miss Thorpe said. "Lady Bar has, I understand, gone to Clinton in readiness for his coming. I'll let you know if you wish."

"Thanks," Julian said, resisting with determination Miss Thorpe's pressing efforts to detain him, and her invitation to visit her and Miss Tascher, who was a captain, at their rooms in Jermyn Street.

But it was Eleanor who telephoned him one morning to tell him that Everard was in town.

Julian found him, after two futile calls, at the Constitutional. In his faded khaki, patched with leather, and spangled like a harlequin's coat with divisional marks, Everard had the serious, far-away look of the men from the trenches. He looked, weather-browned and a little round-shouldered, very tired. He was about to take a snack before catching his train to Clinton.

"I have not yet had an opportunity of offering my congratulations," Julian said as they sat down. "I do so now with all my heart."

"Thanks. I am indeed to be congratulated," said Everard. He went on, with an ecstatic look, to speak of Vera in terms the extravagance of which made Julian blush. "Do you know that she is a genius—in every sense of the word, a genius?" he said, leaning forward with earnestness.

Julian looked at Everard in silence with a profoundly uncomfortable feeling. Could this be the same Everard whose somewhat cynical sanity he had admired? Julian almost expected him to turn his words into a joke. He did not enquire into the manifestations of Lady Bar's genius, but sought to divert the conversation by asking Everard how, since he was so happy in his marriage, he could bear the separation and the risks of active service.

"That can make no difference," Everard said. "Vera would not wish it otherwise. And we are never really apart. I can't explain to you."

Julian was genuinely alarmed. He did not encourage Everard to explain.

"Is it going to last long, the war?" he asked to change the subject.

"My dear fellow, I am not Mr. Hilaire Belloc," Everard said, with a laugh which came as a relief. "Only fools have opinions on the subject." Then with deliberate seriousness: "In a sense, it may perhaps never end. I mean, the change which has come about may continue indefinitely, even after 'peace' comes. It is something bigger than an ordinary war."

Like all the men from the Front, Everard could not be got to talk much about it. He had been mostly in the Ypres salient, he told Julian.

"It's no use trying to describe," he said. "No doubt, many fellows will try to tell what it is like, some day. But you simply can't. It is all so unreal, so much outside ordinary experience, descriptions don't mean anything."

"That is one reason why it is so easy to turn it into a fabulous, idealised, glorified fantastic fiction," Julian reflected.

"The people here talk about the war as they talked about it before it came—without knowing what it means. It is ghastly. But the most ghastly thing about it is that one gets used to it, so that the ghastliness becomes trivial and commonplace. The first time I saw a dead body, lying on the ground, the first time I saw a man die, torn to pieces, my whole being was churned, and I thought I should be haunted by the sight till my dying day. But dead and dying men become a commonplace occurrence, and no one even turns his head to look."

"Just as people get used to the ghastliness which surrounds their everyday life on all sides, so it too seems commonplace and trivial, makes no impression," put in Julian.

Everard looked at him for a moment thoughtfully, then he suddenly said :

"You will have to join."

"I, join? Why? There are half-a-dozen causes for which I would willingly give or risk my life, but the cause of the British Empire is not one of them," Julian said.

"The British Empire, for all its faults and stupidities, is the most decent organisation in what is called civilisation," Everard said.

"Decent?" Julian called to mind his conversation with Eleanor. Decent? If that were decency, he'd like to know what decency was.

"Oh, I know, I know. Nobody knows better than I do what a very little way that decency goes. It is damnable. But Prussian barbarism is even more damnable. The Germans. . . ."

"What are they really like? Over there, I mean," Julian interrupted.

"Haven't seen a single one, except one frightend boy we once caught in a raid. No, no. You'll give me credit for enough intelligence not to share all the nonsense and fury of the Hun-haters. Germans are, as a rule, quite good fellows, simple, rather naïve fellows, much more friendly and frankly sociable than many other people, Frenchmen, for instance. But the fact remains that with the Germans you haven't got to scratch so deep as with most other so-called civilised Europeans to find the barbarian, the brutally ferocious barbarian."

"Nothing to do with race," Julian interposed. "All a question of history. The Germans were busy exterminating one another in the Thirty Years' War while Western Europe was growing out of the Middle Ages. They missed the Renaissance, and had to catch up hurriedly with Western civilisation, like the Japanese. In a sense, they have remained parvenus, retaining the barbaric ideals of insolent force, of brute power, under the veneer, always ready to crack on the slightest strain."

"Race, or history, the fact remains. And German domination would be very much more indecent than British domination."

"The lesser of two evils is not exactly the sort of cause for which one is inspired to lay down one's life. Is England's relatively more decently disguised rascality an argument?"

Everard laughed. "Damn you and your logic. Of course it isn't. But one doesn't live by arguments. You will join, you will be drawn

into the current, because there is no other water to swim in just now.
You will be drawn into it because all else, reason, argument, escape, is
impossible today. You will be drawn into it because time is standing
still, and you cannot live in a vacuum."

Everard had to catch his train. Julian accompanied him to Padding-
ton in a taxi. They stood a few moments saying good-bye on the dark
station-platform. Everard, with his heavy webbing pack slung on his
back and leaning on a birchwood stick, seemed weary.

"We will meet again in France," he said as he took his place in the
compartment.

At last the long-awaited letters from Russia came. Julian knew at
a glance when he saw Zena, as he returned after a day of aimless wandering. She had been crying; her face was drawn and flushed. She
read out to him her mother's letters, translating the general drift of
them. There were two: one, a long one, of merely general news. Nothing very particular. Daria spoke of the generally deplorable state of
things, the incredible incompetence and corruption, the general scramble
for profiteering loot, army contracts paid for several times over and
the goods never delivered, the fears of famine, with grain piled up all
along the Siberian railways.

"Exactly the same as here," Julian said with a shrug. "It isn't Russia
that breeds profiteering plunder and corruption. It's something else—
the system."

Daria spoke about her hospital, the appalling misery that so little
could be done to relieve even in part. Epidemics were raging, dirt-and-
misery plagues. The doctors and the newspapers called them influenza.
It was really typhus. Every sort of difficulty was placed in the way of
her work. It wasn't patriotic; it attracted attention to things that had
better be kept out of sight at the present time. Daria went into long
details. The work was very heavy. Nadia was helping bravely, working
unsparingly.

Then Zena passed on to the other letter. It was only a brief hurried
note written some days after the other. Nadia was down with typhus.
There was no occasion for grave alarm, Daria said, but at the moment
she was very ill.

"I must go at once," said Zena. She had already telephoned the embassy. There was a courier leaving from Newcastle in three days. Her passport was all in order.

"Of course, we will go at once," Julian said. It was too late to go that evening to the Foreign Office to see about a passport. He would go first thing in the morning.

He had a great feeling of relief now that the decision was taken. The blank uncertainty of the last weeks had been intolerable. It was all right now. He looked forward to going to Russia. Formerly he had viewed the prospect with some diffidence and hesitation. The strange distant country, so different from all he knew, the inclement climate, the unknown language. He would have felt as lost there, he imagined, as Zena did in England. But now . . . England itself was so different from what he had expected. He felt almost as much a stranger as did Zena. He had all the while the same sense of constraint and uncomfortable stuffiness which he felt in his mother's flat in Brompton. All England smelt to him of cat's piss. He was in haste to be away from England, to breathe freely. The further, the better. He would have gone to Shanghai.

He hastened to Downing Street next morning as early as he decently could to get the passport formalities over. The spruce official to whom he was referred was delightfully courteous and amiable. He helped Julian to fill in the form of application, and remembered Julian's father's name. There were some documents with his signature in the archives, he said. He knew also of Mr. Welby Penmore, who was expected shortly from Petrograd.

"You are almost one of ourselves, Mr. Bern," he said, smiling pleasantly. "In your case, of course, one can dispense with many formalities. When do you propose to leave?"

Julian explained he had to leave in three days.

"Three days? That is very short notice, Mr. Bern. The issue of a passport takes in the ordinary course of things about ten days or a fortnight. However, I will see to putting the matter through specially. I will see that it is brought to the attention of the Foreign Secretary at once. I will see to it myself. You can count upon receiving a reply in time," said the courteous official. It was a pleasure to deal with gentlemen, after all.

The next days were of almost joyful excitement, the weight, the constraint lifted. Julian and Zena busied themselves doing some necessary shopping. It was almost the old joy. They talked about the journey by way of Christiania, Stockholm, and Helsingfors, with amused anticipation. Julian wrote to Viola, explaining. It was running things rather close, that silly passport business. But one could trust British officials; they kept their word. One must give them credit for that. But on the morning before they were due to leave, no reply had yet come.

In the evening, an official envelope, marked O.H.M.S., arrived. It contained only a letter signed by some "obedient servant," informing Julian Bern, Esq. that, much to the Foreign Secretary's regret, it was deemed inexpedient in the present emergency to grant his application for a passport to Russia.

Julian dropped limp under the blow. He should have gone to headquarters. His aunt, Lady Penmore, could have got the matter through. There was not a moment to lose. It could be arranged yet. The train did not leave King's Cross till early in the following afternoon. Zena sought to comfort him.

"Don't worry, drujok," she said, soothingly. "There is another courier leaving in about a week. I can well wait a few days longer. It won't make so much difference. Don't worry."

Julian rang up Lady Penmore. By good fortune, she was in town. She answered the telephone herself. Could he see her at once? He had an urgent favor to ask of her. She would wait up for him, she said.

He hurried in a taxi to Half-Moon Street. He found his aunt in a little parlor on the second floor, reading through tortoise-shell rimmed glasses a book about "England's Sacrifice."

Putting down her book and taking off her glasses, she at once began to speak before he had had a chance to explain.

"I may as well tell you at once, my dear Julian," she said, "that it is quite impossible for me to do anything for you. Quite impossible. My own situation is, let me tell you quite frankly, exceedingly serious. Those Russian scoundrels, who are letting us down so disgracefully, are taking no steps whatever to fulfil their financial obligations. I always had a premonition that one could never trust Russians. Events have shown that I was right. I have not received one penny from Russia since the beginning of the war. And, of course, not one penny from Germany or from Belgium. Even the London investments are doing badly. I have two houses empty. Mr. Notice tells me that it is impossible to collect rents, owing to the scandalous moratorium of that fellow Lloyd George. Notice also talks of competition, though I do not understand what he means. Then, the income-tax is doubled. In fact, my dear Julian, I am just now almost entirely dependent upon your uncle's pay and some slight acknowledgment made by the Government for the use of the house for national purposes. You see that it is no use expecting any help from me."

"But I have no intention of asking you for money, Aunt Aurora," said Julian.

"Oh? Why didn't you say so before? What, then, is it you want?"

"I want you to use your influence at the Foreign Office to obtain a passport to Russia for me." Julian briefly explained to his aunt the situation, and showed her the letter he had just received in answer to his application.

"I think that they are perfectly right," Lady Penmore said, after glancing at the letter. "I don't see at all why you want to go to Russia. Your place is here, with all the other young men of your age who are defending their King and country. And, by the way, I am bound to say that Princess Hruzof has behaved very rudely. Very rudely, and, I may say, ungratefully after all the kindness I have shown her, going out of my way, for your sake chiefly, to introduce her and make her feel at home. But I suppose one cannot expect manners from Russians. However," she went on, dismissing the subject with a tolerant shrug, "that is none of my business. I cannot understand your determination to go to Russia, but I wouldn't dream of interfering in your affairs. You are exactly like your poor father, most foolish. I dare say that business of the passport can be arranged, since you are determined. As it happens, Welby is expected at any moment. Indeed, he should have arrived—on a special mission from Russia. We are trying, that is, Welby and the British Government are trying, despite the way the Russians have let us down, to put Russia on her feet again. Welby has great influence, very great influence. His word carries weight in official quarters. I have no doubt that he will be able to arrange the affair for you. I shall write to him, so that he may get the note at the Foreign Office as soon as possible. And I shall telephone, if I don't see him first, to make an appointment. I will let you know."

Two days later, Julian received a message informing him that Mr.
Welby Penmore would be at liberty to see him, and making an appointment at the Foreign Office for the afternoon.

For a moment Julian did not recognise Welby, so much had his
cousin changed since they had last met. His flabby adenoidal countenance had hardened into a solid, somewhat sallow mask, well under control, and eminently adapted to inflict the most stony snubs. Welby Penmore had aged considerably in appearance. His reddish hair, which had
been wont to stand up rebelliously in parrot's feathers, had grown prematurely thin, and was now carefully smoothed over denuded calvaria
which imparted a domelike importance to his brow. The bearing and
motions of his gaunt figure had acquired a corresponding self-command.
Improbable as it might have seemed, Welby had become, in appearance
at least, a "pucka" diplomatist.

When Julian was introduced into the stately oak-panelled room, Mr.
Welby Penmore was gravely seated before a large leather-covered and
brass-bound table, toying with a letter-opener. He at once rose to meet
Julian with appropriate bright and cheery cordiality.

"Hello, Cousin Julian, so jolly to see you, by Jove! Quite a long
time, what? And how are you getting on?" he said, waving him to a
deep leather armchair.

"I am getting into slight difficulties with red tape entanglements, and
have come to ask if you would be so good as to help disentangle them,"
Julian said.

"Why, of course," Welby said cheerfully. "Red tape is not so formidable as it looks, don't you know. There's usually some way—among
gentlemen—of getting round it. I'm sure we can dispose of your difficulties. Now, what is it? I am entirely at your service."

"I want to go to Russia," Julian said.

"To Russia? Russia?" Welby repeated in a tone which suggested
not only surprise, but the gathering together of threads of unspoken
thought. "Why the deuce do you want to go to Russia? I can tell you,
having, as you know, just come from there, that it isn't quite the most
desirable place of residence at the present moment. Everything there is
at sixes and sevens. A bally awful mess. One's not even quite sure
that one might not have some difficulty any day about getting one's
tucker. Fancy any one wanting to go to Russia, now! Wouldn't

mind, myself, if I never saw the damned place again." While speaking, he had pressed a button on his desk, and in a moment a black-coated official appeared at the door. "Excuse me one second," Welby said, without waiting for Julian to reply, and going up to the official who stood at the door, he spoke a few words to him before returning to his seat. "What the deuce do you want to go to Russia for?" he repeated.

"I wish to accompany Princess Hruzof there, a lady whose name is, I believe, not unknown to you," Julian said.

Throwing back his head, Welby gave a prolonged low whistle. *"Cherchez la femme,* what? Princess Hruzof, by Jove! So that's it, is it? Congratulations, my dear chap! Oh, oh! Ah, ah! You dirty dog!" And with an unpleasant leer he leaned forward, making a lunge with his hand in the direction of Julian as though to poke him in the ribs.

Julian ignored Welby's jocularity.

"Princess Hruzof, who is at present in London, is returning to Petrograd," he said. "She has, of course, her passport, which has been visaed by the Russian minister and the Foreign Office. I have applied through the usual channels for a permit or passport for myself, but my request has not, for some reason, been granted. Your mother thought that, since luckily you happened to be in London, you might perhaps be able to get the matter settled."

The black-coated official had meanwhile unobtrusively returned, deposited a file of papers in a blue folder on the table, and silently retired. Welby resumed an air of gravity.

"I may tell you that it is, just now, not at all an easy matter to go to Russia," he said, leaning back in his chair and placing the tips of his fingers together, "not at all an easy matter. The journey is, I can testify, not a comfortable one. I have done it three times lately, and even travelling in an official capacity, it is bally uncomfortable. Got an awful tossing this last trip between Bergen and Newcastle. There was some talk of old Kitchener himself going over to Russia to try and straighten up matters there a bit. But the uncertainties of the journey are such that it has been thought best to put off the trip for the present."

"The risks and discomforts are, of course, my own concern," Julian said.

"Quite so," Welby agreed. "But I'll tell you quite frankly that, although passports for Russia are not often asked for, our people are very reluctant to issue any. I'm speaking to you, of course, in absolute confidence. There's such a confounded lot of underhand dealing with the Boche going on over there, you see. Perfectly appalling. Anything that is said in Petrograd goes over somehow straight to the Huns. One might as well issue permits to go to Germany as to go to Russia."

"I've gathered something of all this, and that's why I've come to you, thinking you might perhaps be able to get round the difficulty," Julian said. "You can at least vouch for my not being a spy or anything like that."

Welby smiled. "If you were in the service, there would be no difficulty in sending you over under some pretext or other. If you were in khaki, I dare say I could get you tacked on to the military attaché. But . . . to go as a private individual, with no particular reason that one can give, is a bally awkward matter. Look here, old chap, between us there is no need for official eyewash," Welby went on in a confidential tone. He took the file of papers which had been deposited on his table. "We have here, I don't mind telling you, a few confidential notes concerning you." Welby, looking down his nose, glanced over the papers and cleared his throat. He hastily put aside a note which was among them and which he had just received from Lady Penmore, requesting him to see that Julian be on no account granted a passport to Russia. There were also a couple of lines from Viola Foster to the same effect, which had been enclosed in his mother's letter. Passing to some typewritten sheets, and clearing his throat anew, Welby went on. "Er, yes. Let me see. You were in Berlin last July. You attended pacifist anti-war meetings. You associated with German socialists and with that silly woman, Eleanor Astley, whom you have been meeting again here in London. It is believed that you hold pacifist, anti-war, and socialist views. And so forth. My dear fellow, I'm not discussing. That has nothing to do with me. A chap is bally well at liberty to hold any views he likes. I am merely showing you, in your own interest and in strict confidence, that the F.O. is kept pretty well informed."

"So it seems," Julian said, flushing. "Your people must have been going into my affairs pretty closely. I had no idea I was such an important person."

Welby looked at him with a suavely ironic smile.

"We keep a pretty close eye on every one, especially when his occupations are not accounted for by public service in the present emergency," he said. "You perceive that there would naturally arise some hesitation in permitting you to go to Russia at a time like this, when that confounded country is riddled with German pacifist agitation and activities, when information is everywhere leaking out to the enemy, and all the efforts of His Majesty's Government are scarcely able to keep Russia up to her obligations toward the Allies. You have been at one time or another in contact with Russian revolutionaries, it seems," Welby said, glancing again at the papers. "There is no harm whatever in that, no harm whatever. It is even conceivable that situations might arise that would render it desirable to encourage the activities of those gentlemen. One never knows. But . . ."

"I am, in short, to understand that it is not possible for me to obtain a passport to Russia?" Julian said, breaking in.

"I'm afraid that's practically what it amounts to," Welby said. "I'm most frightfully sorry, old chap, don't you know," he added, after an impressive pause, regarding Julian with an expression of compunction. Julian leaned forward with his hand to his brow in a gesture of despair. "Most frightfully sorry. It's a damned shame I can't help you and that charming Princess. A bally shame. I know how you feel about it, old man. I have myself. . . . But there you are, what? If I were you, I should persuade the lady to remain quietly here, in jolly old England, for the present. It's a bally sight more comfortable than in Russia, I can tell you."

Julian rose abruptly, feeling it unnecessary to prolong the interview. "Thank you all the same, Welby," he said, holding out his hand.

"Most frightfully sorry, old chap," Welby kept repeating, as he followed Julian to the door. "And by the way, I shouldn't, if I were you, try to do anything about it, slip over by way of the continent, for instance, or anything like that, don't you know. Our people keep their eyes wonderfully wide open nowadays."

At the hotel, Zena was awaiting him. She knew before he had spoken. A pall, as though already she had been far away, was upon her while he recited, with slow detail, his interview. Zena listened, motionless, listless.

"What will you do?" he asked, looking up, when he had finished.

"I must go, dear." Her voice seemed to come from afar.

A sudden shattering within him obliterated all things.

"When?" he asked, breaking a heavy silence.

"By the next courier. It leaves on Saturday," she said.

A fury mounted within him, as though in hatred, as though he would kill her. Then, as he was about to speak, the tenseness fell. She was right, he knew she was right. It was he who was being unreasonable. But he did not speak, in his resentment.

Zena went slowly over to him, knelt, her arms about him. She spoke with a different voice, no longer distant, close, close to him.

"Dear, dear, don't you see? It was in joy, in beauty and joy that we loved. Now . . . there is no longer any joy, or beauty, or what, in sheepish mockery, the world calls romance. The world has changed. Our love must needs change also. Long ago . . . long ago, do you remember? I told you I was no heroine, not brave, not noble. I am not strong enough for tragedy. And this England! I hate this England where all, all is sham . . . where even people's emotions turn to sham . . . where this thing, this war, even, is made a show. . . . It chokes me, chokes me, this England."

In his darkness, the tenseness was relaxed. He kissed, in silence, her hair. She was right, wholly right. He wished he could have accounted her wrong, have vented on her his protest, the protest of his whole being against the unjust thing—impersonal, intangible, that was slaying him.

"We shall be together again," she said. "Oh, I know we shall be again together. I know it, I tell you."

He kissed her, briefly, rising, taking a pace or two.

"Listen," she said. "We have five days yet. Five days till the courier goes. Five days all our own. Let us forget, forget, forget everything for five days."

Julian smiled back with bitter, sceptical tenderness.

Strangely, the intolerable strain broke down, actually, in what seemed a new joy, so unwonted had it become, in those last days. Strangely, so intolerable was the overhanging shadow that, almost, Julian forgot it—those five days. They went away. It didn't matter where. They found a quiet inn in Hampshire and for an instant the thought that she was there, his, obliterated the overhanging horror.

The illusion, the inconceivable illusion, lasted till the very last evening, when they went together to a little restaurant in Soho, and laughed over trifles. It persisted till the last good night.

The next morning, Julian hastened to Claridge's. The world still existed. He was about to see her.

Zena was sitting ready, dressed for the journey. She had ordered oysters and champagne. Julian could not taste them.

She sat very stiffly, very pale, her lips trembling.

"Please, let us not say much," she said.

It was an agony. Her presence, the sound of her voice, were an agony.

A servant came to say that the gentleman from the embassy was waiting downstairs. The man took the morocco dressing case and the rugs. When he had closed the door, they rose. Scarcely did they dare to kiss.

Zena arranged herself before a mirror.

Her voice was already as from another world.

"Wait a while before you go down," she said, "wait till I have gone." Then her hand was on the knob of the door. With a last look, she said: "Good-bye."

Julian stood with muscles taut to prevent himself from dropping limply on the floor. He counted the seconds, dazed. With an effort he left the room, descended the carpeted stairs, noiselessly, like a ghost.

In the hall a friendly clerk greeted him, smiling:

"Splendid news from the Front, this morning, sir," he said.

Julian did not trust himself to unclose his lips.

The car had not yet left. Porters had been arranging the luggage. Zena had just entered the car. The courier from the embassy was holding open the door, giving directions. As the man turned round, Julian saw his face. It was Pravduski, the violinist.

Julian staggered into a side-room. There was a taste of salt in his mouth.

Was it possible so to suffer? In the days of the Renaissance men carried a dagger which they called "misericord." Was there no "misericord" in the world when suffering transcended all limits? Deliberately, considerately he desired death. He had always been an optimist.

He had been, if ever man was, a lover of life. Again and again he had given life the benefit of the doubt. Once more life had betrayed him.

It would be absurd to kill oneself when death was stalking abroad. In that game of death, that fantastic, maniacal convulsion of an insane world, he might as well satisfy a last curiosity.

And so Julian joined up.

IV

"Better I go for the nurse, eh?" Keetje said.

All day Viola had not been feeling well. But towards evening she had been so much better that she had not asked, as she had intended, Mrs. Scrone, the cook, who went home at night, to tell Nurse Doylan. In the middle of the night the pain had again been so violent that Viola had got up, and was pacing up and down the room. It seemed to relieve her a little.

Keetje, hearing Viola move, had come in, a coat over her nightdress, her feet in red felt slippers.

"Wait. Perhaps I can hold out till daylight. But you had better put on some clothes," Viola said.

But she had to lean over the footboard of the bed. She uttered low, stifled moans. Her back felt as though it would break.

"You can't go, child. It is pitch dark," she said, when the pain had passed.

Only a few lights dimmed with blue paint were lit in the town, and none on the Aldwick road, because of the Zeppelins and submarines.

"I can ask Connie, next door, to go with me," Keetje said.

But as she was about to leave the room, Viola's pain became so sharp that she cried out. She threw herself across the bed and lay groaning. The pain did not leave her. She asked Keetje to bring a towel. The bed was soaking wet. Viola was lying doubled up, her drawn-up legs stiff. Keetje, as she arranged the towel as best she could, was reminded of the dead horse in the street at Antwerp that lay like a capsized wooden horse with its legs out.

Curious and a little frightened, Keetje stared as she tucked the towel under Viola. The skin bulged, enormous, as if it must tear. The lump moved when Viola cried, and then remained a while motionless. There was a whitish film bulging, and white flakes under it, floating like the snow flakes in the old glass paper-weight. Viola was moaning, with her lips tightly closed, straining, her face red. Yellowish water was dribbling from her. The lump seemed to have moved forward; the white thing looked like hair plastered down with soap. Viola gave a great scream, and the head slipped out, purplish red, wizened, covered with white cheesy flakes. Keetje held Viola's stiff leg. The baby dropped on to the bed, its face crisped and convulsed, its drawn-up fists clenched spasmodically. Its chest heaved, struggling, till it gave a little cry.

Viola had sunk exhausted. "Is it all right?" she asked.

"I think so," said Keetje, "but it is all covered with cheese."

Almost afraid to touch the little red, doubled-up thing, she arranged it in the towel, where it lay with eyes shut, breathing quietly. The long bluish white, opalescent cord, twisted like a braid, attached to its belly, hung limply from its mother.

"It is a man," said Keetje

Viola had stopped groaning now. Keetje gave her some water.

"I shall be all right now. You can go with Connie and fetch Mrs. Doylan," she said.

Mrs. Bern came down to stay with Viola—"to help her," she said. She added, in truth, greatly to the labors of the house and was terribly in the way. She had to have a cup of tea with a piece of toast before going to early mass, and a glass of sherry with a biscuit afterwards. Mrs. Bern sat in beatific fruition of vicarious maternity, bestowing advice, rehearsing the fruits of her experience. Boys had to have their napkins changed more often than girls. They should be primrose colored. When the baby had the wind, it should be laid on its stomach and given a few drops of dill water.

Little Harry had his father's fair hair and blue eyes. He was attired like an idol, in embroidered satin and lace. His layette and cot would not have been unbefitting a prince of the blood royal. Viola was, what with her special pension and gratuity, and some trifles of property that had come to Harry by bequest, fairly comfortably off. Nothing was too good for the ritual service of the baby. A room had been specially decorated and furnished as a nursery. Viola had her mother's large dark eyes, now dilated with a concentrated intensity of maternal passion, verging on unreasonableness.

The fierce blind force of life! What cause for exultation could there be in the bringing of one more human being into the world? So Julian thought when he, belatedly, came down to inspect his nephew. The Church might rejoice in one more stupefied soul, the British bourgeois empire in one more defender. The pulpy little creature's non-existent mind would presently unfold through the inculcation of chimerical fables and superstitions, would be stocked with the ideas by means of which it would think, feel, and battle, not one of which would have the remotest basis in reason or reality. Those inculcated stupidities would in all likelihood be for ever ineradicable. Should any glimmer of struggling intelligence survive the process, he would spend his life tortured by the interminable and futile conflict. Poor little pulpy Harry! About to become, in all probability, an insufferable little maleficent sham. Rejoice! Rejoice rather in the climacteric maniacal crisis of insanity, in the purifying carnage of poor sweet, bestial fools. The bloody carnage wipes a little dirt off the face of the earth. Rejoice where thou bemoanest; bemoan where thou rejoicest.

Julian's mother and sister beamed gratification and approval at seeing him in khaki. The uniform made good, wiped out certain unuttered disapprovals and reproaches. They could be proud of him now. (The bloodthirsty women!) And how the change had told on him already! There was a new strength in the brief decision of his words and the strength of his silence.

"Whilst in a state of temporary insanity,"—such would have been the verdict had his first impulse taken effect. Was there no jury to brand in like terms the delirium of his later decision? He had, in the crisis of his sick mind, thought to plunge, as one leaping with closed eyes into dark waters, into the maniacal Walpurgis night of death. He found himself instead grotesquely cabined amid the puerile activities of training camps. The monstrous thing could not even be dignified; it needs must, even in criminal folly, be ludicrous and mean.

It was the current belief among the recruits of the New Armies that the war would be over long before the deadly monotony of the puerile routine that went on from day to day, as though in itself an end.

He foregathered in the reek of unmitigated masculinity with boys, ranging from eighteen to forty-five, innocently arrested and sterile:

moronoi, mature aments. He found himself ignominiously set back to school, in a last anticlimax of indignity, relegated to a manner of premature senile infancy. Even though he had fraudulently curtailed his age by some three years, he felt embarrassingly mature among those babes. Nor could he wholly conceal his maturity. The nice Public-school boys would intuite hinterlands of unspoken thought which they interpreted as superior wisdom, and would at times inadvertently address Julian as "sir," as though he were a superior officer.

Darkly within glowered the final calm fury of reposeful despair. It ached with numb anguish grown familiar, the dear wound bleeding. He had received letters, forwarded from Bognor. The Pole, Pravduski, had been arrested at Stockholm, caught red-handed copying the diplomatic correspondence for transmission to Berlin. It had been a ghastly coincidence, she had lengthily explained. It might be true— or she may have been lying. What matter, sweet phantasm, what matter? Sooth or lie, can death touch the past? Can aught that is past touch death? Abide sweet memory.

Moira! In hours of freedom, Julian breathed the solitude of the barren moors, carrying, mayhap, a Greek elzevir in his pocket. Ye had sung in serene calm of horror and despair, of fate and folly, amid the delirium of war—

"Shall my thought lie concealed? It flieth from me, blowing like a bitter sea-wind before the prow, the wrath of my heart swollen with rancor, horrible and divine."

Mr. Hugh Viney, happening to catch a sight of the Greek page, desired to discourse with Mr. Bern concerning the discovery of new religions that would save the world.

"The sole breath of salvation ever vouchsafed the world, Mr. Viney, blew from Ionia when it set religion once for all aside, and Europe was born."

"Ah, Ionia? Cometh not all wisdom from the East?"

Language can but communicate to the hearer the repercussion of his own thoughts. My words shall be obscure unto thee, Mr. Viney. *Mirate il mistero che s'asconde sotto'l velame delle parole oscure.* "Can an idea move the world?"

"Why, sir, Christianity."

"Not Christianity, but revolt moved the slave throngs against tyrannous oppression to destroy it. It gave topical expression to the Day of Wrath, till it provided in turn oppression with a new weapon. Strife of possession and despair of dispossession, not ideas, destroyed a world, as now, in their contention."

Mr. Viney wondered respectfully, cogitating meanwhile the wisdom of Mrs. Annie Besant.

With fierce obduracy, Julian grimly, unsparing of sinew and spirit, mastered the military puerilities. The tense wrath within vented its violence in drills, route marches in columns of four, schemes in extended order, musketry practice. In his hardened flesh the blood tingled, tempering anew the force of futile will. He outdistanced requirements in his enquiries, dipping into Clausewitz and Jomini, Kuhne and the later Frenchmen. His instructors distinguished Mr. Bern by their esteem, holding him up to the young gentlemen of the O.T.C. as a soldierly example. Colonel Rische ffolliot Willis, D.S.O., one time instructor to the forces of H.R.H., the Maharajah of Guanipur, now commanding the young gentlemen in training, honored Mr. Bern with his confidence over whiskey pawnee and cheroots, and intimated the hope that, following upon his special recommendation, Mr. Bern's commission would bestow upon him a full lieutenantship.

On evenings off duty, the young gentlemen required Mr. Bern's company on visits to the attractions of the variety show and the whores in the neighboring town, festive with the unwonted influx of khaki and polished buttons, and prolific in provisions for the entertainment of heroes. Mr. Bern's outward semblance acceded with due goodfellowship to the convivial instigations, he being by general repute a good sport, though retaining a strange sobriety in the revels.

Young Mr. Burd, sometimes known as the Babe, whose conspicuous minority cast doubts upon the veracity of Orderly Room records, lost his virginity on one of the festive occasions. Young Mr. Burd's virginity supplied for several weeks a topic of light conversation and pleasant wit in the young gentlemen's mess. Young Mr. Burd's aunt provided the young gentlemen's mess with weekly parcels of Dundee cake and home-made jam, accompanied by copies of the *Church Times*.

Mr. Bern, with Mr. Viney, Mr. Dummer, and some others, were in due course of time beloved by the King and honored with his commission. They received orders for transfer to Depot (Officers, drafts) First Fifth Mercian battalion on Salisbury plain. Young Mr. Burd was at the like time honored by the King, but had, on M.O.'s orders, to be transferred to C Hospital with a clap.

The Fifth were in France, presumably in full strength.

"This stinking hole may be your home for duration," the young officers were hopefully informed by Captain Albemarle Percy Inglis, who, after a long convalescence from a bullet wound in the buttocks, had just been returned for duty, class A. "Better than being on the other side, anyhow, what?"

Captain Inglis made no secret of his distaste for active service. He had, after the comfortable Blighty received during his first week in France, managed by bold and tireless wangling to spend six glorious months amid the pleasures of England. He confided to Julian some particulars concerning the "crummy lot of girls" whose favors had assuaged the tedium of his convalescence. Captain Inglis was downcast at the failure of his more recent efforts to elicit a further extension of his convalescent leave, but was not without hope of the outcome of further endeavors to obtain an appointment as bombing instructor at depot.

Among other occupants of H and I huts, for officers (drafts), was Lieutenant Roger Fullison, who had come all the way from the Argentine to rally to the defence of the empire. Mr. Fullison, whose father was a Yorkshireman and his mother a "gallega," had a swarthy countenance and Latin nonchalance, which justified the appellative of "Caballero" by which he was generally referred to among the young officers, and interspersed his English with the South American variety of Castilian speech, which came even more naturally to his lips. The Caballero gave, with the help of a horrible gramophone with red tulip tin funnel, bequeathed to the mess by a former occupant, now on the roll of honor, demonstrations of the Argentine tango, from which Captain Albemarle Percy Inglis derived considerable advantage, acquiring with much sedulousness new and graceful steps which could not fail to impress some of the crummy lot of girls whose acquaintance he was privileged to enjoy. The absence of feminine partners in H and I huts somewhat marred the choreographic studies of the young officers.

"When I have had a good talk with the Old Man, we'll have a run up to town, and have some fun, what?" Captain Inglis proposed to Mr. Bern and the Caballero.

Mr. Bern, being on duty as orderly officer when Captain Inglis and the Caballero obtained leave to carry out the expedition, was unable to accompany them. But he was, during the week following their return from the metropolis, entertained with detailed reports, including sartorial and anatomical particulars, of the successful raid.

"Ripping time, what?" stated Captain Inglis, glancing to the Caballero for confirmation.

"*Mierda! Habrase visto!*" exclaimed the Caballero.

"Those two girls we picked up at the 'Ship,' what? Working at the W.O., don't you know. Diggings in Jermyn Street. While the one played the piano, we danced in turn with the other. Nothing on but their little wisps of chemmies, what? Had a ballum raucum, didn't we?"

"*Pues, una boda!*" the Caballero confirmed.

His father, a wealthy ranchero owning illimitable acres on the Rio Colorado pampa, was making pots of money from hides and frozen meat. The Caballero confided in a sentimental mood to Julian his nostalgia for the glorious freedom of the "camp," the endless rides on "fletes," in poncho and chambergo, to the confines of the Cordilleras; the revels among the gauchos and peons by the "quinques" fires or at the posada of the estancia, when the guitarists sat on horses' skulls, and the men and women danced the "cueca"; the luxury and pleasures of Buenos Aires, where his father had a palace on the Esmeralda and kept a stable of polo ponies.

"Thought I'd be getting into the cavalry. But it appears they've no longer any cavalry in this *mierda* of a war," he said.

"What the deuce made you come over?" Julian enquired. "Felt you had to lay down your life for the flag and the empire, I suppose?"

"Empire *mierda! Me ne cujo!*" the Caballero replied. "Why I came over? *Quien sabe?* Damned if I know. Because I'm a bloody fool, I suppose. Sport, perhaps, you know. War, the original of all sports, and all that sort of rot."

Lieutenant J. Bern directed the military exercises of the 5th Mercian (drafts and reinforcements) in the bull-ring, on route marches, musketry practice, strategic attacks on dummy trenches, and bayonet exercise on pendant sacks in the effigy of sons of the Fatherland. He led details and reinforcements to C of E Church parade on Sundays, and lectured them upon soldierly duty, reading out from "Infantry Training"—

"The moral qualities to be developed by a soldier include self-control, self-respect, patriotism, loyalty, pride of race, and a high sense of humor —as you were—of honor. The growth of these moral qualities will be fostered chiefly by environment, and it is the duty of all ranks to assist in this object by their conversation and example. The value of the co-operation of the Army Chaplains' department in this connection should not be lost sight of."

Lieutenant Bern would unaccountably absent himself from festive evenings, raucous with the sound of the gramophone in H and I huts, and canorous speculations as to what might be—

"If I were the only boy in the world
And you were the only girl—"

to take further exercises on the more desolate portions of the plain.

Mr. Viney would at times offer to accompany him.

"Noisy young fellows, are they not, Mr. Bern? It becomes a bit trying for people like you and me, who are inclined to serious thought."

Against the scarlet streaks of a bloody sunset, the trilithons of Stonehenge stood outlined, and were descried with emotion by Mr. Viney, who sought Mr. Bern's opinion concerning the science of the Druids.

"Do you think, Mr. Bern, that the Druids derived their knowledge from the Egyptians?" queried Mr. Viney.

"Or from the sapience of the oak, which being impregnated by the rays of the moon, turns mistletoe, which in turn causes kine and women to be with child. The Druid Merlin, the founder of Stonehenge, caused the stones to move over from Ireland, whither they had been conveyed from Africa by giants, as we are informed in the Triads, in order, as Geoffrey of Monmouth tells, to mark the sepulchre of Constantine, buried there by the side of Uther Pendragon. Although the temple be elsewhere attributed to Aurelius Ambrosius, the successor of Vortigern. And from the oak of Sein, great Merlin, thither waylaid by nine Druids and enchanted by the Lady of the Lake, gave forth oracles, as reported by Pomponius Mela, and confirmed by the immortal bard—

> " 'When bawds and whores do churches build
>   Then shall the realm of Albion
>   Come to great confusion.'

This prophecy Merlin shall make; for I live before his time."

In the city of Salisbury, Julian came upon "Colonel" Thorpe, who was down on an enquiry into the conduct of some Canadians having their camp on the Plain. The Dominion contingent had had to be withdrawn from France on account of alleged danger to our allies. Near the venerable records of Druidic science, the night had, it was charged, been rent by the screams of a damsel in distress. Four gallant oversea troopers had hastened to the rescue, and had discovered one of their company engaged in attempted rape upon a V.A.D. employed in a nearby army bakery, with whom he had formed a platonic friendship. Seeing the difficulty which their comrade encountered from the young woman's resistance, the lads of the maple had promptly lent their aid, holding the lady's limbs and gagging her mouth, thereafter sharing the spoils in turn. "Colonel" Thorpe had been called to watch the case in the interests of the V.A.D.'s and to testify as to their morals. She was staying at the deanery, in the cathedral close, the Dean's wife being active in assisting her to maintain high standards of purity in the feminine corps.

"It is a great responsibility," Miss Thorpe said. "But Lady Bar is most particular that no effort should be neglected to uphold the good repute of the unit. She was down the other day to talk with the Dean on the subject."

From Miss Thorpe, Julian learned in the course of a pleasantly civilised meal at the George—remains of Roman wall in the lounge and fine double ale—that Everard had received a D.S.O. for distinction at Neuve Chapelle. Julian had missed the announcement. Like most of the young gentlemen, he had dropped into the habit of never reading the papers, and shared the general ignorance as to the progress of the war. Was there a war? All quiet on the Western front. Artillery duels. A war of attrition.

"When I was out at the front . . ." Miss Thorpe said, "at Etaples, I mean. . . ."

"I beg your pardon."

"Sir Douglas Haig told me that the great offensive in the spring will be the biggest battle in history."

While young officers were at mess one morning, a chit was brought from Orderly Room informing Lieutenant J. Bern that the Secretary, War Office, London, required his immediate presence. The announcement caused much surmise among the young officers.

"K. of K. wants you on the G.S., Bern, what?" suggested Captain Inglis.

"Or they're going to make you G.O.C., *mierda*," put in the Caballero.

The adjutant was unable to cast light upon the matter. The order was to report at the War Office, B.J., 369.

Julian, less agitated than his mess mates, slumbered in the railway compartment to Waterloo. At the War Office, a pathetic crowd of men and women filled the dark, dingy hall where casualty lists were posted up. A queue lined up to the desk where a blue liveried porter handed out forms to fill, stating their business, and distributed slips of yellow paper on which he scribbled figures to the boy scouts and girl guides who moved in and out.

Julian, when his turn came, presented his orders.

"Here, Jimmy, B.J. 369," called the blue-coated official without raising his head, to a boy scout who stood by disengaged.

After a route march along interminable staircases and corridors, Julian was introduced into a room where a handsome young staff captain with a carefully trained, silky moustache and a high-pitched Public-school accent, was engaged in sipping coffee, smoking cigarettes, and looking at the *Vie Parisienne*. He greeted Julian smilingly with a cheery "Good morning."

"I'll see if the general is disengaged. Won't you take a pew? Do," he said, and went into an adjacent room.

The general in whose presence Julian was presently ushered turned out to be no other than his Uncle Horace. He was resplendent. His riding-boots armored with enormous spurs and his sambrowne shone like mirrors. Two rows of brightly colored ribbons adorned his tunic. Sir Horace's hair, now glowing white, was no less highly polished than his boots and buttons, and his face was red from long weathering on the golf course. General Sir Horace Penmore had been occupied, when Julian was introduced, in playing a game of solitaire, which was spread out on the large green-covered mahogany table before which he sat. He greeted Julian with inarticulate sounds which were the perfection of amiability, and out of which presently emerged occasional key words.

"Er—er—wh—what? Jolly decent of you, my boy, er what? to have joined up, what? Jolly decent, by Jove. Take . . . er—a pew—er. The old country, what? And all that?"

After a considerable amount of nervous vocalisation, and clearing of his throat, Sir Horace settled down to communicate the purport of the business which had led him to require his nephew's attendance.

"I hear . . . er . . . you've been writing a book about bugs and things, what? Sorry haven't had time to read it. So busy, don't you know. But fellows have been telling me it's jolly fine. Er . . . jolly fine. Er . . . well . . . hm . . . hm . . . Where was I? Oh, yes. You know, over there in the Dardanelles, flies have been killing more of our fellows than the Turks, what? Shit fever, don't you know, and all that. Positively dying like flies, our fellows, because of the flies. Well . . . er . . . Kitchener was saying to me the other day: Horace, we ought to do something about it, what? And one of the fellows said we ought to send out some fellow to lecture about flies, don't yer know? Eh, what? And I thought to myself, by Jove, you're just the very man for it. See, what?"

Julian sat impassive while Sir Horace delivered himself with some difficulty of the lengthy oration.

"I don't really know anything about flies, sir," he said, while Sir Horace was taking breath.

"Tut, tut, my dear fellow, you're not quite used to the army yet . . . er . . . what? Nobody wants you to know anything about flies. We have some demn lance-corporal who used to work at the museum in Cromwell road, who knows all about flies. He can write all the paw-waw for you and tell you anything you want to know. What I mean to say is it's about the demndest cushy job I ever heard of, what? The demndest cushiest job. By the way, I believe the flies are all gone.

Season over, what? No responsibility or any demned thing like that. Old Saxford . . . you know old Saxford, I believe? . . . has placed his yacht at our disposal, the *Nereid*. You just go down to Alex, take the yacht, and just take it round for a cruise pawwawing about flies as long as you like. Eh, what? Cushiest thing I ever heard of. Know Cairo? Jolly lot of fellows there. Fine golf course. Heliopolis, eighteen holes. Jolly sight cushier than sitting in this demned office, what? Jolly glad I thought of you, my boy, what?"

"It's frightfully kind of you to have done so, sir," Julian said.

"Tut, tut . . . not a word, not a word, my boy. Always do the best we can for our own people in the army, what?"

"But, Uncle Horace, I'm very sorry, but I don't think I can accept."

"Er . . . er . . . what?" said Sir Horace, sitting up in his chair.

"The fact is I joined up with the idea of going to the Front."

"The Front? The Front? Demned unhealthy place from what I've been told. Sort of place a fellow would like to keep away from."

"Awfully sorry, Uncle Horace, but that's the way I feel. Of course, if it's an order, sir, I have to obey. But I'd rather not."

Sir Horace, genuinely hurt and indignant, assumed a purplish color and his brows appeared more shaggy.

"All I can say is that you're a demned fool, a demned fool!"

He, however, restrained his excusable indignation at Julian's unsoldierly behavior, and so far mastered his feelings as to close the interview with the dignity becoming a gentleman and a soldier.

"By the way, do you happen to know anything about this demned game? I've had five goes at it and can't get the demned thing out."

The incredible rumor was circulating in depot that the 5th Mercian, (drafts and detail) were shortly to proceed to France. Some weeks later the report was confirmed by orders from Western Command to stand by in readiness for overseas service. Outworn articles of clothing and accoutrement to be replaced from issue at Q.M. stores, iron rations and field dressings to be drawn, together with thirty rounds of ammunition, and identity discs checked, and where necessary renewed. Ten days later orders came to the 5th Mercian (details and reinforcements) for embarkation at Newhaven, under Captain A. P. Inglis, in command, and Lieutenant R. Fullison, second in command. A subsidiary order directed Lieutenant J. Bern, Second Lieutenants Viney, Dummer, Mellin, and Burd—discharged from C Hospital—to proceed to Aldershot for duty.

Captain Inglis, greatly perturbed, made a last desperate appeal to the adjutant and C.O., who, yielding to his insistence, granted him an interview at I A.M. in his pyjamas. Captain Inglis alleged symptoms of imperfect circulation in his lower extremities resulting from injuries sustained in action. But Captain Murphy, R.A.M.C., after inspecting Captain Inglis's buttocks, pronounced them A I, and Captain Inglis's offer to resign the privileges of seniority were without effect upon the plan of campaign.

Accommodation for young officers (drafts) being overtaxed at Aldershot, Mr. Bern and the other young gentlemen were billeted at Farnborough, at the Queen's, the manager of which establishment had recently been shot as a German spy. A large service passage at the back of the stairs had been converted into a dormitory by the erection of sacking partitions and wire-netting bunks. The accommodation was familiarly known as the rabbit-hutch. It was already occupied by a number of young officers unattached for the time being, and redundant with animal spirits.

Here were six weeks spent in complete idleness, the outlet afforded for distraction by drills, route marches, and exercises being denied, and leave sparingly conceded, owing to the fiction that the young officers were standing by in readiness for service at an instant's notice. Night was made hideous in the rabbit-hutch by young cubs yelling their guts out, drinking whiskey from bottles which strewed the floor and playing poker till the small hours. Julian, having exhausted the picturesque aspects of Aldershot and environs, spent hours stretched out on the rabbit netting endeavoring to make up for lost sleep. The attendant maidens of the establishment took deep interest in the defenders of their country, and from his wire bunk, Lieutenant Bern heard in adjoining compartments the respiratory gurgles, groans, sighs and slaverings, and the sounds produced by the intimate friction of epidermal and mucous surfaces, which attend the congress of the sexes.

Second Lieutenant Pearce, an insufferable fellow, who rushed round, flushed with whiskey, arrogantly elbowing opposition out of his way, was the ringleader of the riots in the rabbit-hutch. He was dead drunk when, much to Lieutenant Bern's relief, he received orders for France. Pearce stole Lieutenant Bern's shaving brush. Julian had to buy another at the Army and Navy Stores, Aldershot branch, for ten shillings and sixpence, a poor substitute for the silver-mounted one which formed part of a dressing set bought on the Croisette, at Cannes. Zena had given him the present the day they had gone to Mentone. How sweet her look when she gave it! At the Alexandra, at Carnioles, when they had lunch at a table by the window, she said she liked the way he ate. Curious idea. It was the first time he really knew. *Eritis sicut deus, scientes bonum et malum.* Did it really all happen? Or had he dreamed that other life? Woman's love. My God, how melting sweet! The old helpless formulas came out to voice the unutterable. Oh, God! Dushka! Drowning men saw their whole past, they said. Was he drowning?

"Stop your yelling, you damned, imbecile young cubs! Stop it, I say, or I'll report the whole lot of you, you abominable young idiots!"

Silence. No one offered reply. Lieutenant Bern looked dangerous. His hand twitched in the direction of his revolver holster.

At long last! "To proceed to Folkestone for embarkation and report to O.C., L.o.C., Echelon, Boulogne. Twenty-four hours' leave."

Julian went over to Bognor to say good-bye. Viola was tenderly solicitous. She gave him Harry's field glasses and prismatic compass, returned to her by the War Office. Little Harry was expecting a tooth. Was it so long a time? Time, time stood still. Scarcely did Julian know the date. His mother gave him a medal of Our Lady of Loretto. Her eyes were moist when he left to catch the train to Waterloo.

Mewing gulls balancing on the Channel breezes; rainbows flickering on the blown spray; the white cliffs fading behind indigo mists. How exhilarating it always was to leave England! There were Salvation Army women on board singing hymns, and Y.M.C.A. men in spurious khaki. Two grey torpedo-boat destroyers scuttled back and forth as far as Gris Nez. The crazy roofs of Boulogne crowding down the spur of the cliff, etched against a pale sky, the blown clouds scattering sunlight and shadow. . . .

At the wharf an R.T.O. shouted through a megaphone: "All drafts forward to the station. Find your kits there. Hurry up." Julian showed the R.T.O. his orders.

"Move on forward. Wait a minute. What division? Don't know? Report at L.o.C. Orderly Room, Boulevard Saint Boove. Military police will show you. Pick out your kit and dump it anywhere here."

A cheery K.O.S.B. captain with whom Julian had exchanged a few words on the boat whispered to him as he passed by: "Hang on to your kit like hell, old man, or you'll never see it again."

Julian and the young officers rescued their kit from the loaded lorry. A French porter with a barrow offered to take charge of it. They followed him to the Boulevard Sainte-Beuve.

As a boy, Sainte-Beuve obtained his one memorable glimpse of the great Napoleon at Boulogne in the act of making water against a wall.

Boulogne in khaki. Grey ambulances with red crosses rushing round on the cobbles. Military police with red covers to their caps directing traffic.

At Orderly Room a corporal, a supercilious, politely impertinent despot, informed Lieutenant Bern and the young officers that it was unnecessary to report to C.O. or adjutant. Handed out orders to proceed to D camp, on Wimereux road. A.S.C. lorry would call for kit.

By Napoleon's column, the young officers vegetated in idleness in a crowded hut for several weeks. Viney, Dummer, and Mellin had never been on the continent. Young Mr. Burd had been to Paris once for a week at Easter with his aunt. Cafés in the Rue Victor Hugo and shops selling smutty books in English rather exciting. Young Mr. Burd caught another dose of the clap, and was sent to hospital.

Deadly, almost maddeningly intolerable, was the interminable idleness. Lieutenant Bern and young officers of 5th Mercian had apparently been completely forgotten. Were they to remain in this concentration camp for the duration of the war? Daily, other officers received orders to join their units and departed for the Front. The personnel of the camp was several times completely renewed. Lieutenant Bern and the young officers became the oldest inhabitants.

There was suddenly great excitement in the town. A big battle, it appeared, was raging. Trainload after trainload of wounded began to pour in, a continuous stream. The French population crowded silently round the railway station and the hospitals to see the men borne on stretchers, wrapped in bandages, some blood-soiled. The streets were blocked with ambulances. The hotels and the casino, converted into hospitals, were full. One caught glimpses, through the large panes of the casino, of surgeons and nurses moving in the baccara room, turned into an operating theatre.

Lieutenant Bern, his endurance at an end, called at the Orderly Room, one afternoon, in an irritable mood, and demanded to see the C.O. He defied the politely impertinent corporal who arrogantly sought to oppose a determined resistance, saying that it was no use disturbing the C.O. He must await orders.

When Julian had almost forcibly intruded into the presence of the officer, a youngish man with florid face, very elegantly clad in slacks, silk socks, and a starched shirt under his tunic, the gentleman broke out irately.

"What are you doing at D camp? You should have joined your unit three weeks ago. Why the hell didn't you report before? Corporal Jenkins will give you your orders."

Corporal Jenkins, whose direction of the movements of the B.E.F. had never before been challenged, made out orders for Lieutenant Bern and young officers.

"Say, Freddie, d'you know where the Fifth Mercian are?" he enquired of a lance-corporal with an elaborately dressed head of hair and the stump of a cigarette behind his ear, who was tapping at a typewriter.

"Fifth Mercian?" Lance-corporal Freddie repeated, looking up dreamily, "I think they're 63d."

Orders directed the Mercian officers to be at the central station at eight o'clock punctually. It was a great hustle to get there and obtain transportation for the kit in time. The train in which the young officers were accommodated in a dilapidated first class compartment steamed slowly out half an hour after midnight.

Stiff and aching from attempts to sleep in unnatural postures, pillowed on packs and valises, they found themselves at dawn meandering at a leisurely pace among green fields. They passed a road edged with an endless perspective of poplars, a farm where a French peasant in "bleu horizon" and a forage cap was pitchforking manure, smoking a pipe. A welcome sun warmed their cold and stiff limbs.

"Pretty country, France, isn't it?" remarked Mr. Viney.

The train came presently to a stop at a place which seemed to be nowhere in particular. There was no station, not a habitation in sight. Nothing but numerous sidings. Some one called out for everybody to detrain.

There was a general scramble of men, a hauling of packs and valises, a din of oaths and jocular remarks.

"Where are we?"

"Clapham Junction. Change for Crystal Palace."

"Lor' Blimy, I've lost me bleeding kit."

"It's all right, Bill. I've got your pack. Pull up your trousers."

From a closed van marked: $\frac{Hommes\ 40}{Chevaux\ 8}$ issued shouts and a stream of foulest language.

"Order there. Stop your bloody yelling, will you?" called a gunner sergeant running up to the scene of the disturbance and addressing the closed van.

From its depth the flow of eloquence continued.

"Bugger yourself. You wouldn't 'alf yell, you wouldn't, if you was wedged in between two fucking hosses."

"Entertainment for man and beast," smiled a young R.T.O. who was standing by, wearing his tunic and sambrowne over pyjamas.

"Where do we go now?" Julian enquired of him.

"What division?"

"Sixty-third."

"Corby. That's your train over there. The one to the left. Starting in half an hour."

"What's the name of this place?" enquired Mr. Dummer.

"Cæsar's Camp."

"Corby, where's that?" Mr. Viney queried of Julian.

"Corbie, probably. A nest of heresy. Father Ratamnus denied the miracle of the mass, *De Corpore et sanguine Domini,* as against Radbertus Paschasius. The Benedictines of Corbie Abbey first spread scholastic learning in Germany. Founded Corbia Nova, on the Weser. Progenitors of German pedantry, which writes itself in the old French

blackletter brought from Corbie, since styling itself German. German
Kultur. Remaining scholastic to Kant and onward."

With delight, hot coffee and ham sandwiches were obtained from a
Y.M.C.A. canteen. The spirits of the young officers and their chilled
insides revived.

The train by which they proceeded steamed eventually into a big
station, then steamed out of it again.

"Amiens," Julian remarked. "Pretty good going. We're half an
hour from where we started off last night."

Towards noon they arrived at Corbie.

A large convoy of German prisoners, several hundreds, were en-
training. They looked smart, marching in quick step under their own
N.C.O.'s escorted by guards with fixed bayonets.

"By Jove! Looks as though we were winning the war," said Mr.
Dummer.

"Just had a big show, you know," said a young officer in a Kilgarry,
with whom they got talking. "We're almost through. Be in Germany
in a week or two. The cavalry is standing by to go into action. Open
warfare now. It's the beginning of the end."

"We'll just come in at the finish," said Mr. Viney.

At the R.T.O.'s office Lieutenant Bern presented his orders.

"Fifth Mercian?" the assistant R.T.O. queried. "Why, there's no
such thing. Not in the 63d at any rate. Ever hear of the Fifth Mercian?" he enquired of another officer. After some research through piles
of dog-eared files, the assistant R.T.O. informed Lieutenant Bern that
the 5th Mercian were in the 36th division.

"Just a clerical error, don't you know. Figures got reversed. You'll
get a train back to Boulogne about twelve o'clock tonight."

V

WHEN the 5th Mercian had been warned for service in France with the first drafts of the New Armies, an impressive ceremony had been enacted at the factory of Messrs. W. H. Foster & Co., at Leicester, for the purpose of the presentation by the staff of a sword of honor to Captain Laurence Foster, the son of the managing director. The head-foreman of works had, in artless words, made a little speech expressing the loyalty and devotion to the firm of all the employees and hands, through whose contributions, which they had gladly consented should be retained out of their pay, the weapon had been purchased. The speaker made a touching reference to the recipient's younger brother, Captain Harry Foster, who had heroically made the supreme sacrifice on the field of honor. He also dwelt on the scarcely less heroic and patriotic example set by the honored head of the firm, Mr. William Foster, who had been one of the first to place his factory at the disposal of the country, and who was now giving another son to the cause of England, Justice, and Right.

After the recipient had very briefly expressed his thanks, Mr. William Foster addressed the gathering. His voice was tremulous with emotion and his eyes dimmed with moisture. The report of his speech occupied two columns in the *Leicester Mail*.

None indeed, he said, could know the extent and magnitude of his sacrifice. But he had always placed duty before selfish interests and personal feelings. No selfish consideration would ever stand in the way of his doing his duty, his whole duty, in the cause of King and country, which was the cause of God. The men had also done their duty. How could they do otherwise when England was calling her sons to the defence of Right, the defence of the weak and the oppressed, the defence of small nations? He was proud that the workmen of his factory had so nobly answered the call. Every man who could be spared, consistently with the efficient carrying on of the work—the sacred work, he might be permitted to say—which, setting all meaner tasks aside, the factory had undertaken in the service of the country and the army, had joined the colors. The speaker felt bound to add some words in recognition of the self-sacrifice and patriotism shown by the women and girls, who had stepped nobly into the breach to set free their men, husbands, fathers, brothers, for the service of the country, even though they must naturally be content with a lower scale of pecuniary remuneration. Mr. Foster concluded by dwelling with stirring eloquence upon the unique demonstration of selfless national unity which England, inspired by the ordeal of battle, was setting to the world. There no longer were differences of party or politics, of classes, of workers and employers, of rich and poor. "Today we are all brothers, standing shoulder to shoulder in the defence of Right, all equally prepared to confront in that sacred cause and in that of England and the King, every sacrifice and every danger."

The stirring allocution produced its effect upon the emotions of the audience, which repeatedly broke into cheers, although many eyes, especially among the women and girls, were moist with tears.

Only in one member, perhaps, of the assembled company did the ceremony and the display of eloquence which attended it give rise to different emotions. The recipient of the presentation was filled with shame. He has spent a large portion of his emotional life in feeling ashamed; ashamed of the whole ambient world in which he lived and moved; ashamed of himself for being inextricably bound down to the fictions which make up that world, and which serve to cover its callous and unscrupulous selfishness; ashamed of lacking the courage, or the power, or, to put it more correctly, the individuality to break the bonds which bind men to lies. In a previous portion of this chronicle he so completely effaced himself as to violate, wittingly enough, accepted artistic standards. In candid truth, I should not have the heart to write about myself. Does any one? Is not so-called autobiography more brazenly fictitious than any other fiction? We set apologies for ourselves, and give out the fake as self-portraiture and self-confession. I had come to know well enough the falsehood and meanness of the insolently smug world in which I had grown and lived. Yet so truly had it nurtured me that I was, whether I willed it or no, a part of it, and if anything in me had succeeded in growing to independent individuality, it barely availed to discover to my consciousness the sham which that world was, and which I, its nurtured product, was doomed to be. I was unequal to throwing off the nurture, the fashioned substance out of which I had been kneaded, and which had come to constitute my "individuality." Individuality! It makes individuality impossible, that narrow shackling world which, from cradle to grave, constricts the faked mind and the faked heart with hoops of steel. It renders individuality impossible, that world which, with supreme cynical irony, prates of "individualism," which with supreme effrontery proclaims itself the defender of individualism. I, Laurence Foster, am one of its "individuals." I have therefore no individuality, and the utmost effort of veracity of which I am capable is to have, at least, no illusions on the subject. I am a miserable English Middle Class man, a *petit bourgeois*. Why, then, should I write about myself? I shall continue, therefore, to keep my own insignificant personality as far as possible out of the present narrative, except in so far as such an intrusion is absolutely unavoidable.

At the time of the ceremony to which I have just referred, the relations between my father and myself, which had for some time been growing increasingly strained, had reached the climax of an open outburst. When I left the university my father had been anxious that I should join him in the conduct of the business, hoping that I might in time succeed him in the direction. But the whole thing was unspeakably repulsive to me. Knowing the conditions under which the work was carried out—I had studied some economics at college—I felt utterly humiliated in the presence of our workers. When, some time before the outbreak of war, my father consulted me about the considerable fall in returns which was taking place owing to American competition and the increasing use of silk, natural and artificial, and told me that a substantial cut in the wages of the staff would be necessary in order to maintain the rate of dividends, I replied by handing over to him the shares in the company which had been allotted to me, so that the proceeds might be employed to make up the deficit. From that time I endeavored to maintain myself by the contribution of articles to various papers and magazines. I was beginning to establish the foundations of a relative pecuniary independence from my family when the war suddenly put an end to the prospects of my literary career. My mode of writing could not well adapt itself to the purposes of patriotic propaganda, the only form of literature then remaining. My father had, immediately on the declaration of war, obtained large Government contracts for the manufacture of webbing for military equipment. The factory had been enormously extended. The men, except such foremen as were indispensable to the conduct of the works, had been bluntly told to "enlist or go." Cheap female and infant labor was now obtainable in abundance. It now everywhere replaced male labor. Wages were cut to less than half. Hours of work were extended without limit. From the very beginning of the war, colossal profits were accumulated which rose higher and higher, and my father's fortune was, even in the early period of the war, multiplied tenfold. He was once more anxious, especially after my brother's death at the Front, that I should join him as junior partner in the business, and resign my commission in the territorial battalion with which I had for some time been associated. For once, I was moved to speak out my mind.

"I do not wish ever again to touch one penny coming from your infamous sweatshop," I burst out in a flush of anger. "Henceforth, if I survive, I shall provide for myself."

The scene took place in my father's office at the factory, immediately before the presentation of the sword of honor.

Like the men, I had no choice but to "enlist or starve."

A few days later the battalion was in France. Our first months at the Front proved an unexpectedly welcome and almost exhilarating liberation from the atmosphere of constraint and falsehood in which we had been living at home. We were in the Fleurbaix sector, one of the quietest parts of the line. Glancing through my diaries of the period, I smile on finding references to "incessant firing," "violent bombardments." Such expressions, though our inexperience did not realize it at the time, were but rhetorical figures. The enemy seemed to observe the convention "live and let live." Never during our three months' occupancy did he let off a salvo of more than five shells, which appeared to be about his daily ration of "hate." Our village billets were pleasant and within easy access of the agreeable little towns of Estaires and Armentières. We got the impression that war was far jollier than peace.

We were soon disillusioned when, from the nursery of the Fleurbaix sector, we were transferred to the canal bank at Ypres. There we learned what a bombardment meant, the ceaseless spitting of enfilading machine-guns, the proximity of trench-mortars, and not least, gas. The old P. H. helmets were still our only protection against the latter. I once saw a man mad with the suffocation and pain cut his throat with his bayonet. The winter of '15–'16 completed our tempering. The liquid mud in which we stood behind our meagre sandbag breastwork reached above the thigh-boots with which we were tardily supplied. We came out of the purgatory seasoned warriors, but the battalion was, like Paddy's knife, made over when we took the southward road from Poperinghe. It was once more, and even more completely, decimated in the shambles of the 1st of July. A few days later, the reduced remnant had again been cast into the furnace at Thiepval. It was but the skeleton of a battalion which crawed wearily back from the Ancre to the village billets that had been allotted to us at Brigade reserve.

Yet no sooner had we reached the comparative security of the "back" than the ghastly reality was well-nigh forgotten, and our animal spirits became engrossed in the delight of feeling our four limbs sound and in the consciousness that life still held possibilities of joy. The men set to making themselves as comfortable as possible in the battered grange where the companies took up their quarters. The bare, brick-floored billets in the farm houses of the dilapidated village seemed sybaritic luxury. We exulted in the sense of wellbeing that followed a shave and a sponge tub, in the promise of sensual comfort held out by the sight of our sleeping valises spread over wire stretchers by our faithful batmen, in the delicious smell of cooking which pervaded the mess and tickled our expectant appetites.

At battalion headquarters, cheerful with the light of candles guttering over bottlenecks, Corporal Saunders was unpacking the mess hamper and aligning a formidable array of live bottles on the dresser. Captain Scrutch, R.A.M.C., was skilfully compounding "trinities," *secundum artem,* mixing two vermouths and the gin in *partes equales,* much to the appreciation of Padre Cramp, who through all tribulations clung to the mess cart like Faith to the Rock of Ages. Major Sotty, temporarily in command—the C.O. having gone down with a grazed shoulder wound sustained at Auchonvillers—declared, after the third whiskey and soda, that he felt better.

"Wait a moment, Weeney," he said to the adjutant, who had come in to submit the casualty returns for signature, "this requires some preparation," and poured himself out a fourth whiskey to fortify himself against the worst. The Major inspected and countersigned the dismal documents in silence, confining himself to a prolonged sniff by way of sentimental comment.

"Well, there's this comfort that they can't very well send us back into the line again. Practically no battalion to send; one company wiped out, t'others short of a platoon or two, and scarcely any officers left to carry on," he remarked, taking another gulp to restore his equanimity after the ordeal.

"There's four reinforcement officers reporting for duty, sir," announced Captain Weeney.

"The devil there are," said the Major with another sniff, dejected at the sudden shattering of his hopes. "What do the buggers look like?"

"Pretty good stuff, sir. A bit green, of course," the adjutant said cheerfully.

"Hm. Bring them in."

Clicking to attention as they saluted, Lieutenant Bern and second Lieutenants Viney, Dummer, and Mellin were presently introduced.

Privates Swan, Hogmore, and Frittle, of B company, having procured sundry fragments of timber and a short piece of tarred felting, were industriously employed in effecting temporary repairs to the roof of their billets where a large gap, caused by enemy shell-fire, let in the winds of heaven and the sight of the stars. An old French peasant in a black blouse stood by the midden in the yard, remonstrating against the misplaced industry.

"*Hoheh, dites donc, messieurs, de quoi vous mêlez-vous là haut? N'y touchez pas, nom d'un nom d'un nom, à mon trou de marmite. C'est ma propriété. Ah ça non, par example, pas de réparations. C'est le gouvernement qui va me les foutre, les réparations.*"

The old gentleman was greatly put about lest any interference with the war-battered condition of his barn should detract from the plausibility of the bill for damages and compensations which he was looking forward to presenting to the Government when the war was over.

His expostulations were met with irrelevant retorts from the industrious rank and file:

"Non compris, old prat face. Keep your hair on, Mooshoo. Compris, bugger off!"

A smiling gallery of other ranks was standing about, listening to the interchange of diplomatic views. Attracted by the debate, the commander of B company was seeking to pacify in inadequate and halting French the irate proprietor, when he caught sight of Lieutenant Bern, strolling over to report for duty.

"Here, Julian, just in time! Your French is better than mine. Explain to the citizen that his barn will be restored to him in a thorough state of dilapidation."

"Ces messieurs desirent qu'on leur fiche la paix, et que vous ne leur cassiez pas la tête. Ne vous en faites pas. On va vous démolir votre grenier, monsieur, vous pouvez être tranquille."

The man, delighted to find an intelligible interlocutor, was disposed to continue the conversation, but meeting with little encouragement, went off shrugging his shoulders.

"Turned up at last, old man," I said, shaking hands. "Been expecting you. Everard told me you were due. Seen him at Brigade?"

"No. He was up the line."

We wasted as few words over strange meetings as over tragic partings.

"He should have gone down after that gassing we got last December on the Canal, you know. Instead, he took a few weeks off at Lady Irene Sexborough's and dodged the doctors. They took him on at Brigade," I said, while I settled Julian in his billets and procured for him the services of Private Hooge, the batman of poor Dibdey, who had gone West that morning. "Mr. Pluckley, Mr. Shakespeare; Mr. Bern," I introduced.

"How d'y do?"

We were settling down in company mess to further exploration of news, when Inglis broke in considerably perturbed.

"Well, I'm damned! Have you heard the latest, Foster? They've got the brazen cheek to ask us to find a wiring party. It simply can't be done, what? There's only the thirty crocks that were left in reserve, and a dozen reinforcements green from the bull-ring at Rouen. Brigade wants sixty. And I suppose that, just because I stayed behind to keep the home fires burning and defend the lines of communication, I shall be expected to take the party up. Can you beat it? When we've just come out of a show. That puts the kibosh on it, what?"

The runner from Orderly Room came with the chit while Inglis was still seeking words to voice his indignation.

"I'll take the wiring party up," Bern said.

"Nonsense, man. You've this moment arrived. You need a rest and a couple of days to get the hang of the ropes."

"I'd like to stretch my legs, and am fresher than any of you," he said.

He was insistent. To make a long story short, after conferring with the adjutant and C.O., Bern got his way, much to the relief of Captain Percy Inglis.

I gave Julian a few pointers.

"You'll have a lorry as far as crucifix corner, Lens I, 6, 8254. Got it? There's an R.E. dump in the quarry, where you'll pick up wire, pickets, and mallets. Sergeant Day will be in charge. Will show the way to the sap head. Yorks and Lancs, who took over, will find guides. There will be a sapper to direct work. All you have to do is to hand over the party to him. It shouldn't be much more than an hour's work. Fritz doesn't usually interfere."

After a snack, Julian set out on the last lap of the journey, begun almost a year since, to that thin line which ran across the face of Europe, where the crust of civilisation had burst, exposing the raw wound of murderous savagery.

From the rail-head, that morning, the row of yellow observation balloons, the rumble of gunfire had roughly outlined its direction. The torn up roads, bordered with camps, huts, ambulance stations, ammunition dumps, canteens, latrines, Salvation Army rest rooms, were encumbered with surly, slatternly military traffic. Heavy lorries bumped over the ruts, caterpillar tractors hauling heavy guns daubed red and green with futuristic designs rattled and rasped like cement breakers, horse limbers jogged, and ambulances threaded their way through the slower traffic. A French battery of seventy-fives screened with netting and brushwood fired intermittently with short, sharp reports.

Julian and the other officers had obtained a lift to their brigade on an A.S.C. lorry loaded with bottles of liquor. An engaging young staff lieutenant had offered them tea and provided a car which deposited them with their valises at the reserve billets, where Captain Albemarle Percy

Inglis was keeping the home fires burning in expectation of the battalion's return from the line.

"Whereabouts is the line?" enquired Mr. Dummer, surveying the surroundings with interest.

Inglis, who sat dejectedly on an ammunition box, jerked his thumb over his shoulder.

"Over there, behind those bits of hills. A good toddle from here, but too near for my liking. You can get all the excitement you want in this stinking manure heap of a village. It gets crumped two or three times a week. Damned unhealthy, if you ask me. A crump hit the Y.M.C.A. canteen last week and laid out a cook and a Bible-reader."

The lorry with the wiring party now wound down the silent and deserted road between black shadows of undulating country and clumps of trees massed against the starry sky.

They pulled up at an evacuated and ruined village. From a cellar opening screened with a blanket glowed a light. The lorry driver consulted a gunner who emerged from the sand-bagged entrance in response to his call.

"Quiet enough just now, mate. But the heavies will be having a stunt in a few minutes," the man said. "Nasty corner, this. 'Tain't exactly Piccadilly Circus. A blooming brass hat came streaking up the curve in his car this morning while a few coal-boxes was dropping round. The chaffer pulled up 'ere for some water for 'is engine, and it wasn't until then 'e noticed that 'is fare was sitting in the back of the car with no blooming 'ead on 'is shoulders. Laugh, I wanted to, 'e looked so bloody funny. I'd drop your passengers hereabouts, if I was you, mate. It's easier to get to cover when you're riding Shank's naggy."

Sergeant Day agreed. The party, Bern and the sergeant leading, marched down the macadam that curved down to the river. Over the heights on the other side shimmered a whitish glow like a phosphorescence. Silent flares went up over chalky clifftops. All was silent but for the occasional crackle of a machine-gun.

Suddenly the valley burst into flame and thunder. Red flashes poured from the mouths of the guns and lit up the scene and the batteries, massed three deep. The torrent of noise echoed from the bluffs and shook the night.

By the time the party had reached the quarry, the firing had ceased as suddenly as it had started. There was no reply from the other side. The night was again still and silent. Small parties moved to and fro under the shelter of the bluffs, while the R.E. material was being picked up from the dump.

In the approach sap they were held up by a ration party. The line of men carrying sacks had come to a standstill, blocking the trench. Loads were dumped on the side while the men leant back.

"Get a move on, over there," Sergeant Day called out, after they had stood some moments.

"'Ow c'n I move, sergeant, with the 'ole B.E.F. front of me? I ain't the Roosian steam roller," came a Yorkshire voice.

In the darkness a chatter of voices rose from the crowded sap.

"Pass the word. There's party wunting to get by."

"Can't stick 'ere all night, blocking gangway."

"Hey, wot's 'olding up party?"

"Quartermaster sergeant can't find foocking headquarters."

"Got into wrong trench."

"This 'ere lead to Elgin Avenue?"

"Take first sap to right."

"Hey, wot you doing there?"

"I'm waiting for a taxi, mister."

"We're being buggered about, we are."

"Give us a fag, mate."

A voice sang:

> "Pack up your troubles in your old kit bag,
> And smile, smile, smile,
> While you've a lucifer to light your fag,
> Smile, boys, smile."

"'Igher up, there."

"Fook 'igher yourself."

"Are you wiring party?"

"Naw, thank Gawd. We're the bloody infantry. Didn't you know? We's 'aving our photo took."

> "What's the use of worrying? It never was worth while.
> So, pack up your troubles in your old kit bag
> And smile, smile, smile."

"Eh, what are you?"

"Rootions."

Julian and the sergeant clambered out into the open and went ahead to find out the cause of the obstruction. Two men with slung rifles came down.

"Are you the guides?"

The tail of the ration party was shunted into a cross trench. With their coils of wire slung over the iron stakes, the men toiled up, puffing till they reached the main communication trench under the slope of chalk mounds honeycombed with dugouts screened with ground sheets and blankets. There was a cheerful activity and a smell of frying rashers, consequent on the arrival of rations.

Further on, the trench was in places blown in. The men clambered with their loads over the collapsed chalk. To the right the sloping hill was covered with shivered stumps.

The remains of the trench lost themselves in the pocked lunar landscape, striped with a gridiron of derelict saps. The starlit sky and white chalk gave an illusion of luminosity, but details were hard to distinguish a few yards off. The place smelt of chloride of lime, like a latrine.

The guides went ahead, walking too quickly for the loaded men, stopping a while, now and then, for them to catch up. They leapt into a cross trench.

"Our support line, this morning," said Sergeant Day.

Underfoot it felt strangely soft and cushioned after the crunching of the chalk and gravel. The bottom of the trench was padded with dead bodies. They were lying face down like a row of skittles, their khaki and equipment neat and clean. No one commented. The guides hurried on. Julian and the working party followed, stepping on the backs and rumps of the dead.

In the firing line, the sentries stood silent, their rifles laid across the sandbag parapet. The runners made enquiries, briefly, as they passed.

"Two bays off to right. Got a fag?"

Other wiring parties were at work on the tape line. The young R.E. officer took over with few words.

While the men worked, Julian paced the parapet.

In the deceptive, diffuse luminosity one could not see across. The

star-lit sky seemed blinding. The Great Bear was low over the horizon. Movements were felt in the darkness rather than heard or seen,
as of insects in the night. A rifle cracked some way off. A machine-
gun rattled lazily and was still. The heavy breathing of the men working on the wire could be heard. A flare went up, dazzling, showing only
still slant shadows. In a shell-hole lay a dead German, his belly swollen, his big boots sprawling over the rim. The night air was chill.

Down the trench came three officers. One said "Good evening" as he
passed.

"The brigadier," Sergeant Day whispered to Julian.

The third officer stayed behind speaking to the sergeant on duty in
the traverse. He stopped again as he came up to where Julian stood on
the parapet and looked up into his face.

"Good evening," Julian said. He could not see the officer's face for
the shadow of his steel helmet. He had red staff tabs on the lapels of
his tunic. The officer sprang on to the parapet and shook hands. It
was Everard.

"You haven't lost much time, old man," he said.

"Have I been doing anything else?" Julian gave a dry laugh.

"I shall be looking in at your people tomorrow." He cast a look
round. "This bit of line will have to be straightened out." Long-legged,
he strode beyond the wire, glancing about quickly. The machine-gun
rattled. There was a ping of bullets. Everard examined the shell-
holes.

"See that machine-gun?" he said, as though about to stroll up to it.
Bullets were singing softly about their ears. "You'd better make a
mental note of the position, if you haven't got your prismatic. You
may find it useful to remember it."

"I hope you have good news of Lady Bar," Julian said, when the
singing had stopped.

"Vera is doing marvellous work," Everard replied. "She was conferring with your aunt in London yesterday."

"You have received a telegram?"

"No." Everard looked vacantly for a moment across No Man's
land. "As a man of science, you have probably enquired into the phenomena of telepathy?"

Julian caught his breath. He answered off-hand.

"I must admit I have never given much attention to the subject."

"But you are acquainted with the facts?" Everard persisted.

Had it come to this? Was madness in the air of this madhouse?

"Since every molecule in the universe must needs affect every other, there is nothing at variance with a scientific conception in the notion of telepathy. Capella, yonder, affects the molecules of my brain." His heart bled within him.

"I am glad you think so. Vera has gone into the matter thoroughly. But I must catch up with the brigadier. Cheerio till tomorrow." And, slipping back into the trench, Everard strode along.

Bright sunlight glowed over the village, filled to capacity with troops out from the trenches. The canteen by the partly demolished church was driving a brisk trade. Orders to polish buttons and clean up had been strictly enforced by company sergeants major. Major Sotty, an old territorial, who owned a prosperous grocery business at Hungerford, was a stickler for ceremonial drill and was exacting as to the men's appearance.

Fullison had gone off with Captain Scrutch, the M.O., who exercised the functions of mess president, to Acheux village, where there remained a native shop. The Caballero made large acquisitions of perfumery and toilet articles. His valise and pack were ballasted with bottles of eau de Cologne, quinine hair lotion and brilliantine, tubes of almond-scented shaving cream, perfumed soap and other preparations of Messrs. Roget and Gallet, which, he said, were remarkably cheap.

"The Caballero's billets stink like a bally whoreshop," Mr. Mellin remarked. "I could scarcely get to sleep. By the way, do you know, Bern, that the Babe has turned up?"

Young Mr. Burd had reported for duty that morning, having been somewhat summarily discharged from hospital. There was a shortage of subalterns. The Babe, with his usual vivacity, found everything frightfully jolly. Julian had to share sleeping billets with the young gentleman, who decorated them with erotic postcards by Raphael Kirschner and pictures cut out of the *Vie Parisienne*.

"I say, it's a bit thick, what? They're sending us back into the line day after tomorrow," Captain Inglis informed, blowing into the mess and helping himself to a whiskey. "What do brigade think we're made of? The Brigadier is pawwawing with the Major this moment. Old Sotty's batman had to get him up from his bunk when the Old Man came. Sotty's liver is giving him fits. The brigadier has that bally brigade captain with him, of course. A damned slave-driver, that fellow. Just because he's a lord, he rules the whole bally brigade. Those fellows living in confounded luxury at a château while we're going over the top! I'd like to see his Lordship swining it in the damned trenches, what?"

"Captain Bar has more guts in his little toe than you in your whole belly, Captain Inglis," barked out Julian, flushing.

"Oh, I say. I didn't know he was a friend of yours, Bern. Sorry. Didn't mean anything, I'm sure. It's a fellow's privilege to grouse a bit, what? Damned few other privileges we have. A damned fine soldier, Captain Bar. Sorry, don't you know. Have a whiskey?" Inglis said, full of conciliatory apology.

He drank a second double with himself as a placatory libation.

The slight passage of arms was terminated by Everard's entrance into the mess room. He sat down on a rookee chair and filled a pipe, declining the proffered whiskey.

"Sorry you fellows can't be given a spell out," he said. "It's pretty rough, I know, but it can't be helped."

"I suppose there's no chance of leave, is there?" asked Inglis.

"Leave, man! Do you realize, my dear fellow, that the British Expeditionary Force has been reduced to almost exactly half its total effectives in the first twelve hours of the present operations?" said Everard.

"But we won, didn't we?" suggested Mr. Pluckley.

"Did we?" queried Mr. Shakespeare.

"We were to have been in Bapaume on the first of July," smiled Everard sadly.

"The leather bumpers at G.H.Q. are as much at home in this business as fishing skippers on the bridge of a Dreadnought," said Inglis.

"The French on the right let us down, of course," Everard said, "and they're at us to relieve the pressure at Verdun."

Mr. Viney raised his eyes from his volume on the philosophy of the Upanishads, and, perturbed in his inward vision, decided to pursue his meditations under God's heaven, pensively wandering down the Varennes road, where buzzing planes scoured angrily the azure infinities dotted with white puffs of smoke by the "archies."

"So it's back in the line tomorrow?" interrogated Inglis.

"I'm afraid so. Only two days' interrelieving with the Duke of Wellington," Everard said as he rose.

"Fall in!" The men in the yard donned their equipment and picked up their rifles.

"Platoon—'shun! Right—dress! Platoon, by sections—number! Form —fours! Form—two-deep! Stand—at ease! Stand—easy! Platoon— 'shun!"

Sergeant Day saluted Lieutenant Bern. "Platoon present and correct, sir," he said.

"Platoon—slope—arms! Move to the right in fours, form—fours! Right, quick—march! Right—wheel! . . . March easy!"

With rifles slung, the battalion filed down the road. The sun was broiling. Julian's steel helmet gave him a headache. He must procure, when he got the chance, one of those patent linings, like that Everard had. They were sold at Hawke's in Saville Row. Through Authuile Wood the road was in places encumbered by dead horses and a dead Ford ambulance twisted into scrap iron. A machine-gun was enfilading.

"What tune is Fritz playing?" called a wag in the ranks.

"Mademoiselle from Armenteers," another voice replied.

"Silence in the ranks!" thundered the C.S.M.

The left file in front of Julian had the heel of one boot neatly shot off from under him.

"Pick it up there. Left, right . . . left . . . left."

While we stood in the narrow approach trench a salvo of Black Marias came over, landing short in a meadow to the left. Young Mr. Burd hoisted himself up on to the parapet to enjoy the spectacle. He had not seen a shell-burst before.

"Keep your head down, there, you fool," called the Major.

Lush grass, with cornflowers, poppies and saxifrages, was deep over the sides of the sap, unused for some time. Two white butterflies danced above the long halms, delicate against the dotted sky where round clouds cast moving shadows over the fields.

The small salient newly acquired from the Germans, who surrounded it in very intimate proximity on three sides, was cramped and crowded. At one place, where we shared a sap with the Boche, only a steel sniper's shield separated us from our neighbors' premises. By sliding aside the sight, a glimpse of the enemy could be obtained, not twelve yards away.

The deep timbered dugouts had a peculiar odor. *Fetor germanicus*. It was still more potent where two German corpses had got built into the parados. Their blue trousers showed among the sandbags over their soggy rumps. The sanitary corporal sprayed two tins of chloride of lime over the offensive portion of the wall.

In the middle of the little salient, a sloping cavern plunged into the bowels of the earth. Common report had it that the place was mined, and we were, throughout the three days of our tenancy, in cheerful expectation of being blown up sky high at any instant. The intelligence officer who had established a listening post there took fiendish pleasure in not committing himself to a denial of the rumor.

Our worst fears proved, however, unfounded, and the lines were in too close proximity for use of high explosives. Trench mortars putting over a few "minnies" and strange winged missiles, which the men called "flying devils," that fluttered over the trenches following a devious and impredictable course were, besides rifle fire, the chief sources of annoyance. But snipers were active. Near the most forward bay a warning notice was posted. One had to duck on going round the corner. The sentries were provided with periscopes, and the Lewis gunners— tall men, for they were Lifeguards—crept round bent double along the low parapet to seek their emplacements.

While Julian was making his first round at early stand to, accompanied by young Burd, the boy must needs peer over. He dropped back instantly with a bullet through his head. They buried him near the approach sap, where the butterflies fluttered. The contents of his pockets —two hundred and seventy-five francs, a letter from his aunt, and a packet of pornographic postcards—were forwarded to nearest relative.

Our turn was normally peaceful and uneventful.

We settled down to the monotonous round of interrelieving—three days in various sectors of the trenches, three days out in various billets. The routine of Armageddon could be as dreary as that of camp and barracks.

"What about your paradigm of sports, Señor Caballero?" Julian asked Fulliston at mess.

"I was a bloody fool to give up polo. Damned little sport about this sort of thing. *Mierda!*"

Routine tempered by death and dread. At each turn of trench duty men died—an inglorious death, without enthusiasm, without heroism, not from confronting human opponents, but from scrap iron and chemicals.

"I don't mind taking my chance over the top," said Second Lieutenant Pluckley, "but there are times when I object to the supreme sacrifice." He was obsessed with a special fear. He was in terror lest the supreme sacrifice should be consummated in a latrine. Pluckley ran out holding his breeches whenever any crumping started while he was seated over the honey-bucket.

Human values had reverted to the crude, primitive exaltation of physical courage—coupled with how much moral cowardice. Yet there was no reticence or shame in the open avowal of fear. It was, among the young officers, accounted rather good form to expatiate upon abject funk, and no modesty was shown in confessing to cold feet, the admission serving to vent, while disguising through jocular exaggeration, the haunting state of terror. "I've got a perfectly awful attack of cold feet today," some subaltern would declare in answer to enquiries concerning his health.

We went one morning, Julian, Inglis, Fulliston, and I, down to the transport lines to get our mounts for a ride over to the Field Cashier at Bouzincourt to draw battalion pay. The Caballero burst into loud protest every time he had occasion to bestride the army mount that had fallen to his lot.

"Do you call this a horse? This critter, this screw? The beast is not fit to be sent into a corrida. That *sinverguenza* who calls himself my groom brings me this moke, this *burro,* this *rocinante,* this *caroña,* with the most solemn air. 'Your charger, sir,' says the impudent fellow. Charger! *El caballo de guerra de Usted.* I wouldn't be found dead near the brute within ten leagues of the pampas."

The Caballero was very nearly rid of the unlucky animal that morning. While the grooms were fussing round, the horse lines became the object of Fritz's attention. A crop of fifteens started peppering the paddock. The second landed in the further lines; six horses lay in a heap, plunging and kicking; the rest stampeded, followed by the transport men. In a moment the paddock was deserted. Julian remained in the middle of the field, lighting a cigarette, and strolled leisurely over to where we were flat on our stomachs under the lee of a bank. He was so tickled by the appearance which Captain Percival Inglis presented as he lay under a limber, with mouth agape and eyes starting out of his head, the very picture of terror, that he doubled up with laughter.

I remonstrated. Everard had warned me to keep an eye on Julian. "He is inclined to be reckless," he told me.

"The target is about four acres. By an easy arithmetical calculation, the chances of a hit are about two thousand to one," Julian replied. "Were my emotions wrought upon by chances of two thousand to one, I should have stayed at home—where the odds are only slightly better."

After visiting the Field Cashier, we stopped at an estaminet. It was a parching hot day. The dram-shop had been invaded by Australian troops, who were just over from Egypt, and we found it almost impossible to approach the bar, thronged as was the place with husky giants in grey shooting-jackets and rough-rider hats. The proprietor and his wife were desperately endeavoring to defend their stock, which was being looted by the colonials. Catching sight of English officers, the distracted little man beckoned us over to his bedroom, whither he and his family were being forced to retreat and barricade themselves against the bandits.

The man poured forth his lamentations, while he produced for us, from under the bed, some bottles of refreshment which he had succeeded in rescuing.

He had, he told us, gone in to Amiens the day before and had brought back with him a cask of "stoot," in anticipation of the antipodeans' arrival. The Australians had smashed the cask open with an axe, and were engaged in bathing in its contents.

"What will you?" said the little man earnestly. "They are of course convicts—forçats." He believed the "Aussies" were just out from Botany Bay.

Under the influence of the liquor Inglis's spirits began to revive from the shock they had sustained that morning.

"You did look a damned funny sight, Percy," the Caballero admitted. He burst into song:

> "When to evade Destruction's hand,
>   To hide they all proceeded,
> No soldier in that gallant band
>   Hid half as well as he did."

Inglis joined in good-humoredly, and the estaminet keeper's bedroom rang with the lyric echoes.

> "In enterprise of martial kind,
>   When there was any fighting,
> He led his regiment from behind,
>   He found it less exciting."

Such was Inglis's appreciation of the estaminet's resources that, when we set back towards our billets, he was incapable of bestriding his charger, and we had to enlist the assistance of an A.S.C. lorry, the driver of which undertook the safe delivery of Captain Inglis at his company's quarters.

A few days later, Colonel Henry Frisham Cator, D.S.O., rejoined the battalion, having recovered from the abrasion which he had sustained. Colonel Cator was, as he was careful to let it be known, a regular, a Sandhurst man, and it was with some sense of derogation, tactfully but distinctly indicated, that he found himself in command of a territorial unit. His promotion had been interfered with by the circumstance that he had, during the earlier part of his career, in India, seduced the wives of two of his commanding officers. But for the scandal, Colonel Cator would, as he not infrequently hinted, have had a brigade. He was sometimes familiarly referred to among the subalterns as Forny.

The colonel was in depressed spirits on his return. He attributed his mood in part to having "the wind up." The decimation which the battalion had suffered during his absence, and the fact that he was now surrounded with unfamiliar faces, were not calculated to cheer him. But the chief cause of his melancholy was, he said, the loss which he had sustained of his favorite Irish setter, Toby, which had died of old age while the Colonel was on sick leave. Colonel Cator lamented with

Major Sotty, while taking over and fortifying himself with liberal potations of whiskey.

"Hate having to make the acquaintance of new fellows, Sotty," he confided to his second in command. "Rankers, I suppose. Some fine fellows in the old mob, all the same. Trosley still with D company?"

"Reported missing at Thiepval. They found bits, I believe. But no identification," said the Major.

"Do you know, Sotty, I swear that dog knew we were out for the last time when we went on the twelfth for the opening of the grouse. Poor shooting this year. Scarcely any fellows. Got a new man in A company, I see."

"Young Longbottom stopped a five-nine on the third."

"*Ars longa, vita brevis,* as we said at school. The poor tyke came and licked my hand. You would have thought he was crying. What's become of Dillcot?"

"Got the body all right. It was that second stunt."

"I had him since he was a puppy. You never saw such a lurcher. Worked a hedge from both sides and never failed to land a rabbit. I'm too tender-hearted, I know. Who's doing B company?"

"Foster is still there."

"Plodding fellow. Very conscientious. But damned uninspiring. Has no imagination. Well, I suppose I'll have to get used to the new temporary sahibs."

Colonel Cator, it turned out, had married a cousin of Dorothy Coston. On comparing dates, Julian found that they must have met at Cranne Hall. The Colonel at once conceived a high opinion of Julian.

"I saw at once from the way you sat a horse that you were a pucka wallah," he told Julian. "Between ourselves, no ranker can ever sit a horse. A fellow who knows horseflesh is almost the same as a pucka soldier, what?"

Dorothy herself, Julian learned from Colonel Cator, was now married ti an army man, a Captain, now temporary Lieutenant-Colonel, Luseley.

"Got a place over in Ireland, I believe," the Colonel said.

The rumor went round shortly after Colonel Cator's return that the battalion was to be in another show. The news was received with considerable elation by the young fellows who had joined up since the last decimation.

"We've been doing nothing but three days in and three days out, and dirty fatigues," groused Mellin. "Are we a dashed pioneer battalion? Every unit except ourselves has had a stunt."

"You're in a precious hurry, young fellow," said Fulliston. "You'll be getting it in the neck soon enough. *Tienes tiempo de sobra.*"

"I didn't join the Ally Sloper Cavalry, did I, Caballero?" insisted Mellin.

Among the more seasoned veterans the prospect was viewed with different feelings. There was an appreciable lowering of the tone of hilarity at company quarters. Captain Albemarle Percy Inglis in particular manifested considerable alarm. He sought the advice of Captain Scrutch, R.A.M.C., concerning the condition of his heart. Inglis had, he said, peculiar sensations in that region.

"I am sometimes scarcely able to get my breath, and you could knock me down with a feather," he explained, while holding up his shirt for the M.O.'s ausculatory investigation.

"I could knock you down without one," declared the burly and unsympathetic medical officer. "What's the matter with you is too much whiskey."

Inglis was resorting more and more to whiskey to drown his apprehensions, and reports were frequent concerning the irregularity of his attendances on parades. Major Sotty agreed that whiskey formed a part of necessary munitions of war. But the colonel was compelled one morning to issue a chit summoning Inglis to headquarters to explain his absence from rouse parade. Captain Inglis excused himself by casting the blame on the quartermaster, whose duty, he pleaded, was to provide the officers' latrine with bumf.

"It was quite impossible for me to attend," he declared, "until I had received your chit, sir."

The anticipated "show" was put off from week to week.

At officers' conferences, the colonel had gone carefully over the dispositions. Companies were to stand to arms thirty-five minutes before zero hour; B company on the left, C company on the right of the forward trench. A and D companies to stand in the support position. Artillery preparation to begin five minutes before zero, the forward sections to advance in echelon immediately after the lifting of the first barrage. The immediate objectives consisted of the first two German lines, which were imperfectly consolidated among shell craters, and depended chiefly for their first defence upon two machine-gun positions located at points marked J and K on the trench map. The attacking sections of A and C companies, to be supported if need be by others, were to move forward in half-right and half-left directions respectively, converging in two main sections upon emplacement J, the attack on K taking place simultaneously on the left in the same formation. After the capture of the front-line machine-gun positions, sections from B and D companies would mop up and consolidate, supported by Lewis guns, while sections of A and C companies leap-frogged to the second line.

Three times the battalion had gone into the line expecting to go over the top, and three times the orders had been washed out. The wire, it was said, was imperfectly cut, or the divisional artillery was otherwise engaged, and wanted to perfect its range. It was none too comfortable a piece of line. The Germans, badly entrenched and with their right flank in the air, were nervous and assiduously kept up the ritual of morning "hate," their guns strafing pretty continually our tumble-down trenches. Headquarters and Orderly Room had been blown in, fortunately without any more serious casualty than the burial of a cook, who had to be extricated, warning having been given by two shorts.

On our fourth trip to the sector, we had remained six continuous days. Major Sotty was furious at the complete exhaustion of headquarters' supply of whiskey. Saunders, the mess corporal, was ordered to procure munitions immediately at all cost. The corporal dashed off in search of the Johnny Walker necessary for the carrying on of hostilities. A good deal of dirt was coming over at the moment. Corporal Saunders was killed by a direct hit in the first communication trench.

Everybody was worn and weary by the unwonted extension of trench duty when orders were received that the attack should take place on the morrow, zero hour being 4 ack emma.

After a final inspection of his men, checking rifles and supplies of Mill's bombs, Julian tried to snatch a couple of hours' rest in the stifling dugout. He fell into a fevered and restless sleep.

He was awakened by the faithful Hooge, who brought a tin of tomatoes by way of breakfast. In the shallow firing trench the sections were in position. There was little speech and no jesting. Faces looked ashen in the grey light. Teeth chattered. Men shivered, but it was not particularly chilly. Scarcely any man looked another full in the eye. Some gulped down the remains of their rum ration.

"I can't hold myself any longer, corporal," private Frittle whined.

"Be quick, then," called Corporal Blean. And the man went behind the sacking screen near a traverse to let down his trousers.

Major Sotty and Adjutant Weeney passed quickly along the lines, giving a last glance round, checking the dumps.

Sergeant Tonk went up to the major. Captain Inglis could not take command, he said.

"He's very bad, sir."

Stifling futile and inadequate imprecations, the major and the adjutant hurried to the near-by funk-hole where Inglis was lying. He was snoring, dead to the world.

They shook him violently.

"Good God, man, you know what this means? A court martial, and worse."

"Go to hell! Go and bugger yourself!" Inglis grunted without opening his eyes.

It wanted six minutes to the artillery zero. With the help of the sergeant, they dragged Inglis out and dropped him unconscious on to the firing step.

"Just hoist him up on to the parapet, presently, and shove him over. You understand? I'm afraid you'll have to take charge, sergeant. There's no time to get another officer. You know the orders?" said Major Sotty.

"That's all right, sir. I can manage all right," said the sergeant.

"Better for the blighter to get shot by German bullets than face a firing squad," said Major Sotty to the adjutant.

Julian peered at his wrist watch in the dim light. Three minutes and thirty seconds, and the barrage would begin. One . . . two . . . three . . . four. . . . In one of those counted seconds time was obliterated. The moon spread out its fan on the Tyrrhenian sea; olive groves waved over banks of violets; russet firs stood on the slope of the lush hills, like soldiers on parade. A great peace in the great stillness. Forgiveness, forgiveness . . . *in articulo mortis*. His lips moved slightly. How small the things that had seemed to matter! Peace and sweetness ineffable. . . .

A piercing hiss overhead. Two, four, twenty . . . innumerable crashing explosions. A deafening tumult, howling viciously, rending the air, crashing in a continuous tempest. The ground rocked. Cries, calls for stretcher-bearers, amid the tumult. In the pandemonium a scream at his side: "Mother . . .!" Mellin rolled over, his hands clutching, his eyes staring, astonished. He crumpled and lay still, staring astonished with glassy eyes, his hands clutching the air.

The watch marked fifteeen seconds to go. The show had started from the wrong side half-a-minute sooner. Efficient, the German information! Difficult to make out the added tumult of our own guns, or to note their lifting.

Julian stiffened his muscles, strained his eyes. Everything was rocking, his brain stunned. He blew his whistle and leaped on to the parapet. Four men dropped as they rose. Julian plunged forward, the stream of bullets hissing. He dropped flat into a shell-hole.

"You there, sergeant? Good egg."

"Aye, aye, sir."

Sergeant Day was holding a Mills bomb. The pinging bullets hissed all round, spattering like rain. Julian peered to the right for a sight of Inglis and his section. No sign of them. The machine-gun which was their first objective was turned full on Julian's section, sweeping the sector. Were any of the men still alive? Julian felt an almost irresistible impulse to leap up and be done with it. Was anything worth the hesitation? At the moment the whole ghoulish stupidity seemed so excruciating that he laughed aloud. He laughed, laughed. He would have leapt forward laughing. The poor fellows, if any were still alive! Tensely, desperately, he controlled his muscles, as one resisting the fascination of the abyss. He watched for the swerve of the machine-gun to take another leap forward. Where the devil was Inglis? There seemed to be no one about. A bullet struck his helmet. His nostrils were full of chalk and dirt. His mouth was dust-dry. Some one was going across to the left. He caught a glimpse of Viney, gaunt and haggard, slowly moving forward, leading his section. What a funny sight he looked! No sign of Inglis, confound him.

Suddenly Julian saw him, standing almost in the middle of No-Man's land, bare-headed, shouting, gesticulating, brandishing his revolver and letting it off at haphazard. He staggered forward, lunging towards the machine-gun. Men sprang up after him. Hand-grenades exploded. Inglis stumbled forward, discharging his revolver. A shot smashed the jaw of one of the Germans who were manning the gun. The rest, taken by surprise, did not have time to swing the gun round. They put their hands up as Inglis, tripping, fell forward and lay like a sack across the barrel of the machine-gun.

Julian had sprung forward, making straight for the trench. The machine-gun on the left was silent a moment, the men manning it hesitating whether to enfilade over their own men. During the second's hesitation, Mills bombs showered over them. From the support, a huge Boche wearing a leather bombing apron rose and threw stick-bombs which dropped short. Julian drew a Mills from his pocket and tore the pin out with his teeth. He threw it at the German. It exploded in his face, which, when Julian next caught a glimpse of it, looked as though a jar of raspberry jam had spilt on it.

"Good cricket, sir," he heard Sergeant Day say at his elbow.

As Julian leapt down into the trench, a German sergeant stood before him stiffly at attention. He reminded Julian of a German waiter. "*Guten Tag, Herr Unteroffizier! Alle Waffen abgeben.*"

The support line collapsed in the confusion.

When, that evening, after relief, we had got back to camp—we were under canvas in Acheux wood—the Brigadier came round, looking mighty pleased. Despite the big odds and the German anticipation of the attack, we had reached our objectives. It was chiefly getting that gun which had won the show.

We had some trouble in getting Inglis down from the line. The mess cart had to be sent for. Julian and I went to help his batman to get him into his bunk. Major Sotty came round some moments later.

Bloated, with blood-shot eyes, Inglis was an awful sight.

"Now, look here, Major," he said in a thick voice. "Can't you give a fellow a chance, for once? I know I should be bloody well court-martialled. Drunk on duty. But . . . you know . . . hang it all . . . How the hell did I get here?"

"Who's talking about a court-martial?" Major Sotty chuckled. "It was jolly fine the way you got that machine-gun, old man."

"M'chine-gun? What bloody m'chine-gun? What the deuce . . .?"

"May I come in?" It was the Brigadier, stooping at the entrance of the tent. Inglis made a pathetic attempt to sit up on the edge of the bunk in an attitude of attention. "Please don' move, Captain Inglis. Feeling a bit knocked out, what? I don't wonder at it. I merely wished to shake hands with you and to congratulate you. I'm putting you up for a V.C., and I'll see that you get it. Please don't disturb yourself. Just rest as long as you like and take good care of yourself, Captain Inglis. Can I send you over anything from brigade? A little supply of whiskey, what?"

VI

THRONGS of officers and other ranks, khaki and *bleu horizon,* broken loose for a few hours from the grime and grimness, imparted to the rue des Trois Cailloux a festive animation which the narrow cobbled street had not known for centuries. Army lorries had been plying from the fighting zone, bringing troops on a day's leave. Our party had been provided with a staff-car for the joy ride. After long weeks in the trenches and back-of-the-line billets denuded of civilian life and women's presence, the prospect of a few hours in even such a dingy little French provincial town as Amiens had all the glamor of a schoolboys' outing.

Rosy-cheeked subalterns rushed the patisseries, eating éclairs, babas au rhum, macaroons. They bought picture postcards, and stared at the tawdry inutilities displayed in the shop fronts. The rubbish might have been, after the long weaning from "civilisation," luxury displays in the rue de la Paix.

The fish-shop where an attractive blonde presided over the caisse was, Everard informed, assiduously patronised by the Prince of Wales, who had suddenly acquired a taste for fish and domestic marketing.

"He was a shy, pasty-faced lad when he first came over," Everard said. "He has got his baptism in the messes of Amiens. The fellows rag him unmercifully and get him drunk. Last time I saw him, he had one boot off, and was being conveyed, hilariously comatose, into a car. No heir to the British throne ever enjoyed such an upbringing. One wonders how he'll ever manage to settle down to the prescriptive imbecility of a Victorian throne. Simply hates the idea, I'm told."

Everard restrained us from entering the little restaurants where young officers were crowding in for a beano, and led us up a side-street to an hotel, where the cuisine was, he said, not to be outdone in Paris. The chef was from the Café Anglais. The place was patronised by the high command of both allied armies, and served as a social meeting place of amicable liaison between the French and English staffs. At a large circular table at the further end of the dining room sat a number of French and English generals. The commander of the Fifth Army was there with two brigadiers. He confined himself mostly, owing to the limitations of his colloquial French, to wearing a permanent smile, while a young staff officer by his side kept him informed in whispers of the drift of the conversation.

Notices on the walls warned: *"Les oreilles ennemies vous écoutent."* But although the distinguished gathering, who were lighting cigars over the coffee and liqueurs, might present the appearance of an allied council of war, enemy ears would have gathered little of strategic value from the conversation. One of the British brigadiers, not a little proud of his linguistic accomplishments, led the colloquy from the English side, and was singing the praises of the fare of which the company had just partaken.

"France is invincible in the culinary field, *mon général,"* he said, addressing a stout French general, one of the heroes of the Marne. "We in England are not only incapable of doing anything approaching to that *sole normande* or that *caneton à l'orange;* we are not even able to cook peas—*petits pois.* Our troops are constantly suggesting to orderly officers that our peas should be utilised in the present emergency as shrapnel."

The French generals chuckled politely.

"Mind you," declared the hero of the Marne, "I am not one of your chauvinists in culinary matters as are some of my less informed countrymen. I for one do not fail to appreciate your English cuisine. *Mon Dieu,* your rosbif, your saddle of mutton which melts like butter in the mouth. And your biftek with *pommes* chips. *Honneur à la Tamise!"* he said, smacking his lips. "None of our chefs can imitate your joints and your grills. You are past masters in cooking meat. But you do not know how to cook vegetables. Those peas, for example. What do you do with them? You tip them into a pot of boiling water, *et voilà!* Now, *mon général,* those *petits pois* which you have so nobly appreciated, are the result of quite as elaborate culinary art as the *sole normande* and the *caneton à l'orange."* He went on to describe with the gusto of a connoisseur the details of the process. The selected young peas were to be placed in a casserole with half a dozen button-onions, the heart of a lettuce cut into quarters, a *bouquet garni* of parsley, chervil and savory, a pinch of salt, a spoonful of sugar and as much fresh butter as will melt in a minute. More butter should be added later after the liquid—only as much water being used as barely to cover the peas—has been reduced by slow boiling. "There are two schools of opinion among our culinary artists," said the French general, "which differ as to whether the boiling should be slow or quick, and the lid be placed on the pan or not. The great controversy is still raging."

The British generals were duly impressed with the revelation of those mysteries, and courteous international self-depreciations were exchanged.

"We are mere barbarians, *mon général*," said the brigadier.

"*Mais non, mais non*," the hero of the Marne insisted. "I will not admit it. Look you, I have tasted most cuisines in Europe. All, all west of the Rhine and south of the Alps, are, each in its own way, agreeable. English, French, Italian, Spanish cooking—each excels in some particular fashion. But once you cross the Rhine or the Danube —ah! *mon Dieu!* The Germans do not eat, they merely feed, and one must be endowed with a leather stomach to derive nourishment, and not mere wind and indigestion, from the abominations they devour. It is nothing short of a criminal atrocity which cries to Heaven for vengeance. And the barbarians are absolutely unteachable. In Vienna, where the most gruesome culinary crime is rampant, and they have no notion of cooking even an egg or a potato, they have the inconceivable effrontery of referring to their pigs' fodder as '*die gute Wiener Küche*' —the good Viennese cooking." The hero of the Marne waxed indignant and eloquent. "This war, gentlemen, is being waged between the people who can cook and those who can't, those who know how to eat and those who don't. It is a war for the defence of civilisation, that is to say, of good eating."

"The weightiest justification of the war that I have yet heard," Julian, who had been listening to the discussion of the Allied council, remarked. "Nothing goads national sentiment to fury like culinary differences of taste. The English populace, always dull to political issues, was wont to be roused to martial ardor by the reminder that the French were eaters of frogs and snails, or the Germans devourers of sausages. The foundations of national prejudice are dietetic."

Everard had acquaintances among the French staff. He exchanged polite remarks with some officers who were dining at an adjoining table. A captain with a marvellously cultivated fan-shaped beard joined us for a few moments. On noticing that Julian almost spoke French, he addressed his remarks to him, while Everard was talking with a divisional staff-captain, and despite the warning notices, grew more confidential than was usual in inter-allied conversational intercourse. Punctilious civility excluded as a rule genuine frankness between French and English officers. This was partly due to English ignorance of French rank badges, a deficiency which several army orders and circulars had failed to remedy. English officers and other ranks commonly passed by a French general without attempting to salute, held back by the uncertainty in which they were as to whether he might not be a bandmaster. Julian himself had felt confused on one occasion when he discovered that the smart salute he had bestowed on a person whom he had taken to be a field officer had been addressed to a *"pharmacien."*

The bearded staff captain, whose appearance was more suggestive to English eyes of an astrologer or an alchemist than of a soldier, politely expressed his admiration for the achievements of the British troops. They were wonderful, he said, considering that they were not, like the French, real soldiers, but an amateur army. The offensive would have been a great success had the British been able to keep pace with the French.

"In the south we had carried our objectives, and our cavalry was patrolling in front of Péronne," he said. "Unfortunately you were unable, if I may be so frank as to say so, to afford us adequate support."

After the French captain had rejoined his friends, the young divisional red tab who had been talking with Everard turned round with a smile at the Frenchman's claims.

"Those French fellows make even worse muddles," he said, "—inconceivable muddles. You couldn't find worse staff organisation anywhere. At the outbreak, there were not nearly enough rifles to go round—some two millions, when something like twelve millions were needed. Many units went out against the Boche armed wih all sorts of queer gaspipes, fowling pieces, sports blunderbusses, museum specimens. They had practically no ammunition for their seventy-fives. They fired dummy shells used for artillery practice so as not to give

away their desperate plight. And the bright fellows in the Government
had enlisted nearly all the men at Creusot's, so that the factory was
practically closed up. The medical mobilisation material was found to
have been completely plundered. They had to procure iodine and thermometers from chemists' shops. And you should see some of the army
orders I've seen. Abso-bloody-lutely unbelievable. During the Charleroi show, divisional orders came in mentioning assembly points which
were, since several days, in enemy occupation, and setting down orders
as though for a parade without a mention of possible fighting. At
Verdun, though they had ample notice of the intended attack, no preparation whatsoever had been made. One strand of barbed wire in front
of the forts, believe it or not. Practically no trenches; no support line
of any sort. Not a thing had been done to provide lines of communication. There was nothing, I tell you, but the old puff-puff single line and
a road which broke down in a few days under the traffic. Don't you
come grousing about British staff work. The French organisation is
chaos. Guns have to be got, if at all, from one department, and munitions from another."

"For that matter, even the German command muddled things stu-
pendously," Everard said. "They lost the battle of the Marne, and
probably the war, through sheer staff incompetence and bungling. When
a yawning gap was left between their first and second armies, the operations of co-ordination were left entirely in the hands of one young
lieutenant. Tannenberg has cost them the war. The Russians say that
they saved Europe. It is difficult to contradict the claim."

"The fact of the matter is," said the fellow from Division, "that the
new, gigantic, mechanised armies are quite beyond the power of control of any general or staff. The essence of all strategy is the ability
to alter a plan and adapt it to changed circumstances at a moment's
notice. That simply can't be done with modern armies. With such un-
wieldy armies, one can only prepare for one definite plan. It takes
months, or years to prepare it. It is out of the question to prepare for
even two or three of the dozen alternatives which predictable circumstances may demand. And the chances are that what will actually happen is the thirteenth alternative that could not be predicted. So that,
between fairly evenly balanced forces, the chances of being able to
carry out the prepared plan are infinitesimal. And when the plan fails,

there's no doing anything about it. Except dig in for a war of attrition. Modern war is bound to be trench warfare. The old war of movement is now impossible. It's like trying to play polo on elephants."

Everard had business with the Town Major. He left us to wander about the town, and said he would join us later at the Café de la République.

Hungering for literary pabulum after the mental aridity of the long fast, Julian dived into a bookshop. It was stocked almost exclusively with works of devotion and Catholic propaganda. There were numerous publications on the miracles of Lourdes, Lisieux, and other wonder-working shrines. With the unctuous manner of a sacristan, a salesman offered *The Secret of the Cure of Diseases by the Invocation of the Holy Virgin, for the First Time revealed by the most Reverend Father Calot, S.J.* Prominent were lives of the sainted Joan, the new patroness of French catholic chauvinism, and books glorifying the heroism of the seminarists and priests in the French armies—"Heroes of the Cross." The shop was frequented by black-cassocked priests who, from their proprietary manner and the vendors' deference, seemed to be the directors of the town's literary commissariat. Julian acquired a life of Robespierre, which set forth the satanic nature of the revolutionist and his compeers.

"I had underrated their worth," he said with a smile. "By the undying hatred poured upon their memory may that worth be truly measured. Tell me who are thine enemies, and I will tell thee who thou art! History is perhaps the real foundation of judgment."

"What of biology?" I queried.

"I formerly gave too much attention to biology, influenced by the fiction of the individual, and the meaningless fable of history seemed but a tale told by an idiot. Now that I perceive the course of human affairs to be governed by laws as inflexible as those which rule the motions of the stars, I derive satisfaction from following the inevitable effects of stupidity, mendacity, predatory greed, and ignorance to their rigorous and inevitable conclusion. Sow lies, injustice, expedients, compromises, and you will reap ruin and catastrophe."

"Is reason ever at the helm of events?" I said.

"Wherever reason has been able to build, the achievement has been perennial and invincible. One flash of revolt, six thousand years ago, in

Asiatic Greece, against oriental mysticism and unreason, and Europe has been created. The Hellenic seed of reason has flowered over and over again despite Plato, despite Christianity. One abortive revolt in the French eighteenth century against social iniquity, and revolution will not be stilled, though it be drowned a hundred times in blood, till iniquity be put down."

Mr. Viney, who had joined us at the bookstore, desired a copy of Ruskin's *Bible of Amiens,* but could obtain a French translation only, passably done in truth, with an introduction by a certain Monsieur Marcel Proust. When we had driven up, the cathedral, with its two uneven towers, loomed alone visible, like the stranded carcass of an antedeluvian monster above the clustering undergrowth of houses round its base. But from the meander of narrow streets it was not seen, and we had to enquire the way.

"One of the wonders of Gothic architecture," murmured Mr. Viney in hushed awe as we stood craning our necks to look at the *'Beau Dieu d'Amiens,'* and at the souls of the damned being tortured by grotesque devils on the tympanum.

"We are in the heart of the Gothic wonderland, Mr. Viney," said Julian. "Here, in Picardy, the core of Merovingian France, did the Christian Church, creeping up from Rome and the Provincia, first fasten its talons into the flesh of Europe. The first Defender of the Faith, the bandit Clothwig, had his lair at Soissons; Charlemagne, the armed missionary of the Church, at Noyon; while the later Merovingians, of infamous memory—'it would not be easy to find more vice and less virtue'—favored Laon. Hence did Peter the Hermit lead his vagabond rabble against the Saracen who was restoring culture to barbaric Christian Europe, and, returning from Palestine loaded with holy relics, among which the severed head of the Baptist, here enshrined, built Gothic cathedrals with imaged façades after the likeness of Greek iconostases. Flowing down the course of the Somme, from Noyon, Laon, and Soissons, to Amiens and Abbeville, a stream of wealthy Cistercian abbeys and Gothic cathedrals testified to the power and plunder of bishops and abbots. The cradle land of European culture, Mr. Viney. Upon this blasted soil, as in Germany, the renaissance of Hellenic rationalism never seeded."

"Christianity remains, I see, the red rag to your bull," I smiled.

"Thank you for assuring me that I retain my sanity. When I become tolerant of the cancer of European culture, see that the bullets do not again miss me."

Julian glanced over Mr. Viney's guidebook. "Ruskin declares, I see, with due enthusiasm that the wonder of Gothic was built 'for the purpose of enclosing or producing no manner of profitable work whatsoever.' Well said, old psalm-singer. Should Europe ever become rational, its sons will be hard put to it to adapt this lumber to any use or service. The temples on the steps of which the Greeks were wont to sun themselves have unfortunately proved adaptable to every public use. Muslim mosques radiate joy and light to whatever purpose they may be turned. This wonder of Gothic, this dark and dank medieval dungeon, does not answer a single human purpose or express a human joy. It has no aim other than to browbeat, crush, awe, and terrify, no message but of abjection, subjection, and prostration. Look at those undressed men and women chained like galley-slaves, drawn by leering devils into the pit. The central theme of pictorial decoration of the French Dark Ages. 'Undressed' I say, for there is no joy or beauty in the nakedness of those worms who are ashamed of their vile bodies."

In the dark nave, with its tawdry plaster ornaments, we came upon some of the French generals whom we had seen at the Hôtel du Rhin. The Commander of the Ninth French army, General Ferdinand Foch, was crossing himself and genuflecting with abysmal piety before each plaster saint surrounded with candles and paper flowers. He sank with joined hands on a praying stool before the shrine of Saint Firminus, his bowed head displaying a nodular brown skull, suggestive of a fossil relic, streaked over by thin strands of unctuous hair.

"The Church militant!" Julian smiled.

Having distinguished itself by the conquest of twenty yards of shell-holes, and more particularly by obtaining the award of a V. C., the 5th Mercian was the recipient of favored treatment, being allotted the best billets and the quietest trenches during the period of general slackness that followed the fizzling out of the Somme offensive. Pleasant weeks were spent in walking tours through the Artois country, varied by agreeable sojourns in Old-World towns and delectable villages and châteaux. In our memories, dulled by the monotonous variety

of our passive peregrinations in accordance with the schedules issued
by divisional staff, topographical names and chronological order faded
as though writ in water. Like trippers from some Wild West state,
abysmally ignorant of every historical or geographical association of
European localities, rushing on a conducted tour, we were unable to
recall a week later where we had passed, where we had slept a few days
before. Only pictures without location in time or space survived in our
recollection of those stagnant days. What was the name of the village
where, one evening, we were entertained by the pretty schoolmistress?
Where was that pleasant French château, so-called by courtesy, being
in truth a two-storied country house set in the midst of its park, where
we enjoyed such luxurious hospitality? The owners, an old-style
French nobleman and his daughter, remained secluded in two rooms
of a distant wing, and were only glimpsed as they took their daily exercise in the alleys of the park, attired in deepest mourning for the three
sons of the family killed in the earlier months of the war. The stately
parqueted rooms were given over to the use of the English allies, and
an old servant brought us daily presents of choice wine and of fowl.
Whereabouts was the tumbledown farm where we were sheltered one
rainy night, and, as the battalion moved off next morning, Captain
Weeney discovered he had left his trench-coat behind, and, going back
for it, asked the buxom farm wench in his rudimentary French whether
she had seen *"une capote anglaise?"* Whereat she discreetly invited
him upstairs. Undulating woodland; rivers and canals bordered with
rows of poplars; little towns, awakened from their secular sleep by the
momentary contact with the men from the trenches; forgotten provincial towns that looked like eighteenth-century aquatints; canvas-camps
on lush grass aroused even in the simple hearts of our sentimental
Tommies emotions of the picturesque, leaving detached memories.

In the fading twilight, the day's march once brought us to the wooded down-slope of a little valley, in the deep shadow of which glowed
a blacksmith's forge. Above it rose the battlements of a castle to which
the billeting officer directed our steps. We passed the barbican and
crossed the moat over a port-cullissed drawbridge, and entered the court
of the machicolated keep, flanked by posterns, pepper-box turrets and
bartizans, surrounded by corbelled and embrasured curtaining walls,
strengthened by pointed flanking towers. An aged serving-maid, in a

quaint white cap with flapping wings, preceded the officers to their quarters, bearing a branched brass candlestick up the stone steps of the twisting stairs, *"pour éclairer la montée à ces messieurs."* Our sleeping berths were in vaulted chambers, groined with ogival mouldings. The deeply splayed windows overlooked the rounded tops of the neighboring hills and the chimneys of the little burg clustered at the foot of the manor. Flights of cheeping swifts flitted in the evening sky about the age-stained towers. Alcove couches hung with faded and threadbare arras, worm-eaten chests of carved wood, basins and ewers of copper, praying stools and receptacles for holy water, formed the furnishings, unchanged since ancient days.

Three ladies, of the indefinite and changeless age of old maids, though the youngest might still be in her thirties, were our hostesses, zealous, with high civility, of our comfort, though reserved and seldom seen except when crossing the yard every morning and evening to betake themselves to the chapel. The curé, a jovial-faced peasant, was their familiar and liked to grace the mess with his company.

"We are well accustomed to the English," said the hearty priest. "We went, you know, many of us with your King Edward."

"With King Edward VII?" asked the colonel, surprised.

"I mean King Edward III. We of Picardy went, many of us, with him to Crécy, not being at that time over friendly to King Philip of France. Ever since, we are looked upon as half English. There is much English in our speech, I am told, from long usage. For instance, the animal which the French call *'lapin,'* we call 'rabbit'; we say 'cat' rather than *chat;* your word 'town' is quite intelligible to us, for it is our 'ton,' or 'tun.' "

Julian was appointed deputy to thank our hostesses for their hospitality. He praised the beauty of their manor.

"Oui, c'est un bon castel," said the eldest sister; 'a good castle,' meaning a serviceable fortress. "The Prussians would not easily take it," she said with a mild, confident smile.

The room which Julian occupied was, he was informed, "the duke's room," and he supposed at first that the reference was to the ducal owner, who might at the moment be absent. But it appeared that the "duke" was Duke Charles of Burgundy, who had at some time occupied the room in the course of his campaigns against King Louis XI. The latter had also been a guest at the castle, and had been lodged in the room now occupied by the colonel, which was known as *"la chambre du Roy,"* and was, his hostesses informed Julian, always kept in readiness for a royal visit. For the ladies, although properly speaking Burgundian in their allegiance, admitted, as a sort of concession, their loyalty to the crown of France. As for the Revolution and the present republican government, which was regarded by them as continuous with it, it was a mere incidental and transient disorder, scarcely worthy of being taken into account. The present wars—the ladies, who spoke an antique sort of French, referred to *"les guerres,"* "the wars"; the present campaign being vaguely confounded with the war of 1870—were the result of the lack of government in France and also of the persecution of the Church due to the influence of M. Voltaire. These were, however, modernities of little importance. The ladies expressed their gratitude to the King of England for sending his troops to the assistance of *"le Roy"*—they pronounced the word "Roy" as it would be pronounced in English.

The young officers, as well as Mr. Viney, were deeply impressed by their brief residence at the ancient château, and even Private Hooge, Julian's batman, was moved to express archæological and esthetic emotions as he brought Julian's tunic and sambrowne belt in the morning, with the buttons polished and the leather shining like a mirror.

"You should see the chimney in the kitchen, sir, and the cellars. You would think you was in church, in a cathedral. Remind me of steel-engravings I've seen in an illustrated Shakespeare. Place is a regular mooseum. It's a liberal education, sir, to see a place like this."

"My dear Hooge," said Julian, sipping his morning tea, "beware of the false fascination of picturesque antiquities. It may be a liberal education, but it is also an obstacle to liberal intelligence. The fifteenth century, where this place belongs, was savage, ignorant, brutal, and altogether abominable. You would do better, my dear Hooge, to acquaint yourself with the twentieth century, and to look ahead. To turn your face backward is a form of cowardice and desertion. See King's Regulations."

"You are making a frightful mess, Viney, with your damned tub," observed the Caballero. He was lounging, glossy and perfumed, on his bunk, his breeches unlaced, a pair of exotic *zapatos* on his stockinged feet, engaged in reading *Flossie, A Venus of Sixteen,* acquired from a hawker of pornographic literature at Saint Pol. Viney, modestly screened by a towel hanging over the backs of two chairs, was in his green canvas tub, lathering his person. "Hey, Spragg! . . . Spra-a-ag! Clean up the mess Mr. Viney is making. You know, Viney, you can get a real hot bath, in a real tub, at the convent. One franc, fifty centimes. Wonder whatever made the nuns install a bathroom? Unusual. And place it at the disposal of the officers of His Majesty's Expeditionary Force? Had a most luxurious tub. The sister quite a jolly soul. Stood there talking after she had run on my bath. Didn't seem disposed to retire. Wonder whether she intended to stay and assist in rubbing the old back. Bet she would if I had tried it on. I'm a bloody fool. Always repent moral impulses. The still small voice. Spaniards go mad at the idea of fun with a nun. *Una muenca.* Catholic idea, you know. Bride of Christ. Give horns to our Lord Jesus Christ. Deadly sin. Wasn't exactly a beauty, the sister, but a hefty enough country wench. *Una cantonera morena.* Curiosity. *Mierda!* Wish I'd tried it on. Minorites, they are. Fun all the same, a Minorite nun *en ropas minores. Hacer zancadilla con une muencita redonda de cucharros y cobuda de panza!*"

"Oh, dry up, with your dago jabberwocky. Don't take away that towel, Spragg," exclaimed Mr. Viney, rising from the waters, anadyomene.

"I wasn't addressing you, Mr. Viney without a vine leaf. I was addressing my remarks to Mr. Bern, who is a scholar. A queer fish you look, Mr. Viney, in your pure naturals. Fancy a girl wanting to go to bed with that!"

"Dry up, I say, or I'll hit you," Mr. Viney said, blushing and enduing his khaki shirt.

"Dry yourself up, you irate lamb. You have assumed the virile toga ere having parachieved the desiccation of your backside and appurtenances. Have you read this book? It would have an uplifting influence upon you. The blighter has arguments that would make you retract. *Hay muchas buenas cosas fornicarias.* By the way, Bern, you know that old Forny sends his compliments and invites us all to dine in town. Wants to make the acquaintance of the ladies, does old Forny.

Great lad. Remember the schoolmistress at that hole of a place? Kissed her as though he had been sucking an orange. Application at headquarters for a job at the base. Forny heard there were some ladies of considerable accomplishment in the town, the place where you get the Moët et Chandon at six francs the half-bottle, you know."

"The young woman at the Chapeau Rouge?" queried Bern, looking up from the *Life of Robespierre*.

"No, not that one. You mean the one with the baby? *Es cosa rica. Guapa de veras*. But she's a snob. *Se ha puesto muy copetuda*. Swollen head. When the Germans were through here, Prince Rupert of Schweinbauch, who was in command of the division, issued orders that the prettiest girl in the place should be brought to him to solace the tedium of the night. The choice fell upon Mademoiselle of the Chapeau Rouge. Prince Rupert was killed the following day at Le Câteau. Ever thereafter Mademoiselle and her people have conceived so exalted a pride of caste that she thinks herself too good to mingle with the common herd. She is minded to make a good marriage with a wealthy '*industriel.*' Her father counts on becoming *Maire* after the war."

Julian had noted the new suburban residence which Mademoiselle's father was having built. We were quartered near a little Artois town which retained picturesque architectural memories of sixteenth-century Spanish occupation. Though it lay within half-an-hour's footing distance from the trenches, and the Germans could without opposition from our thinly manned line have walked into it—as they in fact did not long after we had left the sector—the town appeared to continue its normal life, and was indeed enjoying unprecedented prosperity owing to the presence of its British defenders. Only here and there, on the outskirts, had a stray shell demolished a house or two. Next to one of these, the host of the Chapeau Rouge was having a new, pretentious-looking villa built, and as Julian passed the place, he had seen workmen sitting on the scaffolding finishing off the plaster decorations of the façade which bore in large figures the date, 1916.

The sector of trenches we occupied during our fortnightly turns of duty was, from long occupancy, endowed with all the comforts of modern trench luxury, and we betook ourselves, when our turn came round, to our cosily appointed dugouts as we might have resorted to a week-end bungalow. The line was approached through pleasant orchards which still bore fruit, and the neatly revetted trenches ran through a demolished village which had been the scene of one of the B.E.F.'s first futile offensives. Above the levelled ruins rose as conspicuous landmarks a Singer sewing-machine and, by the demolished church, a crucifix. The latter had probably been re-erected by pious hands, like the "Lady of the Limp" on the steeple at Albert, a miraculous madonna said to bleed when struck, which pious French sappers had firmly secured with wire cable in its pendant position.

So pacific were our relations with our Germanic neighbors across the way that we seldom suffered more than an occasional casualty or two from the accidental dropping of a trench mortar bomb or a minnie. The only serious loss of lives during our occupancy of the sector was caused by Captain Scrutch, the medical officer, an indefatigable collector of war souvenirs, who had sought to detach the nose-cap of a dud shell with a hammer and chisel, and had been blown up to fragments, together with a lance-corporal and four other ranks.

On another occasion a young divisional officer was permitted to amuse himself by arranging a gas attack, and his cylinders of obnoxious gas, after remaining, despite general protests, aligned for a week near the first support trench, while waiting for a favorable wind, became uncorked, almost compelling us to evacuate our comfortable quarters. The delinquent tock emma wallah was sent down to carry out his nefarious experiments at Etaples, out of danger to the fighting troops.

Accidents such as these scarcely disturbed the even tenor of our warlike activities. From our observation posts, ingeniously camouflaged, of which the most picturesque was named after Heath Robinson, we could observe the peaceful activities of our neighbors, the arrival of ration carts and of the postman, to the delectation of the good Fritzes, who gathered round smoking long porcelain-bowled pipes.

"Not half bad, the jolly war," Mr. Dummer remarked, giving voice to the general opinion.

"Wait till the winter and the mud, my boy," I said. "And you don't know the Salient."

"Remember Belgium! No damn fear of any one forgetting it, who's been there," the Caballero confirmed. "We're just being fattened up for the slaughter, like those Indian gods who were given a good time before having their throats cut."

To some the very deadliness of that uneventful peace was more intolerable than any hardship or danger. Julian, who had borne himself stolidly, and even with a certain morbid exhilaration, during the strenuous days of July, was now visibly fuming.

"As bad as solitary confinement, which drives men mad," he let out once. "I feel bedrugged, bemused, mind and spirit rotting. And the worst is that there is no escape. It is not here alone. It is everywhere the same, wherever one might be. Europe is in a state of suspended animation. Time is standing still, nothing is happening or can happen."

"Nothing happening! Crickey!" exclaimed Shakespeare, overhearing the last words. "The biggest war in history, that's all. And there's a chap who complains that nothing's happening."

Julian considered for some moments the infant, murmuring under his breath:

> "He that outlives this day, and comes safe home
> Will stand a tip-toe when this day is named."

Then, aloud, repeated: "Nothing at all. For the present, nothing except this war can happen. And after? Have you any faint notion of what you will do, Mr. Shakespeare? Or you, Laurie? Or I? Wherein we are neither wiser nor less wise than any of our statesmen, rulers, or philosophers. No one is able to turn a thought to what will follow, to what lies behind the war's dead wall, which shuts off the horizon. Before, everybody—you, Shakespeare, you, Laurie—looked out into the future, into life spread, vaguely maybe, but interminably before you, for the future would be set upon the same stage as the past. But any one who should suppose that things will begin again where they left off, that the thread will be picked up where it was dropped, is a lunatic. The change will be so great that none is able to think of it, much less to provide for it. None can think ahead beyond the dead wall. The intelligence of Europe, the life of Europe, is at a standstill."

Almost never, among us, were politics mentioned. Though no restrictions were placed upon our receipt of newspapers, scarcely ever did we see any, mostly because we were indifferent as to procuring them. The pictures of Bairnsfather in the *Bystander*, and feminine forms in the *Tattler* and *Vie Parisienne*, sufficed us. The war itself interested us little. We knew but vaguely what took place beyond our immediate sector.

Remote rumors reached us of Rumania's entry into the war and of Mackensen's sweep over the country. Julian learned of the death of the old Austrian emperor from a scrap of newspaper in which some of the Caballero's purchases had been wrapped. There were the mimeographed "Divisional Information" sheets, currently known as "Comic Cuts," which depicted the horrible plight and demoralisation of the Central Powers and the triumphant achievements and brilliant prospects of the Allied Forces. Even the simplest readers were moved to mirth at the naïveté of the communiqués. There was the unvarying "latrine rumor" of an imminent "big push" that would end the war.

Not that the officers, old or young, and the temporary gentlemen at the Front were wholly devoid of political convictions. Their views were indeed so definite as to be to all intents unconscious and automatic. They had no particular reference to the war or the immediate situation, but were the unvarying politics of decent Englishmen, fixed, unalterable, and eternal. It would no more have occurred to any of them to regard those politics as possible themes of discussion than to enter into an argument about the Ten Commandments. They were hence nothing to get excited about. Divergence from them was only possible in a cad, and like the table manners of a cad, was not so much morally reprehensible as ridiculous. The political creed of decent Englishmen was completely represented by *Punch;* deviations from it were a subject of derision and hilarity rather than of serious indignation.

It was therefore exceptional for post-prandial conversation to take on a mildly political turn, as it did on the occasion of the little party which Colonel Cator gave at the *Lion d'Or,* instead of degenerating, as it usually did at such times, into an exchange of smutty anecdotes. This may have been due in part to the obvious desirability of retaining in so deliberately mixed a gathering a larger measure of dignity than would have been demanded by custom in a mess of pucka gentlemen. But despite the easy time which the battalion had lately enjoyed, the personnel had, as usual, gradually been changing. Inglis, having gone on leave for his investiture by the King, had for one inscrutable reason after another obtained extensions of leave to which there seemed to be no limit. He had been unable to keep his first appointment at the Palace. "Was abso-bloody-lutely blotto," the Caballero, who had accompanied him, reported. The King had had to be put off twice. Burthrop had found his way back to the line after a long convalescence from trench fever. Several fellows, ranging from a Rugby boy to a draper's assistant, who had formerly served as lance-corporal in Kitchener's first army, filled up the gaps.

"A pretty mixed mob the army is becoming," remarked Colonel Cator to Julian in an expansive mood, as they were out for a canter in the Nieppe forest. The colonel had just had one of his hunters sent over, his previous charger, also from his own stables, having contracted the staggers, and having had to be shot. He had asked Julian to accompany him while he tried out the hack. "Would rather sit down in an office at Whitehall than trust my fifteen stone to a G.S. hairy," he said. "A remount wallah offered me a ghora that I wouldn't put between the shafts of the Maltese cart. This is a useful enough plug and safe to hack, but not a patch on the grey mare. Was too good for the field, of course. A good looker, standing sixteen hands, and as sound as a bell, but for a slight noise that, however, never stopped her. A straight mover and could park her like an Indian cow pony. Would stand at attention for hours on end. This fellow's just up from grass. Brushed his near hind and had to be put in a Yorkshire boot. But seems all right now, though perhaps a little speedy-cutting. We'll soon wear that down over here. Well, as I was saying, not one of those fellows can sit a horse. Should be in the *shutur suwar,* the camel corps, don't you know. Fulliston? Why, my dear fellow, he's a dago cow-puncher. No form, sir, no form. His heels are always in the air above his toes, has a forward seat from looking for the pommel of a bronco saddle, and positively no hands at all. No sir, not a horseman."

Colonel Cator was sorely troubled as to what the British army was coming to. But despite the wound to his deepest feelings inflicted by the unavoidable presence of rankers and persons like Hinchpin, the draper's assistant, in the battalion, he was all the more anxious not to display his feelings, and to uphold the tradition of equality among holders of the King's commission. The dinner he gave at the little inn of the town was indeed expressly intended to set an example to the confounded rankers and bounders which the necessities of the present emergency had caused to be admitted to the company of *pucka sahibs.* But it was at the same time desirable that those impassable barriers should, even in the very act of setting them ostensibly aside, be unmistakably indicated, by abstaining from giving full rein to the conversational licence which is admissible only in the genuine equality of pucka gentlemen.

The unwonted seriousness which the after-dinner talk assumed—notwithstanding an unsurpassed vintage of Gevrey-Chambertin, 1904, the Moët et Chandon, 1911, and, most delectable and exhilarating of all, a rare Yquem, 1896 (the stock of the "Lion d'Or's" cellar being remarkably rich and select)—was perhaps due in part to Colonel Cator's disappointment in the young ladies of the house, of whom he had heard glowing reports from Major Sotty and Captain Weeney, but whose charms turned out not to be of the kind which he, the colonel, had expected in Frenchwomen of their class. Our hostesses, Mademoiselle Germaine and her younger sister, Léonie, favored us indeed generously with the pleasure of their company while expertly supervising the service of the banquet and later consenting to join us, after the King, proposed by Major Sotty, had been drunk.

"The King was over again inspecting, I hear," remarked Shakespeare in a whisper to the Caballero as the company sat down again in silence. "He fell off his horse."

"I took over a picked twenty-five from our mob to Abeelee for inspection by the King, when we were over at Elverdinghe," the Caballero recalled. "He fell off his horse."

"Gentlemen, the ladies!" proposed the colonel. "No, Sotty, I'm not going to tell that story."

"The ladies!! Bless 'em."

"For they are jolly good fellows . . . !!"

On the stone hearth Julian's glass broke to splinters. Which gallant example meeting with the colonel's enthusiastic approval, it was followed by the remainder of the company.

"I will tell you a story," said the colonel. "No, not that one, Sotty, not the one you mean. It is the custom, gentlemen—as we say, *mamool,* with regiments in India—to give a banquet in honor of a new officer, whatever his rank, who joins the regiment. The newcomer is the guest of honor and is seated on the right of the Commanding Officer, who makes it a point to devote his attention to the guest and show him every courtesy. When we were stationed at Hoshiarpur, a newly commissioned youth of humble origin who had been at first attached to a sapper corps was transferred to our mess. The usual ceremonial *khana* was given in his honor. He sat on the right of the C.O., who addressed his conversation to him, and was served first. While we were yet at the soup, the *khitmutgar* (the waiter, you know) offered him ice to cool the wine-glasses. The poor mut, who had never before eaten in a gentlemen's mess, was painfully embarrassed, having no notion of the purpose of the proffered ice. *'Kuch burf lehogeh, sahib?'*—'Will you take some ice?'—said the khitmutgar. In desperation the poor wretch helped himself to ice and dropped it into the hot soup. A general titter, rippled round the table. But the C.O., quietly continuing the conversation, as the khitmugar offered him the ice, dropped it in the most natural manner into his soup. Every one followed his example. The ruined soup was well worth the lesson."

Having, with somewhat cumbersome tediousness, delivered himself of his didactic anecdote, Colonel Cator drank the hostesses' health. But, in truth, the presence of the ladies, instead of imparting to the convivial exhilaration the pleasantly erotic touch for which the colonel had been prepared, exercised instead upon the conversation that decent restraint which used, in England, to be thrown off in the last moments of conviviality at the migration of the ladies to the drawing-room. Mademoiselle Germaine, a tall blonde, elegantly gowned for the occasion in rustling grey charmeuse and adorned with substantial jewelry, had paid several visits to England, and not only spoke fluent English, but had acquired a sense of English manners which would have enabled her to hold her own at a gathering at Cranne Hall. She and her younger sister, Mademoiselle Léonie, who, although more timid and less accomplished, was effectively chaperoned by Mademoiselle Germaine, joined us with unembarrassed gaiety, and the elder sister, being a passable pianist and vocalist, entertained the company with selections from the "Bing Boys," and with popular ditties such as, "Oh, it's a lovely war," and "When there isn't a girl about," besides encouraging the young officers to join her in old favorites like "Three blind mice," and "There is a tavern in the town." Mr. Pluckley, who had a sonorous baritone voice, favored us with some "Indian Love Lyrics," and his rendering of "Pale Hands I Loved" elicited much appreciation.

It was, nevertheless, quite evident that it would have been as much out of the question for Colonel Cator to invite the young ladies to sit on his knee, as if the dining-room of the Lion d'Or had been the drawing-room of an English country house.

The colonel later expressed in confidence to Major Sotty and Julian his conviction that Mademoiselle Germaine was a German spy, a charge which he was, indeed, in the habit of levelling, without much discrimination, against any of the French population when, for one reason or another, they did not entirely meet with his approval. The fact that Mademoiselle and her sister continued to reside, flaunting considerable affluence, in a town immediately under German gunfire was, in Colonel Cator's estimation, sufficient evidence of the treasonable nature of their purposes, and the suspicion was more than confirmed by the young lady's frequent trips to England and her familiarity with English affairs. In the present instance some color might, by a strange coincidence, have been lent to the colonel's suppositions, by the fact that some time afterwards, a few days after the sudden exit of the two sisters, a German attack took place which resulted in the occupation of the little town and of the whole district by the Germans.

Mademoiselle Germaine's acquaintance with current English affairs was indeed considerably more up-to-date than most of us, who had not recently been home on leave, might claim to possess, and it was in consequence of some remark of hers that the conversation was led to assume an unwonted political turn. The lenient and easy-going manner in which conscientious objectors were being treated in England would, she said, fill the French with amazement, and would never be tolerated in her country.

This was a sore subject. For however much pucka soldiers like Colonel Cator might deplore the humiliation inflicted upon a gentlemanly army by the admission of all manner of rag, tag, and bobtail into its command, they at the same time regarded, with some apparent inconsistency, any opposition to conscription as the most heinous of treasons. Mademoiselle's remark had therefore the effect of fanning to flame the loyal emotions of the company.

Mr. Viney took it upon himself to observe, in defence of English toleration, that the liberty of the subject was more respected in England than in France. But Major Sotty, whose grocery business at Hungerford was doing an enormously extended trade in army contracts and in supplying whiskey to officers' messes, could not refrain from some asperity in the expression of his patriotic sentiments.

"Liberty!" he snorted. "That is but a catch-word of those blasted agitators, mostly foreigners, to appeal to so-called workers. Workers! A worker is a blighter who goes on strike. Liberty means liberty to go on strike. Let those damned shirkers come over here and try to go on strike. We'd soon teach them. No eight hours' day in the army."

The Rugby boy signified like a gentleman his approval. "More pay and less work. That's what they're always striking for. Perfectly disgusting!"

"When we had a working party of pork-and-beans," said Mr. Shakespeare, "and they were set to filling and carrying sandbags for the front-line parapet, the blighters shouldered three bags at a time. Our fellows were disgusted. 'No, you don't, Antonio,' they said—they called every Portuguese Antonio—'one sandbag per man is the rule here. We don't want no blacklegging.'"

"Have you heard, Monsieur le Major, that they are actually sending Monsieur MacDonald and Monsieur Henderson to France on a conducted tour of the front?" asked Mademoiselle.

This was too much. The major's face, already congested, deepened in hue.

"A pretty government we have, with old 'Wait-and-see' pandering to dirty traitors. No wonder we're a long time winning the war. Ramsay MacDonald and Arthur Henderson! German agents, as everybody knows. They'll be sending that fellow Bernard Shaw next. I know where I would send such perishers. Line them up and shoot them!"

"Come, come, Sotty, you must not get excited. *Sab karo, sab karo!* You're not taking your wine well," said the colonel, filling his glass with Château Yquem. "It will do the blighters good to see with their own eyes the hardships we go through. Damned good stuff, this, what? Mademoiselle, my compliments. Your cave . . . Pardon, your *'cave'* deserves a military medal. Can't say I've tasted better at Jules's or Odonino's. My father knew a good Burgundy. Did a little on the side. No derogation, you know. Used to say that there hadn't been a good Burgundy since 1879. Though, of course, the great vintage of 1865 has never been equalled. He sold a bottle of genuine Romanie-Conti, thirty years old, to a Russian grand duke for five thousand guineas."

"Ought to be shot. Blasted German spies, Ramsay MacDonald and Arthur Henderson . . ." the major was still murmuring.

"Now, now, Sotty, try a little Moët et Chandon; Yquem perhaps a little too heady for you. There. Bubbly not so liverish, what? Let's hear what Bern has to say. He's a bit of a politician. Why, man, you haven't opened your mouth the whole evening. You haven't been drinking. Shame upon you. You remind me, don't you know, Bern, of a colt I once had, far too serious for his age. Sire a bit stale, you see. You can always tell a colt or a filly that's by an old sire. Drops his head, and hangs his gib. Inclined to silent meditation. Bet your father —no offence, you know—had sown his wild oats before you were born. Thought so. Now, forward. *Agehburho!* Philosopher and scholar. Tell our friend Sotty not to be so bloodthirsty. Unbecoming of a soldier. Pronounce judgment, Bern. Should the sacred perishers, Ramsay MacDonald and Arthur Henderson, be shot at dawn?"

"Not yet," said Julian.

"What do you mean? Not yet?" glared the Major. "Are we to wait till the blasted traitors have sold England to the Huns, the Sinn-Feiners, and the Trade-unionists?"

"Now then, Sotty. You are befuddled, if you will excuse my saying so. Your sense of humor is blunted. You don't see the joke. Bern is quite right. Not yet! Ah, ah, ah! Very good, Bern. Now, Sotty, listen. I will explain to you. The government are not such fools as you would make out. I have been told on good authority that the Comic Opposition led by Messrs. Ramsay and Arthur—blast their traitor souls—is entirely run by the government. Know how they got the Comic Opposition together? They sent down the Strand, where the Variety agents have their offices, and booked the whole troop of eccentric comedians for the duration. A comic newspaper proprietor was engaged to write them up, and the blighter Bernard Shaw himself was got to contribute the gags. Now d'you see? It keeps the people in good spirits. Keeps up their morale. No deuced danger of those fellows of the Comic Opposition ever being taken seriously by the public common sense of the British people."

The colonel's wit excited general hilarity. The Rugby boy had to be smartly smacked on the back by Shakespeare, as he choked over his wine. Mr. Hinchpin dropped all his h's, and the Caballero pretended to pick them up from under the table, taking occasion to attempt liberties with Mademoiselle Germaine's ankles, which were, however, sharply withdrawn. Pluckley was trying out his French on Mademoiselle Léonie, who, through unacquaintance with the English language, had been unable to take part in the general conversation. But Mademoiselle Germaine sending her on the pretext of reinforcing the ranks of bottles, the young lady took occasion to retire as the atmosphere became increasingly hilarious. The somewhat embarrassed decorum which, in the earlier part of the banquet, had chilled the spirit of the younger subalterns, was rapidly thawing.

Mr. Hinchpin, somewhat wounded by the Caballero's jocosity, confided in an aside to the Rugby boy that, although he might not have enjoyed the benefits of a classical education, he was born a gentleman, and knew better than did some people how to behave in the presence of ladies.

"When we was training at Marsden, the C.O. 'ad us at a party where several very nice lydies was invited. Was fond of telling funny stories, was the C.O., just like the colonel 'ere. The lydies laughed so much at one of 'is stories that one of them, who was sitting next to me, broke wind rather loudly. So I says, says I, thinking to spare the poor young thing's feelings, I says: 'Beg pardon, lydies,' as though the accident 'ad 'appened to me, like. And when we took leave, she came up to me, did the young lydy, and she says to me: 'Mr. 'Inchpin, you're a gentleman.' Very nice and lydylike they was."

Mr. Pluckley was once more touched to song by the happy vintage:

"Old MacDonald had a farm in Ohio-io-io,
And on that farm he had some dogs, in Ohio-io-io.
Bow-wow, wow, wow, wow. . . ."

The round was taken up by the young officers at the lower end of the table. The farm animals barked, yapped, howled, mewed, purred, bayed, brayed, neighed, bellowed, mooed, lowed, grunted, snorted, crowed, clucked, cackled, gaggled, gobbled, guggled, and cooed.

"That fellow Parts, in my platoon, is pestering me to recommend him for promotion to lance-corporal," said the Rugby boy to Adjutant Weeney. "Says he can't bide no longer being addressed by the sergeant as 'Private Parts.'"

"Her privates we," said Weeney.

Mademoiselle Germaine persisted in her condemnation of the British Government's excessive leniency towards conscientious objectors. The Major was growing purple. But the colonel intervened, addressing himself with a gallant gesture to the hostess.

"We are more subtle, Mademoiselle. The long-haired conchies are quite useful fellows. They are serving their King and country by making laughing-stocks of themselves. Is that not so, Bern?"

"The conscientious objectors have been the founders of the British Empire," Julian said.

"Eh, what? You have the advantage of me. It is above my head. Unfold your meaning, sir philosopher."

"When England was about to enter the war against the northern states of the American Union, the conscientious objectors of Lancashire refused to handle the southern slave-owners' cotton. The distracted millers forced the government to change their policy in order to save them from ruin. Canada, which was about to join the American Union, was generously granted self-government, and thus became the first self-governing Dominion. The glorious, free British Empire was thus founded, thanks to the conscientious objectors of the Lancashire mills."

"Ingenious, very, Bern. An ingenious argument. For all that, of course, you would not, as a gentleman, have taken sides with the damned Yankees, would you, Bern?" the colonel earnestly asked.

"Were taking sides needful, yes," Julian said.

"Fight on the side of the Yankee bounders? Never!"

"Oh, oh, oh!"

"Ohio-io-io!"

> "And he had some cats in the farm in Ohio-io-io!
> Miao . . . Miao, miao, mia-o-io!"

While the caterwaul went on, Colonel Cator, by this time very bloodshot, stared with dropped jaw. Then, suddenly recovering, burst into hoarse laughter, smacking his thigh.

"I see it, I see it. Sotty, you damn fool, Bern is pulling our legs. He's a philosopher and all that, but he's first and foremost a born soldier, don't you see? Wasn't thinking of politics, was thinking of strategy. And what more magnificent strategy was ever seen than that of Ulysses S. Grant? You haven't been to Sandhurst, Sotty. You haven't gone into it as you should. Man, Cold Harbor, Chattanooga! Double and triple feints that not even the commanding officers could tell from the attack. Never anything like it, not even Napoleon at Quatre Bras, though that was a masterpiece. Now, look here, Sotty. Pay attention. See, here, the bottle of Moët et Chandon? That's the army of the Cumberland under Thomas, bottled up in Chattanooga. The *rootee* over there is the Tennessee River, see, bending round like this. This fork is Missionary Ridge, and this knife Lookout Mountain, with Bragg's Confederates entrenched on the top and across the valley. Hooker is here at the bend of the river, and Sherman, just over from the Mississippi, is higher up by Chickamauga Creek. Is that clear, Sotty?"

"As mud," mumbled the major.

"Wait. Let's have it down on paper. Any one got a piece of paper?"

"Will this do, sir?" Hinchpin said, producing a battered trench map.

"Thanks. Now look here. How are you going to attack Bragg sitting round you on those hills? Mark, three detached numerically inferior bodies of troops. Three feints. First Sherman on the right wing, whose map is wrong and mistakes a hummock for the ridge. But the second attack holds Bragg's left at Tunnel Hill. Thomas's feint on the centre turns out a smash, a veritable Battle of the Marne. Then comes Hooker over on the left. Battle in the Clouds. The surrounder surrounded. Eh? Magnificent, what? None of your pure frontals, you see, but bigger than a frontal. I tell you, Sotty, that fellow Grant was a genius. Then the final campaign. Sherman's march to Savannah."

"Chattanooga! What an amusing name!" said Mademoiselle Germaine. "Let me have a look at Chattanooga, please."

The colonel passed over the paper to Mademoiselle.

"And in his farm he had some pigs in Ohio-io-io!
Frr . . . grrr . . . grrrr . . . grr . . . oio!"

"Nothing would induce me to fight under a Yankee bounder," the Major was declaring. "England, England right or wrong!"

Shade of General Royden!

"And so say all of us!"

The Caballero bent over Julian's ear.

"La chica se la ha puesto en la media, la mapa."

"I am surprised to hear you express so disloyal a sentiment, sir," Bern said. "Do you mean to suggest, Major Sotty, that England is ever wrong? Am I to understand that you are of opinion that England was in the wrong when opposing tooth and nail every liberal reform against feudalism on the continent, when stoutly supporting the noble Bourbons and the *émigrés* against the French Republic, against Italian and Spanish liberals? Are you implying that England is wrong in her upholding support of Irish landlords? That England was wrong in her support of Southern slave-owners? Are you hinting, Major, that England was not right in marshalling the Empire to the assistance of the Jo'burg Jews against the Boers driven from the Cape? A most disloyal sentiment, Major. England is never wrong. English policy is invariably dictated by concern for the eternal moral principles, to the neglect of all selfish interests. England is the Defender of Right and Justice."

"Take that, Sotty," said the colonel, who was by now inclined to be somewhat drowsy. "Have you any more of that Château Yquem, Mademoiselle? Sotty, do you hear? Reconsider your sentiments. The soul of England is always right. The moral conscience. The playing fields of Eton. England fights for the triumph of right and justice among all peoples."

"If I might add a word," said Mr. Viney, whose voice was a little tremulous, "I should like to say that England is fighting for right and justice among the German people also. I mean, sir, we are not fighting the German people, but the Kaiser, junkers, bankers. We are fighting, I mean to say, for the liberation of the German people."

In a back room, reserve forces of choice vintage stood aligned on the sideboard by the horse-hair sofa, ready to go into action. Mademoiselle Germaine felt herself suddenly gripped from behind by strong arms, and an audacious hand entangled among elastic suspenders and flimsy silkeries searched insolently.

"Ah, cochon! Vous êtes fou, tout de même . . . ! How dare you, sir, how dare you? Let me go," she hissed, struggling and twisting like a cat in the Caballero's arms.

"Not until you have paid ransom, Mademoiselle," smiled he, drawing out from under the hem of Mademoiselle's silk stocking Hinchpin's trench-map.

"I regret to differ from you, Mr. Viney," said Julian. "I regret, I say, not to be able to see eye to eye with you in the matter. Did you come upon the Kaiser or the junkers, or the bankers in the Leipzig redoubt, Mr. Viney? You came upon the German people. Who mans the guns and points the rifles? The Kaiser or the German people?"

"They are compelled," Mr. Viney said.

"Compelled? Compelled? Sixty million people with machine-guns and rifles in their hands, compelled? Compelled by a handful of colonels and bankers? As well might you say, Mr. Viney, that the French are compelled by Monsieur Poincaré, that we are compelled by Mr. Harmsworth and Mr. Lloyd George. Are you compelled, Mr. Viney? Are we compelled?"

"No!!!"

"Here we are, here we are, here we are again!"

"Britons never shall be slaves!"

"If we are compelled, then are we an army of cowards!" Julian said.

"Fooled by their rulers," Mr. Pluckley observed.

"Folly is no defence, else were every criminal blameless. Murderers are hanged, be they fools or sages. Kaiser, junkers, and magnates make war with the full assent, consent, and participation of the German people in arms, or the German people would turn their arms against them. Their folly in not doing so no more attenuates their act than the idiocy of their war-lords is ground to hold them guiltless. Cowards or fools, the people it is who make war and at their door the bloodguilt lies, seeing that they are free to shoot war-mongers should they be so minded. Are we fooled by our newspaper lords? Heaven forfend. (No, Laurie, I am not drunk. My pulse as yours doth temperately keep time and makes as healthful music.) We are fighting the German people, and no plea can sever the guilt they bear, no sophistry. This is a war of the people."

"Do you deny it, Sotty? A war of the people, by the people, for . . ."

("Be quiet, Laurie, don't chip in.) If the people be fools and cowards, then is it well that the earth should be swept clean of ten million fools and cowards."

"Kill more Germans, that's what I say. We are a nation of gentlemen, do you hear?

> "If you can dream—and not make dream your master;
>   If you can think—and not make thought your aim;
> If you can meet with triumph and disaster,
>   And treat with the impostor just the same;
> If you can bear to hear the truth you've spoken
>   Twisted by knaves to make a trap for fools . . ."

Nodding heavily, Colonel Cator mumbled inaudibly.

"When old Forny begins reciting '*If*,' he's terribly boozed," said the Caballero, resuming his seat. Then he whispered in Julian's ear amid the noise: ". . . *Y hay que ver como la he espetada!*"

"Fools and cowards!" Julian sank back into his chair. "And I, too. Fooled to the top of my bent."

VII

IN THE late afternoon light slanting over from Selsey Bill, the trim lawn was sabbatically serene. Its peace was broken only by the noise which little Harry made, prattling loudly to himself and booing and whooping. He was riding a hobby-horse, waving a wooden sword with destructive effect on the bed of geraniums.

"I'se killing Germans!" he informed Julian presently, running up to him, and standing, with pouting fierceness, before him. "Has oo killed many Germans, Uncle Oolian?"

"Don't know, sonny. People no longer fight on horseback with swords."

"I'se got a gun too," little Harry asserted.

"Even guns are not worth much now," said Julian. "Killing is done by machinery, with big engines."

"Buy me an engine for killing Germans, Mummy."

"Yes, darling. I will buy you a tank," said Viola. She glanced up at Julian, conscious of his disapproval.

But he said nothing.

"We were once near La Bassée," he said, later. "I went up to the place where the Goorkhas attacked. The old breastwork is still distinguishable, constructed entirely of bully-beef tins. I picked up this Goorkha knife, thinking you might perhaps like to have it."

"Ah, the old *kukri*! Aren't they funny? The Gurkhali wallahs use them for anything, cutting wood, carving their food, picking their teeth. It will do nicely for the curio stall at the hospital bazaar. The men are awfully clever at making things out of souvenirs, shell-noses, cartridge cases, badges. Such pretty inkstands and paper-weights, they make. Olive and I are looking after the stall. The *kukri* should fetch quite a lot."

"Olive" was Miss Glamrood, a dreadful creature of uncertain age, attired in butterclothy, untidy things to represent youthful fluffiness.

135

Viola was now hand in glove with the lady and her brother, Herbert Glamrood, a widower with two young daughters. The Glamroods were constantly about the house, with an air of familiarity and possessiveness. They and Viola called one another by their Christian names.

On the evening when Julian had arrived on leave, Mr. Glamrood, a lanky fellow, with undefined mutton-chop whiskers, gold-rimmed spectacles, and a smile which wrinkled the whole of his face and displayed equine teeth, welcomed him with benevolent hospitality.

"Ah, back home from the Front, Lieutenant? No place like home, is there? We hope that you will have a really pleasant rest," Mr. Glamrood bleated in a tone of benign patronage. "I may have to go over to France myself, shortly," he informed Julian. "We are about to make some great improvements there. We are establishing a temperance canteen, with a reading and recreation room, where the boys can play draughts and read the best papers, and we hope to arrange a series of lectures."

The palace of delight was to be erected at Rouen, Mr. Glamrood said in answer to Julian's enquiry as to which sector had been chosen for its location.

The editorial "we" which Mr. Glamrood was in the habit of affecting had reference to a local religious body which held its meetings in a corrugated iron shed that bore in large letters the words: "The Church of the Friends of Jesus." Mr. Glamrood, who was by profession an estate dealer, was its animating spirit. The services were conducted by the Reverend Simon Loughley Spender, formerly a Church of England clergyman. Julian, who was in the habit of dropping in occasionally at the "Pig and Whistle" for a glass of ale—none but watery refreshments being provided at Viola's house—learned from the barman that Mr. Spender, who was also in the habit of frequenting the house, had left the established Church in consequence of charges of indecent exposure which had been brought against him.

"Mind you, I ain't exactly what you might call a Puritan myself," the barman confided. "But I calls it a bit thick, don't you, sir? when a dirty old man goes showing his prick to a lot of kids at the Sunday School."

The police had, at the instance of the ecclesiastical authorities, dropped the prosecution, but Mr. Loughley Spender had, at the suggestion of the bishop, resigned his living and retired from the ministry on grounds of poor health. Having made the acquaintance of Mr. Glamrood, he had accepted that gentleman's offer to conduct an independent church. This had long been a cherished scheme of Mr. Glamrood's, who found no difficulty in raising sufficient funds for the purchase of a piece of land which had long been on his hands.

Viola, whose Catholicism was not bigoted, had now got into the habit of attending the Reverend Spender's, or rather Mr. Glamrood's, church.

"Viola likes our services very much," said Miss Glamrood. "They are so bright and cheerful."

"We are strictly unsectarian and undenominational," bleated Mr. Glamrood. "I hope, Lieutenant, that we may see you at the church next Sabbath. You should not miss it. The minister is having a special service for men. You need not feel any shyness about coming. Every one is heartily welcome, and all pews are free."

On another occasion Mr. Glamrood expressed to Julian his gratification at "the effects which the great trial and test of the war was having upon all people. The splendid change that is taking place in France, for instance, the spirit the French are showing."

"At Verdun, you mean?" queried Julian.

"No." Mr. Glamrood put on a grave look. "I mean the splendid revival of religion in infidel France."

"Herbert has been so helpful," Viola told Julian. On several occasion Julian found Viola engaged in earnest talk with Mr. Glamrood, and the conversation was changed when Julian entered the room. It appeared that most of Viola's affairs were being managed by Mr. Glamrood, who had been advising her about investments. She had purchased a whole row of villas. "Now is a splendid opportunity for investment in real estate," he said. "There will be an enormous rise in values as soon as the war is over."

Viola seldom referred to the past. Her abstention from any expansive or confidential abandonment made unconstrained intercourse difficult. Not that she was insensitive or devoid of deep feeling. Perhaps it was the very strength of her emotions which made it difficult for her to disclose them. She had been genuinely excited when Julian arrived on leave. Her eyes had sparkled with excitement.

"I felt so proud when I saw your name had been mentioned in dispatches," she had said.

But it was difficult to tell what, and how much she felt. Even in regard to little Harry, Viola showed very little manifestation of emotion. Julian never saw her hug the child or evince any extraordinary outward signs of tenderness. Yet her maternal preoccupation verged on morbid extravagance. The child was disgustingly spoilt. He was never reproved when in outbursts of temper, to which he appeared subject; he wrecked his toys, delighting in wholesale destruction, struck and bit his nurse or deliberately spilt porridge or ink on the furniture.

"Doctor Survace says that he is very highly strung," Viola said.

The doctor was generally in attendance two or three times a week, although young Harry, plump, sturdy, and rosy, presented the picture of exuberant health. His mother said, however, that he twitched in his sleep, and was subject to nightmare. Whenever he sneezed, he was immediately put to bed and his temperature was taken. Viola had a whole nurse's outfit and a library of works on infant hygiene. Harry's temperature, his pulse, respiration, and weight were regularly charted. There were weighing scales in the nursery and a close eye was kept on the thermometers, which were placed in every apartment. The nursery had to be kept day and night at an unvarying temperature. Doctor Survace laid down diet charts, and special health foods and expensive preparations were obtained from Fortnum and Mason's. Viola got it into her head that Harry had a tendency to bandy legs, although Doctor Survace assured her, after repeated examinations, that the conformation of the child's limbs was perfectly normal. The doctor had, however, in order to satisfy her, to arrange a consultation with a Harley Street specialist, who recommended electric massage, and Harry went three times a week to a nursing home to have his legs rubbed with a sponge attached to an electric wire.

Viola had now got a special nurse for the boy, "a highly trained qualified nurse," she said. She confided to Julian that Keetje had of late proved far from satisfactory. The Belgian girl, who had now developed into a decidedly attractive young woman, insisted more and more on going out, and sometimes, when she went up to London to see her parents, absented herself for several days at a time, far outstaying her leave. Moreover, Keetje had grown, Viola complained, very pert, answering back in the rudest manner when reproved.

Julian, though he was spared the spectacle of such minor domestic commotions, did, in fact, notice a remarkable self-assurance in the girl's manner.

"I suppose you'll be returning to Belgium after the war, Keetje?" he asked her.

"To Belgium? Not if I know it," she replied.

"You then so much prefer England?"

"It offers greater scope," said Keetje. "Where there is more money, there is more rascality."

"You are quite a philosopher, for a chit of a girl," Julian smiled.

"Chit of a girl, indeed!" Keetje said. Her pronunciation made him regret he had used the expression. "I'm over eighteen now, and if a girl does not know how to put two and two together by then, she never will."

Julian went up to London for the remainder of his leave. More complete solitude could be found, as he well knew from not very remote experience, amid the crowds of London than even the domestic slumbers of Bognor could afford. He had looked forward to enjoying the privacy which life in the field rigorously denied. But Julian was, this time, deceived in the expectation. Circumstances had changed. The war had entered upon a new phase on the home front. The assumption of gravity and austerity of the early days had given place to another and opposite mood. What had been an unimagined novelty had, by continuance and habituation, become in turn the normal tenor of existence. To the younger generation at least, the strange, humdrum peacetime conditions of pre-war days were already becoming legendary. The young people found it as hard to imagine a return to that stuffy, outmoded world as it had previously been to become accustomed to the cataclysmic change of the war. Under the charter of slogans such as, "Keep smiling," or "Are we downhearted?" and of the duty of stimulating by general cheerfulness the morale of the country's heroic defenders, the pretence of solemnity had been set aside and had largely given place to the undisguised enjoyment of the new conditions.

Throngs of women and girls who hurled themselves into "war work" revelled in a new and consecrated emancipation passing the dreams of suffragettes. To give the heroes from the trenches a good time was part of their patriotic duty. On his first landing at Folkestone, Julian had been set upon by a bevy of respectable bourgeois matrons and young women on canteen duty, who had descended upon him with the leers of whores. No impropriety attached to their similarly accosting the khaki heroes in the street in a manner which recalled the solicitations of painted women. "Oh, the dear! Just fresh from the trenches!" smiled fashionably dressed women and sweet young things as Julian passed them in Pall Mall. The carefree youths and temporary gentlemen on leave were ready to respond to the patriotic solicitude of the new wild women. Many of them were, for the first time in their lives, in possession of a cheque-book, the abuse of which by the utterance of uncovered cheques—a frequent enough occurrence—was leniently regarded. Home-leave was a chartered occasion for throwing open the floodgates of revelry and riot. The absence of formal parties—townhouses being for the most part made over to the wounded and convalescent—turned the tide of pleasure into hotels and restaurants, and the multiplied night-clubs where sumptuary and curfew regulations could be evaded. The more private seclusion of the war-working bachelor girls' *garçonnière* rooms replaced the drawing rooms of Mayfair. The London night echoed with the saturnalia, despite the gloom of the darkened streets, with their scanty lights obscured with smears of blue paint as a provision against air-raids.

Pluckley, whom Julian came upon at Short's, told him that Inglis, being somewhat squiffy, had followed a bit of a skirt one night half-way down Great Windmill Street, which was pitch dark. On his pursuing the fluttering allurement into the glare of a lighted bar, its wearer turned out to be a sturdy sergeant of the Black Watch!

Julian, who had looked to his home-leave as an occasion to recuperate amid the creature-comforts of civilisation from the strain of field conditions which, however hardened one might become, wrought a cumulative wear and tear of which one was not always fully aware until the tension had been relaxed, had little desire to participate in the unleashed gaiety. But he was not permitted to indulge his mood.

He had put up at the Savoy, which offered attractive special terms to officers of His Majesty's forces. The very first time he entered the luncheon room he was seized upon by Mrs. Luseley, formerly Dorothy Coston, who impressed him for her table. She was just up from Ireland, where her husband, Colonel Luseley, was stationed, and had come for a few days in the company of Sir Trevor and Lady Gluff, with whom the Luseleys had been spending a hunting season in County Wicklow. The Gluffs, Anglo-Irish country gentry, had brought over their daughter Phoebe, who, determined to do her bit, had obtained a clerical post at the Ministry of Munitions. She was accompanied by her bosom friend, a Miss Tooley, Daphne Tooley, usually called Ultima.

"We had a perfectly delightful season," Mrs. Luseley said. "The hunting is much better than in the Midlands. Phoebe is the champion horsewoman of the county. You should see her put her mount to a stone wall or five-barred gate."

Miss Gluff was a very handsome dark blonde, with the fresh complexion of a country girl, and Irish at that, and her dark check tailor-made outlined superbly significant forms. But she seemed painfully shy and reserved. During the whole of lunch she scarcely spoke a word. Lady Gluff explained in excuse of the young women's gaucherie, that it was their very first visit to London.

Julian asked whether the disturbed state of Ireland did not interfere with sport. Colonel Luseley, as he vouchsafed explanations, snorted like the misguided war-horse in Job.

"They don't usually interfere with hunting," he admitted. "But the most dastardly assassinations of British troops are daily being committed by those cowardly murder-gangs who call themselves the Republican army. Directly after that disgraceful Easter business in Dubin, things were pretty quiet in the country generally, which gave no support to the anarchist rebels. But since the executions of the traitor leaders, all those dirty Irish are showing the most unreasonable unfriendliness towards us. Only the other day one of our officers was brutally murdered while shooting down some peasants who had been found in possession of arms. Troops peacefully patrolling towns are intolerably insulted and booed. Our men show an admirable patience and forbearance. But at Ranelagh a patrol which was being jeered at by a mob of women and children lost patience, and fired, killing one woman and three children. The officer who was in command was found murdered in his room by those blackguards—in retaliation, they said. It makes one's blood boil. They have no idea of clean fighting. They fire on R.I.C. men and troops from behind cover, the cowards."

"Isn't it a rule laid down in Infantry Training always to fire from behind cover, if possible?" Julian could not refrain from remarking.

Sir Trevor thought that Colonel Lusely was rather too hot in his indignation.

"People get too excited over politics. After all, there will always be good hunting, whatever happens. So what does it really matter?"

Mrs. Luseley had a baby. She had given up the idea of professional singing. She was interested to hear that Julian was in Colonel Cator's battalion.

"A very old friend of ours," she said. "You surely remember meeting him at Cranne Hall. He was Captain Cator, then. Mrs. Cator was Helen Hogson, one of the Hogsons of Hogston, cousins twice removed of mother, whose grandfather on her mother's side was a Hogson."

Mrs. Luseley expressed regret that the Gluffs and herself were obliged to return to Ireland the following morning.

"We might otherwise have taken you around a little to meet people. I know how you feel, coming back from the trenches. It is nice to see a lot of people when one is on leave, isn't it?" she said to Julian as they passed into the lounge. "The Gluffs are a very nice family. Related to the Gluffs of Grantham, don't you know. You will find Phoebe and Daphne very nice girls. Of course they are a bit awkward. Country-bred girls, you know. I hope you can look after them a bit and make them feel at home. So brave of them to come to London to do war work, don't you think?"

Julian was not particularly anxious to cultivate the young ladies' acquaintance. It was a bit too much to expect of him. He made, on the contrary, a point of avoiding as far as possible having their company inflicted upon him, and made long detours through the corridors of the Savoy in order to minimize the risk.

Gladly would he in like manner have evaded the incitements to riot that poured upon him, in the form of invitation cards and telephone calls from unknown ladies. The frivolous vivacity of war-time London seemed on a level with the promiscuity of billets and trenches. Julian bethought himself of looking up Eleanor Astley, and betook himself with that intention to Lady Castle's in Chesterfield Gardens. He found her apartment abuzz with the chatter of a numerous company consisting mostly of young women, and likewise including Mrs. Montague-Douglas, Captain Inglis, V.C., and Pluckley.

"I keep open house on Thursdays," Lady Castle, who displayed a kindly pleasure at seeing him, explained to Julian. "When I say 'open,' that is meant almost literally. People nowadays admit almost any one who rings the door-bell. Complete strangers walk in. Every one who is still in Town does it. Any officer on leave is welcome, and the young women come on the chance of meeting them."

Eleanor, Lady Castle regretted, was in Switzerland. There was now no lack of employment, and finding that her work was no longer required, Eleanor had wished to escape from the war atmosphere.

"The war is all the rage now," Lady Castle observed. She spoke with good-natured tolerance, tinged with regret, of what she regarded as her niece's aberrations.

Mrs. Douglas took possession of Julian. Her activities had become largely transferred from the secretarial work of the W.W.W.C.C. to a more social sphere. She was at present interested in a feminine foundation, the Sybil Club, of which Lady Bar was the patroness, and which was for the present palatially lodged in Bar House. Mrs. Douglas insisted on dragging Julian there one morning for lunch, masculine guests of members being, in special circumstances, admitted on tolerance within the walls of the exclusively feminine fortress. The trend of the after-luncheon conversation seemed, however, not altogether to support the stringent interpretation of sexual barriers.

"What's to become of a surplus of some two milion women matrimonially unemployed?" asked Ursula Dickleman amid the clouds of cigarette smoke. "I see that some one seriously suggests in the dignified columns of *The Times* that Bastardy Laws be repealed and all disabilities on illegitimate children removed. Ronald McNeill, M.P., appeals in the *Morning Post* to religious bodies to promote the patriotic cause of fornication 'by coming forward with an honest and courageous pronouncement' that unmarried mothers should be treated with no scorn and that their infants should receive 'a loyal and unashamed welcome.'"

"Quite right too!" said Pamela Porter, the niece of Canon Eustace Fuge. "The Government should adopt the proposal put forward in the House to pay the separation allowances due by the unknown fathers of war babies."

"Or should, as many are advocating, legalize bigamy," said Mrs. Cosmo Smythe (née Felicia Kendrick).

"Or organize contraceptive assistance," said Rachel East, an authoress, the acidulous sharpness of whose tongue and pen was gaining a growing popularity. "I shall insist, *après la guerre finie,* that a monument be set up in a conspicuous site to the women and girls who have fallen during the war."

"There are some things the Controller can't ration," cried in chorus Ursula Dickleman, Cora Manners, and Joyce Ryde.

The women appeared to appreciate to the full the luxurious commodity provided for their foregathering by the generosity of Lady Bar. They sprawled, with legs crossed or unceremoniously elevated in the downy depths of chairs and couches, smoking cigarettes, drinking liqueurs, and displaying the more seductive luxuries of their attire. While the prices of the necessities of life soared to fabulous heights, luxuries had become unwontedly cheap. Bread had gone up to ten times its pre-war price, but oysters and champagne were more accessible than they had ever been. A new efflorescence of feminine luxury was conspicuous, and contrasted with the sobriety that had been modish in the early days of the war. Furs and osprey feathers were general. Silk stockings, which had up to then been a refinement, had become indispensable, and were associated with a novel shortening of skirts—for greater freedom and convenience in war-work, it was said—and high buttoned or laced boots of variously colored kid. Mrs. Montague-Douglas retailed to Julian the expert comments of Sylvia Chantrey.

"You know, by the way," she said, "that Sylvia was married the other day? A banker of the name of Jameson—Jacobson before the War. The wedding was at St. Margaret's, Westminster. Quite a grand affair. Sylvia's bridal dress was gorgeous. She wore a profusion of orange blossoms and carried a huge bouquet of lilies. Margaret Melway was chief bridesmaid. Clever girl, Sylvia. She's given up doing her golliwogs and chronicles, feeling that they were in danger of becoming a little dated. You were an ass to quarrel with her. What business is it of yours if she chooses to amuse herself in her own way? Oh, yes, no use raking up old stories. Well, modern girls make fun, Sylvia says, of the respectable back numbers who still wear drawers. I grant you, it is difficult to foresee the consequences of the revolution. Women no longer can undress, however much they take off."

Lady Bar was shortly expected in Town, Mrs. Douglas informed Julian. She would doubtless take the first opportunity of communicating with him, and seek to provide him with a good time.

Julian could have readily dispensed with the attention. Despite precautions, he could not avoid stumbling upon Miss Phoebe Gluff and her friend Daphne as he passed through the Savoy lounge. The young ladies did not, however, seem to be at a loss for company. They were drinking cocktails with three or four young fellows in khaki slacks.

"Hello! Do come and muck in with this mob," called out Miss Phoebe as Julian tried to get by with a casual greeting. "Ultima is fixing up a binge at the White Owl tonight, with Bob, Jack, and Freddie, who are digging in our shop. It's the best dive in town."

"Your 'shop'?" Julian queried.

"No, the Owl. They've got a posh bar, with bags of funny cocktails. And they give you a gasper with every swill."

"Some look like gaspers, but have ooja-thingumajigs rolled up inside," put in Miss Ultima.

The simple country girls appeared somewhat more sophisticated than Julian's first impressions of them had led him to suppose.

"You do not find the work at your office overtaxing, I hope?" he enquired.

"No blooming fear. We chuck it on the tick of four," said Phoebe. "You can bet your boots we made sure the berth was velvety before we put in for it. I got old Dotty Luseley, who's not a bad egg, but is, of course, most fearfully prehistoric, to touch a City Johnny she knows, a Mr. Simpson, who runs the jolly show at the M.O.M. financial and exchange department. Phoebe and I simply had to jerk out of that putrid hole, over in Ireland, you know. Governor and Mater tried to put the kibosh on it. They're such dreadful back numbers, poor dears."

"We just had to cut it," Miss Ultima said. "The hounds and the geegees are topping and all that, but a girl can't stay buried in Rathrum for the duration, can she? Only half-a-dozen fierce frumps and a few dugouts are left to play round with now. This child was not going to stick it. Simply could not. Would have driven a girl dippy."

Ultima announced in high glee that Jack was getting a W.O. car. "We can take a jolly joy ride to somewhere after we've cut the dive," she said.

"How posh!" exclaimed Phoebe. "Ultima and I have taken digs in Jermyn Street," she informed Julian later. "But we have to wait in this pub for the two old girls who are kipping there now to show a leg. You must stagger over and have a squint at us when we've shaken down. And, of course, you're dribbling round with us and the boys tonight, aren't you?"

Julian was unable to accept the invitation. He had received, from some complete stranger, a ticket for a box at Chu-Chin-Chow, and had asked Pluckley and Inglis. They were bringing along Cora Manners and Joyce Ryde, whose acquaintance they had made at Lady Castle's.

In the middle of the performance, loud reports were heard. The noise drowned the music. Oscar Asche came forward to reassure the audience, but without waiting to listen to him, every one trooped out, and in a few seconds the theatre was empty. Inglis had gone deadly pale.

It turned out, when they had reached the street exit, that the alarming noise was not due to an air raid but to a sudden thunderstorm.

They took a taxi and drove to the apartment near Berkeley Square, which Miss Manners and Miss Ryde occupied. A provision of bottles was produced. Miss Joyce Ryde turned on the gramophone. An hour later Julian slipped away, while Pluckley and Inglis were assisting the young ladies to change, for greater choreographic freedom, into pyjamas.

Lady Bar telephoned one morning, asking Julian to dinner, at Jules, where she was staying. He had not met her since her marriage. He had avoided doing so, and felt some discomfort in facing the ordeal. But it was inevitable, and Julian was anxious, for Everard's sake, to be amiable.

When, after Julian had waited some moments in the drawing room of her suite, Vera appeared, holding out with a mixture of flurry and hesitancy a jewelled hand which had manifestly never been set to a stroke of work, it would have been difficult to believe that she had not been born to the purple. The amiability of her manner was as correct as the subdued richness of her toilette.

"I have been looking forward so long to this meeting. Why did you not let me know you were in Town?" she said in a tone of smiling reproach. "Such a dear friend of Everard's! I had hoped that we might have had you down at Clinton when he was over last, but furloughs never coincide. I am so seldom in Town. I have given up Bar House, you know, for a women's club. And it is just by chance that I heard you were up."

"Did not Everard inform you?" Julian queried.

"I have not heard from him for some days," said Vera.

"Do you mean that the telepathic correspondence is interrupted?" he said with an ironic smile.

She looked at him doubtfully for a moment. "Ah, he has spoken to you about it?" she said. "I know that you are a hardened sceptic. I must convert you. But let us sit down to dinner, first. We can talk better at table."

A choice meal, light and relying upon quality rather than over-abundance, was exquisitely served in the private dining room. Vera set herself to play the hostess, and did it, Julian had to admit, to perfection. She continued to harp, however, upon her craze.

"I wish I could take you to one of our séances," she said. "I am afraid I shall not have time. I have only a day or two in Town. But Mrs. Montague-Douglas might."

"She frequents a medium?"

"Oh, not a medium exactly. At least, not a professional medium. Her friend lays no claim to special training, but she has power. She consents to hold a séance, now and then, at the Sybil. I must arrange for you to be present at one. You would form your own opinion. I was surprised. I heard things which I thought nobody but myself knew."

"From the medium?"

"No, no. It is difficult to explain. From . . . the evocation."

"You saw an evocation?"

"No, not exactly. There was nothing to see, you understand."

"You heard a voice, then?"

"I did not hear a voice, exactly. It is so difficult to describe. You see, I was conscious of a presence."

"But what you said you heard? Those things that no one but yourself knew?"

"Well, I had just a feeling about them. I did not exactly hear them. Now, I should like to know how you explain that?"

"What?"

"Well . . . that . . . that thing."

"What thing?"

"The thing I was conscious of. Now, don't be impatient. If only you could see for yourself."

"But you have just told me there was nothing to see?"

"I mean . . . Oh, I know you are prejudiced. But you shouldn't be, you know, until you have investigated. That is what I resent, people condemning without proper investigation. It is so unscientific. It is not worthy of your scientific mind. If you dismiss it, how do you explain it?"

"You haven't yet told me what you want explained. There are, of course, plenty of things that one cannot explain. . . ."

"Ah, that's just it. More things in heaven and earth. . . ."

"Quite so. I do not, for instance, profess to be able to explain all the tricks of an illusionist. It suffices to know that they are tricks. I do not attempt to explain to a demented person his delusions. If the inmate of a lunatic asylum were to inform me that he has had a conversation with Jesus Christ, I cannot prove to him that he hasn't, nor should I dream of wasting my time in attempting to do so."

"So that is, candidly, what you think about all those . . . phenomena, those . . . experiences? Don't mind telling me frankly what you think."

"Frankly, then, my dear lady, I think that they are the clotted quintescence of balderdash, and I am pained and ashamed at our so-called civilisation which permits of the human mind sinking thus into the realms of cretinism."

Vera flushed, but showed no offence, and smiled as she said:

"I suppose that you have been telling Everard that I am a fool."

"I have not hinted such a thing, nor should I dream of speaking of you to him with anything but respect."

She looked pleased and genuinely grateful, and extended her hand towards him.

"Thank you. Do you know, Everard thinks so highly of me that at times I feel terribly afraid . . . lest he should be undeceived. I am glad we have really met at last," she said. "Pity that I cannot remain longer in Town. Everard has often told me not to fail to give you a good time when you should be on leave. I shall see that you get tickets and invitations. Tell me anything you would like me to do. Are there women . . .?"

There was an insinuation in her smile that struck an unpleasant note. "No, thanks," Julian said. "There is nothing."

It was no queasy austerity or scruple that held him. But the way-laying of life and thought at such a time from the issues of life and death which convulsed the world sickened him. The discrepancy between the wartime dissipation and the tragedy which jeopardized all, froze the joy of life and became repellant. The hunger of the men from the trenches for that joy—and how potent was that hunger none was readier to acknowledge—was being unconsciously exploited in the khaki delirium of the prevailing licence, to dope and drown thought, to set out of sight the issues for which men bled and died. It was that contrast which rendered nauseous the saturnalia of the young women.

The less boldly emancipated got married in indecent haste. They hurried to the Registrar's office with the young subaltern home on leave whom they had just met, and to whom, after a one-night honey-moon, they bade farewell at the leave train, perhaps never to see him again. Or the boy-friend to whom a girl had been vaguely engaged for years, waiting, and prepared to wait indefinitely for the position of assured security that should justify a prudent, well-to-do bourgeois marriage, rushed now recklessly to the altar before the boy returned to France. England was full of young war-brides, of young war-widows, who had only known the ecstasies of married life for a day.

Claudine, Lady Cope's daughter, had got married one afternoon that she had been up to Town to shop. The temporary gentleman was, it turned out, a salesman in an Italian warehouse. Lady Cope's prayers that he should be promoted to the roll of honor were only partially ful-filled. The heir to the Cope estates got off with a spinal wound which rendered him a permanent invalid. Claudine was expecting a baby.

Julian received an invitation from Sir Anthony and Lady Fisher to attend the wedding of their daughter, Paula, to Captain George Packer, M.C., of the King's Own Lancashire Light Infantry, at St. George's, Hanover Square. The bridegroom was, as the engraved card informed, the son of William Packer, Esq., of "The Cedars," Sefton Park, Liver-pool. Julian had several times met the boy, and the happy consumma-tion of a long childhood companionship was not unforeseen. George had obtained special leave, and was returning to France the day after, Paula herself informed Julian in a bright and friendly little note which accompanied the invitation. Her mother had insisted on a full-blown church wedding, befitting the social status of Sir Anthony and Mr. Packer, who was a cotton merchant of considerable substance. Thus Paula was to be married with more ceremony than most of the innumerable war-brides, and numerous invitations had been sent out. Julian, whose leave expired some days before Paula's wedding, obtained without difficulty a week's extension.

On the evening before he should, according to original arrangements, have been returning to France, there was an air-raid—a genuine one, this time.

Julian had undressed and was getting into bed when sirens blew and telephone bells rang. A sound of voices, swelling to a hubbub, came from the passage.

He slipped on a dressing-gown and looked out of the door of his room. People were streaming towards the lifts and stairway, attired in a variety of makeshift garments, women and girls in opera cloaks and wraps, men in dressing-gowns, army great coats, and British warms over their pyjamas. From the stream that flowed down the corridor came a chirping purl:

Oichowpuffththrellnersemowdshickenfindherpahmasowwwowaindowhowow icycumlongullsiceyerntoocuminohicysttheredengerowowwwownowrthucuminth swayowwwowkwhitasowwowowbeeslebowrdownthnowowwowqwytspiltmbew tsleepoicyherrowpowowmasloonfurrcl owkoicysuprsurwdinthsellawowwerva bandtowhowowjollycumoneryoogellsddoonnowwoowoowicyicyoicyow

The purling stream flowed down the stairs and the overcrowded lifts, thinning down to a rearguard of stragglers till the passage was empty. Last came Miss Phoebe Gluff, strolling leisurely down, in a fluffy evening cloak of pink velvet trimmed with swansdown.

"Hello, there you are! Aren't you coming down to the jolly cellars with the rest of the hippodrome?" she asked, stopping before the door of Julian's room.

"Why? One takes bigger chances every day. The likelihood of a Boche bomb hitting this particular room in the whole of London is not so great as that of being run over when crossing Piccadilly," Julian said.

Phoebe raised her eyebrows in total assent. "That's exactly what this child feels. They make an awful fuss about the air-raids. One has never heard of any one one knows being hit. Rot isn't it, getting cold feet. People pretend 'cause the others do."

"You're not afraid then?"

"Me?" Phoebe shrugged her shoulders. "I say. I'm not nuts on staggering down, myself. Looked in the other night when they had an alarm. Fearfully boring. We stayed half an hour down there, freezing. What about snuggling down here a while? Much more comfy than the nasty cellar. D'you mind awfully if I drop into a pew for a few secs?"

"Not at all," said Julian, holding open the door.

Phoebe settled down in an armchair. "Got a gasper?" she asked.

Julian reached for the matches on the bedside table and held a light for her cigarette.

"Thanks. Excuse my things. I've only got a nightie on," she smiled.

"Don't mention it. You look stunning."

"I expect it's a sell as it was last time," said Miss Phoebe. "They mostly are. People are so absurdly jumpy. They set up an alarm every time some Zep or plane is seen hovering round somewhere on the east coast. Then all the chumps make a dive for the cellars. Mostly for the girls to show off their pretties and 'jamas, and to have a cuddle in a corner."

"I suppose so," Julian said.

"You and I are not so green. But most of those boys are ninnies. Ultima has gone down with Jack. I couldn't catch up because I couldn't find my nightie."

Explosions were heard, muffled in the distance, and noisy volleys of antiaircraft guns.

"There's a raid on all right this time," Julian said. "But it sounds a good way off. They mostly go for the East End, where the munition factories are."

Phoebe sat quietly smoking, dangling a bare foot in a pink satin slipper. Other explosions followed, considerably louder.

"That sounds nearer," she said, blowing a long puff.

"No nearer, probably, than the City," said Julian.

Then suddenly came a tremendous crash. The windowpanes rattled as though they would break, and the whole place shook.

Phoebe jumped up in a swish of silk. Julian sprang to the window and, drawing aside the curtain and blind, looked out.

"It was on the Embankment, I think, near Cleopatra's needle," he said.

As he spoke, the electric light went out.

"Wait a moment," he said. "The matches are on the bedside table, and I have a candle."

He groped in the darkness towards the table. Instead, his hands encountered the warm smoothness of firmly modelled flesh. Miss Phoebe Gluff was naked.

Paula Fisher called up Julian on the telephone, the evening before the wedding.

"We are frightfully worried," she said. "Mother and I came up yesterday, and Father should have come by the six twenty at Euston. But there is no sign of him, though it is past midnight. I've just telephoned up to Liverpool. They say, at the house, that he had left. I can't think what can have happened. There is no train in the morning that could bring him in time. What can we do?"

"I'll make what enquiries I can, and let you know directly," Julian answered. "Let me have your number."

He jotted it down, and rang up Scotland Yard.

"Lieutenant Bern, Savoy Hotel? We were just about to ring you up, sir. Hold the line a moment, please," answered the official.

After some moments, another voice called.

"Lieutenant Julian Bern? This is Inspector Woods speaking. You were enquiring about Sir Anthony Fisher? Could you come at once to Judd Street police station?"

"Certainly. Is something very wrong?"

"I'm afraid so, sir. I'll be at the police station, sir."

After ringing up Paula to give her a preparatory warning, Julian hurried in a taxi to Judd Street.

It was an unspeakably squalid and ghastly business. While they went round to a little hotel near Euston Square, the inspector gave Julian the outline of the sickening story.

About half-past six, Sir Anthony had, it appeared, taken a room at the hotel, a disreputable house frequented chiefly by prostitutes. He was accompanied by a young woman. Half an hour later the woman ran downstairs in great dismay and told the proprietor that the gentleman was dead. The proprietor immediately rang up the police. The coroner was now holding an enquiry. A note had been found in the deceased's coat pocket addressed to Julian at the Savoy Hotel, together with one of the invitation cards to the wedding of his daughter.

The coroner, a medical man, happened to be acquainted by name with Sir Anthony and also with Julian through their work, which he admired. The circumstance much facilitated the unpleasant business, and in a preliminary private talk with Julian, who was required to identify the body, the coroner assured him that he would do his best to avoid the tragedy being made public.

The woman, a miserable pasty-faced little slut, who was terribly upset, said the gentleman, who was quite unknown to her, had accosted her at the corner of the Euston Road. He had given her two pounds. She took him to the hotel, where she was known to the proprietor. The first she knew that anything was wrong was when the gentleman suddenly breathed strangely and turned blue.

After consultation with another medical man, the coroner returned a certificate of accidental death from heart failure.

Julian broke the news as best he could to Paula and Lady Fisher. Paula was married quietly next day at the Registrar's Office.

The same evening, Julian went down to Bognor, where he had one or two things to pick up.

Viola told him that she intended to marry Mr. Glamrood.

"You are a fool," Julian said. "But I know perfectly well that it is useless for me to say so."

While, next morning, Julian was shaving, Keetje, who was pottering round with the fire, told him she was leaving.

"I don't altogether blame you," Julian said. "But what are you going to do?"

"Oh, there is no difficulty about that," she said. "Could go now to a dozen places. But no more waiting round on women for me! Besides, there is no hurry. I have a little money."

"Been saving, eh? Provident girl!"

She hung round, dusting and pottering about, rather unnecessarily, Julian thought. Having scraped off the lather from one side of his face, he turned round and looked at her interrogatively, meaning to hint gently that he would prefer to be left alone while he finished dressing. Keetje stood where she was, looking at him.

"Well? You'll know me another time," he laughed, unwilling to speak more harshly to the girl.

Keetje, however, did not move. "Did you get any letters out there . . . from Russia?" she asked.

"No," said Julian, sharply this time and frowning a little. What the devil did the child mean by making so free?

"Two letters have come for you. I think Madame put them in the fire," Keetje said.

Julian was taken aback. For a moment he stood looking at her, his razor in his hand. She had a quiet self-possession about her, as though she would not be easily snubbed.

"Another came the other day," she said, without moving. "I did not give it to Madame. Here it is." She drew a crumpled envelope from the pocket of her apron and handed it to Julian. "I thought that perhaps . . ."

"You did quite right," Julian said curtly.

"I hope. . . ."

"Yes, yes. Thank you," Julian repeated. He opened the door of the room and held it, signing to the girl to leave him.

"I think you had better tell them at the Russian embassy to keep them," Keetje said, as she left the room.

Julian looked at the familiar handwriting, the long, feminine hand. He laid the letter down on the top of the chest-of-drawers and went on shaving.

When he had finished dressing, he took up the letter and looked at it again. It was rather thick; many sheets of thin paper, evidently. He could guess well enough what the contents would be like. Vain, unprofitable wistfulness, regrets over the unrecapturable, the irreparable. What was the use? Julian stood leaning over the mantle-shelf, before the crackling fire, holding the letter, between his finger and thumb, over it.

Bah! It was cowardice, shrinking from his own feelings.

He sat down and slowly tore open the envelope.

VIII

No REPLY to my last two letters, drujok. As well might they have been prayers addressed to Almighty God. People keep on praying, however. I have faith. Not in prayer . . . but in something else. The other night, at the Mariinski Theatre, Madame Nejdanova was trilling: *"Arturo, il cruel termine serbato al nostro amor!"* I was sad, but I did not flinch. For I have, I think, a new strength. Suffering! Any one who is not suffering today is to be pitied. He must needs be a hopeless fool. Our pangs and personal uncertainties are dwarfed by the tremendous uncertainties of a whole world that cannot answer the simplest questions.

So I will not send you sighs of futile wistfulness, dear. I am merely going to write as though I were keeping a private diary, in the hope that it may fall into your hands, and not, as diaries are prone to do, into the hands of those who one would least wish should see them.

I have been in St. Petersburg—I mean Petrograd—since June. Nadia is staying on at Kniajeskii Pokoi, our place near Kursk. The hospital work would be too heavy, in any case, for her. But I think there is also another reason for her staying. A certain Andrei Varachin is in the habit of calling pretty frequently. He is a pleasant enough young man, very quiet and serious, and a bit romantic. He used to write poetry and articles in the *Apollo* and the *Novoja Doroga,* a literary paper conducted by the Merejkowskis. I had come upon Andrei once or twice at Peters, where he used to frequent the salons, and more especially the reunions of the symbolist group of poets which were held in the huge apartment of Viacheslav Ivanov, opposite the Taurid palace. Andrei Bely, Alexander Blok, and the poetess Anna Akhmatova, the author of the *Chetki,* which every one knew by heart, would be there. Well, Andrei Varachin was especially attached to Mikhail Kusmin, Fedor's favorite poet, who used to sit in Ivanov's salon, rouged and with painted eyebrows, and talk about Italy and Goldoni. He talked to me about Mozart, whom he considered the greatest composer of all time. I said that I always wanted to open a window, when I heard Mozart, to get a breath of fresh air. It is the same feeling I had about all that poetry—it made me want a breath of air, of naturalness, of something real.

Andrei Varachin has now given up poetry, and writes articles for the liberal papers which are published by a group of rich Moscow merchants. Nadia and I met him at the house of Madame Zolvchin, an agreeable and cultured woman, who is president of the local branch of the Red Cross in the Kursk Government. Her husband is a rich merchant, and an active member of the same group of influential liberals, or Cadets, as we call them, to which Andrei is attached. We came upon several of them in Ida Zolvchin's house. I was put in mind of the masons in Tolstoï's *War and Peace*. George Evgenevich, Prince Lvov, is their great man—a prominent member of the Duma and president of the Union of Zemstvo and Town Councils. A charming, most affable, kindly gentleman. (Though one is conscious that he never forgets how affable and kindly he is!) He has spent his life being good, and thinking out plans for the improvement of the conditions of the people. Once he went over to America to study the conditions among immigrants there, who become so happy in America, with a view to shipping out thousands of mujiks to improve their condition, or at least to avoid doing anything about improving it at home. He is a great disciple of Count Tolstoï. "The Russian mujik," he said to me, "is essentially good. All that is needed is to develop the good qualities of the Russian soul by appropriate conditions." Andrei keeps telling us how frightfully good George Evgenevich is. (And I keep thinking what your Doctor Johnson said about the paving stones of hell!) Prince Lvov also says, and Andrei repeats, that the mujiks are essentially democratic. I asked him what he meant, and whether he supposed that the color of political opinions was inherited like the color of hair and eyes. You see, drujok, that I have profited by your lessons. Andrei was distressed at my frivolity. I felt rather sick at all the goodness and kindliness, as though I had been on a diet of treacle and molasses.

Nevertheless, Prince Lvov and his Moscow friends, the millionaire Knovalov, Nekrassov, and Kerenski—that little spouting lawyer—hold that the essential goodness and democratic disposition of the Russian people cannot be properly brought out till the Tzar, and especially the Tzaritsa, are got rid of, and they had a little plan for deposing the Tzar and shutting Alix up in a convent. Prince Lvov went to the Stavka (the General Headquarters) at Mogilief to confer with General Aleksiev about the matter, and all arrangements were completed, down to the last detail, for the *coup d'état,* but Lvov fell ill on the very day when they were to have been carried out. Andrei says that George Evgenevich was poisoned, but I think that it was the prospect of passing from fine words to action which made his belly ache. "Like some of the pregnancies of the Tzaritsa, which ended in wind," mother said to Andrei, who was horribly shocked.

But since coming back to Petrograd, I have felt more disposed to believe that some great change is coming. Matushka was anxious I should help her in the hospital. She has great difficulty, as I told you, in running the hospital. Every obstacle seems to be placed in her way. Nurses are difficult to get, and expect to be paid double for working in a civilian hospital where there is no honor and glory or romance. All the women are, of course, doing nursing now, from the Tzaritsa and the little Grand Duchesses, who have their own hospital at Tzarskoie Selo, down to our friends of the Riviera. Stephanie Merjeski and Princess Eugalicheva had uniforms designed by Worth's, trimmed with d'Alençon lace. At the beginning of the war, all the women and young girls of Petrograd society rushed to the military hospitals, which, owing to the difficulties of transport and the lack of ambulance trains, are situated much nearer to the fighting line than is usual with you. There were some very unpleasant incidents. The soldiers, who could not understand that ladies and young girls should want to wait upon them, imagined that they placed themselves at their disposal for their entertainment, and in several hospitals all our amateur nurses were raped. That does not, however, seem to have abated their enthusiasm for nursing wounded soldiers. But when they hear of Matushka's hospital for civilian women and children, they are scandalised, and consider it something unpatriotic and almost seditious. Even Cousin Pasha, who is in the Commissariat Department at the Ministry of War, lectures Matushka gravely. Doctors are as hard to induce as nurses to work in our hospital. The chief of our medical staff is old Doctor Jivotef, who had retired from his fashionable practice among old ladies suffering from the effects of rich feeding and from nervous complaints, to whom he used to prescribe rest-cures in the Crimea and electric massage. Strange to say, he has remained, nevertheless, remarkably human.

I must admit that my heart sank the first time I saw my old rooms, the bedroom I occupied as a girl, every little luxurious detail of which I had grown to regard as almost a part of myself. It is now filled with two rows of iron beds, from which look up discolored and distorted faces. When I looked in at my bathroom, they were washing an incredibly dirty old woman—at least I thought her old, but I learnt afterward that she was not so very much older than myself. Her yellowish, wrinkled body was all covered with red and black spots. Lice! I had never seen lice before. A nurse was picking up with a pair of tongs the rags they had just taken off the woman, to send them to the disinfecting oven. What used to be my private boudoir is a children's ward. Old Jivotef says he is discovering some most interesting diseases among the children! There is a little boy that does not seem to have any bones; you can tie his limbs up into knots as though they were made of india rubber. Another is covered with scales like a fish, and another has the skin of his body almost black. To see the Nevski palace filled with all that ghastly humanity, that one scarcely knew existed, gives one the impression that the drains have burst and the drain-waters are rising from the subsoil. Will they go on rising?

To please Matushka, I set to work, supervising the admissions and discharges, taking over as much as possible of the administrative work so as to release the professional nurses. I was glad enough, at first at least, to escape when occasion offered from all that squalor, which made me physically sick, and to breathe once more the breath of civilised life. It all goes on as usual, civilised life—the dances, the dinners and restaurant parties, the gala functions at the Mariinski Theatre. If anything, more than usual. People say that one must keep up the spirit of the people and the soldiers. Marie Milovskaïa gave a great ball in aid of the Red Cross. To see the Milionaïa street blocked with luxurious limousines, the bright uniforms and tail coats, the women covered with diamonds and furs, one could hardly have supposed that all was not right. They speak of the great lack of men, and in the country one notices it—the haggard faces of women everywhere. One also sees women working on the tramways, in the shops, the offices. But the absence of men was certainly not noticeable at Marie's ball. Officers on leave from all parts congregate in Petrograd, so that there are more than one has ever seen before. The war department has taken over the Astoria Hotel for the use of officers. There are also a great many new people that one did not see before. Cousin Volodia, Prince Vladimir Alichief, took me. He was full of indignation.

"Disgusting, the people one comes upon everywhere nowadays," he said. "Do you see that fat, greasy swine, with the face of a goat, who goes round smiling at every one? God knows out of what gutter he has sprung. He is making millions selling rotten flour to the army, while the mujiks in Little Russia are burying their grain rather than sell it for a song, and enough wheat lies rotting all along the Siberian railway to feed the world."

I thought of the bread queues, which are getting longer and longer. Volodia pointed out a man who makes army boots out of cardboard, and another who sold the same lot of old German rifles six times over to the War Department. But somehow, it was not the sight of those vulgar persons which shocked me. Nor that things and people looked different, as Volodia complained. I was shocked, rather, to see that they looked so much the same as ever. Yet everything had a different flavor. I was not so much disgusted at the vulgar profiteers as at the extraordinarily handsome young men in their uniforms, filled with vanity and brutality. Even Volodia, stiffening to military rigidity and protruding his chest on which hung the striped yellow and black ribbon of the cross of Saint George, repelled me. The lovely toilettes and jewels of the women looked suddenly to me like the cheap and vulgar frippery of a *café chantant*. All the splendor and gaiety seemed shabby and ridiculous, like stage dresses and scenery seen close, in daylight. The women's dresses all at once seemed to me to be in very bad taste.

Yet the scene and the people were really the same, they were what I had been used to all my life. They had not changed. But you know how certain colors which are delightful in themselves are changed when set by the side of others that kill them. I have sometimes had an evening ruined by the upholstery of a room being out of harmony with the dress I was wearing. So it seemed then. I kept seeing the rows of beds in what used to be my bedroom and my boudoir, with the drawn, blotchy faces of the women, and their haggard, staring eyes, and the rags covered with lice. And I felt a little sick at the sight of the studiedly expensive frippery, the carefully tended skins, the soft white hands of the women. The fixed smile on Marie Milovskaïa's made-up face was awful. She looked like a harlot.

I caught sight of myself in a mirror. I was too much like all the other women at the ball. And it made me shudder.

"It is disgusting!" said Volodia, beside me.

"Yes, it is, isn't it?" I said, following the train of my own thoughts, and, for an instant, not realising that his exclamation had reference to quite other things.

"It's the unspeakable people who are appointed to rule the country," he said. "People like that fellow Stürmer. All decent persons, such as Samarin, Kharitanov, Polivanov, Ignatiev, have been dismissed one after the other to make way for the incompetents and traitors whom that devil of a horse-thief, Rasputin, chooses to appoint. What can you expect? He got Grand Duke Nicholas destituted from the supreme command and sent to the Caucasus because Nicholas threatened to hang him if he showed his face at the Stavka."

Volodia said that the Grand Dukes—there are sixteen of them in Petrograd at the moment—plan to dethrone the Tzar and arrest the Tzaritsa—the *"Niemka,"* the Boche, as they call her. They say that they can count upon four regiments of the guard now in Petrograd to support them. So it is not our liberal friends alone who are plotting revolution. Indeed, everybody is talking about it as if it were inevitable. On the bookstalls, books about the dethronement of Tzar Paul I are having a great vogue. The chorus of detestation against the Tzaritsa is almost universal. They say she is in league with the Germans. That is probably not true. But she is so insane, with her beastly monk, that the Germans have no difficulty in getting all the information they want. She has a copy of the secret Staff map with the disposition of all the troops, and consults with Rasputin over it, and the scoundrel blabbers everything he knows and more when he is drunk— which is pretty often. The advance in Galicia was arrested owing to such information. They declare that it was some drunken confidence which caused the death of your Lord Kitchener. At Marie Milovskaïa's I talked with Madame Sukomilanava, the wife of the Minister of War, whom I thought the most beautiful as well as one of the most charming and intelligent women there. A few days later both she and her husband were arrested for espionage.

I now prefer not to go out, and to work at the hospital. I don't do it because of pity or charity, or anything noble like that. I don't pretend to be anything but selfish. I do it, first, to please Matushka; and then I feel a need of cleaning up things, of cleaning up all that disgusting misery and dirt. I confess that I am so obsessed with the idea that I even dream about it. When I have nightmare I dream that I am in a room which is being flooded with foul drain water and that I am sweeping it, and sweeping it out with a broom. But the water comes in as fast as I sweep it out, and if I stopped sweeping for a moment, the flood would rise and drown me.

Most of the women and the older children that come to us are like brute animals. Their eyes stare stupidly. They seem even too stupid to complain or to feel their misery. And when they recover sufficiently to go back to their terrible hovels, they kneel and kiss my hands, or my shoulders, Russian fashion. It is disgusting; even their stupid, servile gratitude is disgusting.

Some of the younger women and older boys are different. They are sullen, as if some great anger were brooding within them. One day, while I was in the receiving room, a woman came, brought in by a young girl. The woman had fainted, the girl said, in a bread queue where she had been standing for several hours. We had absolutely no more room. I asked Doctor Jivotef to have a look at the woman. After examining her, he said that there was nothing much the matter with her: "Only general exhaustion and malnutrition." After having been given some food and having rested a while, she could be sent home, he said. (I thought of what Doctor Jivotef would have prescribed for one of his old patients suffering from "vapors." A trip to the Crimea with two nurses in attendance!)

"Thou wilt give Matriona Vasliscaïa a bed, and keep her there until she is well," said the girl who had brought the woman in. She was a sturdy-looking girl of about eighteen, with great dark eyes that had a wild and defiant expression. She spoke in a sharp tone, using the unceremonious "thou."

"But there is not a bed available," I said to her.

"Where dost thou sleep, then, Zena Ivanovna?" the girl retorted, looking at me straight in the eyes. "Who has more need of a bed, Matriona or thou? Give up thy bed to Matriona, if thou hast no other."

The nurse who was on duty in the receiving room flushed at the girl's insolence, and told her, sharply, to speak respectfully or hold her tongue. But I stopped her. The girl was right; the wretched old woman had more need of rest than I had. We managed to put up another bed for Matriona in what used to be my room.

The girl, who is called Maïa, came every day to enquire about the patient.

"Is she a relative of yours?" I asked Maïa.

"Matriona is the mother of Mikhail Katinief, who was sent to Galicia with the Pavlovski regiment," she said. "He worked in the Putilov ironworks, but was put into the army three months ago, and since then his mother has had no one to support her."

I remembered watching the departure for the front of the Pavlovski regiment, in which Volodia Alichief was adjutant. Although they no longer went in for the great send-offs which they used to give the troops at the beginning of the war, they made the departure of the Pavlovski the occasion for a display, for it was one of the last of the crack regiments to leave the capital. As they marched off from their barracks on the Marsovoje Pole to the Nikolaï Station, the whole route along the Milionaïa and the Nevski was in bunting and filled with people cheering and throwing flowers. Yet it was only a pretence, for almost all the men of the metropolitan garrison had long since been drafted to the front, and there is, in fact, precious little of the old army remaining. The Pavlovski had always to consist entirely of men of a certain height, with Kalmuk noses and red mustaches. Absurd tradition! But the Pavlovski which I saw depart had been recruited from the workmen in the iron and munition factories and sent into the line with a couple of months' training.

Volodia was back in Petrograd a few weeks later with a flesh-wound in the thigh, and after spending some months in Grand Duchess Xenia's hospital for convalescent officers, got some post or other at the War Ministry. He was decorated with the Cross of Saint George. I did not hear much from him about the campaign. He shrugged his shoulders when I asked him about the regiment. "Wiped out," he said.

But I heard a little, later.

The little savage Maïa, though she did not deign to express any thanks, was clearly grateful for the care we took of the old woman, and became a little less distant in her manner towards me. With rest and good feeding, Matriona soon looked different. She is a gentle, kindly old woman. When she was ready to leave the hospital, I saw that the room in the tenement, in the Vyborg district, where she lives, was provided with some comforts, and that she should be supplied with food. Maïa, who lives with her and looks after her, worked in a boot factory. But they had a strike. The women were being paid two and a half kopeks per day, and the boots, which are for the army, are mostly soled with cardboard. There was trouble with the police, and Maïa, who was very active, was arrested, with several other girls. I managed, through Cousin Pasha and some other friends, to have her set free, and now she helps with the rough work at the hospital. (I am becoming quite an *intriguante!*)

One evening, when we had driven in the ambulance to return two convalescent children to their homes, Maïa said she was going to a meeting of the council, or *soviet,* as they call it, of the factory. We were in the wretched district on the further side of the Alexander bridge. Maïa asked me if I should like to come. I smiled, but the girl's large eyes were so earnest that I had not the heart to make fun, and I accepted, to humor her. It was an atrocious dirty, dark evening, with a drizzle mingled with snow, and a cold wind blowing from the direction of Lake Ladoga. After leaving the car at a corner, we went up a squalid side-street off the Simbirskaya. We passed two policemen who were pacing up and down, with their fur collars turned up. They looked at us with an amused smile, recognising me, I suppose. The meeting was in an abandoned garden which was strewn with rubbish and broken pots. It was too pathetic for words. About fifty men and women stood shivering in the rain and sleet, stamping their feet to keep themselves warm. Several men addressed the meeting, and I must confess I scarcely paid attention to what they said. But I couldn't help noticing one speaker, who was a little more eloquent than the rest and said that they must be ready to seize power and take the place of the Duma. I could hardly keep from laughing. The notion of those half-frozen wretches talking about seizing power was too ludicrous. It reminded me of an article I once saw in the *Bognor Advertiser,* in which the editor said: "We warn the Tzar of Russia that the people of Bognor will never tolerate negotiations for a separate peace." I felt a little ashamed for poor Maïa's sake and thought she must be embarrassed at my witnessing such a pathetic display of futility. The two policemen outside, who had been sent to keep watch over the dangerous revolutionists, were again smiling ironically as we passed them.

One evening Maïa returned to the hospital after she had left, and asked to see me.

"Zena Ivanovna, Mikhail has come back," she said. "He is wounded. Thou must take him in the hospital. Order an ambulance and I will bring him."

"But, my child, you know that we don't take wounded soldiers. There are plenty of hospitals for them. The authorities will see to him," I said.

"No, no. He must come here," said Maïa. "He cannot go to one of their hospitals. He must come here, I tell thee. He came away from the front."

"You mean he—deserted? Do you know that we could be sent to prison for sheltering a deserter?" I said.

Maïa laughed. "They sent our people to prison for merely saying 'Down with the war!'" she said. "If they get Mikhail they will shoot him—as they have done already."

"He was shot by the Germans, you mean," I said.

"No, by the Russians. It was Captain Alichief who ordered the machine-guns to be turned on the battalion when they refused to attack," Maïa said.

I talked the matter over with Matushka. We had two old men, cases of broncho-pneumonia, in the little room that used to be Nadia's boudoir. I sent an ambulance car with Maïa. When they brought Mikhail Katinief, the man was in a terrible state. Doctor Jivotef shook his head after he had examined him. There was an abscess in the pleura, and a bullet, the doctor thought, in the muscles of the spine. After some days, they operated on him. We said that the wound had been received when the police fired on the strikers at the Putilof ironworks. Old Doctor Jivotef smiled with good-natured incredulity, but Miasnikof, the young surgeon who operated, who works at the large military hospital in the Serpuchovskaia—we had to pay him a large fee to induce him to undertake the case—was inclined to turn nasty. Mikhail lay between life and death for ten days, but recovered. Miasnikof showed him the bullet he had extracted.

"This came out of a German gun, my man," said the surgeon.

Mikhail examined the bullet curiously. "I did not know that the Germans used Vickers guns," he said coolly.

Miasnikof got confused. It was a Vickers machine-gun bullet of the British pattern supplied to the Russian army and police, quite different from the long, slender bullets of the German Maxim guns.

I heard some time later from Mikhail how the battalion of the Pavlovski regiment, which had been given such an enthusiastic send-off, had, as Volodia had informed me, been "wiped out." From the time they had boarded the red train, the men to whom flowers and kisses had been thrown by the women on the Snamjenski Square were as cattle sent to the slaughter. During the interminable journey they were crowded in the goods vans. Whole days went by without any provision for a regular meal. At the stations the men rushed the steaming *kipiatok* boilers to make tea, which they drank with their dry rations. They arrived at the front exhausted, and straightway were ordered to prepare for going into action. Division after division was being thrown into the hell of the German gunfire, as fast as the red trains brought them, without even giving them time to recover from the horrors of the journey, regardless of the cost in lives, so long as some commanding general could gain personal credit for a futile success. Let me try to tell you Mikhail's story.

On the first order to advance, nearly a third of the men of his company were killed or wounded within a few minutes of their getting to their feet from behind the meagre cover scarcely higher than a plough-ridge. As those who had survived turned back, another wave was sent on, driven by their officers, who struck them with the flat of their swords, and trampled over the dead and the screaming wounded. Mikhail and the other survivors crawled back to a wood a little distance in the rear, where a field kitchen served rotten meat floating in greasy water. They could see the worms in the meat. After four hours so-called rest, the officer in command, Captain Alichief, gave order to re-form for another attack. No one moved. Mikhail says they had not plotted any concerted action; indeed, they were too tired and wretched to speak at all. But when the captain gave the order, all stood still and shook their heads, acting as one man. The captain swore, stormed, and threatened. But all the men remained silent, and as the officer threatened them with his revolver, there was a light in their eyes which made him think twice before going farther. He went off to report to the colonel. Presently he returned with the colonel and several other officers, and called out *"Stroisya, smirno!"* The men drew up, dirty and haggard as they were, and stood at attention while the colonel harangued them. He spoke first in a tone of kindness, calling them *"rebiata,"* children, and repeating some of the old formulas about "the honor of Holy Russia." But they were not mujiks to be fooled by hollow words, and some asked under their breath: "Where is Holy Russia, and where is she to be found and her honor?" And when he asked: "Will you make a last effort?" several shouted: "No, we will not," and all joined them, shouting: "We will not." Then the colonel flushed and frowned and spoke in another tone of "insubordination" and of "the discipline of the army." But the men stood in silence, while the colonel and the other officers withdrew. And presently, Mikhail says, they saw that the hollow clearing in the wood where he and the others stood was surrounded on three sides by troops: Caucasians! They could tell from their black fur *papachi* and their long *cherkeskas* that they were Caucasians. And from all sides, except that which faced the front line, machine-guns were pointed at them. The captain and the lieutenants of Milkhail's company stood in front and shouted: "Battalion *fperyod!"* Mikhail says the men did not speak a word. He himself was filled with a mixture of fear and anger, but I think the anger was greater than the fear. Automatically he and the others clutched their rifles and looked to see they were loaded. A voice gave the order to fire: *"Pli!"* and from three sides the machine-guns began to rattle and splutter. Men fell in rows, crying and cursing. Mikhail knelt down, taking steady aim, and fired. Captain Alichief fell. Mikhail's bullet had got him. The machine-guns continued to splutter. Mikhail felt a sharp burn in his side and lost consciousness. When he came to, it was dark night, and all around him the hollow in the wood was filled with dead bodies. So, that was how the third battalion of the Pavlovski regiment was "wiped out."

After crawling some distance, Mikhail was picked up by some stretcher-bearers. He was put into a train full of wounded. Friendly order-lies helped him to get off before they got to Petrograd, and he reached the house of a peasant, where he was nursed for two weeks. Then the peasant took him at night in his cart to the city.

Mikhail, who is a big, powerful man, recovered quickly after the bullet had been extracted.

One day a young lieutenant came and asked to speak to Matushka. He had two soldiers with him, with fixed bayonets, who remained in the hall, while the officer was shown into the little office where Matushka works. He apologised for the character of his visit and for the intrusion of the armed escort.

"I deeply regret the painful duty which has been assigned to me," he said, "but it is thought that your Excellency is, unwittingly, of course, sheltering a deserter. You have a man of the name of Mikhail Katinief in this house, I believe?"

I had left the room on some excuse to warn Mikhail and to conceal him somewhere. But Maïa had already forestalled me. Matushka showed the lieutenant round the house. The two soldiers made a somewhat perfunctory search. But there was no trace of Mikhail. He had left by a back door as soon as the soldiers had appeared.

Two days later we received a visit from Cousin Volodia. He lounged in his usual nonchalant manner into the little room which Matushka uses as a private sitting room, and after some general talk and a good many sneers about her hospital, he said:

"You know that you will end by getting yourself into trouble, Daria, collecting all this riff-raff and pampering them, at a time, too, when so many brave defenders of Russia, so many gallant officers are needing care and attention! It can only be regarded as outright treason. It encourages the *svolotch,* the *canaille.* And Heaven knows they are getting presumptuous and insubordinate enough. But it seems that you are not satisfied with encouraging sedition among the rabble. You have, I believe, been sheltering a deserter from the army. You know, Daria, to what you are rendering yourself liable?"

"To be stood before a firing-squad. Have you come to arrest me, Vladimir Sergeivich?" asked Matushka. "If so, I am ready."

Volodia laughed—an uncomfortable laugh.

"Come, come," he said, "you know very well that no one is going to interfere with you. But all the same, it is a pretty serious matter, harboring a deserter. This man, Mikhail Katinief, was here. You do not deny it. He is not only a deserter, but a particularly dangerous fellow. Has been spreading sedition in the army. In my own battalion, as a matter of fact. I could tell you all sorts of things. But, in short, you must be good enough to tell me where he is to be found. Doubtless you can help. He apparently escaped when a party was sent here to arrest him the other day. A search at his home has yielded no result. The man must be apprehended, and you can doubtless give information that will help to do so. Where is he?"

At the moment the door opened, and Mikhail stood in the doorway. "Here," he said.

Volodia gave a slight start, but quickly resumed a calm manner.

"Ah, very well," he said, rising stiffly. "In the name of the Military Governor and the Divisional Command, Private Katinief, consider yourself under arrest until you are handed over to an escort." So saying, he stepped over to the telephone which stood on a table nearby.

But before Volodia had reached it, Mikhail had sprung forward, seized the receiver, and torn it from the wire.

"In the name of the Soviet of Soldiers of the Pavlovski regiment, Captain Vladimir Alichief, consider yourself under sentence of death as a vile murderer, until you are handed over to a firing squad!" he said.

Volodia, flushed crimson, faced the man rather magnificently.

"*Smirno!* Stand at attention before your commanding officer, you swine!" he shouted, and at the same time gave Mikhail a violent cuff on the cheek.

In another moment Volodia was on the floor, with Mikhail on top of him, his knee upon Volodia's chest and both hands at his throat. Volodia's eyes started out of his head and his face turned black as the other man strangled him. We thought Mikhail had killed him.

"Stop, Mikhail, stop," I called.

Mikhail looked up with a smile. Slowly relaxing his grip, he felt Volodia's pockets and from one of them took out an automatic pistol, which he put into his own pocket. Then, shaking Volodia like a rat, he let him go.

"For the sake of these ladies, you can wait a while longer for the undeserved honor of the firing-squad," he said, getting up.

In silence we watched Mikhail back slowly toward the door. Opening it, he stood for a moment before it.

"You can send your people to look for me whenever you please," he said with a smile. "My address is: The Central Committee of the Soviets of Soldiers, Workers, and Peasants. I hope that we may meet again, Captain Alichief." He went out, closing the door behind him.

Volodia rose slowly to his feet. Then, going up to a large mirror hanging on the wall, adjusted with leisurely care his collar and dishevelled hair. There were red marks on his jaw and throat, but otherwise he was very pale. Then he turned to us with his usual careless and superior manner.

"You see, my dear Dasha," he said, "the sort of people you have been encouraging. A pretty state of things it would be, did we not keep such gentlemen in order. And if they were to become our masters!"

Matushka stood, superbly impassive.

"Do you think it can be prevented?" she asked. "Shooting them down with machine-guns does not appear to be sufficient."

Do you remember, drujok, that time in Berlin, when you were minded to throw up all for what you thought worth while? I said nothing at the time, and I thought you were being rather foolish. But all the same I admired you for it. Perhaps people like Maïa and Mikhail are also being foolish. I don't pretend to see what they can do, or to hope much from anything they can do. But I admire them, all the same. They are men and women; they are real and living. My people, people like my cousin Volodia or Marie Milovskaïa are disgusting. Disgusting! And so, I feel something of the same mood in which you were when you wanted to throw up all for what you thought was real and worth while.

I prefer to be working here at the hospital to seeking shelter at Kniajeskii Pokoi or in the Crimea. It gives me more satisfaction. I am still being selfish, you see. No one can tell what will come of it all. All the things we took for granted, as stable and unchanging, are rocking under our feet. But in all that uncertainty I feel absolutely certain—you may smile at my feminine intuition—that we shall be before long together again. I know now that we are together in our deepest feelings and thoughts.

. . . .

After reading Zena's letter, Julian sat for more than an hour without moving. Then, he gathered together his few belongings, put them in his pack, and after taking leave of Viola, departed.

I X

THE winter trailed interminably on the frozen fields of France. From bare war-battered billets, chilled by the glacial breath that drove through broken panes, the troops shambled over icy roads to the frost-bound line. There was little fighting. The desultory crackling of machine-guns, an occasional volley of five-rounds rapid, the lazy booming of the guns using their daily ration of ammunition at dusk, served chiefly to indicate the presence of the opposed entrenched forces. But though casualties were few—Viney, who was caught by a stray bullet in the forearm, and went down the line with a Blighty, was the only one among the officers of the battalion—the companies were thinned out by exhaustion and cold. Sentries froze at night in the fire-bays, despite sheepskin-coats and Balaklava caps. The men were made to walk in turns down the duckboards to the sap-head, where hot water and axle-grease were available, to keep their feet from freezing, and they were given soup.

"More men are being evacuated from the B.E.F. with trench-feet than were sent down with wounds during the whole Somme show," informed Captain Burr, the M.O. who had succeeded the self-exploded Scrutch.

The draughts sent from depot to fill the vacant files presented a desolating appearance: men of fifty and over, who looked even older, the combings of slums and workhouses, haggard and worn, crippled with rheumatism, flat-footed, afflicted with asthma, hernias, varicose veins. The colonel stormed at the medical officer.

"What the devil do you mean, Doc, by passing such a bunch of crocks for service? Can't expect a battalion to fight with graveyard stiffs, can one?"

The M.O. had addressed repeated complaints to the Brigade A.D.M.S., he explained, but without avail. "You've got to take them," he had been told. "There's nothing else to be had."

"When I think of what the British army once looked like!" the colonel lamented. "I used to laugh at those damned slouching Frenchies and dagoes that looked like nothing on earth by the side of our bouncing Tommy Atkins. Now I feel positively ashamed that the Frenchies should see our troops. I came upon a Jock, the other day, a Seaforth, no bigger than Tom Thumb, who was so bandy-legged he could hardly walk. When the durgan got off the duckboard to let me pass, he—'s fact—toppled down."

The '16—'17 winter was the turning point of a great change. It broke the war-spirit in the field. Gone were the last traces of the thrill of adventure, the blind dash after novelty. The old slogans could no longer galvanize; nor could the talk about a "spring offensive" and a "breakthrough." To be done with it all; to escape, to escape from the attrition that lay close to madness, was the haunting, pervading thought. If the truth were known, few, save in the highest ranks, had not been haunted by the thought of escape at all cost. Self-inflicted wounds multiplied to an appalling extent. Men laid the muzzle of their rifles on their feet and fired, or held up their hands over the parapet as a target to German snipers. Three large hospitals in France were filled with S.I.W's. Medical and commanding officers blinked with conniving mercy at these acts of despair. They had not the heart to call down the rigor of military law upon companions in misery. All hostile feeling towards the occupants of the opposite trenches, on the other side of no-man's land, had long vanished. The poor Fritzes were also fellow-sufferers. When some scared, half-starved deserter or prisoner happened in our trenches, he was an object of spontaneous tenderness. To what purpose, to what end all this misery? Men asked the question and could not answer it. Often, as Julian viewed the dumb dejection and despair in their faces, he marvelled that they did not mutiny, refuse to be any longer driven. Others—the Germans, the French, Italians, Russians—were beginning to murmur and to chafe. Were the English the supreme cowards? It was chiefly the cheap, superficial, sentimental kindliness in the attitude of officers towards their men—the traditional English paternalism toward social inferiors, which stifled mutiny in their hearts. The Higher Command recommended enhanced observance of that attitude. Sops of creature comforts were lavished upon the troops, abundant rations, rum-issues, cigarettes, and, above all, leave freely granted.

After four timeless months that seemed an eternity, Julian had to admit to himself that he looked forward to the time when his turn should come round again. Not that he was greatly attracted by the delights of "Blighty," by the licence offered to joy-starved men escaped for a brief spell from the limbo of the trenches, but he felt, like all others, the maddening craving to escape, were it but for a respite, a physical ravening, like the prisoner's desire for the day of liberty.

"If you only knew it," said Burr, the medical officer, who had just been on leave, "you're better off here in many ways. We're not on short rations, at any rate. You won't get a cut of roastbeef like this on the other side. Two and a half pounds of meat a week is the allowance, and four pounds of bread. Potatoes are, practically, not to be had. And no sugar. People have to draw in their belts, I tell you, that the army may be fed. And the old folks are dying off like flies. There are more people going West than Fritz's guns have done for during the whole war. 'Flu' they call it. If you ask me, it's malnutrition and cold."

One day a message came in the trenches, with the admirable efficiency of the field postal and telegraph services, to inform Lieutenant Julian Bern of his mother's death.

"Be off at once," insisted Colonel Cator. "We'll see to fixing up any red tape, old man. Brigade have sent round to say they have a car to run you up to Boulogne."

Mrs. Bern had died after only two days' illness as the result of a chill caught while attending early mass. Julian arrived in time for the funeral. Herbert Glamrood was attending to all arrangements. He took an early opportunity, after the ceremony at Brompton Cemetery, to broach delicately the question of the estate. From her savings in the old days, Mrs. Bern had had a very modest competence, invested mostly in consols. There was a will dividing the estate equally between the children, and appointing Julian executor.

"If, in present circumstances, you would rather that I should see to the necessary formalities, and relieve you of all trouble, I would gladly undertake to do so, for your sake, you know. If you would care to give me powers of attorney in the matter . . ." Herbert Glamrood bleated.

"Do as you please," said Julian, and signed the paper which Glamrood held in readiness.

His mother's death was but a deepening of the sense of gloom and tragic futility. Julian could not pretend to himself that her release at this time counted as a vital loss. He recalled, with a heart-grip, the solicitude that had surrounded his childhood, the letters that were wont to soothe his nostalgia when he was at school, and bade a reverent farewell to the resting spirit.

Tenderness and love! It needed more to rescue the world.

He had ten days special leave. This time he would guard more resolutely his solitude. He hid himself in a shabby Bloomsbury lodging house, albeit it was somewhat more expensive than the Savoy.

In duty bound, he paid a visit to his Aunt Aurora. She had sent a wreath, with a note to Viola excusing herself from attending the funeral, on grounds of poor health. Lady Penmore looked, in fact, considerably aged as she sat wrapped in a shawl by the fire in the little sitting room, which was pervaded with an odor of rancid cold cream. She was distinctly more subdued in her manner, a change which was an improvement, and made her seem more human, Julian thought.

"I find that I have to take things more quietly," she admitted. "Poor Betty wore herself out running about as she did, at her age. This dreadful winter has been hard on us older people. And things are very depressing—very depressing. Much worse than people are told or realise. At one moment there was only some three weeks' supply of food in England. Those U-boats are playing havoc with the shipping. People would get a shock if they knew the figures. If America does not make haste to do her plain duty, God knows what may happen."

Welby was at Half-Moon Street when Julian called. The cordiality of his greeting seemed intended to efface any unpleasant recollections of their last interview.

"I was awfully cut up, don't you know, not to be able to do anything for you that time," he began.

"That's all right. It doesn't matter at all," Julian said.

Welby had left the embassy at Petrograd, and was engaged, Julian gathered, on special missions. Again Julian was struck with the enhanced importance which his personality seemed to have acquired.

Baron Rubinstein was also on a visit to Lady Penmore, but appeared to be chiefly interested in an exchange of views with Welby. He spoke with his usual ingratiating courtesy and serene smile to Lady Penmore, seeking to reassure her. Some members of the Government were, he said, alarmed at the exhaustion of the Allies' gold reserves. But the circumstance was in itself a guarantee of American co-operation. "Blood is thicker than water," he remarked with some apparent irrelevance. He was convinced, he said, that neither America, nor even Germany if it came to that, could afford to see England's credit seriously imperilled.

"Those Americans! To think that we should become indebted to them!" exclaimed Lady Penmore.

The baron mentioned that he had just been speaking to Mr. Arthur Balfour, who was deeply interested in the Zionist plans for a national home for Jews in Palestine. The enthusiasm caused by the exploits of the modern crusaders who had liberated Jerusalem and the Holy Places from the Turkish yoke went a long way, the baron said, to revive the public morale and to counteract any depressing effects resulting from the apparent stalemate in the West.

"The archæological exploration of Palestine and the Bible lands of Western Asia," he remarked, "will be afforded precious opportunities by the operations of our troops. It has already yielded results of the greatest interest. There are, I have been assured by competent archæologists, indications that important oil deposits exist in Mesopotamia. Mr. Balfour assured me that, even in the present strenuous circumstances, the British Government would not lose sight of the interests of science."

"You bet they won't," said Welby.

While Lady Penmore enquired from Julian about Viola, on whose new marriage she, strangely enough, passed no comment, Baron Rubinstein engaged Welby in private conversation, and they passed into the adjoining room, which Welby used as a smoking room and occasional study when he happened to be staying at Half-Moon Street. Presently a maid came to inform Lady Penmore that the committee of the Women's Auxiliary Workers was awaiting her pleasure downstairs. Julian rose to leave, but Lady Penmore pressed him to remain a while longer. She would not be detained very long, she said, and wished Julian to have an opportunity of more talk with Welby.

"He has now very great influence," she said, "very great influence. You might find it of use."

Julian dropped into a seat by the fire. Presently Welby opened the door between the two rooms in order to admit the warmth. He glanced round as he did so, but did not see Julian, who was hidden by the back of the deep armchair into which he had sunk. While he awaited his aunt's return, Julian could thus not help hearing the conversation which was taking place in the adjoining room.

"The importance of Mosul is not likely to be overlooked by the Government," said Welby. "You were, I think, in partnership with the Deutsche Bank, Baron, in regard to certain concessions which were obtained from the Turkish Government?"

"Negotiations had been taking place between the British and the German directors of the Turkish Petroleum Oil Company as to their respective rights in those concessions," said Baron Rubinstein.

"Which negotiations assumed a somewhat more heated form in August, 1914, and were not without influence upon England's generous decision to defend the rights of small nations," Welby said.

The baron chuckled and murmured something in agreement.

"Well, we haven't got Mosul yet," said Welby. "But the trouble is that we have had to promise Mosul to so many different people. Sir Henry McMahon, the British High Commissioner in Egypt, has solemnly promised it to Sherif Husein and his son Feisal who, goaded by the stirring Oxford eloquence of that crank Shaw, or Lawrence, or whatever he calls himself, are leading the Arab tribes to the conquest of national independence."

"Sir Henry is one of our directors. The importance of the engagements he has taken, with our consent, toward wild Bedouin tribesmen must not be exaggerated," said the baron.

"Quite so. The French kicked up an awful row, I believe, about our crusading enthusiasm in the Holy Land while they were being hammered down at Verdun," Welby said. "They had to be pacified, naturally. Our plenipotentiary, Sir Mark Sykes, has concluded an agreement with Monsieur Georges Picot, the representative of the French Government, promising Mosul to the French. So you see it is a little awkward. An Englishman's word is as good as his bond, England always keeps her promises, and all that. But I'm damned if I see how we're to do it. You're damned lucky not to be an Englishman and not to have to bother about moral ideals."

"The defence of British interests is the highest moral ideal," said the baron smoothly.

"I can assure you that every step is being taken to protect them, even farther afield than Mosul," said Welby. "For instance, that expeditionary force which is being got in readiness to secure the Baku oil-fields against any possibility of damage. Should the Turks or the Germans threaten the region, material aid to our Russian allies will be forthcoming."

"Perhaps," put in the baron, "it is even more probable that such aid may be called for against the Russians themselves, should labor disorders, which are rife in that region, render it necessary to guard British property."

"You are jolly well right," Welby agreed. "And I have a notion that the British Government is not altogether averse to seeing such troubles arise. We have promised Constantinople to Russia. We must keep our promise—by seeing that Russia is not in a position to call upon us to redeem it. We are therefore not likely to do anything that might thwart any German action calculated to foment trouble in Russia. The Russian revolutionaries who swarm all over Europe can expect no countenance or assistance from the British Government. But that is not to say that we shall place difficulties in the way of such assistance if it should come from Germany."

"At the moment our most urgent anxiety is in regard to the Bessarabian oil fields," said Baron Rubinstein. "Should they fall into the hands of the Germans, as the sweeping advance of General Mackensen gives every reason to anticipate, no apprehension need arise as to their safety. There is every ground for hoping that some adjustment may be arrived at as to the proprietary rights when the final settlement comes to be discussed. I have in fact already approached some former business associates in Germany on that point, and am given to understand that no serious difficulties as to a friendly settlement are to be feared. The real danger is that the Rumanians should, in their retreat, cause our industrial establishments irreparable damage rather than let them fall unimpaired into the hands of the Germans. That is a danger which it will be difficult to avoid."

"You mean that the German advance should, as far as possible, be facilitated?" said Welby, after a pause.

"Or that, at least, no serious effort should be made to oppose it," the baron said quietly.

"As for instance, the reinforcement of the Rumanian operations by the two army corps which have been promised by Russia?" said Welby.

"Or an advance from Salonika in their support," said the baron.

There was a moment's silence.

"I understand that every pressure is being exercised on the French to give General Sarrail no encouragement and to prevent him from interfering with the German eastern advance," Welby went on. He cleared his throat. "It is a delicate matter. There is much unreasonable parliamentary and public opinion demanding that the Salonika armies should do something. The British Government is doing its best to . . . er . . . to insure that they should do nothing."

"It is adopting a threatening attitude towards King Constantine, and encouraging M. Venizelos," Baron Rubinstein said, argumentatively.

"Come, come, need I point out, my dear Baron, that the external attitude which the Government is obliged to assume and its actual attitude are two different things?" said Welby. "As a declared ally of the Kaiser, Tino must needs be openly frowned upon. But do you suppose that his activities would have been enabled to be so effective a brake upon General Sarrail and the Salonika army, had he not enjoyed effectual support? King Constantine is cousin german to the King, and no English Government will ever, except in direst extremity, support such antidynastic and republican interests as are represented by M. Venizelos. The Italians are in the same case. They will have nothing to do with Venizelos. Russia stands even more firmly by the side of Constantine. Grand Duchess Helena, Tino's sister-in-law, a tenacious and ambitious woman, will not tolerate Russian opposition to the Greek dynasty. Although French popular opinion is violently opposed to Tino, M. Briand can be counted upon to co-operate with England in ensuring the inactivity of Sarrail. M. Briand is much under the fascination of that charming woman, Princess George of Greece, a Bonaparte princess."

"Quite," murmured Baron Rubinstein. "I see. Well, in order to assure the best protection of our interests on the Dnieper, Germany should be made aware of our good offices as regards her eastern expansion in the Balkans and even, should circumstances turn out insecure in Russia, in the Ukraine."

"And in return Germany will . . . ?" queried Welby.

"Germany will, I believe, make no undue effort to reinforce Turkish resistance in Syria," said the baron.

"Quite. But the negotiation is a delicate one," said Welby.

"I have reason to think that a representative of the Deutsche Bank is medically advised to spend a short holiday in the Bernese Oberland," the baron said.

"And how much would the Deutsche Bank be prepared to pay?" asked Welby.

"To the negotiators? Probably a hundred thousand pounds," said the baron.

"The probability should be secured by a previous deposit," said Welby.

"That, doubtless, could be arranged, provided sufficient guarantee be added to an authoritative signature by a detailed statement of the distribution of the forces in the regions concerned," the baron said.

"The chief risks of our branch of the public services are that we must be prepared to be disowned by the executive powers. More chances are taken in Switzerland and other pleasure resorts than in the trenches. And without the glory," Welby said.

"But with more substantial rewards," the baron remarked.

Having disposed of her committee, Lady Penmore returned to the sitting room. Welby, as he and Baron Rubinstein joined her, cast a glance of surprise at seeing Julian. Julian returned the look impassively.

"Do you know," said Lady Penmore, "that the land workers are selling potatoes at threepence three farthings a pound? Yet they are not to be bought anywhere at less than tenpence a pound. Well, I am dining tonight on mashed swedes. This profiteering is scandalous. Prices should be regulated. They are not."

"Prices are regulated by the economic laws of supply and demand," said Baron Rubinstein. "Economic laws cannot be abolished."

"Profits are too large," said Lady Penmore.

"They are as large as can be obtained. They always are," said the baron.

"Lloyd George professes to control them," said Julian ironically.

"He is not doing so," Lady Penmore said.

"Mr. Lloyd George told me the other day that if a stop were put to profiteering, the war would be brought to an end. Large profits are indispensable to entertain patriotism," said Welby.

After the baron had taken leave, Welby turned to Julian and spoke to him with considerable sympathy of the hardships of the winter campaign.

"Do you still wish to go to Russia?" he asked.

Julian stared into the fire. "No," he said.

He declined his Aunt's invitation to share her meal of mashed swedes.

Julian looked up Viney, who was in hospital at Saxford House. Despite his mysticism, which Julian always found irritating, Viney was in many ways more civilised than most of the wild young cubs among the officers, and Julian, though he sometimes snubbed him unmercifully, was not without appreciation for the lad. He was an Eton boy and had been at All Souls at the outbreak of war. After all, the mental foundations of every Englishman were mystic. How could that be otherwise when all English upbringing and intellectual influence were expressly directed to eschew any contact with reality? The English mind was a work of fiction, which could exist only on fictitious foundations.

Viney was looking better than Julian had ever seen him look. He was unable to conceal his physical appreciation of the luxurious ease in which he was basking. The room he occupied was an old boudoir of Lady Irene Sexborough's, and was filled with floral tributes like the dressing room of a prima donna. It was Viney's second day up. With his arm encased in plaster of Paris and supported by a sling, he sat in state, receiving his visitors. His father and mother were with him when Julian called. They had heard of Julian from their son, and, with grave earnestness, manifested their pleasure at making his acquaintance.

The elder Mr. Viney was in special constable's uniform, which gave to his short-bearded, spectacled, and earnest countenance the look of a Salvationist. He was a gentleman of considerable substance and influence in the Midlands, being managing director of a well-known insurance company and an alderman of the City of Manchester. Mr. Viney was also a justice of the peace, a liberal, free-trader, single-taxer, anti-vivisectionist, anti-vaccinationist, a total abstainer and a vegetarian. In the course of conversation he informed Julian that he was also an atheist.

Mrs. Viney, a little woman with eager, intelligent eyes behind a pince-nez, was an able helpmate of her husband, whose views and interests she espoused, considering, however, that he was disposed to underestimate the importance of women in the growth of intellectual enlightenment. She had collaborated with her husband on a number of works on social subjects and municipal administration, which had been published by a firm of non-conformist booksellers in Bloomsbury.

After the first exchange of obvious remarks concerning the satisfactory progress of the patient, the unsatisfactory progress of the war, and a suitable exchange of personal compliments, Mr. Viney, Senior, led the conversation to more general themes.

"I am in reality a pacifist," he said. "I felt, at the beginning of the war, considerable scruples about Robert enlisting. But I have come to perceive that the present emergency is exceptional. We are in fact fighting against war and militarism. We are fighting, as has been well said, to make the world safe for democracy. This is a war between democracy and the abominable principles of dictatorial authority under which the less enlightened nations of Europe are groaning. This war is going to sweep such barbarous abominations once and for all off the face of the earth. It will mark a new era of freedom and true democracy. Much as we deplore the terrible sacrifice involved, it was perhaps necessary for mankind to go through this appalling experience in order that the eyes of people should be opened once and for all."

"If one could only believe that people did profit by experience," murmured young Mr. Viney, his eyes on Julian.

"Ah, there is no fear of their not being opened this time! Mankind has been blind enough, and stupid enough in the past. But not now. No possibility of their ever again swallowing the humbug of perorating politicians, militarists, priests, press lords, and profiteering financiers. No sir! Never again," said Mr. Viney, Senior. "Democracy is going to assert itself, and the last survivals of medieval tyranny, unscrupulous capitalistic exploitation, dictatorial oppression and propaganda will melt like mist when the smoke of battle clears. It is a fight worth fighting, a fight which is going to redeem and reawaken the moral conscience of mankind."

"Until the next war, Pater," said young Mr. Viney, turning to Julian, as if by way of apology for his father's somewhat aldermanic eloquence.

"But, my boy, there are going to be no more wars, I tell you! No one will ever be able to fool the people into war after this. Democracy will compel every government to settle all international disputes by arbitration. There cannot be the slightest doubt about it, can there?"

"Of course not," put in Mrs. Viney, answering for Julian who sat in silence, bowed with hopeless despair before the blind paralysing of the human mind by the fanatical superstitions of liberal moral idealism. What would Baron Rubinstein have to say to Mr. Viney? he wondered. "But I think," continued Mrs. Viney, "that women will have to be granted a large share of authority in the task of preserving peace. They are better fitted for it than men. Have you heard about our Ethical Society of Manchester, Mr. Bern?" she asked. "We are demanding that ethics should be taught in all schools."

"What ethics do you propose to teach in your schools?" enquired Julian.

"Why, ethics . . . just ethics, you know. The elementary principles of ethics," Mrs. Viney explained.

"Mother has just given me this beautifully bound copy of Spinoza's immortal work," said Viney, exhibiting the volume. "You are familiar with it, of course, Bern?"

"I remember having an acute attack of Spinozism, many years ago, in my nonage," said Julian. "I did not again come across Mijnheer Spinoza until I picked up a copy of the *Ethica* among the guide-books and catalogues of tulips in a hotel at The Hague." Julian spared the worthy atheists a more detailed account of his feelings. He had been aghast at his own former simplicity. Could this have once been mistaken for intellectual courage—this pathetic muddle of age-old fallacies and delusions, this opiate of Christian resignation, this self-centered concern for personal salvation? *"Sub specie aeternitatis,"* indeed! What had the soul of man, which was the outcome of humanity's social development, to do with eternity? "Eternity" was merely a refuge of escape, witting or unwitting, from the world of living realities—a funk-hole. The liberal philosopher who, like all mystics, sought refuge in eternity, was not a hero, but a coward. He sought to save his soul; but his soul could not be saved apart from the world which produced and conditioned it. "The wise man is scarcely ever moved in his mind, and always enjoys true peace." The wise man? The blinded fool, rather, stands aside from the eternal battle which is the growth of the world's soul and his.

And only some two hundred and fifty years ago, this farrago of subterfuges and evasions was the best that honest intellectual courage and "independent" thought could achieve! It drew down upon itself anathemas for its boldness. "Cursed be he when awake and when asleep, standing or sitting. . . ." *Eppur si muove!* Truly the world had moved, the human mind had grown. There were still plenty of Spinozas, to be sure, of infantile liberal minds, like the worthy Vineys. But it scarcely occurred to any one to account them courageous, or independent. The battling world had moved; it had moved from the Jew Spinoza to the Jew Marx. "The mind is disabled in proportion as it is furnished with inadequate ideas; it is restored to power in proportion as it has access to adequate ideas." Well said, poor inadequately furnished liberal philosopher!

"Being curious to see the dwelling of the liberal philosopher, I made enquiries from the hotel porter," Julian told the Vineys. "He suggested the telephone directory. A gentleman whose acquaintance I made at the Rijksbibliotek sent me to the Pavelioengracht. The lady who answered the door seemed to misunderstand my request to be allowed to visit the house. After asking me to wait a while in a back room, she introduced several buxom young women in scanty attire. Symbolic fate! The home of the worthy liberal philosopher had become a brothel."

Mrs. Viney did not think Julian's remarks on the liberal philosopher in the best of taste, being somewhat out of harmony with the sublime ideals which his heroic name suggested.

As Viney's people were about to take their departure, a nurse came to announce another visitor. It was Mrs. Cator, the colonel's wife, who made it her duty to call upon any officer of her husband's battalion, in hospital in London. Mr. and Mrs. Viney were sorry to miss the opportunity of cultivating the acquaintance of the colonel's wife. They had promised to attend a lecture at the Bloomsbury Ethical Society's rooms on "Vegetarianism and Peace." They therefore excused themselves after shaking hands with Mrs. Cator.

Mrs. Cator sailed in amid a purl of fluffy luxuries, chirping chatter, and smiles. She kissed Viney on both cheeks, and beamed on Julian as he was presented to her.

"Well! I am bucked to meet you. I've heard so much about you from Henry. I must have a pow-wow with you presently, but I must first attend to our wounded hero. How's the poor game arm? You're looking top notch today, isn't he, Mr. Bern? Nurse says you're doing spiffingly. See, I've brought you a few flowers, some chocs—don't eat too many at a time, you know—and here are some *Sketches* and some *Vie Parisienne* and all the leggy magazines. What's that you're reading? Pugh! Put away that stuff, my dear boy. What you need to do now is to buck up and have a good time. I'll tell you what. I've got a scheme. I'm going to take both you boys round for some tucker with me at a dinky place. Oh, I'll fix things up all right with nurse. It won't do you any harm, and will do you no end of good. Where's that nurse? Ah, here's the bell. Nurse, I'm going to run away with your patient for a tiny wee bit of spree. What? You'll have to ask the assistant matron? All right, you ask her from me. Say it's Mrs. Henry Frisham Cator. I'll be responsible for bringing back your patient safe and sound. They have to make a fuss, of course, these hospital people, but they're all right if you know how to deal with them, and take them the right way. All right, is it, Nurse? That's topping. What does the matron say? Back by ten o'clock? It's fearfully early. But I suppose for a first outing that will have to do. I swear on the book I'll bring the patient back by ten. Now, that's all fixed up, see? Put on your sambrowne—here, let me help you. I'm quite used to it. I always inspect Henry before he goes out on parade and fix up his harness. Poor Henry has about reached the last hole of his sambrowne. I don't know what to do with him, he's getting so fat. You fellows must be doing yourselves pretty well in the mess. I know all about it. Living on the fat of the land while we poor women at home are being rationed. Well, we'll have a little splurge for once. It's not a bit of good going to the ordinary restaurants. They won't serve officers with more than five bobs' worth of tucker. It's absurd to expect a big grown soldier to survive on that. At the White Owl you can get anything you want. And besides, they know me and will do anything if I give them the wink. No, Mr. Bern, I won't accept any excuses. I am the C.O. this evening, and you've got jolly well to obey orders. Don't try and tell me you've got so many engagements you can't put off the girls for once. As a matter of fact, I had promised to go to Phoebe Gluff and Daphne's, who are having a cocktail party at their flat. Frightfully jolly girls, aren't they, Mr. Bern? Yes, I know. Dotty Luseley told me all about you. Besides, I'm sure we must have met before somewhere, Mr. Bern. I wonder if you could get some one to call a taxi, Nurse. Thanks awfully. Now we'll go somewhere where we can talk. I've got such a lot I want to say to you, Mr. Bern. But I haven't yet had an opportunity to say a word. Got a taxi? You're a darling, Nurse. Now, come along, boys. Isn't this jolly?"

Mrs. Cator was distressed at finding that, owing to the unreasonably early hour—it was only half-past eight—the subterranean resort where she entertained her guests had not yet awakened to life. The crowd of subalterns and smartly attired young women at the tables round the dancing-floor was as yet relatively sparse and sober. By the time that, under the influence of refreshments and ragtime, the spirit of revelry had risen to a more accelerated tempo, and fresh crowds filled the room to capacity, it was the curfew hour, and Mrs. Cator had to redeem, though with a slight unpunctuality of half-an-hour, her promise to the inexorable hospital authorities.

"It's really too bad," she said. "But this is only a first outing, a preliminary canter, just to try out the old legs, isn't it, Bob? Another time, I shall arrange things better, have a talk with that matron of yours. For this once we must call it a night, I suppose, else they might not let me take you out again. It's scandalously early, and I shall yet have time to barge into Phoebe's party. I expect it's just getting under way. You, of course, Mr. Bern, have no need to be so strict about observing the beauty-sleep order. We'll just take Bob round to his hospital, and after we have seen him tucked into his little beddy-bye, we'll look up the girls."

Mrs. Cator's enticements, however, met with a determined resistance on the part of Julian. Pleading fatigue, he said he would remain a few moments longer and retire early.

"Oh well, it will be for another time, then," said Mrs. Cator. "It's been so nice to have a talk with you." (Julian had scarcely opened his mouth except to put food into it.)

The table at which they had dined was in a corner under a gallery, the low settees which ran round the wall of the room being more comfortable than the chairs. From the recess, dimly lit by a shaded lamp, Julian was favorably situated to escape observation. On the stage, four men and two young women in pierrot costumes sang, each in turn, alleged comic songs and sentimental ditties. During each entertainer's turn, the rest sat in a row nursing their hands and looking bored, like choir-boys during a sermon. The troupe was just back from a tour in France where they had been giving entertainments in the back billets. Their humor had the ingenuous, lady-like delicacy of *Punch,* and mingled patriotic sentiments—"Half-a-mo', Kaiser"—with respectable suggestions of naughtiness which might have served to adorn the wit of a curate at a mothers' meeting. There was a character-sketch of a long-haired "conscie" which excited much laughter. The troupe enjoyed a great reputation in England—"a ripping show." The performance was concluded by a melodramatic sketch in the trenches—barbed wire against a lurid sky; the silent watch; Bairnsfather's "Ole Bill"; the public school spirit and Oxford accent in mud and khaki; the girl I left behind me. Most touching and inspiring.

After the show, the floor filled with fox-trotting couples. Julian sat sunk in rep cushions and reverie. Rome burned to ragtime. Orpheus safe at least from the assaults of the wild Menads. He would not turn round. Not for Eurydice. *Che farò senza Euridice?* Eurydice: Far-reaching Justice! Eurydice or Europa? Gone are the pleasant groves of Armida's gardens. Far-reaching Justice, I will not look back upon thee.

"Good evening, Mr. Bern."

What the . . . ? Who the . . . ? A young woman had come up to him. Dismissing the partner with whom she had been half-heartedly fox-trotting, she had come straight up to Julian. She was blonde, decidedly good-looking, elegantly, perhaps a little over-elegantly, attired. Julian stared at her blankly for some moments.

"So, you don't know me?" she said, with a faint mocking smile.

"I . . . don't quite . . ." he stammered. Then he exclaimed: "Good God! You're not Keetje!"

The girl smiled nonchalantly, showing little surprise at his surprise. "May I sit down?" she asked.

"By all means."

"Thanks. Do you mind if I order something? George, bring me some champagne cup," she said to a passing waiter.

Julian looked at her, amused. Could this be the little street-urchin he had picked up in Antwerp?

"You appear fairly prosperous," he said.

"Oh, quite. I stuck it long enough doing scivvy, didn't I? I should like a cigarette. Thanks. I said I could always manage, didn't I?" she said, after Julian had given her a light. "I took a job, here, entertaining, after I left Bognor."

"You mean on the stage?"

"Oh, dear no. Just making myself agreeable. Encouraging the boys to drink champagne. I wasn't going to wait on any more women. Not I."

"So you're on the staff of this establishment?"

"Not now. Don't need to be, now. Got plenty of money. Uncle Marcus, who has been doing very well, gave me lots of money. Came in very handy at first."

"Your uncle is in England, then?"

"No. He's in Belgium. Still selling all sorts of things. Buys things in Holland and sells them to the Germans. Buys from the American Commission for the relief of the starving Belgians, food, flour, and so forth, and sells them to the Germans."

"A precious scoundrel this Uncle Marcus of yours."

"Oh, an awful scoundrel. Like everybody else." Keetje looked drolly at Julian. "Do you know of any business man or any politician who is not an awful scoundrel?"

"No, I don't," Julian admitted. "But I don't quite understand. How does this uncle of yours manage to send you money from Belgium? I also once used to receive money from Belgium. But since the war . . ."

"Oh, I haven't had any money sent. I've been over to Belgium two or three times," said Keetje.

"You've been to Belgium?"

"Nothing very hard about that. Lots of people go backwards and forwards. But it is a little risky now for most of them. The Germans have become pretty strict. They've electrified the barbed wire all along the Dutch frontier, so that a good many poor devils have got electrocuted. None of that sort of thing for me. I go comfortably by train in a first-class carriage. Just told the Germans, the first time I went over, that I was going to visit my uncle in Brussels. They were quite nice, and one of the officers happened to know Uncle Marcus. So there was no difficulty. None at all. Coming out is more difficult. They have to be more careful letting people out of the country. There's such a lot of correspondence going on. But I told them I wanted to pay a visit to my grandmother at Zuylen, in Zeeland. So they were quite nice about it. Of course, with all the spying that's going on, everybody who passes across the frontier has to strip to the skin. I have a rather good figure. So, I suppose, the German captain at Antwerp rather enjoyed it. Hope he did. Anyhow, I never have much trouble."

"But what about getting over to Holland? You have to have a passport or something."

"The first time I went over, I hadn't a passport, and they did make rather a fuss." Keetje looked round. The music had stopped and the floor was deserted. There was nobody near, but she lowered her voice. "But what with my speaking the language of the Cheeseheads and having relatives in the country," she went on, "it was soon fixed up. Now, however, I have all the passports and papers I need."

"How do you manage that?"

Keetje smiled and puffed at her cigarette a while.

"I met a relative of yours here," she said.

"A relative of mine? What the devil do you mean?"

"No, not the devil. Mr. Penmore."

"Welby Penmore!"

"Yes. He fixed it all up for me."

"I think I begin to understand. You're employed by the Intelligence Service."

"Sssh! Not quite so loud." Keetje cast another quick glance round and leaned forward with both elbows on the table. "I happened to make Welby's acquaintance in this very place. It was soon after I came back from my first trip over to Belgium, and I told him about it. Just to make conversation, you know. He asked me if I would care to undertake some more little journeys over. And so . . . ."

The music had started up again, drowning her words.

"I see," said Julian, after a pause. "So Mr. Welby Penmore thought —very shrewdly—that your talent for getting across frontiers might be put to profitable use?"

"It's much easier, of course, for a girl than for a man. And they haven't got many in England. English girls are too stupid. Look at the mess those nurses in Belgium made of things. They always have too many moral and patriotic prejudices and all that sort of thing. So that they can't be intelligent."

"And you have none of those sentimental moral scruples?"

"No fear. It makes things so much easier. It's great fun, besides. And one meets so many different people. I met another friend of yours the other day."

"The deuce you did. You seem to have been following the track of my social acquaintances. And who is this mutual friend of ours?"

Keetje had thrown off her air of nonchalance. Her blue eyes were now serious.

"A man called Ogonin," she said.

"Ogonin?" Julian thought for a moment. "Oh, yes, I know whom you mean. A somewhat polynymic gentleman."

"Neither pollymimic, or whatever you call him, nor a gentleman. He's a Communist."

"You met him in Belgium?"

"No, here in London. He was having difficulty in getting away. He wanted to go to Switzerland. So I soon fixed him up, with a pass number, and got him over to Paris. One can do quite a lot in the service." Keetje hesitated a moment, and flushed slightly. Then she spoke hurriedly, as if a little embarrassed: "Welby stopped you going to Russia. But if you still want to go, it can be arranged."

"Thanks. Mr. Penmore has already made me the same offer. But I do not very much care to go in the service of—scoundrels, as you yourself say."

Keetje folded her hands on the table and leaned towards him, almost touching him. He could smell her perfume and see the light down on her cheek. She smiled mysteriously.

"But you will want to go in the service of—the Revolution," she said.

"What revolution?"

"*The* Revolution. It is going to start in Russia."

Julian looked mistrustfully at the girl. She was an agent of Welby Penmore and of the Secret Service—though she seemed frank enough. He was not going to speak unguardedly.

"That remains to be seen," he said, making a move to indicate that he was about to rise.

Keetje rose, looking at him. "Well, if you get fed up with the silly old war, you can let me know. Ask the barman for Katie."

It was with a sense of pleasurable relief that Julian returned to France. It was good to leave behind him the world of meanness and intrigue, of blind stupidity, of frivolous and flashy mirth— that world which, far more truly than the combatants at the Front, was the maker of the shambles. By comparison, the uncivilised isolation, the inconscience, the dull futility of the field were restful and clean. The battalion had been moved to a more northern part of the sector. As commonly happened, Julian had some trouble in reaching his unit. He was wrongly directed, the railhead to which his pass took him was at a considerable distance from the battalion location. He had to cover the distance as best he could, lorry-jumping part of the way, and walked the rest. The flat country lay still and deserted under the wintry sky. In the dark ploughed fields was no life. Along the straight poplar-bordered roads he met scarcely any vehicles or men. A great stillness lay over it all, like a great peace. Julian found it pleasant to stride in the keen, frosty air, to throw off the impressions of his leave. The stillness and quiet continued till he found he was quite close to the line. Only a dull rumble of distant guns indicated its proximity. The men in billets were mostly huddled indoors round hearths and fire-buckets, with blankets spread over the windows for warmth. Julian felt as though he were back to a peaceful retreat.

The Germans had fallen back slightly on new positions, and the line taken up by our division, after contact had been established, was relatively quiet. Both sides were kept occupied consolidating, and the work was welcome to keep warm. The snow had melted off, and a hard frost had set in. The line was thinly held by posts in firebays at some distance from one another. In some places the parapet was very low, and on one occasion when Julian was returning along the fire-trench with Everard, from an inspection of the wire, a volley of bullets came singing sharply very close to their ears.

Everard, who had, during the previous two or three months, been away a good deal, having been engaged on liaison work at Division and at G.H.Q., and later having gone on leave, now came up pretty frequently to the battalion in the line. He was supervising the preparation of a raid, which had been ordered to obtain an identification required to complete Divisional information records. With his usual thoroughness Everard made elaborate preparations for the operation and came over frequently to survey the ground. The raiding party of some thirty men was under the command of Pluckley, an R.E. officer being in charge of the Bangalore torpedo party that was to cut the wire.

On the appointed night, every detail had been gone over and checked. The men, their faces blackened with burned cork, and looking like nigger minstrels, were waiting to move up to their positions until the moon should set. It hung low over the wooded heights behind the German line, casting a greenish light over No-man's-land. Everard had come to inspect the last preparations and to await the result of the raid. He and Julian sat, waiting for the hour, in the support line, where a small gravel bluff hollowed out into a recess provided cover, while it afforded at the same time a view of the flat expanse beyond the wire.

Everard lit a pipe.

"Did I tell you I came upon Viney's people?" Julian said, breaking a long silence.

"His governor is quite an important person among the radicals, I believe," said Everard. "Will be in the next radical Government probably, should there ever be one."

"He's an awful ass. A sort of Christian atheist," said Julian. "Viney is at Saxford House, in Lady Irene's boudoir. Haven't seen her since— since before the war. She must be no longer quite a chicken. What on earth does she do? I mean, how is it she's not married or something?"

Everard had a dry smile and a slight shrug. "Independent sort of girl. I fancy she's not very keen on marrying. I've heard some gossip about her taking to aviation—or aviators. But she's too shrewd to give much handle to talk."

They relapsed into silence. All was still. No-man's-land was particularly broad in the sector. The German line stood out clearly against the dark background of the woods. The setting moon cast its last rays across the flat expanse which glittered with patches of hoar-frost. The scene had a romantic look. In the stillness a tenor voice could clearly be heard in the German line singing the *Preizlied* from the *"Meistersinger."*

"May be his swan song, poor devil! In another half-hour . . ." Julian said.

"You're being sentimental!"

"Sentimental, you call it. It's all horrible, the killing!"

"Huns have got to be killed—in self-protection," said Everard.

"Protection of what?"

"Of decency, of England." Everard's voice was cold.

"Decency! D'you call England decent? The American President asks England to state what she's fighting for, and she can't do so because it would sound too obscene. England's fighting for dictatorship on the seas, for the overland way to India, should she one day be compelled to keep her word and abandon Egypt, for oil, for exploitation, for profits. That's all very well. All so-called nations that are but the instruments of privilege and profit do the same sort of thing. But England pretends to be fighting for the freedom of small nations, for democracy, for I know not what fine phrases. England is more obscene than the barbarian Hun. She dare not show her naked rascality."

"English democracy provides the means of keeping down human rascality," said Everard, sharply.

Julian had an impatient movement of scorn. "You're talking like Mr. Viney, Senior. English alleged democracy provides the means of perpetuating rascality through imbecility. It provides the means for keeping down revolution."

"Of substituting evolution for bloody revolution, rather," said Everard.

"Ah, it's you who are sentimental now, and humanitarian. Huns have got to be killed for the protection of rascality, profit and privilege, but blood must not be shed to put profiteering and rascality down. You, the privileged rulers, have shed seas of blood to conquer empires. When the political and economic interests of cliques of profiteering exploiters are at stake, you do not count lives. Daily you shed blood like water in defence of property. But as soon as the liberation of the world from oppression and the poison of lies which oppression needs to defend it from intelligence are at stake, you turn soft-hearted, lily-livered, humanitarian, and moral. You who stand knee-deep in blood cry out that revolution must be effected without the shedding of blood—by Democracy. If that's the humanitarianism you stand for, you're a damned hypocrite!"

"You could be shot, you know, for what you say," Everard said coolly.

"I could be shot—and would be, gladly. A thousand times more gladly than for the fraudulent infamy which calls itself England," Julian said. "Do you remember my once putting forth the hypothesis as to what would happen to the English mind were it forced to consider its foundations? Well, it is happening. And the result is panic-stricken clutching at every form of mystic superstition—spiritism, table-rapping, crystalgazing, Christianity, palmistry, Wisdom of the East. That's the nemesis of building on sand—on conventions, as you said then. It was a long time ago, wasn't it. Oh! I've been silent, consuming my own smoke too long. It's about time to speak out, to revolt against all the fulsome pretence. . . . Your wife treated me to some of it. I told her she was a fool."

Everard flushed. "Julian, will you please . . ." he began, rising to his feet.

At that moment the divisional artillery-fire broke the night's stillness with a sharp volley, drumming the German front line. Flare signals went up. The massed fire opened out after a couple of minutes to form a box-barrage round the raid area.

"They're off," Everard said.

The explosion of the Bangalore torpedo was heard and seen. Then nothing more. It was now pitch-dark. It seemed but a few moments before voices were heard in the front line as the raiding party returned. The gun-fire had stopped, only a few flares went up on the other side, and all was still again and silent.

Everard and Julian hurried down the trench to get the news. The returning party was already some distance down the communication trench before they caught up to it.

The raid had been a complete success inasmuch as an identification had been obtained, a German boy who appeared to be mentally deficient. Not a man was "missing." Corporal Pipkin reported that they had at first captured a sergeant, but the German had drawn his automatic after surrendering, and had had to be killed. A post of four had been killed. The corporal had thrown a petrol can with a Mills bomb attached down a dugout. "A lot of yelling was heard and sheets of flame shot out," he reported. "The results appeared to be satisfactory."

Pluckley had got a leg smashed by the explosion of one of his own bombs. It was a comfortable "Blighty." He was in high elation, beaming and laughing as he lay on his stretcher, ready to be taken down the line, receiving congratulations and taking leave. Sergeant Walsh was also going down with a flesh wound of the arm.

As the party were going down the trench, a bombardment of fifteens started.

"Their usual backchat for the raid," Everard said. "We had better wait till it is over."

They lingered in the first support line. The bombardment died down. Everard peered over in the direction of the firing trench.

"Hello, what's up? I believe they're raiding us now," he exclaimed.

Drawing out their revolvers, Everard and Julian half crawled, half sprang forward over the top. In the firing trench the sentries, taken by surprise, had been rounded up by a German officer and half-a-dozen men, and were already being led off over the parapet. He was rapidly looking round the bay, glancing into the cubholes screened with ground-sheets.

"This way, please. Move on," he said quietly in perfect English as though he were a London policeman directing traffic.

A sergeant and two men ran up from the next traverse. Julian and Everard sprang forward, firing their revolvers, towards the officer. At the same moment a crump dropped in front of the support line. Everard staggered forward and dropped with a low groan. Julian, neglecting all else, knelt down by his side.

The sergeant sprang on the German officer. The latter emptied his automatic, and the sergeant, getting a shot point blank in the chest, fell dead. The two men who were with him knocked the officer down and knelt on him. The other Germans were by this time halfway across No-man's land, with their prisoners, and had disappeared in the darkness.

"Where are you hit, Everard?" Julian asked. His voice shook.

"Not sure. My leg . . ." Everard lay clutching at his left hip. "Have you got some opium pellets?"

By the time Captain Burr had come up with stretcher bearers, Julian had managed to clap on a field dressing. There was scarcely any blood, and only a small tear in the breeches.

"The artery is all right, so far," said the medical officer, "but the femur is splintered."

After tying a rifle to his leg and waist, they moved Everard down towards headquarters.

"If I should peg out, look up Vera, old man. I wanted to . . ." Everard was in great pain and very pale. "Are you all right?"

"I'm quite all right," said Julian, pressing Everard's hand. "So will you be. I'll look you up next time I am on leave."

After Everard had gone down, Julian looked in at the Orderly Room, where the German officer had been taken. He was sitting nursing his left arm, which was wounded. Turning to Julian he said with a harsh laugh:

"Well, you see they've made a soldier of me, after all."

Julian looked at him. He was a fair-haired youth with spectacles.

"Prince Christian of Heuchelmund!" he exclaimed.

The German laughed.

"What has become of your brother, Prince Egon?"

"Killed at Verdun," said Prince Christian.

Julian turned away. The meeting and the memories it stirred up were unwelcome. Confound the Huns! Confound Armida's gardens!

On returning to his dugout, Julian felt his left leg very stiff and painful. He could hardly get down the trench and descend the steep steps. He asked Hooge to help him off with his puttee. It was soaked in blood. There was a bullet wound in his leg.

X

THE man with the grey mustache who occupied the other bed sat propped up on his elbow to watch the proceedings, while Julian was being changed into blue-striped pyjamas and given a perfunctory wash. The nurse, a tall, very English-looking blonde, with a swift, self-assured, professional manner, conducted the proceedings with the expert modesty of a music-hall artist. After she had taken Julian's temperature and tidied away his pack and belongings in the locker, she left the room with a frou-frou of starched skirts, informing him that the major would be in presently to see him.

The man with the grey mustache continued to stare at Julian.

"Are you bad?" he asked.

"Not at all!" said Julian.

"Thought so," said the man. "They send only flesh wounds, trench fevers, shell-shocks, and lead-swingers here. Real cases go to Boulogne so as to be handy to the ferry."

Having apparently satisfied his curiosity for the present, the man turned his face round to the wall.

Julian hoped the fellow was not going to be a nuisance. He would have preferred complete privacy. But that was too much to ask. It was delightful enough as it was. He lay back savoring the ineffable beatitude of the clean bed, the down-soft pillow, the odorant freshness of the glossy laundered sheets. It was a room in what had been before the war a fashionable luxury hotel overlooking the sea. The wide-open window let in a balm of salty air. Sensual wellbeing entered through every pore of his body, penetrated to every molecule, as a positive, overwhelming sensation which blotted out all other feeling and thought. Had it all been so strenuous, then, that the commonplace material things, the unnoticed comforts of everyday life should assume a disproportionate value? No wonder they beamed with pleasure, the young fellows like Pluckley, when they went down with a Blighty!

Julian had vigorously protested when Burr, the M.O., notified by the faithful Hooge, had sent him down. Go down with a scratch like that?

Julian felt thankful now to the cheery doc for ignoring his perverse stoicism. It was strange to be carried on a stretcher down the sap up which he had toiled, broken with fatigue. He had been whisked off in an ambulance to the Casualty Clearing Station, where he had been put to bed in a marquee. The smoothly sprung ambulance train had brought him that afternoon to the coast, doing in half-an-hour the journey which the troop trains usually took two or three days to cover.

In the marble entrance-hall of the pre-war luxury hotel, the stretcher cases had been aligned. The walking cases in their muddy boots and faded khaki straggled in. Julian had been amused to note how they took trouble to look the part of wounded heroes, overdoing it somewhat. They looked mighty sorry for themselves, drawing long faces, like truant schoolboys nursing a cut finger with tragic gravity. Dare say they felt more like dancing and singing for joy. The M.O.s glanced at the label tied on to each case, and called out numbers to the orderlies. The quartermaster sergeant collected and checked the kits. Tin hats and ammunition were confiscated.

Julian had had a look at his label: S., for stretcher-case; G.S.W.; Cp. Fr. fibula R.; AT. AT stood for the nasty big needle they had stuck into his belly at the C.C.S.—antitetanic serum.

And now here he was with no other care or duty but to lie abed, to be waited upon, tended, pampered, fed.

The medical major, a foolish-looking old gentleman in spectacles, with a white overall over his new-looking khaki, came in presently with the nurse. He merely glanced at Julian's label, and scribbled something on the chart.

"Do you like beer, porter, whisky and soda, or wine?" he asked. Then, "We'll have a look at you tomorrow."

"What diet has he given him, Sergeant Major?" Julian's room-mate asked the nurse when the major had gone.

"Chicken," the nurse said.

The man leaned forward conversationally.

"The chickens here have four legs, you know," he said to Julian. "They come from Australia, in tins. Still, they do you pretty well. Chicken includes soup, fish—quite good soles—two veges, custard and prunes or tart. Here, Sergeant Major, offer the gentleman a gasper," he said, holding out a tin of goldflakes.

"You're not supposed to smoke before dinner, you know, boys. Hide them till the Matron comes round," the nurse said, passing the gold-flakes to Julian.

"Not a bad sort, the sergeant major," the man said after the nurse had left the room. "All eyewash, of course, that pretence of being straight Jane and no nonsense, and turning up her nose when the breeze blows fresh. She's had her skirts turned up more than once, I can tell you. Those women have to put on those cornstarch airs, else . . . Fellows positively go mad, you know, at the sight of a skirt when they come out. There's no holding them. When we came off the Peninsula on a hospital ship, after nearly nine months without so much as a glimpse of a frill, almost every damned nurse on board got raped within two hours of our boarding the ship."

"You were at Gallipoli?" put in Julian, enjoying the cigarette.

"Yep. By the way, we haven't introduced ourselves. My name is Spirido."

"Mine's Bern. Three pips, I suppose?"

"No, a crown."

"Sorry, sir."

"Oh, dry up. There ain't any blooming ranks here. Where are you from?"

"Fifth Mercian."

"I meant in civil life. I suppose you're a gentleman. I'm a professor."

"Oh, eh? Indeed?" Major Spirido's person and manner did not exactly suggest academic pursuits.

"Yep. English literature, and mathematics."

"Eh? Ah! What Varsity?"

"Waramarangu."

"I beg your pardon?"

"Waramarangu, New South Wales."

"Oh, you're an Australian."

"Well, I'm with the Tommy army now, although I was with the Aussies on the Peninsula. I'm a gunner. Was in command of the Waramarangu artillery long before the war. We have an arrangement in Australia for an occasional exchange of officers with the Tommy army. Something like a sort of Rhodes scholarship, you know. I was due to join the R.H.A. just about the time this show started. But the red tape took about a year to unwind. So I went off with the Anzacs, and it wasn't until some time after the evacuation that I got notice to proceed to Shoeburyness for instruction. Instruction, mind you! I'd instructed every gunner in Waramarangu. Could give the johnnies at Shoeburyness a few points in cabalistics. But they treated me as though I had been the wild man from Borneo. Stared at me through their monocles, and pretended to find fault with everything I did. Wanted to teach me how to ride a horse! You can bet I could have shown them some riding! I stood it as well as I could for a while, then one day I just went up to the C.O. johnny and told him exactly what sort of an ass I thought he was. Would you believe it, the damned fool laughed, and asked me to have a whiskey and soda, and said he believed I was right. What can you do with people like that?"

The mock-chicken dinner which the orderly brought presently justified Major Spirido's recommendations.

"Not too bad," the major agreed on Julian signifying his approval. "The fellow who runs the kitchen is a Yorkshireman who used to be a French chef in a hotel in London. He does pretty well, but has to be kept up to the mark now and again. On the whole I've found this place about as good as any in France. And I've tried most of them. The Boulogne hospitals are too rushed during the season. Le Touquet is too big. Etaples and those places round G.H.Q. I can't stand at any price. The M.O.s and nurses have swollen heads on account of all those brass hats about. Here it's quite homelike and friendly, especially just now in the off season, and the cooking is better than in most places. I haven't tried Lady Irene Sexborough's, which is only for toffs."

"You have been often wounded, then, Major?" Julian asked.

"Me? Only once. Just a bit of a scratch on the Peninsula. Didn't trouble to go down with it."

"You're sick, then?"

Major Spirido did not answer at once. "Eh, there, Wilkie, you son of a gun, come along with that coffee," he called out to the orderly in the corridor. Then, lighting a cigarette, he turned round to Julian with a queer look, and, blowing a long puff of smoke, said: "Neuritis."

Wilkie brought in the coffee and cleared away the trays.

"I had the distinction of being the only casualty when we evacuated the Peninsula," continued the major after Wilkie had gone. "In my indecent haste to get on to the lighter, I tripped over some cases of champagne which we had to abandon to the teetotal Turk, and sprained an ankle."

"And it still troubles you?" Julian enquired.

"Not exactly. They put me up at a delightful place when we got to Alex. Know Alex? That place at the end of Ramleh. Anyhow I had plenty of time to think things over a bit during the three months I was there. Yep, I jolly well thought things over. And when my ankle got well, I found I had come to my right senses, and developed neuritis."

Major Spirido looked round at Julian and burst into a guffaw of laughter.

"A jolly M.O. found it out for me. It's neuritis of a nerve they call Tiberius and Titus."

"*Tibialis anticus,*" Julian suggested as an emendation.

"That's the fellow. You've not had it too?"

"No, but I've heard of it. But how on earth do you manage?"

"Manage, my dear fellow? Manage! If you have just a tuppeny worth of savvy, you can manage any blooming thing you bloody well like in this army. Go where you like, do whatever you like. When the docs here have a medical board on me and suggest sending me to Blighty, I just say: 'No, my dear fellows. I prefer staying over here for the present, if you don't mind.' So they say: 'All right, Major. Any particular place you'd like to go to?' And I may say: 'Number 4 or Number 23,' as the case may be. And that's all there is to it. I'm thinking of going to Switzerland for the summer. They have an arrangement, on the q.t., to send officers to pleasant sanatoria there. Don't care much for Blighty. At Shoeburyness, after I had called the C.O. an ass, he and I became quite chummy. His name was Sir Thomas Wandworford Sop-Smith. Took me to his club and even introduced me to his wife and family, mentioning that I thought him an ass, which gave them a big notion of my intelligence. After I had had a good look round England, I thought I'd like to see what things were like over here. I saw all I wanted to in a few weeks. So I just got my old Tiberius and Titus, see?"

"I see," said Julian.

"Look here. I can see from your face that you're not a fool," Major

Spirido went on. "Fools have smooth faces with silly smiles. You don't get those lines on your face at your age when you're a fool."

"Thank you," said Julian.

"Don't mention it. Now, Bern, you can't tell me that any one in the senses that God gave him prefers to spend the duration in the abominable mess that we've had a taste of rather than in a decently comfortable place like this, where he is bedded, well fed, waited on by a passably neat lot of women, all for the same pay and at the expense of His Majesty, the British Tax Payer. Any one who says he does is just a damned liar. Mind you, I'm not saying anything about the chance of being blown to bits. I don't suffer from cold feet. It's embarrassing to talk about those things oneself, you know. But when we landed on Gallipoli I got pretty well to the top of Gaba Tepe, and if there had been any diggers somewhere near behind me, the British would be in Constantinople today. I've got a D.S.O. Not that it means very much. They give D.S.O.'s to most field officers. Officers under field rank get M.C.'s. Padres usually get V.C.'s. It all goes by rule of thumb. But it isn't because I've the wind up that I prefer being comfortable to being uncomfortable. It's just plain horse sense. In a ghastly mess like this, the best thing to do is, of course, to stay out of it and make a pile. Plenty of fellows are doing that. Don't blame them. A regular gold mine, this war. But I'm not very good at swindling, myself. It takes a lot of scheming and bothering, and I'm too lazy. Besides, I am fundamentally honest. No, don't laugh. I am. Well, if you're not profiteering over the war, the only thing to do is to be in the army. That's no reason, though, why a chap should go soldiering when he can spend the damned wartime in comfort on the same pay. And why the devil should he? Why should he, I ask you?"

Major Spirido's confidences were interrupted by a visit from the assistant matron, Miss Privett, a prim and starchy lady wearing gold spectacles, who, escorted by Nurse Coleman, was making a formal round of the newly admitted patients to express to them official sympathy, the matron being slightly indisposed. Miss Privett hoped that Mr. Bern was comfortable. She hoped, with a prim smile, that Major Spirido continued to be comfortable.

The assistant matron's visit was shortly followed by Nurse Coleman's final vesperal attentions, before she went off duty for the night. Julian and his room-mate sucked thermometers, were exhorted to further ablutions, and reminded that lights should be turned out at ten o'clock.

"All right, all right, Sergeant Major," said Major Spirido. "I'm not going to talk any more tonight. Who's on night duty?"

"Nurse O'Brien. Good night."

Julian decidedly suffered more physical exhaustion than he had realised. His sleep, untroubled by subconscious anticipations of rouse parades or stand-tos, was deep. He dozed off again, after the night nurse had awakened him at an unearthly hour to take his temperature and attend to his morning toilette. To his relief Major Spirido did not disturb his repose, and only after breakfast had been brought in and a first cup of coffee had been partaken of, did he say "Good morning."

The sun was shining over the steel-grey Channel. A clean, fresh breeze bellied out the white curtains.

"Quite pleasant here," Julian remarked, lighting a cigarette.

"Not bad—

> 'Charmed magic casements opening on the foam
> Of perilous seas in faery lands forlorn—,' "

said Major Spirido. "As I was saying, I prefer to stay over here, myself. In England you're liable to have silly old D.M.S.'s poking their noses round and suggesting medical boards."

"Why, I can fancy I can see the white cliffs quite clearly," Julian said. "Of course it must be an illusion or a mirage."

"True dinkum it isn't. We're some hundred feet above sea level. The visible distance is the square root of h by one minute seventeen seconds, which being corrected for the dip by ninety-seven seconds, the difference in the coefficients being due to refraction, gives you well over the twenty-eight miles or so that separate us from perfidious Albion."

When Captain Pender, R.A.M.C., a young man with a pleasant smile and a pince-nez, investigated Julian's injuries, the wound in the patient's left leg had almost healed. It was therefore found necessary to make a new one, considerably larger, the X-ray examination having shown that, although the bone was not completely fractured, there was considerable roughening of the periosteum over the lower third of the fibula. Julian was sick for two days from the ether, and had to endure considerable

torture from Captain Pender's efforts to prevent the wound from heal-
ing by stuffing it with iodoform gauze. Having made good progress
despite the treatment, he was, at the end of four weeks, permitted to
sit up a little.

Long before that time, Major Spirido had decided to assume slacks
and to explore the place's possibilities of entertainment. He brought in
some of the acquaintances which he had made among the convalescent
officers to see Julian, with the suggestion of a game of poker, a proposition which Julian firmly rejected. Spirido's chief associate at the
moment was a Captain Chantalow, who occupied the adjoining room.
He was a blond youth with a regulation Charlie Chaplin mustache and
certain pretensions to elegance, indicated by the tightness of his sambrowne belt, which caused his tunic to puff out about his hips like a
ballet-dancer's skirts. He also wore a tooth-paste-advertisement smile
which served to display the perfection of his denture. Captain Chantalow had indeed come down from the line expressly for the purpose of
obtaining the services of a capable dentist, having been alarmed by the
prevalence of pyorrhea in the trenches, an affliction which would have
endangered the oral perfection of which he was not unjustly proud.
Captain Chantalow was looking forward with much elation to invalid
leave in England, which he was shortly to enjoy in order to complete his
convalescence from dental treatment.

"In another week I shall be in dear old England, with the dear little
wife and kid," he exclaimed in irrepressible sentimental excitement.

He took occasion to produce from his pocketbook snapshots of his
wife, a young woman with a rotund face which might have been carved
out of a turnip, and of the one-year-old baby which appeared to take
morphologically after its mother. Chantalow usually took the first opportunity of exhibiting the photographs to any new acquaintance, and
his room was decorated with several more framed photographs of the
same subjects.

"Is that the kid's face or its arse?" enquired Major Spirido after a
scrutiny of the picture which he had seen several times before.

"You dried-up old bachelor!" smiled Captain Chantalow. "He has
no children," he said, turning dramatically to Julian.

"Shouldn't care to take my oath on that, Macduff," said Spirido.
" 'O, I could play the woman . . .' "

"You dirty old man," put in Chantalow. "The little night nurse, by the way, was all honey. Such diddies!"

The major sucked the end of his mustache.

"We'll take him round when he's got steady on his pins," he said, nodding sideways to Julian.

"I don't think you will," Julian said.

"Those French girls have some tricks!" said Chantalow. "The art is in its infancy in England. Remember those squarepushers we picked up, Spirido? But there's no place like England, for all that."

"There isn't," the major said drily. "The Old Kent Road, the Waterloo Road—'Good evening, darling!'— Bermondsey, Bromley, Tooting Common."

"What do they know of England who only London know?" postulated Chantalow with a display of pearls.

"Nothing," said the major sententiously. "There's Chatham, Liverpool, Walton, Manchester, Birmingham, Leeds. Were you ever in Leeds? No place like it anywhere on the five continents or in the Golden West. The people in Hell can't commit suicide, but I can't make out why the people in Leeds don't."

"Spirido, thou hast no soul. The English countryside, the lanes and fields, the peaceful villages, thatched roofs, ivied towers, moors, and downs. . . ."

"The advertisements of Carter's Little Liver Pills and Cadbury's Cocoa. What say, Bern?"

"I was thinking whether we are supposed to be fighting for the thatched cottages, the lanes and fields of England, or for Manchester, Birmingham, Leeds, Threadneedle Street, Tyneside, and Glasgow," said Julian.

"What are *you* fighting for, Chantalow? Tell us. Be the only man in the B.E.F. who knows what he's fighting for," burst out the major.

"For hearth and home. A little home . . ."

"One of a hundred and seventy-two identical jerry-built little homes in your suburban road."

"And a little family."

"One of a hundred and seventy-two in the hundred and seventy-two identical semi-detached desirable villas, without counting in the little night nurse, and the squarepushers."

The tooth-paste advertisement of Captain Chantalow's smile continued to glow undimmed by any asperity from the belittling of his ideals. He suggested adjournment to a place of refreshment in the little town, followed, maybe, by a visit to "that little girl I came upon last week."

After a delay which appeared to him unnecessarily cautious, Julian received permission to go out for a walk with the aid of a stick. He experienced an extravagant delight in the freedom. Major Spirido and Captain Chantalow accompanied him on his first outing to pilot him among the attractions of the place.

The scope which the little seaside resort afforded for exercise and entertainment was limited. The sandy beach, interspersed with outcrops of rock, was a poor one. Bathing, Spirido remarked, was unsafe. He pointed out the place where, some months before, one of the nurses had been drowned, having been drawn into the whirlpool which eddied among the rocks. It was several hours before they recovered her body. A row of villas, only a little larger than kennels, incredibly ornamented with polychromatic façades, which made them look like the cardboard sets of a musical comedy, straggled along the sea front. Each bore, conspicuously inscribed upon it, some sentimental designation, such as, Sans Souci, Mon Désir, Miramar, Le Rêve. In front of the villas ran a miniature promenade paved with figured colored tiles, which had become invaded by sand and had fallen into a state of neglect and dilapidation. One house at the further end of the row had been wrecked by a bomb in the course of an air-raid, the little place having on two or three occasions been visited by German "Gothas."

Three or four of the tiny villas were occupied by visiting French and Belgian families. The pathetic pretence of a seaside holiday season which their presence imparted to the beach had a ludicrous effect amid the deserted and dilapidated conditions of the place. The ladies sat in lounge chairs, doing needlework or reading novels, and kept an eye on the children who, with their garments tucked into bathing-knickers, played with buckets and spades. One villa was, according to Major Spirido's information, occupied by the widow of a French colonel, in deep mourning, with her sister. Another harbored the family of a small Government official from Paris. In another was a numerous Belgian family, mostly women, whose Rubenesque forms were not without claims to attractions, which they carefully cultivated by a considerable display of elegance and expert cosmetic care.

In the little main street which ran parallel to the row of villas, half-a-dozen shops offered a meager choice of provisions and barest necessities, and a *papeterie* catered to the higher needs by providing English literature of which the circulation was prohibited in England. There was not a possible café or estaminet in the place, and when the convalescent officers desired refreshment or a quiet corner for convivial conversation or a game of cards, they were in the habit of resorting to the house of a lady who offered furnished rooms to let—"*Appartements meublés*"—and, as a card in the window notified, was further prepared to supply "Afternoon Tea" to English visitors.

Thither Major Spirido proposed they should betake themselves after the possibilities of the *plage,* and to some extent the strength of Julian's legs, had been exhausted. The lady of the tea-shop, a quiet and respectable-looking French bourgeoise, whose appearance suggested that she had seen better days, welcomed the English officers with motherly kindliness, solicitously enquiring as to the progress of their health and asking by name for news of other convalescent officers whom she had had the privilege of meeting. Madame Mignon, that being the lady's name, after attending to their wants, conversed with her guests in broken English after they had come to the end of their French, which they made a point of displaying with some ostentation during the first greetings, but usually discarded after a while. On finding that Julian's French lasted out better than was usual with his companions, Madame Mignon, after serving tea, addressed her conversation to him, while Captain Chantalow was engaged in giving Major Spirido further confidential particulars of his amatory adventures.

"You must find it rather hard, I should say, to let apartments here in these times," Julian remarked to Madame Mignon. The house appeared, indeed, to be entirely empty.

But Madame Mignon found, she said, nothing to complain of. Her best rooms, on the first floor, "*un très-joli appartement,*" were, she told him, permanently reserved by "*le général.*" "One of your great generals," she said, "a very nice old gentleman—*ah! mais très gentil.*" The general, whose name Madame Mignon did not mention, saying indeed that she did not know it, was, she informed him, in the habit of coming regularly every month to spend a week-end, which might sometimes extend to ten days or a fortnight. Every second month, his wife, a very nice lady, *"une très grande dame,"* came over from England to see him and keep him company. On the alternate occasions, when the general was not expecting his wife, he was joined by a little lady from Paris— a very nice lady, *"très gentille."*

Captain Chantalow, having come to the end of his erotic confidences, handed round a snapshot photograph which he had just received of his house in England. Madame Mignon expressed her admiration for English taste and comfort and the devotion of that wonderful nation to the home.

"The stately homes of England," Spirido murmured sarcastically.

Chantalow took occasion to show Madame Mignon the photograph of his wife and offspring which he carried about with him, and which she had already seen several times, but politely admired once more.

Madame Mignon had presently to excuse herself, some visitors, two ladies, friends of hers, having dropped in to see her. They passed through into the kitchen for a talk with Madame Mignon, while she busied herself there. Spirido and Chantalow had expected to be joined by another officer from the hospital, who had promised to meet them, and on whom they had counted to make a fourth at bridge. As, however, no one turned up, they proposed to go and look for him in one or two haunts about the town where they thought they might come upon him. Julian, feeling slightly fatigued from his outing, said he would remain quietly for a while in Madame Mignon's front room before returning to the hospital. Spirido and Chantalow accordingly set forth without him.

Madame Mignon expressed regret that they should have departed so soon, and, after they had gone, suggested to her friends, who were partaking of *café-crême* in the kitchen, that they should come into the front room and sit there a while to keep Julian company. The ladies, who appeared very shy, consented after some hesitation, bringing their coffee along with them.

"Mademoiselle Adélaïde and Mademoiselle Amélie," said Madame Mignon, by way of introducing the ladies, "were consulting me about the investment of some money in the new Victory loan."

The two ladies were of pleasant appearance and, like Madame Mignon, were attired in the sober black uniform of French bourgeois respectability. Mademoiselle Adélaïde was, moreover, in deep mourning, and wore the funereal weeds assumed by the French on the decease of any relative, however remote. She had, Julian learned presently, lost a brother in the war.

In reply to Madame Mignon's observations, Julian said that such securities, floated by an appeal to patriotism which could not be betrayed, might be considered absolutely safe, being backed not only by the credit of the French Government, but by that of the Allies.

The ladies were glad to hear him express the view.

"But supposing the Germans were to win?" asked Mademoiselle Amélie.

"That is, to say the least, exceedingly unlikely," Julian said. "A war of attrition such as this depends in the last resort upon the resources and credit at the command of the combatants. Even in the event of the Germans obtaining some signal success, even should they, let us say, occupy Paris and even London, there can be no doubt as to the ultimate result."

Mademoiselle Adélaïde wished particularly to be assured that should she desire at any moment to realise her capital there would be no difficulty in her doing so. She explained that it was her intention, after the war was over, to open a little commerce of articles of devotion. She had an uncle in Paris, in the Saint Sulpice district, who had an important manufacturing business for the production of devotional statuary, crucifixes, and rosaries, and Mademoiselle Adélaïde proposed, when the dreadful war was over, to open a shop of such articles in Cambrai, where she came from and where she had a brother who was a canon of the cathedral. She was, she confided, strongly attracted to religion. Had she been free to follow her own inclination, she would have entered a convent. But her second brother, who had been killed early in the war, had left a young widow and two children who were quite destitute, and she, Mademoiselle Adélaïde, felt it to be her duty to work and help provide for them.

Julian learned that Mademoiselle Amélie was also from the invaded territory. Her father was, or had been, Prefect of Police in the little town from which she came. She herself had been a teacher of music.

In answer to some of his questions, she gave some account of the hardships which the French population endured under German rule, but
Mademoiselle Amélie's resentment was not so much directed against the
Germans as against the French officials who, anxious for their own advantage to stand well with the German Kommandantur, conducted themselves with callous tyranny towards their fellow-citizens. The *maire*, a
M. Morpiaux, who was entrusted by the German authorities with the
carrying out of their decrees and the collecting of levies in money and
in kind, was the particular object of Mademoiselle's denunciations.
Under the pretext of carrying out German orders, the *maire* and his
friends had set to plundering the population. The gang, who provided
themselves with free food-cards, lived without cost on the fat of the land,
while the majority of the inhabitants remained miserably short of food
and fuel. Monsieur Morpiaux had obtained authority to administer the
contributions granted from the American Relief Committee. Most of
these he kept for his personal use and that of his friends or sold to the
Germans. The gentleman used and protected his despotic authority by
wreaking vengeance upon all recalcitrants and patriots.

"Poor old Marquise de Lusas, who had ventured to bring complaints
against M. Morpiaux's shameless depredations, was the particular object of his vindictiveness," said Mademoiselle Amélie. "She and her
two maiden daughters, pious gentlewomen, the elder being about thirty
and her sister a couple of years younger, were almost unable to obtain
any food or fuel, and the poor women starved and shivered in their
château. One day the German Kommandantur issued an order for the
registration of all women of loose life, requiring them to be medically
examined and confined within close houses. The mayor, who was entrusted with the carrying out of the order, drew up a list according to
his fancy and had it posted up. On it appeared the names of the shoemaker's wife, who was rather handsome, of the two school teachers, and
of the Mesdemoiselles de Lusas. Neither protests nor petitions were of
any avail. M. Morpiaux alleged as sufficient ground that in the earlier
part of the war, German officers had been billetted in the château. The
poor ladies were forcibly placed in a *maison de passe,* and the mayor
himself, on the pretext of inaugurating the institution, was the first to
outrage them. Since when, they have served for the entertainment of
German officers."

Mademoiselle Amélie said that her people were still near Cambrai. At least, so she supposed, for her efforts to get into communication with them had failed. She had applied to the Red Cross, which undertook to communicate with relatives in the invaded regions. But to no purpose. It was all very sad. Mademoiselle Amélie, somewhat overcome with emotion, passed her handkerchief across her eyes.

Julian expressed his sympathy with the ladies, and remarked, to console them, that they had at any rate cause to be thankful that they were able to put by money, though he did not presume to enquire into their business, and were thus in a position to be of assistance, sooner or later, to their relatives. "The war has at least offered women unprecedented opportunities," he remarked. "They are everywhere in business and industry, taking the place of the men at the front. There is no lack of occupation for them."

"Indeed there is not," said Madame Mignon. "There are scarcely enough women to cope with the demand for their labor, although the whole of French womanhood may be said to be mobilised. The numbers of those who were in business before the war has become multiplied nearly tenfold, and they are being joined every day by young women of good bourgeois families who had previously no experience of business, and no thought of earning money. But such good money is being earned now that it would be hard not to avail oneself of the opportunity, n'est-ce-pas, Adélaïde?"

Mademoiselle Adélaïde agreed. Even those who had no actual need were glad enough to be able to make a little pocket-money by occasional war-work. "All do it. Many make without difficulty clear profits of six thousand francs a month. Angélique," she said, turning to Madame Mignon, "puts aside as much as ten or even twelve thousand. Of course, she is a very hard worker."

The women continued to discuss the possibilities of making money. It was much easier now that opportunities were more or less organised. "Of course," said Madame Mignon, "it is the big people, les gros, who get the lion's share. I could tell you of some who had not a sou at the beginning of the war and who are now worth millions. There will be many new fortunes after the war."

"That is what is making the war last so long," Julian said. "The enormous profits of war industries and trade."

"After all, one cannot altogether blame the *toilers,* the *propriétaires,* Monsieur," Mademoiselle Amélie said. "Every one tries, in one way or another, to make the most of opportunities, the *petites gens* no less than the *entrepreneurs.*"

Mademoiselle Adélaïde remarked that business was so much more profitable in the English "zone." "Therefore, every one flocks there," she said. "The English are so generous, not niggardly like the French, who haggle over *sous.* And they are also so expeditious in what they do."

Julian judged that it was time for him to make his way back to the hospital, and rose to take leave of the ladies. Madame Mignon regretted that he was so pressed. She even ventured to assure him, if she might do so without presumption, that the general's room, which was at present unoccupied, was at his disposal, *"si Monsieur désirait s'amuser quelques instants."*

"On pourrait faire des petites cochonneries," Mademoiselle Adélaïde, modestly lowering her eyes, suggested.

A few days later, the matron of the hospital offered an afternoon tea-party to the medical and nursing staff, to which the walking patients, whose conditions permitted them to attend, were graciously invited. The social function took place in one of the spacious salons of the former hotel, the tall French windows of which opened onto the sea terrace, and which served, now, with only a few decayed remainders of its once luxurious furnishings, as a general sitting room for the nurses when off duty. Julian imagined the appearance of the place when, in its days of glory, it had been peopled with such crowds of wealthy idlers as had frequented the pleasure resort, of women, both old and young, engaged in displaying to one another arrogantly expensive attires, waited on by staffs of deferential menials, and dawdling, dancing, or flirting in bored fashion, while the string band played on the terrace. Now the salon was filled with professional women, middle-class spinsters, accustomed to a hardworking life, for the most part distressingly "capable," socially dull and sexually unattractive. All of them would have been shockingly out of place among the pre-war denizens of the hotel, and some would have been relegated to the servants' hall.

Endeavoring to make himself agreeable to the good matron and the senior sisters, Julian found it distressingly difficult, despite his conscientious efforts, to sustain the stream of conversation, which threatened, at every moment, to stagnate like ditch water, and only managed to preserve a spurious appearance of vocal resonance by endless enquiries into the composition of the tea, requests to pass round the sugar or the tarts, and recommendations of the Dundee cake. The worthy sisters, brought up on the atrocities and famine of English "institution" fare, were totally lacking in any appreciation of civilised sensuality and discrimination in respect of nutritional amenities. One of the young doctors, whose pre-war experience had been confined to that of a ship's surgeon on a liner running to South America, and to whom Julian, during a pause in his exhausting efforts to kindle the conversational fire among the ladies, had hinted something about the notorious culinary deficiency of English medical institutions in general, related how he had once been shown over a hospital in Rio de Janeiro by a courteous Portuguese confrère, who, after taking him round the wards and operating theatres with profuse apologetic acknowledgments of their deficiencies, as compared with the up-to-date appointments of English hospitals, beamed with sudden pride as he showed his visitor into the kitchen. "Here we have our revenge," the Lusitanian physician had exclaimed, "and can claim to be as far in advance of your institutions as you are ahead of ours in the aseptic perfection of your surgical appointments." The place was redolent with the aroma of tomatoes, green and red peppers, bay, thyme, sage, and marjoram, cinnamon and other spices, the rich scent of sauces and crackling roasts, and exhibited arrays of turkeys basting on the spit, and luscious sea-food simmering in wine. "After all," the young doctor remarked, "my dago friend may have done more for the restoration of enfeebled human bodies by his culinary attentions than we are able to achieve by the surgical means at our disposal."

Major Spirido, Captain Chantalow and the other guests looked uncomfortable and bored in the midst of the sisterly gathering, any disposition to levity on the part of the younger nurses being checked by the presence of the matron, the assistant matron and senior sisters, so that the officers' attempts to fall back on banter with Nurse Coleman or Nurse O'Brien met with little response. Conversational resources were further limited by the unwritten law of the times which excluded references to war experiences, or indeed any too particularised allusion to the war. But while the combatant officers were precluded by the convention from drawing upon their experiences for conversational material, the same rule did not apply to the medical staff. As happens in most medical gatherings, the young doctors drifted into talking "shop," and gathered in small groups exchanging accounts of their cases, the marvellous results obtained by their personal methods, and the respective merits of the latest types of splints and wound treatment. Captain Pender was holding forth on the results which he had obtained in cases of fracture of the collarbone by an arrangement of splints and suspending cords which he had devised and which immobilised the patient in an attitude resembling that of the Laocoon.

The matron and sisters fell back on reminiscences of their pre-war experience and of the various institutions where they had worked. The matron, who had received her training at St. Thomas's, maintained the superiority of that institution against Miss Privett, the assistant matron, who claimed the superiority of Bart's, whence she originally came. Miss Privett had, it came out in the course of the reminiscent discussion, served in a Manchester infirmary under Miss Edith Cavell, who had been matron there at the time.

The mention of Miss Cavell seemed to afford Julian an appropriate opportunity of joining in a conversation in which it would otherwise have been difficult for him to enter. The enormous publicity which had been worked up over the case, far from dying down after more than a year, had assumed the proportions of a mystic patriotic cult, and the martyred nurse had become in the popular legend a national heroine, a sort of English Joan of Arc. Many people seemed to be under the impression that one of the main objects of the war was to avenge the foul murder of the sainted martyr. The sinking of the *Lusitania* and the slaying of Nurse Cavell were indeed depicted in cartoons and posters, side by side, the one as the final ground for the entry of America into the war, and the other for England's determination to pursue to a finish the crusade against Teutonic barbarism symbolised by the brutal assassination of the nurse, who had come to embody the highest ideals of humanity and mercy and whose death was freely assimilated to the crucifixion of Christ. Nurse Cavell societies had been founded, and there was already some talk of erecting a worthy monument in commemoration of the martyr who stood for the English virtues of Mercy, Charity, and Humanity as opposed to the bestial vices of German brutality.

Julian naturally assumed that the cult would be particularly rife among the women of the heroine's own calling, some of whom had been her actual associates, and for whom that cult would not only be expressive of patriotic emotion, but likewise of professional pride. In venturing to refer to the canonised nurse, Julian, therefore, made a point of assuming the tone of reverence which was generally prescriptive.

"You must feel it a great privilege," he said to Miss Privett, "to have been personally acquainted with Nurse Cavell."

Julian was not a little surprised at the manner in which his remark, which seemed at once to attract general attention among the sisters, was received.

"Not at all," answered Miss Privett sharply. "She was a fool."

The matron turned to Julian with a patronising expression of commiseration.

"You surely are not taken in, Lieutenant Bern," she said, "by all this absurd nonsense about Edith Cavell? What else would have been done in England or in any other country in the like case? On her own admission, Miss Cavell concealed from the authorities and sent out of the country nearly two hundred enemy combatants. Scores of people have been shot in England on mere suspicion of enemy activities that did not amount to a fraction of those charged to Miss Cavell. Of course from the English point of view her activities were patriotic. But you cannot expect the Germans to take the same view any more than our own people do when they find a German with a wireless apparatus or catch him trying to leave the country. The Germans did no more than what is the universal usage of war. Indeed, they were particularly lenient, weren't they, Miss Privett?"

The explanations given by the matron for the enlightenment of Julian's supposed simplicity were accompanied by general indications of approval from all the nursing sisters assembled round the tea table.

"I told Edith that she was an idiot, and that even if she didn't mind

being shot as a spy, she had no business to make us all share the same
fate," Miss Privett said. "The Germans would have had a perfect right
to shoot us also."

"You were with Miss Cavell in Brussels?" Julian asked, interested.

"Miss Privett and Nurse O'Brien were both at the Berkendael Infirmary at Brussels, which, when the war broke out, was turned into a
Red Cross hospital," the matron explained.

Several other nurses contributed remarks of the same tenor as the
matron's, intended to dissipate what they supposed to be Julian's naïve
illusions concerning the Cavell case. It was evident that, on account of
the tone of his remark, they had conceived a poor opinion of his intelligence.

Julian withdrew after a while to the terrace and joined one of the
groups of young medical officers who stood discussing the treatment
of wounds with Dakin's Solution.

"I rather put my foot in it, didn't I?" he said.

"When you mentioned Nurse Cavell? Rather," said Captain Preak,
the late ship's surgeon. "Miss Privett hates any reference to the affair."

"I was rather interested to hear the sisters' views about it," Julian
said. "It is so different from what one would have been led to expect."

"Oh, if you want to hear about it, you've only got to ask Captain
Staubberg. Here, Staub, have you met Lieutenant Bern?" Captain
Preak said, signing to one of the medical officers. "He is interested in
that Nurse Cavell business."

"I sure am glad to meet you, Lootenant," said the gentleman addressed.

Captain Staubberg was an American who, like many other transatlantic medical men who had come over during the early months of
the war or had happened to be in Europe at the time, had joined the
Red Cross and been later transferred to the British Medical Services.
Doctor Staubberg was, properly speaking, an apothecary or druggist.
But, owing to the pressing need for medical men, little attention was
paid to the exact qualifications of those who offered their services.
Doctor Staubberg had, in fact, been employed as dispensary assistant in
the very institution, in Brussels, conducted by Miss Cavell. He laughed
over Julian's surprise at the nursing sisters' attitude.

" 'Course you can't expect those Janes who are in on it to lap up the

stuff dished out to the folks in England," said Captain Staubberg.
"Same as the eighteen-carat ballyhoo about cheerful heroes all in a
buck-fever to have their guts ripped out by the Boche can't cut mustard
with you buddies at the front. Mind you, Lootenant, I'm not sticking
up for the Huns. They sure can be goddam brutes, and I could tell you
some, though I haven't seen any kids with their hands chopped off or
any crucified Canucks. But I'll say the lousy hypocrisy of the Britishers
gives me a bigger pain in the neck every time than even the beastliness
of the Boche."

Captain Staubberg seemed to hesitate at being drawn into giving particulars, and glanced round to assure himself that none of the nurses
was within hearing.

"I can't give you all the inside dope," he said. "But they wouldn't
have set up all the holler if they hadn't been fair mad over the cave-in
of their Intelligence Service in Belgium. I'll say those birds in the I. S.
are a mighty dillingery bunch. They had the thing organised from A
to Izzard. Never showing the peak of their beaks, neither, but passing
the buck all the time to dolls and Belgians. The Cavell woman was
just one of their employees. Prince Reginald de Croy, who has cousins
all over the Boche army and among the Austrian archdukes, was the
paymaster general, but you can figure that the dough didn't come out
of his pants. They had a whole staff of guides and agents to help the
gang make the Dutch frontier. Recruiting, your noospapers call it! It
was a regular daily mail service run on skedule between Belgium and
the War Office, London, England. And you Limies have the kite to
belch and beller when the Boche did something about it! It makes me
want to puke. They rounded up some thirty-five guys and floozies, but
they never could lay a claw on the bosses. The Germans kept the gang
in the hoosegow at Saint Giles around three months, and had full-dress
trials. I'd like to see the Britishers go as easy as that! It's a cinch they'd
have had the whole bunch bumped off the next morning, and you'd
never have heard a squeak. In the end only the Cavell dame and Baucq
got sent up. The others did a term or got a floater. The *Allemans* didn't
even run in the staff of the Cavell drum. 'Course they couldn't touch
me, being an Amurrican citizen. And it's mighty sweet they were to
Amurrican citizens in those days. But even the two other Limey
nurses, Sister Privett and Nurse O'Brien, who were in an honest-to-

God sweat when they had to gaze at the melody, didn't get jugged, though the Boche had a line on them and kept a close shadow on the Janes."

"They eventually managed to get away from the country, it seems," Julian said.

"Yep. It was me and the United States Ambassador, Brand Whitlock, that got them clear after a while. You can figure that after the show-down I stuck pretty close to the Amurrican legation. Got myself tacked on to their staff as a kind of medical officer. Due to my tie-up with the hospital and speaking the German language I got the job of seeing the calico out of the country. I guess the Boche was just as glad they faded as having them around covering the news and mailing it home. So we got them shipped off to Holland. I was the guy that took them round to Antwerp. But the captain in charge wasn't going to let any mail through, and after all their duds and scanties had been gone through with a fine-toothed comb, the Janes had to peel down to hide and hair. Well, Sister Privett is rather a cold biscuit, but I'll say the old girl looked goddam funny in nothing but her gold specs. But, O Boy! Nurse O'Brien is a calf's lesson in curves. You'll know now why they're not so keen on the story. I'll tell the world they were stunned when they saw me, after a good many months, walk into this outfit."

With friendly solicitude, Captain Pender sounded Julian, some time later, as to his wishes in regard to invalid leave.

"Not that we wish to hurry you off," he said apologetically, "but now that you are able to get about a little, you would perhaps like to go to some convalescent place in England. There are some very nice ones, Cranne Hall, for instance. Whenever you feel inclined, we can have a medical board and arrange the matter."

Julian had no desire to go to England. He asked the doctor whether he could not be sent to Lady Irene Sexborough's hospital.

"The Sexborough hospital? That is rather difficult to get into. However, we will telephone and enquire whether they have room," said the doctor.

"Thank you. You might mention my name," Julian said.

The application was at once granted. Major Spirido was filled with envy when he heard.

"I am making arrangements for my villegiatura in Switzerland," he said. "I believe Lady Irene sees to those things. You might put in a word for me."

The following day an ambulance car was sent for Julian and, after a drive through the pleasant Norman country, he reached the luxurious château situated in the middle of a large park, which Lady Irene had rented. Unfortunately she was away, having had to go over to London on some business connected with the hospital. Julian was received by the assistant directress, the Honorable Margaret Purcell, who in the absence of Lady Irene spared no pains to minister to his comfort.

An atmosphere of feminine luxury pervaded the place. The nurses were society women who enjoyed their masquerade in becoming uniforms, under a young matron who evinced a rooted dislike for the garb of her profession and a taste for elegant toilettes. The work of the nursing staff was not onerous, the patients being well advanced in their convalescence and requiring little in the way of treatment. The only cases demanding much attention were a brigadier, an assistant director of medical services, and a padre, who required daily urethral irrigations, for which operation a male orderly had been detailed.

Julian had a luxurious bedroom, the windows of which afforded a view over the park and a glimpse of the sea, and a sitting room which he shared with an airman who had had a bad smash. There were golf-links on the grounds, which, however, only two or three of the patients were able to use, tennis-courts much patronised by the nurses, and the sitting rooms were provided with ping-pong sets, gramophones, and pianolas.

Julian abandoned himself to the torpid idleness which the place was expressly designed to encourage. He was a good deal weaker than he had realised. His exhaustion from the strain of the last years was made more evident in the relaxation of that strain. His leg still pained him, and he was obliged to use a stick.

The Honorable Margaret Purcell, commonly referred to among the nurses as the Honorable Peggy, regretted that Lady Irene should be away.

"She will be so disappointed," she said to Julian. "Had to hop over to London about some tiresome proposals of the dear old things at the

War Office who want to take over the place. Irene will not, of course, hear of it. She flew over only the other day on one of the buses. An old patient who is at the airdrome close by offered her the ride. But we are expecting her back any moment."

The Honorable Peggy affected a somewhat mannish manner, wore tailor-mades of masculine cut, and a monocle, and was in the habit of smoking cigars. The attention which she paid to Julian was, he gathered, a privileged distinction which he owed to his being an old acquaintance of Lady Irene, for the Honorable Peggy was not as a rule in the habit of associating much with the patients, and showed a preference for the company of the younger nurses, with whom she would sometimes play tennis attired in flannel trousers. She was, Julian learned, a close friend of Lady Katherine De Nivelle.

"Kattie, you know, now lives in Paris," the Honorable Peggy informed him.

"Nursing or canteening?" Julian asked.

"No, just staying. She does not care for war-work, and finds it pleasanter than at home, where every one has to pretend to be doing his bit."

"How noble of her! My estimation of Lady Kattie is enhanced," Julian said.

Among the patients at the hospital was a novelist of considerable reputation who, having joined the Artists' Corps, had been wounded in both legs, and hobbled about on two sticks. He had been an inmate for several months. Julian, who had read one or two of his books, was interested to make his acquaintance.

"I should imagine that you would find this a delightful place in which to write," Julian remarked to the novelist as they sat one morning on the lawn partaking of chicken-broth.

"As a matter of fact, I feel very little inclination to do so," said the novelist. "The disturbing atmosphere of the war is not favorable to literary creation."

"I should have thought that the war would, on the contrary, afford a mine of inspiration."

"You are mistaken," replied the novelist. "People do not like and do not want to hear about the war. They read books which will draw their minds away from the subject and from any form of actuality.

My publishers tell me that my books are having a gratifying sale at present. They deal, as you may know, with social life in the most refined circles, with, of course, a mild love-interest which never departs from the plane of beseemingly controlled emotion and distinction. A book making allusion to the war would scarcely be tolerated at present by the English public. It is an unpleasant subject, and the purpose of creative fiction is to engage the reader's mind on pleasant themes and to draw it away from unpleasant ones."

"I had supposed that war had been, since the days of Homer, a romantic theme," said Julian.

"That was when people were in general unfamiliar with it, and inspiring and colorful pictures of heroic combats could safely be drawn at a distance," said the novelist. "But the times have changed. I have no doubt that in the course of a few years, when the war can be viewed from a distance, it may be used incidentally in creative literature. But it will have to be done with great judgment. Were one to speak of the war according to the best English literary traditions as an occasion for exhibiting the heroism of the combatants, the spirit of the playing fields of Eton in the face of the supreme sacrifice, such treatment, if too heavily insisted on, would be apt to fall short of that modicum of plausibility which is indispensable in a work of fiction. If on the other hand, one should attempt to capture something of that reality, the result would be not only unpleasant; it would be unpublishable. At least in England. It would amount, in fact, to treason, that is, it would be controversial, for it would invite people to think, and pure art would thus be debased to the vulgar level of propaganda."

"To discourage thought and to turn it away from reality, may these not also be regarded as forms of propaganda?" Julian remarked, but did not deem it worth while to enter further into unprofitable comment. The novelist merely smiled from the heights of Oxford scholarship at the paradox.

Lady Irene blew in without warning one afternoon. On hearing that Julian was there, she ran up to his sitting room before even removing her hat and coat and, using the freedom sanctioned by current usage, greeted him with a hug and a resounding kiss.

"Why, Julian! So you're in my charge," she exclaimed. "Not too bad, I hope? I heard all about you from Everard. We'll look after you all right. Well, this is delightful. Have some tea sent up, will you, Peg? I'm simply dying for a cup. Have had absolutely nothing but two sandwiches and some chocs since I left Hendon."

She threw off her cloak, and after an elaborately approvisioned tray had been brought, went on talking brightly, while consuming cup after cup of tea, sandwiches, and cake.

"Yes, I saw Everard. Pretty bad, if you ask me. That gassing he got before and neglected has affected his heart. Oh, nothing really terrible to fear. But the war is over as far as he is concerned. Some suppuration in the pelvis. The doctor told me that the what-d'you-call-them vesicles are affected. It will go pretty hard with Everard."

"I boiled over a little just before it happened. Had an outburst of truth-telling . . ." Julian said.

"Yes, yes. But Everard has forgotten all about that. Said you saved his life. Was terribly concerned when he heard you had been wounded. But now let us talk about yourself," she said, after indicating that she felt refreshed and moving from the tea-table. "No, thank you, I don't smoke. Fancy . . . how long is it since we met? Don't tell me; it would make me feel too old. And you, you look older . . . the trench face. Don't I know it? Poor boy! What beastly hard luck that I was not in England when you came over. Yes, I heard, I know. I could have made things so different for you . . . and for her. Ah dear! *Nessun maggior dolor che ricordarsi de' tempi felici nella miseria.* You see, I was frightfully busy. This place, which I got up when there was scarcely a hospital in France, isn't of much account now. The Government want to take it over, but I think I'll keep it as a haven of rest. But in the early days, when they hadn't even got proper ambulance trains, it came in very handy for the really bad cases which they were afraid to send over. We were really frightfully busy then. All the same, if I had only known, I could have smoothed things over."

"Better, probably, as it is," said Julian.

"Tut, tut. You used to talk like that before. Everything has, I know, grown frightfully difficult to disentangle. But, after all, the important thing is to live. . . ."

"Live!" A wry laugh crisped Julian's face. "I once loved life. I sought to pick out all the beauty, the love-worthy things of life, of humanity—I loved them to intoxication. Now! You say I look changed. It's not the trenches . . . only. Something within me has snapped, dried up, and chokes the rest of me. Before! Before! None of us is what he was before this. None ever will be!" His head drooped in a great abandonment. Then, after a long silence, he recovered himself, speaking with studied casualness. "Forgive this outburst, Lady Irene. I have been silent so long . . . hiding my aloneness, that I have almost forgotten human speech."

Lady Irene looked at him awhile, her eyes caressing him with silent sympathy.

"The first thing is to get you thoroughly well," she said. "I'll have Doctor Forsher let me know exactly how things are. Worn nerves, he says, cry out for . . . oxygen, he calls it. His way of putting it. I'll tell you what we'll do. I have to run over to Paris. They want me to take over the arrangements for the Swiss sanatoria cases. I'll take you with me. Peg wants to look up Kattie. To shake off the war-must, to get it out of your system, that's what you need. To live. . . ."

X I

DRIVEN in daredevil style by the French chauffeur, the Rolls sped along the poplar-bordered roads, and reached Paris in a little over two hours. It drew up in the rue Castiglione, before the hotel where Lady Katherine De Nivelle had her apartment. The Honorable Peggy had arranged to stay with her. Lady Irene and Julian went up for a few moments to greet Kattie, who had grown somewhat fat and flabby, but retained so much of her grace and charm that one almost overlooked the decay of her figure. She pressed her visitors to stay to lunch, but Lady Irene declined.

"I am ravenous," she said, "but I have reserved a table at the Meurice."

As Lady Kattie was seeing her and Julian back to their car, she stopped for a moment in the hall to salute a friend, a very beautiful, foreign-looking woman, who was just taking leave of another lady.

"Mrs. McLeod," she informed Lady Irene. "All the French officers are mad over her. The poor soul is very worried. She wants to go back to Holland to her people, but has no end of trouble getting her papers."

Julian thought he had seen Mrs. McLeod before, but could not recall where. But he recognized the lady who was with her, though she drew up the collar of her mink coat as he passed. It was the hostess of the Lion d'Or, at Estaires, Mademoiselle Germaine. He heard Mrs. McLeod say to her, as she was taking leave: "You will take good care of the baby, will you not?"

At the Meurice, the church-like peace of the breakfast room was almost oppressive. The place was patronised by English ladies, so unspeakably swell that scarcely any one knew them. Most of them had come over on the pretext of visiting male relatives, but in reality to escape the retirement of deserted country houses and the boredom of committee meetings. Their composed dignity did not permit of their public conversation extending beyond laconic remarks or rising above a muffled murmur. The awed waiters took elaborate precautions lest the unseemly rattle of a plate should break the Sabbath stillness of the meal-time Pax Britannica.

"There are livelier places in Paris," Lady Irene apologetically admitted to Julian, lowering her voice to a whisper. "But this is so respectable."

She bowed from a distance to Lady Haig, who had accompanied from G.H.Q. the Marshal, called to a conference at Compiègne, and to Princess Arthur of Connaught, who was over with her sister, Princess Maude of Fife, to see their cousin, the Prince of Wales, who had run up the previous day from Amiens.

"I shall have to pay my respects," said Lady Irene, "and give you your freedom."

Paris did not, like London, make a show of the war. There was no decking out of every activity in the shrill ostentation of understated moral virtue which is indispensable to English public behavior, no nonchalant hysterics about "the jolly old war." The *permissionaires* from the front went inconspicuously by, unnoticed, intent on repose in the seclusion of *la famille,* or on slaking in even greater privacy the war thirst for a draught of happiness, the soldier's hunger on his way to death for woman's flesh. Everywhere were *mutilés de guerre,* legless, armless men, hobbling on crutches or swathed in bandages. In the rue de Rivoli, Julian passed a brilliantly uniformed staff officer who had a cork leg, a glass eye, and articulated artificial hands of chromium metal. He looked like a mechanical robot. The women who replaced the men, in offices, in shops, buses, to a far larger extent than in England, did so without heroics or hysterical ostentatious good humor. Because the war was viewed with more realism, life seemed more normal in Paris than in London. Because "business as usual" was not a slogan, business proceeded more naturally as usual.

Only among the foreign crowds which flowed from every allied country to the boulevards, the Champs Elysées, Montmartre, was the bacchanalian spirit let loose. The Paris which thrived on its reputation as a caterer of pleasure thriftily enjoyed a war-time season. Cafés, restaurants and night clubs overflowed with British khaki, with colonials from the wilds of Canada, South Africa, New Zealand, and the Australian bush, eagerly obtaining for the first time in their lives a glimpse of luxurious dissipation. Big cheery Americans, in painfully new uniforms or civilian attire, the vanguard of the coming transatlantic legions, awakened the echoes with the guffaws of their laughter and staggered round, drowning unquenchable thirsts. Bevies of trim girls from the Golden West, who had long forestalled the cry of "Lafayette, we are here," Red Cross nurses, volunteer relief workers, ambulance drivers, stenographers, purred in every feminine variety of American intonation. Unwonted uniforms met the eye, Italian, Serbian, Rumanian, Portuguese. The augmented hosts of French harlotry, in full field equipment of frippery, were mobilised to meet with overwhelming effectives the foreign invader.

In the Café de la Paix, the tumult recalled a railway station on a Bank Holiday. Temporary gentlemen, in discolored khaki from which the trench mud had been patiently scraped off, released their pent-up spirits in an expansion of potatory and amatory exuberance. Bounced about by shouting subalterns and eager whores, Julian stood amid the hubbub glancing round for an available seat, when he was hailed by Fulliston who, perfumed and manicured, sat at a table with three tarts.

"*Mierda!* See the conquering hero come, now sufficiently restored from glorious wounds to join the Paris front, *por Dios!* Congratulations. How the devil . . .? The blighters at G.H.Q. are mighty chary of Paris leave, fearing, they say, the effects of the pleasures of Capua on the morale of His Majesty's troops."

"You have, nevertheless, contrived to wangle . . ." Julian began.

"Shsh! I am here on business," said the Caballero with an important air of mystery. "I will explain it all to you by and by. *Aqui hay que tener cuidado.* Meanwhile, fill the cup. Garçon! Bring another battery of Heidseck into action. Mesdemoiselles, let me present to you the flower of British chivalry—a hero, *un brave.* Lieutenant Bern captured in single combat a cousin of the All-highest Hun, a prince of pure Hunnish blood royal."

"Oo! Zen the guerre vill soon be over! Vat a pity!" said one of the whores.

"The jolly old guerre vill continue for the duration," said the Caballero, filling glasses all round. "The Boches are demoralised, the French immortalised, the British immobilised, and the Belgians demobilised.

Bern! Let me present to you, O knight of the mournful mien, these noble damsels of the joyful rump. Mademoiselle Kiki, Mademoiselle Nini, and Mademoiselle Fifi."

"I don't like the Belgians," said Mademoiselle Kiki.

"Les Belges, les Belges, ce sont des maqueraux;
Ils couchent avec les femmes pendant la guerre!"

she hummed.

"Quite right too! What else is the good of the bally war?" the Caballero asked. "Chin chin, Caballero de la Triste Figura. Pardon my suspicions, I believe you do not sufficiently couch with the ladies. The fault should be remedied. I will presently introduce you to a charming lady, an old acquaintance of ours. Don't rack your pensive brains. You would never guess. Our hostess of the Lion d'Or."

"Saw her this morning," Julian said.

"Caramba! You are a sly dog, Señor. You are a dark horse. You will, I vouch, see more of her. I have an appointment with the lady in twenty minutes. We will . . ."

Julian descried the bulky form of Major Spirido perambulating with the help of a stick in search of a seat. He introduced the Australian, briefly accounting for the acquaintance, and Fulliston, ordering more refreshments, made room for him by taking Mademoiselle Fifi on his knee.

"Ah, *mais,* you are not going to leave us to see another lady. *Ah ça non,*" said Mademoiselle Kiki.

"You are going to take us to dine at Prunier's, vill you not?" said Mademoiselle Fifi.

"And then vee vill go to the Thélème. Vill vee not, *mon petit choux?*" said Mademoiselle Nini.

"I don't think vee vill, my little Brussels sprout," the Caballero said gently, but firmly.

Major Spirido was meanwhile giving an account of himself to Julian. He was staying at a hospital on the Champs Elysées, where they specialised in nerve injuries.

"Quite a dinky and friendly spot. Privately run by a chap who likes to do the thing in style and has a commendable taste for pretty nurses. Thought I'd like to have a dekko at Paris before booking for Switzerland. Benevolent lady who looks after diggers with a taste for Alpine scenery is attending, I believe, to my reservations."

"The benevolent lady is at present in Paris, occupying herself with your welfare, Major," Julian said.

"Ah! You have, I hope, commended me to her. I should like to meet the lady, to tell her . . ."

"Chance may favor your desire."

"Vee must go to the Thélème, chouchou," Mademoiselle Fifi was saying. "It is formidable."

"Not tonight, my dear. My friend and I are retiring toot-sweet according to plan to new positions," the Caballero persisted. "I am sorry, Major," he added, turning to Spirido, "that important business robs me for the moment of the pleasure . . . I hope . . ."

"I trust I may . . . the pleasure. Bern, should the benevolent lady wish . . . I am in the habit of haunting Maxim's bar towards the sacred hour of the apéritif," Spirido said.

"Ladies don't," said Julian.

"Oh, vee vill go viz you to Maxim's, Monsieur le Major," said Mademoiselle Kiki.

"Coals to Newcastle," said the Caballero.

"Are you very rich, Monsieur le Major?" enquired Mademoiselle Nini.

"Simple sapper said to flapper:
Compris promenade.
Cautious flapper said to sapper:
'Ave you leetle money?
Simple sapper said to flapper:
Napoo, je suis stoney,"

recited Spirido.

"Oo oo! Monsieur le Major is a poet!" said Mademoiselle Fifi.

"No, my dear, I am a mathematician," said the Major.

"A madematician! Vat is dat?" asked Mademoiselle Nini.

"A géomètre, as you say," Spirido replied.

"Ah! Un géomètre. How terrible!"

"The love of knowledge is greater than lechery," said Spirido. "Your immortal Jean-Jacques resolved a problem in mathematics when about to engage in the delectable deed. Whereupon the link of love failed him. The disgusted lady counselled the sage to stick to mathematics and forswear women."

"I do not understand," said Mademoiselle Kiki.

"No author is ever understood, my dear," said the Major. "I have written books on geometry. The critics have said that I was a born poet, but no geometrician. I have also written poetry. The critics have said that I was a great geometrician, but no poet."

The Caballero signalled to the vestiary attendant for his British warm. A renewed chorus of protestation rose from the ladies.

"But, dar-r-r-ling, you vill give us a *petit cadeau,* vill you not? Vee 'ave devoted ourselves all ze afternoon to your entertainment," said Mademoiselle Nini.

"You have drunk five bottles of Heinseck. How much commission does this peaceful establishment allow you?" said the Caballero.

"Oh, not very much," said Mademoiselle Kiki.

The Caballero slipped hundred franc notes into the sirens' receptive palms. Taking renewed leave of the Major, who appeared disposed to bibulous repose in the ladies' company, Fulliston and Julian elbowed their way to the swing doors.

"As hard to shake off as leeches. Bloodsucking vampires. Should have got away half-an-hour ago. Most important business," he said in staccato tones as they reached the pavement.

"Business of State?" Julian enquired.

"No damn bloody fear. I'm not in the Intelligence Service. Still in the Bloody Fool service." As they strolled down the Boulevard des Capucines, the Caballero confided, linking his arm with Julian's: "My old man in Buenos Aires wrote saying he had a contract for leather hides with the French Government. The *sinverguenza* of an agent offered merely a fair price. Did you ever hear of such barefaced impudence? Naturally the governor suspected foul play. He wrote asking me whether I could slip over to Paris and look into the swindle. I must say Division, when I applied through the proper channels for Paris leave, was jolly decent, though at first disposed to raise difficulties. Saw the point, however, when I told them how things stood. At the Ministry of Armament, in the Champs Elysées, where I got hold of Monsieur Loisy, the minister being engaged on a strike conference, I found that the Frenchie Government was paying exactly eighty times the price offered to my old man. No less than twelve middlemen getting their chisel out of the plunder. The goods were originally contracted for to an officer in the Commissariat by a hairdresser in the rue St. Honoré. Everybody, concierges, waiters, pimps, message boys, barmen, whores, are selling goods to the Government. Any sort of goods, from underpants to airplanes. The trouble arises, of course, when it comes to producing the goods after they have been sold. Well, I've succeeded so far in eliminating four rapacious Frenchmen out of twelve, and have good hopes. . . . Will benefit the paternal exchequer by some millions, my boy. *Mierda!* I think I've found at last my true vocation. Should have gone into business."

"But how do you perform the miracle of loosening a Frenchman's grip on pelf, of wrenching plunder out of his talons?" Julian asked.

"Ah, ah! That's where the fair lady of the Golden Lion comes in. Came upon her by chance in a bar. We turn off here," said the Caballero as they passed the shop with the figures of Germans sitting on chamber-pots.

"A somewhat dangerous association. The lady is, as you know, a German spy," Julian said.

"Precisely. That is why she proves so helpful. Don't you see? She knows she is utterly in my power. Ah, ah! I treat her like a thing, a damned door-mat, wipe my boots on her, see? The only satisfactory tender relation, by the way. Do just as I please with her. She answers the rein and the spur like a well-broken gaucho pony. She, on the other hand . . . Listen to this. She, being involved in all sorts of shady transactions with French officers and officials . . . do you follow? . . . has exactly the same lien on them as I have on her. Now do you twig? The firing post at Vincennes for her if she proves recalcitrant with me; the same for the Froggies if they don't do what she asks. The Froggies whom she requested to release their plunder on the contract stormed and swore, but they were at her mercy. And Germaine's mercy is colder than their cold feet. A scrumptious piece of rascality is the lady. You will see. She is at present engaged in ticking off the chief rascal in the little transaction, a deputy in the French Chamber, a noted patriot. The scurvy fellow, one Monsieur Aristide Bouchon, is proving, it seems, a troublesome fish to land. Is wriggling like a hooked trout. But Germaine has quite enough against him to send him up before the firing-squad ten times over. I'm impatient to learn the progress of the sport. Here we are. You will, by the way, find her friend entertaining. A sugary morsel of a flapper. Not more than eighteen, I should say. But very *farouche,* a very fortress of virtue, notwithstanding the deceptive appearance of her sporting manner, I warn you."

"You mean Mademoiselle Germaine's sister, Angélique, I suppose?" Julian said.

"Sister be mucked! Germaine's sisterly relations are subject to alteration without notice. This time. . . . But you will see for yourself in a moment. My boy, we are going to have some furious fun!"

They entered a small hotel in the rue Caumartin. The bar to the left was blatant with bare lights and clanged with the uproar of Anglo-Saxon mirth and intoxication. A big Canadian, red in the face, was shouting:

"It's those lousy Russian buggers we ought to be fighting, I tell you. Hand and glove with the Boche. Are you blooming Britishers going to stand by while they insult and maltreat the King's own cousin?"

"I say, I *say,* old Mapleleaf, you're foo."

"Foo yourself! Where would you Tommies be without us, I'd like to know. What price Vimy Ridge?"

> "You can't find a woman in a bully-beef can;
> If you can't get a woman, get a clean . . ."

"Old man, give us a gasper, will you?"

To the right, the large lounge at the foot of the stairs was so dimly lit that the unhabituated eye could scarcely pierce the penumbra of its recesses. It was almost deserted. In a corner a young subaltern and a wily Frenchwoman carried on in whispers a pecuniary-amatory conversation.

From another dark recess stepped forwards Mademoiselle Germaine, tall and dignified, in a rustle of silks, a mink cape over her shoulders. She was even more *grande dame* in her bearing than on the previous occasion Julian had met her. But she looked nervous and very pale, and shot a quick startled glance at Julian when she saw him.

Fulliston addressed her sharply in low tones:

"You need not mind my friend, whom you have already met. Is the business settled?"

"Not yet," said Germaine. "He has promised to let me have an answer within two days."

"Why two days?" asked the Caballero. "What the hell is the meaning of this dodging? Why could you not bring him to book at once, you bitch? I suspect that you have been up to some trickery of your own. We shall soon see." He was raising his voice.

"Not here, please," said Germaine, glancing round anxiously. "Let us go upstairs, if you wish to talk."

"Talk! I am damn well going to put you through some paces, my lady. We are going to make a domiciliary and personal perquisition. And woe betide you if we lay our hands on any compromising indication. Do you understand? My friend here will assist. Have a good look at her. A rather appetising piece of goods, what? Wait a few minutes till you see her stripped. A croup like a thoroughbred mare. Lead the way. Forward, quick, march."

"Cad! Brute!" hissed Mademoiselle Germaine from between clenched teeth. She flashed fiercely at Fulliston, but after a moment lowered her eyes like a cowed tigress. Scowling, she took a step towards the stairs.

At the moment, Julian felt a hand on his arm. Turning sharply, he saw Keetje standing beside him.

"Just one moment," she said with deliberate nonchalance. "Captain Fulliston, you will please sit down here and discuss quietly anything you wish with Germaine."

"Well, I'm damned!" the Caballero exclaimed.

"Very likely," Keetje said coolly. "Have you a cigarette, Mr. Bern? Thank you."

"What's the meaning of this?" Fulliston said.

"I shall shortly be calling at the British Embassy. Indeed, I am a bit late for my appointment," said Keetje. "If I should mention your name, Captain Fulliston, the Provost Marshal might take it into his head to poke his nose into your affairs. It would be annoying. He might ask disagreeable questions. You will find it much more convenient to stay here quietly if you wish to discuss any matter with Mademoiselle. No one will disturb you. If Mr. Bern cares, he and I can have a talk, meanwhile, up in my room."

"Mierda de Dios! Well, I'm . . ." spluttered the Caballero, looking from Julian to Keetje in perplexity. With a shrug he moved over with Germaine to a corner of the lounge.

Keetje led the way up the stairs, Julian following her along the creaking passages. She showed him into a dingy room with soiled wallpaper, orange with black and red stripes and blue flowers, in the best French style, and a patched threadbare carpet.

"Excuse me for bringing you to my room," she said. "You need not fear that I have any intention of seducing you. But the accommodation in this place is somewhat limited and privacy for conversation difficult to secure."

She drew aside a framed colored print of the Emperor Napoleon III with the Empress Eugénie, and carefully examined the torn wallpaper behind it.

"The next-door room is empty at the moment. It is a pity in a way. I might have shown you some amusing sights, if the lady who occupies it had been entertaining a visitor," Keetje said with a cynical smile.

"This, I gather, is a brothel?" Julian said.

"All French hotels are. Even the swellest. I shouldn't care to answer even for the Meurice, where you are staying with Milady Irene Sexborough."

"You are damnably well informed," Julian said, scowling.

"It is my business. Please take a seat," she said, pointing to the only armchair. "I will sit on the bed."

"How the devil do you know . . . ?" Julian began asking.

Keetje laughed. "Simple enough. Did not you come upon Germaine this morning at the Hôtel Lotti when you called on Lady De Nivelle?"

"You're a rather clever chit of a girl," he said.

Keetje, dangling very high-laced boots over the edge of the bed, and smoking her eternal cigarette, smiled back roguishly.

"Rather," she said.

"I thought I also recognised the lady with whom Mademoiselle Germaine was," said Julian.

"Very possibly. She used to give exhibitions in Oriental dancing. Called herself Mata Hari," said Keetje.

"I saw her in Berlin."

"She will have some difficulty in getting back there."

"You seem to be playing a pretty dangerous game, chit. Double spying, are you?"

"Not the way you mean."

"You know, of course, that this Mademoiselle Germaine is a German spy?"

"She is one of the chiefs of the Boche service in France. Her real name is the Comtesse Mathilde de Richepin. She is a great patriot."

"Patriot? What nonsense are you talking! Isn't she a Frenchwoman?"

"She's a royalist. The royalists hope that the French Republic will be overthrown."

Julian laughed. "What's patriotism?"

"The bunk, as the Mapleleaf boys say."

"It's a pretty fishy business that you've got yourself mixed up with, all the same," Julian said.

"What business isn't? Welby says I'm invaluable. What will he say when he knows of my today's haul?" Keetje drew from her blouse a sheet of thin, minutely folded paper. "Almost a complete list of French and English sailings and the location of nearly every battalion in France. Mrs. McLeod is very clever. But she's got badly scared. She passed on the baby to Germaine for safe keeping. Germaine, who has the wind up almost as badly, passed it on to this child, who is on her way to Switzerland and promised to pass it on to the German High Command. I don't think."

"Is Mr. Welby Penmore in Paris?" Julian asked.

"No. By the way, he is Sir Welby now. Your uncle died a week ago. Welby will be Lord Penmore when the war is over."

"I suppose you are his mistress," Julian said.

"You suppose wrong," she replied without indignation. "Not for want of being asked. But at present, it does not suit me. I want much more. And now I must report at the Embassy. As I have to change, you perhaps had better join our friends downstairs, who will have finished their disputes by now."

Lady Irene was kept busy taking over the arrangements for the transfer of suitable cases to the Swiss sanatoria in conjunction with the Swiss Red Cross, and in obtaining the necessary information. She called on Madame d'Haussonville, the president of the French Red Cross, Madame Carnot, president of the association of the *Dames Françaises,* and several other ladies. They were, unfortunately, at the moment, ex-

tremely busy with the Bazaar which was being held at the Ritz in aid
of the military hospitals. The most helpful informant in the matter
with which Lady Irene was concerned was, she found, a Mrs. Latterly,
who had been managing most of the business connected with it, knew
Frau Schultess, the wife of the Swiss president, and was shortly going
to Switzerland herself. She would speak, she said, to Frau Schultess
and to the president of the Swiss Red Cross, and was extremely solicitous and obliging in assisting Lady Irene. Mrs. Latterly was an American by birth, though a British subject by marriage, but had long been
divorced from her third husband, and had taken up her residence in
Paris, where she had a luxurious mansion in the Avenue Henri
Martin.

At the Ritz bazaar a further opportunity was offered of meeting
all the benevolent ladies and many of Lady Irene's old friends. The
occasion was eagerly seized to enjoy a social gathering which recalled
some of that brilliancy to which one had become unused, and which
now seemed a distant dream of the past.

"It's the only place in Paris which is warm enough for us to wear
décolleté evening dresses," said Wanda O'Toole, a daughter of the
Marquise de Montenotte, to Lady Irene.

"Coal is almost unprocurable, you know," said Princess Sutzo,
who lived at the Ritz, and whose handsome shoulders were the cynosure of Monsieur Marcel Proust, who haunted on her account the
corridors of the hotel. "It has been cornered by the Comité des Forges
to raise prices. Fortunately, Mr. Capel, who is in charge of the distribution of English coal, has an apartment here for his 'petite amie,'
'Coco' Chanel, and does not wish her to suffer from chilblains. She's
taken it into her head to start a shop for knitted jumpers, which are
all the rage."

The princess was helping at the food stall, where she was selling
patés de foie gras and Cambridge sausages.

Lady Kattie turned up late. She looked very discomposed when she
sailed in with the Honorable Peggy.

"Poor Kattie has, I'm afraid, taken to snow," Lady Irene told Julian.

"Such a terrible thing has happened," Kattie said. "They've arrested Mrs. McLeod. I saw it all. An inspector and two plain-clothes men
came to the hotel. They took the poor thing away in a taxi."

Lady Irene endeavored to console Kattie by taking her to buy some of the exquisite lingerie which the saleswomen, the Marquise de Pracomtal and the Duchesse de Levis-Mirepoix, were displaying. She herself bought, from Baroness Henri de Rothschild, at the antique stall, an emerald and diamond ring which, she was assured, had belonged to Queen Marie Antoinette. It bore the arms of Austria and the French lilies and the poinçon of Cartier. But the sensation of the bazaar was the animal stall, presided over by Princesse Guy de Faucigny-Lucinge, where, besides black Pekingeses, Siamese cats, and monkeys, two lion cubs were for sale. One was purchased by Mademoiselle Chanel and the other by the Comtesse de Salverte.

The bazaar was a huge success. Lady Roper Parkington, the secretary of the Montenegrin Red Cross, who was with Princess Anne Galitzin and Monsieur Islavin, the diplomatic representative of the court of Cetinje, told Lady Irene that she had just received a cheque for five hundred thousand francs from Baron Rubinstein and another from Monsieur Henri Deterding. The Princesse de Chimiez suggested that an even more brilliant financial success could be secured for the humanitarian cause by having an exhibition of tableaux vivants, as they had had in London recently—"only a little more French." The princess, who had formerly been a star in burlesque shows, in New York, had given an exhibition of "plastic poses" at the Folies Bergères. People had paid two hundred dollars and more for a stall.

In the pastel-colored supper room, Monsieur Isvolski, the Russian ambassador, sat with Grand Duchess Anastasia of Mecklenburg-Schwerin, the mother-in-law of the German Crownprince, and Princess George Vivesco, the habitué of the Hohenzollern court and the Kiel regattas. Blonde and Germanically insolent, she was proclaiming in a loud voice that the Allies might as well admit that they were beaten. They could not hope to cope with German efficiency and military power. She was on her way to Bucharest, she said.

"Treason in high places is quite safe," observed Lady Irene. "The rascal Isvolski, whose functions and status are not at present very clear, is gorged with German money. The Italian Government, who are afraid the Allies may conclude a separate peace with Austria, are also liberally supporting him."

"He needs the money," Lady Kattie said. "Never has a penny of his own, and since the beginning of the war has led the life of a pasha, surrounded by a seraglio of women."

Kattie needed distraction, she said. And snow; her supply had run out.

"Let us go to a boîte," she proposed.

The "Thélème" proved more boring than the Ritz. But, catching sight of Major Spirido, with the Caballero and two English nurses, Julian took the opportunity to introduce him to Lady Irene.

"Have you made the acquaintance of your protégé, Lady Irene?" he asked.

"Which? The one with the neuritis?" she smiled. Julian had already given her some private information about the case.

Spirido was taken unawares and at some disadvantage. His courteous alacrity in rising at Julian's invitation imperilled his equilibrium.

"You behold me, gracious lady, sorrily afflicted," he said. "My means of support are impaired. My birchcane has unfortunately become mislaid, lost, purloined, or abstracted."

"I had been officially informed that you were a walking case, Major," Lady Irene banteringly remarked.

"Alas, I fear you may think me unworthy of your charitable interest. I will not conceal from you, gracious lady, that I have been seduced by agreeable company into abusing the kindly laxity of hospital regulations. I have been induced to ingurgitate an overdose of tonic potation. I am, I fear, somewhat whittled, if I may so express myself, a trifle raddled, in short, cut."

"A passing indisposition, Major," smiled Lady Irene. "I trust you will shortly recover your full health amid the silences of the eternal hills."

"*Ueber alle Gipfeln ist Ruh!*" Spirido cited, growing rhapsodic.

"A damned untruth," Julian said. "The peaks of intelligence which pierce the mist-racks of unveracity and imbecility are not peaceful. He who dwells there is vowed, like Prometheus, to unceasing anguish."

"You are, I believe, right. I was but quoting an ornate platitude. Like the majority of his countrymen, Goethe was eminently proficient in imparting to platitudes a specious air of profundity."

"The sleek-headed Olympian courtier is a much overrated old gentleman," Julian said. "His fame has, like all things Germanic, been puffed up by barbaric bluff, which seeks compensation for the sterile barbarian's seething sense of inferiority."

Lady Kattie tipped the waiter, with a request for "reniflette," and was presently supplied with a matchbox filled with the precious snow.

A nude dancer, lithely moving in langourous poses, offered the prefigurement of joy to eyes that had looked upon death. The war chartered new licenses and tempered police prudery, relaxing morals in the interests of morale.

When a gentleman pimp approached with the offer of a private entertainment, "tout-à-fait spécial," Lady Irene, with an indulgent smile, turned enquiring eyes upon Julian. He shrugged his shoulders:

"Coney-catching codgery for Anglo-Saxon gudgeons!"

But the Caballero, whom Major Spirido had rejoined, inclined a favorable ear to the proposal, and the two nurses sufficiently indicated, with the reserve of Englishwomen of good family and refinement, that they were not incurious.

A bedraggled female with yellow tousel and eyelids painted green sang in a raucous voice:

> "Eux! dans leurs bureaux d'affaires,
> Dans leurs bordels et dans leurs bars,
> Font la politique et les guerres.
> 'Guerre jusqu'au bout et à outrance,'
> Qu'ils disent, 'Allez-y, les gars,
> Pour le salut de la France'—
> La France à Eux—
> les Merdeux!
>
> Eux! Ils m'ont pris mon homme.
> Il est crevé sur la Somme,
> Pour le salut de leur peau,
> Pour le salut de leurs négoces,
> De leurs poignons, de leurs tripots,
> De leur bombance et de leurs noces—
> Pour Eux, pour Eux—
> les Merdeux!
>
> On la leur foutera, la guerre,
> A ces cochons, un de ces jours,
> La véritable dernière.

On se battra, gars de France—
De la vraie—et pour toujours,
Jusqu'au bout et à outrance—
Mais contre Eux—

                  les Merdeux!"

"A dull show," said the Honorable Peggy, yawning.

As they were leaving, Lady Irene graciously took occasion to renew her assurances to Major Spirido that she would bear in mind his medical requirements. They came upon him, with Fulliston and the two nurses, who were getting into a taxi, to pass, at the Caballero's suggestion, an hour or two in an unpretentious, but discreet, little hotel before returning with their patient to the hospital.

Lady Irene had, in point of fact, forgotten to mention the major's case when she had interviewed Mrs. Latterly. She rang her up the following morning with a view to securing early accommodation for the major. There would be no difficulty, Mrs. Latterly replied over the wire. Could Lady Irene look her up in the course of the evening? Mrs. Latterly was having a few friends. She would be delighted if Lady Irene cared to come, bringing with her any one she pleased. Mrs. Latterly begged Lady Irene to excuse the informality. She was a very active lady, being engaged, in addition to her numerous benevolent undertakings, in feminist political movements directed toward pacifism. She happened to have no other time free that day.

After a late dinner at Larue's, preceded by one or two apéritifs, and accompanied by choice vintages, with a few fine liqueurs to assist digestion, Lady Irene, with Kattie, the Honorable Peggy, and Julian, betook themselves accordingly to the Avenue Henri Martin. Mrs. Latterly's salon was humming like a beehive with the buzz of chatter, stimulated by the circulation of potent cocktails. There were one or two men—a French journalist of Irish extraction, Monsieur de Tara, and an English gentleman from Shanghai. The more numerous feminine portion of the gathering was American, with a sprinkling of French literary, political and journalistic ladies.

Mrs. Latterly, taking Lady Irene aside, disposed in a few minutes of the object of the call.

"The case should be sent," she said, "to Professor Schurkmann, in Zürich. You have doubtless heard of him, my dear Lady Irene. No?

He is perfectly marvellous. Uses a new magnetic method he has discovered, a sort of rod charged with a particular kind of electricity.
Rhabdo-therapy, it is called. He influences directly the aura of the
patient, you know. I shall get my secretary to write at once to the wife
of the Swiss President, and shall let you know before the end of the
week."

After presenting some of the ladies—Miss Ella Wapburn, her secretary, Mrs. Cosmelly, a great temperance advocate, Valentine Thomson,
editor of a feminist journal—Mrs. Latterly informed Lady Irene that
she was engaged in establishing an international league of women,
which would shortly hold a monster meeting in Switzerland in order to
bring pressure on all Governments to stop the war. "The voice of the
wives and mothers of the world will be irresistible," she said. She was
in communication with German, Austrian, and Scandinavian pacifist
ladies.

"You know, my dear Lady Irene," said Mrs. Latterly, "that the German Government has made overtures, apart from Chancellor Beth-
mann-Holweg's declaration in the Reichstag last December. Only the
other day a lady came from Belgium to see Monsieur Briand. She had
been told by Lancken, the civil governor, in Brussels, that the German
Government was prepared to enter into negotiations at any time. The
young Emperor Karl is positively determined to have peace. On the
recommendation of Cardinal Piffl, he has vowed to build a new church,
should his dearest wish be granted. His brothers-in-law, the Bourbon
princes, Sixte and Xavier, are going and coming between the Quai de
Béthune and Neuchatel, where their mother is living, and are about to
go to Vienna. King Alfonso, who is a true lover of peace, has also sent
proposals through General Denvignes."

"Who left the said proposals in a taxicab, where they were picked up
by a lady of the Comédie Française," put in Monsieur de Tara.

"The French comedy. How appropriate!" exclaimed the feminist
editress.

"Monsieur Poincaré is favorably disposed," said Mrs. Latterly. "But
that skeesix, Lloyd George, made a date with Baron Sonnino at Saint
Jean de Maurienne."

"The City won't hear of peace," said Monsieur de Tara. "Royal
Dutch is soaring sky-high. The Manchester cotton merchants are do-

ing a fabulous trade with Holland, and so are Vickers. Everybody is happy."

"Haig is making a fortune in whiskey," said the temperance advocate.

"It is time we affirmed the rights of peoples to dispose of themselves," declared Mrs. Latterly, with noble liberal intonation.

"You may affirm all the rights you like. But the only rights you cannot interfere with are the rights of property," said Monsieur de Tara. "You cannot prevent people from making money. That's anarchy, communism, or . . . what is it those Russian fellows call it now?"

"Bolshevism," put in Mrs. Salsidge, Daughter of the American Revolution.

"People have a right not to be made the tools of Governments ruled exclusively by financial interests," Mrs. Latterly went on airily.

"And how are you going to prevent financial interests from ruling Governments?" smiled Monsieur de Tara. "What else are Governments but the servants of financial interests? This country is ruled by the board of directors of the Bank of France, an association of two hundred gentlemen, who are likewise the directors of every financial, industrial, or commercial interest of any importance in this country. They are—France. Monsieur de Wendel, or von Wendel, the president of the Comité des Forges, was called upon the other day in the Chamber to show cause why he should not stand before a firing-squad. He is sending weekly trainloads of steel to Switzerland to manufacture German guns, nickel to cap German bullets, cyanamide to manufacture German explosives. The manager of this profitable export department of his is a German, whose father is at the present moment the head of a business in Berlin. Monsieur von Wendel can, of course, shrug his shoulders at the denunciations of his accusers. He scarcely deems it worth while to answer them. And you talk, my dear lady, about affirming the rights of the people. Have you no idea whatever of how the world is made?"

"I have been assured by a military authority of the highest competence," said the Comtesse de Détuyeau, "that the German army would have been smashed at Charleroi but for the sacred immunity enjoyed by the strategically situated iron furnaces of Briey, controlled by Monsieur de Wendel and his friends, and strictly protected from

gunfire by an express order from G.H.Q. acting on the command of
the French Government. An aviator who ignorantly dropped a bomb
on the Germans occupying Monsieur de Wendel's factory was repri-
manded and disgraced."

"But do you mean that nothing can be done about such colossal
treason?" asked Mrs. Latterly.

"Nothing whatsoever, my dear madam. Unless one were to turn
. . . what do you call them again? . . . Bolshevik, and the people acquire
the right to manufacture their armaments for themselves and not for
Monsieur von Wendel and the Germans, to be the proprietors of their
own coal, food, cloth, land. And the only means of acquiring those elementary rights is to turn the machine-guns against the Messieurs von
Wendels and their Governments. But when you do that you stand an
excellent chance of being shot down yourself as an enemy of civilised
society," said Monsieur de Tara, helping himself to another Manhattan.
"The representatives of Schneider, Vickers, and Krupp settle the whole
of our politics, and incidentally of our lives, in pleasant conversations
which they openly hold over their wine at the Grand Hotel at Lucerne.
One of the leading directors of Krupp, being in a hurry, recently visited
Paris on business. The French Government of the great patriot, Poincaré, courteously provided the distinguished visitor with a bodyguard
for the protection of his person against wrong-headed people."

Lady Kattie and the Honorable Peggy, bored with the intolerable
dullness of political conversations, wandered from group to group in
hope of more entertaining converse, refreshing themselves with a cocktail at each pause. The French journalistic ladies were discussing the
book of Barbusse, which there was some talk of suppressing, and the
Jeune Parque of Paul Valéry. Mrs. Oswald Chew, of Chicago, talked
with Miss Enos, the fashion expert from London, about the trend
towards simplicity in clothes.

"But much more silk is being worn," said Mrs. Chew.

"Yes, because cotton is now fetching fabulous prices," Miss Enos
said. "It is needed for explosives. So that silk, which is being dumped
by the wily Japs, is coming to be more economical. Isn't that so, Mr.
Chatters?"

She referred to the English gentleman from China, who was sitting
close by in the inglenook with Miss Ella Wapburn, whose legs ap-

pealed to his sense of proportion. He had made a huge fortune in cotton, Chink labor costing but a few bowls of rice.

"But we must have some more cocktails," said Miss Wapburn, shapely and efficient, rising to procure the refreshments as Kattie and the Honorable Peggy sat down.

Mr. Chatters, young, with fleshy lips and dilated eyes, had been telling her his life story. He had, immediately upon the declaration of war, transferred his residence and capital to Shanghai, so as to be as far as possible from the field of glory. Only the attraction of a huge deal with the German Government had drawn him to Europe, on a flying visit, and he was impatient to be back among the delights of the Chinese Babylon.

Miss Wapburn returned with a tray of Whiz-bangs and cigarettes. "Mr. Chatters finds Paris as dull as ditchwater," she said.

Chatters had gone so un-English as to make no claim to moral virtue. In Shanghai, police interference with enjoyment was negligible, especially since the war, and the continuous supply of women from all parts of the world, American, English, Russian, Hungarian, Spanish, was unending. Chatters had his own private pastime-house on the Hang-Chow road. No matter what woman caught his eye and fancy in the hotels, on the Bund, the Shanghai Club, at Sun-Yan's, he had but to make a sign to one of his Chinks, and the next time the lady went jin-rickshawing on the Foochow road she was whisked, gagged, into a junk, and served to him the next day at his pleasure place. He had all manner of fantastic Chinese modes of erotic entertainment, perversions, and bestialities.

Lady Kattie was curious about opium-smoking establishments. While Mrs. Latterly and Monsieur de Tara were rambling on, she and the Honorable Peggy concerted with Miss Wapburn and Mr. Chatters as to an agreeable way of concluding the evening. After the termination of the consultation, Kattie exchanged with Lady Irene a smiling glance as a signal to cut short the tedium of the visit.

"It has been so delightful," Lady Irene assured Mrs. Latterly, taking leave.

"So early. Not yet twelve o'clock. I shall have the tiresome papers ready in a day or two. My secretary, Miss Wapburn, will see to . . . Er . . . I hope . . . So good of you. . . . So charmed to have made . . ."

The party, augmented by Miss Ella Wapburn and Mr. Chatters, crowded into the car.

By the Trocadero, strange Mongol faces peered from behind barbed wire and machine-gun nests. Bayonets gleamed in the night, where the Annamites mounted guard.

"They don't trust French troops any longer in Paris. Four divisions refused to return to the trenches, I hear," Chatters said.

Sizzling sparks shot from the wireless of the Eiffel Tower.

"That poor Mrs. McLeod," said Lady Kattie.

"Where are we going?" Julian enquired.

"To Hing-Shu's fumery," somebody said.

"Of course, the little scapegoats can't be let off, else the big game . . ." A bump threw Julian on to Lady Irene's shoulder.

"The national interest . . ."

Rue Tholozé, the Abbesses' road, the Moulin de la Galette. Julian felt dazed and sleepy. Twinkling, varicolored lights of Paris below. Pencils of light wheeling in the inky sky above the Mount of Martyrs, and the white sugarloaves of the Sacred Heart of Jesus, rising in insolence above the Ville Lumière to celebrate the crushing of the Commune.

"Stoppez!"

All alight and walk through deserted, narrow-winding streets. Heard only are the swish of skirts and the click of Louis seize heels on the trottoir.

"Mind where you step."

"It means money."

They come to a standstill before a yellow-painted door. Chatters gives a discreet knock. A snagmouthed harridan uncloses the postern. In Indian file, they thread, groping in Cimmerian darkness, along the narrow vestibule. An orange glowlight points to the steep stairway. There is a stuffy smell of size, sumach, and sandalwood.

"Par ici, par ici," mumbles the harridan.

"Which way? Pardon, did I . . .?"

A door opening suddenly dazzles with sudden glare. Before the cinnabar-lacquered bar-counter sit three French soldiers in grey-blue capotes, and two Annamite Chinks. The poilus glance slowly round at the incomers.

"Qu'e'qu' c'est qu'cette gadouille de chipies?"

"Chiée d'Angliches pour s'appuyer une muffée de bleue et un coqueli-cot. La gruerie veut s'aplatir."

The Chinks veer slit-eyed pokerfaces towards the women.

From behind the bar comes sliding forward Hing-Shu, in black-braided blue coat, his parchment face drawn tightly over two prongs of cheekbones, and utters low, sibillant sounds.

Mr. Chatters casts his eyes round, landing them on the Chinaman's inscrutable optic slits.

"Tsew yen fang."

Hing-Shu returns a comprehending nod and lightly strikes a brass gong.

A panel slides open. A dim antechamber limned with cranes and lotus-blooms leads to another chamber tapestried with figured hangings and furnished with low, cushioned saffian couches and tchuotse tables of black wooden fret. A carved lanthorn sheds a rosy-tinted glow. Joss sticks smoulder in a ting cresset of brass before a niche, wherein squats a gorbellied figure with egg-shaped head, nodding monotonously. Silken scrolls inscribed with tao-te-king bird characters proffer unconned lore.

Silently a small Chinese girl in beeswax-colored coat and trousers appears from out the folds of a hanging. Hing-Shu snaps out peremptory syllables:

"Ya teoo! poo-oh li pei ji ke, shang yu yen tsiang!"

The yellow girl, her arms folded across her breast, bends to the ground.

"Khen khao," she replies in low silvery tones.

"Noe-noe chih shin."

"Khen khao."

Chatters transfers money-notes to Hing-Shu's long slender hand. Silently and noiselessly the Chinee and the yellow girl vanish. Presently the yellow girl returns bearing cruses and goblets of opaline liquid. All sit to sip the iridescent liquor.

"Wormwood," the Honorable Peggy says, with a grimace.

"And the name of the star was Absinthios. And the third part of the waters became wormwood, and men died because they were made bitter," Julian intones.

Bitter!

"I thought this was a hopjoint," says Miss Ella Wapburn.

"No choicer in Paname," Lady Kattie remarks.

Dimness dowsed the glims. Dimly Julian saw Lady Irene's eyes shine like black stars. Faintly he heard murmuring voices, the murmur of music, as of tristful catlings stroked by fair hands of hoa-niu flower-girls.

"Where is ...?" Miss Ella Wapburn questions.

Tristan's wail—

> "Isot ma drue, Isot m'amie,
> En vous ma mort, en vous ma vie."

"Where is ...?"

The yellow girl holds the edge of a limned tapestry aside. All, save Lady Irene and Julian, disperse in various directions.

Miss Ella retires discreetly, but without mauvaise honte, along a likely passage. Thank God, from whom all blessings flow! And it so happened that Sir Chatters, urged by the same touch of nature that makes the whole world kin, sought likewise solitude and seclusion. *Die Blase ist der Spiegel der Seele,* as German science vouches. Miss Ella Wapburn, so urgent was her need, neglected to consolidate her lines of communication. Wherefore did the foe find her in full retreat, her unguarded rear exposed. Miss Ella Wapburn flushed. The ungallant foe, forcing her to deploy in extended disorder, engaged her at close quarters.

Severally or by twos, all are accommodated in the seclusion of curtained bunks, and closets with lacquered panels inscribed with the trigrams of the Male and the Female principle, and the six auspicious jui tokens.

Julian and Lady Irene remain before the joss. The yellow girl brings trays bearing yeng-tsiang pipes of orange wood, with red clay bowls, yen-hauck needles, kow-ten lamps with perforated glass globes, tsha knives to clean the pipe cakes, and hop-toys of buffalo horn enclosing the gow-hop. She rolls the pills and roasts them over the blue flame of the lamp.

"No dope for me. I will face fate without blindfold," says Julian. "I shall strike down all poppyheads with the sceptre of reason."

"Fudge! It would need more than fifty pills to dim it," says Irene.

The curtain is drawn over the black-satined bunk.

The tristful catlings wail.

"It is to be noted that, according to the Triads, as transmitted in the bestiaries of love of Master Hubert de Franconnet, Iseult of the fair hands sought refuge in Lyonnesse, Tristan's realm, located, as you know, in the Scilly Islands."

"Don't be silly!"

Faintly out of the distance floats the crystal murmur of a childish voice, wilting like lotus stems.

Kneeling motionless before the joss niche, her hands upon her knees, the yellow girl interprets monotonously—

> "Months go by, years slide backwards and disappear.
> Musing, I shut my eyes and think of the road
> I have travelled and of the springweeds
> choking the fields of my house."

"What skills it? I say. Skylla, daughter of Nisos. Europa's son, Minos, seduced her with armlets of Kretan gold. And she drew from her father's brow the lock of red hair whereon hung his life."

The voice wailed low to deathly languor—

> "Today we will drink the cup of supreme pleasure together,
> Tomorrow we will part beside the river for ever."

Away, away, awake.

> "My bowels are broken within me,
> Island of the White Water-flowers."

"Those girls stayed to tea for two hours in my sitting room. They are so nice. I was bored rigid. Had to stretch my legs by taking a walk in the Tuileries gardens. Maud came to farewell Captain Carnegie, of the Scots Guards, who is going to India as military aide-de-camp to the Viceroy."

A catgut snapped harshly. The voice broke into a cry—

> "There were men yesterday on the walls of the city.
> There are ghosts today on the walls of the city.
> . . . .
> . . . . Not yet is the killing ended."

Julian raised himself on his elbow and bent over the recumbent form of Lady Irene.

"And for those styes of rapine, high in name and power, called England, France, for that festering foulness that beggars the breath of denunciation, men give blood and lives in the shambles, that infamy may fatten more. For this, for this . . ."

"Persons who have attained the years of discretion are supposed to be acquainted with the world's pigstye," said Lady Irene. "As it was in the beginning, it is, and ever . . ."

"Per saecula saeculorum!"

He rolled another pellet on the needle and toasted it on the blue flame. It swelled to a rubbery sponge. After placing it in the bowl, he drew a long breath.

"Sickly sweet, yet soothing."

His throbbing brain was stilled to a great clearness.

"What you say is either true or untrue." A long stillness fell upon the world. "If it be untrue, it is more foolish than the tragic folly of the Panurgian sheep that go leaping to their slaughter." A great wave rose, surging blood-red. "If it be true, if it be true . . . then . . . discretion, sense, sanity, honor, decency, have no more meaning than the gibbering of a madman in a padded cell. If it be true, nothing matters. Ah, ah! Nothing matters, nothing, nothing, nothing. Do you hear? Nothing. Let's murder a Chinaman for fun. Let's set cock-a-hoop. Let's run amok. Let's strip and run out into the middle of the street to fornicate. Ah, ah! And be apprehended for an offence against public morals. Ah, ah! Against the morals of the pigstye. By the majesty of the law. By a moral world! Ah, ah, ah! Nothing matters . . . if such things can be . . . for ever invulnerable."

From a figured panel, Pu-t'ai, god of lechery, leered, holding the peach that ripens in three thousand years.

Lady Irene held out her large, luxuriously tended hand, considering the ring of Marie Antoinette, and watched the stones glitter in the faint gleam of a yellow glowlight.

"It was given by her mother, Maria Theresa, to the archduchess before her marriage . . ." Her words halted vaguely in a swooning pause.

Julian leant over to scrutinise the jewel more closely. Floating trails of smoke swayed and trembled back and forth, dissolving into

coiling loops, and tossed up like great flowers, or forms that stained
the fancy with awful seduction, sweeping, as in the purple caves of
sleep, the chambers of the brain.

". . . twenty years before the storming of the Bastille."

Julian's hand rested inadvertently on Lady Irene's gastrocnemius.
Her drawn-up limb stretched out in slow languor. Under Julian's motionless palm, the sheathing silk gave place to the warm living meat of
the powerful ham.

An ear-rending shriek pierced the stagnant night.

"What was that?" cried Lady Irene, startled.

"The uprooted mandrake's cry that makes men mad. Madness has
rent the heart of the world." Julian, striking his brow, drew welsh-
combing fingers through his hair. "And you would mend it with a
haunch of venery!"

Rising, he tore the silken hanging and reeled across to the joss niche.

"NOTHING MATTERS! Dost thou hear, thou idiotic old Sinic
sage, Kong-Fu-Tseu, Fu-Hi, Hing-hong? Nothing matters. Stop nodding thy ancient imbecile capsheaf, I say. Sit not upon the ancient
mountain of Mehru in judgment over thy betters."

The joss-magot crashed to shards from his lacquered nook, his vacu-
ous belly shivered.

"Not a turd in thy guts, not a thought in thy poll, thou vacant tala-
poin! No chyle in thy Catayan chitterlings, no presence of mind!"

Again a screech, horrible and protracted.

"Where are the others?" asked Lady Irene.

The yellow girl appeared.

"Come with me, lady, come with me. I will take you to your friends,"
she said.

Drawing aside an arras, Julian reeled forward. His steps, muted by
thick pile, wended along dim passages and chambers shot with dark
nooks. From out the darkness streaked with heavy clouds, a Chinaman's cat-like eyes, red from the reflection of a cresset's glow, stared
at him unseeing. The beat of muffled gongs rattled in the distance.

Men lay in stupor. Hob-nailed soles protruded, pigeon-toed, from
under a saffron drugget. A poilu was stretched full length, his prone
face pillowed on folded arms. Another breathed heavily, huddled in a

corner, his chin sunk on his chest decorated with the Croix de Guerre
and palms. A one-armed man, holding up his quivering stump, lay un-
braced, untrussed, on cinnabar red cushions, starkly rigescent.

Julian slid open a paper-panelled door. The curtain of a closet,
stitched with demoniac tao-tieh ogre figures and five-toed Lung dragons
shooting arrow-pointed tongues, drooped, partly detached from the cor-
nice, and white limbs and fingers seemed to creep and tremble among
monstrous shapes. Stretched upon a disorder of strewn draperies and
cushions, entwined arms and legs quivered with quick spasms. Lady
Kattie's breasts lobbed over the omphalos of her creased belly.

A thousand gongs clanged, shaking the place with their tumult.
Bursts of ghoulish laughter cackled without. Over a spinach-colored
door, a yellow lantern swayed, casting livid flashes of flickering light.

Pushing open the door, Julian found himself on a small brick platform. The city lay below, immersed in darkness, illumined only by the
lurid reflections of red clouds. Like a stream of fire the Seine coiled
between dark banks. Spokes of white light wheeled giddily, shooting
back and forth in the conflagrated sky. Guns boomed and rattled from
all sides. Shells flashed and exploded in the clouds. Machine-guns
cackled overhead. At intervals the throb of motors pulsed, waxing and
waning. From a torn cloud-rack issued a flock of black-winged planes.
It wheeled back, scuttling, as the beams of the searchlights converged
upon it.

The tumult above swept on, rattling panes and shaking tiles, like a
gust of broom-bestriding Brocken-hags riding to Sabbath.

Steps led down to a yard, gutted with shards and offal. A shingled
penthouse leant over, dragging down after it a batten fence. Rats
scurried and squeaked as Julian made his way to the street. It was
deserted.

He threaded winding lanes and alleyways. A toothless night-hag
was sounding with a stick a refuse-bin, driving off raiding rats. She
turned steel-grey eyes upon Julian as he passed, offering him an unspotted virgin. A girl thrust her head out of a window and looked up
at the sky. She beckoned, calling:

"*Viens donc, joli petit Anglais.*"

A salvo of gunfire broke from near by. A hissing nosecap struck
the roof of a house with a clatter of tiles.

Down a cobbled street came some soldiers, arm in arm, singing:

> *"Debout les damnés de la terre . . .*
>
> *. . . .*
>
> *S'ils s'obstinent, ces cannibales,*
> *A faire de nous des héros,*
> *Ils sauront bientôt que nos balles*
> *Sont pour nos généraux."*

They staggered down a flight of steps.

"Cré cochon de Poincaré au poteau!" shouted a hoarse, drunken voice.

Near the Butte, an open patch of ground planted with phthisic trees overlooked the grey sea of houses. On a gas lamppost with lantern askew was a notice headed: "Commune de Montmartre."

The tumult was abating, swept southward towards Montparnasse and Malakof. The explosion of a bomb flared up near the Val-de-Grâce. The domes of the Invalides, Pantheon, and Institut stood out against the red sky.

Julian leaned his elbow on the stone parapet. There was a man, a couple of yards away, looking down also. He turned sharply, and Julian saw his face in the light of the street lamp.

"Hic et ubique, old mole?" Julian said.

The last gunshots sounded in the distance. There was a silence. Sirens and bugles signalled the "All clear."

"From the Front?" the man asked.

Julian carelessly nodded. "You?"

"To the Front." The man stood up silently, shifting round. "The real one. Here where we are standing it began fifty-six years ago. The guns of the National Guard defended the Commune of Paris from this spot. The day has come, the Day of Wrath."

Rows of lights appeared along the lines of the boulevards.

Looking over, Julian murmured:

> *"Dies irae, dies illa,*
> *Solvit saeculum in favilla."*

Raucous peals of laughter rose from the Place Blanche. Julian turned round to the man, wearily.

"You murdered Nevidof," he said.

The other repressed a bitter laughter.

"You speak of murder, of murder . . . now! You speak well the language of the murderous throng, murderer and judge. You murdered . . ."

"Oh, yes! A Chinaman, Rousseau's Chinaman," Julian said carelessly. He saw the face of the German at Thiepval Wood turn to raspberry jelly. There was a short silence.

"To mention an unimportant detail, I did not kill Nevidof," the man said.

"The evidence . . ."

"Circumstantial."

"The maid identified the revolver as having been in the possession of Princess Nevidof."

"Erroneously. Here it is. You see the initials, Г. H., on the ivory butt? Nevidof killed himself. Not that it matters."

"No. Nothing matters. The moralisers red-handed. The judges convicted habitual criminals."

The man moved up, leaning back on the stone parapet.

"Nothing matters in a sham world that is finished. And it is finished because nothing matters any more. Its values are exploded. This time we, of the Commune of the New World which fought here, are going to strike at the roots. So long as one rootlet is left all strife is vain. The Day of Wrath is also the Day of Judgment. I am on my way to help make a new humanity. Good-bye, fellow-traveller. We shall meet again."

Julian stood awhile leaning against the cold stone, bathing his aching brow in the cool night air. He descended along the steep streets towards the Boulevard de Clichy. A few belated revellers were strolling home. At the Place Pigalle, he met Fulliston.

"I'm a bloody fool," said the Caballero. "Been wasting my time with wine and women. Should have kept an appointment I had with that bitch. She swore she'd bring the scoundrel of a Frenchman to book this evening. Come, let's go to the hotel."

They roused a sleeping taxi-driver and drove to the rue Caumartin. Another taxi-cab drew up as they arrived. Keetje, swathed in furs, was just paying off the driver.

"A nice time of night to be calling. Too late. Germaine has left," she said, as the sleepy night-porter opened the door.

"Hell! what do you mean?" cried Fulliston, following her, with Julian, into the hall.

"Get me a glass of porto wine," said Keetje to the man. "I'll have it in the lounge."

"Very well, Mademoiselle," the man answered.

"Here! Has the lady in number seventeen left the hotel?" Fulliston asked the porter.

He was a thin, grey man, in a green baize apron. He glanced at the key-rack.

"Her key is not there. The Demoiselle must be in her room," he said.

"Good. You see? Has any one called for her?" Fulliston asked.

"There was a gentleman for Mademoiselle. He's left some time ago," said the man.

"Right. I'll go and see."

The porter turned on a light in the bar and fetched the port wine. Keetje sat down and lit a cigarette.

"I hope she's got away. I warned her to," said Keetje. "So you've just met Comrade Ogonin. Saw him just now. I'm getting him and a few others over to Switzerland. You see, I can be of some use."

"Can't get her to answer," said the Caballero, returning. "Come, bring the key and open the door."

"But, Monsieur, I can't go opening the doors of occupied rooms at this hour," the porter said impatiently.

Fulliston handed him a hundred-franc note.

"Come on and be quick. It is important," he said.

Shrugging his shoulders, the man took the master-key from the drawer of the office desk. With flat-footed gait, he led the way up the creaky stairs. Fulliston signed to Julian to come also. Keetje stayed in the hall, sipping the port wine and smoking.

The sleepy porter opened the door of the room.

"*Voilà, Monsieur,*" he said, holding the door open. Then, as he glanced in, "*Ah! Nom de Dieu!*" he cried.

Across the tumbled bed lay the naked body of the Comtesse Mathilde de Richepin. Her glazed eyes stared horribly out of her head. A twisted scarf was round her neck, discolored with a livid, purple mark. The room was in disorder, the drawers emptied out on the floor.

When the police came, they seemed to make light of the matter. The inspector did little more than glance round perfunctorily. Leaving a plain-clothes man in charge, he said a truck would come presently to take away the body.

"*Deuxième Bureau*," said Keetje, draining her glass.

XII

MILD sunshine fell on the turquoise waters and the skirting shores. Cloud-high above the hills and the Rochers de l'Enfer, the white expanse of Mont Blanc was mirrored again as though in the depths of the lake. On the opposite bank the spires of Lausanne stood up like needles, and, at the extreme bend, Chillon thrust out its pinnacled dungeon over the waters.

Like Saint Bernard, when of old he rode his mule over the same shores, the idle-seeming crowd that glanced carelessly at the view from the terrace of the Grand Hotel at Evian was mostly occupied with other thoughts than the picturesqueness of the landscape. The place was one of the busiest in Europe. It was the advanced post, on allied territory, of international intrigue and transactions. The opposite shore was neutral Switzerland. The ferry-boat plying between Evian and Ouchy served as one of the main vehicles of communication between the belligerent countries. Among the visitors on the French shore many watched it with anxious eyes, awaiting the arrival of messages, or hesitating before embarking on the perils which the brief passage across the still waters might hold out for them.

Princess George Vivesco was surrounded by a number of elegant military-looking men, who appreciated, more than her blonde beauty, her influence with the German Government. She was on her way to Bucharest, as she informed them, to dine with General Mackensen and his staff. Captain Chermakof, lately of the imperial Russian horse-guards, was deputed to sound the views of the German high command as to what their attitude would be should the Russian provisional Government be imperilled by labor uprisings, and to ascertain if possible whether the German authorities would be willing to give passive or active assistance to General Kornilov should he be called upon to defend the Government. He also desired to induce the German authorities to refuse assistance to Russian revolutionaries abroad seeking to make their way to Russia.

"Although the Kaiser's Government might benefit from social anarchy in Russia," he pointed out, "yet the danger of Germany being infected with revolutionary doctrines outweighs any transient strategical advantages which might be obtained."

The little town was full of *évacués* from the occupied regions. A pathetic-looking lot, for the most part; thin, ragged and famished, old men and women, children, some nuns. The municipality and charitable associations organised relief, distributions of food. People crowded round them to hear the tale of their sufferings, the long starvation, the German brutalities, the endless difficulties in obtaining permission to pass through Switzerland, after having been stripped and searched.

The more fortunately endowed had been spared many of those sufferings, and were basking on the terrace of the hotel. The Countess d'Oultremont had just "escaped" from Belgium for the third time. It was generally understood that she was the bearer of peace proposals from the German general staff to Monsieur Ribot.

Mrs. Latterly was plying her with exhortations. The Women's International Peace Congress which she was on her way to attend would pass a resolution, she said, demanding that the French premier and Mr. Lloyd George make the terms of the proposal public and give it their most favorable consideration.

"Monsieur Ribot is very old," the countess said. "I do not think that he will be so much influenced by women. Though there is no telling what old men will do. Monsieur Clémenceau who is seventy-seven is, they say, much influenced by women, especially your beautiful American women."

A group of men stretched on lounge chairs were smoking their cigars in silence, broken only by occasional remarks.

"Good morning, Baron," called out one of them as Baron Rubinstein came walking slowly in their direction. "How are you feeling this morning?"

"Ah, a little better, I think, thank you," said the baron. "My toe still gives me a good deal of trouble. The doctors say that I have been eating too well and prescribe diets for me. But I must confess that I succumb easily to temptation. I don't think this *Source Cachat* is all that it is cracked up to be."

"Not as good as Marienbad, eh? Ah, when will those good old days return?" said the other. "We all have to suffer in one way or another through this confounded war."

"Yes, we all have to suffer while trying to do our bit," said the baron with a sigh, letting himself down cautiously into a lounge chair.

"Congratulations, Baron. I have just seen in the paper that the French Government has made you a commander of the Legion of Honor," said another of the men.

The baron made a depreciative gesture.

"I could very well have dispensed with their rosette, my dear Sir Raphael," he said. "I refused it repeatedly, but they were insistent. Said it was a political duty." Baron Rubinstein had just made a gift of a million francs in aid of French combatants blinded in the war.

"Do you think, sir, anything will come of all this peace talk?" asked, after a silence, a famous journalist whose pen-name carried almost official authority.

"We must all hope for the best," the baron said.

"Hum! I hope that those hot-headed politicians will not rush us thoughtlessly into a hasty peace," said Sir Raphael. "Too sudden a change is apt to dislocate the markets."

"That is true," Baron Rubinstein said. After a moment he added with a slight twinkle in his eye: "I do not think they will do anything rash."

The journalist started up, interested.

"But, sir, attrition has almost reached its limits on both sides," he said. "The people in Germany, as you know, are starving. And our own food-supply is at times very precarious. The U-boats . . ."

"Aï, aï, aï!" cried the baron with a grimace. "I beg you to excuse me, gentlemen, but that confounded toe of mine gives me at times some really nasty twinges. Food shortage," he continued after the lancinations had subsided, "is not a very serious matter from a military point of view so long as the army can be well fed. It may, of course, increase discontent among the people. That is the real danger. But so long as the army can be decently nourished, there is little danger from popular discontent."

The journalist was, however, persistent. There was very considerable discontent in the French army. Not one man out of five could really be trusted, the French authorities said. There were, he had been recently informed, no less than fifty thousand French deserters at the moment in Barcelona alone. Even the English were not immune from disloyalty, he said. "When Sir William Robertson asked the other day for a new combing out, Lloyd George told him that if this were done the possibility of revolution would have to be faced."

"Did he really say that?" asked the baron, sitting up a little. "Ah, but those politicians are always timid. Lloyd George is an alarmist. The English people will never have a revolution . . . or an evolution. They are too . . . well-behaved. Of course, should any real danger of revolutionary unrest develop, whether in the Allied countries or in the Central empires, it would be necessary to put an end to the war. But such a calamity does not appear to me for the moment imminent. Until it becomes so, there is no reason why the war should not be continued."

"It is costing a deuce of a lot of money," remarked one of the men, who had not yet spoken.

"England's credit is practically unlimited," said the baron.

"What about Germany's?" put in the journalist.

"The credit of a large country like Germany remains good, even in defeat," the baron said. "It may become frozen for a time, but that merely calls for higher rates of interest. It is still a good business proposition."

"I am glad to hear you say so, baron," said Sir Raphael Mendel, who had just completed the delivery of a large munitions contract to the Swiss Government.

The Lausanne boat was just berthing. Most of the visitors stood watching with interest the arrival. The men rose from their lounge chairs and went over to the balustrade.

Near where they had been sitting, Julian and Major Spirido were left almost alone. They were to cross over to Switzerland on the boat, when it made its return trip. At Lady Irene's suggestion, the medical board in Paris had recommended that Julian should have a complete rest in the Swiss mountains. The prescription coincided with his mood. The necessary formalities had been arranged without difficulty, and he had come down from Paris with Mrs. Latterly and Major Spirido.

They sat in silence. Spirido was reading. Occasionally he burst out into a chuckle. Julian glanced at him, questioning with a look the cause of his mirth.

"Listen to this," said Spirido. " 'The common question is, What have we been fighting for all the while? The answer is ready: We have been fighting for the ruin of the public interest and the advancement of the private. We have been fighting to enrich usurers and stockjobbers. The nation begins to think these blessings are not worth fighting for any longer. Since the monied men are so fond of war, they should furnish out the campaign at their own charge. It was in their power to have put an end to the war. And this is what we charge them with as answerable to their country and posterity, that the bleeding condition of their fellow-men was a feather in the balance with their private ends.' "

"Who is the graceless Marxist traitor?" asked Julian, his lip curling to an ironical smile.

"The dean of Saint Patrick's, Jonathan Swift," Spirido replied. "History . . ."

"Now then, no platitudes, if you please, Professor! History repeats itself, but upon altered planes. The chimney catches fire time after time, till one day the house is burnt down. The heart aches, year in and year out, and one day it breaks."

"Optimist! Hoping for something to burn up or break. The tragedy is that nothing breaks. The world goes on smouldering; the heart of mankind goes on creaking, creaking. Over there, at Chillon castle, even so pedestrian a soul as Charles Dickens visioned the great Mystery."

"The mystery of the eternal hills?" queried Julian inattentively.

"Damn you, no. The great mystery, I say. Having been shown the charred stakes where men had in the good old days been burnt alive by pious liberals, he marvelled how and why the world had been spared and tolerated by its Creator and had not long since been dashed to fragments."

"If man does not soon dash some portion of his infamy to fragments, I too will doubt his divinity," said Julian.

Some of the visitors had gone down to the landing-stage to obtain a closer view of the arriving passengers. The examination of passports and papers, in the temporary offices erected for the purpose, occupied a considerable time. Those who had been looking for some sensation, such as the arrest of a suspected spy, were, this time, disappointed. The last passengers presently passed through the barriers and the cordon of police and detectives. The onlookers came strolling back to the hotel. Among them was a young woman in a mink coat. Julian had not happened to notice her before. It was Keetje. She stopped a moment, leaning over the granite balustrade of the terrace, apparently interested in the view. After some moments she went into the hotel.

Baron Rubinstein, slowly limping, moved over, when she had gone, to where Keetje had been standing. The balustrade on which she had been leaning was marked with two little chalk crosses. Rubbing them off with his hand, the baron turned to Sir Raphael Mendel, and said, as though continuing their conversation and summing up the conclusion of his thoughts:

"As I was saying, there will be no peace negotiations as yet."

The men strolled back into the hotel. The journalist went to the smoking room to write an article while ideas were fresh in his mind.

"I see our gracious guide distributing gratuities to rapacious porters and waiters, and directing her attention towards her charges," said Spirido.

"I am ready," said Julian.

> "—And whatever sky's above me,
> Here's a heart for every fate,"

Spirido chanted.

The inquisitorial ordeal before embarking was passed successfully. Mrs. Latterly flourished her British passport with golden crown, lion and unicorn, with an American's pride and faith in the supremacy of British prestige. A young woman who faced the inquisitors after Mrs. Latterly's party proved less fortunate. She was led away by two gendarmes.

"She's for the execution post, poor thing," said Spirido.

After a short navigation, the ordeal had to be repeated on Helvetic soil. The officials at Ouchy were more numerous, more inquisitorial, and less amiable. Mrs. Latterly's loud American voice rose gradually to its highest pitch as the papers were scrutinised and criticised by various officials with dilatory suspiciousness. A British official and a representative of the Swiss Red Cross devoted some time to the investigation of Major Spirido's credentials. A dispute arose over Julian's.

There were minor technical flaws, the British official discovered, in some of his papers, in one of which he was stated to have been born in the eighteenth century, which appeared improbable. His name had not been previously notified. He was moreover attired in mufti, whereas the regulations required that he should present himself in khaki, and Julian was unable to produce his identity disc. Mrs. Latterly's voice assumed a more pronounced American intonation as her impatience rose.

"I'm telling you, officer, that Lootenant Bern is in my charge and I'm going to see him through or know the reason why," she said, "if I have to call up the legation and get the ambassador down to iron out all this baloney. In America . . ."

"I'm sorry, Madame, but the gentleman will have to return by the boat till we have made further enquiries and received instructions," said the impassive official.

Julian himself sought to pacify the lady, saying he was willing to return to Evian and await instructions.

While the argument was proceeding, Keetje, who had been reporting to one of the British officials, came up.

"Mr. Bern is with me," she said.

The inquisitor looked at her for a moment, exchanged a glance and a nod with his colleague, and turning to Julian, said:

"Pass on, sir."

Keetje disappeared in a taxi, and it was not until they met again at the Lausanne station, Mrs. Latterly having by then recovered in part from the surprise, not unmingled with indignation, caused by the young woman's interference, that Julian introduced them.

"I suppose you are attending the Women's Peace Convention, Miss Dools?" she asked.

"Yes," replied Keetje with a look of sweet simplicity which caused Julian and the major inner jubilation.

"Belgium is being represented by a strong delegation," said Mrs. Latterly. "The tragic voice of martyred Belgium rising in accusation shall rouse the conscience of humanity. We shall be sending a full report of the Convention, with copies of its resolutions, typewritten in every European language, to every government. The voice of justice and humanity will make itself heard."

"Oh yes?" said Keetje, whose accent automatically mimicked her interlocutory environment.

In the federal capital's uninspiring Germanic neatness, Julian whiled a few days. Spirido was in no haste to place himself under the care of Professor Schurkmann.

"And you? What are you seeking here?" he asked Julian as they lolled on the Kleine Schauza.

"Solitude," Julian replied.

"The quest romantic! The silence of the hills lifted towards heaven in perpetual mercy, as Ruskin revealed to the Victorians," Spirido chuckled. "There they are," he said, pointing to the outspread range of the Bernese Oberland, "and here are they all neatly labelled for you: Wetterhorn, 3703 meters, Faulhorn, 2685, Schreckhorn, 4030, Finsteraarhorn, 4275, Eiger, 3874, Mönch, 4105, Jungfrau, 4166. Railway to the summit, restaurant, pension from fifteen francs, running water, h and c, all modern discomforts."

"Far from the maelstrom of mendacity and mendacity-swallowing stupidity. I would hear myself think. I seek an issue, like a trapped rat, which not finding I shall go mad. Do not gibe. By all that's real, do not gibe. You are hale, you leadswinging cynic. I am desperately sick."

"There is no issue. Therefore are we all mad. You will be tamed and doctored into hebetation by a mad world."

"May I die first!" said Julian.

Before the cinemas, stood pictured the glorious victories of the invincible German army. Posters headed in Gothic characters: *"Deutschland über alles!"* informed of the desperate plight of England and France and of the duplicity, brutality, and cowardice of the Allies. The Swiss burghers steeped in German Kultur entertained no uncertainty as to its supremacy and that of German arms, and as to the victorious issue of their defence of civilisation. Their cause was the more righteous for bringing to peaceful Helvetic citizens a stream of wealth passing the dreams of hotel-keepers, despite the closing down of the chocolate factories, the consequent prevalence of unemployment, and outbreaks of unrest in Zürich.

Exotic figures haunted in groups the Bubenberg Place and the arcades of the Old Town—French and Belgian peasants and workers from the occupied regions, Polish, Hungarian, Czechs, and Balkan escapers, and earnest-faced Russian revolutionary exiles. The latter held meetings in the People's House, setting forth to stolid Swiss comrades and dishevelled internationals fantastic plans for the creation of a socialist state in Russia that would shake the foundations of the capitalist world, schemes so extravagant and ludicrous that they were frequently received with derision and shrugging shoulders, and the civic authorities deemed it advantageous to allow the subversive speech-making of the hair-brained aliens to convict them out of their own mouths of patent absurdity.

Spirido, who had strolled into one of the gatherings, in a hall in the Lengstrasse where the stage was still set with paltry scenery from a recent amateur performance, rocked with laughter as he reported to Julian.

"One of their chief fellows outdid all other gospellers in silly nonsense," he said. "As though a handful of seedy starvelings could turn the tide of centuries so that the people might labor for themselves and not for their masters!"

The women's congress to bring about permanent peace was a much more serious affair and enjoyed the hospitable patronage of the federal authorities, which placed a hall at the disposal of the lady delegates and opened the proceedings with addresses of welcome and encouragement delivered by Colonel Hauser of the federal army, expressing sentiments which did honor to the high ideals guiding the policies of the Republic. Attending the meetings, Keetje got there in touch with one of the German delegates, a Frau von Schroeder, who had been designated to her as the accredited courier of the Frankfurt branch of the House of Rubinstein and of the armament firms of Essen. Keetje was the bearer of an important mail for the lady, having reference to various financial transactions and to proposed contracts for the supply of cotton, saltpeter, glycerine and other necessities to the German firms. To the various conditions enumerated in the documents of which she was the bearer, Keetje added on her own behalf that the documents themselves should not even be delivered until Frau von Schroeder should have communicated with her chiefs and obtained pledges that the Russians now in Switzerland should be granted free passage through Germany to Stockholm.

In the Street of Righteousness—*Gerechtigkeitsstrasse*—Julian and Spirido were sitting before steins of watery beer in a tavern decorated with biliously colored Alpine pastorals, bibulous mottoes in Gothic characters, and chamois heads, where the apple-faced Fräulein wore her red and black corsets outside her chemise, when Keetje, mink-coated, tripped in with Frau von Schroeder, a pale, dark woman with nervous, hollow eyes. Keetje introduced Julian to her as Sir Welby Penmore's cousin and Major Spirido as his military aide-de-camp. Frau von Schroeder plunged at once into a stream of appeals and explanations, out of which Julian could make neither head nor tail.

"Have patience, sir, and consider the difficulties in the way of what you would have me do. Unless I go back to Germany how can I explain or persuade? And if I go back empty handed I shall assuredly be dismissed or punished. I am a poor woman. . . ."

And so forth, *und so weiter*. While the German woman was abjectly pleading, Keetje, who stood a little behind her, plied Julian with telegraphic winks and nods. Pretending to be au courant of the matter, whatever it might be, and assuming a stern tone and manner, Julian said curtly:

"All this does not concern me, Madame. The conditions demanded must be complied with. Else no reciprocity is to be expected."

"Write out a telegram now," said Keetje.

"But I have not my code," said the Frau.

"I have it," said Keetje, producing a card from her handbag.

Frau von Schroeder stared at her a moment with her nervous eyes, then with a helpless gesture submitted.

"Write it out first in clear," said Julian.

Pen and paper being produced, the Frau drew up the message and submitted it. She then laboriously set to coding it.

"I will help you," said Major Spirido. "I am expert in codes."

"Good. We will now take it to Christopher Street," said Keetje, when they had finished. And the two women tripped out of the tavern.

When they had gone, Spirido burst into laughter.

"Well played, sir comediante! You have settled the fate of Europe," he said to Julian.

Julian politely smiled at the inane jest.

"The Convention has turned out a triumphant success," Mrs. Latterly announced. "It marks an era in the history of world-peace. I am sending our fourteen resolutions to Washington, D. C., to President Wilson. Colonel House, whom I know well, told me the President is most interested. You do wrong not to have attended the meetings, Mr. Bern. Such intelligent women. You should have heard the Austrian delegate demonstrate the folly of war."

"A lady clearly possessed of penetrating insight," Julian observed.

"We are going to agitate for a League of Nations," continued Mrs. Latterly, impervious to irony.

"Shade of my father! What is a nation?" queried Julian aloud.

"A nation? Why it is . . . a nation, of course," elucidated Mrs. Latterly.

"Do you mean a government?" Julian sought to elicit.

"The government of the nation, the national government," Mrs. Latterly defined.

"The secular arm of the detainers of economic power," glossed Julian.

"A government of the people, by . . ." Mrs. Latterly began.

"There can be no government by the people, were it an elected government of angels or red-hot Jacobin devils, unless the people have previously taken the precaution to hang the holders of economic power," Julian threw out.

"But this is anarchy," Mrs Latterly protested.

"No, Madam. It is physics," Julian said.

"We are going to abolish secret diplomacy," Mrs. Latterly announced.

"Lying in the open, so to speak," Spirido put in.

"To uphold the rights of small nations," Mrs. Latterly continued.

"The rights of Japan against China, for instance. Of Italy against Abyssinia, or against Spain, let us say," Julian mused, unamused.

"Those principles will be laid down at the Peace Conference," Mrs. Latterly assured.

"Then is there no hope," Julian moaned.

"You undervalue women's intelligence, Mr. Bern," Mrs. Latterly observed.

"I undervalue liberal intelligence, be it masculine or feminine," he said.

"I had hoped that you, being a scholar, might have addressed a few helpful words to the Convention, giving your view of the outcome and effects of the war," said Mrs. Latterly.

"Wild horses would not draw it from me," said Julian.

"Our last sitting was marred by only one painful incident," Mrs. Latterly said. "One of our delegates attempted to commit suicide."

"I no longer have the slightest doubt about women's intelligence," said Julian. "What is the sagacious lady's name?"

"A great English lady. The Honorable something or other. What is her name, Ella? Ashley, or something like that."

"The Honorable Eleanor Astley," Miss Wapburn corrected.

"Where is she? Here?" asked Julian.

"No. It was at Oberhofen, on Lake Thun. She threw herself into the lake," said Mrs. Latterly.

"Is she . . .?"

"Oh, all right, I believe. They fished her out in time," said Mrs. Latterly.

Julian rose and grabbed his hat.

"Where are you going, Mr. Bern?" Mrs. Latterly asked.

"To Oberhofen," Julian replied.

He had no difficulty in obtaining information. As he landed, the hotel porter with melon-shaped Prussian face was able to supply all particulars, in porter-English, steadily refusing to use his native German.

"English lady who threw herself over the wharf? Yessir. Know her very well. Came over by the 8:20 boat from Thun. I was standing at the door looking round for passengers. Saw the lady standing alone at the end of the wharf after all the other passengers were gone and the boat was going back. Thought to myself: funny her standing there. Was getting dark. Yes, know her quite well by sight. Stays at the Helvetia. A little hotel. Not much of a little hotel. Not like here. This is a house of premier rank. Best cuisine in the town. Charges moderate. Pension from twenty francs. Special terms for long stay. Hot and cold water in the whole rooms. The lady? Oh yessir. Well I go in to sort the mail. Baron Schmelling in number six very particular to get mail at once. Well, I came to the door again after I had sent the mail up to number six, and I saw the lady was not there. And the boat, sir, was coming back towards the wharf. And they were throwing ropes over and Lebensgurteln, what you say. And there was people running up the wharf. Oh, all right sir. Brought her up all wet. Water bloody cold this time of year. Season very bad. Worse we had since years. Yes, lady all right. Know what women are, sir. Silly nonsense. Affair of heart, probably. Bet your boots. Cold water very good for silly women when they are taken that way. Saw Doktor Spitzbubi this morning. Told me the lady was quite all right. Very good doctor. If you should have need of medical services at any time. . . . No the lady is not at the hotel. Went over to Grindelwald this morning. Porter fellow at the Helvetia told me. Rather silly fellow. Speaks very bad English. Not like I. Those little hotels cannot pay for real porters with good education. Yessir, he said Grindelwald. Chalet there where they take English ladies en pension. Often goes there. Not much good. The Bear Hotel a very good hotel. Same management as this. But now taken by Red Cross for wounded officers of Allied countries. Lots of wounded officers. War very bad for Allied countries. Cannot fight like Chermans. You American, I guess. Oh, I speak American O.K. Very great pity for America to come into the war. Very great pity. But war will be finished before your folks can come over."

Julian proceeded by the creeping, toy-like train to Grindelwald. The whole valley was submerged in a sump of dank mist, which dripped, oozed, and sweated from every object. Nothing was visible beyond a few yards. A few people under guttering umbrellas, with drops of water standing out like dew on every thread of their clothing looked on stupidly at the arrival of the train. The trees dripped. The white cement cube of the Bear Hotel was visible below the railway station. It had assumed the now familiar appearance of a war hospital. One caught glimpses of patients, cases mostly of gas poisoning, lying huddled in blankets on the verandahs and of nurses wrapped in navy-blue cloaks and shawls. On the high side of the road were a few small pensions with highly colored and ornamented fronts, and their names —"Bellevue," "The Alp Panorama," "Sunnyside"—painted in large Gothic letters on the sodden, oozing, damp-blistered plaster.

Julian walked along the single road that ran through the village. The mist swirled round in waving trails, growing thicker. The rush-

ing sound of a torrent was heard in the depths of the valley below.
The village tapered off in a straggling row of small wooden chalets
with verandahs. Colored postcards and Edelweiss were exhibited for
sale in the groundfloor windows, and notices offering rooms to visitors.
On the verandah of one of the chalets, Julian saw Eleanor Astley lying,
swathed in rugs, in a chaise longue. She saw him at almost the same
moment, her face lighting up with surprise and pleasure.

"Why, this is a surprise," she exclaimed when he had joined her.
"How . . .?"

"I heard in Berne, and at Oberhofen found you had come here," he
began.

"Oh! I am utterly utterly ashamed of myself," Eleanor said, flushing. "Is any situation more humiliating, undignified, ridiculous than
that of a person who has bungled a feeble attempt to make an end of
it?"

"I have been in that situation for three years," he said.

Eleanor remained silent a few moments, then stammered explanations.

"I don't know what made me. I don't think it was premeditated at
all. . . . It came over me all of a sudden as I returned to Interlaken
from that futile congress. There seemed nothing to be done! Everything had become blank . . . blank . . . intolerably, maddeningly blank.
Oh, I can't explain."

"I understand well enough," Julian said. "It is that we are not alive.
No one is, or can be, really alive. I often wonder they don't feel it
more than they do. They get drunk, or dance, or make love . . . have
a 'gay time.' Just to make themselves believe they are alive. The
young fellows who joined up in this war business did it in just the
same way as those who get drunk and dance tangos . . . for the same
reason, to make themselves believe they are alive. Excitement, they
call it. Excitement is the only thing which can make them forget that
they are not alive." He paused a while, and then went on as though
thinking aloud. "It will be even worse when the war is over. People
will feel more clearly that all the old values they looked for in life have
come to an end, have become ridiculous. Even ivory towers of refuge
are in ruins . . . devastated regions. They rested on the supposition
that the individual can save himself, save himself by shutting him-

self up. As though every individual soul were not built up of the materials drawn from the social world. Even egoism has become impossible."

Eleanor nodded, though only half apprehending his meaning, resting as it did on too radical a discarding of the most profoundly ingrained ignorances promulgated by millennial education.

"It is good of you to have come," she said.

"I had intended to have come here in any case," he said, with a laugh at his own plump discourtesy.

She asked about his being in Switzerland. He explained.

"I have six weeks' leave," he added.

"There is a clean room in one of the chalets . . . the last one. Quite nice souls. You will be comfortable, I think," she said. "I'm all right now. It . . . it does me a great good . . . your having come."

The weather continued abominable. Outdoors was nothing visible but mist and rain. Where were the famous mountains? The peasants made huge log fires which crackled pleasantly with an aromatic smell of pine. One sat by them, drying one's damp clothes. Julian and Eleanor usually had their meals together at one or other of the cottages. The old people where Julian lodged were good, hard-working souls, with the blessed peace, patience, and contentment of cattle. The idyllic happiness of sheep awaiting slaughter, which fools hold up as an ideal to thinking man. The daughter looked after the lodger business, insisting on speaking English, which, it must be admitted, she spoke remarkably well, considering she had learnt it at the village school.

"A strange place to come to for recuperation of body and mind—in a fog," Julian remarked. "I suppose you came here for solitude? I too. It is, of course, a delusion. People imagine they are isolated, while, in truth, they carry the whole world with them into the desert— all that has been pumped into their brains by what they have heard and read, by human history. The English when they took to invading Switzerland fancied that their sublime emotions came from the mountains, when in fact they came from Mr. Ruskin. And the asses who talk about self-expression, the expression of their precious little selves, imagining that all the erroneous platitudes they have learnt, or learnt to revolt against by means of other platitudes, are their selves, their individuality, and that they are great artists! We fancy that by coming here we've got away from the war. Have we? The war is with us, were we to climb to the top of Jungfrau."

"Yes. This dreadful war," Eleanor said.

Julian knit his brows, impatient at the platitude.

"Oh, let me hear no more futile whining about 'this dreadful war,' " he said. "You used to go in for statistics, the statistics of your Webb friends. How many people were killed in so-called peace-time by the ruthless rapacity of those same powers that have made the war? Have you not seen whole populations in the Midlands, in the East End, the potteries, the black country, the Welsh mines, maimed, misgrown, deformed, stunted, so that they look a different race from your tall, pink, prosperous Englishman? They die prematurely, and their lives are scarcely better than death. The war-murder is more spectacular, that's all. But any doctor will tell you that the epidemic of influenza due to underfeeding and underwarming brought on by the profiteers has killed many times more English than the guns in France and Flanders. I'm not saying that the war isn't dreadful. But I do say that when I hear the constant slush about this dreadful war and the glorious dead and the maimed heroes, while not one word is breathed about that other dreadful war which has been going on, not three years, but centuries, it turns my stomach. Tender humanitarian emotions are all very well. But they become disgusting when they are selective, when they are rigorously selected according to the interests of the established rule of rapacity. I should be more moved about starving Belgian children if something were said about the hundredfold numbers of starving British children done to death by British chartered profiteers. All our emotions are falsified, turned into lies. Let me hear about the horrors and atrocities of the war that is daily and ceaselessly waged, of the murder that is continuously going on, and I shall be ready to talk about the horrors and atrocities of 'this dreadful war.' "

"War is an added horror. Because one cannot stop other horrors is no reason why one should not strive to stop the horror of war," said Eleanor.

Julian smiled at the ingrained liberal sophistry, arming himself with patience.

"One cannot because the one and the other are parts of the same thing. The war is the outcome of the ruthless greed for licenced personal profit which murders and starves daily for the sake of cheap labor and dividends. You cannot put down the one without putting down the other. It isn't the war-slaughter itself which is disgusting; it's the cause of it. The war is a lie. The people who are made to give their blood and lives are told that they are fighting for noble causes, for inspiring principles, for their countries, when they are fighting for the profits of a handful of exploiting enterprises. Supposing that instead of being the result of organised profiteering greeds, the war were truly a war for the liberation of mankind from that organised exploitation—would you, then, cry: 'Stop the war'? You would cry instead: 'On with the war, to the last drop of blood.' It isn't the fighting that is horrible; it's fighting for lies and infamies. Fighting is more necessary now than ever, fighting against lies and infamies, not for them."

Eleanor listened in silence while Julian poured out his mind in soliloquy. After a pause, he burst out laughing. She looked up at him.

"What are you laughing over?" she asked.

"Do you remember . . . ? It is some years since, I'm afraid . . . when you were good enough to desire my company at the opera on condition that I listened and did not talk? The tables seem to be turned."

Eleanor smiled, flushing, a little embarrassed. By the telepathy that sometimes takes place between interlocutors, Julian was conscious that she was thinking of other conditions which Eleanor had laid down at the time. He had no intention of breaking them, those conditions. No desire to make love to her. It was long since he had talked at his ease to a sympathetic and fairly intelligent listener. Eleanor was at least a good listener. For years Julian had got into the habit of locking up his thought in mystifications, obscure language and words used intentionally so that he could be true to his thought without being understood. And so he found it restful now to talk—or be silent—without fencing and being on his guard.

He was sorry, besides, for Eleanor, and there was a likeness in the defeat of their lives.

During intermissions in the deluge, they went for walks along the pine-bordered road by the Luschine, which foamed and roared over its bed of granite. At the head of the covered wooden bridge, under the crucifix, a monstrous cretin, with ashen apelike face, toadlike eyes, and lolling tongue, was in the habit of sitting. He had burst into a hideous laugh at sight of them, the first time they had come upon him. His horrible guffaw, multiplied by the echoes of unseen walls of rock, mingled with the tumult of the torrent, and seemed to come, like the gibbering of a thousand hidden demons, from the vault of driven mist. Eleanor had shrunk back with a shudder.

"A pinch of iodine would have made a human being out of that idiot monster," Julian remarked. "Preventable. Human idiocy is preventable, needless. That's what makes it infuriating. If one could go on believing that it was 'human nature,' 'the natural fallibility of reason,' the 'changeless order of things'—if one could still believe those interested explanations, one would resign oneself to—cynicism, barren, mocking cynicism. But we now know that those phrases are apologetics, subterfuge lies to hide the fact that human stupidity is the intentional outcome of 'education,' propaganda specially intended for the protection and perpetuation of the existing . . . 'order.' "

" 'Bourgeois ideology,' the Marxists call it," put in Eleanor with a smile.

"They speak an ugly language. But it serves a better purpose than our traditional English, pure and undefiled, sodden in every syllable with . . . 'bourgeois ideology,' " Julian said. "A pinch of honest, disinfectant iodine would make their stupefied 'human nature' impossible, their wars impossible, their crucifixes. . . . A sad come-down, their resigned crucified god, from his Greek prototype, crucified Prometheus, defying the gods and greater than his tormentors."

"If one could be sure that Prometheus would one day be unchained!" she said. "I went to that women's congress, to which some one invited me, because it seemed as though anything, anything aiming at peace were not to be despised. And then the appalling, inconceivable silliness of the whole thing, those poor creatures babbling in the void, their complete, but complete, ignorance of the most elementary and patent social facts, their unconsciousness of any reality. . . . It all overcame me with the hopelessness, the futility of any striving. I felt beaten, defeated by the monstrous, invulnerable, triumphant forces, crushing me, laughing at me . . . like that idiot monster. That is why. . . ."

One morning when Julian awoke, he was dazzled as he looked through the wide-open window. The sky was bright cloudless blue. The peaks of the Fischerhörner stood white against it, the glacier dropping in a cascade of diamonds to the green alp. The sheer granite wall of the Eiger towered overhead, bearing dazzling snowfields on the shoulders of its buttresses. Eleanor called to him from the road as he was dressing, and they went up the Wengern, gathering meadow-flowers at the foot of the Maiden, to the tinkling sound of cowbells from the herds grazing on the lush grass, by the edge of the ice-world.

Eleanor was childlike almost in her joy, as though in release and rebound from the unspeakable depths into which she had sunk down to the very gates of death. And also because—Julian was aware—of the man-friend by her, that had come unexpected into her prolonged retirement. He continued serious, warding off the fugitive physical spell, the transient semblance of joy, fugitive like that Alpine sunshine that might in an instant darken to gloom. Was it not, too, a blinker?, an ivory tower of self-deception? He knew the woman's thought, even in her silence, and waived it sternly aside.

Besides. . . . No, there was no need for Eleanor to renew her old request. No need at all. Deep down, Julian knew. . . . He had ruthlessly, persistently thrust the image, the memory of happiness, aside, crushed it back into the very depths, turning quickly his mind aside whenever it came up. Perhaps it was partly craven shrinking from the pain. But for all that, he did not deceive himself. He was conscious that it was there, the memory, gripped fast to the very roots of his being.

He went on pursuing the theme of their talks, warding off the personal, continuing the soliloquy of his mind, striving at clarification.

"As a matter of fact, the deep urges that rule us are not egoistic, self-regarding at all," he said. "What is the supreme tyrannical, physical urge of life, of animal life? The reproduction of the race. The world of vegetable life consumes itself in the fulfilment of that urge, and the plant dies to sow the seed of a future season. *Sic vos, non vobis.* All animal life confronts danger, starvation, death to the same end, that future generations may live. Ideals, fatal to the individual, precious to the race, are the only things that men and women will sacrifice themselves and die for. If we are unable to disinterest ourselves from the issues of the social world in which we belong, if the war and the human fate which it lays in the balance pursues us even here, and paralyses our concern for purely personal issues, that is not idealism, it is the very stuff of which is made that 'human nature' which people are in the habit of adducing in excuse of greed and brutality."

Eleanor caught in Julian's words the reply to her own questionings.

"Have you news from Russia?" she asked hesitantly.

He intentionally misunderstood her question. He made a vague gesture.

"None can tell as yet. The end of brutal Tzarism—which, by the way, our English tories are lamenting. Certainly an event of importance. But what is taking its place? The usual junta of money interests and their moralising liberal lackeys performing their function of clothing sordid rascality in the garb of high inspiring sentiments. Just as in any other 'democracy,' in England, in France, in America. I've heard that the exiled fighting revolutionaries here are going back to Russia. They have great hopes of fighting the pecuniary-liberal machine, I gather. Have we not heard the story before? Nothing new about Russia, as far as I can see."

"Some women I met in Zurich wanted me to meet them, the Russians. But I shrank," Eleanor said. "Was feeling too disenchanted. And then their talk is all of tactics of violence."

"Excellent!" Julian said, with some impatience.

They walked over to Lauterbrunnen, returning by the valley of the Zwei Luschinen. The sunshine was partly dimmed in Eleanor's eyes, the childlike gaiety of the morning subdued—by the thought, she supposed, of the horror without which no good could be won.

The next day they climbed up the goat path to the Fischer glacier. They were in the upper ice-world. The séracs of the ice were like emeralds, and the dazzling snow-fields stretched, immense, on the curving laps of the Mönch and Jungfrau. An effervescence coursed in their veins, intoxicating like champagne, from the keen air and the exercise, and the utterness of the solitude and silence. The illusion that the unseen human world below was very small and remote was almost complete. Bareheaded, Julian bathed body and mind in the empyrean and the sheer vastness. He forgot at times that Eleanor was by his side.

Unused as she was to the physical effort, he had had to help her over the ice and rocks, and instinctively she clung to him.

"It is very peaceful, all the same. Is not solitude a solution—mitigated solitude?" she said.

"*Egoïsme à deux?*" he said with a bitter smile. The phrase made him wince, when he said it, from its meanness and the memory. "Not in the Day of Wrath," he murmured to himself, without troubling to expand his meaning.

They reached the summit of the ice-stream, looking out upon the Place of Concord. Then suddenly the scene changed. A curling tongue of cloud which had licked round the summit of one of the high peaks waxed with incredible swiftness, like a released jinni, to a black, angry globe. Then to a billowing host that swept over sky and fleeing mountains, drawing over them a black curtain. Julian and Eleanor turned back hurriedly from the head of the moraine as the anger of the rising wind raised a fierce cry, and the light turned to eerie green, swiftly deepening to ghostlier lividness. The brooding wrath of the storm burst as they reached the other side of the glacier. They stood on a ledge of rock, panting and exhausted from the scramble over the jagged jaws of ice crevasses. Stinging, sleety rain began to fall, swept by hissing gusts of wind. Darkness deepened, and exploding thunder bounced, growling, from cliff to cliff and rolled down the echoing valleys. As the tumult rose, thunderclaps multiplied by endless reverberations seemed to break from all sides. Julian was reminded of the gunfire on the Ancre. The blackness was rent by the quick quiver of lightning-forks, and ropes of fireballs dangled for an instant across the darkness. In the momentary flashes, the shrouded phantasmal forms of three peaks hanging in the clouds fleeted by like giant ghosts. The rain was now a beating torrent cast up again, foaming, from the ground, and the walls of rock. The air was sizzling with molecules charged with electricity. In a moment, Julian and Eleanor were drenched to the skin as though their bodies had been naked. They groped, and scrambled among the boulders, seeking a downward direction, making little headway.

The darkness was now complete, impenetrable. Julian had to feel the ground at every step, with his foot or alpenstock, to avoid stepping into the void. Eleanor followed, clutching at his arm, stumbling. Loose stones crumbled underfoot, swept away by the rushing ankle-deep water.

"I can go no further," she said, exhausted.

They were against a ledge of rock. It might be at the head of the path. Julian shouted, but could not hear his own voice in the tumult.

"Stay here," he said. "I will go ahead to seek help. The goatherd's hut cannot be very far."

He went on, following the downslope of the ground, clinging closely to the ledge of rock that rose on his right. Several times he just missed stepping into the void, unable to find a foothold. In the utter darkness and helpless solitude, a sense of fear came over him, which he had not experienced under fire. He stopped a while, leaning back against the rock. Far away he caught sight of a glow of orange light. It might be the hut. It disappeared. After a while the light, two lights, re-appeared nearer. He shouted again, and presently an answering yodel came up from below. Guided by the movement of the lights, he picked up the direction of the path, from which he had strayed on to the sheer rock. Presently he saw the forms of the people coming up towards him. As they came near, he saw it was Spirido, with the idiot boy, carrying lanterns.

"Came over this morning," the Australian explained, "and was told you had gone up in the mountains with a lady, and no guide, no ropes, no nothing, you damn fool. When the storm came thought it was about time to fish you out of the Fischerhorn 'lifted towards heaven in per-petual mercy.' That damn fool Ruskin! Mr. Idiot here showed the way at the request of the little landlady, some nephew of whom he is. She says he is quite good-natured, save for occasional outbreaks of ungovernable rage. Like most of us! And what have you done with the lady?"

They went on, Julian turning back, to look for Eleanor. Spirido strode along, cooeying, with his cherry cane among the rocks, forget-ting all about his game leg, so that Julian and the idiot boy could scarcely keep up with him. They found Eleanor by a boulder in the moraine. She had tried to follow, but the ledge of stones crumbled under her, and she had slipped down into the moraine.

The idiot boy laughed loud—from joy, Spirido interpreted, at find-ing the lady.

Eleanor was humiliated by her weakness, a weakness, a hopelessness of mind as of body. But she was quiet, uncomplaining, grateful when they came to her with the lights.

"I'm afraid I cannot walk on the rough stones. I think my ankle is twisted or sprained," she said.

Julian discussed how best they should carry her. But Spirido loaded Eleanor across his shoulders and carried her, performing feats of mountaineering, up to the goat path and all the way down, and back to the chalet.

The women there solicitously tended her, prepared a hot bath and got hot-water bottles, and put her to bed.

Julian, after a tub and a change, felt rather braced up, the blood tingling within him, by the day's adventure.

The next day was bright and clear again after the storm, and the mountains sparkled in the sun. Eleanor felt no worse for the breakdown, but had to lie up to nurse her ankle.

It was Easter Day. The country people and the children were tricked out and beribboned in bright colors. Church bells echoed throughout the valley and there was a procession. Many people had come over from Berne and Lucerne for the holiday. Spirido coolly proposed a walk to the "Place de la Concorde," meaning the Concordia Platz, the meeting-place of the glaciers, up in the mountains. Julian had had enough of the icefields for a day or two. While Spirido went off by himself, he strolled quietly up the Wengern, glad enough to be alone.

The sound of church bells rose from the valleys all round, from Lauterbrunnen and the Luschinen, like noisy children's toys. On the alp Julian passed two men sitting on a rustic bench, with their backs turned, and when one of them suddenly looked round, it was Ogonin. With a wave of his hand, Julian answered his salutation, but did not stop, going further on to sit on another bench facing the pyramid of the Jungfrau.

Presently Ogonin came up to him, alone.

"*Christos voskres!*"—'Christ is risen,' Julian greeted him jestingly with the Russian Easter greeting.

"In a figurative sense, you speak perhaps more truly than you know," Ogonin smiled. "This day may mark the resurrection of a dead world."

Julian noticed, he fancied, a change in the appearance of the man, a quiet confident strength, as of one whose mind and body are firmly poised. "We are going to Russia. All is now arranged and a passage allowed us through Germany. We should have left a day or two ago, but for these Easter holidays."

"I had, I think, something to do with bringing about the arrangement," Julian remarked with a sarcastic smile.

"So I heard. And I have come to thank you," Ogonin said.

"Oh, pray don't mention it. It was quite unwittingly, and I don't know what it's all about," Julian said, with a shrug.

"If you should care to come to Russia with us," Ogonin said, "there would be no difficulty. We are permitted to go in any number."

Julian remained silent a moment, looked at the avalanches on the flanks of the mountain, which seemed, at a distance, like the dust thrown up by a sandfly. A wistfulness gripped him suddenly at the heart. He thrust back the hesitation.

"No," he said.

"My friend was so overwrought with the stress and strain of these last days, with the excitement and impatience, that I got him to come up here for a few hours. Shall I ask him to speak to you?" Ogonin said simply.

Julian raised his brows. Why should he want to speak with the man?

"Who is your friend?" he asked.

"Our chief. The living leader of Revolution," Ogonin said.

Julian made a vague gesture, which Ogonin took for an expression of consent, as he left him.

Presently Julian saw coming towards him with quick steps a little man, squat and broadchested, with solid face, a vague goatee and dome-like crown, part of baldness, part of brow. From the impression of efficient energy which he gave, one would have taken him for a business man, a German or Russian industrialist or banker, maybe. He had the business man's mannerism of toying with one of the buttons of his waistcoat. But his clothes, though clean and decent, were crumpled and neglected, and had never, obviously, come in contact with a pressing iron.

He shook hands with Julian heartily, coming close up to him and looking straight into his eyes. His eyes went through Julian, seeming

to sound and measure at a glance the very depths of him. Those eyes!
They had none of the melodramatic magnetism of the hypnotiser, no
suggestion of pose, an absolute candor rather, yet Julian felt at once
overwhelmed by the spell of their impressiveness. They were the eyes
of a man from whom all lies had fallen, all pretence, and had the strength
of a great clarity.

"You are an Englishman?" he asked in German. He excused himself, saying in clumsy English: "I do not speak the English language
very well."

"Alas!" Julian replied in answer to his question.

The man had a gay, bright laughter.

"Your misfortune, not your fault," he said. He sat down on the
bench by Julian's side. "Nationalism is one of the frauds of capitalistic
imperialism," he went on. For a moment his eyes became dreamy. "I
am a Russian. I am on the point of returning after long years of exile
to Russia. When I shall land on the frozen soil of my native land,
when I shall once more hear the Russian speech about me, shall be
surrounded by familiar Russian things, by the Russian people, I shall
be moved—deeply moved. It is that emotion which capitalism fraudulently exploits. Capitalism substitutes for it chauvinistic patriotism,
that is, blind subservience to a State, a government, which is but the
tool, the armed weapon of capitalistic rule, its means of making war,
either on foreign countries, to extend the field of exploitation and
the appropriation of raw materials, or on the people themselves. It is
patriotic loyalty to that abomination which the bourgeois ideology of
capitalistic countries substitutes for the very natural sentiments of affection we feel for the habitual surroundings and associations of our
youth."

"I have long perceived the fraud," said Julian. "I quite share your
indignation, your fury."

The man had again his light laugh.

"Ah, but those are big words!" he said. "We do not go in for fury
and indignation. The liberals are concerned with emotions; we are
concerned with facts. The bourgeois language intentionally confuses
differences of opinion as to tactics, as to what is to be done. But as to
facts there is simply intelligent interpretation or ignorance, taking the
facts into account or ignoring them. You would not speak of the

theory that the earth is flat, or that it is the center of the solar system, or of the theory of special creation as opinions. They are simply forms of ignorance. In the same manner the theory that there is no class struggle, that the private ownership of the means of necessary production and the exploitation of the producers for private profit can continue indefinitely once the producers have become able to perceive the facts, that is, have become class-conscious, is not an opinion, but ignorance, generally wilful ignorance. We keep on explaining the facts to the workers deceived by capitalistic ideology, but we revolutionaries no longer discuss them. We are concerned with tactics, with the means of bringing about the change. Our immediate task at present is to help transform the imperialistic war into the social war. The liberals speak of this being the last war, the war that shall make war impossible. In a sense they are right. It is the last imperialistic war on a large scale. Any future war will inevitably be a social war because the workers will be class-conscious and can no longer be deceived by the fraud of chauvin patriotism."

"But how is imperialistic war, as you call it, to be changed into social war?" Julian asked.

"It can only be done through the dictatorship of the proletariat. That is the point. Not giving the proletariat, the workers, the poorer peasants, a voice in the State, together with bourgeois liberals, populists, social democrats and all the defenders of capitalism—that is, democracy—but the *dictatorship* of the proletariat, with the force of the State, the police, the army, under its rule, and not under the rule of capitalism. Not liberty, in the social democratic sense, but dictatorship."

"But that is not socialism. I thought you aimed at founding the socialist State," Julian put in. "You don't think that the socialist State can be established?"

"No. Not now. We are in a stage of revolution, that is, in a state of war. Even if revolution triumphed completely in one country, or in half a dozen, while capitalism ruled in the rest of the world, the social revolution would be in a state of war, of ruthless war to death. The whole capitalistic world would fight it, by arms, by propaganda, by relentless and ceaseless plotting, by corruption, by every available and imaginable means. Treason and sabotage would be sewn through corruption in the very heart, even in the governing head of the revolutionary State. It would be in a state of war, external and internal, till the last trace of the capitalist system is swept off the face of the earth. You cannot defend revolution by democracy, that is, by allowing the enemies of the revolution and all their dupes full liberty to plot and scheme against it, and to wreck it. As well might you claim now in your England full liberty and democratic privilege for German spies, plotters and saboteurs. What would your liberal democratic government say to that? No, we cannot establish the socialist State in one country. What we have to establish is something entirely different: a ruthless war dictatorship. Not liberty, but discipline. But alongside that beastly dictatorship and bureaucracy, which the workers will be bidden to obey and hate, the organisation of the socialist world, of the workers, of production, will be building. And when that is complete, when capitalism has no longer the power to sap, to attack, and to plot, then let the workers, whether of hand or brain, smash that monstrous thing and let them establish true freedom and true democracy."

There was no designed eloquence in the man's speech, no brilliancy. He was not concerned with producing any effect by means of words, but with the concrete expression of his meaning, only. His language, his use of stereotyped slogans and uncouth terminologies—"capitalistic imperialism," "petty bourgeois ideology," etc.—which served as a kind of shorthand, jarred at times on Julian. But there was in his manner a simple, easy directness, careless of mere allusion and indirect implication, as of ornament, betokening the clarity of thought that comes of its complete digestion, which was more impressive than studied appeal. Julian had the feeling, while he listened to him, that his own mind bathed in clarity of thought and purpose.

He tried to express his own doubts, and the man tirelessly explained, without condescension or impatience.

"But how are you going to move, to influence, to lead the huge, inert, ignorant mass of the people?" he asked.

"We do not propose to influence or lead them," the man said. "It is they who will lead and influence us. You are thinking in terms of the usual bourgeois demagogy. In that scheme of things the people have to be hypnotised and carried away by eloquence, fine sentiments, persuaded against their own feelings and sense, in other words, deceived, as they have been by ultra-patriots and social chauvins in order

to be sent to the slaughter in defence of the economic interests of ruling classes. We are not demagogues"—he always said "we," not "I."
"We shall direct the people because we shall express their own will. We
are not concerned with 'persuading' them."

They sat talking till the flush of the alp-glow colored the white peaks,
and as he listened to the man, Julian felt as though the ground grew
more solid than ever it had been in the path of his spirit. They walked
back to where Ogonin was sitting. Julian took leave with a sobered,
fortified feeling. A new strength had been imparted to him.

"There is nothing in the world I more heartily wish than your success," he said, shaking hands, humbly, almost reverently.

He avoided seeing Eleanor except briefly to enquire how she was.
Her ankle gave little trouble; she was feeling well. Next morning he
came to take leave. Eleanor was sitting on the verandah in the sun.
Spirido was with her. She had fought her own inward battles, and was
composed. Julian mentioned his meeting with the Russians, but only
briefly. One could not report the language of the New World without
raising clouds of misunderstandings. Julian felt it a sort of desecra-
tion to say much.

"I shall be returning in a few days to England," Eleanor said.

"England is a good place to have the corners knocked off intelligence,
enthusiasm, and all that," said Spirido.

"And you, are you going to Russia?" Eleanor asked again, looking
at Julian.

"No. I am not worthy," he said.

"When they have established Utopia there perhaps?" Spirido
chuckled.

Julian was impatient at the flippancy. The cynicism of mere nega-
tion was as stupid as the fraud of liberal idealism.

"Perhaps when the war will have begun," he said. "In the West it
is not war."

XIII

EAST of Poperinghe the B.E.F. wears a different face. A drawn, grey look is on the countenances of the men, as though the shadow of dissolution were already upon them. There is no singing on the march or in camp, no jest or laughter, and little talk. For this is the inferno of the "salient." Here is no relaxing of tense nerves, no zone of shelter and safety. It is always zero hour. For rest and relief the troops have to move back beyond the Belgian border. Groans are heard in the ranks as the macadam of France gives place to the cobbled Belgian roads. Remember Belgium!

Past Vlamerdinghe, with its church steeple cloven in two by shell-fire, lending it the silhouette of twin Gothic towers, the straight plane-bordered road to Ypres is the Oxford Street of the Front. Four lines of traffic move continuously along it in both directions. Military police with red brassards regulate the circulation. Intercalated in the streams of lorries, limbers, guns, march ingoing and outgoing columns of infantry. Returning units in soiled khaki, unshaven, haggard, glance grimly at the incoming battalions as they pass. A company of Canadians, with maple leaves painted on the sacking covers of their tin hats, is coming out. A staff car, flying a divisional banner, wants to get past. "Sorry, sir," says the sergeant of police, saluting the general whose monocled face expostulates from the window of the car. The staff car drops behind an R.A.C. lorry which is bringing back a wrecked airplane.

An unremitting rumble of shellfire mingles with the rattle of the traffic. Crumps are dropping in the distance to the left. The corner of a little Belgian château with pointed roof goes up in dust and flying debris. No one takes notice.

For its ten-minutes-before-the-hour rest spell, the battalion falls out into the ditches. There is a huddle of bell-tents along the road. Officers in shirt-sleeves stand looking on at the passing traffic, smoking their pipes. Six German planes in squadron formation, the black crosses visible on their wings, are being pursued by the white puffballs of the "archies." The crash of a bomb is heard over to the right.

Tramp, tramp, tramp. The booming of gunfire becomes louder. We are coming up to Ypres. The railway station, which has a bad name, is given a wide berth. The space before it is deserted, but for the red-capped policeman warning off the traffic. The bulk of it bends round to the left, skirting the town. The tank of the gasworks, tilted on its twisted uprights, has a comic, tipsy look.

The battalion's billets are in the old cavalry barracks—what's left of them. Half the building, which surrounds a large barrack square, is a heap of rubble; the other half a battered ruin. But there are large vaulted cellars. The companies grope their way down, along the catacombs. A supply of candles is issued. The men throw off their packs and equipment, and spread their ground-sheets on the uneven floor of pounded brick-dust. They have the frightened, stupid look of cattle driven into the pens of a slaughterhouse.

"Goin' to 'ave us buried alive now," remarks Private Chirpin, an oldish man with a grey mustache, who sits down in a corner, too tired to shake off his harness.

"What's the matter? Feelin' done up?" asks Corporal Jutson, kindly.

"A bit, Corporal."

"Was you at medical parade this morning, if you're not feeling fit?"

"Aye, Corporal. The doc gave me a number nine. But it ain't that there's nothin' much wrong. To tell the God's truth, I'm fed up, Corporal. Can't no longer. The wife and kids . . . you know."

"Aye, aye, I know, all right, mate. Buck up, old man," says Corporal Jutson, helping Chirpin off with his pack. "It ain't going to be so bad. We're only doing forty-eight hours in this line. Then you'll get a rest in brigade reserve."

Headquarters mess is in a cellar with a trestle table. Two empty whiskey bottles serve as candlesticks. Quartermaster Plumtree has come up with the mess cart.

"Division have only provided two mules for the rations, sir. We'll need two more."

"Can't you wait a moment before bothering me with your damned requisitions? Confound you. Petty! Corporal Petty! Where the hell are you?" The colonel and Major Sotty sink on the bench by the table.

Captain Inglis, V.C., has come up with the quartermaster, to report for duty.

"Hello, Inglis, found your way back, have you? Had a good time?" the colonel greets undemonstratively the returning hero. "Corporal Petty! Some whiskey and glasses. Look sharp. Damn you, don't drown the stuff with your Perrier. So, you've got back? You should have stayed over at Houtkerque with the baggage. Plumtree is going back to camp. But since you're here, I suppose you'd better take over C Company, eh, Weeney? Young Stringer will hand over, what?"

"Very good, sir," signifies Adjutant Weeney, who has some chits from brigade. "Division wants returns of specialists before the attack, sir."

There are rabbit-wire bunks in the officers' quarters. Crumps are dropping round viciously at regular intervals. Every now and then the crash of shattered masonry is heard, and the place rocks. It seems foolhardy to go to sleep here.

"They drop mostly on the other side of the yard," Major Sotty remarks optimistically. "A Belgian working section was wiped out the other day while the men were asleep."

Inglis pours forth his troubles into inattentive ears. Every expedient to prolong his sojourn in his native isle had at last failed.

"Rotten luck, what?" he laments.

His audience wraps itself up in blankets. Fulliston is morose and ill-disposed to talk.

"Got raided once, Bern, you know," Inglis informs.

"Yes, I saw. Gothas."

"No, police. The blighters, instigated by some damned officious assistant P.M., blew in at one of our little parties with those girls near Berkeley Square. You know, the ones we met at your friend's in Chesterfield Gardens. Alleged that our lady friends were insufficiently clothed. Rotten lie. Cora and Marjorie weren't clothed at all. Damned interference, what? Disorderly house and all that sort of rot. But when the inspector noticed the old wine-colored ribbon on my tunic, he saw he'd made a mistake. Was quite decent. Assured us the little affair would be settled without any annoyance."

"Where did that one go?" asked Pluckley, starting up. A crash louder than the rest shook the place and the candles blew out.

"That's just the stuff Fritz puts over on the square."

"You know that Mrs. Cockburn with the red stockings, don't you, Caballero?"

"Shut up, I want to sleep."

The heavy drug-like sleep of physical and nervous exhaustion settled over the company, they slept amid the unceasing noise and clatter as though on a ship buffeted by the storm. The air laden with brick-dust and the smell of sweat was choking.

Julian was surprised to find himself still alive when the first rays of daylight filtered down through the cellar window.

The men are cleaning their rifles and greasing the bolts. After inspection, some of the young officers stroll out to have a look at the Cloth Hall, familiar from the pictures in the illustrated papers. Shells drop at regular intervals. Military police are posted at the main points. An ambulance dashes across between two explosions. Some streets have been cleared of debris, and wind between mounds of rubble. Among the heaps of brick and mortar are fragments of quaint carved Flemish gables. On a collapsed pediment may be read in ornamented wrought iron the date: 1616.

Out through the Menin gate and along the Menin road. Shells come whining over and burst among the remains of the battered town. By a corner of the town-wall, the moat is still filled with water from the Yser Canal. A swan floats lazily over it.

The battalion is straggling in loose double file. It has left the road, and is now on the vast wasteland that shelves towards the ridges. Tramping along the trodden paths over outcrops of rock, or following the log-road over mires of mud. The ground is strewn, every square yard of it, with the debris and wreckage of war—rusty coils of barbed wire, broken wheels of limbers, twisted rifles and bayonets, cartridge clips, helmets, gas-masks, accoutrement, rotting leather, bandoliers, boots. In the lee of a stony ridge an old German gun emplacement lies shattered. Huge blocks of concrete hang over the gunpit, where sprawl four swollen German corpses. Their braided blue uniforms make them look like musicians in a German band. The ridge beyond is honeycombed with dugouts. A halt is called in the lee of the rise.

The colonel and officers are hospitably received at the headquarters of the Leicester battalion that occupies the dugouts. Whiskey is served and cigarettes lit.

"Well, fancy seeing you here, Cator," says the Leicester colonel. "Last time we met was at Cranne Hall. Remember that run we had with Fernie's? That was a pacer, that hack you rode."

"Got her over here now."

"Well, I'm blessed. Chin, chin!"

"Pretty cosy place you have here."

"Not bad. Fritz strafes it now and again, but he knows the house he built for himself and that he can't do much damage. How's Mrs. Cator?"

For a while we are all good fellows.

"Do look in on your way back," the adjutant tells Inglis after the fourth whiskey is disposed of. "Awfully bucked to have seen you. Cheerio and good luck."

We push along the railway bank. As evening draws near, the gunfire grows livelier all along the salient. We seem to be marching right into it.

The colonel looks very red and bloated; his eyes bulge out of his head.

"Any one got any whiskey?" he calls.

Trosley runs forward with his water bottle. Colonel Cator, squatting down on his haunches, sucks at it avidly.

The battalion is moving in single file along the track. The head of the column becomes lost to sight behind a rise in the ground. They are shelling the track; the Germans have got the range exactly. A shell bursts straight ahead. That one must have surely dropped in the middle of A Company. Another and another, at quick intervals. We tramp on, steadily. The next shell bursts just behind the ridge in front of us. There are cries and screams. Private Chirpin rolls over and over down the bank, screaming. Both his legs are blown off. He lies at the bottom, moving the mangled stumps. The torn muscles twitch violently and the blood is spouting in big jets.

"Help! Help, for God's sake! For mercy's sake, help! Oh, my God!"

The column marches on. It is useless to stop. We must get over the ridge before the next one. The M.O. glances down at Private Chirpin. Nothing to be done about it. Tramp, tramp. We are over the rise. The bodies of two men are lying across the track, horribly shattered. We step over the mess of torn flesh and scattered intestines. The next shell bursts behind us. We breathe more freely.

The track rises steeply. Down on the left, out of the mire of mud, emerge the heads of two horses. Struggling desperately, they are slowly sinking, inch by inch in the liquid mire. Some wagon or limber sunk there. Only the heads of the horses are visible above the mounting mud. Their nostrils quiver, bloodstained. Their eyes, their soft, liquid, animal eyes, filled with terror, yet gentle, seem to beg and beseech. Those guileless, desperate eyes!

"Hello, Bern, what are you up to?"

Julian has fallen out and is scrambling down the bank. He draws out his revolver. Leaning over a broken plank, he fires two shots into the horses' brows.

"Those eyes, those eyes! Men are fools and cowards. Those beasts are guiltless."

Heavy shelling is taking place all along the ridge. A tall staff officer, followed by a runner, is stalking along.

"Where's headquarters?" asks the officer of a group of men.

"Over there, sir, near where that man is sitting," answers a young lance-corporal.

The man, grey and old, is sitting motionless on a ledge of rock, leaning on a spade. He has a strange, unearthly look. As the officer passes by him, he notices that the back of the man's head has been blown off. The inside of the skull shows, yellowish white with purple lines, cleaned out of brain.

"Colonel Cator there?" calls out the nice Eton voice of the officer.

A grunt comes from the bottom of the trench that runs round the large pillbox. Colonel Cator and Major Sotty are crawling on all fours. Their purplish faces with bulging eyes wear a look of abject,

undisguised terror that is comical. The whole vicinity is being peppered with five-nines.

"Hell of a place, this," growls the colonel.

They crawl into the pillbox followed by the staff officer. Inside it is
a roomy enough round cave of reinforced concrete.

"Brigadier sent me over to see that you have all you want and are
comfortable," says the staff officer after they have had one or two
glasses of whiskey and the colonel and major have somewhat regained
their composure.

"Oh, quite," says the colonel unenthusiastically.

"Enough plum and apple jam, and all that?" asks the Red-tabs.

"Ask the bloody quartermaster," growls out the colonel. "Now, out
with it. What's the news?"

Red-tabs laughs pleasantly.

"The brigadier would like you to come, sir, with the company com-
manders, as soon as you're out, to see the relief map for the show.
Awfully pretty. Made by one of our corporals from airplane photographs. Put in a lot of work. All the bushes made out of the shavings
that the champagne comes in. And little lead Boches in field-grey. Very
realistic, don'tyerknow."

"Humph! Is that all?" grunted the colonel.

"You'll be going into the show a bit earlier than we expected, sir,"
Red-tabs went on. "Afraid there won't be time to take the battalion
out for rehearsal. You see, five or six brigades have been wiped out
first go. And the G.O.C. is frightfully keen on the job, don'tyerknow.
Says cost is no object. So we'll only be able to take you out to Vlamerdinghe for a few days."

"Looks as though we were in for it," the colonel says.

"I'm afraid so, sir," says Red-tabs smiling. "And, by the way, the
brigadier wants that return of specialists as soon as possible. You won't
need any. It's a straightforward go. Have you got a gas sergeant?
Sergeant Hordie would have been just the man for the school at Divisional bull-ring. Pity he went down. And you think . . . ?" he says,
turning to Captain Burr, the M.O.

The doc shrugs his shoulders.

"Hard to prove. Besides, if you were to track all the self-inflicted . . ."

"Strange. I can't make it out," says the staff captain. "Sergeant Hordie didn't look like the man who would put a bullet through his arm, did he, Foster?"

"They're getting a bit fed up, every one of them."

"Say what you will, Sotty. It isn't the old regular army. These chaps haven't got the guts," the colonel says.

After relief had been reported complete, Julian went up with the others to the front line, a straggling line of small posts. One officer was to remain with each of the two companies on duty, while the others took up their quarters for the night in the line of pillboxes lower down on the ledge of the hill. It was relatively quieter in the firing line. The occasional splutter of a machine gun indicated the position of the corresponding German posts.

Julian walked back over the broken ground. The sun had just set. From the high ground the whole land sloping down to Ypres could be seen. The silhouette of the ruined Cloth-Hall tower was distinguishable on the horizon against the red sky. The eye ranged from the flooded country of the Yser in the north to the heights of Kemmel and Mont des Catts in the south. Never probably had human eye looked before upon such vastness of desolation. Over the whole prospect was not one leaf or blade. Mile after mile the earth stretched out black, foul, putrescent, like a sea of excrement. Not a sign of animal or vegetable life; none of human life either, for it hid itself underground, and only the dirt spouts thrown up by missiles of death, bursting like mephitic bubbles over the foulness, gave visible indication of its presence. But everywhere the detritus and garbage of the murderous madness. It was one vast scrap heap. And, scattered over or sunk in the refuse and mud, were the rotting bodies of men, of horses and mules. Of such material was the barren waste that stretched as far as eye could see. It was not a desert of nature, a waste land of rock or sand, but what had lately been a fertile and smiling landscape, green and luxuriant, peaceful and pleasant, covered with waving fields, pastures, gardens, orchards, strewn with villages and farms. It stank, lurid and blasted in the poisoned air.

Julian, with Inglis, Sergeant Trutton, Sergeant Day, and Corporal Shortable, took up his quarters for the night in a "pillbox" on the Zonnebeke railway line. They crept through the low opening into the cylinder of concrete. A narrow ledge ran round three sides of the interior. The middle of the pillbox was a pit filled with greenish black water from which rose an intolerable stench.

"There's two dead Germans in there," Corporal Shortable informed.

All five sat on the concrete ledge and a couple of planks laid across the stinking water, taking turns at stretching out their legs.

Outside the storm of shellfire grew fiercer as the night darkened. It was unceasing. Only the shells that burst quite near were heard as separate explosions against the continuous roll of the tempest. Some burst just outside the pillbox. They alternated with crumps which sounded a few hundred yards away. Two guns were firing at intervals of three minutes at the two pillboxes on the lower slope of the ridge, the one in which the men were sitting and the other, some five hundred yards further on.

"Come in, you runners, we can make room," Julian called to the men outside.

"We're all right, sir. We're in the lee. The crumps drop on the other side," Lance-Corporal Beddoes called back.

The five men sat in silence, in dull, stupid silence. Inglis sat staring blankly, his mouth slightly open. Corporal Shortable was holding a guttering candle.

The last crump was quite near. They've got the range exactly. Then the other on the next pill-box. Three minutes, another nearer still. It must have hit the corner. The whole place shakes and rocks. One can hear the crumbling cement. A direct hit and all will be over. Three minutes. That one dropped a bit short. The next crash has hit the roof. Julian feels as though he had been struck on the head. The pill-box quivers and creaks. Another direct hit will finish it. Like that one they passed coming up, with the four German gunners. They will look like that. They will be all mixed up with the two dead Germans in the greenish black water. It is inevitable. The five men sit, saying no word. There is nothing worth saying. Corporal Shortable lights another candle from the stump of the one which has burnt out. They sit waiting for the next crash. Will it be the last?

Julian did not feel afraid. He asked himself whether he was afraid. No, it was curious, but he really did not feel in the least afraid. He felt terribly uncomfortable, and weary. But not, as far as he could make

out, afraid. It was the end. There could be no doubt about it. It was
not a question of chances this time. The German battery was deliberately aiming at the pill-box, and they had the range exactly. Had it on
their map. It was their job, to smash that pill-box, if they took all night
to do it. Question of mathematics. Damned poor gunnery, by the way,
that they hadn't yet made a job of it. Spirido would have had something to say on the subject. Well, it had to come. The sooner it was
over, the better. It was this waiting in the condemned cell that was
nerve-racking. Julian's mood and thoughts had none of the solemnity
appropriate to the occasion. Considering this was his leave-taking of
life, of the world, the last moments he would spend in this world. Inevitably. None of the drowning man's retrospect. Was it necessary, all
that solemnity? No thoughts to rethink. He had thought pretty well
all his thoughts to a dead end. Life? He had, after all, had as good a
life as most people and a better one than many. There was not much to
regret. He had often been very foolish—like everybody else. But he
had come to see things pretty clearly, he had grown out of the Days of
Ignorance. That was what he valued most in his life. He would have
liked to live to see how things would come out of this crucial crisis, this
turning point in the growth of Europe, of humanity. That was the
chief reason he had to regret that he had to die now. What was the
date? Seventh of November, 1917. He wondered what was going on
in Russia, whether the dreams of the man he met on the Wengern Alp
would come to anything. And, over there in Petrograd. . . . How was
she faring? So many partings of separate lives! Death was only another parting—much like the others. There was nothing to be done
about it. If only those gunners would get on with their job, and be
done with it. It was intolerable, this waiting. The shell-bursts were
now all very near, just missing the rocking, cracking cement pill-box,
or grazing it. Every three minutes. Now. That one dropped a little
beyond. Three more minutes. Nearly got it that time. There was a
crumbling of cement. The red light of the candle trembled, and nearly
went out.

Then it happened. An instantaneous, fulminating crash, stunning,
deafening.

It was some seconds before he was aware of what had happened.
During an appreciable duration of time, consciousness was obliterated.

There was complete silence. The candle had gone out. Darkness and complete silence. Julian became slowly conscious that, as far as he could tell, he was all right. He was alive. That was surprising. He was not hit. No sound or movement was to be heard in the silence that followed the deafening explosion. No one said a word. Corporal Shortable began fumbling for a match. Then, in the darkness, Sergeant Day gave a low groan, and began whining in a childlike voice:

"Oh, my God! I'm hit. Oh, my God!"

When Corporal Shortable had got the stump of candle lit, Sergeant Trutton was seen nursing his right leg, groaning and complaining.

"It hurts, it hurts awful!"

Sergeant Day was moaning, in great pain.

Inglis was staring blankly, motionless. He had not moved.

Lance-Corporal Beddoes put his head in at the door.

"Are you all right, sir?" he asked.

"Two hit, I think," said Julian. "You outside . . . ? You must come in now."

"We're all right, sir. We were on the other side. It dropped just at the door. Shall I go for the stretcher-bearers, sir?"

"No. It's no use. They can't move any one through this crumping."

Julian ran his hands quickly over Sergeant Trutton's leg, and tested the bones.

The thigh-bone cracked and moved disjointedly as he handled it. The sergeant kept whining like a child.

Sergeant Day lay back with eyes closed, groaning.

"For God's sake give me some opium. I can't bear it."

Julian and the corporal, who was holding the candle, undid the sergeant's clothes. They could find no wound.

"Where's the pain?"

Sergeant Day pointed to his groin.

There was a tiny wound on the groin.

"Give me some opium, for God's sake."

Julian gave the sergeant his pellets of opium.

Inglis sat staring without saying a word. Julian and the corporal got the two wounded men stretched out on one of the ledges and over the boards. It left very little room for the others to sit.

They bound Sergeant Trutton's leg to a rifle, and he was quiet, saying he felt better. Day was groaning and kept asking for more opium.

"May I hold your hand, sir?" he asked.

Julian held the large, rough hand of the sergeant. The physical human contact comforted him. The conventional separation of rank and class was almost bridged.

"What were you in civil life?" Julian asked.

"Foreman in Mr. Foster's factory. Captain Foster's father, you know," said the sergeant. "A very kind gentleman is Mr. Foster. Was good to the workmen. It was a lovely speech he made when the battalion left for France."

Ye gods! The hallucination of the servile mind!

"Married?" Julian enquired.

"Yes, sir. Wife and two kids. We was very happy. Wife now working in the factory to keep the home fires burning. Could I have another pill of opium?"

"You've had a lot of opium. Try and bear the pain a while longer," Julian said.

Outside, the tempest of shell-fire continued. Crumps came very near and one or two rocked the whole pill-box with direct hits, blowing out the candle in Corporal Shortable's hand. But Julian no longer timed the explosions. He thought no more about them, but only of the interminable time till daylight. His wrist-watch marked a quarter to four. His whole body ached and he could not move, sitting cramped on the wooden board, holding the sergeant's hand. The night seemed interminable.

At last a pale grey light began to filter through the shattered opening of the pill-box. It was so welcome that when, a while later, Julian went out into the ashen dawn, it seemed to him a beautiful morning, as though a spring day had been breaking upon the gladness of green fields. The pale, feeble sunshine felt delightfully warm. There was a deep hole, a half shell-hole, before the entrance.

As the light grew brighter, the firing quieted down and then stopped altogether. It was the usual breakfast-time truce. Stretcher-bearers came down, and with some difficulty, Sergeant Day and Sergeant Trutton were lifted out.

"Good luck, Day," said Julian, shaking the sergeant's hand. "You'll be all right. Have a good time."

"Thank you, sir. You have been very kind," the sergeant said as the stretcher-bearers started off down the railway bank.

Captain Inglis stretched himself.

"I suppose I'd better have a look round at my company for stand to," he said. They were the first words he had spoken that night. "Meet you again at headquarters for breakfast."

Julian was off inspection duty that morning. He went to headquarters for a snack of breakfast. It would be welcome. The old man with the back of his head blown out was still sitting leaning on his spade. He was a landmark.

Colonel Cator and the major were busy with the ham and eggs. How delicious it smelled.

"Sergeant Day and Sergeant Trutton have gone down, sir," Julian said.

The colonel gave a slight grunt and went on with the ham and eggs.

A runner came from C Company and spoke to the adjutant.

"Captain Inglis was caught by a stray bullet in the front line, sir. In the neck. Death instantaneous," Weeney announced.

The colonel finished the ham and eggs.

"Petty! Bring some more tea," he called. "I told you you'd have to get a larger tea-pot. Do something about it."

We straggled back at dusk by platoons. The relieving battalion of Middlesex had had a bad passage, and our opposite numbers turned up desultorily at intervals of several hours. One of their companies had been practically wiped out, as it had fallen out for rest by a ruined farm. We passed it on our way out. A shell had dropped plumb in the midst of them. The men lay, knelt, sat, or stood, propped against the battered wall in the attitudes in which death had instantaneously caught them, with the looks of supreme terror still on their faces. No macabre imagination of painter ever conceived a like fantastic spectacle of horror. We tramped past in silence, only glancing sideways at the scene.

We were quartered in an open bell-tent camp, with a couple of elephant dugouts for mess and orderly room. Space was at a premium in the area overcrowded with troops, confusion prevailed in the arrangements, and for several days we moved from camp to camp. It rained unintermittently and the sodden ground of the camps was a mire of mud. Tents had to be taken down at dawn and set up again at night, because of the squadrons of cruising Gothas which peppered the camps with bombs. We lost six men and an N.C.O. as they paraded before the Orderly Room for guard duty.

Orders and instructions poured in for the attack in which we were shortly to take part. We no longer spoke of a "show," our language had become more sober. The gloom which hung over the battalion deepened; the last flickers of forced levity died out; profane language largely gave place to a shy sentimentality. Each was oppressed with thoughts too private and solemn for utterance. Rumors had reached us of the place against which wave after wave was being thrown through seas of mud, to the attack of the ridge. Of a Yorkshire battalion which had gone in some days before, only a handful had returned. A Canadian contingent which had been hastily called upon to replace them, had been reduced in a few minutes to heaped-up mounds of corpses.

One-third of the officers was to remain in reserve at Red Rose Camp, near Vlamerdinghe, where we had been drawn back for a perfunctory preparation. To my disgust, I was among those chosen to stay out, and Julian was to take charge of the company. I made every effort to have the arrangement altered, and in response to my insistence I was told I could settle the matter with Bern. But I found Julian irritatingly indifferent. Since his return to duty from convalescent leave, he had been more than usually silent and apathetic. He shrugged his shoulders when I broached the matter.

"I joined up three years ago to take my chance, didn't I? To leave it to fate to decide. I have since seen no reason to change my mind. No reason whatever," he said. "There's nothing, anyhow, that any man can do to turn the blind tide that is sweeping us along. Is there? Show me if there is. If there were any hope of cleansing even a little of the filth in which we are sinking, I should be eager to live a hundred years that I might see it done and have a hand in it. But . . . As things now appear, there's no vital difference between a hundred years and a hundred hours or minutes. No reason to try to interfere with one's unimportant personal fate."

He looked at the matter in the same manner as he had done a few nights before in the pill-box at Zonnebeke, when he thought his last hour had come. Without much emotion, one way or the other. That indifference appalled me more than his former mood of contained wrath. There was no changing his resolve.

"Your life is much more likely to be possible than mine," he said.

He gave me some letters. One for Violet, another for Everard, and one for Russia.

"See to sending them, please, if, as the chances are, I go West."

"It's pretty difficult to get a letter through to Russia. I hope I won't send it. If I should, I'll see that it gets through by diplomatic channels. Have you seen the news? It seems the Communists have wiped out the Kerenski crowd and are ruling the country."

"For how long? We know what happens to Communes. They end at Père Lachaise. I met one of their leaders in Switzerland. I was impressed. A clear thinker. But thinkers are never men of action. Perhaps I was a fool not to go with them to Russia, as they offered me the chance of doing. Some old notion about not liking to be called a deserter. And so . . . I have deserted! No use going back upon it now. I'll just take my chance, Laurie."

Even the brief respite upon which we had counted was abruptly cut short. An urgent order came one evening from Brigade to proceed to our positions before Bellevue spur. Two battalions of the 147th Brigade called for immediate relief.

After a short spell at Lancashire Farm, where a couple of hours' sleep was snatched, the battalion set out on the long route march. The night was pitch dark, and there was a continuous fine drizzle. For hours the men trudged along the single line of grids. In the darkness they stumbled off the duckboards and sank ankle-deep in mud. Every one was dead tired, plodding on as in a dream.

It was faintly light when we reached the assembly point. We were late. The battalion on our left had already taken up its positions. Another battalion which was to have taken part in the operation had lost its way, and never turned up. There was just time for the companies to move forward to their jumping off positions before zero hour. After a few minutes, while the details and reserves were throwing off their packs at Calgary Farm, the artillery barrage opened out. They were off. Less than ten minutes later the whole thing was over.

Wounded began to pour in. The divisional field artillery, unable to move up close enough through the sea of mud, had been firing short.

It had wrought havoc in our own ranks. The wire was uncut. The troops struggling through mud and tangled scrub up the ridge, dominated by an amphitheatre of heights lined with machine-guns and rifles, had been mowed down. Few had reached the wire. Not one of the company officers came back.

We spent the interminable day, till relief should come, bringing in wounded under heavy machine-gun fire and deadly sniping. The ambulance service had completely broken down. The wounded lay on stretchers on the floor of the farm building and around it, in the open, and could not be evacuated. The ration party could not reach us. We seemed cut off from all communication.

The young staff captain who had made out the orders and whom we had met at Zonnebeke, came up to view the situation. He had never seen the place before. He broke down, actually weeping.

"If I had known what it was like, I would have refused to write out the orders," he said.

A New Zealand battalion relieved us in the middle of the night, and what was left of ours straggled out in small parties. When we reached X camp, at Saint Jean, Adjutant Weeney sent out provisional casualty returns to brigade.

"Officers killed:—Captains Wanford, J.; Spater, F.; Gougher, A.; Lieutenants: Shakespeare, W.; Pluckley, J.; Fulliston, F.; Second Lieutenants: Hordie, W.; Tupper, F.; Melrose, M.; Sordyce, D.

"Missing:—Lieutenant, Bern, J."

I remained behind with Hooge after relief. The New Zealanders, big, cheery fellows, full of energy and confidence—unlike our own worn, weary men—gave us some welcome food. In the small hours, when all was still, Hooge and I crept up to the German wire, on the side where B Company had made its advance. So many bodies were lying about that it would have taken hours to have a look at them all by the light of the small flashlight I was carrying. Some were lying in heaps, piled one on the top of the other. We found Fulliston's body entangled in the wire. We could not find Julian's.

I returned the next night from Saint Jean camp. The New Zealanders had made their attack. The slaughter had been even more terrific than that which our battalion had suffered. The cheery colonials who had entertained me the night before were lying about, literally, in pyramids of corpses. A truce was being tacitly observed on both sides. Stretcher-bearers, with lanterns, were bringing in the wounded and clearing away the dead. There had been casualties among the Germans also. On the higher part of the ridge, near the wire, they were also removing wounded and dead on stretchers. I moved freely in front of the German positions. I even spoke to a German stretcher-bearer. After getting him to give up his automatic, I asked him if any British officers had been taken prisoner. He said there were no prisoners. The search proved again vain.

XIV

AFTER Passchendaele, the reorganised 5th Mercian battalion lost any identity it had retained with the unit to which, since the beginning of the war, I had been attached. Colonel Cator was transferred. Major Sotty, after commanding the battalion for a few weeks, had to be sent down with an attack of delirium tremens. Adjutant Weeney developed heart trouble and was invalided. New officers, a raw-looking lot, clerks and shop-assistants mostly, took the place of the dead; drafts of men, old, infirm, and unwilling, the outcome of the last ruthless combings, filled the ranks. Sergeant Day had died a few days after his transfer to hospital.

The months dragged on, desolate and disheartening. We were still in the Ypres salient, terribly depleted of men—at times only a thin line of troops in the front trenches guarded the hard-won ground—when the big German offensive broke out. I was knocked out by a shell splinter at Mont des Catts.

I was too ill and worn to enjoy the tardy luxury of hospital nursing. I had three operations. The splinter, imbedded in the muscles of the back and the capsule of the right kidney, set up suppuration. For many weeks I lay in a high fever, with spells of delirium. There is a blank in my memory of those days. I have no recollection of how I got to the large London hotel, turned into a hospital, where I gradually came back to consciousness, too weak to speak to my mother, Nora, and my father, who came to sit by my bed.

My father was kindly and sympathetic and spoke with suitable gravity the correct and expected words. He was in reality enormously proud and pleased. As was the case with many people who had relatives at the Front, the fact that in the course of over three years I had escaped being wounded had been felt to be somewhat disappointing and humiliating. My father was particularly elated on account of the D.S.O. which had been bestowed upon me, and, even while I lay between life and death, he could not help betraying the excitement with which he looked to my going before the King for the investiture.

He was indignant at the unmanly and unpatriotic suggestions concerning a conclusion of peace before the knockout blow had been dealt and the German Kaiser brought to trial before a court martial. My father had no patience with such weakling talk.

"This country means to fight to a finish," he would repeat. "It is a sacred duty which we owe to the glorious dead and a just demand after all the sacrifices we have made."

My progress towards recovery was extremely slow. Months passed by before I could leave my bed. Few, besides my own people, came to see me. Viola even did not come. Nora, who kept me posted in what minor gossip she thought might be of interest to me, mentioned that the Glamrood household was unspeakable and that Viola was having a ghastly time. But Nora did not go into details, preferring evidently to avoid the subject. Once Mrs. Cator blew in with flowers. But mine was not the sort of case on which she cared to lavish her wounded-hero-worship. There seemed little likelihood of her being able, as yet, to give me "a good time." I was, moreover, no longer in her husband's battalion, and Mrs. Cator's activities as the lady bountiful were now transferred to the colonel's new unit which, as she did not fail to inform me, was, this time, a pucka "regular" battalion, though she omitted to mention that Colonel Cator was only second in command. The change enabled Mrs. Cator to move in higher circles. But the ladies in the Guards were, she could not help mentioning, insufferable snobs.

Eleanor Astley came once. She wished, of course, to hear particulars concerning Julian's fate.

"He was, after all, only posted up as 'missing.' Surely there is hope that he may still be alive," she said.

I could give her little comfort.

" 'Missing' means that the body was not found, and that there are no witnesses to his having fallen. The circumstance can cause no surprise, since practically the whole of his company was wiped out," I said. I told her of my search on two occasions. "Naturally, in the conditions in which it was carried out, the negative result proves nothing. You know that in an attack, we wore ordinary issue khaki, so that officers are undistinguishable by their uniform from the rank and file. The place was strewn with bodies, many being heaped one on the top of the other. There is nothing surprising in a search carried out in the night, by the light of a flashlight, and under the very nose of the enemy's posts, having proved fruitless. It was some considerable time, after the Canadians had carried the positions on the ridge, that any complete clearing of the ground became possible. Also, poor Julian was very careless about his identity disc."

"But he might have been made prisoner," said Eleanor.

I shook my head.

"The German stretcher-bearer to whom I spoke said that no prisoners had been taken. I grant you that no implicit faith can be attached to the declaration. But as a matter of fact, there was no hand-to-hand fighting during the attack. The wire was, as I saw for myself, absolutely untouched. None of our men got across it, or had the slightest chance of doing so. They were mowed down by machine-gun fire, and the Germans themselves did not come out in the open and made no counter attack. There is therefore little likelihood of their having captured any prisoners."

"Then you think there is no hope?" Eleanor said after a silence.

"To be quite frank, I am afraid it is useless to delude oneself with false hope," I said.

Eleanor sat in silence, while the tears welled up in her eyes. She took leave, after she had sufficiently regained her self-control, not trusting herself to speak further.

Even while I was compelled to remain lying on my back, I had caused enquiries to be made through the Red Cross. There was no answer for months, and when they were further approached for information, they replied that no trace of Julian Bern had so far been found, but that they were pursuing investigations. Later, when after the cessation of hostilities, several thousand of officers who had been prisoners in Germany were rapidly repatriated, no trace of Julian was forthcoming, and I soon gave up what glimmer of hope might remain.

I was still in hospital, though allowed to take occasional outings, when the Armistice came. The whirlwind of the mafficking mob caught me up and swept me off my still insecure feet as I was struggling to effect my escape and boarding a homebound bus at the Shaftesbury Avenue corner of Piccadilly Circus. A party of subalterns, entire strangers to me, taking a mean advantage of my manifestly feeble condition, forcibly commandeered me, and dragged me down with them to the Carlton, where they held an orgy in the palm court. The ringleader, a young hopeful from a city battalion of the Middlesex, smashed a magnum of Mumm over the spike of a German Pickelhaube, lit cigarettes with Bradburies, and scattered round a bundle of five-pound notes for the benefit of the Swiss waiters. I effected my escape when the riot was at its height and my captors were too obfuscated to notice.

The streets were scarcely less tumultuous. Surging crowds decorated with Union Jacks bawled, to the added sounds of tin trumpets, whistles, hooters, and exploding maroons. In Wardour Street a bonfire had been lit, and the Kaiser and Admiral von Tirpitz were being burned in effigy. Munitionettes were dancing round, singing: "Knees up, Mother Brown," and "Rule Britannia." Some Belgian soldiers joined lustily in the British patriotic song, substituting, owing to their imperfect knowledge of English, their own words in Flemish. I understood enough to make out that the sentiments voiced in their version were not an exact rendering of the proud declarations of the original refrain, and that *"Britannia, küss mein kloder!"* had little reference to the rule of the waves. "Hurrah for brave little Belgium!" shouted the crowd in appreciation of the Belgians' participation in British patriotic elation. The girls bestowed embraces promiscuously on unknown soldiers and policemen. I was myself seized, much to my embarrassment, in the arms of a handsome blonde young woman who had been a chief instigator of the Belgian chorus. After sonorously saluting me, the young lady, with her arms still about my shoulders, fixed her eyes on my badges.

"You belong to the Mercian regiment!" she said. "Are you by chance of the 5th battalion?"

"That is, or was, my unit," I replied.

"Then you knew Julian Bern," the young woman said.

"I have known him for a very long time," I said.

"You are not, by any chance, Mr. Laurence Foster?" she asked.

On my returning an affirmative reply, she told me her name was Keetje Dools, and asked me to take her into a bar.

While we were making our way to the saloon, I was trying to recollect in what connection I had heard the somewhat unusual name and at last thought I had placed it.

"You used to be with my sister-in-law, I think, Mrs. Harry Foster? Julian Bern's sister," I said.

"Yes. I was skivvy in her house at Bognor," she answered, with a queer ironic smile, narrowing her eyes and wrinkling her nose, as we sat down to glasses of port wine. Then she said suddenly, "Have you seen anything of old Lady Penmore lately?"

I said that I was still in hospital, had not long been up, and had paid no calls as yet. I had not seen Lady Penmore.

"Why? Is she a friend of yours?" I asked with some surprise.

"On the contrary," said Keetje. "The old bitch has her knife into me. On account of Welby."

I then remembered something Julian had once dropped about Welby Penmore having employed the girl on some work connected with the Intelligence Service.

"Is Sir Welby Penmore . . . ?" I began. "I was going to say, 'a friend of yours.'"

Keejte ignored the interruption.

"She says she'd rather see Welby shot dead than married to me," she said.

I gave an involuntary start.

"Well, if you see her you can tell her that I don't very much care whether it's the one or the other," she went on. "But if I don't marry him he certainly will be shot, or at least be picking oakum and eating skilligolee."

"You had better tell Lady Penmore yourself," I said, laughing. "I am not in the habit of interfering in other people's affairs."

"Oh, I wouldn't speak to her if you paid me," said Keetje. "But I'd like her to know, all the same, what sort of a precious scoundrel is her Welby."

I did not venture to dispute her view, but saw no reason for pursuing the subject, and before we parted made some reference to Julian.

"I have a feeling that he will turn up," Keetje said.

"Alas, life has little regard for the convention of a happy ending," I said.

"Yes," Keetje agreed. "Life is a filthy business."

Although I had no particular reason to call on Lady Penmore, it so happened that, not long after my interview with Keetje, I received from her a note couched in very friendly terms, in which Lady Penmore excused herself on the ground of her state of health for not having visited me in hospital, and said that she would be glad if I would at any time call upon her.

My father was now a frequent visitor at the Half-Moon Street house, and seemed to be on very friendly terms with the hostess. His fortune had become many times multiplied. He had received an O.B.E. shortly after the khaki election on the occasion of which he had made considerable contributions to party funds. Our old house near Leicester was given up, and my father had acquired Cranne Hall, which came into the market, as Lady Coston found it too expensive to keep up, and too large for her personal use since Dorothy's marriage. She had come to live in London in a small flat near Baker Street. Dorothy was still in Ireland, where Colonel Luseley was actively engaged in combating the Sinn Fein guerillas.

Lady Penmore, whom I found very cordial, desired me to use my influence to persuade my father to buy the house in Half-Moon Street. She had offered it to him, she said, and he already happened to have a considerable mortgage on it, but was hesitating, saying that both he and my mother preferred a county life, and doubted whether he would have much use for a town house. Lady Penmore thought that, even should my parents choose to live at Cranne Hall, the house would make a very suitable residence for myself. I ought to get married, she considered, and hinted that she could undertake to find a desirable match for me.

I told her that I had no intention whatever of giving up my freedom. This was true in more than one sense. For, although I now kept on good terms with my father and there had been no reference to the dispute which I had had with him at the time of my departure on active service, I was nevertheless more firmly resolved than ever to be entirely independent of him, not to accept his renewed suggestions of partnership in the business, and to earn, as best I could, my own living. Lady Penmore had therefore an altogether false impression of me as a man of substance and prospects, and I sought my best, without entering into details, to disillusion her.

In the course of our conversation, Lady Penmore could not help alluding to her disgust over Welby's plans.

"I have no doubt," she said in an assumed tone of indifference, "that I shall be able to arrange a very good marriage for him. There is my old friend Lady Irene Sexborough. There has been some unpleasant gossip about her, which, doubtless, is quite destitute of any foundation. That comes of her staying so constantly abroad. It is not good form. As I have told Irene several times, she should, despite her hospital in France, have shown herself more frequently in England. However, now that this tiresome war is over—which, by the way, I am beginning to think was a mistake from the first—(we have, after all, far more in common with the Germans, who are not such bad fellows as people would have had us believe, than with the French)—now that the war is over, everything will arrange itself little by little. It is certainly about time that Irene got married; it is the best way of putting an end to silly gossip. And she has always been very fond of Welby. At the present moment he has some perfectly insane infatuation for I don't know what little foreign adventuress—something quite unmentionable and impossible, a street-walker, I think, picked up from goodness knows what gutter. Oh, I'm not really worrying very much about it. Those things are liable to happen, and are quite all right so long as they don't go too far. I suppose I shall have to see the creature and give her a cheque, although I can ill afford it at the moment."

Penwood, the house in Hampshire, had, of course, upon the death of the general, gone to Sir Welby, who was, I gathered, doing very little to assist his mother, whose financial situation was extremely embarrassed. He was at the moment in Paris in some advisory capacity in connection with the Versailles peace conference

I remained in hospital in London for a much longer period than would normally have been the case at an earlier stage, when I should, in the ordinary course of things, have been transferred to one of the numerous country houses that had been placed at the disposal of the medical services as convalescent homes, but of which the owners were now in somewhat of a hurry to regain possession. The transformed hotel where I had been treated was itself about to revert to its former use, and the wounded officers who still occupied it were encouraged to make all speed in getting well and were gently made to feel that they were somewhat of an encumbrance. The days of wounded-hero-worship were definitely over.

Eventually I went over to spend a few weeks at Cranne Hall, where a room was reserved for my use and the services of a nurse retained, while the rest of the war patients were being transferred or evacuated into civil life, and my mother was busy having the place redecorated in the Italian Renaissance style. Fortunately my progress, following the last operation, was fairly rapid, and, after a while, I seemed to be none the worse for the damage wrought by the German shell splinter.

I lost no time in setting about finding an occupation. There was no urgent haste, for my accumulated army pay, my gratuity and wound pension secured me for some time against pressing financial need, but I was anxious to assure as early as possible my independence. My pension was renewed from time to time after the formality of attending a medical board. But I received a communication from the War Office offering me a round sum in discharge of all further claims. The sum seemed at the time attractive by comparison with the dribbles of the paltry dole I was receiving. I therefore, like many others in the same case, made my way to a Nissen hut in St. James's park, where a distinctly discourteous N.C.O. in shirtsleeves made me sign a paper, counted out to me a bundle of five-pound notes, and as good as told me in the name of my beloved country to go to the devil. It was not until later that I realised what a fool I had been and to what extent I had been mystified and cheated.

My intention was to resume the literary and journalistic activities which had been interrupted by the war. My father, after giving up all hope of persuading me to enter the business, suggested that I should go on the stock exchange, and proposed to use his influence with Baron Rubinstein to procure me an opening to a lucrative position. Mrs. Cator, whom I met once again while calling on Lady Coston, offered a suggestion for my entering the wine business, which the colonel, who was at the time with the army of occupation at Cologne, intended to take up on retiring from active service. He had a very good connection in prospect, his family having been in the trade for generations, but his health had become so impaired by the hardships of campaigning—his liver was, the doctors said, in a terrible state—that he would almost

certainly require the assistance of a younger partner. I, somewhat fool-
ishly and quixotically, turned down those attractive propositions, and
looked up some of my old pre-war associates in Fleet Street, several of
whom still survived. I found them excellent and helpful fellows, and
they assured me that there would be no difficulty in obtaining a job on
one or more of the better papers. They said complimentary things about
the quality of my work having, before the war, attracted the attention
of editors, who would be only too glad . . . etc., etc.

Again, I proved unbusinesslike in not pressing the matter at once to
an issue, under the pretext that I should wait, as I could afford to do,
until I had fully recovered my health. In reality I wished to complete a
trifling novel, the writing of which had helped to while the weary days
during my long convalescence. I consulted Mrs. Montague-Douglas as
to its merits, if any, and as to the best means of publication. She had
directed her activities once more towards literature, and had now
founded a sort of writers' club, the Penmen's International Literary
League, known for short as the P.I.L.L., which was meeting with a
considerable degree of success, and was about to establish foreign
branches, in Prague, Valparaiso, Yokohama, and Seattle. The immediate success of the P.I.L.L. was largely due to its having practically
absorbed the Sybil Club, and thus having from its inception the advantage of a large membership of fairly lively young women who knew not
Victoria and the moral stuffiness handed down from her remote age.

Mrs. Douglas, after perusing my manuscript, pulled a wry face and
bluntly told me I should never make a novelist. My style, despite labored
attempts to be "modern," was distinctly pre-war. I had committed every
possible error in construction, mingled the method of personal narrative
with that of omniscience, and offended against every standard and
principle of fiction. Although I had some qualms about the realistic
treatment of some portions, which I feared might be thought cynical, I
was informed that I was fulsomely moral and sentimental. In short, I
had the conceit thoroughly knocked out of me and, despite my feeble
attempts at self-justification by saying that I knew of no way of judg-
ing in such matters what would please people except by writing what
pleased myself, I had to recognise in general the justness of the criticism
and that I was little better than an old fogy.

Notwithstanding her unsparing censure of my book, Mrs. Douglas generously exerted herself to find a publisher for it. This was no easy matter. I had inevitably embodied some of my war experiences. But people did not wish to hear about the war. It was bad enough to have had scarcely any other topic of thought and conversation during four years. Now that it was over, they wished above all things to forget about it and looked for agreeable literature which would help them to do so and to return, mentally, to the normal life of a world that had returned to normal. For they supposed that things could return to normal, and be as though the war had never been, as an incident that was now closed, leaving the world to resume its course where it had left off. When a daring young publisher eventually consented to consider the book, he found himself confronted with baffling difficulties. Some people were, innocently enough, mentioned by name, and a lawyer had to be engaged to investigate the risks of actions for libel which such mentions invited. Once set to work, the lawyer conceived suspicions that every character in the book might have some foundation in reality and that the originals would jump at the chance of obtaining several thousand pounds damages by bringing claims which, as is well known, are invariably upheld by an English court, provided the claimant occupies a sufficiently respectable social position. The attorney further discovered that allusions to sexual relations, which it is difficult to avoid in an attempt to depict life, were not treated in the unreal manner which has been prescriptive in this country for a century and a half. Such a departure from the best post-Shakespearean English usage and tradition exposed the book to suppression on the ground of obscenity. Those legal dangers did not so much arise, as was explained to me, from particular offences as from the opportunity which they afforded to bring the weight of legal displeasure to bear upon a book which, in its general tone and implications, was felt to be out of harmony with established English ideals, such as the divine superiority of the English race and the eternal character of its established institutions and tacitly recognised conventions, the love-inspiring excellence of royal personages, and the Public School virtues which animated the conduct of every decent Englishman, in a word, a book which was un-English in its outlook or, what amounts to the same thing, betrayed some measure of realistic intelligence.

Those difficulties saved, as a matter of fact, my literary career from being wrecked at the very outset. For by the time my unfortunate excursion into the realm of fiction saw the light, I had had an opportunity of establishing my respectability as a writer, and the peccadillo of my novel was leniently overlooked and attracted no attention whatever.

Perceiving in time my mistake, I hastened to accept the favorable offers which the generous intercession and recommendations of my journalistic friends procured me. At first my contributions took the ostensible form of columns of dramatic criticism, which, however, according to the conventions of English journalism, merely afforded me an opportunity to write on any subject I pleased, since there exists neither drama nor criticism in England. I had so far profited by experience as to develop a mode of expression which made it quite impossible to discover that I had any opinions or ideas whatsoever. A little practice enabled me to state facts without vouching for them and without letting it appear that I either believed or disbelieved in their authenticity, and opinions without betraying whether I approved or disapproved of them. I was thus able to say in print a great deal of what I wished to say without committing myself to having said it. The method procured for me a reputation for balanced judgment, objectivity, and impartiality, and was much appreciated by editors of even the most violent and blatant newssheets, which were thus furnished by my articles with clear evidence of their unbiased and broadminded policy, however hysterical might be the ravings of their leading articles, however fraudulent their doctoring or manufacturing of news.

For obvious reasons, I saw little of my former companions in arms, as I did not belong to any society for psychical research, and led a fairly laborious life. But I found one morning among the letters which my articles sometimes caused me to receive, one from young Viney, who was now occupying a post as teacher in some non-conformist college in the Midlands. He said in praise of my writings things which made me blush and which I could never bring myself to repeat. Had I been so foolish as to believe them, I might have imagined that I was to be regarded as the most profound thinker and most brilliant writer of the age. But I found that his undeserved praise was elicited by the very faults I had most striven to avoid, and by views which he ascribed to me, and which were the exact reverse of those I held, and the chief object of my contempt and disgust. Viney understood in a literal sense expressions and passages of which, I had supposed, the ironical tone could not but be manifest, and accepted as significations of approval references to what I had intended to hold up, by subtle implication, to the reader's scorn. I had first lamented my lack of skill and my incapacity to express myself clearly. But I very soon learned that, however lucid and direct any writing may be, it is never understood unless it confines itself to reproducing current clichés of thought with which the reader is familiar. To express a point of view which is in any degree original and personal is to court misunderstanding. This is only natural, for the great majority of readers and of reviewers being as good as illiterate, they are not prepared to undertake, in addition to the labor of spelling out his text, the task of dwelling upon an author's meaning and seeking to apprehend it, when it is not identical with what they are accustomed to read in their papers or have been taught at their colleges, unless, indeed, in the few cases in which he has acquired such a swollen reputation as to be interpreted and explained by others.

The judicious manner in which I presented my copy elicited expressions of admiration from my fellow-journalists, who conceived an altogether exaggerated notion of my wisdom and talents. They were in general the most excellent fellows. I soon discovered that their intelligence and the clarity of their views bore no relation to the stupidity and perverse muddle-headedness of what they wrote. The majority of the writers on the starkest reactionary newssheets, which were able to pay the highest fees, made me gasp, when conversing in private, at the red-hot radicalism of their views. Having in one of my articles been unable to forbear from some covert indication of my contempt for the brazen cynicism with which a certain notorious rag, appertaining to what our American cousins denote as the "tabloid press," consistently espoused the worst causes and poured forth contumely and slander upon every defender of right and justice, I received from the editor of the foul publication an invitation to lunch with him and one or two friends at the Cock. I found him a jocund and intelligent man. He was a large, rubicond Irishman, exuding genial good-fellowship, and as sharp as a needle in the shrewdness of his judgments. The tabloid editor heartily complimented me on my article, expressing entire accord with its tenor, and enunciated views in the course of conversation so unconventional that I was made to feel that I was little better than a back number.

"That we are a pack of prostitutes goes without saying, my dear sir," the editor said. "What about it? Isn't everybody? If you live within the system, you've got to be either a prostitute or a fool. Most people manage to be both. It's like the women, be they whores or wives— unless they are economically independent, which merely means that, like ourselves, they are prostituting themselves in some other manner. Can you blame them? Moral condemnation of whores comes from insufferable wowsers with non-conformist consciences, police-court and assize judges, and the like criminal cretins. Mind you, a salted whore feels humiliated only when she's not getting enough money and can't afford to be as expensively tricked out as some disgusting honest woman. The commerce of her vile body, to which she in time learns to attach but little importance, preserves intact and undefiled her spiritual independence and self-respect. Same with us. Business, which is always vile, is entirely dissociated from intellectual conscience. The thoroughgoing and unbridled prostitution of our filthy pens leaves our spirits free, our mental honesty unspotted. Trouble arises only when the dissociation is not clearly observed and realised. Your dilettante intellectual who imagines that he can combine sincerity, or art, or what you will, with bread and butter, and inject some pinch of honest thought into what he writes for money—he is the real worm. He can't do it. Consequently he has to squirm and wriggle, limed in shameful compromises. And in trying to serve both God and Mammon, he succeeds in serving Satan only till his own worm-soul is choked in brimstone. Whereas we. . . ."

"Crawford, you're the perfect Jesuit," said Baffles. "You'd argue the horns off the devil that black is white and white black."

"That's my trade, damn it!" laughed the editor, and quaffed noisily at his tankard of three X. "Tell me, whom do you account the more respectable, that finished and complete fool, the American Messiah, Wilson, with his airy talk of Cloudcuckooland, Leagues of Brigands to stop robbery, open diplomacy, disarmament and heaven knows what other moonshine, all of which would strike him with paralytic panic the moment it were transferred from the realm of blather to that of action; or the avowed scoundrels, the Tiger and Welsh welsher, and the rest?"

"Miao-o!" said the black cat, smelling the odorous fumes of the steak-and-kidney pie, and rubbing a wheedling silky flank against the editor's uncreased pants.

"Pretty pussy!" said editor Crawford, dangling a titbit over her moist muzzle. "You agree, do you not? Ever an eye on the main chance, without surrender of one jot of independence. You will not eat from my hand? There, then, have your way, you incorruptible votary of self-determination."

The mainstream of gabble directed by the editor, following the path of hydraulic least resistance, drifted to politics, while backwaters of neighborly dialogue gently rippled with amatory breezes.

"It is marvellous; it is amazing; it is almost admirable," the editor was saying.

"What is?" asked a spectacled youth of curate-like appearance, a journalist from the D.T.

"That it all goes on," said the editor, "goes merrily on, as though the bottom had not been knocked out of it. As though this world fit for heroes and made safe for democracy had not exhibited to the universal eye every bloody indecency of its inside. As though the post-war world were still the pre-war world. It goes on as though nothing had happened. Like the doughty little knight of the story who had failed to notice that he had been killed, and went on fighting although dead some time. I say it is incredible. Anybody with a pinch of gumption would have laid his shirt that the game was up. I for one would have taken my oath on a stack of Bibles that by the present calendar date the whole of Europe, including the adjacent island of Great Britain, would be throwing up barricades and hanging the boss, Northcliff, to the cranes of Carmelite House. But no sir. It still goes on, ye gods and little fishes, only more so."

"Met you, I think, at the P.I.L.L.," said my neighbor, an ex-sub, now on the *Morning Post,* who still wore his B.E.F. Charlie Chaplin toothbrush.

"Possibly," I said. "I regret that at the moment . . ."

"Remember, you were with Pamela Porter," he said.

"The niece of my old friend, Canon Fuge," I said.

"Sporty lass," he went on. "Saw her home. Felt her silk stockings in the taxi. *Das Ewig-Weibliche zieht uns hinan,* as brother Fritz says.

Quiffed and double-quiffed her on the polar bear that guards the sanctity of her hearth."

"Just look at the enormous reserves of power!" said the quasi curate. "Take England. First in the field of trade, of colonial imperialism, of industrial revolution. Pretty well a century ahead of all other nations in capitalism. John Bull can live a damned long time on his own fat, even were he unable to get a mouthful to eat. But for all that. . . . It doesn't alter the fact that we haven't the monopoly any longer, that we've become a debtor nation, that the command of the sea isn't what it used to be, nor king coal, nor India. Everybody knows that though England can bluff, and bully and bilk almost any other nation, England isn't a patch on what she used to be. Old Rep, of the *Times,* was telling me the other day that he asked one of the French general johnnies who was the founder of the British Empire. The froggy had several guesses —Dizzy, Queen Bess, and so on. No, says old Rep, the founder of the British Empire was Joan of Arc. See?"

"Smart fellow, Rep," put in Baffles.

"Awful ass," went on the curate. "England has never had any luck on the continent."

"What about Waterloo?" queried the editor.

"That was a battle, not a conquest," countered the curate. "England, which like every other country dreamed at one time of continental conquests, was driven from the continent once and for all by Joan of Arc. Wisely gave it up, and went off instead to conquer the rest of the world, at a time when other European nations did not care two straws about savage islands. Came the industrial revolution, made possible by the plunder of India, came cotton, raw materials, imperial markets. England was everywhere, and the rest nowhere."

"After that, had to wangle her a job in the Ladies' column. Couldn't get her out of the Old Man's waiting room. Pushing girls, those lady journalists," my neighbor remarked.

"We've been diddled by the French at Versailles," said Baffles.

"You fellows are all at sea," said the tabloid editor, who had, during the last few minutes, transferred his attention from the conversation to the steak-and-kidney, and drained his tankard in preparation to re-entering the field of discussion. "Bring us another half-pint, Frank," he said, turning to the waiter. "A damned good brew. Might almost be pre-war."

"Getting a bit better, sir," said the elderly waiter, smiling. "Though it isn't yet what it used to be."

"Now look here, we're not in the editorial office. You're talking in terms of the old pre-war politics. That's all very well for the editorial columns, but there's no need to turn tail out of school. The political axis of the world has shifted. *'News havong changey toossau,'* as the French say. The treaty of Versailles. . . ."

"An insane truculent creation of colonels and French generals, insuring war in our time, O Lord!" said Baffles.

"That's what you tell the public. Usual eyewash. What else did you expect? Can anything peaceful come out of Galilee? The Versailles treaty is just what all such treaties are. Robbers' sharing of plunder, England taking, of course, the lion's share. And no provision whatever for its enforcement, so that it may conveniently be regarded, like all such pompous documents, as a scrap of paper. Not half truculent enough, if you ask me. You fellows are, according to plan, serving up Versailles as a scapegoat to the public and blaming the French. That's all according to plan, as I say. But the real crime was not the treaty of Versailles, but the Armistice."

"Bloodthirsty fellow!" cried the curate.

"No, I'm not bloodthirsty," said the editor. "But what, pray, was the purpose of the war, of the bloodshedding of our golden youth without count of cost, of the sacrifice of our golden throne as the world's creditor nation? The face value, I mean, the ostensible purpose. To beat the Germans, if I am not mistaken. England shall not sheathe the sword. . . . And after four years, we have, voluntarily, and at the moment that the consummation was in our very grasp, turned aside from it, wilfully abstained from it, withheld the sword which we had unsheathed, when it was at the enemy's throat. We have cut short the war at the instant when the end was at last in sight. Instead of imposing peace in Berlin, we have restored nineteen-fourteen at Versailles. Why? Why, I ask you? Because another issue, more vital than the crushing of the barbarian Hun, had arisen. Because the Hun, to whom we had signified our refusal to parley unless he kicked out the All-highest and the saber-rattling Junkers, and was made an honest man, was about to turn Bolshevist. Therefore, and for no other reason, was the war hastily cut short in the betrayal of the Armistice, and peace patched up. We took the Hun to our bosom, we speeded to the aid of the Junkers and their Shadyman lackeys, we returned to them their machine-guns and prisoners, that Communism might be put down and Liebknecht and Rosa Luxemburg assassinated. Exactly as Bismarck returned to the monstrous gnome, Thiers, and the unapprehended swindler, Jules Favre, Bazaine's gallant traitor army, that Communism might be drowned in Paris in a shambles of blood. The great Jesuit Hun-swallower, Foch, who had sworn not to sheathe his sword save in Berlin, proposed immediately an alliance with brother Hun, to march on Moscow. Who put an end to Armageddon? Who brought the war to a conclusion? Not the goose-stepping legions of the Kaiser; not the Allies; not the Yank innocents abroad—but the Russian Bolsheviks. Hey there, Frank, another tankard of that sweet nutbrown!"

While the editor was moistening his throat, knitting his brow, in preparation for a resumption of oratory, his audience maintained a respectful silence, broken only by the murmur of inaudible sidewhispers.

"Ghastly for those Tzarist hot-house flowers, that Bolshevik blast," Baffles remarked in my ear. "Last came upon one in Antwerp in 1914. A pearl of price, by Jove. Was with a very agreeable fellow. Bern, I remember. Wonder what's become of him?"

"Killed in action at Passchendaele," I said.

"Too bad. As I was saying. . . ."

"All those crocodile tears we shed editorially now over the poor old Hun—mustn't be too hard on him, you know—are just a nice little transition to prepare our volte-face. England's always been pro-Hun. The French, the traditional antagonist. Now that, for a brief moment, France is apparently cock of the walk on the Continong, it's our turn to befriend poor little hard-done-by Germany. Versailles truculence all eye-wash. Make Germany pay. As though there were the least chance of Germany ever paying. Make Germany sign. As though Germany's signature to a scrap of paper was ever worth the ink it was written with. We've done our best to keep the French from imposing conditions too hard on poo-oo-oor Germany. As though any means were provided, except beginning the war all over again, to enforce those conditions. You mark my words. Two decades shall not pass before we shall have helped poo-oo-oo-oor Germany to be a more truculent, arrogant, murderous, and aggressive pest and abomination than she ever was under Kaiser Willy or Barbarossa. *We*'ll see to that. *We*'ll see that nothing is done to hinder brother Hun from setting Europe on fire again. We'll wash out the Versailles treaty and every grain of the Pyrrhic victory won by our glorious dead. That's going to be England's task during the next two or three decades."

"You've got a vivid imagination, Mr. Crawford," said Baffles, laughing.

"Better than to have none at all, like the poor muts who swallow your stuff and mine," said the editor.

"Why the devil should we set up the Turk's head again, after knocking it down?" queried the D.T. curate.

"Why? Because, as I was telling you, the axis of politics has shifted, as it has never done since the year 4000 B.C., when this madhouse of a world was created. Because the old pre-war politics that you've been talking are finished. Dead as the dodo. The war has been a war to end politics. The last war for the old politics. Another motive, far more momentous, now overshadows and eclipses all paltry squabbles about frontiers, markets, spheres of influence, and all the litter of demoded diplomatic lumber." The editor assumed a comic solemnity, and impressively declaimed in pondered tones: "A haunting spectre stalks over Europe—the spectre of Communism."

"Pah! That's Marx's Communist Manifesto, of more than seventy years ago. A bogey to frighten children with. The spectre is not dangerous," said the curate.

"Whether it be or no, the powers on the stock-exchange, and the powers behind the stock-exchange think it is—which amounts to much the same thing. Stoutness of heart is not the leading virtue of Europe's shepherds or of the sheep that look up and are fed up. They are haunted to lily-livered ecstasy by the spectre which they bid us scoff at in public. And every act of policy internal or external is henceforth shaped by the one sole cynosure of their terror-stricken souls. The old immediate interests count no longer, the old policies are dated. Am I talking through my hat? Ask Monsieur Pichon, the French foreign minister :—

'The sole aim which preoccupies the Allies is to extirpate Bolshevism.'
Ask our F.O.:—'If an end is not put to Bolshevism in Russia at once,
the civilisation of the whole world will be threatened.' Ask Winnie
Churchill. Frenchmen are ready to hail the hereditary enemy with,
'Heil! Heil!' Austrian Jesuits are ready to lick the boots of any blue-
bearded organ-grinding Hightalian, so the spectre may be averted.
England is even ready to barter some of her empire. The empire, the
command of the sea, the life-line to India, everything can go phut, so
only the spectre, the dreaded spectre can be laid. Have you watched
Spain?"

"Not particularly. What about it?" said the D.T. "Heard of rioting
in Barcelona as everywhere else. Not much news in that."

"No. But they have inaugurated a new way with labor. The soldiery
are not wholly to be trusted, the police are unequal to the task, and the
slow ways of justice are unreliable. Gangs of assassins have been
formed, professional bandits and bravos, and young men of good family. The *'somatenes,'* as they are called, are armed by the Government,
furnished with cars and machine-guns, and provided with a strategic
leader, General Martinez Anido. They kill, they kill, without trial, rule,
or scruple. A method much in favor is to arrest liberal thinkers, pro-
fessors, and the like, or trades-union leaders, and set them free. The
notified bravos await them at the corner of the street on their exit from
prison, and shoot them. Pogroms, without consideration of sex or
age, are started in the workers' quarters. The Spanish method is generally admired in well-thinking quarters as the coming substitute for
the eyewash of democracy. The Italian Government, the Swiss Federal
Council, have sent commissions to enquire into the new admirable method, and have a mind to imitate it. England will offer no moral indignation such as is aroused in her noble humanitarian heart by the self-
defence of revolution in Russia. Watch Spain!"

"What is really happening in Russia?" I enquired.

"Winston's little war. Poor Winnie has no luck. Whatever war he
makes is a disaster. Antwerp, Dardanelles, and now the forsaken *Mur-
man,*" the D.T. said.

"Come away, away, children!" murmured the *Post* sub.

The editor raised his shoulders in a French gesture.

"Posterity shall know," he said. "We can't. Nobody can get there, or hear therefrom, and the truth about Russia is unprintable, as the atrocity writers of Stockholm and Helsingfors say. Of one thing only are we certain. Bolshevik Russia is the hidden hand that henceforth sets the stage of Europe's contemporary secret history—the only real one, the external show that still babbles of imperial or democratic politics and national diplomacies being mere eyewash and camouflage. Our bread-and-butter, boys. The bill, Frank! No, it's my shout."

Having arrived at much the same conclusion as the editor, that the issue raised by the Russian revolution reduced all others to insignificance, I had neglected no occasion to inform myself on the subject. But the only available information at the time was such as was furnished by the press, of which I append a few haphazard samples—

Wallowing as they have been in the very depths of abomination, and going from crime to crime under the hypnosis of an "idea," they recoil before their own misdeeds . . . and at the first sign of organised retribution will come repentant to submit to authority. The Allies must render effective support to the opponents of Bolshevism.—*The Times,* Jan. 1, 1918.
. . . Bolshevism as a religion cannot last, because its aims are purely material.—*Daily Telegraph,* Jan. 11, 1918.
The rule of People's Commissars is the rule of usurpers who have seized the reins of government by sheer brute force and are using them in order to realise their policy of fantastic Communism.—*The Times,* Jan. 24, 1918.
RUSSIA REAWAKENING . . . the heartfelt disgust of the Russian nation at the result of their twelve months' spree. A new spirit is coming over the nation. Even the Russian workman is undergoing a radical metamorphosis. . . . They begin to recognise that brain counts for something, and they have doubts as to the wisdom of their leaders who have too plainly been using the masses for their own advantage.—*Morning Post,* April 1, 1918.
BOLSHEVISM IS NEARING ITS END.—*Morning Post,* 1st May, 1918.
PETROGRAD REDS FLEEING . . . the people of Petrograd, especially the workmen, who were recently armed by the Bolshevists for the defence of Petrograd, have turned upon their oppressors. A desperate battle is going on in the streets.—*Daily Mail,* May 24, 1918.
EXECUTIONS BY WOMEN—MORE CRUEL THAN MEN. . . . Nearly one hundred executions are known to have been carried out by these murderesses.—*Daily Mail,* June 26, 1918.
RUSSIA'S REVOLT AGAINST BOLSHEVISM—MOVEMENT SPREADING.—*Daily Telegraph,* June 27, 1918.
BOLSHEVISM ON ITS LAST LEGS—REPORTED FLIGHT OF LENIN.—*Morning Post,* Sept. 6, 1918.
Russia in her agony is crying aloud for help and we must respond to the call. She cannot emerge from the chaos into which the war and revolution

have plunged her without foreign assistance. . . . There is reason to believe that in this country there is subterranean Bolshevist propaganda going on.—Sir George Buchanan, British Ambassador to Russia, in *The Times,* Sept. 7, 1918.

LITVINOF ARRESTED AT GOLDER'S GREEN—WORSE THAN FRENCH TERROR—SOVIET'S MANUFACTURED VICTORIES. . . . The Red army is so weak that it is only able to hold its front against the Czecho-Slovakians because the latter move always slowly. . . . The Bolshevists are unable to get troops.—*The Times,* Sept. 11, 1918.

PETROGRAD BURNING—INDISCRIMINATE MASSACRE PROCEEDING IN THE STREETS.—*The Times,* Sept. 12, 1918.

There is a general saying among the people: "The British will come to help us."—*The Times,* Sept. 16, 1918.

BOLSHEVISTS DEFEATED—OFFICERS DESERTING TO BRITISH.—*Morning Post,* Sept. 18, 1918.

BOLSHEVISM UNMASKED—LENIN AND TROTSKY GERMAN AGENTS—DOCUMENTARY PROOFS.—*The Times,* Oct. 18, 1918.

The Allied powers plan to form an economic ring around Bolshevism. . . . As for the character and the acts of the Leninite tyranny, we may cite the most recently published pieces of first-hand evidence . . . the character of the hideous cruelty with which the Tzar and his family were done to death. . . . The result . . . is described by the apologists of Leninism as "majority rule" (Bolshevism), though they are good enough to allow that it is, on its own showing, a class despotism. . . . Its central principle is that the proletariat is entitled to wield absolute power over the community, and the group of illiterate dupes whom the leaders have inflamed to the ends of blood-murder are doing as they have been taught. How can any sane man talk of a settlement of Europe and an establishment of peace while demanding that nothing shall be done, even in the way of self-defence, against this scourge. . . . Any peace which allowed Russia to continue to exist with her present abominable government would be no peace of justice. —*Daily Telegraph,* Jan. 1, 1919.

It is only waste of time to give further information. . . . The only question is whether the various countries are prepared to make an end of Bolshevism or not.—*Daily Telegraph,* Jan. 10, 1919.

REPORTED ARREST OF LENIN—Travellers who arrive here from Moscow report that Trotsky has arrested Lenin and assumed a dictatorship.—*Morning Post,* Jan. 10, 1919.

FLOGGED INTO FREE LOVE—The decree for the nationalisation of women has been put into force and commissaries of free love have been established in several towns. Respectable women have been flogged for refusing to yield.—*Daily Mail,* Jan. 17, 1919.

M. Miliukof and his colleagues of the Russian delegation now visiting this country are doing their best to enlighten British opinion as to the true nature of Bolshevism. They find, to their surprise, that some people are still inclined to take the view that the Bolshevik system should be given a fair chance. . . . Our position is that Bolshevism is the blank rejection of ordered government and civilisation and that there will be no tranquillity in

Europe until it is destroyed root and branch. . . . The menace of 1789 to Europe was negligible compared to that which now confronts us. . . .—*Daily Telegraph*, Jan. 17, 1919. (Leading article.)

Petrograd is considered doomed. What means doom to Lenin's adherents will of course be salvation to the remaining inhabitants of the tortured Russian capital, and that is undoubtedly the majority. . . .

Under Bolshevik administration all in the city are starving to death, save those upon whom the ruffians in power depend. . . .

It is strange to any one with even a little knowledge of history, to hear this death-gang of ruffianism and folly compared, as it has been lately in certain quarters, with the rule of Revolutionary Committees in France a century and a half ago. . . .

Fifty million Russians refuse categorically to make any compromise with beings whom they do not regard as human.—*Daily Telegraph*, Jan. 25, 1919.

BOLSHEVIK ATROCITIES—It is credibly asserted that not one child above 12 months has been left living in Perm. . . .

BOLSHEVIK TERROR—A NEW SERFDOM—It is quite certain that the armed force of the Bolsheviks cannot offer any serious resistance to organised and well-armed pressure.—*Daily Telegraph*, Feb. 1, 1919.

LENIN PREPARED TO SURRENDER TO ENTENTE.—*Daily Telegraph*, Feb. 3, 1919.

LENIN INCITING TO PILLAGE AND ASSASSINATION.—*Daily Telegraph*, Feb. 4, 1919.

The situation is getting more terrible every day, and Helsingfors is filled with Russian officers who have fled.—*Daily Telegraph*, Feb. 6, 1919.

CITIES OF THE DEAD—DREADFUL PLIGHT OF MOSCOW—The Bolsheviks are withdrawing their troops from Petrograd. The remainder of the population, only now about a half million, are threatened with certain death if no outside help comes. . . . Moscow has suffered more than Petrograd. It is like a city of the dead. . . . There are only a few schools open. . . . The churches have no priests.—*Morning Post*, Feb. 11, 1919.

TRAGEDY OF RUSSIA—EFFECTS OF BOLSHEVIK MISRULE—TERRIBLE SCENES—. . . The Bolsheviks could not rely on support from any class if there were any intervention. . . . There is no real revolutionary feeling among the workmen. . . . All plants, factories, cinemas, and theatres have been "nationalised," which really means confiscation . . .—*Morning Post*, Feb. 18, 1919.

LEADERS' DISSENSIONS. . . . Trotsky, Bukharin and Zinovieff are pulling in one direction; Lenin and Chicherin in another.—*Morning Post*, March 22, 1919.

(Paris.) A powerful press campaign is going forward with the object of swaying public opinion in the direction of a military expedition to combat Bolshevism in Eastern Europe and the journals are picturing vividly the sinister consequences to the civilisation of the world which the spread of the anarchist movement would engender.

BOLSHEVIK MONEY—It has been ascertained beyond a shadow of doubt that the Russian Bolshevists are giving large sums of money . . . millions to newspaper propaganda.—*Daily Telegraph*, March 9 and 11.

The Bolshevik régime is nearing its fall.—*Daily Telegraph,* March 14, 1919.

LENIN AND TROTSKY AT LOGGERHEADS—Lenin and Trotsky, as is doubtless known in Allied countries, have come to a definite break.—*Morning Post,* April 2, 1919.

RUIN OF RUSSIA—BARBARITY OF THE BOLSHEVIKS— . . . The children go to school because they get a free meal, but in one case even this had to be stopped because the children contracted venereal disease through the filthy condition of the utensils used in serving meals. . . . It is noted that the Jews figure very largely in the Bolshevik organisations.—*Morning Post,* April 4, 1919.

THE BREAK-UP OF BOLSHEVISM— . . . we . . . have . . . no other motives but to see order restored and the Russian people put in a position to choose their own form of government.—*The Times,* leader, May 5, 1919

The women workers in the Treougolnik factories were particularly violent and thrashed the Communist labor leaders, who were endeavoring to harangue the workers. For the first time the cry was heard in the streets of Petrograd, "Long live Kolchak, our savior!"—*Daily Telegraph,* May 12, 1919.

The problem of Russia remains a cardinal factor in the future of the world. Until it has been satisfactorily settled there can be no assured peace, no real League of Nations. . . . She is seeking to liberate herself from the monstrous tyranny which the Bolshevists, with German aid, have fastened upon her. The statement of Mr. Bonar Law on Tuesday holds out the hope that at last the Allies may be meditating a bolder application of the principles on which their efforts to aid the Russian fight for freedom must be based. . . . We believe that it will speedily strike down the bloodiest and most brutal tyranny which Europe has witnessed for a hundred years.—*The Times,* May 16, 1919.

THE BOLSHEVIST DECLINE— . . . No one, however prejudiced, can keep up the pretence of regarding the Bolshevists as even a de facto government of Russia, and the last has surely been heard of the idea of negotiating with them.—*The Times,* May 21, 1919.

GREAT DEFEATS OF THE BOLSHEVIKS—PETERHOF CAPTURED—LENIN WANTS AN ARMISTICE— . . . Lenin has sent Admiral Kolchak a request for an armistice with a view of opening up peace negotiations.—*Daily Telegraph,* May 26, 1919.

FALL OF PETROGRAD IMMINENT. . . . Of great interest and importance is the reported capture of Peterhof.—*Morning Post,* May 28, 1919.

BOLSHEVIK ATROCITIES—None of the cities regained from the grip of Bolshevism presents so deep an interest as Perm. . . . Is it surprising that the whole population of the region is determined to exterminate the Red peril? . . . Of course, not all the Permians, even of the educated classes, resisted the blandishments of Sovietism. Some bourgeois families did not scruple to give their daughters in marriage to the People's Commissars. But the day of reckoning dawned when the Whites entered the city. The guilty parents and brides received twenty-five strokes with the lash.—*The Times,* May 28, 1919.

TORTURED PRISONERS—BOLSHEVIST DEVILRY—FIENDISH ORGIES—The Commissars nightly made merry while the Bolshevist, Chinese, and other ghouls were revelling in a more ghastly manner. Comrade Edward played the piano or the mandoline while the tortured were screaming. There were round-ups of girls, who were ostensibly mobilised for communal work, but were violated by the Commissars and their subordinates.—*Morning Post*, August 5, 1919.

LENIN'S POWER WANING—The rulers of Russia at present are the most extreme reds, real anarchists. The most powerful man in Moscow or in Russia now is the Lettish painter, Peters, well known in London in connection with the Sydney Street affair. Trotsky also is not in Moscow and is no longer powerful.—*Daily Telegraph*, August 14, 1919.

CHILDREN MURDERED—It is learned from a very reliable source that the Bolsheviks have completely devastated and ransacked the stanitzas of the upper Don district. . . . The population has undergone unspeakable cruelties; children were killed in their cradles, old people were burnt together with straw. . . .—*Daily Telegraph*, August 22, 1919.

SCARED BOLSHEVIKS—A NARROW MAJORITY—LENIN FOR SURRENDER— . . . The Bolsheviks have actually considered the question of capitulation, a ballot of 200 votes being taken. Trotsky, Radek, and Chicherin, who are against surrender, received a majority of only 12 votes. Lenin and Kameneff are in favor of giving up the game. For obvious reasons the news of the ballot was not announced.—*Daily Telegraph*, December 15, 1919.

XV

"Mnie vsio ravno—stradat il naslajdatsia
K stradaniam ya privik uje davno,
Gotof ya plakat i smieiatsia:
Mnie vsio ravno, mnie vsio ravno!"

(Pain or joy—it's all one to me,
So much and so long have I suffered, I
Am ready to laugh, am ready to cry:
It's all one to me, it's all one to me!)

THE soldiers who stood drinking at the bar joined occasionally in a verse, while the landlord of the *traktir* sat playing the accordion and singing, swaying from side to side.

"Friend or foe—it's all one to me,
It's all one to me, it's all one to me!"

"Come along, children," said one of the soldiers after a while. "That Grand Panjandrum of a *vachmistr* has an English watch which is always ahead of time. If we're half-a-minute late for evening inspection, there's no telling what trouble he'll make for us."

They gulped down their vodka and prepared to leave. The one who had last spoken handed the landlord a note. The little landlord examined it curiously, holding it in both hands.

"It's a good brand-new rouble printed in Stockholm," the soldier said. "Come along, you damned Bolshevik, give me the change."

"Bolshevik! Me?" the man laughed out a little artificially. "That's a good one. Why, I'm a properly baptised Orthodox. Bolshevik? Do I look like it? Look at my nose. They wanted me for the Pavlovski regiment, I've such a Kalmuk nose—if only I'd been taller."

He handed the soldier some *patioki*—five-kopek pieces—out of the till. As the soldiers walked out, swaggering in their long-skirted coats, he held the door open for them with ingratiating grins, and stood, after they had passed, calling out:

"Long live the saviors of Holy Russia!"

They went off at a swinging pace along the road, singing:

> *"Marsh, marsh,*
> *Generale nash,*
> *Raz, dva, tri,*
> *Russkie pali!"*

The voices died in the distance. After closing the door the host walked back to the bar, where the serving girl, a stolid-looking wench with a brightly colored handkerchief round her head, was washing up the glasses.

"*Kradeki!* Damned thieves!" he murmured.

He turned round to the three men who were seated at a table near the stove eating cabbage soup and drinking tea in silence. They were the only guests left, and the host, who had been watching them from the corner of his eye while he sang, had not yet had an opportunity of satisfying his curiosity in regard to them.

They were a sorry-looking lot. The two older ones had unkempt beards and sallow, haggard faces. The younger looked also weather-beaten and haggard and had a several days' growth of bristles, but his features were finer and clear-cut. All three were wearing much worn and patched military coats, buttoned up to their necks. From the portions of nondescript clothing which appeared in places from underneath, one was led to suspect that they didn't have much on under their overcoats. One of the bearded men had his legs swathed in sacking tied round with string. They were eating the steaming *chshee* greedily, like very hungry men.

"From the front?" asked the landlord cheerily.

"Yes," replied the man with the rag leggings, "or rather . . . er . . . no."

The host burst out laughing at the incongruous reply.

"You seem to be a bit mixed up, friend," he said. "That's something like the way I answer when they ask me if I am a Partisan or a Volunteer."

"German prison camp," said the other bearded man.

"Oho! I see. So? Just got over, eh?" said the musician. "Must have had a pretty rough time? Hard going, eh? Where were you?"

"Near a place called Tilsit," said the chief spokesman of the three.
"Lots of us came away. Germans didn't seem to mind."

"And how did you come over here? By train?" enquired the host,
eager for information.

"Got a ride on a train now and then, but mostly had to walk. People
gave us food and let us sleep in their barns, here and there. Then we
got lost in the woods. Three days. Thought we should never get out.
And only little more than a half loaf of bread among us. Then at last
we got out, not very far from here."

"So? Have some vodka. Look as though you could do with a drop,"
said the host. He gave an order to the girl.

The two older men gulped down the vodka eagerly. The younger
man sipped his. But the firewater did not make them much more talkative. They spoke with difficulty, in thick voices, like men who have not
spoken for a long time. The younger man did not utter a word.

"I thought they had done away with vodka," said the man who had
last spoken, and who seemed more intelligent than his bootless companion.

"Oh yes, the Bolsheviki did forbid it, but all the same . . ." The
host winked and smiled knowingly. "And then we're no longer under
the Bolsheviki."

The three men looked up, seeming rather perplexed.

"Then there are no more Soviets here?" asked the one who acted as
spokesman.

"There won't be any very soon," the little man said with a shrug.
"Looks as though their goose were cooked." He glanced round to
assure himself that no one had come in. There was only the girl, washing glasses behind the bar, looking cow-like. "Mind you, I think
it's a pity, myself. Those officers from Stockholm and Reval are disgusting swine. The Soviets couldn't do much, to be sure, with the
country as it is. No food, no railways scarcely, no nothing. But they
did try their best to do what the people wanted. These swine don't give
a damn for the people. Treat them like dogs, and worse."

The others remained silent, expressionless. The little man was
disappointed at the difficulty of carrying out a conversation with
them.

"What's your regiment?" he asked.

"Ziechanowski," said the spokesman. "But the comrade here," he added, pointing to the younger man, "is not Russian."

"Indeed? *Nemesh,* I suppose?" the host said, turning to him.

The man spoken to gave a quick nod before the others had had time to answer.

"We've had plenty of Germans round about here," the host said. "There's a chap who is more or less with the army here, but over on the side of Latvia, called Colonel, or General Bermund. He dresses up in a Georgian *cherkesa* all covered with daggers and bandoliers, and calls himself a Caucasian. About as much Caucasian as I am! Ah, ah, ah! This Herr von Bermund is in command of some twenty thousand good sons of the Vaterland, all fitted out in Berlin with Caucasian uniforms and crosses of Saint George, and good Mauser rifles, who have been taught to yell the *Boje Tzara khrani* with a *nemesh* accent on every occasion. The boys here are not very fond of Herr Bermund and his German Caucasians, as they themselves are under the English, though between you and me, they hate the English like poison."

The three men did not seem to be much interested. After a silence, the fellow with the rags round his legs asked suddenly, looking down at them:

"How could I get a pair of boots?"

"A pair of boots? Oh, yes. Lost your boots, have you?" the host said.

"Traded them to a German for half-a-loaf of bread," said the other.

"So? By the way, you fellows ought to have another helping of *chshee.* Here, Maniacha, bring some more *chshee* for the comrades here, with nice lumps of meat. Do you good, eh? A pair of boots, you want," he went on, looking down at the man's legs. "You should have no difficulty in getting a pair of boots. There are quite a lot of Yupin in the town over yonder. You go round, my friend, and look for a Yupin who has a pair of boots you think might suit you. Then, you just knock him on the head, see? and take the boots." The little man laughed good naturedly. "Or," he went on, "if you don't feel up to killing a Yupin, you can find plenty of dead ones. They shot a batch of thirty only two days ago, and all the Bolshevik commissars. Make them dig a big pit, you know, and line them up along the edge. Then, bing bang! They make them take off their clothes first. But the Whites have plenty of good English clothes and boots. So maybe if you go round to the field on the other side of the town where they do the shooting, you may quite likely pick up a pair of boots. They'll be shooting another batch today, I think. Where are you going?"

"Comrade here wants to go to Petrograd," said the more talkative of the men, pointing his thumb at the silent young man.

"Petrograd, eh?" the other repeated. "You should have no difficulty in getting to Petrograd. You've only to follow the army. They'll be there tomorrow or the next day, or the day after. But look here, whatever you do, you'd better go and report to some one, you know. And be sure to say something about Holy Russia, and God save our Little Father, and Confound the Bolsheviki, and all that sort of thing, you know. Else . . . you might get it pretty hot. You just tell them how you've come over from Germany to save Russia. Tell them your regiment. If you don't make it all right with them, it will go hard with you, and the comrade here won't need no pair of boots."

The man who had done most of the talking glanced at the other two, and they moved to leave.

"How much do we owe you?" he said to the landlord, pulling out of his coat pocket a knotted rag wrapped round a few coins.

"Oh, that's all right," the host said. "I'm being robbed right and left just now with paper roubles printed in Stockholm or in Berlin which will probably never be worth a kopek. But all the same, I'm not going to take anything from you fellows. You'll need all the kopeks you have."

"Thank you," said the two bearded men simply. "Is it far to the town?" one of them then asked.

"Not so very far, after you've crossed the bridge. It's a straight road after that, and you just follow the main street to the square. And mind you report at once to the first sergeant you see, and say you have come to join up, as I told you. Else . . . You look more like Partisans than 'saviours of the country,' you know. Look like nothing on earth, in fact. So that you'd stand a poor chance if they just picked you up."

The three men left the *traktir,* and walked in the direction of the little town. Dry snowdust was blown by gusts of wind into drifts on the frozen road. A dark-red and lilac sky glowed in streaks under a slanting bank of grey clouds in the west, over the tops of the fir-woods through which they had wandered for the last three days. They felt better than they had done for a long time, with the vodka and the hot *chshee* in their stomachs. But their feet were horribly painful, especially the bootless man's, so that they could not swing out in military step. They passed a silent sawmill, about which lay stacks of cut timber covered with an icing of frozen snow, and then, turning to the left, crossed the wooden bridge over a stream with steep banks. They reached the outskirts of the little town. The wide, uneven road continued, with patches of round cobbles among the deep ruts, between two rows of wooden houses painted green and yellow, which stood at a lower level than the road. It was as still and deserted as the country road. As they walked on, they met a few peasants in sheepskin coats and fur caps, and two long narrow carts with high, green-painted *dugas,* drawn by shaggy little horses.

The main square was filled with a jumble of standing vehicles and horse-lines littered with straw. There were *arba* carts, limbers, field-kitchens, and four field guns. Soldiers in khaki greatcoats, in *cherkases* and high fur caps, sat and stood about. Some were singing to the accompaniment of an accordion in an old tramcar. There was a good deal of coming and going before the inn, a brick building which occupied one side of the square, while on the opposite side was an old monastery, with onion-shaped domes crowned with gilt crosses. The soldiers took no notice of the three men. They were awaiting the call to the cookhouse, and were too occupied thinking of their meal to bother about the strangers. The three men stood in front of the double flight of steps that led to the inn, uncertain what to do.

While they stood there, an officer, wearing a monocle, with a collar of mink fur to his coat, and shining spurred boots, came out of the hotel, and stood at the top of the steps, drawing on his fur-lined gloves. He stared at the three men.

"Sergeant!" he called out.

An enormous sergeant, with padded chest, and the skirts of his greatcoat sticking out below his waist like those of a woman, rushed out at the door, and, saluting, stood at attention, snapping out in stentorian voice the regulation:

"Rad staratsa vashe visokoblagorodie!"

"Who are those men?" asked the officer.

The sergeant looked round, fussed and flurried.

"I don't know, High Wellborn."

"Find out. Bring them here," the officer said.

The sergeant rushed down the steps and called the men, half leading them, half pushing them up the steps, and telling them to stand at attention before the officer. The latter looked them up and down with a cold stare through his monocle.

"What regiment?" he asked with a sardonic curl of his lip.

"Ziechenowski, thirty-fifth division, *vashe visokoblagorodie!*" said the spokesman of the three. "Just arrived, ready to serve, High Wellborn!"

The smart manner in which he snapped out the answer and stood at attention evidently impressed the officer, whose expression relaxed.

"Just arrived, eh?" he repeated.

"From the German front, High Wellborn, to serve Holy Russia," the man said.

"Take them, Sergeant, and try to find some clothes for them. You can put them in the cookhouse or transport, or something for the present," the officer said.

The sergeant saluted once more the High Wellborn and reiterated his readiness to serve. The officer strolled down the steps and crossed the square, over to the monastery.

The three men were led by the sergeant into the hotel yard, which was encumbered with field-kitchens, baggage, and other paraphernalia, and into an outhouse where some soldiers were sitting drinking glasses of tea and smoking cigarettes. The sergeant's fussy and flustered manner relaxed when he was out of sight of the officer. He told the men to sit down on the ground and wait, and asked one of the soldiers to give them glasses, so that they might help themselves to tea from the samovar. At the other end of the outhouse was a table at which other sergeants and non-commissioned officers were seated talking, and sipping glasses of tea. The big sergeant who had brought the men in talked in undertones to another sergeant, pointing to the men, telling him about them. Presently the second sergeant, a lean young man with sleek black hair, got up, looking bored, with a long cigarette between his lips, rummaged in a box containing papers, pulled out a notebook and a pencil, and sitting down before a packing-case, signed to the three men to come to him.

"What's your name?" he asked one of the men.

"Katajev, Andrei Ivanovich," answered the man.

The sergeant wrote down particulars.

"And you?" asked the sergeant turning to the man who had no boots.

"Gurudin, Simon Macarovich," the man said.

When the younger man's turn came, Katajev said:

"If you please, Sergeant, the comrade does not speak Russian."

"What? What the devil's the meaning of this?" said the sergeant.

"Do you speak German?" asked the stranger.

The sergeant spoke a little German.

"You are German?" he asked.

"No, English," the stranger said.

"Are we supposed to enlist any confounded foreigner in the Russian army?" the sergeant grumbled. "Sergeant Stavoski!" he called, and as the other sergeant came over, he asked him what he was supposed to do.

Sergeant Stavoski said that Captain Chermakof had said to take on the men, so they'd better be taken on. After all, the English were allies. Anyhow, the matter could be gone into when they were in Petrograd. There wasn't time for much fuss now. Captain Chermakof had complained that they needed another orderly to wait in the mess. The Englishman would do. Sergeant Stavoski had better send the fellows to the quartermaster, get them cleaned up a bit, and get some boots for Gurudin. The other sergeant shrugged his shoulders, lit another cigarette, and directed the men according to Sergeant Stavoski's instructions.

The sitting room of the hotel was not luxurious. Soiled and torn green plush armchairs with broken springs, a rickety round mahogany table bearing the imprints of the glasses which had stood upon it during three régimes, and charred at the edges by cigarettes. On the walls remained fragments of hastily torn down revolutionary proclamations and posters, which had been replaced by an old fly-soiled oleograph of the late Tzar and Tzaritza garlanded in oak leaves and crowned with the double-headed eagle, and, on the opposite wall, an ikon. The frosted glass doors communicating with the dining room had one pane broken.

They were wide open, letting in a stale reek of food. At the long table, which had been partly cleared by turning aside the soiled tablecloth, some of the older officers, among whom side-whiskers were still in fashion, were sitting round an outspread map, discussing in low voices. In the sitting room several younger officers surrounded Princess Scharowski and Nathalie Nersterski, talking mostly in French.

"Not quite so bright as the Grand Hotel at Stockholm," Nathalie said, casting a glance round the room. "But when I think that we are so near Petrograd, I can put up with almost anything. Dear old Peter! To think that we shall be there again in a day or two! '*Lubliu tieba, Petra tvorenie!*' I love thee, O creation of Peter!" she declaimed from Pushkin's *Brass Horseman*.

The young officers were flushed with excitement also, at the presence of the women, whose evening toilettes and feminine perfume lent a festive air even to the dingy surroundings. Princess Scharowski and Nathalie had arrived that afternoon from Narva. The young officers called to the orderlies to bring more champagne.

"God bless our holy cause!" cried a handsome boyish lieutenant who was not more than eighteen or nineteen, raising his glass.

All rose and sang a verse of the imperial anthem.

"Alexei Georgevich has just come from Petrograd," said Lieutenant Velikof to Princess Scharowski, presenting another young officer.

"What? You have been in Petrograd?" she exclaimed.

"I have never left it, except for short excursions across the Finnish frontier," said the young man. "For two years I have worn the abominable Soviet star and the filthy uniform of the Red Guards, and sung the Internationale. Oh, I am not by any means the only one. The Red army couldn't get on without us. Half the officers on the other side are patriots. One of them brought his company of two hundred men over to the lines of the White army before Pulkovo yesterday and had them all shot. Our men are everywhere, in the railway services, the post and telegraph, the commissariat. We have even a man on the general staff of the Red army, and another on the Cheka. Some are presidents of local Soviets."

"To our heroes!" Princess Scharowski cried.

"To the rebirth of Holy Russia!" said Alexei, responding to the toast. "May St. George, the holy martyr, lead us to victory!"

"Are you not coming to join us, Sandro Yaroslavich?" called Nathalie Nersterski to Captain Chermakof, who was in the next room discussing with the senior officers, over the map.

"In a moment, Natasha," he called back, turning round and interrupting an earnest speech punctuated by gestures with a pencil on the map.

The boyish lieutenant was recounting to Princess Scharowski the entry of the army of liberation into Krasnoje Selo. Cheering crowds had filled the streets, shouting: "Long live our saviours!" as the troops marched past the theatre where the Tzar used to attend the imperial ballet, the lines of the Preobrajensky guards' summer quarters, and the carved wooden villas of the officers. The clergy, singing, had brought out the holy ikons. Women knelt, crossing themselves. Others threw flowers, which the field boots of the troops crunched as they marched over the cobbles.

"How thrilling!" said Nathalie with genuine emotion. "A foretaste of the triumphal entry into Petrograd. Mila and I have come to see it."

Captain Chermakof, leaving the elder officers, came up, adjusting his eyeglass, and sat down beside her.

"We are not likely to get many flowers there," he said, "unless we can manage to bring with us plenty of flour."

"Oh, don't be so gloomy, *churok*," said Nathalie. "Do you think we shall be in Petrograd tomorrow?"

"You are not at all likely to be there, in any case, Natasha," said Chermakof. "We shall have to fight our way, step by step. Petrograd is full of barricades and barbed wire. If all goes well, if the English silence the guns of Kronstadt and Krasnaia Gorka, as they have promised to do, if the attack on Pulkowa, on our right, succeeds, if we break through to the coast and disengage our left flank, we might possibly reach the outer suburbs tomorrow or the next day."

"What a lot of 'ifs'!" said Mila Scharowski. "You are not cheering."

Chermakof raised his shoulders.

"War is made up of 'ifs,'" he said. "And if tomorrow does not bring a smashing victory and clear the Oranienbaum coast, we might as well return to Stockholm, and you adventurous ladies had better hurry back to Narva and Reval as fast as you can."

"You are indeed encouraging, *churok,*" said Nathalie, tears almost starting to her eyes. "We thought to give you a nice surprise and cheer you on to your triumphal entry into Peter, and this is how you receive us."

"I for one refuse to be upset by your gloomy mood, Alexander Yaroslavich," said Mila. "How can a ruffianly rabble, the scourings of the Wyborgska and the Petrograd factories, stand up against our magnificent troops? They look so smart in their new English uniforms! Why, look even at that orderly who has just filled my glass. He looks like an English gentleman. Do you know, he curiously reminds me of one I met at Nice."

"We'll make the cowards run, don't you fear, Princess," said young Lieutenant Velikof, "and send them jumping down the cliffs into the sea, like Gadarene swine."

Chermakof glanced at him nonchalantly, puffing at a cigarette.

"Swine, if you like," he said, "but, as a soldier, I must give even the devil his due. They are not cowards. Their artillery fire is rotten, but they can fight. In the last attack I saw a company of them march against a tank. They didn't even take the trouble to duck. They got decimated, of course, but enough of them reached the tank to climb all over it and ram their bayonets through every opening. They captured it without firing a shot, with nothing but cold steel."

"They are driven by their Bolshevik Jew masters," said Princess Scharowski.

"Unfortunately, they are driven by an idea," said Chermakof. "It is we, who should be inspired by every noble idea, the rescue of our country, Holy Russia, honor, religion, duty, who are unable to unite, and are always divided. At Reval, it was disgusting. All the beasts of prey, the profiteers, the sharks, some of whom we saw at Stockholm, immediately turned up, intent only on plunder, speculating on paper roubles, filching on army contracts, on the supplies furnished by the English, exactly as in Petrograd in the last years before the breaking up. And everybody thinking of his own advancement only, scheming for posts, offices, jealous of everybody else. They formed a phantom Government, you know, with sixteen cabinet ministers, with their ministries in their hotel bedrooms. A minister of Commerce, a minister of Industry and Public Health, a minister of Internal Affairs with only a couple of villages to govern, a minister of Marine with only one old out-of-date gunboat, and so on. Those scoundrels of Excellencies, who licked the boots of their English paymasters, had the impertinence to give, at their bidding, their official 'recognition,' if you please, to the independent states of Finland, of Lithuania, Latvia, and even White Russia, unblushingly signing away the heritage of Peter the Great. And we, of the Tzar's guard, had to receive the orders of the English, who treated us as though we were niggers, issued their commands, and went off to fish salmon. The Germans established at Helsingfors laughed at us, their 'general' Bermund, disguised as a Georgian, ignored us, the wild Batka, Bulak Balakhovich, and his Cossacks carried on a guerilla war of their own, refusing to co-operate with the Volunteer army, and even the dirty Letts, jealous of the independence of the puppet state carved out of Russian soil by the English, stand by with crossed arms, and will do nothing even to safeguard our lines of communication. Every one is thinking of himself only and is betraying Russia. Whereas the accursed Bolsheviks . . . they at least sink their quarrels for the time being, for what they account their common cause." Chermakof frowned darkly. "If we are beaten, it won't be by superior armaments or military tactics; it will be by superior *morale.*"

"But we are not going to be beaten," cried Nathalie Nersterski. "Here's to victory!" she called, raising her glass.

"To victory!" cried the young officers. "Bring more champagne!"

A little later, Lieutenant Velikof was bowing over the long white, jewelled hand of Princess Mila Scharowski, bidding her good night at the door of her room. With a gurgling laugh, she passed her hand round the back of his head and, drawing him to her, pressed his mouth against her red, sensuous lips. She opened the door, and intoxicated with joy, the youth followed her into the room.

"Say that you believe that we'll soon be in Petrograd together, *churok,*" said Nathalie Nersterski, as Chermakof rested his head on her small firm breasts. He smiled, covering her body with kisses.

"We shall," he said, springing out of the bed, and tearing himself away.

Long before dawn the town was full of movement. In the square only a few carts and kitchens, and a litter of straw and horse-dung remained on the soiled, frozen snow when the grey daylight had broken. The guns had gone forward to positions outside the town. Baggage trains were moving with their units. Companies marched at the slope, swinging their arms and singing. Others were falling in and forming on the square. There was a going and coming of Cossack horsemen and officers. Katajev, Gurudin, and the stranger were packing headquarters luggage and loading it on to *arba* carts. They were to follow, with the field-kitchen and baggage, a company which stood formed before the inn.

As they were about to move off, a noise of scuffle came from the other end of the square, in front of the monastery. Soldiers were dragging two men in shirt sleeves, with their hands tied behind their backs. Other soldiers were adjusting ropes to two wrought-iron lamp brackets which projected from the wall of the monastery. As the nooses were passed over their necks, the two men cried out in loud voices: "Long live the Revolution! Long live the Soviets of workers and peasants!" Their voices were choked off, and the two bodies dangled before the monastery wall, as the company moved off.

Gurudin was driving the *arba,* seated on the luggage. He had not been able to procure boots that fitted his swollen feet. Katajev and the stranger marched beside. After passing through streets of wooden houses, they came out on the open plain. It stretched dead flat in all directions. A low skyline of buildings and the onion-shaped steeples of churches showed in the far distance at various points. Also, rounded tree tops. And beyond them, in places, a pale, steely streak of sea. In the mist that hung over it, the forms of ships could be made out.

Troops were already in extended order to the left, in long lines curving in the direction of the sea. The company to which Katajev and his companions were attached was on the extreme right. There were machine-gun positions in front, and field-guns behind the troops. The baggage train had been ordered to keep close behind its unit, so as to be ready to move when the general advance should take place. They were on a cross-road leading to the main coast road. Two *sotjas* of Cossack cavalry had galloped forward, reconnoitring. Groups of officers in advanced posts were observing with field-glasses. As the company was lying at rest and the sergeants were busy forward, one of the men in the rear rank fell out, and laughingly asked Katajev for a bottle of vodka. After looking round to make sure that none of the officers or *vachmistri* was looking, Katajev drew a bottle from one of the boxes on the *arba*. The men called out their thanks, laughing, while the bottle was being passed round.

The sound of singing rose from the extreme left and gradually extended along the lines. They were singing the Russian military prayer. The chorus of deep, rich voices was impressive. The stranger recognised the hymn from having heard it in Tchaïkovski's "*1812.*" A *krestny-klod* procession, headed by bearded popes with high rimless headgear and embroidered stoles passed along the lines, carrying ikons and ornate gilt crosses, some bearing the double eagle. Officers and sergeants accompanied them, bareheaded. As they passed, chanting and making the sign of the cross, the officers and men in the ranks knelt and crossed themselves.

The procession was a long time passing along the extended line of troops. Before it had reached the right flank, gunfire started on the extreme left. Officers shouted orders. A detachment of Cossacks came riding back at full speed. Two of the horses fell, rolling on the ground with their riders.

No enemy was visible, but one felt his presence, hidden in folds of the ground in the distance. The shelling on the left became more and more violent and extended towards the centre of the line. Field guns at the back answered. Units moved forward, lay down and fired, advancing by short runs. Machine-guns rattled. The fighting was nearly all on the left, a considerable distance away from the battalion at the extreme right, but all the companies were now standing by to go into action. The engagement gradually extended to the centre. There were casualties. A shell exploded in the middle of a company as it was advancing. One could now see the machine-guns flashing from behind cover. The whole left and centre were engaged. Companies advanced, wavered, men dropping under a hail of bullets, and stopped or fell back in disorder.

There had been so far no shelling and no action on the right. The order was now passed for the companies on the right to advance. The machine-guns rattled; some were moved forward. The companies extended, wheeling round to the left, and fired three volleys of five rounds rapid. The Reds could now be seen leaving their cover and advancing on the centre, stopping now and then to lie down and fire. The White troops were falling back. The more distant troops on the left could not be seen for the confusion and smoke. The officers shouted the order to charge, exhorting the men. Two of the popes, holding up ikons, ran forward shouting before the troops. One company moved forward, slowly, hesitatingly, towards the flank of the Red troops attacking the centre. The other companies stood still. Captain Chermakof shouted the order to his company to advance. They stood still. Brandishing his revolver, he came back, and went up to the first file, repeating the order. The man did not move. Chermakof fired point blank, and the man fell. The man next to him raised his rifle high and drove his bayonet into Captain Chermakof's belly.

One of the popes had fallen and crumpled up, hit by a shell splinter. The other ran back, bareheaded, holding up a gilt cross, shouting to the men. A man raised his rifle and shot him dead. Then the men began shooting all the officers, who stood, about half-a-dozen of them, in front. They fell one after another. A fat colonel doubled up and somersaulted like a shot hare.

Katajev ran forward and took off a dead officer's boots, planting his foot in the officer's crotch as he pulled the boots off. He also took the greatcoats off two dead soldiers, picked up some automatic pistols from the officers, and ran back to the *arba* with the booty.

The Reds were now coming forward in force, driving back the main body in disorder. A body of Red cavalry came at a gallop towards the right companies. The men held up their rifles reversed, shouting:

"Long live the Soviets of Soldiers and Peasants!"

The Red horsemen slowed up and approached, smiling. The rout of the centre and left was now complete. Bodies of Red infantry and cavalry were pursuing them in the direction of the town. The companies on the right, which had at first been somewhat behind the main body, now found themselves forward among the Red reserves, which were coming up. Presently a motor-lorry came up along the road, into which White officers were hoisted by Red Guardists with fixed bayonets. A second lorry arrived.

"Get in, comrades, we'll give you a lift. No doubt you're tired," called out a Red Guard.

The men, who had given up their rifles, crowded into the lorry.

Katajev, who had come up with the *arba,* unyoked the nag, and with a rope tied the *arba* to the back of the lorry, to the amusement of the men.

"You'll need some new springs on your limousine, comrade," a Red Guard said, laughing.

The lorry full of men from the White company and several Red Guards started off down the road with the *arba* in tow. The lorry with the officers had to wait while some more were being brought up. The lorry and attached *arba* bumped and rattled over the broken road ploughed up with deep ruts and puddles. Presently they reached the main road and the going was a little better. The road skirted the grey, misty sea. From the *arba* to which they clung, Katajev, Gurudin and the stranger could see the main body of Red troops occupying the little town, and red flags being hoisted. On the right of the road were the bare trees of dismal, neglected-looking parks and gardens, and decayed mansions with Greek peristyles of peeling plaster columns.

Shortly after they had passed Peterhof, near the monastery of Saint Sergius, a group of about ten men in khaki greatcoats came from behind some trees on the shore side, and stood in the road. They looked enquiringly at the lorry as it approached.

"What news?" called out one of them.

The light was getting dim, and the details of their uniforms were not easily distinguishable at a distance. The men on the road also peered at the occupants of the lorry to make out their uniforms. As the lorry slowed up, and the men on the road saw the high fur caps and new coats, they raised a shout, and some of them tore off the large red cockades they were wearing on their greatcoats. The voice of the man who was at the head of the party was heard as he came up towards the lorry. It was an English voice, speaking English.

"By Jove, they're Whites," he said.

The lorry had stopped. From the *arba* cart, the stranger jumped off and went towards the man who had spoken. He was a red-faced colonel in British uniform.

"You are mistaken, sir," said the stranger. "These are not your White friends. But there is at least one Englishman among the defenders of the people, and he has no scruple in shooting you down as he would vermin."

Before the colonel and his companions had had time to recover from their surprise, the stranger, drawing an automatic pistol, discharged it at the colonel.

The Red Guards in the lorry had meanwhile raised their rifles and opened fire. As the colonel fell, five others dropped to the ground. The rest ran back, firing revolvers. They disappeared in the dark among the bushes.

"Prievoskhódno, tovarish!" called the Red Guards, clapping the stranger on the back.

They drove on in the dim light. The skyline of roofs, chimneystacks, domes and spires of Petrograd sprawled over the flat plain. They passed through silent and deserted suburbs. At the Narvaskaïa, a barricade of barrels, paving stones, corrugated iron and barbed wire blocked the road. A sentry post of sailors guarded the barricade. The lorry had to meander through side streets to reach the old Preobrashenskii barracks. As it was turning sharply into the Nikolajewskaïa, the rope which held the *arba* in tow broke, and the vehicle capsized on the curb of the sidewalk.

Katajev, Gurudin and the stranger picked themselves up. A crowd was gathering as the news of the rout of the enemy spread and detachments of cavalry and motor vehicles began to return. The attention of the occupants of the lorry had been drawn by the scene as they approached the central parts of the city, and they had not noticed at the moment the disappearance of the *arba*. The three men walked along the Ligovskii canal to the Nevski, now called the Twenty-fifth of October Prospect.

In spite of the late hour, the whole population seemed to turn out into the streets which had, only a short while before, been like the deserted streets of a dead city. Lights appeared at the windows, which had previously been kept dark from fear of the English airplanes. The barricades and obstructions were being removed to clear the way for the returning troops.

"I never thought they would ever be coming back, did you, comrade?" a man said jovially to Katajev as they stood looking on from the sidewalk.

The returning detachments of Partisans which people had gathered to see and cheer had not the appearance associated with victorious troops decked up for a triumphal march. There were horsemen on small, shaggy mounts, the harness of which, as well as that of the teams of the carts of all shapes and sizes that did duty for limbers, was patched with rope and cord. The men had no uniform except large red rosettes and badges indicating their units. They were attired in a variety of civilian clothes and wore all sorts of headgear, fur caps of all shapes, tweed caps, soft felts. Some even wore bowlers. They were unkempt, worn, tired, serious. The stranger looked on curiously. He had seen the armies of many nations parade in the glamour of drilled military smartness. But he had never been moved, as he was by the sight of these extempore soldiers. For there was in the faces of those tired, unkempt men a grave, determined look which made the set faces of drilled battalions on parade seem mean and paltry. They were not made soldiers by the orders and the discipline to which they conformed, but by the purpose which they lived. He was reminded of the volunteers of Valmy and Bunker Hill, and he joined in the cheers of the crowd with an emotion that was spontaneous.

The detachments came from the Krassnoje Selo front and were returning to rest at the Pawloski barracks, on what had been the Field of Mars, but was now known as the Field of Martyrs. After they had passed, the three men strolled down the street in the same direction. At a corner near the Kazan cathedral there was a disturbance. Two officers in Red Guard uniform were being led off by militiamen. They had been trying to blow up an ammunition store. A crowd in which was a large number of women sought to lynch them. The four militiamen in charge of the prisoners were trying to keep off the crowd, but were being hustled, and the prisoners, who had been knocked down, were being kicked and beaten by the women. A patrol of sailors supervened, and rescued the officers, getting them away in a closed lorry.

Katajev and Gurudin were hungry. They had eaten only a small loaf since morning.

"Where are the barracks of the 5th City Defence Regiment?" Katajev asked the man who had spoken to them. He had noted that the militiamen in the lorry in which they had come wore the badge of that unit.

The man scratched his head. He did not know. A militiaman to whom he referred said the 5th Regiment were in the old Arakschevki barracks. It was a long way away, in the Jekaterinskaïa, near the Smolny.

When they got there, the sentry was puzzled.

"But who are you? You don't belong to the regiment," he said.

"No, but we came with them from the front, from the other side of the front," Katajev tried to explain.

"Then you are prisoners," said the sentry.

"Yes, comrade, we are prisoners," Katajev said.

"Comrade Captain, here are some prisoners who want to be taken in charge," the sentry called to an officer.

The officer decided they were to be admitted. Their case would be examined later.

He called to a militiaman in the guard room, who led the three men to a large bare room full of soldiers. There they found again their companions of the lorry, both the prisoners who had surrendered and their guards, as well as many other militiamen and a group of sailors. The new arrivals had been served large bowls of *chshee,* which they were eating ravenously and noisily, holding the bowls between their knees. Katajev, Gurudin, and the stranger were given portions of the cabbage soup, which had large pieces of meat in it.

The militiamen and the sailors were standing about and sitting on benches, chewing sunflower seeds. They were all talking and questioning eagerly the men who had just returned.

"It's the first real battle that I've been in," said one of the men, wiping his mouth with his sleeve. "I was a clerk before the revolution. And do you know, it wasn't as bad as I had imagined."

"It would have been very different, comrade, if we hadn't had those big guns of Krasnaïa Gorka behind us," said another. "The English gunboat was firing at them and all along the coast, but the sea was a bit choppy, so that their firing wasn't much good. Never hit anything."

"Anyhow, I expected regular soldiers who had been in the war to fight better," said the other. "They just seemed to be driven on by their officers and *vachmistri,* and when one started running, they all started running."

"We should be after those swine right up to Narva and Reval," said one of the sailors. "I'm sure we'd soon settle those wretched Esthonians and Letts. Comrade Trotsky is all for pushing on and taking the offensive instead of letting all those damned White Guards get back to safety and get ready to start all over again."

"Yes. And a pretty mess we should be in if we did anything like that," said a militiaman. "As if we hadn't enough on our hands for the present and for a good many years to come. The English and French would be only too glad if we attacked and invaded another country. The moment we gave them the excuse, they'd say we were committing aggressions, and we'd have all the capitalist countries about our ears, and the revolution would be done for. Whereas now they don't dare to make war on us openly, but only by arming the Whites, because they're afraid of their own people. No, no, Comrade Lenin knows what he's doing. No aggression, only defence of the revolution. Afterwards when we've repaired some of the damage, and built up the socialist state and a strong Red army to defend it . . . even then, we shan't attack any one. We'll just wait for them to attack us, which they'll do sooner or later. Let them, then, if they dare. It will be the end, not of the revolution, but of their precious civilisation of rascality."

The next morning all the men who had been with the Whites were taken before a regimental council and questioned individually. The president, a corporal, questioned Gurudin and Katajev, and took down their records.

"The comrade is English," Katajev said when the stranger's turn came.

"English? Ah, the English, it is difficult to trust them. They are implacable enemies of the Soviets," said the president.

Several men, who had been with the party in the lorry, and who were sitting round the room on benches, rose and related the conduct of the stranger when they had met the English officers near Oranienbaum.

The president listened attentively, but remained cautious.

"The English are very cunning," he said.

The man who was sitting on the president's right spoke German. He questioned the stranger. The Englishman's name was Julian Bern. He had been taken prisoner on the Western Front.

The president and the other members of the council consulted together.

"He had better be sent to the Cheka," was their decision.

There was an exchange of telephone messages, and long waits. The Special Commission, or Cheka, as it was called, was very busy. The case of the English officer could not be considered until the following day. He was to be sent up to report in the morning.

With the German-speaking member of the regimental Soviet and Katajev and Gurudin, who were now decorated with red rosettes and acted as escort, Julian went to the old police building in the Gorochovaïa, where the Petrograd Cheka had now its seat. The sentry at the door directed them to the second floor. They had to wait over half an hour in a bare room bordered with benches till an official of the Cheka was ready to see them.

He was a powerfully built man with black hair and eyes, obviously a workman. The report of the regimental Soviet had been sent in, and he studied it and looked perplexed.

"But what do you come to do in Petrograd?" he asked, the militiaman acting as interpreter.

Before Julian could answer, a militiaman entered with a message.

"Comrade Khatinief, the Comrade Commissar of the Central Committee has come from Moscow and wants to speak to you at once," said the militiaman.

A man in black leather jacket and pointed Astrakhan cap entered the room as the militiaman was still speaking. Wasting few words on a brief greeting, he spoke to Khatinief about an officer in the Second City defence regiment who had tried to pass over to the Whites.

"This sort of thing is happening too often," he said. "At least eight officers out of ten from the Tzarist army who are employed by the Soviets are monarchists, and are either engaged in treason or waiting for an opportunity. We have been too lenient. Our generosity has cost thousands of good lives. We wanted to keep the cause of the Revolution clean, and we were not concerned, as is infuriated reaction, with vengeance, punishment, or hatred, but with defending the Revolution. We must be ruthless, as the peasant is ruthless in defending his food-crops against vermin. The mendacity of reaction will not fail to besmirch our task, and to announce to the world atrocities and terrorism, however lenient and generous we may be. It is useless and fatal, that generosity. Tzarist officers and plotters must be eliminated at all cost. The training of proletarian officers must be accelerated."

"At this very moment, comrade, I was puzzled what to do with an English officer from a German prison camp, who came over to us the other day from the White army," Khatinief said.

"An English officer?" said the commissar, frowning. "There can be little hesitation what to do with an English officer trying to insinuate himself amongst us. You should see how the English papers are still ramping about that naval attaché who got shot down at the English embassy. You may not believe it, but they have the effrontery to speak of it as a 'murder.' I should like to know what they would do with a naval attaché of ours, or of any other country, who had arranged, as did this Cromie, to blow up the whole fleet of the country to which he was diplomatically accredited! Too bad of us to prevent him, wasn't it? No, Khatinief, there can be no trifling with generosity towards English plotters. Make short work of it with your English officer. Where is he?"

"There he is, Comrade Ogonin," said Khatinief.

During the conversation which had interrupted his interview, Julian and his escort had, at a sign from Khatinief, retired to a bench at the further end of the room. Commissar Ogonin had stood with his back turned to them. He turned round sharply as Khatinief spoke and looked at Julian, then went up to him and gazed into his face.

"So, we have met again!" Ogonin said in English, with a short laugh.

He returned towards Khatinief.

"Comrade Khatinief," he said, "leave me to deal with this Englishman. I happen to have come upon him before."

"Gladly," said Khatinief. "I have enough to keep me busy, heaven knows. Here is his examination."

Khatinief left the room. After reading through the papers he held in his hand, Ogonin told the militiamen that they might go and, taking Khatinief's place at the table, signed to Julian to be seated.

"What do you wish to do in Russia?" he asked him.

"To fight, for once, against the real enemy, so as to indemnify myself for having during three years campaigned against windmills," Julian said.

"Good," said Ogonin. "But, as a foreigner, you could give but one more rank and file to our armies. We have no lack of men, we have millions of them. It is arms, munitions, equipment, transport, food, everything that we lack. A short while since, you could have been of great service, when Petrograd and the surrounding country were swarming with English agents. Now they have pretty well given up the game, so far as the northern front is concerned. They are turning their attention once more to the south, after having been driven out of Baku. It may be that an occasion will arise when you may be of service." Ogonin paused some moments, looking at Julian. "I have learnt in a hard school to judge men," he went on. "I believe you are to be trusted, and that your urge to fight the real enemy is sincere. For you understand that the enemy we are fighting against is not the enemy of Russia alone, of a power-born state, of a régime, but the enemy of humanity and of everything that is of worth and fraught with hope in humanity. But in that hard strife each has to fight with different weapons. Yours are neither the weapons of the proletarian militiaman nor those of the plotter and secret agent. You will remain with us and see. Then you will return to the West and tell them. For the present, remain with the Second Regiment of defence. In a day or two, I shall send a messenger to you. I will, now, give you a few words for the commandant, and a personal safe-conduct that will spare you any trouble."

Ogonin wrote the papers, gave them to Julian, and, shaking hands, dismissed him.

"So they have not shot you, comrade," said Katajev, laughing, when Julian returned.

He and Gurudin had lost the haggard and wild appearance which their countenances and attire had presented; their beards and hair had been trimmed down, and hollows of their eye-sockets had filled up. The militia troops in Petrograd were resting after the hard fighting and tension of the last months, and those which were being incorporated into the Red army that was being formed had moved to Moscow, where reserves were being massed to face the attack threatening from the south. There were police duties to be performed, the rounding up of White conspirators, who had swarmed into the old capital to co-operate with the army of General Yudenich in expectation of its victory. There were perquisitions for arms, of which large stores had been found hidden in cellars and under parquet floors. Julian was in general excused from those duties, and was free to wander about the city. He saw little in it to correspond with the dreams of splendor which he remembered having, as a boy, entertained. The Tzarist capital was indeed a city built for all-powerful rulers, consisting of huge and innumerable palaces, barracks, government offices, prisons, and fortresses. All gave evidence of boundless wealth and scanty taste. Without the glint of gold-braided uniforms and the glitter of luxury, without the hieratic savage pomp of mystic autocracy and its church, without the pageantry of extravagant and reckless pleasure, it must needs always appear a dead city—for it is the city of a world that is dead— being voided of those purposes for which, exclusively, it had been raised upon the marshy plain at the cost of 200,000 lives, by chained serfs bringing into material existence with their blood the caprice of a demented tyrant. The vast open spaces of the "prospects" and squares, intended, like the boulevards of Baron Hausmann, for the evolutions of the troops necessary to dominate the mob, must continue deserted-looking no matter how many millions of citizens they may contain.

On all the open spaces, in front of the Isakskii cathedral, on the palace square, squads of men were drilling, workmen in caps, men in bowler hats. A mixed, pathetic-looking lot. But no one could have thought them ridiculous as recruits always look when first drilled in civilian clothes. They were too serious and earnest for one to laugh at them.

Leaning on the massive parapet, Julian stood musing on the Neva bank. The line of palaces, with their garish daubing of chalky red, yellow, green, and white, which imparted a barbaric note to the stately mediocrity of the Germanic barroco, now presented the aspect of carcasses where rapidly encroaching decay followed the extinction of the last spark of life. Most of the façades were pocked with the marks of bullets and had broken window-panes. The plate glass of several of the windows of the Winter Palace had been shattered by the shells from the gunboats on the river. Perhaps from one of those windows, on the night of a court ball, amid the glitter of jewels and uniforms, a girl had looked out on the icy moonlit river and the silhouettes of the fortress of St. Peter and Paul, where the last Romanofs had, a few weeks since, fallen before the firing-squads.

"Which is the Nevidof palace?" Julian asked Katajev as they walked up the Nevski, where a demonstration carrying red banderoles inscribed with revolutionary slogans was passing.

"Don't know," said Katajev. "Comrade, which is the Nevidof palace?" he asked another militiaman who was with them.

"Nevidof? O yes, that's it over there. It's a hospital now. There are no Nevidofs there now," the man replied.

"None?" Julian said.

"No, none," the man repeated.

One morning, in the barracks, just as the midday soup had been taken and cigarettes were being lit, a commander entered the mess room calling out Julian Bern's name. With him was a martial-looking young woman in a leather jacket, short black skirt, high boots, and with a white Astrakhan cap on her head. As Julian rose in answer to his name, she walked up to him, looked him closely in the face, and said:

"*Tui Yulian Bern?*"

"*Da,*" he replied.

"*Idyi za mnoi,*" she said, signing to him to follow.

A car was waiting before the gate of the barracks, into which the young woman signed to Julian to enter. They drove away in silence. Julian had picked up a few words of Russian from the prisoners with whom he had been some time, but it was too rudimentary for conversation, and the young woman apparently spoke no other language. They got out in one of the short streets that open out of the Milionaïa. She rang and, when the door had been opened from above, they went up to the second floor, where a girl with a handkerchief round her head held the door open. In the dark, small hall, Julian was asked to wait a moment, while his companion went in, pushing open a door and closing it again behind her.

After a few moments she returned and, holding open the door, signed to Julian to enter. He was a little dazzled, after coming out of the dark hall, for rays of sun were streaming into the room. After standing a moment at the door, looking with a smile into the room, the young woman closed the door behind Julian.

X V I

Aclear blue star twinkled in the dark sky. Julian had been looking at it for a long time. He did not know how long. There
were black outlines of trees and bushes against the sky. Little
by little he remembered. He shivered. His head throbbed and ached.
He wanted to put his hand up to his head, but could not, at first, raise
his arm. Slowly, with much effort, he moved it; it was stiff and sore.
The top of his head felt clammy when he touched it; his hair was
matted and sticky, as though covered with tar. He looked at his hand.
He saw there was blood on it. He tried to look round. His body was
stiff; it felt as though it did not belong to him. After a while he managed to raise himself a little on his elbow. There was something lying
across his legs. It was the body of a man. There was another body by
his side, lying face down. They were motionless. He touched them.
They were cold, dead. Julian looked round. Gradually his eyes became accustomed to the darkness. There were other bodies all round
him, scattered on the sloping ground on which he lay. Further down
the slope there were whole heaps of them, in mounds.

All was still in the night. There was not a sound, not a movement.
Julian lay during what seemed an endless time. He felt very cold, yet
his head, his face, were burning. He thought he heard some movement
in the distance, a faint murmur as of voices very far away. Peering
into the darkness, he saw the forms of men moving, and flashlights,
appearing and disappearing like glow-worms. He tried to call, but
could utter no sound; his mouth, his lips were parched.

Presently he saw other men moving nearer him, on the other side,
near the crest of the hill. There were four men carrying stretchers.
Another man was walking ahead of them. He now and then turned a
flashlight on to the bodies lying about. Some time later the man with
the flashlight passed close to where Julian was lying. He ran the light
of his torch over the bodies. The light fell on Julian's face. He saw

the man's face and the round German cap with a cockade, which he wore. He was a middle-aged man with scrubby blond beard and blue eyes that looked kindly.

"*Ein Tröpfchen Wasser, bitte,*" Julian said.

The German knelt down, unscrewed the top of his water-bottle, and, supporting Julian by the shoulders, gave him a drink of water. It felt delightfully cool and pleasant, despite the taste of chlorine.

Julian thanked him, as he fell back exhausted.

"*Sind Sie schwer verwundet?*" asked the German.

"*Ich weiss nicht. Mein Kopf . . . Ich habe viel Schmerz,*" Julian replied.

The German had a look at Julian's head. He drew away the body which was lying across his legs, and ran his hands over Julian.

"*Nun, es ist nicht so schlimm,*" he said, and told Julian he would come back presently. He walked off with the stretcher-bearers, who were carrying two German dead or wounded—Julian could not tell which.

He felt too weak to move. The German, who was an ambulance corporal, came back after a few moments. After he had applied a field dressing to Julian's head, he squatted down beside him.

"Ach, this dreadful war," he sighed. "When will it be over?" He chatted a while. He had been mostly on the Eastern front, he said. It was not so bad there. There had been practically no fighting for a long time. Then he asked Julian whether he would like to go to his own stretcher-bearers, who were lower down the slope. He, the German, would help him, if he wished, or call to them. "But you will be just as well looked after in a German hospital. The German doctors are very good. And surely the war will not last much longer, and you will be able to go home."

Julian said he did not care. He thought afterwards he had been very foolish. He did not know why he had not accepted the German's offer to be helped to get back to the British line. In truth, he scarcely knew what he was saying, and had not the strength to will.

"Do you think you could stand up and walk a few yards?" the German asked.

With considerable trouble, and after several attempts, Julian found he could manage to stand, leaning on the German corporal.

"You had better give me your revolver and any ammunition or bombs you may have on you," the German said.

Julian handed his revolver and three Mills bombs that were in his pockets. The German corporal half supported, half carried him through the gap in the wire and to an aid post. A young German doctor dressed his head, and Julian was given a bowl of hot soup. His head felt a good deal better, but he must have fainted from weakness, for he scarcely remembered his being taken down the line and driven to an ambulance station. He was too ill to answer the usual examination of prisoners of war, and beyond getting his name and unit, they did not trouble him for the moment. Only some weeks later, after he had been transferred to another hospital, further back, and had sufficiently recovered to be able to walk, was he told that he and some other English prisoners would have to report before an Army Intelligence officer. . . .

They were in some village in Belgium. The wounded English prisoners, about six of them, Julian being the only officer among them, were taken under escort to the examining officer's office. Near a dilapidated little château they passed a group of higher officers, among whom several generals, standing by, talking. The officers glanced at the prisoners as they went by. An old general in a grey cloak and spiked helmet looked particularly at Julian as he passed. He called the N.C.O. in charge of the escort, and spoke a few words to him. The sergeant came back and told Julian to fall out and follow him. They went up the main alley of the dilapidated garden of the château, passed along the dusty corridor, and Julian was shown into an empty room. The sergeant remained at the door, his rifle at the slope.

After a moment the general who had noticed Julian entered the room and closed the door behind him. Julian recognised General von Dornheim, whom he had known in Germany before the war. The general came up to him and shook hands with him.

"Sit down," he said, as he took a seat before the table. "Are you badly wounded?"

"I don't think so. The doctor said I should be well soon," Julian said.

"Good," said the general. "You will need rest and attention in a hospital. You look worn. Where is Princess Hruzof?"

"In Petrograd," Julian said.

General von Dornheim remained silent a moment. He had spoken with kindliness, but with grave reserve and brevity.

"Would you like to go there?" he asked.

"Yes," Julian answered.

Von Dornheim nodded, and was again silent a moment.

"Very good. The examining officer will see you presently," he said, rising. "I wish you a speedy recovery, Mr. Bern." He shook hands again and left the room.

Julian was treated with special consideration and care, which he owed, doubtless, to the recommendations of General von Dornheim on his behalf. He was eventually sent to a hospital at Stettin, where he spent several months. When completely recovered he was transferred to Tilsit. He was lodged, as prisoner of war, in the old castle of the Teutonic knights. He was the only Englishman there, the other inmates being Russian officers. Shortly after his arrival, the armistice on the Western Front was concluded. English prisoners in Germany began at once to be repatriated, and Julian expected daily to return to England. But the repatriation of prisoners took place chiefly from the Western provinces; indeed, there was none in East Prussia. The attention which Julian had enjoyed suddenly ceased, and he appeared to have been entirely forgotten. The Russian officers, who had treated him with aloofness, left, mostly for Sweden and Esthonia. Near the town was a camp of Russian rank and file. They were loosely guarded, or not at all. They had formed a Soviet of their own, and found their way back to Russia as they listed. It was with them that Julian had mostly associated, and in the company of two of them had crossed the Lithuanian border.

It all seemed very remote, very unreal to himself, as Julian recalled it, recounting it to Zena—a great blank, dimmed and blurred by the accumulated clouding of exhaustion and torpor, the relaxation of all effort in passive surrender tc enforced inactivity; like a wide gulf between the unrealities of the war and the even greater strangeness of the present.

"I feel," he said, "as though I had already lived several lives, distinct and discontinuous from one another, in different worlds. As though I had been different persons. And I look back upon past selves as I might upon some other individual that I had known, but that is a stranger to my present self."

"Yes, you have changed . . ." said Zena, looking back into his stained, life-ploughed face, "you have changed. I, too, for that matter."

She had, Julian also thought. It had been strange that first sudden recovered sight of her. The image of her in his memory had to become adjusted, modified before it could blend with that of the woman who now stood facing him, in her simple white frock, her plainly dressed hair, worn short, with none of the studied elegances that had been part of her in the past. There was more than the passage of years in the change that had come upon her, as the image stamped in his memory recalled her, in the seriousness that had settled upon her features, her subdued manner, the traces of trial in her pallor, the wistfulness in the brightness of her eyes, that seemed expanded and haloed with faint shadows.

She and Julian recaptured by degrees the common memory of their own past selves, similarly transmuted, as if they had, though apart, shared the tempering of trial, of despair. Each found again in the other the continuity of his own being in common wistfulness, and the weight lifted, the heavy stuff, in mutual recognition, in a great release. Not as of yore in the passion of joy, but in a new joy of release from their aloneness, a deeper sense, full of the tears of things, were they urged, homing, to each other's arms.

The growth in Zena through the events that had swept round her life was, in reality, not so radical as, superficially, it might have appeared. She had always accounted with resigned scepticism and essential contempt that world from which she had drawn the opportunities of insubstantial pleasure which it afforded. She felt a satisfaction in the belying of her own scepticism as to its immutable and invincible permanence, a pleasant surprise in the contradiction of herself by the event. Whether the new world that was being born in travail and suffering could hold a trustier promise of elusive happiness, so frail and precarious in the other, remained to be seen. But her mind had mellowed into a tolerance of possibilities and larger hopes.

They talked long with unconstrained discursiveness, bridging the gaps of the years, focussing the present.

Her mother, Zena told Julian, had been asked to continue the direction of the hospital she had established. But it was no longer so greatly needed. Not that there was less misery and disease, but there was greater provision for its care, now that privilege had gone and selective charity, and ostentatious excess of military hospitals and luxurious nursing for officers.

"Matushka preferred to give it up and the old palace, and did not wish even the semblance of privilege. So we moved here. It is part of Pavel Dadianin's house—six rooms," said Zena with a smile. "He is at Kislovodsk, in the Caucasus, where most of our people, who have not left Russia, have withdrawn. I am still working at the hospital, but intend to go south, to Kursk, where they have now greater need. We shall go there, shall we? Come and see Matushka."

They passed through the dark entrance hall.

The young woman who had brought Julian had gone.

"It was Maïa," Zena said. "She is Commissar in the Cheka."

Whatever changes Julian had noted in Zena, he was not prepared for the altered appearance of her mother. But for Zena's words when she led him into the small, rather dark and dingy room, overfilled with shabby wrecks of a splendor that had at its best been tawdry, he would have hesitated before recognising the famously beautiful Daria Dimietrovna, Duchess of Friedland, in the woman who sat bolt upright in a high-backed chair in a corner of the room. The hand over which he bent was bony, prominently veined, and discolored with brown patches —that hand of which the painter Martin had revelled to depict the perfection. Under Daria's eyes were almost black half-circles which outlined the edges of the bony orbit, and, together with the prominence of the cheek-bones, suggested a fleshless skull. Julian's impression was perhaps a little exaggerated by the first shock, as he entered the room. He perceived, as he sat near her and they talked, that the mask at the sight of which he had been startled and almost repelled, was made up of the same features which, in his boyhood, had represented for him the highest vision of dazzling beauty, and which, reproduced in Zena, had become indelibly imprinted in his mind as his ideal of feminine loveliness. Daria's figure, though thinner, retained a good deal of the harmonious dignity of line for which it had been notable.

She greeted him in a voice which, as happens with hens which acquire the crowing tones of the cock, had taken on a masculine depth, but through the harshness of which could yet be distinguished the old undertone of kindliness.

"I am glad," Daria said simply.

In the first embarrassed moments of conversation, Julian inevitably referred to the commonplaces about hardship and courage. Daria overlooked the platitudes.

"I am glad," she repeated in a different connection, "that I have lived to see the crumbling down of all that gilded putrescence, carious with unspeakable iniquity. I am thankful that I have seen the end which I knew to be inevitable. But I can never be a part of the new world that will eventually grow out of present ruin. I belong to that hollow world that is now irrevocably dead. I cannot help it. They used to call me 'Europa,' " she said, with the faint flicker of a smile, glancing at a reproduction of Peugh's statue of the symbolic goddess and the bull, which stood on a table near by. "I shall pass away with the old Europe to which I belonged, thankful that I have witnessed its end."

"But you are not passing, Matushka," Zena said. "You will go, as we want you to do, to Stockholm and to your beloved Paris, and you will still be in the old world to which you are accustomed in spite of your horror of it."

Daria shook her head.

"What are they saying about us in the West?" she asked Julian.

He replied that he knew nothing, that he had not been, for a long time in the West, but in limbo, outside the world.

"Ah, yes, I gathered something from what I had been told. I forgot," she said. "There are such fantastic tribulations in people's lives these days that one ceases to be surprised—surprised at anything. Nobody knows where he will be, or whether he will be alive in a month's time."

Zena insisted again that her mother should leave Russia, should go to Paris.

"Even Maïa thinks that Matushka should go," she said to Julian. "Maïa has been good to us. Mother has done her share, she says. She should go where she can rest, away from all the strife and struggle."

"It is ended, the old world. It cannot be recaptured," Daria said. "What is happening here has changed it for ever. The old Western world will, of course, pretend . . . pretend that it is not changed, that it has not come to an end. One more pretence added to the countless pretences of which it is made up. The pretence will last for a time, for my time certainly. But what are a few years? It is a pretence nevertheless which makes all the other falsehoods seem more false. And the proof that in their hearts the people of the Western world know it, is their haunting fear. All are waging a relentless war against revolutionary Russia, from the outside and from inside, a war that sets aside all rules of war, all international law, all shame and scruple."

"Do you think the Revolution will survive?" Julian asked.

Daria smiled.

"Even if they crush revolutionary Russia . . . the spectre which stalks the old world will not be laid. It is well that you have come," she repeated after a while. "You will see ruin, suffering, strife, famine— but life, not pretence, not the hollow pretence of life. No, my dear," she said, turning to Zena, "I have no great wish to go back to that."

There was a ring at the door, and a tottering old woman, in whom Julian recognised Marusia, came to say that "the lady Commissar" was there.

Maïa came in, booted and belted.

"Kogda vui pojenites?" she said, with a little laugh, to Zena.

Zena laughed and a flush of color rose to her cheeks.

"What did she say?" asked Julian.

"No, I will not tell you," said Zena. "You will have to learn Russian."

She and Maïa talked on a while volubly. Zena interpreted, now and again, to Julian. Maïa thought it would be best if he remained for the present with the city militia, until they should go down to Kursk.

Her work at the hospital, the obtaining of supplies and food, the maintenance of an adequate staff and the organisation of its work occupied a great deal of Zena's time. There were also many other calls upon it. Old Marusia, though she endeavored to keep up the old style in which her pride was involved, serving the meals of *bortsch* and *golubtsi* with as much ceremony as if they had been delicate banquets, and announcing visitors with the stateliness and phraseology of an old-time butler, found it difficult to cope with the service of the little apartment, and Zena, despite the old woman's protests, helped a good deal. She would stand in the food-queues at the co-operatives for hours, and

Julian frequently found her with her sleeves turned up when she had been doing some washing or baking *piroski*.

Countess Farsen, the morganatic wife of the Duke of Kronstadt, who was a frequent visitor at the Duchess of Friedland's, liked to press upon her and upon Zena offers of assistance, much to their discomfort and annoyance. She would send them bottles of wine. The duke's cellar, in his palace at Tzarskoie Selo—now called, as the countess would mention with disgust, Deskoie Selo, the Children's Village—had contained one of the finest collections in Europe, amounting to fifteen thousand bottles. A large portion had been confiscated, but the countess had managed to conceal several thousand bottles of Burgundy and champagne, and was now deriving a sufficient income for her present needs and those of the duke, by secretly selling the wine. Daria would remark in an ironic mood to the countess that the greatest atrocity which the Bolsheviks had committed was not the assassination of the Tzar, but the scandalous manner in which, owing to their barbarous ignorance, they had stood all the bottles of old Burgundy and champagne which they had collected, upright, instead of laying them on their sides, thereby utterly ruining the vintages. Countess Farsen's most trying manifestation of kindly friendliness was her offer of cast-off clothes. She told Zena that she had a couple of frocks which had been scarcely worn and which might easily be altered to fit her. As the countess was a squat and fattish woman of about fifty with an amorphous figure, Zena was unable to conceive of the operation of adapting them to her own use, although she had lately acquired considerable skill with the needle.

The countess could with difficulty forego, amid her present trials, the pleasure of patronising people and of playing the lady bountiful.

Despite the many tasks which occupied Zena, she and Julian managed to be together a good deal. Sometimes they would go in the evening to a theatre or concert.

"On the night when you arrived in Petrograd," Zena told him, "I was at the Conservatoire of Music, seeing Smirnova dance in Gluzunov's 'Salome.' There was, they say, food for only four days in Petrograd. We could hear the gunfire and the English airplanes droning ominously overhead. Every one was expecting the Whites to come at any moment. The Tzarist officers had organised a rising. It is curious how the little trivialities and amusements go on while the fate of the world is being decided. Smirnova danced better than I had seen her do before an imperial audience."

"It is that illusion of the continuity of common life which distorts our perspective of the events in the midst of which we live," Julian remarked. He recalled the sight-seeing parties at the storming of the Bastille.

"When the Winter Palace was taken," said Zena, "I was at the ballet at the Mariinskii Theatre with some friends. When we came out we heard the sound of firing in the direction of the palace square. We drove round to the Hôtel de l'Europe for supper. The Nevski was full of promenaders and the colored electric signs glittered before the cinemas. We saw a couple of armored cars going down the street. At the 'Europe,' Jimmy, the barman from the Waldorf-Astoria in New York, remarked, giving a final 'bottoms-up' smack to his cocktail shaker, that there seemed to be some rumpus going on. Only the next morning did I hear that the Bolsheviki were in power and the Provisional Government prisoners."

Countess Farsen admitted that she had rather rejoiced, at first, over the overthrow of the Provisional Government by the Bolsheviks, being at one with them in her hatred of the Kerenski régime, and not supposing for a moment that the Bolsheviks would be able to maintain themselves in power for more than a few days.

"How can there be order in Russia without a Tzar? Our blessed martyr," she said, meaning the late Tzar Nicholas, "was the anointed of God. Had he shown himself in Petrograd on a white horse and, like Tzar Nicholas I, ordered the soldiers and people: 'Down on your knees, slaves, before your lord and master,' all would have been well. The power of the Tzars who have, during three hundred years, built up and constructed would not have given place to the tyranny of people who only know how to destroy."

She took it for granted that Julian must be acting on some mission on behalf of the British Government.

"You English have let us down," she said to him. "Everybody knows, of course, that you are in league with the Bolsheviks. It was Sir George Buchanan who hoisted them into power. I dare say that the English are now, like Lenin and his fellow-bandits, appalled at their own work. But your Lloyd George has been bought over by the Bolsheviks with the gold they have stolen. Our dear Alexei"—this was the son of the Duke of Kronstadt by his first wife—"had organised everything to hand over Petrograd to General Yudenich. You have no idea what a hero he is. He has been going about in the Red Guard regiments, disguised in their abominable uniform to gather loyal officers and soldiers, who were to arrest the Bolshevik agitators as the liberating army entered Petrograd. The duke had been asked to act as regent governor."

Julian recalled the young officer whom he had seen at the inn at Jamburg.

Zena recovered a good deal of her old brightness. It was a new happiness which they had found, she and Julian, different in many ways from the luxurious happiness of Armida's garden, but even more precious it seemed to them. Julian would meet her at the hospital when she had finished her work there. Zena showed him over what, in the old days, had been her St. Petersburg home, her sitting room, her bedroom, full now of little iron beds. The head nurse, Maria Semeonovna, was a tall, cheerful, capable woman. She had been in Daria's hospital throughout the war. Zena would take her and another of the nurses down to Kursk with her, where they were very short-handed, she said.

Julian and Zena would then walk down together to the Milionaïa. And after the plain, crude meal, they would be alone in her two rooms. Her bedroom looked out upon the quays and the Neva. At night the moon shone on the steely waters on which gunboats lay at anchor, and on the fortress of Peter and Paul. All the pent-up, inhibited heartache and silenced agony of years was released in a new physical joy.

Countess Farsen arrived at Daria's late one afternoon, just as Zena and Julian had come in, and sank down, tremulous and tearful, on the sofa.

"I can hardly get my breath," she said in self-pity, pressing her hand to her fat bosom. "You know, Daria, that I have a weak heart. What do you think those monsters have done now? They've arrested George."

"I am surprised they have not done so before," Daria said.

"Ah, yes. Anything may be expected from such brutes. They have no respect or consideration for their betters," said the countess. "Once before they had come for Alexei. Fortunately he was away at the time with the White army in Esthonia. Now the ruffians have taken away the duke. He, so good, so noble! What harm had he done? They came in the middle of the night. Probably they were afraid lest the people should rise up in indignation. I told the curs that the duke was ill, that he was suffering from his liver, that I would let them have a certificate from our doctor to show that he was not in a fit state to be removed. The chief of the bandits, who tried to conceal his shame and embarrassment under an air of insolence, said that one of their own doctors would examine the duke, 'And we shall take care that he does not get too rich a diet and too much Burgundy,' the disgusting little Jew said with a fiendish grin. George bore himself with so much dignity that I could see the soldiers, who merely act from fear of their tyrants, were impressed. 'I am ready to follow you, you sons of bitches,' he said, after he had carefully dressed and devotedly kissed the holy ikons. I said that wherever my husband went, I should go too. They brought us in a car to the Gorovchaïa. Oh, I am so upset that I have scarcely any breath to speak."

"You are doing very well," said Daria, during the pause in the flow of words.

"After an interminable wait among a medley of people who were sitting round on benches in an anteroom, a man came and called 'citizen George Nikitish.' The duke rose and I hastened to follow him. But they refused to admit me, despite my protests. The man who had come for the duke told me that, if I wanted to make any deposition, I should apply at an office which he indicated on the third floor, and ask to see Comrade Guchberg. Overcoming my disgust at having to humiliate myself by pleading to some dirty little Jew, I obtained an interview. As it happened, the 'comrade' Guchberg appeared to be a trifle more human than most of the brigands, or perhaps he was stricken by his conscience. The Bolsheviks, you know, sometimes recoil in horror before the crimes they have committed and are afraid of the vengeance of God and of the people. The man treated me with considerable courtesy and kindness. 'Why do you torment us like this?' I asked him. 'We have done no harm to any one.'"

"What did he say to that?" asked Daria.

"He looked embarrassed and seemed not to know what to reply," said the countess.

"He said nothing about your husband and your son's recruiting for the armies attacking Petrograd, and plotting a massacre of the people?" Daria asked.

The countess stared, uncomprehendingly. "But what they do is from patriotism, for the good of Russia," she said.

"Perhaps, Pavla Igorovna, the Soviet Government thinks that to keep your husband under lock and key is also for the good of Russia," said Daria.

"The man said he himself had spent many years in prison. An ex-convict, of course, like all those Bolshevik criminals. 'Then you are having my innocent husband arrested merely to revenge yourself,' I said. Guchberg leaned over and took hold of my hand, speaking very gently. 'We do not believe in either revenge or punishment,' he said. On the whole, he seemed rather human for a Bolshevik, but I could not obtain from him that the duke should be set at liberty. The most I got out of him was permission to visit my husband every day and supply him with caviar and chicken. He also allowed me to take away the holy ikons from our palace which has been declared national property. Thinking that it might perhaps be possible to redeem the man from the career of crime into which he had fallen, I offered to give him one of the ikons to place over his bed. 'Thank you, I already have one,' he said, 'the red flag of the Revolution.' 'To me, it is a disgusting rag,' I said. 'Evidently we think differently.' 'Evidently we do,' he said. 'Your ikons are to me the age-long symbols of the crushing down of the minds and lives of the people, the red flag, of their liberation from that intolerable age-long oppression.' "

After further disburdening herself, Countess Farsen asked Daria to use her influence to have the duke set at liberty. Daria considered a while in baffled silence the abyss of incomprehension that confronted her, and after telling the countess that there could be no possibility of her husband being liberated, said she would speak to a member of the Cheka with a view to procuring for the duke the best possible treatment and obtain, perhaps, that his life should be spared.

"You think they will murder him?" the countess asked, in a crisis of agitation.

"There is always the possibility of the Government of a country at war contemplating the application of the final penalty to persons whom it regards as dangerous traitors," Daria explained.

A few days after Countess Farsen's visit, Julian, while at mess in the barracks, heard his name called by one of the officers, who signed to him sharply to follow him. After leading the way to a part of the building which was little used, the officer, a young man with carefully trained dark moustache, showed Julian into a room where another young officer was waiting, and carefully closing the door behind him, addressed him courteously in perfect English.

"We have no doubt," he said, "that, as an Englishman, your discretion and assistance can be counted upon in the execution of the plan we are preparing. It is for the liberation of the Duke of Kronstadt. He has been transferred from the main political prison in the Sherovskaïa to one in the Golodaï Island, where the precautions taken are not so great and where we count several friends. Tomorrow night we are to furnish a guard of three men. You will be one of them. You are not required to take any active part in the business, but merely to assist passively and, if possible, keep the other two men out of the way. We shall be, in any case, in sufficient numbers to deal with them. Our friends will be close by with a car, and at about half-past twelve my friend here and I will come to fetch His Imperial Highness. If the guard is kept out of the way, the whole thing can be carried out without any disturbance."

Julian gave a non-committal reply which, allowing for English usage, they interpreted as satisfactory. That day he made a point of seeing Zena and told her what had taken place. She advised him to do nothing further in the matter and interfere as little as possible when they should come to take the duke away.

"I shall, of course, at once advise Maïa, and all necessary action had better be left to her," she said.

The following afternoon Julian, Katajev, and Gurudin were warned for guard duty at the Golodaï prison. A light lorry took them over at dusk to the island on the smaller arm of the Neva, together with other militiamen who had to reach duty posts in the same direction, and who were deposited on the way. The young officer who had spoken to Julian was in charge of the party. He gave the men their formal instructions in more than usually brusque fashion and returned to the city with the lorry, which took back four men who had been on duty during the day.

No one at the prison paid any attention to the guard. The three men were to take sentry duty in turn at the entrance, while the other two paced the courtyard and main corridor or rested in a small guard room where there were a stove and a samovar for their use.

When the officer had departed, Julian told his companions something of what was brewing. The officers might be expected to come about half an hour after midnight, he informed them, presumably for inspection. Katajev, who, it was arranged, would be on sentry duty at that time, was to let them pass unchallenged. The rest was to be left to the Cheka authorities, who were warned. Only in case no assistance arrived, and the officers sought to leave the building with the prisoner, was opposition to be offered and the alarm raised.

The building remained deserted-looking and silent. It stood isolated amid a flat waste-ground, where there were only bushes and a few clumps of trees, but no other buildings near. It was a dark night. The two officers came, as expected, a little after half-past twelve. They went openly past Katajev, casually asking as they passed him:

"All well?"

"All well," Katajev answered, and let them pass.

The officers went up to the first floor and were absent some time. Julian and the two militiamen looked about outside, but no one was to be seen in the neighborhood of the prison. Julian thought he heard a motor engine running, probably that of the car in which the officers had come, and which seemed to be waiting round the corner of the enclosure wall. Gurudin joined Katajev, with rifle and fixed bayonet, at the entrance. Julian remained in the guard room at the other end of the front corridor, so as to be able to cut off the officers' retreat, should there be need.

Presently they came down with another man in a military greatcoat.

"We are taking away one of the prisoners, whom the Cheka wish transferred to another prison," said one of the officers as they reached the entrance.

Katajev and Gurudin had crossed rifles, barring the door.

"Have you got a *bumaga,* some piece of paper?" asked Katajev.

Uncertain whether to make some excuse or openly to force their way, the officers hesitated. At the moment, some twenty sailors sprang forward from behind the bushes on the opposite side of the road and rushed to the prison door. At their head was Mikhaïl Khatiniev.

The officers drew their automatics and fired. A sailor dropped to the ground. A scuffle took place. Julian and his two companions, springing behind the officers and the prisoner, barred their retreat. The duke drew a Browning from his coat and fired at Khatiniev, wounding him in the arm. At the first sound of disturbance, another party of about ten men ran up from the corner of the building, firing pistols at the sailors. The fray was over in a few seconds. The two officers and the Duke of Kronstadt were overpowered and five of the party who had come up to their rescue were also captured. The rest escaped, running back to their car and driving off at full speed.

The Duke of Kronstadt was transferred to the fortress of Peter and Paul. Countess Farsen was kept in ignorance of his place of detention, and her insistent enquiries and applications to see him were put off and refused. She was daily at the Duchess of Friedland's apartment. It was impossible to show impatience at the woman's interminable flow of laments and tears, seeing that her husband must now inevitably face the firing-squad. Her detailed accounts of interviews with people whom she vilified, while at the same time admitting that they had treated her with kindness and consideration, had to be endured. She had been to see Maxim Gorki in his apartment on the Krowesky Prospect, having heard that he had exerted himself to obtain the pardon of Grand Duke Nicholas Mikhailovich. But the writer, who received Countess Farsen in bed, being at the time suffering from a bronchial cold, could give her no assurance of help.

"Chaliapin, the singer, was with Gorki," she said. "He sat, with his big red face, looking rather uncomfortable, for it was the duke who had launched him in Paris, you know."

One afternoon that Countess Farsen was in Daria's apartment, Marusia announced "the Commissar." The countess almost started out of her skin at the word, which connoted for her arrests and domiciliary searches. It was Maïa. The countess began at once pleading hysterically and in the most abject manner, almost dropping to her knees, to be allowed to see the duke, to have him set at liberty, appealing with extended hands to Maïa's feelings as a woman. It was an uncomfortable scene. Daria and Zena looked at Maïa anxiously, fearing an outburst on her part. But Maïa stood in silence, very quiet, taking the countess's hands and setting her back, with quieting gestures, in the armchair from which she had almost dropped.

"My dear Madame," she said, after a brief silence, when Countess Farsen at last paused, "do you seriously and truly suppose that I, or any other official of the Revolutionary Government, would not be only too glad to spare your sufferings—were it only from pride, to show that we are not as ruthless and heartless as you and your friends have always been, never giving one thought to the thousands of lives you have crushed, the countless widows and orphans you have made, without pity, with only sneers and hatred, and contempt for sufferings and agonies which seemed to you to be beneath your notice? The people have revolted against that cruelty of yours. The leaders of the people have devoted their lives to the task of putting an end to it. Most of them shrink from the exercise of the severity which is necessary to carry out that task. We are at war with you, who have joyfully sent millions to slaughter for no other purpose than the increase of the privileges of the few, and we hate the war that is necessary to put down war. You appeal to my feelings as a woman. If I were without any, if my feelings had not been harrowed by the sight of dear ones unfeelingly done to death, I should not be standing here now as a representative of the people. My duty as such would be easier now if I could restore to you your husband, who has severely wounded my own husband. But my duty is to safeguard that emancipation from ruthless cruelty which the people have won, and it is not consistent with indulging in mercy towards those who endanger that hard-won release from suffering. You call our defence of the people's liberation 'Red Terror'; and you call the defence by a thousand times greater cruelty of the property and privileges of your class 'order.' We, the people, cannot accept your judgment as to what calls for mercy or for hard severity, any more than you can accept ours. It is for us to decide what is necessary in order to save our lives and that which we regard as more precious than our lives."

"Yes. We speak different languages," said the countess.

"True. And it is perhaps foolish of me to argue. That is why we defend ourselves by force," Maïa said.

"Tell me at least where my husband is. Is he in danger?" the countess asked.

Maïa looked at her for some moments before saying very quietly: "Your husband was executed this morning."

With the assistance of Zena and of Maïa, the woman was led to her apartment, near by. Her daughter was informed and her doctor sent for.

Maïa returned to the Duchess of Friedland.

"I had come to inform you of citizen Nikitish's death, Daria Dimietrovna," she said. "That poor woman will probably wish now to leave Russia, where there is nothing to keep her. There is no great objection to her doing so. She will slander, vilify us, and misrepresent us. But so will every one in the capitalist world. But there is a reason why she should not be permitted to leave the country just now. While she is here, Alexei Nikitish will probably try to return. He is one of our most ruthless and dangerous enemies. No opportunity of rendering him harmless must be lost."

"I cannot undertake to act as police agent," Daria said.

"No . . . of course. We must rely upon ourselves," said Maïa.

"I can have no real place in your strife, even if I wished," Daria said. "I, too, think I should do well to leave Russia."

"You can do so, Daria Dimietrovna, whenever you wish. Every facility will be given you," said Maïa.

Zena had been urging more than ever her mother to leave Russia. She was anxious to go down to Kursk, where the provincial and country atmosphere gave an illusion of peace which was impossible amid the agitation and fear which reigned in Petrograd and Moscow, and where also she could do more useful work in the military hospitals. At the same time, Zena did not wish to leave her mother in Petrograd.

"For the people the sufferings of the present time, the shortage of food and of everything, are not greater, or scarcely greater than those to which they have been used. For us, even though we perceive clearly the necessity and the justice of the social revolution, they are very great and mean the loss of everything by which we lived. Matushka ought to go to Paris."

The friends of Countess Farsen crowded round her in the apartment of her daughter, Countess Maria Voruskaïa, where she remained in bed in a state of collapse and self-pity which she did nothing to overcome. They did their best to persuade her that she was in danger of arrest, and to urge her to hide or escape. After she had attended a mass which her daughter had had celebrated for the soul of the late duke at the Cathedral of the Mother of God of Kazan, Countess Farsen accepted the offer of a ballet-dancer, a former mistress of the duke, to move to her lodgings, where the authorities would not be likely to seek her.

There she received the visit of Count Holden, of the Danish legation, which, as formerly the British embassy, and indeed all the remaining foreign legations, acted as intermediary between the monarchist and anti-sovietic plotters in Petrograd and the White Guards abroad. He had been in close relation with the late duke, who had been in the habit of sending through him his correspondence to foreign crowned heads and Tzarist generals, urging them to more vigorous activity and intervention against the Soviet Government. Count Holden had helped many members of the old aristocracy to leave Russia. He came to offer his services to Countess Farsen and to inform her that her step-son was making all preparations for her passage to Finland and that, in a day or two, she would be informed of every detail.

Eager though she was to go, Countess Farsen, engrossed in self-pity, told her friends she doubted whether her strength was equal to facing the hardships of the journey, the drive in the night and bitter weather, and in the fear and danger of detection and pursuit. Daria, who several times visited her, sought to rouse and encourage her. She said at last she would herself go with her and, with profuse demonstrations of tearful gratitude, Countess Farsen was persuaded by the offer.

Zena and Julian protested with the Duchess of Friedland. She had an authoritative pass permitting her to travel freely and in relative comfort by train to Wyborg. But Daria was persistent in her resolve.

"I have no right to privilege," she said.

It was decided Daria should go. Zena would join, as she had long proposed to do, Nadia at Kursk, and all would meet again some day in Paris. The leave-taking was painful, but restrained. It had been arranged that Daria should join the countess at a house on the other side of the Neva, where a friend of the ballet-dancer lived, so as not to excite suspicion. Daria drove there, after dark, one night in a droshki. Thence a cart with two horses, partly loaded with milk cans, and driven by a trusted man, took Countess Farsen and Daria, who sat wrapped in their fur coats, partly concealed among the milk cans, out of the city and on along the Wyborg road.

A northern wind was blowing from the Finnish swamps that froze to the marrow. The night was dark and cloudy. They drove past the private parks of Lanskaia and Count Shuvalov's estate, which had formerly been favorite picnic resorts in the summer, and into the end-less desolation of the swampy country, a dead-level scattered over with stunted pines, single and in clumps and copses. The wind and cold were bitter. In the direction of the gulf, the searchlights of Kron-stadt could be seen sweeping the black water and the coast. There were other searchlights, too, along the coast, at the defence posts, which at times turned the glare of their white beams on the road, lighting up the fugitives in their stark light.

They arrived after what seemed an interminable drive at a small log house that stood in utter isolation at some distance from the main road on the plain, near the edge of a pine wood. There was light at the win-dow, and as the cart drew up a man opened the door, in a military greatcoat, wearing glasses and a black beard. The women dismounted, and when they had entered the house, the man removed his glasses and beard. It was Prince Alexei Nikitish. They had welcome draughts of hot tea from a boiling samovar, warming themselves before the log stove. The milk cart returned to Petrograd. There was a sleigh with swift horses waiting, Alexei said, at the back of the house. The driver, a villainous-looking Finnish smuggler, who was to take them over the border, came in for a moment. Alexei handed to him five thousand roubles, his fee for the work.

As, after they had rested a while, they were preparing to resume their journey, the sound of a car-engine was heard outside. Alexei sprang, lightning quick, to the window and peered out through an opening in the shutter. As quickly he sprang back, bolting the door, seized the countess by the wrist and rushed out by the back door, dragging her after him.

. "Quick! Come!" he called to Daria.

She stood, taken by surprise, hesitating a while. In a moment Alexei was back. Steps were heard before the front door, and a knock. Alexei stood a moment and signed to Daria to come, But as they reached the back door, shots were heard and the sounds of the sleigh horses galloping off. Alexei banged shut the door and drew the bolt.

There was now a violent knocking of rifle-butts at the front door. Alexei drew two automatic pistols from his coat and, through the peepholes of the shutter, began discharging them. The door shook with repeated blows. Two of the planks in the upper panel flew into splinters, and through them at once appeared the barrels of several rifles which fired volleys into the room.

The party of sailors who had rushed up in a motor truck from a post on the coast at last battered down the heavy door and broke in. In the middle of the room lay stretched on the floor, riddled with bullet-wounds, the Duchess of Friedland's body. Nikitish had disappeared.

It was Maïa who, distracted, brought the news to Zena. She herself, informed of Countess Farsen's departure, but unaware of the Duchess of Friedland's, had sent out orders to keep a lookout for Nikitish and get him at all cost.

Zena bore the blow with greater strength than might have been expected. Three days after her mother's body had been buried in the Smolensk graveyard, she and Julian took the train for Moscow on their way to Kursk.

XVII

THE house which the Varachins occupied—an old-style Russian wooden house, painted green, with inside walls of oiled pine— had been the head-forester's in the old Nevidof estate. It was rather too large for Nadia and Andrei and, until Zena and Julian came, the four-roomed extension which had been built to accommodate the head-forester's son when he had married had been closed. Marusia, with one of her nieces, a peasant girl from the former estate, waited upon them. The peasants brought food, of which, in contrast with most other parts of Russia, there was no shortage in the rich dark-earth country. A stream with reedy banks purled at the end of the neglected garden, thickly shaded over by old elms and carpeted with their last year's leaves. Andrei Varachin would at times angle there for trout. The rounded nearby hills were covered with orchards, and the sunset decked them with rich colors. There were few immediate signs in the peaceful retreat of the world-heaving turmoil.

Andrei Varachin now kept aloof from politics. He took no sides, he said. He was wholly impartial—"above the strife," as he was wont to say. Should the rule of the Soviets survive, which appeared, one had to admit, somewhat doubtful, he hoped they would make a good job of the task they had undertaken. The experiment should be given a chance, he maintained. He blamed some of his former liberal associates who had now turned into the most virulent and irreconcilable foes of the Soviet Government. The "good" Prince Lvov, for instance, whose suave broadmindedness and humanitarian tolerance had been the pattern of liberal virtue, had now become a raving maniac in his furious denunciation and immoderate hate. He was in Paris, moving heaven and earth to raise White armies and to goad every country to a crusade against Russia. Andrei blamed such an attitude. Russia should be allowed to work out her own destiny. He, personally, was loyal to the Soviet Government. He had offered his services to teach in the schools which had been established in the district. Andrei gave lessons on Russian literature and readings in poetry. He would invite Zena and Julian to attend the "melo-recitals" which he gave once a week, intoning poems of Pushkin and compositions of his own while accompanying himself with obligatos on the piano, at the school conducted for the children of mujiks by two maiden ladies, Konia and Melania Sladosteia. Culture must be preserved. Having forsworn politics, Andrei had reverted to his former interests. He was hoping to have a volume of verse published shortly. Pure art had nothing to do with politics. It was "above the strife." Art was a thing apart.

Zena was more deeply affected than she liked to admit to herself by Nadia's absorption in her affection for Andrei, whose every point of view she adopted, regarding him, as he was himself disposed to do, as a genius, and Zena felt bitterly the undefined and intangible sense of separation between herself and her sister. The secret bitterness which Zena felt vented itself in irritation at Andrei, his self-approval, his small mutton-chop whiskers, his idleness, his high black necktie and long hair, and the views which he expounded with nervous twitchings of his long, somewhat feminine face and gestures of his tapering hands. She urged Julian to reply to him. But Julian firmly declined. Even to indicate that what was happening in Russia was not a fortuitous effect of local circumstances or an "experiment," but the inevitable outcome of awakening consciousness of realities in the industrialised servile classes, which now rendered impossible the system of slavery on which civilisation had for thousands of years been founded, or to try to show that what Andrei imagined to be "pure art" was more completely drenched in tendentious apologetics than any pamphlet of revolutionary propaganda, would require, he said, the revision of the most elementary conceptions assumed in every word of the views expressed by Andrei, and which he supposed to be detached and impartial. Such views could not be modified by direct argument, but only by a long education. And even such education required special conditions of experience to render it possible and to break down the millennial foundations that had been laid by the interested wishes of a servile society.

Zena was drawn more closely to Julian by what she felt, perhaps somewhat magnified by the intensity of her own feelings, to be a tacit alienation from her sister. He was now all that was left to her of a world which had crumbled about her, burying in its ruins not only the external setting and incidental amenities of her life, but the intimate affections, the very lives to which her own had been bound. In that desolation Zena and Julian felt more closely bound than they had once been by joy and passion. Before leaving Petrograd, Zena had registered, according to Soviet law, the annulment of her former marriage and her union with Julian. The formality, over which they had smiled at the time, seemed now to have for them a solemnity which the most pompous ceremony could scarcely have suggested.

A few of Andrei's old liberal associates had from the first wholeheartedly espoused the revolutionary cause. Among them was Markel Zolvchin, a Moscow merchant formerly a patron of liberal journalism, who had a small country house at Kursk. Zolvchin was an amiable, keen-witted Jew, who had made a considerable fortune. Not only had he voluntarily given up the wealth which, as he freely acknowledged, he owed to the opportunistic use of the capitalistic system's licence to despoil, but had devoted his talents for organisation and management to the service of the Soviets, and it was largely due to his energy that the natural abundance of the district had become utilised to ward off the dangers of food-shortage, both in Moscow and among the hard-pressed troops now fighting in the south. Zolvchin had been appointed People's Commissar in Kursk, and with the assistance of Comrade Sverdof, formerly a retail green grocer in the town, represented the authority of the Soviet Government, and saw to it that the mujiks received a fair compensation for the foodstuffs which they were required to supply and which were transmitted to the capital and to the front.

Madame Zolvchin, the wife of the Commissar, was one of Zena's and Nadia's closest acquaintances in the neighborhood, having been the president of the Red Cross during the imperialist war and having afforded at that time the most pleasant and cultured social companionship available in the place, which boasted few resources in that respect. She was a woman of about forty, but looking younger, though disposed of late to plumpness, whose composed manner and smooth brow under heavy folds of lustrous black hair, parted in the middle, gave her the appearance of a placid and cheerful madonna, with bright, intelligent eyes.

The Zolvchins' house was unfortunately at some distance, on the other side of the Kura River. The nearest neighbor of the Varachins was Countess Groza, the widow of a general, who lived in a small villa, about a verst down stream. She had led a fashionable life in Moscow society. Her two daughters were Zena's immediate associates in the management of the hospital. Anna, the elder, a tall blonde, with serious, capable manner and athletic figure, had been a medical student before the war. She and her sister, Olga, had served as nurses in a Moscow hospital and, for some time, near the front, during the war. They were "modern," self-reliant young women, reserved, but energetic and efficient. Olga was more "feminine" and sentimental by nature than her elder sister, but patterned herself admiringly upon her.

The young women ran the military hospital at Kursk, with the help of Maria Semeovna and the other nurse whom Zena had brought down from the hospital at Petrograd. Two rather raw medical students acted as surgeons. The hospital, a large square building at the extreme north end of the town, was taxed to full capacity by the sick and wounded from the southern front. Typhus and diseases of malnutrition and exhaustion played more havoc among the men than did wounds. The difficult tasks of organizing the supplies of food and medical stores and of fighting insanitary conditions called for much energy and ingenuity on the part of Zena and the two Groza sisters. Large quantities of medical supplies and preserves were generously being sent from America. But the bulk did not reach beyond Poland, which was preparing a large-scale attack on the Soviets, and the rest of the transatlantic bounties found its way to the White armies. Zena would have been at a loss but for Mark Zolvchin's aid. He never considered anything impossible and had an uncanny gift for producing rabbits out of a hat, as it were. Supplies turned up from all over the place. Once a whole wagon-load of English hospital supplies arrived, intended for General Denikin's army, and cleverly diverted by Bolshevik agents all the way from Odessa.

Zena and Julian frequently drove over to the Zolvchins' house in the *brichka,* a rickety buggy drawn by a patient old horse, which served as the usual means of transport. There was about the Zolvchins' house a civilised air of well-being, cleanliness, and comfort to which one had become unused. The Zolvchins had always been endeared to the country folk by their helpfulness and efficient devotion to their cause, and their modest little countryhouse, ensconced on the fringe of the woods on a hill to the north of the town, had thus escaped the anger and envy which had devastated so many of the large estates. It still bore the marks of refined taste and culture, choice pictures and books and snug furniture. Two hefty country wenches were only too glad to labor to preserve its amenities. Ida Zolvchin used to say that she saw no reason why good Communists should make a point of living like pigs and savages. Countess Groza, a large part of whose conversation, when she came over to have tea with the Varachins, ran upon the losses she had sustained, the jewels which she had been obliged to dispose of, spoke with disgust of the comforts in which Mark and Ida Zolvchin indulged, "like Lenin and all those other Jews in the Kremlin, who spend their time carousing, eating caviar and drinking champagne, while they are being entertained by troops of naked dancers." Anna and Olga Groza frequented as often as they could the Zolvchins' villa in order to escape from their mother's conversation and lamentations. Countess Groza had tried several times to reach Kislovodsk, a watering place in the northern Caucasus where most of her old friends were now gathered, but had, much to her daughters' disappointment, been unable to do so owing to the present disturbed state of the country. She was hoping that the "Volunteer" army of General Denikin would before long restore order, and that she would then be enabled to rejoin congenial society.

It was at Ida Zolvchin's that Zena and Julian went chiefly for news of the outer world, life in their secluded surroundings seeming peaceful enough, and almost somnolent, in spite of the fierce struggle which was being raged not many miles away. Ida Zolvchin was inclined, at least so Julian thought, to be somewhat too uniformly optimistic in her views of what was passing. She spoke with smiling confidence of the triumph of the Soviets and discussed the various tasks of organisation, education, recreational and rest institutions, which would have to be undertaken, as though no doubt could exist as to the future, although White armies and foreign intervention were at the time pressing forward from every quarter of the compass and the actual territory under Soviet rule was being reduced to a relatively small circle round Moscow. The news of the advance of the Southern White armies equipped, fed, and paid by England was far from being in harmony with that optimism. Every day the exhausted Red armies were being forced further back by the "Volunteers." The signs of breakdown became at last more and more visible. At first it was the arrival of trains of wounded and sick, most of whom had to be sent on to Moscow, the single local hospital being already overcrowded. Later came straggling parties of Partisans, ragged and starving, some coming by train, others by road, with trails of carts loaded with women and children, and cooking utensils. Many passed through Kursk, and, after having been given food and having spent a night's rest in bivouac in the woods, resumed their march northwards. The straggling, wretched-looking retreating troops became more and more numerous. Some were desperate. A party of "Partisans" once looted some wagon-loads of food which were being sent to Moscow. Mark Zolvchin and Sverdof had trouble in stopping the pillage and in restoring order.

The Whites held Ekaterinoslav. Then news came that they were at Kharkov, only two hundred versts away, and still advancing. Ogonin came down from Moscow. The retreating, demoralised Reds were now pouring through Kursk. There could be no question of defending the place. New armies, well-equipped and organised, were ready, Ogonin said. But they could not be sent south. The defence was being organised further north. He had guns placed on the heights and the cliffs by the river, where the old Kremlin had stood, and machine-gun positions in the monastery of the Epiphany of the Virgin and the Nevidof gardens. But those defences, placed in the hands of small trained detachments, were only for the purpose of covering the retreat of the last units of the Partisan army.

The peace and silence of the country were now broken by the sound of gunfire, which came every day nearer. Even from the quiet cottage of the Varachins the rattle of musketry and machine-guns was heard in the stillness of the night.

One morning it stopped, and Marusia brought the news that the White army had entered Kursk. Zena was anxious to go at once to the hospital, where only the two nurses from Petrograd, Semeovna and Sasonova, slept at night. Endeavors had been made in the last few days to evacuate some of the patients, but it had been impossible to obtain accommodation for more than a very few of them in the trains, filled to the running-boards with retreating troops and refugees.

Julian harnessed the horse to the old *brichka*. They intended to call for Anna and Olga, but met them on the road, also hurrying to the hospital, and picked them up. Avoiding the town, they drove by the road which skirted it on the west. They met a post of White soldiers on the northern road as they turned into it. An officer, who was in charge, stopped them, coming up to them and asking them, politely enough, their business. Zena had put her old passport in her bag and showed it. The officer smiled, clicked his heels and saluted.

"I advise you not to go farther," he said in reply to Zena's explanations. "Still, if you wish to, you may. You will probably find some officers there, who will be able to inform you as to what the High Command propose to do about the enemy wounded."

Leaving the buggy at the top of the road, they went on to the hospital, which was only a few steps farther, at the northern extremity of the steep High street. There were soldiers all round it. On the opposite side of the wide road, smoking cigarettes, stood a group of officers. One of them called out to them in a rough voice, as they approached, telling them to keep away. But Zena went up to him, and when she had told him her name, and that Anna and Olga were the daughters of Countess Groza, his manner became more respectful.

Soldiers were bringing out of the hospital the stores of medical supplies and loading them on to a lorry. Others were carrying tins into the hospital. Shouts and screams came from the building.

To Zena's questions and requests, the officer, a captain, answered with a shrug:

"We take no prisoners. Bolsheviks are brute beasts. The ordinary rules of civilised warfare do not apply to the stamping out of vermin."

Zena turned pale as a sheet.

"But the nurses . . . there are two nurses there . . ."

As she spoke, the screams of women were heard above the shouts of the soldiers and cries of the patients.

Immediately Zena dashed across the road, followed by Julian and the two young women. The soldiers at the door, taken aback, did nothing to stop them as they rushed in. The nurses' room was on the left of the entrance. Zena pushed open the door. She stood, staggering back into Julian's arms, frozen with horror at what she saw. Two of the officers had run across. Seizing the girls by the arms, they forcibly drew them back and out of the building. Julian led Zena back to where the captain stood.

"You had better be more careful," the officer said sharply, "or you may share the fate of your nurses." Then, with an ugly leer, "The men must have their amusement. If we did not let them have it, it would be difficult to keep up discipline. Run away at once, and keep away, or I will not answer for the consequences."

Trembling and speechless, the three women drew back with Julian to the end of the street, and stood leaning against a wall.

Some soldiers were at the windows of the upper floor. Others called out to them from the street. Several soldiers came out. At the back of the hospital, smoke was rising. They were setting fire to the building. In a few minutes sheets of flame burst from the windows. There was a crash of timber. Soaked with kerosene, the building was going up in flames like a dry haystack. The screams of the patients rent the air. Some came rushing out at the door, but were received by the soldiers, killed, or thrust back. Some threw themselves down from the windows. The soldiers below finished them off with their bayonets. One of the nurses, Maria Semeovna, rushed out, almost naked. Four men seized her by the arms and legs, and, swinging her, tossed her back into the burning pile.

A gigantic fellow with his head swathed in bandages, and wearing a long sheepskin coat, came out brandishing a double gallon jar of ether. His coat, beard, and bandages were smouldering, but he staggered forward with blood-shot eyes and a horrible grin towards the group of officers and the lorry full of men into which the stores had been thrown. He had filled his pockets with phials of ether from the operating room of the hospital, which exploded as his clothes caught fire, shooting flames, like squibs, in all directions. The soldiers drew back as he advanced upon them like a walking fire-work. He halted, at a few yards' distance and, swinging the large bottle of ether above his head, threw it into the lorry, where it exploded among the supplies. The men jumped from the burning lorry, wrapped in flames, and rolled upon the ground. The officers sprang aside. The giant dropped to the ground at last, pierced by a dozen bayonets.

Julian led the women away to where the buggy was tied. They drove to Madame Zolvchin's, whose house was not far away. Hardened as they were by experience of grim realities, they were shaken by what they had witnessed. Ida Zolvchin gave them some vodka. Markel had left for Moscow, she said.

"He wished to stay, but comrade Ogonin insisted on his leaving," said Madame Zolvchin. "It is thought his knowledge of local conditions may be of avail to organise the rescue. Ogonin has remained. I wanted to have him here, but he said it would be dangerous for us. He is concealed somewhere in the town."

"But you, Ida Stanislavna? Are you not in danger?" Zena asked.

"Oh, I shall be all right," Madame Zolvchin said with a calm smile. "They do not molest those who preserve outward bourgeois appearances, especially a woman. And the place is so isolated. They will not trouble me. Besides, they will not be here for long."

Madame Zolvchin asked them up to her room on the upper floor. From thence a view of the town below could be obtained, over the tree-tops. The hospital was still burning, the bare outer walls now alone remained standing. The bells of all the churches and convents—there were twenty-three in the town—were pealing joyfully. Down the long broad central street, which sloped steeply and rose again to the Kremlin hill, a procession was moving with golden crosses and ikons, and gold-coped and crowned papas from the cathedral. The Bishop of Kursk and Bjelgorod had already resumed possession of the episcopal palace. The clergy was singing a *Te Deum*. From the Jewish quarter in the eastern part of the town, shouts and screams were rising. Pogroms were taking place.

Zena and Julian and the two Groza girls remained till the afternoon. They drove back about five o'clock. A curfew order had been issued forbidding every one to be out after seven.

The following morning, Countess Groza came round calling on the Varachins in her barouche. She was beaming. Her attire took one's breath away. She wore a blue costume of shot taffeta, with bolero jacket, furbelows and innumerable trimmings, which looked as though it had been taken out of a museum. A gold chain with pendant locket adorned her neck, and she carried a small sunshade with folding handle, although the mild sunshine was scarcely strong enough to take the twang from the sharp air.

"Soon it will be all over. In another week or ten days the Volunteers will be in Moscow, and Lenin, Stalin and all the other Jews will be shot or hanged. Thank God!" she exclaimed in an exuberance of excitement.

Everything was already returning to normal, she said. A reception was being held at the governor's palace and in the adjoining gardens. The divisional general and the new civil governor and their wives would be there. A military band would be playing. All must come with her.

From curiosity, Zena and Julian consented to accompany the silly woman, with the Varachins. Anna and Olga, the countess said, had sent word that they were staying with a friend.

The appearance of the litle town had become transformed with striking suddenness. The Red Square, the neighborhood of the governor's palace, the Nevidof gardens—presented to the town by the late Prince Nevidof—displayed an animation which they had not known for years. One wondered where all the men in bowler hats, starched white collars, and striped trousers, the women holding up with gloved hands the flounces of silk skirts, had sprung from, and where they had lain hidden all the time. To be sure, they looked extremely funny. Even the governor's lady, Madame Krasvianoga, who exhibited on her person, to everybody's wonder, the creations of Parisian couture, looked rather startling, so unaccustomed had one become to such things. Zena had never seen skirts worn quite so short. Madame Krasvianoga had shapely legs, tapering to a fine ankle and sheathed in the finest cobwebs of flesh-colored silk. The lady's legs were the sensation of the afternoon, and quite overshadowed the political and military situation as a topic of interest. She had arrived that morning in a luxurious car, with two maids, innumerable bandboxes, and a dachshund puppy which was supplied with warm milk out of a thermos flask.

An astonishing number of women had come with the army of the liberators. Nadia was introduced to a number of officers' ladies—one was left in some doubt in each case as to whether the lady was a married woman or a whore.

The governor, a stout, bearded general, whose half-closed eyes suggested that he was about to drop off to sleep, stood speaking in a thick voice to each group of visitors as they passed before him, shaking hands with everybody. He recited a little speech, which he repeated in turn to each group of persons, as his audience changed. It was very gratifying, he said, to make the acquaintance of so many good and loyal Russians. Their beloved country was now being rescued and restored. One supreme sentiment united all Russians: the love of Russia, their devotion to their great and holy country. When once order had been restored even the wretched misguided people, the poor dupes whose ignorance had been exploited by foreign agitators, emissaries of the enemies of Russia, would discover that the love of their country, implanted by God and nature in their hearts, was stronger than transient aberrations induced by shallow reasoning. He looked forward to a great and united Russia which would continue to lead, as in the past, the advance of civilisation.

The liberal and broadminded sentiments expressed by the governor elicited the deep approval of Andrei Varachin, who did not conceal his pleasure at the happy change which had taken place. It was proposed to hold some days later a less formal reception at the gubernatorial palace. A gypsy orchestra was expected and several noted singers. Andrei offered to give some readings of poetry.

He came upon, among the younger officers, a kindred spirit, Lieutenant Erdeli, who was, as he informed Andrei, also a poet. His work had been much admired by Grand Duke Constantine, himself a connoisseur, and the author of a religious drama, "The King of Judah." At the suggestion of the Grand Duke, a small collection of Erdeli's poems had been privately printed. The youth was very handsome, and Madame Krasvianoga, developing a sudden interest in poetry, paid a good deal of seductive attention to the young poet and to his companion, Lieutenant Velikof.

Zena and Julian avoided as far as possible mingling with the company, and had declined Countess Groza's offer to present them to the governor and the governor's wife, whom the countess claimed as an acquaintance. They were content to observe the scene as spectators only and from a distance, and went off to sit on a terrace which was raised above the general level of the gardens. Nadia and Andrei sought to dissuade them from their aloofness. One should not allow one's private political views to influence one's social relations, Andrei said. "Such an attitude is a mark of a narrow and prejudiced mind."

The disappointment which Zena's abstention caused Nadia increased when, among the officers whom she met, she came upon their cousin,

Prince Vladimir Alichief. On his enquiring about Zena, Nadia said that her sister was a little indisposed, adding with a significant look:

"I don't think she cares much about mingling with the society that is here."

"Oh, I know Zena from of old," Volodia said. "She is inclined to be a snob. Not that I blame her altogether. Such a mob of impossible people! It is positively ghastly. And one is in duty bound to hob-nob with them and to make oneself agreeable. All the same, I cannot miss the opportunity of seeing my charming cousin."

After a while Volodia, informing himself from Nadia of the direction in which he might find her, set off to greet Zena, and soon discovered her on the outlying spot where she sat with Julian.

After a stiff heel-clicking bow as she presented Julian, Prince Alichief spoke to him with charming courtesy, addressing him in perfect English.

"The Allied military mission, which is now at Kharkhof, is expected here in a day or two," he said. "You may perhaps meet some English friends, Mr. Bern."

The Prince said he was glad that Englishmen should see for themselves the state of things. The people in England and the British Government would then be better able to understand.

"I understood that the British Government was affording you every assistance," Julian said.

"Oh, they are equipping us, supplying us with arms and ammunition, transport, and so forth," said Alichief. "It is the least they could do. It is their business as much as ours, and we are fighting for their interests. But they are not supplying us with enough money. The pay of the troops is in arrear. And that is a serious matter. Unfortunately, the men have little patriotism. Many of them are actually infected with Bolshevist ideas. If they are not sufficiently paid, it is difficult to answer for the consequences. In the desolate state of ruin to which the Bolsheviks have reduced the country, the food commissariat has often been difficult. The men must be allowed to help themselves as best they can, and no doubt they are making the most of the opportunities afforded by the relative abundance of the district."

"In other words, they are descending upon the peasants like a cloud of locusts," said Zena.

"It is needless to put it that way. The confounded mujiks can well afford to pay a little for the protection we are bringing them. No doubt they have been careful to keep plenty of hidden stores," said Alichief.

He hoped that he would have the pleasure of seeing more of Mr. Bern. Unfortunately he had to remain for the present in Kursk to keep the lines of communication clear of bandits and clean up the place a little. The hotel where he was quartered was a terrible hole—positively stinking. He wished he could have gone on with the other troops who were driving the Red rabble north and would soon be occupying Moscow.

"One has to sacrifice oneself, however," he said. "By the way, Zena, Fedor Dimietrovich Hruzof passed through here this very morning. The lucky dog is going on to Moscow."

Zena and Julian excused themselves. They had arranged to return with Nadia and Andrei in good time, and they wished, before doing so, to see something of what was going on in the town.

"I should not advise you to wander about too much unaccompanied," Alichief said. "The men are naturally liable to exuberance after the hard campaign they have fought. One cannot blame them, and they have to be given a little rope now and again."

Alichief offered to accompany Zena and Julian.

In the central quarter, round the Red Square, the appearance of the troops, in their English-made uniforms, and with their stiff, elaborate saluting, contrasted with the tattered, straggling bands of Partisans, with gaping boots, and in disorderly formations, which had recently been passing through the town. Zena wished to have a look at the outlying eastern quarter. Alichief tried to dissuade her, but she insisted. They soon met groups of soldiers who were disorderly and drunk, stopping civilians, rough-handling them, searching both men and women.

"You see, it would not have been pleasant for you to go about here by yourselves," Alichief said.

There were freshly printed notices posted on the walls enjoining the troops to refrain from violence, and to respect life and property. Any suspected person was to be brought before the competent military authorities. But Zena noticed that the order was postdated three days. Alichief smiled as she looked at him enquiringly, reading the date. The notice was in fact equivalent to the proclamation of three days' chartered licence.

The street in which they were ran the length of the town, parallel to the main street, and was bordered with painted wooden houses standing below the street-level. There were soldiers going from house to house. The houses which they had visited looked deserted, and the battered doors disclosed glimpses of wreckage and violence. But from the further end of the street came shouts and cries of terror. Men ran in panic, calling to one another, and people were barricading themselves in the houses. From one house came rending screams of men and women, which struck cold horror.

"I think that we had better go no farther," Alichief said. He went down the path which led to one of the houses near to that where the soldiers were, and, lighting a cigarette, glanced in.

"Would you care to see?" he asked, turning to Zena and Julian with a cynical smile.

Hesitating, they stepped in. There were rills and puddles of blood in the narrow hall. On the floor of the room to the left lay seven bodies, a man and a woman, four girls from sixteen to twenty-five, and a young boy. The man had his face smashed; brain-matter dripped from his nostrils. The girls' bodies were naked. One had her abdomen ripped open. The others showed multiple bayonet wounds. Julian had not seen such grim horror on the battlefield.

"Let us get back," said Zena, sickened. "It is time for us to join Nadia and the others."

The sound of the military band which was playing on the square mingled, as they walked back, with the receding cries of the victims of the soldiers' orgy of violence. People were leaving the governor's party. Many, before returning to the rustic conveyances parked at one end of the square, were directing their steps towards the monastery of the Epiphany of the Virgin, following a group of officers. Some women entered the chapel of the monastery, whence came the chanting of priests, to bow and cross themselves before the iconostasis. But most of them followed the officers towards the open space which extended behind the monastery, on the edge of a high bluff. The overhanging brow of the cliff overlooked the level plain where the river meandered, making several sharp turns and spreading out into backwaters edged with reeds, over which ducks and waterfowl were sailing. There were small farm buildings and clusters of trees, and the quiet waters were spanned here and there by narrow, one-railed footbridges. In the evening light the scene was pleasant and peaceful and reminded Julian of an English country scene. Immediately below was a stretch of strewn boulders, where the cliff had crumbled.

On the open space, facing the edge of the cliff, stood a squad of soldiers and two officers. Presently, from a corner behind the eastern extremity of the monastery wall, emerged a party of soldiers with fixed bayonets. They were leading ten men and three women, loosely tied together, like Alpine climbers, by a long rope. Their hands were bound behind their backs, and they were stripped to the waist. Driven by the soldiers with their bayonets, the prisoners were lined up on the extreme edge of the cliff. Julian recognised a man who had acted as policeman to protect the farmers from plunder, and two of the women. They were the teachers from the school where Andrei had been lecturing, Konia and Melania Sladosteia. They stood, most of them, in sullen, resigned silence, the women overcome with shame at their exposed nudity. The sky behind them was bright with orange sunset lights. Only one old Jew, on his knees, cried and whimpered, imploring miserably.

The crowd of bowler-hatted men and bedizened women from the governor's party were looking on. Several shook their fists and called out insults at the victims, shouting: "Dirty Bolsheviks!" Countess Groza, waving her sun-shade, directed her wrath more particularly towards the two school teachers.

"It serves you right," she cried, "for corrupting children in your Godless school!"

The officer in charge of the firing-squad gave the order, and the men fired. Five only, four men and one of the women were hit. As they dropped to the ground, the line of victims wavered horribly for some moments on the edge of the precipice. Some were striving with instinctive terror to maintain their foothold, while the dead and wounded, hanging over the brink of the cliff, dragged them over. Cries and the thud of falling bodies were heard. The crowd of onlookers rushed forward. At the bottom of the cliff a party of soldiers was finishing off the victims with their bayonets.

The spectators turned back, and joined their friends and their carriages on the Red Square.

"It has been quite a pleasant afternoon," remarked Nadia, as Zena and Julian joined their party. Andrei spoke of the rococo poet, Ippolit Bogdanovich, a native of Kursk, whose statue adorned the square.

From one of the upper windows of the governor's palace Madame Krasvianoga contemplated the beauty of the sunset. She lay stretched on a divan, while young Erdeli, seated at her feet, read out some of his poetry. He paused a moment to comment on the beauty of the scene bathed in the golden and purple radiance. But his eyes were arrested by the prospect which opened to his gaze as Madame Krasvianoga, with careless languor, drew up a shapely silk-hosed leg.

While the Varachins' *brichka* drove home, Zena spoke no word. She was deathly pale. When they had reached the house, she dashed off into her room and broke into a storm of tears. Julian took her into his arms. She lay her head on his shoulder.

"To stand by, to stand by and say nothing while such things are," she cried.

"All our lives we have stood by . . . while men and women were being driven over the cliff," Julian said.

"Let us go, let us go. Take me away from this hell of Russia," she said in a passion of horror.

Julian stood over her, in silence, for a time. Then he spoke gently.

"Why? In the West—in England, in France, in civilised countries— the people, all the nice people, the cultured people, the good people . . . are standing by, while men and women drop down into the abyss. Many of them are shouting insults at them, and old ladies are waving their sunshades in anger. Here, here in Russia, all the people are not standing by. They have left off standing by. . . . That's what revolution means. . . . Honor to revolutionary Russia!"

Countess Groza came over daily to see Nadia and Andrei, attired in startling toilettes, of which she had a collection in her attic, and inviting them to accompany her to parties and concerts at the governor's palace. The Allied Mission had arrived, she said, and the gypsy orchestra. A famous singer was going to give a recital.

Zena refused to go out.

Anna and Olga, also, the countess told Nadia, had the same foolish notion of not joining in social activities. They would absent themselves from home for days, and even nights, at a time.

"Sometimes the girls, after not having been seen for twenty-four hours, will drop in while I am at breakfast," she said, "and sit down as though they had just come from their rooms, without a word of explanation. I have long given up trying to advise them and to exercise a mother's influence over them."

While the countess was entertaining Nadia and Andrei with maternal lamentations and patriotic sentiments, Anna and Olga came to see Zena in her sitting room. Anna, despite the health and strength her sinewy form suggested, looked tired. She dropped into a chair and asked for a cigarette.

"I have not had a cigarette for twenty-four hours," she said. "We have been up all night moving arms and munitions. They were buried when the Reds retreated. We have been distributing them to the peasants."

"Were you not afraid lest you might be detected?" asked Zena.

"Horribly afraid," Anna said. She sat with her legs crossed, in silence, puffing at her cigarette.

"A soldier stopped us once, while we were carrying a box of dynamite cartridges to Comrade Ogonin," said Olga. "We told him they were jewels we had buried so that the Bolsheviks might not take them, and after looking at us a while, he believed us. Fortunately the box was screwed down and he couldn't look inside it. But we had to make a long round to get from another direction to where Ogonin is hidden."

Under the two girls' silent reserve, there was a passionate enthusiasm which inspired admiration. Olga, delicately pretty, with her dark eyes and hair, seemed cut for the part of soft, luxurious grace, but strove to emulate the example of Anna's robust energy.

"But what will you do if the Whites and the Allied intervention crush the Soviets?" asked Zena. "All your courage, and all the fighting, and the lives of those who have been killed will have been in vain."

"Oh, no!" said Anna. "Do you not know what Lenin has said, that no revolution, even if it be crushed, is ever in vain? It gives multiplied strength and intelligence to the next effort. The October revolution could not have been what it was without the lessons of 1905, without the French Commune, and the century of revolution before it. Besides, our revolution will not be crushed. The White Guards and the Allied interventionists will be driven into the sea to feed the Black Sea fish. The English are already beginning to be afraid of burning their fingers, even though they are always careful to use other people's fingers, as far as possible, to draw their chestnuts out of the fire."

What news there was did not seem to confirm Anna's optimism. It was difficult enough to obtain any. A news-sheet, *Golos Naroda*, "The Voice of the People," printed locally, had made its appearance. It gave the communiqués from the White Army headquarters, which announced daily victorious advances. Yet it was some considerable time since it had announced that General Denikin's army was at the gates of Moscow, and even given the hour appointed at General Headquarters for the triumphal entry into the capital. One day the news was current that Moscow had been taken and the Soviet Government was prisoner. But the next day the Whites were still "victoriously repulsing attacks" at Oriel. One seemed to know nothing for certain.

Curious to glean information, Julian once agreed to accompany Andrei and Nadia to a musical entertainment at the governor's palace. The fragile decayed silken wardrobes were aligned before the platform where a fat and conceited-looking pianist, who had the appearance of a eunuch, played Beethoven and Tchaïkovski. Most of the officers, bored, remained on the garden terrace, smoking and drinking vodka. Julian sought to avoid Vladimir Alichief. At the further corner of the terrace were some men in English uniforms, and two in civilian tweeds—evidently the "Allied Mission." Julian strolled in their direction. As he approached them, one of the civilians suddenly looked round at him. There was a look of mutual surprise. It was Welby Penmore.

Welby rose, speaking some words of excuse to his companions, and came over towards Julian.

"Am dashed if I expected to bump into you in this bally God-forsaken place," he said, extending a limp hand. "Ahem! Thought it better not to introduce you to the general. That is, unless you particularly wish. Might—ahem—be perhaps a bit awkward to explain, what? I mean your being here, what? You were posted up, I think, as missing. Not been demobbed, have you? So that, technically . . . what? How the devil . . .?"

Julian said briefly that he had been prisoner in Germany and had come away thence to Russia.

"I see. Yes, of course. And the charming princess?" grinned Sir Welby.

"My wife is in Kursk," Julian said.

"Oh, oh, oh! Congratulations. Well, I'm dashed! Of course, in this bally awful mess, Russian princesses are not exactly what they were, what? If I were you, old man, I'd jolly well make haste to bring her over to England," Welby said.

"I thought that the glories of Tzarist Russia were soon to be restored—with your help," Julian said.

Welby gave a long puff.

"We're a bally long way from there, a bally long way, my boy," he said. He leant his elbows over the balustrade of the terrace and assumed a confidential tone. "Those dashed Russian fellows are a bally nuisance. Always quarrelling among themselves and grousing at us. Between you and me, they'll never amount to much. And their men, the rank and file, they're just a bally lot of Bolshies. They're all infected, all Bolshies. Simply won't fight unless they're paid. It's all we can do to keep them from going right over to the Bolshies. There's only the officers' and cadets' corps that are any bally good. We're a dashed long way from Moscow, I can tell you. We'll be lucky if we can save some of the oil fields. Of course, what we should do would be to send out a good stiff British expeditionary force and settle up with the Bolshies ourselves. That's what we ought to do. But, for one thing, those darned Russian fellows don't like the idea. Want to do the job themselves, so long as we hand over the sinews of war to them. And for another, it's a bally ticklish job to get up another little war just now. The johnnies at home and the demobbed fellows have had enough to last them for a while and are none too keen on starting again just at present. We don't want to have the same trouble as the Frenchies are having at Odessa, the men going Bolshie and just bally well turning the noses of the ships homeward. Then there are all those dashed liberal and socialist blighters at home, kicking up the

most unholy row about everything—the blockade and Winston's little
wars. So that it's quite impossible to have a proper settling up with
the Bolshies just now. We'll have to bide our time. But now's the
time for you and the charming lady to hop it. We've got some decent
tubs down in the Black Sea ready to take over passengers, and I could
arrange the whole thing for you so that you'd get a cushy passage,
don't you know. . . ."

Julian thanked Welby for his kindly offers, and said he would talk
them over with Zena.

"By the way, old man," Welby went on, "you might perhaps need
some money. I don't suppose you're terribly flush, what? Well, one
could always arrange for a few Bradburys, you know what I mean.
As a matter of fact, I'm supposed to be in charge of the cashbox.
But I'm bally careful how I dole out the tin to those Pa-Ruski blighters. Waste of good money, I call it. So that, if you make up your
mind to take a passage, you needn't worry about pocket-money. . . .
I'll tell you what, old man," Welby said, drawing nearer, as though
in an impulse of still closer confidence. "I know, of course, about
your queer Bolshie ideas and all that. Well, as I say, that sort of thing
isn't so frightfully serious in a fellow like you, you know what I mean.
Once a gentleman . . . what? But what I mean is, you might find
things a bit awkward to explain with the W.O., don't you know. What
were you doing in Russia, and so on, what? Not that I couldn't fix
that sort of thing up for you all right. Always stand by one's own
people, what? I've a plan to make it all straight. These bally Russians don't know how to do things. Their Intelligence is rotten. You
wouldn't believe it. They haven't got any names. Have been in such
a dashed hurry to dispatch the Bolshies, that they haven't got the
foggiest notion who's who. Now, you could, I've no doubt, give a few
names. Just, you know, as a pretext to put you down on the Intelligence
Service strength. A mere matter of form. You see what I mean?
Everything would be explained and you'd pocket a pot of money besides, what?"

Julian controlled his impulse to let fly his fist in Welby's face, and
gave a curt, non-committal "Thanks."

"Of course it's for you to think the matter over. Save you a lot of
trouble when you get back to England, you know. You can let me

know. I'm not sure how long I'm going to be in this bally hole. So let me know soon. Well, frightfully bucked to have seen you, don't you know," Welby said as they parted.

Crossing the terrace to go out by the nearest gates of the garden, Julian, his mind preoccupied with the conversation he had just had with Sir Welby Penmore, forgot to take the precautions which he had observed earlier to avoid meeting Prince Alichief, and walked right into him as Vladimir was leaving a group of other officers. The prince advanced eagerly to greet him and enquired whether Zena was at the palace.

"I intended to have called on her and Madame Varachin, and had been looking forward to the privilege of meeting you again, Mr. Bern," he said. "But we have been very short staffed, and my duties have been rather heavy and left me little time. Will you remember me to my cousins and tell them that I will shortly give myself the pleasure of paying them a call?"

Julian replied to the prince's politeness with suitable insincerity, assuring him of the welcome which Zena would, he knew, loathe to have to give him, and regretting that, having stayed somewhat later than he had intended, he felt obliged to return home and deprive himself of the pleasure of the prince's conversation.

As luck, good or ill, would have it, the Varachins' minute drawing room was unusually filled with company when Vladimir Alichief rode over, bringing with him two other officers. Madame Zolvchin, who was not now in the habit of going out much, had come, and Countess Groza was, as usual, there. Her two daughters had, this time, accompanied their mother. Prince Alichief excused himself for having taken the liberty to bring two fellow-officers, but Nadia was manifestly pleased at the unwonted affluence of company in her salon, and Countess Groza was in a flutter and flurry of excitement.

Volodia presented his friends, Captains Bochkovich and Gaganin. Zena, Julian and the two Groza girls at once recognised Captain Bochkovich as the officer with whom they had had to do on the morning when the hospital had been set on fire.

In presenting Madame Zolvchin, Nadia made a point of dwelling upon the social position which she had occupied under the old régime at Moscow.

"You remember, Volodia, Markel Zolvchin, the famous Moscow banker, don't you?" she said. "Ida was the local president of the Red Cross during the war."

Countess Groza also showed eagerness to dissociate Madame Zolvchin from her questionable present associations.

"Like most of us, poor Zolvchin has been robbed of every kopek by the Bolshevik brigands," she said. "The magnificent house on the Dreskii and all the lovely art collections, all gone. But, thank God, we can now look forward to resuming occupation of our old homes soon. When will Moscow be delivered, Prince?"

"We have been obliged to postpone the date originally chosen, Countess," said Prince Alichief, "owing to difficulties of transport arising from the ruinous condition into which the roads and railways have fallen during the period of Bolshevik misrule." The White army was in fact experiencing considerable difficulty in revictualing. Having plundered the country behind them, supplies had to be brought up from the Crimea along the single line of railway. They were experiencing a shortage of munitions. "We could, of course, now take Moscow at any time," said Alichief. "But General Headquarters have not yet appointed a definite date."

"I had intended," Countess Groza said, "to go with my daughters to one of the watering towns in the Caucasus. It has been terrible here for the poor girls, in all the chaos and horror of the Red terror. But now that order is likely to be so soon restored in Moscow, we have decided to wait."

Madame Zolvchin maintained her smiling Madonnalike serenity in face of the enemy. Captain Gaganin, a slightly older man than the other two officers, and inclined to stoutness, appeared to take particular interest in Madame Zolvchin. He sat conversing with her, while sipping his tea and consuming smoked-salmon zakuska, expressing his surprise at not having met her at the governor's parties and pressing her not to deprive future festive gatherings of the privilege of her presence. Gaganin had the thick, moist sensual lips of a satyr, and looked at her, while he conversed, with lascivious goggle-eyes.

Anna and Olga had wished to retire on the arrival of the officers, but Zena had persuaded them to remain. They sought to efface themselves as much as possible, staying in a corner of the room and not joining in the conversation. But both Bochkovich and Alichief insisted, with punctilious courtesy, on paying considerable attention to the young women. Captain Bochkovich made, somewhat clumsily, excuses for the manner of their first meeting.

"The circumstances were certainly not such as I would have chosen for making the acquaintance of such charming young ladies," he said with a conciliating smile. "But that was your fault. Women should keep away from the stern work of soldiers."

"That is, I suppose, why you permitted your men to outrage and murder two women who devoted their lives to nursing soldiers, while your brave troops were engaged in the soldierly work of burning alive three hundred sick and wounded men," Anna said, looking defiantly at Bochkovich.

"Oh, oh! I was mistaken in including you in what I was saying about the gentler sex," he exclaimed with an awkward laugh. "You are a combatant amazon."

Nadia and the countess started, alarmed and horrified, at Anna's frankness, and were about to interpose apologies. But Alichief tactfully came to the rescue.

"I attach little importance," he said, "to the morbid attraction which crazy subversive notions seem to exercise on the impulsive minds of some young women. My charming cousin, Zena, is also, I believe, somewhat of a red amazon. Such eccentricities are not serious in persons of good birth. Good blood is of more importance, and divests foolish opinions of real danger. Your Bolshevik friends, my dear young lady, are for the most part Jews."

"That should not be surprising," said Anna. "The Jews, accustomed to use their wits, are often the only intelligent people among an illiterate population of peasants and idiotic aristocrats."

"Thank you for the compliment," said Volodia, laughing.

To the general relief, the officers gave no sign of being ruffled in their good humor by Anna's uncompromising manner. Before they left, Prince Alichief said, saluting the two sisters:

"I detest Bolshevism with an undying hatred, but for such charming Bolshevik amazons as you, my sentiments are wholly different. My friend Bochkovich and I hope to have the pleasure to continue the argument on another occasion."

News came a few mornings later that the railway viaduct over the river had been blown up. Julian and Zena had heard the explosion in the night; Marusia brought them the news with their breakfast.

The same afternoon Marusia came to tell Zena that a peasant girl who had come to the door selling cucumbers asked to speak to the barinia. When Zena, a little impatient at the unnecessary annoyance, went to the door, the girl, wearing a colored handkerchief round her head, stood stooping over her basket, offering her goods and mumbling indistinctly after the manner of the peasants. Suddenly she raised her head and looked at Zena straight in the face. It was Maïa.

"I have come chiefly to look after Ogonin," she said. "He got a leg shattered in the explosion of the bridge. It was he who blew it up. He is hiding at a comrade's, in great pain. He should be moved to a safer place."

Zena and Julian went at once, with Maïa, to Countess Groza's. Anna and Olga were at home. A plan was concerted. An old peasant who had known Ogonin in the old days gladly offered to take him in his *isba,* which was not far. The difficulty was to get Ogonin moved. By superhuman efforts he had dragged himself along the ground, when he was hurt, but he could not walk. It would be difficult to get him moved, unseen, whether by day or night.

Countess Groza had, in the attic of her house, some uniforms of her late husband, which she kept religiously. Anna and Olga chose one, with epaulettes, medal ribbons, a greatcoat, sword, and other oddments. The horse was put into the barouche, the girls telling their mother that they were going to buy some things in the town. They took, besides the uniform, bandages and dressings with them. After his leg had been fixed in a splint, Ogonin put on the late general's tunic, decorations, and epaulettes, the greatcoat and the cap braided with general's marks. He was helped into the carriage. They drove through the main street of the town. The soldiers and sentries they met stood at attention, saluted and presented arms. Ogonin chuckled heartily over the joke.

News was beginning to come through of the victorious advance of
the newly formed Red armies. No mention of it was made in the official communiqués or in the *Golos Naroda,* but Madame Zolvchin
and Maïa received frequent information from Partisans who, disguised as peasants and hawkers, now easily passed through the lines.

Growing signs of demoralisation became apparent among the Whites.
A general atmosphere of anxiety prevailed at the palace. Trains of
wounded arrived which, the viaduct not having been repaired, had to
be transported in ambulances to the other side of the river and re-
entrained. Batteries of field artillery, returning detachments from the
line, bedraggled and dispirited, passed through, going south. There
was a general relaxing of discipline among the soldiers, who became
careless about their attire and about saluting officers. Rumors were
current of outbreaks of mutiny. There were recrudescences of plundering, and of pogroms. The cellars of one of the inns had been
looted by disorderly soldiers and some officers had joined in the riot.

One day Maïa, who frequently changed her abode, but was a good
deal at Madame Zolvchin's, brought word that the advanced guard of
the Red army was now only at a few versts on the other side of the
hills. Ida Zolvchin wished Zena and Julian to come to dine with her
that evening. Comrade Zverdof would be there and Skepner, who
had just come through from Moscow. It would be a little celebration.

"Is it not a little premature to celebrate?" said Zena.

"Markel Zolvchin is expected at any moment," said Maïa. "Local
forces are being organised to act in conjunction with the Red Guards
in driving out the Whites. In a few weeks they will be driven into the
sea."

Zena did not feel well, she said. She had a headache.

"But you must go, drujok," she said to Julian.

Madame Zolvchin had laid herself out to give her guests a pleasant
evening. Despite her outward serenity, she was excited at the prospect of Markel's soon being back, and at the turn which things were
taking. The table was set with candles and precious lace napery, and
laden with zakuska, plates of meat-cakes, sturgeon and other viands,
and the sideboard carried an array of bottles. The partition doors between the dining and drawing rooms had been thrown open, and the
place was brightly lit with lamps and candles.

Anna and Olga were there, and Maïa, who had resumed her black-leather, semi-military attire. Sverdof, Markel's fellow commissar, had come, and Comrade Skepner, from Moscow. Skepner, a stern Bolshevik with dark, Asiatic eyes and grave face emaciated from long sojourn in Siberia, expressed some disapproval of so much bourgeois luxury.

"But, my dear Skepner, I do not in the least admit that Communism should be synonymous with Christian self-mortification," Madame Zolvchin said as they sat down. "What is the aim of Communism, of revolution? Isn't it like that of all human endeavor, happiness?"

"The happiness of the masses," said Skepner.

"Quite so. But you know better than I do that nine-tenths of the world's wealth and opportunities for joy are wasted, like the heat in an open fireplace which goes, most of it, up the chimney. The social world which will put a stop to that colossal waste does not mean less comfort and luxury, but more, infinitely more."

"We are not in a social world yet," Skepner persisted. "We are in a world of war, of bitter war."

"Oh, I know all you could say. The happiness of the few is stolen from the happiness of the many. But this food is not stolen," said Madame Zolvchin.

"Oh, yes it is," said Zverdof with a droll smile. He was a bright-looking little man, with obvious Jewish features, and laughed with gusto. "It is stolen from the Egyptians." Directly upon the arrival of the Whites, Zverdof had astutely offered his services to the commissariat of the White army, and had obtained several contracts for supplies to the "Volunteers." He thus had enjoyed the opportunity of openly collecting produce from the peasants, and had obtained the money wherewith to pay them. On one pretext or another the contracts were only in part fulfilled, scarcity and other difficulties being adduced as excuses. The remonstrations of the White commissariat officers were, now and again, assuaged by deliveries of supplies and by gifts. Zverdof meanwhile directed, without interference, the bulk of his collections by devious routes and channels to Moscow, thus helping to supply the Reds at the expense of the Whites. He enjoyed the joke immensely, and chuckled as he related his astute activities.

Skepner joined in the merriment and, well knowing that Markel
Zolvchin had freely given the whole of his vast fortune to the Soviets,
and that what little of personal possessions he had retained in his Kursk
house was only what could not otherwise be utilised in the district, did
not press his point.

Julian, who though he had made some progress in Russian, was unable to join with ease in the conversation, conversed with Anna and
Olga in French. He questioned Anna concerning her medical studies.
She said how much she had enjoyed them, and what a disappointment
it had been to her to break them off when the war came. She had
heard from Zena of his work in biology, and wished she could become acquainted with it, she said.

Under Anna's self-reliant manner and her bold courage, as when
she had spoken out on the occasion of the officers' visit at the Varachins'
a few days before, was a deep and almost painful natural shyness,
which showed itself in her customary silence, and it was seldom that
she could be really drawn out to speak her feelings with unconscious
confidence.

"Perhaps you have done the better part of your medical studies,"
Julian said to her. "From what I have heard and seen, they begin on
a foundation of science, then they tail off into blind empiricism mingled with dogmatic tradition, and fade at last into humbug."

"Oh, I dare say," said Anna. "I looked forward to a profession
which would give one independence. I don't mean merely economic independence, though, no doubt, it boils down to that. But the sort of
education and bringing up which I should have received, had the matter rested with mother, would have been solely with a view to marriage. As though a woman had nothing, nothing to contribute but her
body. It is disgusting." She tossed her head indignantly. There was
something of fierce Puritanism in her.

Olga said she had been too young when the war broke out to have
the opportunities which her sister had enjoyed.

"That is, I suppose, why I have been drawn more closely to literature and art," she said. "I know it is unreasonable of me, but I cannot
help feeling some regret for all the old culture that will probably have
to go."

"It will wilt in any case of its own accord, because it is so sodden with falsehood at its very roots that it cannot breathe or blossom in the air of a new age," Julian said.

Julian felt sympathy with the tragedy of the old cultures of servile civilisations, built, every stone of them, upon the metaphysical apologetics of servile society, and which most tragically touched women. "They were built round a tyrannous and oppressive conception of women," he said.

Olga—she was only nineteen—looked like a transplanted flower, so obviously belonging to another clime, of gentle grace and delicately decked submissiveness.

The others were devising immediate plans of action. The peasants, now infuriated by the depredations and outrages of the Whites, must be armed and organised, Maïa said. They must be made to feel that the defence of the Soviets was their own defence. A Partisan army could be raised in the rear of the "Volunteers," cutting off their retreat. They must be not only cleared out—to be armed again some day by England, or France, or Germany—but crushed utterly. Skepner disagreed. Such tactics would only goad them to desperate resistance. Whereas . . .

One of the maids suddenly burst into the room, terror written on her face.

"Soldiers, barinia! There are soldiers coming . . .!" she cried.

The rumble of a lorry out on the road, the racing and turning off of an engine, and the sound of voices were heard.

While all got up and stood breathless, Maïa sprang out of the room, glanced through the hall, and rushed back. She was about to speak, signing to the women to follow her, but she had only time to leap out through the French window that opened onto the garden at the back, when five officers burst into the room. At their head was Vladimir Alichief. With him were Bochkovich, Gaganin, and the young lieutenants, Velikof and Erdesi. About twenty armed soldiers filled the hall. Four of them stood behind the officers at the door of the dining room.

The officers' faces were flushed, their eyes bloodshot. There was a swaggering recklessness in their gait.

Alichief stood glancing round with a mocking smile at Madame Zolvchin and her guests.

"You seem to be having a quite pleasant little party," he said. "Champagne, my word! I compliment you on your taste, Madame."

Ida Zolvchin came forward, very pale, but dignified.

"May I enquire, sir, what procures me the honor of this visit?" she asked.

Chuckling ironically, Alichief replied in a leisurely tone of mock courtesy.

"Our apologies, Madame, for the interruption. I regret if we have somewhat unceremoniously intruded uninvited on your charming party. We were, my friends and I, eager to make the acquaintance of your husband."

"My husband is not here," said Madame Zolvchin.

"Ah! Away on some urgent business, no doubt," Alichief said. He drew out a case of cigarettes and lit one in leisurely fashion at one of the candles standing on the table. Then turning to the soldiers: "You will, my children, have a look round the house to confirm the disappointing news that Mr. Zolvchin is still absent. Husbands have sometimes a way of turning up unexpectedly. You will assure yourselves that no dangerous weapons are lying about or are concealed in out-of-the-way places. And, by the way, you may as well investigate the cellar. There seems to be some deuced good stuff here. Bring anything you find. You will have your share."

"Glad to serve, Most-high-wellborn!" the men replied.

While the soldiers were out of the room, the officers unceremoniously made themselves at home, helping themselves to food and drink. Gaganin, coming forward, gravely bowed over Madame Zolvchin's hand, his own straying, as though inadvertently, lecherously over her arm. She shrank back shuddering. The others, Skepner, Zverdof and Julian, stood motionless by. Anna and Olga had drawn back, shrinking, into a corner of the room. "A charming party," Alichief repeated, glancing round at them again. "The delightful young amazons. And our English cousin. But a bit mixed, Madame," he added, glancing at the other two men.

The soldiers returned with grinning faces, bringing in armfuls of bottles.

"No one else in the house, except the two maids, Most-high-wellborn," the corporal reported.

"Very good," said Alichief. "The two maids are your business. The supplies are satisfactory. You can help yourselves, children, to a third of them. And now you will begin by investigating this gentleman," he said, pointing to Skepner. "He looks to me as though he were predestined to be hanged. Search him."

"Can you show any warrant or authority for this perquisition?" Skepner asked.

Staring at him, Alichief struck Skepner a blow across the face. The soldiers seized him, took off all his clothes except his trousers, and bound his hands behind him. They found a few papers in the lining of his waistcoat, among them a pass from the Moscow Central Committee, giving his name and condition: "Iphraim Skepner, Commissar of the People for Public Defence."

"This is interesting," Alichief said. "You will know how to deal with the rascal," he added, turning to the soldiers.

Zverdof was next to be stripped and searched.

"Why, that's the scoundrel who's been cheating our Commissariat," said Bochkovich.

"Looks capable of it," said Alichief. "I don't like his face. I don't like your nose, Abraham. Reminds me of Judas Iscariot."

"We will improve it," said Bochkovich, and drawing out his sword he seized Zverdof by the nose and slashed off the tip.

Streaming with blood, Zverdof fell on his knees. Bochkovich kicked him, and he rolled on the floor, groaning.

Alichief now turned to Julian, who stood motionless with his back against the wall.

"And now, my English cousin," Alichief said, helping himself to a glass of champagne.

"I had better inform you, Prince Alichief, that another cousin of mine, Sir Welby Penmore, is in the British military mission, and that any violence you may offer me . . ."

"Indeed? Sir Welby Penmore is your cousin?" said Alichief, impressed by the information, but maintaining his nonchalant manner. "Unfortunately for you, Mr. Bern, the Allied Mission left three days ago for . . . an unknown destination."

"Any outrage to a British subject is, nevertheless, usually not overlooked," said Julian. "I may moreover have an opportunity of reporting the gallant behavior of Russian officers, and it would make edifying reading in the English papers."

Alichief burst into laughter.

"Though you may think us barbarians, Mr. Bern," he said, "we are fairly well acquainted with the English newspaper press. No English paper will ever publish anything derogatory to the 'Volunteer' Russian armies. Should you manage to provide them with sensational copy, so worded, of course, as not to offend the sensitive delicacy of the good British public, the casting of the parts would, as a matter of course, have to be modified. You see, we are quite conversant with English journalistic usage. The English are, for the time being, our good friends. Are they not, gentlemen?"

"The very good friends of all who combat for the sacred rights of property," said Bochkovich. "Gentlemen, The King!" he added with mock solemnity, raising a cup of champagne towards Julian.

"And the ladies!" shouted Gaganin, raising with tremulous hand his glass towards Madame Zolvchin.

"You see, we are not quite such barbarians as you would make out," said Alichief, whose speech was becoming rather thick. "We are not going to cut off your nose—which is not in the least Semitic. We, on the contrary, invite you to do us the honor of joining in a little merry-making and revelry. But, as a mere matter of formality, you will first have to be searched."

On a sign, the soldiers seized Julian and stripped him to the waist. They produced an automatic pistol from one of his pockets, and handed it to Alichief.

"You see, the formality was not superfluous," said the Prince. "This is a nasty weapon. You will kindly sit down in that easy chair. I hope it is quite comfortable. As an additional precaution it will be better to tie you to it."

Julian was tied down so firmly that he could hardly breathe and the rope cut into his flesh.

"Take away that yelling Yupin and stop him squealing. Cut his throat or something," Alichief shouted to to the soldiers. "And now leave us and enjoy yourselves, children. You have an abundant supply of vodka and two buxom wenches to keep you company."

Dragging away by the feet Zverdof, who writhed in a pool of

blood, the soldiers left the room and closed the door into the hall. The screams of women and the cries and groans of Skepner, who was being tortured, could be heard.

Madame Zolvchin had stood all the while, leaning with her hands against the back of a chair, pale and trembling. Alichief, after quaffing another glass of champagne, turned to her in his tone of mock politeness.

"We have, Madame, from a sentiment of delicacy which you will appreciate, not had you searched by the soldiers," he said. "We will even leave it to you to comply with the formality. Be good enough, Madame, to undress completely."

The other officers stood round her. Gaganin, goggle-eyed, staggered up to her, and laid his hand on her skirts. Madame Zolvchin appealed and implored. But Alichief and the other officers changed their manner from ironic civility to brutality and repeated their command. Madame Zolvchin dropped down on her knees, wringing her hands and begging for mercy. Threatening her with drawn pistols at the same time, the officers laid hands on her. Bochkovich pointed his sword at her throat.

"Don't kill me, don't kill me," she cried, distracted. "I . . . I will do what you want . . . but don't kill me."

Madame Zolvchin rose trembling to her feet and, scorched with shame, submitted amid ribald comment and laughter. Gaganin denuded her of her last garments, and his hands went over her with leisurely lubricity.

Beaten and prodded with drawn swords, she was compelled to dance, while Erdesi played the piano and the others drank and caroused. They made her stand against the hot stove while they subjected her to obscene outrages. After Gaganin had vented his lust and depravities upon her, Alichief and Bochkovich pushed her into the hall, where the soldiers were rioting and raping the maids, and handed Madame Zolvchin to them to do with as they pleased.

Alichief and Bochkovich then turned, leering, to Anna and Olga. The two young women, frozen with terror, had edged towards the folds of the window hangings, in the faint hope of being forgotten and overlooked by the drunken officers. But Alichief drew the curtain aside and all eyes turned to the two sisters.

"Shall we continue our argument?" Alichief asked with mocking irony.

Anna held her younger sister, with her arms protectingly about her.

With scurrilous jibes, Bochkovich said that the fate which they had once escaped had been delayed only to be more exquisitely inflicted.

"You may yet avoid it," said Alichief. "Tell us where we may find your delightful friend, the jail-bird Ogonin."

Anna, her arms still about Olga, looked at her in angulish. Her lips trembled. But Olga cried out:

"Don't speak, Anna, don't speak!"

Julian writhed in the taut ropes which cut into the bare flesh of his arms.

The officers approached the two sisters, gloating with monstrously inflamed lechery over their prey. Appeal, nor prayer could avail. The young women were seized and separated, their clothes tossed up and torn from them.

During two hours Anna and Olga suffered every extremity of shame that unbridled lubricity could inflict, and every outrage. Cruelly, they remained conscious to the last. Till, sated with lust and overcome with potations, the men lay in stupor or slumber, and silence fell on the room.

From the hall still came the sound of riot, the drunken songs and shouts of the soldiers, the moans of women.

Presently, mingled with noise, shots were heard. The accustomed sound drew at first no attention. Then the riot in the hall suddenly stopped. A soldier, capless, his face purple with congestion, burst into the room.

"The Bolsheviks!" he cried.

Alichief sprang up, hastily fastening his belt and drawing his automatic pistol, and rushed out. The others roused themselves, adjusting their clothes, and followed him. Gaganin lay snoring on the floor.

As soon as they were out of the room, Anna, naked, rushed up to Julian and undid his bonds. She took out Gaganin's automatic from the holster of his belt. Julian picked up the one which had been taken from him, and was lying on the table, and put two shots into Gaganin's head. At the same moment the double panes of the French window crashed, and Maïa burst into the room.

"Come with me," she called, rushing through without stopping.

Snatching up what clothing they could, Anna, Olga, and Julian followed her. The hall was empty of men. The four officers and the soldiers had run out towards the lorry in which they had come, and which stood in the roadway. They were met by a well-fed volley from behind the vehicle. Several men dropped. The others ran back.

"To the upper floor, all to the upper floor, you fools," cried Alichief.

All rushed back through the hall and up the wooden staircase. Alichief waited at the foot of the stairs till the others had passed before he went up. While he stood on the stairs, Anna discharged in his direction the automatic which she held. Alichief crumpled up and rolled down the steps. Some soldiers turned back, pointing their rifles. But several Red guardsmen had meanwhile entered the hall, and answered with shots from below. A struggle ensued on the stairs.

Julian and the women followed Maïa to the kitchen. Madame Zolvchin was unconscious, and had to be carried. The dead body of Skepner lay in a corner, horribly mutilated. Zverdof was exhausted from loss of blood. A trapdoor in the kitchen floor led down by a ladder to the cellar. All went down.

"You will be safe here, now," Maïa said to the women. She ordered four Red-guardists to remain with them. "We must now see that Zena and her sister are also safe," she said to Julian.

There was a narrow passage over stacks of firewood, leading from the cellar to the shed where the wood was cut. Maïa and Julian crawled out to the shed. From there they reached the road, avoiding the crossfire between the Red Guards and the Whites on the upper floor of the house. A machine-gun was spluttering from the bank on the opposite side of the road. Under cover of a ditch they crawled up to where the lorry stood.

There they found Markel Zolvchin and the commander of the Red Guard detachment. Maïa exchanged a few words with them. A man started the engine and took his place at the wheel. Twenty others jumped into the lorry with Maïa and Julian.

"You must take one of the machine-guns also," said the commander. "The job is nearly finished here. One machine-gun will suffice us."

The lorry moved off and speeded, bumping on the uneven road. A few hundred yards farther, the road bent towards the river, where a wooden bridge crossed it. Dawn was breaking. As they came up to the bridge, a party of Whites was approaching it from the other side. Shots were exchanged. The detachment of Whites held the bridge-head stoutly. The driver was hit in the arm, and another man took his place. The lorry advanced slowly on the bridge.

"Lie low and hold your fire till we are on them," called Maïa.

After advancing a few yards under a hail of bullets, the driver opened out and the lorry charged, while rifles and machine-guns let go. The Whites were mowed down and fell back. Turning to the right, the lorry sped along the road which skirted the town to the west. They stopped at some distance from the Varachins' house, and left the lorry behind some trees, off the road. Maïa briefly gave directions to the men, and she and Julian went on alone.

Zena was anxiously waiting. She had heard the firing in the direction of the Zolvchins' house. She ran into Julian's arms.

"We heard rumors of all manner of horrors," she said. "That the Volunteers were out of hand, breaking out into pillage and violence."

Maïa remained in the garden. After a while she came up to the sitting room where Zena and Julian were, and where Nadia and Andrei had joined them.

"We have come none too soon," she said. "There is a party of White Guards coming towards the gate."

"Stay where you are," Julian said to Zena and Nadia. "Maïa and I will do the parleying."

About twelve soldiers stopped at the gate. The officer who was with them spoke a few words to them and, lighting a cigarette, strolled up the path. Julian went forward towards him.

To his surprise, he recognised Prince Hruzof. Fedor stopped with a gesture of mock surprise, and the two men remained standing, facing one another at a few paces' distance.

"Ah, ah!" Fedor exclaimed. "I did not expect to have the pleasure of meeting my old friend, Mr. Bern, here. So, you have, with true gallantry, followed my wife into the wilds of Little Russia."

"You are also probably unaware that the lady you refer to has obtained a divorce from you and is my wife," Julian said.

Fedor burst into laughter.

"A cat marriage, eh? The holy sacrament of the Bolshevik communism of women. That is a good joke. For the moment, however, I am but mildly interested in Bolshevik matrimonial arrangements. My present business is to protect the national armies against any tricks from your Red friends. The fact that this remaining vestige of poor Nevidof's estate has become a nest of Bolshevism has too long been tolerantly overlooked. Stronger precautions are now being taken. It is my strange and painful duty to place my own wife under arrest and to make sure that her associates will not be a menace. The times being, unfortunately, unsuited to civilities, I shall use the shortest and surest methods."

So saying, Fedor Hruzof, still waving his cigarette in one hand, drew out with the other his automatic pistol and fired straight at Julian. Thanks to a quick movement on Julian's part, the shot missed him. At the same moment another shot was fired immediately behind Julian. Fedor Hruzof swayed a second or two, fell, writhed for a moment, face downward, on the ground, and was still.

The soldiers, who had been standing at the end of the garden path, rushed forward. But before they had advanced many steps, a machine-gun rattled from behind the hedge, enfilading them. Red-guardists sprang forward from the bushes on either side, finishing off the survivors.

After watching the scene, which did not occupy many seconds, Julian turned back towards the house. In the doorway Maïa was standing. In her arms was Zena. She had received a wound in the shoulder, evidently from the shot which Fedor had fired at Julian.

After they had taken her to her room and undone her clothes, it was found that the bullet had grazed the collarbone. The wound was bleeding freely, but Julian was able to ascertain that the artery had not been injured. Field-dressings were obtained and applied, and Zena's arm bandaged to her chest. She looked better, after the dressing; her color returned, and she smiled, propped up in bed. She felt no pain, she said. The wound had felt like a burn, but she was fairly comfortable.

It was impossible, in the circumstances, to obtain medical aid at the moment. But Zena felt so well that there appeared no urgency.

The town and district were being evacuated by the White army. The Reds were in occupation of all the northern heights, and the Whites retreating under cover of the guns which had been moved to the other bank of the southern river and of rearguard positions in the northern quarters of the town and the railway line.

Julian, who had gone into the town on the chance of being able to procure medical assistance, found the Red Square and the roads leading to the railway in the turmoil of a hurried exodus. The governor's wife and other ladies, with their maids, baggage, servants, and lap-dogs, were leaving in motor-cars. Departing lorries were filled with members of the Gypsy orchestra, cooks, with their kitchen batteries, and other followers. Several battered Ford cars were transporting the bishop and a bevy of popes.

Countess Groza came over to the Varachins' house. She was in more sober attire than she had lately donned. The countess was so upset over her own troubles that she had very little attention to spare for Zena's condition. She was uncertain whether she would be able to obtain a place in a train.

"They are having a train to Perekop this evening for civilians," she said. "But is is impossible to secure a place, and the train is leaving from the other side of the river at some impossible hour. I don't know how I shall get there with my luggage. Things are disgracefully managed, I am told. I could never wait a whole day for another train, as they asked me to do."

The countess did not even mention her daughters. On Zena enquiring whether she had news of them, she said she had none.

"The girls choose to live their own lives, you know. They take no notice whatever of what I say," she complained. "They have never wanted to go away. If it were not for them, I should have left long ago. I have sacrificed myself for them. But now I can do so no longer. I have done my best for the girls. Now I can no longer be responsible. Since they wish to stay, they must learn to do without a mother's care. I believe they are staying with that Madame Zolvchin. They have not even taken the trouble to let me know or to look me up."

Nadia tried to break very gently to the countess something of what had happened.

"They have been through a terrible experience," she said. "Julian was there when the house was attacked."

But the countess interrupted her.

"Oh, I have heard some rumors. Those Bolsheviks! It is terrible to think of the things they do. I warned the girls. What could they expect, consorting with Jews. They commit all sorts of atrocities, the Jews. They are obliged to by their religion, you know."

Zena seemed to be making good progress. In the evening of the same day on which the countess called, Anna came. She was very pale and looked several years older. But her manner was even more self-possessed and calm. She had heard that Zena had sustained a wound, and she had come to see her. She examined the injury carefully. Then sat a while talking with Zena. Anna was, naturally, reluctant to say much. Madame Zolvchin was very ill, she said. They proposed to send her as soon as possible to Moscow. She would probably require an operation. Olga was in bed, but very brave. She had wanted to come out with her sister, but Anna had refused to let her. It came out that Anna had been most of the time with the Red Guard troops, in the posts on the bank of the northern stream. Her calm broke down for a moment, and she said, with clenched teeth:

"I wanted to shoot White Guards . . . to kill . . . to kill."

She spoke to Julian, after leaving Zena.

"It was a very near thing," she said. "A hair's breadth lower and the main artery would have been injured. As it is, there seems to be nothing serious. But there is a dulness at the apex of the lung, which I can't account for, and she is a little feverish. She ought to be seen by a competent doctor. I will see what I can do to get one."

Fighting was going on in the streets. Detachments of the "Volunteer" army were trapped in the town by the blocked exit caused by the destroyed railway bridge. They were trying to hold off the Red Guards till they could retreat. One party from the Officers' Corps was holding out in the main street, entrenched in a baker's house, with machine-guns at the windows. The advanced guard of the Reds was forced to draw back for cover.

Presently a crowd of peasants, armed with old pattern rifles, fowling pieces, some with scythes and pitchforks, made their appearance, debouching from side streets in the rear of the Cadets. They had a long peasant's cart, an *arba,* with them, pushed by men, on which was a machine-gun. Zverdof, his face bound up, and Ogonin, crouching on his splintered leg, were manning it.

Even though caught between two fires, the Whites were able to hold their opponents off for a while. Their machine-guns swept the crowd of peasants. Inexperienced, not knowing how to deploy and take cover, and thinking only of charging in serried ranks, the peasants presented an admirable target. As a number of them were mowed down, the rest wavered and a panic took place, the peasants rushing back for cover into the side streets. Only the arba with the machine-gun was left in the middle of the street. Scattering and bending low, a party of White officers rushed in and pounced upon it. Zverdof was killed. Ogonin, unable to stand or walk, was dragged back to where the group of Whites was massed in front of the bakery. While they continued to hold off the Reds with machine-gun fire, some officers, taking the rope from the pulley over the baker's cellar, hanged Ogonin to the crane. With the noose round his neck, he called to the Red Guards and the peasants:

"In the name of the workers and peasants of the whole world, charge and give no quarter!"

The Reds rushed forward from both sides. Peasants hacked down officers with their scythes. No quarter was asked or given.

Less than an hour after the Red Guard army had established itself in the main part of the town, Maïa brought a physician to see Zena, a famous professor from Moscow. He spoke guardedly to Julian, after he had examined the patient. There had been some internal hemorrhage, he said, a clot over the pleura and some infiltration. Careful nursing and watching would be needed. There was a possibility of pleural infection, of pneumonia.

For several days Zena's condition did not seem to give cause for alarm. It remained apparently unchanged. But a day or two later the threatened inflammation declared itself. Zena became more feverish and her breathing difficult. She became very ill. At times she was delirious and spoke of going to Reizenfels. Then the fever dropped, but not completely, and the evil did not resolve itself in a definite crisis. Zena was very weak.

At night Julian sat up by her bedside. She would wake refreshed after a sleep, and say that she felt quite well. She asked for news. The victory of the Soviet armies was greater than all hopes. The hosts of reaction and European intervention were being swept, literally almost, into the sea. The mean bourgeois crowds, the aristocratic refugees of the Crimea and Caucasus, plotting for their own selfishness only, were now scrambling on to English and French boats at Sevastopol and Odessa. Revolution had repulsed the world, leagued to crush her, and had now gained a breathing-time to build up a new world.

"I am glad," said Zena. "It is what you wished you might live to see."

Nadia and Maïa took turns with Julian to sit up with Zena. There was no great change in her condition. At times she seemed quite well and cheerful. But she was becoming weaker; her breathing difficult. The doctor would not give definite assurances. . . .

Julian sat by her, in the shaded light of the oil lamp. She had had one of her long, restorative sleeps, and awakened refreshed. But she was so weak that Julian had to hold her up while she drank some water.

In the utter stillness of the night, propped on pillows and holding his hand, she asked suddenly:

"Tell me, drujok, am I going to die?"

He did not dare to answer. He could not break with words of vain pretence the solemnity of the silence.

She was shaken with a little sob, tears flowed on her pale cheek, and her mouth twitched. Julian was about to speak, to explain.

"Oh, I know, of course, I know. I don't mind. It is better so," she said, shaking off the spasm. She smiled at him after a while, pressing his hand. Then she spoke very quietly in the great stillness.

"It is best," she repeated. "The battles of the times that are coming will mean more to you than my love, will be worthier of you. I could have no right place in them. I am too much of the old world that is dead. But you know that I have never really loved it. I used to think that it was because I hated people, crowds of people. I knew it was silly and ridiculous. Then I learned that it was murderous and odious. Yet I cannot be of the new world because I looked to the joy of life, and am not strong enough for the joy of strife. The joy of life . . . We have had a taste of it, have we not, dear? It has been short. But is not all joy thus? And now it is past, and in a little while I shall be past. It is well that I should go . . . with the joy and the love still in me, dear. You . . . you will fight, if not with your arm, with your spirit. And you will fight better without me. One cannot have both, the joy and the strife.

"You had better leave Russia, dear. It is a foreign land to you. It has become almost a foreign land to me. You must go back, dear, somewhere in the torn old world where you can fight the old fiends . . . ignorance, hypocrisy, selfish greed, fanaticism . . . and await the day. Help Nadia and Andrei to get back. Open that drawer on the right of the chest, drujok. You will find what is left of my jewels. Keep them. They will serve immediate needs.

"I know you will choose the better part. I have always admired your loyalty to your intelligence, dear . . . even when it seemed weak and wavering. I have always loved you for it. And I believe it has not been in vain."

Maïa came to give Zena her medicine. She insisted that Julian should take some rest.

"Good night, dear," she said.

At the door, Julian turned back again.

Zena put her arms round his neck. They were still a while in a long embrace.

"Good night, my love," she said.

Julian had had no sleep for two nights. He dropped into heavy, leaden unconsciousness, wrapped in a blanket on the sitting-room sofa.

Maïa had to shake him, almost, in order to rouse him at dawn. He could hardly rouse himself, overcome with slumber. Maïa stood at the door of the bedroom to let him pass. He muttered some enquiry.

"Is she . . .?"

Maïa did not answer, looking motionless into his eyes. He burst into the room. He dropped on his knees without a word by the bed and buried his face in his hands. Her eyes were still open, lusterless. Her teeth, her row of pearls, looked dull and soiled in her unclosed mouth. Her head lay a little to one side on the crumpled pillow, as though she had dropped off to sleep, very tired.

XVIII

THE glory of a May morning had tempted me out for a stroll in the direction of the Park. One of those London mornings it was that wield a spell of spring richer and more potent in its way than the gaudier radiance of southern climes, from contrast, maybe, with months of grime and greyness, or from a velvety quality of the air touched with sea-haze, which makes the grass grow more lush and clothes the sheep with softer wool in England.

I had finished work. That is to say, I had just put the finishing touches to a couple of articles I had been engaged on, and felt righteously satisfied with the result. As I stood before the glass, giving a final tug to my tie and cuffs, and the proper suggestion of a rakish tilt to my grey homburg, I was, I must admit, however unwarrantably and childishly, in a mood of self-approval which rightly disposed me to enjoy care-free the weather's witchery.

Sauntering down Piccadilly, I was put in mind, oddly enough, of a like spring day, ages ago—like a coward I shrank from reckoning exactly how long, lest the result should make me feel unconscionably old—when I had driven to Park in Lady Penmore's carriage with Julian Bern. The lapse of time must have been expressible as a vulgar fraction of a century, baulk as I would the brutal truth of figures. Certainly it had been in another age. There had been the same spell in the air, the same suave ambience of people placidly poised on a secure sense of the stability of their fortunes, liking to do themselves well, and to put away all disturbing glimpses of realities which they believed could not touch them. Was it the smell of the violets offered by pavement hawkers which brought back the long forgotten scene to my mind, as odors are apt to do with uncanny vividness?

How much, even to the external eye, had changed! The luxurious mansions of Mayfair, whence the womenfolk of the world's rulers were wont to step into their immaculate carriages, now bore for the most part large wooden boards over their entrance porches, announcing that they were for sale. Many were being pulled down, and the steel skeletons of many-storied "American" hotels were running up. In the shop-windows, still attractive as always to men's eyes, the price-tickets were often marked in dollars. I could recall a time when "tourist" was synonymous in Europe with "English," and only penniless countries like Italy counted catering for the foreign visitor as an "invisible import." London was now making its spring preparations, not as of yore for "the season," but for "the American season."

The men I passed in the street were, as ever, well dressed, but in a more informal manner. I recognised former "brass-hats," toddling round to their clubs in very effaced "civies," and I caught sight of several faces under brimmed felts, which I remembered having seen in France or on the Salient, at relief time, now pathetically fallen from khaki glory. Mostly, they avoided recognising one another. It was a little humiliating. As I turned suddenly from a shopwindow, a man called out: "Hello, old man!" It was a moment or two before I recognised Weeney, our adjutant, under a bowler hat in a blue serge suit.

"Getting on all right?" he asked casually.

"Not too bad. And you. Got a berth?" I said.

"Selling cars," he replied. "Just on my way to catch a bird. Well, ripping to have had a squint at you again, old top. Toodle-oo!"

Meetings with our companions in arms were, as a rule, not much more elaborate and protracted.

The Park looked comparatively deserted. The ladies one met promenading lap-dogs had about them an unpleasant suggestion of gentility which had seen better days. Loafing men in tweed caps and knotted scarfs had invaded the once sacred precincts where a man would have felt embarrassed without a silk hat. Along the Ring Walk the chairs were mostly empty or stacked up. On the benches were rows of men. They sat listless, one against the other. Most of them were slumbering, their heads drooping on their chests or shoulders, their hands in their frayed pockets. They looked as though they had been there all night.

I looked into their faces as I passed, with morbid curiosity. They were the men who had returned to a land fit for heroes. Some had obviously been officers, young subalterns. The boyish public school faces, tanned and worn, the clothes, once smart, now soiled and torn, were recognisable. The sight had for me an unhealthy fascination. I went along peering indiscretely into each face. There was a blond, curly-headed boy, one of those young Greek gods from 'Varsity, I felt sure, sitting next to three simple-faced, heavy-featured Tommies. At the other end of the same bench was a man with grey, lined, worn face, thrown back, as he slept with his mouth open, his coat collar turned up over his collarless shirt . . . A quiver ran through me as I looked more closely into his face. I looked again. I rubbed my eyes to be sure I was not dreaming. My God, could it be? Yes, there was no doubt. It was Julian.

I walked back and forth a few paces, trying to make up my mind what were best to be done. He looked starved. It was obvious that the first thing needed was to give him to eat. The situation would need careful handling. To come to this pass he must have carefully avoided people, a dozen people whom he could easily have gone to. I approached him gently, touching him on the shoulder.

"Hello, old man," I said in as casual a voice as I could command.

Julian did not at first open his eyes. As I called him again, he slowly glared at me with a scowl. He muttered something and shook himself a little, then, without changing his position, mumbled in a sleepy voice:

"Hello, Laurie." He yawned and half closed his eyes again.

I felt unspeakably silly, stuttering, and scarcely knowing what to say.

"Ahem! I say, what about going round for a snack at Duke's," I said. "We . . . er—can have a private room, you know."

"Duke's? Quite a third-rate cuisine, old chap," Julian said, stretching out his legs a little. "Am surprised at you. Not a patch on Jules."

"Right oh! Hooray! We'll drop into Jules," I said, so glad that he took it that way that I got more and more idiotic.

Julian hadn't moved from the bench. He rose slowly and stretched again.

"They make those seats confoundedly uncomfortable to spend the night on," he said. He stood stiffly, looking round at the other men, who were still slumbering. The Tommy who was sitting next to the curly-headed Greek god roused himself a little.

"Could you move along a little, sir?" he said to the Greek god.

They shifted their position and dropped off to sleep again.

Julian smiled.

"That's his batman," he said, pointing to the Tommy, who had settled down again with his head on the Greek god's shoulder. "I say, old man, do you happen to have a few loose half-crowns about you to give those chaps? I don't happen to have much change, myself, at the moment."

"Rather. Here you are," I said, handing him my silver.

Julian divided up the coins and slipped a share into the pocket of each of the sleeping men.

I hailed a taxi and we got into it. There was so much to ask that I did not know where to begin. I said so. Julian agreed and said we'd better put it off till he had had some food.

"Where do you come from, anyhow?" I asked.

"From the threshold of another world," he said.

"I dare say," I replied, misunderstanding him. "I meant . . ."

"From Russia," he said.

As we got out of the taxi, I tried unostentatiously to make whispered arrangements with the manager at Jules for a private room.

"My friend has just arrived from a German camp," I said, nervously trying to explain Julian's bedraggled appearance.

I could have spared myself the trouble. Julian sauntered in with the air of a pasha of three tails. It takes a damned lot of balance to enter Jules's without a collar, with a doubtful shirt, Continental clothes more than frayed and soiled, and shoes that had originally been yellow. Any one who can carry it off must be a super-swell—so, at least, thought the awed waiters. They spent themselves in deferential solicitude, and I overheard a sleekly groomed old gentleman, who was trailing a County family after him, enquire, impressed: "Who is it?" I felt uncomfortably dowdy and absurd beside Julian.

"Where's your place for some sort of a wash and brush up?" he asked the manager.

"Excuse me, I'll be back in one moment," I said, as he was engaged in ablutions.

I ran round to Turnbul and Asser's to purchase a soft shirt. That shirt of Julian's really worried me. "Our latest design, very exclusive," the shopman said, showing me the article, which I snatched up, running back with it to Jules's lavatory.

As we settled down at a table, I looked tentatively at the menu for suggestions. But Julian took charge.

"Pardon me, old man," he said, "but I probably know more about this sort of thing than you do. I've got to go gently," he said, turning to the head waiter, "having eaten nothing to speak of for a week. *Truite au bleu*—that ought to be quite good here, your fish is living, of course? But with melted butter, I'm not able to cope with *sauce Hollandaise* as yet. Then I'll have some *poulet sauté Marengo*—and tell the chef not to forget that hint of 'Marseilles vanilla.'"

We ate in silence, mostly, and leisurely. When the coffee and *fine* were served, and Julian had lit a cigar, he began to talk, slowly, in a low voice. The place was empty. We were left to ourselves.

" . . . .
. . . . From some Grand Duke's hothouse in the Crimea, Maïa managed to procure a sheaf of roses. They scattered them over the Red flag with which, in their indulgent interpretation, they had honored the coffin. It was lowered into the grave we had dug in the garden of Krestianiskii Pokoi."

He remained for a long time silent, the muscles of his face working.

"She was very sweet," he said.

After a while, he resumed his narrative.

The long journey to Paris, where he left Nadia and Andrei, had been uneventful. It was at Folkestone that his troubles began. He had no passport and no papers, and had a good deal of trouble in accounting for himself to the officials gathered in force to protect from contamination the purity of the political views of the people of Great Britain. After five hours' communication with War Office records, it was readily established that Julian was still, technically, an officer holding the King's commission, that he had been mentioned in dispatches and decorated with the Military Cross. But there were circumstances to be explained: how he had not been repatriated together with other war prisoners in Germany, how he came to be on his way from Russia, and what he had been doing there. The chief immigration officer and the various officials questioned Julian with the courtesy and scrupulous fairness of manner of British officials, which nowise prejudices firmness in their action or deflects its course. He was requested to regard himself, pending further investigation, as under arrest in his hotel.

During the two days he was thus confined, policemen and plain-clothes men were unobtrusively stationed in the hotel hall, or stood about in front of it. An immigration official visited him from time to time on the pretext of questioning him on some particular. On the third day after his landing he was convened to the chief immigration officer's office, where a gentleman from the Southern Command (Intelligence) had come down expressly to interview him.

Captain Paradise was a tall and handsome young man with serious face. He greeted Julian as a brother officer, apologising for the trouble he was being put to, and offered him cigarettes.

"Of course, you know, Bern," said Captain Paradise, after the whole story had been gone over once more, and notes taken, with a gold pencil on a block, "the whole purpose of this passport business and all the fuss is to keep track of Communists. There is, I ought to tell you frankly, some . . . er . . . suggestion . . . Oh! I suppose, quite erroneous—that you . . . er . . . have communist sympathies, so to speak."

"The suggestion," said Julian, "is perfectly well founded."

"Er, yes, I see," said the captain, with a slight maidenly blush, but without change of tone or expression. "Have another gasper, will you?" He fumbled with his gold lighter to offer Julian a light. "These damned things are always going wrong. Paid a good price for it, too, at Dunhill's."

"I can venture a shrewd guess at where the suggestion comes from," said Julian. "Should be surprised if it did not originate from my worthy cousin, Sir Welby Penmore."

Captain Paradise laughed. "I didn't know the skipper was your cousin. Between you and me and the lamp post, Sir Welby is a bit of a . . . er."

"Shite," Julian suggested.

The captain blushed.

"Well, to come down to business. Did you give away any military secrets while you were in Russia?"

"Yes," Julian said.

"Ah? What did you tell them?" asked Captain Paradise, applying his pencil to his notebook.

"That the English staff were a pack of bloody fools," said Julian.

"That's not a secret. That's common knowledge," the captain said. "You have not to come to England on any special mission from the Soviet . . . er . . . Government?" he asked.

"Alas, no," Julian said.

"You do not propose to engage, for instance, in Communist propaganda?"

Julian looked at the handsome boy with a flicker of a smile: "We are all engaged in Communist propaganda, my dear sir," he said. "You, for instance."

"I?" Captain Paradise queried.

"You are at the present moment engaged in propagating the deadly fear in which your employers hold the diffusion of intelligence regarding social facts. Have you not just told me that the whole machinery of obsolete international barriers, which the British Government at one time indignantly denounced as an affront to liberty, has been set up again owing to that panic fear? What propaganda!"

Captain Paradise smiled. "You have not answered my question," he said pleasantly.

"Yes, I have," said Julian. "Whether I will or no, what remains to me of life will be a propagation of changed knowledge which neither you nor I can control. The answer is in the affirmative."

"I see," said Paradise.

"Glad you do," put in Julian.

"I am directed to put one more question to you," said Captain Paradise. "Are you in favor of changing the British Constitution?"

"Utterly," Julian said.

"I see. Ahem! You place me, I must tell you frankly, in a very awkward position. Personally, having had the pleasure of making your acquaintance, and knowing that you are a soldier and a gentleman, I do not think that you are at all dangerous."

"Please do not humiliate me," Julian said.

"At the same time, my duty would be to keep you for the present under arrest. I shall have to consult . . ."

At the moment a policeman entered the office with a telegram.

"Official, for you, sir, from Intelligence Department," he said, handing the missive to Captain Paradise.

The captain opened and read the telegram, and handed it to Julian. It read :

LIEUTENANT JULIAN BERN TO BE GIVEN FULL FREEDOM STOP
NO FURTHER ACTION   PENMORE

Julian took a dingy lodging in Mecklenburgh Square. From a sense of moral obligation, he wired to Viola at Bognor, giving her his address. He could not bring himself to visit her in her new household. Viola came to him by the next train.

Her haste was not, it appeared, wholly due to natural concern and affection. Julian's telegram had found her in the midst of an acute crisis, the culmination of a long tale of wretchedness. Glamrood had become, since their marriage, more and more exacting and tyrannical. He was in the habit of beating Viola on the slightest pretext, and even as what he considered to be a wholesome disciplinary measure. Every evening he would read aloud from the Bible to the assembled household, exhorting them to repent of their sins. His zeal for their mortification frequently took the form of administering fustigations to Viola and all the children, with a birch rod. More than by her own humiliation, Viola had been distracted at Herbert Glamrood's treatment of little Harry, on whom he was particularly fond of venting his brutality. Daisy and Meta amply benefited from their father's and aunt's favoritism, and used their advantage to act spitefully towards little Harry, who was now over six years old. Glamrood's cruelty had become greatly intensified since the termination of the Reverend Loughley Spender's association with the "Church of the Friends of Jesus," in distressing circumstances. Miss Olive Glamrood had discovered that the reverend gentleman was habitually guilty of indecent assaults on her young nieces. Herbert had, since then, been conducting the services himself.

The state of things had been brought to a head, only a few days before, when Viola, on unexpectedly entering the nursery, caught Daisy and Meta engaged in vicious practices with little Harry. Distracted, Viola had, there and then, taken Harry to a friend of hers at Littlehampton, intending to arrange for placing him in a private boarding school. When she had returned in the evening, Herbert Glamrood was in a raging fury and there was a terrible scene. He maintained that it was the "Hell's brat," Harry, who had been corrupting his daughters. Herbert had maltreated Viola brutally. It was while she was still collapsed from the maltreatment that Julian's telegram had arrived. She left the house at once, intending never to return to it.

She proposed, she said, to stay with her friend at Littlehampton until she could make arrangements for Harry and obtain some employment for herself. Glamrood had secured legal ownership of every penny she possessed, except a tiny supplement of her pension which she had managed to keep from his knowledge. Unfortunately the quarterly instalment, minute though it was, would not be due for some time. Viola asked Julian if he could let her have a hundred pounds or so to meet immediate needs.

"I feel too ashamed to go to Nora Dingwal or Lady Foster, who would doubtless be in a better position to help," she said. Viola hoped to be able to repay the money some time. She proposed to learn shorthand and typewriting and to lose no time in obtaining a situation.

Julian had not the heart to inform her of his own pretty desperate situation. There still remained a few of Zena's jewels—very few. Nadia had asked him to assist her in Paris, and it had taken the larger portion of the jewels given to him by Zena to do so. Asking Viola to wait, he took a turquoise and diamond ring which still remained to Attenborough's office, and brought the proceeds to Viola.

Like so many thousands of others, Julian himself had to look for a "job." The pursuit was to be during the coming years the general occupation of mankind.

He had at first imagined, with a simplicity which afterwards made him smile, that his own known scientific work might be regarded as qualifying him for some teaching post, if not in one of the universities, at least in some school or other. Julian occupied himself answering various notices of vacancies for the teaching of biology, which appeared in the scientific journals. The applications involved a good deal of painfully undignified correspondence to obtain appropriate testimonials, and also the purchase of several copies of his own work for presentation. Nothing came of it. One appointment for which he applied rather hopefully, a chair of biology in a small university in Wales, was obtained by a young fellow whom he remembered quite well. Julian used to coach him to help him get through his "Mays." The youngster was such a totally hopeless duffer that he was generally regarded at 'varsity as mentally deficient, and he obtained his pass after many years by tiring out the examiners. He was now doing rather well, and on his way to becoming a leading authority in the world of science. He had been sent out in charge of an expensive expedition financed by an American millionaire to make a biological survey of the island of Juan Fernandez. His book, giving an account of the expedition, and indicating the strictly monogamous habits of the stray cats and goats with which the island is peopled, incidentally confirming the Biblical account of Noah's Ark, was by way of becoming a classic.

Julian, while walking along the Strand one morning, came upon Major Spirido. The Australian was attired in a shabby morning coat and bowler hat, and carried an attaché case and a stick, dragging his foot from long habit. He looked like an old-clothes man. But he professed to be in high spirits and prosperous. Spirido had given up his academic duties in Australia.

"England is too damned funny," he said. "Thought I'd like to enjoy the joke a while longer. What are you doing?"

Julian answered the ghastly question.

"Oh, you should soon get the matter settled. There are really plenty of jobs if you know how to find them," said Spirido. He was at the moment an insurance agent. "I know a chap who's a corker for finding jobs. He had the very thing for you. Nearly took it on myself. We'll go round to his office. It's just round the corner."

The job, which was still available, proved to be canvassing for advertisements in a provincial paper.

With set face Julian told in few words of his gradual lapse into the daze of utter solitude and penury. He gave up at last the futile and manifestly absurd attempt at job hunting. The lodging he had first occupied in Mecklenburgh Square, he relinquished for a cheaper room in Islington. Soon he could not even pay the few shillings of his weekly rent.

He braced himself for one last humiliation. There existed, he had heard, a charitable branch of the British Legion for the assistance of ex-officers in distress. It was under the immediate patronage of Earl Haig and the Prince of Wales. In the dismantled and dust-eaten mansion where the institution was housed in Eaton Square, a fat sergeant in shirt sleeves, seated on a box of unpainted wood at the door, gave

Julian, without looking at him, a ticket with a number and a form to fill up. The man's manner would have been accounted insultingly contemptuous by a stray dog. Julian was shown into a closet where seven other ex-officers, even more piteously shabby than himself, sat crowded without speaking or raising their eyes to one another. After over two hours, the boy returned and shouted Julian's number and, racing up four flights of stairs, showed him into an office where a major in civies sat at a desk. The major treated him with gingerly courtesy which was rather more humiliating than the brusqueness of the sergeant. After the interview, Julian waited another three hours in the closet. He was then led to a garret at the top of the house, where another major delicately informed him that it had been decided to allot to him the sum of twelve shillings and sixpence a week for six weeks so as to afford him an opportunity of making a further search for employment.

The charitable assistance broke the last shred of Julian's spirit and self-respect. He now went out only at night. After the fourth week he did not trouble to collect the allowance granted to him. The weather had suddenly become milder. It was pleasanter out in the parks at night than in the evil-smelling dinginess of his room amid the squalor of Islington. He did not return there.

The bitter smile called forth by squalid humiliations died on Julian's lips. We both sat in glum silence. I think I looked the glummer of the two.

"But why the deuce did you not look up some one?" I asked after a while.

He looked back at me wanly.

"There are times when the depths of a man's being are too dark and, like some obscene thing, have to be concealed from the eyes of his fellows. His reserve of strength fails him at such times to play the comedy of appearances; a shred of pride forbids him to expose, even to the trustiest, his dissolution. Animals hide themselves in the darkness of some hole. At such time man must be alone."

I nodded, understanding.

"By the way, Laurie," he said, suddenly rousing himself, "you know I wouldn't have accepted this splurge. I know Jules's prices. But, look here, it's my shout. I still have something left." He pulled out of some recess of his coat a pearl necklace and held it out in his hand. "I've hung on to this till now. But . . . what's the good? These sentimental things are like old photographs. One looks and looks at them till they no longer mean anything, till they obliterate rather than revive memory. It's utterly foolish to hang on to a souvenir, a dead, meaningless fetish." He looked at the little heap of fine pearls in the hollow of his palm. "We'll take it round . . ." He stopped, I think, from fear of breaking down. A nasty convulsive twitch crisped his face.

"Don't talk nonsense, man," I said. "I'm rotto with money, and Jules's bill is a very trifling thing to pay for the good fortune of picking you up. My God, I really believed you were dead. We'll fix up things all right, you'll see. You've got through your bonus and all that, I suppose?"

"Bonus?" Julian asked blankly. "No, I haven't drawn anything."

"Do you mean to say . . .? Good God, you must have several hundreds of pounds due to you." Really, Julian was exasperatingly impractical. "We're going to see to that right away," I said.

We took a taxi and drove to Cox's. They said that there was, to be sure, a considerable amount to Mr. Bern's credit. They could not tell at the moment how much, but would be able to do so by the following day. Meanwhile, if Mr. Bern wished to draw a hundred pounds or so, he could have the money at once.

I knew of a room in York Street, clean and spacious, on the sixth floor and therefore quiet. It was fortunately vacant, and we took it.

During the next few weeks I busied myself ruthlessly extracting from the War Office every imaginable penny. I even put in a claim for travelling expenses from Russia. After the manner in which I had myself been diddled, I was armed with experience and utter unscrupulousness. The War Office always surrenders to determined bluff. They alleged that there was no record of Julian having been wounded at Paschendaele. As his company commander, I was able to defeat the subterfuge and to obtain a substantial wound gratuity and even a trifling pension.

"You are determined to make a filthy capitalist of me," Julian bantered. "You are a wizard to make all this fabulous wealth materialise."

"We shall at least be able to look round systematically for that elusive 'job,' " I said.

In my determination to leave no possible spring of cash untapped, I bethought myself of enquiring from the publishers of Julian and the late Sir Anthony Fisher's book whether they had not some royalties to his credit. Despite the savage official criticism and studied silences, the book had, I gathered, attracted considerable attention in various quarters. It had been taken up incongruously but enthusiastically by the Theosophical Society and the British Vegetarian Association, as also by the Seventh Day Adventists, who thought they detected in it some striking confirmations of the prophecies in the Book of Daniel. The work had even been laid down as a prescribed textbook in the University of Waramarangu. It had been very favorably referred to in the *Church Times* owing to its being understood to contain criticisms damaging to the Darwinian theory, and the report had spread as far as Tennessee, where the Fundamentalists were suggesting an American edition.

Messrs. Mackintosh admitted that they had had small, but steady sales of the work, and that the edition was, in fact, practically disposed of. After some weeks they furnished, at my request, a statement of accounts, which was, however, so involved that, having received no training as a chartered accountant, I was unable to make head or tail of it. The net outcome of the document was that, according to the publishers, Julian owed them the sum of £317 : 14 : 9.

Julian received one morning a much-travelled letter, which had originally been addressed to his one-time bank, and had taken nearly three months to reach him. It was from Nadia. She and Andrei had decided, the letter informed Julian, to move over to London. Nadia was about to open a millinery establishment in Sloane Street, and she asked Julian to help introduce her among aristocratic acquaintances whose patronage might form the nucleus of a clientele. He went down to Sloane Street, turning over in his mind, with bitter amusement, how he should disillusion Nadia of her misapprehensions concerning his influence with the aristocracy of fashion.

To his relief, Julian found that assistance was not needed. Several Daimler and Rolls-Royce limousines were standing in front of Nadia's shop, and uniformed footmen were exercising lap dogs on the sidewalk. He, later, came upon paragraphs in the society papers making reference to the vogue current among leaders of feminine elegance for the millinery production of Grand Duchess Isidore, now engaged in trade under the name of "Nadia." On entering the establishment, a young saleswoman informed him that Madame was at the moment engaged with a client, but that word would be sent up to her that he wished to see her.

Nadia herself, holding a hat in her hand, presently came to see him, smiling.

"What a coincidence!" she exclaimed. "When your name was sent up to me, I was engaged attending on Lady Penmore. She asked me to bring you up at once to the fitting room."

Julian was considerably surprised that Lady Penmore should, at her age, be ordering hats in a new fashionable establishment, for he happened to know that his aunt had for the last twenty years been in the habit of procuring her headgear, which had not varied in style, from Jay's. It turned out that he had been under a misapprehension. The gorgeously gowned lady whom he found awaiting him in the mirror-lined boudoir strewn with feminine hats was not his Aunt Aurora, but Lady Welby Penmore.

"I've been searching for you high and low for umpteen months," Keetje said. "Even had Scotland Yard on the job. You certainly know how to keep yourself in hiding. You have the making of a good conspirator."

"Am I 'wanted'?" Julian asked.

"Not by the police. But I wanted to have a few words with you," Keetje said.

"So did I," Nadia put in. "The post-office took nearly three months to find him."

"I'm afraid I can't spare you your brother-in-law today, Madame. I'm taking him to lunch with me at my house right away," Keetje said. "Please send me those twelve hats along. I must see which of them I can wear with my frocks."

With swift authority that excluded parley, Keetje swept Julian away into the waiting Daimler. As she reclined at his side on the cushions of her limousine, upholstered in blue silk, the firm reliefs of her figure were moulded as by the sculptural ripples of a Greek peplos, in the exquisite softness of luxurious webs, and she dangled a leg sheathed in a film of rose gossamer. Keetje looked back at him with a touch of irony in her narrowed eyes, while her elaborately manicured hand, studded with emeralds and diamonds, toyed with a rope of pink pearls.

"Do you know that but for me you would probably be languishing in the Tower of London?" she said. "Fortunately, Welby's intentions concerning you came to my notice, and I made him send that telegram that set you free."

"Thank you," Julian said.

"Don't trouble," Keetje countered, with a pout at the summary expression of his gratitude.

"Are you taking me to meet your charming husband?" Julian asked.

"No. He's lunching at the House of Commons," said Keetje.

The car stopped before her house at Queen Anne's Gate. During the tête-à-tête luncheon, which was served with exquisite elegance in the panelled breakfast room, Julian felt somewhat restrained by the presence of the butler and hovering footman from speaking of personal relations. But his embarrassment did not appear to be shared by Keetje, who talked about old Lady Penmore, whom, to her surprise, Julian had not looked up since his return, not feeling able to bring himself, even from a sense of duty, to appear before her in the circumstances in which he found himself. Keetje was therefore able to impart to him a good deal of information concerning his aunt.

"Welby has behaved quite abominably towards the old lady," she said. "He has not provided her with a penny."

Lady Penmore was now living in a boarding house at Earle's Court. Keetje, forgetting the hostility which Lady Penmore had manifested towards her, had secretly assisted her. She had herself taken over the Bloomsbury property, which had been standing empty or with unpaid rent during the war, and had rented it in the names of Belgian acquaintances of hers, capable business women and expert manageresses, who had at once raised the tone of the property, importing Belgian girls and engaging efficient touts who worked in the hotels frequented by American visitors. The returns from the houses had almost been doubled, thus greatly easing Lady Penmore's financial straits. The

Maida Vale properties, after having been renovated in a similar manner, with special attractions catering to the tastes of old gentlemen, had been very advantageously disposed of to the Church Army.

Keetje enquired about Viola. She had lost sight of her for some time, she said. Julian indicated that his sister had experienced considerable hardship since leaving Bognor for family reasons. Viola had for some time acted as canvasser for a firm selling vacuum cleaners. Of late, however, she had somewhat improved her position, he understood, having obtained, through Lady Bar, a temporary occupation, correcting the spelling and grammar for a famous popular novelist.

After coffee had been served in her private sitting room, and Keetje, lounging in an easy chair, had lit a cigarette, she delivered herself of the view that the absurd notion that money was to be acquired by work was a superstitious fraud disseminated in the interests of capitalistic exploitation.

"There are but two ways of acquiring money adequately," she said, "swindling and lechery."

"If that be so, you seem to have exercised considerable proficiency in those arts," Julian observed, glancing round.

"Yes," said Keetje. "Welby has done most of the swindling. He has robbed both Peter and Paul, the British exchequer and its clients, that is, most of the assassins and robber-chiefs in Europe, to say nothing of the widows and orphans whom, with the assistance of Baron Rubinstein, he has despoiled on the Stock Exchange. He has even robbed Baron Rubinstein himself. A clever fellow, Welby. A chap who can rob Jews, Greeks—he made a fine thing out of arming them against the Turks—and Welshmen—he diddled Lloyd George—deserves admiration. Says one should always rob both sides, thus neither can lodge complaints in regard to the other. I have sacrificed a lot for Welby."

"Your virtue?" Julian derisively asked.

"On the contrary, I kept it—which is harder," she said. "Insisted upon holy matrimony—with all the solemnity of duly secured legal settlements."

"You love your husband?" asked Julian.

"I detest him. Having now reaped the rewards of continence, acquired wealth and a name with a handle, I do not purpose to continue the sacrifice. Though he is fiercely jealous," she said.

Keetje questioned Julian on Russia. But there was little he had to tell her on which she was not already informed through Welby and Nadia. Nor did he care to speak before her of things sanctified.

"Sale vie," she said, after sitting mutely respecting his silence as he stood leaning against the scrolled white marble of the mantle.

Julian turned towards her as if awakened from a dream to awareness of her presence. She rose suddenly and going up to him put her arms round his neck and kissed him. Taking the caress as a token of sympathy, Julian did not repel it.

At that moment the door opened noiselessly and Welby stood in the embrasure. His face grew white and then purple. Keetje, as he entered, turned her head round, but did not draw away her arms from Julian's shoulders. Welby came up, choking with rage, and catching her by the hair, pulled her away.

"Bloody filthy trull!" he hissed.

Her hand flew to his face with a resounding blow which left the pattern of her fingers on Welby's cheek. He staggered, holding his face. He then picked up from a side table a Sèvres vase and swung it over her head. Julian caught him by the scruff of his coat, shook him, and flung him sprawling to the floor among the broken china.

Keetje kicked him under the jaw, in the ribs. She stamped her feet on his belly and chest, picking up her skirts to her waist for more vigorous action of her powerfully muscled legs.

"You worm . . . you filth . . . you lump of scoundrelism . . . you . . . you Englishman!" she shouted, bending over him and hitting his face with one of her shoes.

"Hell cat!" he cried, groaning. "You'll pay for this."

"Just try any tricks and you're for the chokey and the oakum gang, and you know it, you dirty blackguard," she shouted back, spitting in his face.

Julian, not thinking it expedient to remain while they murdered each other, left the room.

Weeks and months passed. Julian remained sunk in a state of apathy which, I must confess, at times alarmed me. He could not be persuaded to see people, scarcely to go out. For days at a time he would not leave his eyrie that looked over the roofs of London and the river.

He wrote, I believe, a good deal. Sometimes he would hand me some pages, suggesting I should offer them to some magazine or other. But they were couched in language so obscure, as though they were notes meant to be understood by himself alone, in some inner language of his own, utterly careless of being apprehensible to others, jealous rather of concealing his thought as he concealed his person from the world, that I found it difficult to place them, though I did succeed in getting a friendly editor to accept one or two under the impression that their theme was something entirely different from what it was in reality.

Though I avoided in general troubling Julian with such matters, I was meanwhile scouring for a solution of the sordid problem of his livelihood. Mrs. Cator, whom I had met again, renewed her suggestion of a partnership in her husband's wine business. Colonel Cator had, thanks to his previous connections, made a very good start with it, but the business was, I gathered, going to pieces, as the colonel had taken more and more to drink, and was scarcely ever sober.

When I did venture to mention to Julian some clue I had been following up or to discuss possibilities, I found him so entirely indifferent and uninterested that I almost lost patience with him.

"After all, you know, facts have to be faced," I said, with some irritation. "The bit of W. O. money is not going to last for ever. Hang it all, you've got to live."

"Why?" he placidly questioned.

"Please come down to earth. Consent to be a little realistic," I said, decidedly nettled.

He looked at me as though amused, and broke into a dry laugh.

"Don't you perceive, my dear Laurie," he said, "that it is you who are lamentably lacking in realism. Do you seriously and soberly visualise me as transacting the sales of wine, or sitting in front of a ledger? Stop dreaming. This business of looking for a 'job' is perfectly ridiculous."

"Ridiculous? My dear fellow, it is vital. One has to swallow one's pride, you know," I said, nearly at the end of my patience.

"Come, come, don't get angry," Julian said, smiling. "You misunderstand. It is no question of pride. Were I in a position to perform some real work, some real productive service, the meanest and most irksome task would be a joy to me . . . a joy, do you hear? I would sweep the streets with a light heart. But that same task done, not for general service and common good, but under compulsion, under the compulsion of fear and hunger, for private profit solely, would profit neither myself nor any one who hired me. I am supposed —I say intentionally 'supposed'—to have risked my skin for this system of hired service, this England. England expects every man will do his duty. This precious England now expects me to beg the alms of a 'job,' of a slave wage. To compete, in answer to advertisements, for a clerk's desk against two hundred other applicants. That is moral England's idea of equity. I know very well the answer I would get for being a rebel against that equity. I should be told by fools that I am a rebel because I am a misfit. Of course, I am. To be anything but a misfit in a society so constituted is to be a scoundrel or a fool. No matter what hired work I might offer to undertake in the service of that system, any one with a spark of gumption would know at a glance that I am utterly incapable of doing it—that I am neither a scoundrel nor a fool. Don't you see that this pretence of seeking a 'job' is the foolishest of puerilities?"

He was serious now, and I did not find it easy to counter his argument.

"You exaggerate," I said. "Of course what I have in mind is not any 'job' but a suitable employment, one in which your qualities, your intellectual honesty would be of avail."

This time Julian burst into loud laughter.

"Good God, Laurie, have you been drinking?" he exclaimed. "The supreme purpose of England is precisely to put down intellectual honesty. At one time it used to be sent to Smithfield. England now adopts subtler, but no less effective means of carrying out what is the vital purpose of every policy calculated to defend it—the suppression of intellectual honesty. And you would suggest that I should be paid for committing the unpardonable sin. Come, come. . . ."

In turn I laughed, and said something about writing.

"The last resource of honorable misfits—the Word—

> 'You taught me language, and my profit on't
> Is I know how to curse.' "

Despite his savage moods and slings, Julian showed more docility than might have been expected.

He came upon Andrei in Nadia's shop, where he had called to offer his excuses for the abrupt interruption of his former visit. Andrei was in high spirits. He had contributed to several magazines and papers articles on Russian poetry, and later on Russian affairs generally. They were in great request on account of their dispassionate and impartial tone, and had attracted considerable attention. An American newspaper magnate who was over in London had just offered to take Andrei's articles for a large syndicate of newspapers in the United States for which he was the agent. Andrei at once offered to introduce Julian to Mr. Julius D. Burgher, the American gentleman, and had little doubt of the very satisfactory results which would accrue from the acquaintance.

Julian had already, as a matter of fact, written things embodying some of his experiences in Russia, and had offered them to several magazines. But the editors had, on various grounds, declined them. He gave Andrei some of his manuscripts.

Two days later, Julian was jubilantly advised by Andrei that Mr. Burgher had asked them both to lunch with him at the Ritz, where he was staying.

Mr. Burgher was very genial.

"I am real pleased to make your acquaintance, Mr. Bern," he said. "My friend, Andrew, here, has told me great things about you, and I could hardly wait to see your script. Gee, but it's swell stuff! Sat up half the night reading it and couldn't put it down. It's the very sort of stuff we've been looking for. My, but I'll say you can write some, Mr. Bern. A born newspaper guy, that's what you are. Seem to know just what folks are after. Now, we're going to have this thing fixed up right now, Mr. Bern. I'll get my secretary to tap out the contract, as soon as we've quit eating. We're going to make a big thing out of this. You'll let me have some particulars about your background and a photograph for our advance publicity. Andrew told me something about your great work. Biology, I think you call it? That's about health foods, isn't it? Mr. Julian Bern, the world-famous international authority on Biography. Julian, my boy, you're fixed up. We'll take ten thousand words a week with all syndicated rights. That'll be two thousand dollars. Biggest newspaper combine in the world, you know. We'll talk the details over in a moment. There will be a little bit of editing to do. You need not trouble yourself about that. We've got some slick guys who'll see to all that. They'll adapt your stories for our public over in the States, which you, being a Britisher, can't be expected to know. For instance, where you tell about those atrocities, and fine stuff that is, it'll have to be made over a bit. I mean, where you say Whites, we'll have to put Bolsheviks, and so on. We study our public first. As I say, it can easily be done by changing a few words."

"Yes, it's a mere detail, Mr. Burgher," said Julian, "and hardly worth discussing. Nor is any contribution on my part to your newspapers. Good morning." And he walked off with his manuscript.

I received a note from Everard asking me for Julian's address. He was never seen in London now, living in close retirement at his country place, and only asking now and again a few people for a week-end, when complete solitude became oppressive. Everard had learnt only lately, I suppose through Vera and Lady Welby Penmore, of Julian's return. He wanted us both to go down to Clinton Abbey. Julian assented without enthusiasm when I told him.

I was glad for him of the change. It would do him good. I noticed a relaxing of his features, almost an expression of tenderness, as the train glided through the garden-like Midlands. A car met us at the station. The stillness of the vast lawns and centenarian trees, so deep that the flutter of a bird's wing, the tapping of a woodpecker's beak, woke disturbing echoes, was almost sepulchral. We had noticed, as we drove through the village, surviving patches of the tiny war allotments on the common, where rows of potatoes and turnips were still being grown. But the ancestral park of Clinton Abbey preserved inviolate the secular dignity of its vast solitude.

Vera received us brightly at the entrance steps, running down to greet us, looking the perfect chatelaine in the freshness of a cream-colored gown with gold ornaments. But there was a tired, pinched look on her face and her eyes were unhealthily dilated. She had not the vivacity which Julian had remembered, and one could see that the cheerfulness of her welcome was graciously assumed.

Everard met us, throwing open the door of his study and exclaiming, as we were following Vera up the broad flight of carpeted stairs. There was emotion under his restraint, and the forced gaiety of his greeting. Though Julian had been prepared to find him much changed, he was shocked by Everard's appearance. He looked almost an old man, thin and with hollows in his waxen face that showed up the cheekbones prominently. He walked with difficulty, stooping a good deal, and using a stick with a rubber cap over the ferrule. A lift had been installed for his use, as he had trouble in negotiating the stairs, and his apartments were on the first floor. In the library, lined with richly bound books, a great desk littered with papers bore testimony to Everard's studiousness. He exchanged obvious remarks with Julian. When Russia was mentioned, there was a quick crisping of his features.

"An earthquake, not a revolution," he said.

"Does it need less than an earthquake to bring down the ruling powers of the servile state?" I put in, unable to conceal my impatience at the inconsistency of the change which had taken place in Everard's attitude.

But Julian quietly nudged my elbow, glancing at me with a look that said: "What is the good?" while Everard spoke of curbing economic dictatorship of financial interests by the power of a strong patriotic government which should unite the forces of the nation without subservience to the interests of any class. Such a revolution, he said, might take place in England.

"It probably will," said Julian with a smile.

Everard was inclined to pursue the subject, but Vera, who had accompanied us, offered to show us to our rooms, as a hint that we should not stay.

"Well, it is splendid to see you again safe and sound," Everard said to Julian. "We must have talks . . . by and by."

"Everard gets so easily tired," Vera said, as she led the way.

"It is a long while since I was in civilised surroundings," Julian remarked when we were alone. "I had almost forgotten the perfect smoothness of English comfort, of English service. Servants are an English invention. In other countries they are human beings."

I had just dismissed hurriedly the servant who had come to unpack our suitcases, thinking uneasily of the scanty contents of Julian's. While I was putting out my things, I looked, with some embarrassment, through the communicating door into the adjoining room which Julian occupied.

"By the way," I said, "I threw these things into my bag. An extra dinner suit I happened to have. We're about the same build. Thought that perhaps, as you hadn't had time . . . you might, you know . . ."

"Thanks, old man," Julian smiled, "but I've an unreasonable rooted objection to borrowed plumes."

As I was insisting, and trying to persuade him, I was made still more uncomfortable by Sawyer knocking at the door.

"I came to fetch your dinner clothes to brush them, sir," he said to Julian.

"I haven't got any, Sawyer," Julian said brutally, laughing.

"Look here, Sawyer," I said, "I was just trying to persuade Mr. Bern to wear my spare suit. He won't hear of wearing borrowed clothes. You give the ruling."

"Well, sir, a nephew of mine who waits at Claridge's Hotel, told me that the two young Bourbon princes who came over in 1914 to enlist, not being allowed to serve with the French army, were in the same case as Mr. Bern, sir, when they were asked by the King to dine at Buckingham Palace. The manager found two waiters about the same size as Their Royal Highnesses, and Their Royal Highnesses went to dine with the King, dressed in the waiters' clothes."

"There now, are you more snobbish than a Bourbon?" I asked Julian triumphantly. "You decide, then, Sawyer, that Mr. Bern should wear my spare suit?"

"It isn't for me to say, sir," Sawyer said. "If I might presume to give an opinion, I believe, sir, that Mr. Bern should wear whatever clothes he will feel more comfortable in."

"Excellently judged, Sawyer," Julian said. "I shall go down in the herring-bone tweeds I am wearing."

The place was an old Tudor mansion with haphazard Georgian alterations and additions that had grown with a view to solid comfort, fitting itself to the well-being of successive generations that had done themselves well within the seclusion of its walls, and with little concern for the preservation of architectural congruity and "period," or for mere ostentation. Yet the owners had been people of cultivated taste, obviously. The house was full of priceless treasures, pictures—several Van Dycks and a world-renowned Sodoma—a library containing unique manuscripts from the old Clinton Abbey of the Austin Frairs—there were remains of it on the grounds. One Earl of Bar had been an enthusiastic Hellenist, had travelled in Greece at a time when such a journey was a voyage of exploration. There were marbles and exquisite figured urns, brought back by him from Aegina, Eleusis, and Samothrake.

How long would this growth of limitless wealth and leisure, built upon the clay foundations of the servile order, survive? Julian mused. The age-old foundation was crumbling, the superstructure irrevocably doomed. A few decades more, perhaps, and it would go the way of the Austin Friars' Abbey.

We were the first arrivals. The other expected guests were driving down in their cars. Vera had tea served on the lawn, very simply, for us two and herself. She made excuses for Everard, who was in the habit, she said, of having his tea brought up to his study. It was particularly desirable that he should not overtax his strength, unused as he was now to the fatigue of seeing much company. They were expecting the Marquis of Sware. Lord Sware, a former Viceroy of Ireland, was at the moment one of the most commanding figures in English politics, and the hope of the Conservatives, who were looking forward to their return to power, unhampered by the compromise of the Coalition.

"I do so hope," Vera said, "that Everard may, despite his poor health, be able to give the country the benefit of his great intellect. To think of the people who are directing the destinies of England! Such incompetence, such weakness! How invaluable would Everard's guidance be, could it be made available."

Unfortunately, with the breaking up of the Liberals, the Opposition, which would be represented by the Labor Party, would be entirely in the House of Commons. Everard was more than ever fuming over the disabilities imposed by his title, which confined the sphere of his possible activity to the Upper House. Lord Sware was in the same case, and the Conservative leadership would have to pass to the City or the industrial Midlands.

"I am boring you with politics," Vera said apologetically to Julian who, with his head thrown back against the wicker chair, followed the ascending curls of blue smoke from his cigar.

"Not at all," he said. "I have always been interested in archæology, you know. My first hobby—the ruins of Rome."

"To be now revived amid the ruins of England?" I said, completing his thought.

"Oh, England is a long way yet from ruin," Vera protested.

"It is a delightful dreamland of expurgated fiction," Julian said.

We strolled under the trees.

"It's such a pleasure for Everard to have you here," Vera said. "It will do him good. He's a very sick man. To old friends like you, I can speak freely. You know the terrible injury that has resulted from his wounds? He would not admit it, even when the doctors told him. When he realised . . . it was terrible! You can't imagine the ghastly scenes. He would cry like a child, with rage, roll on the floor, screaming, howling like a madman in the middle of the night. I did not know what excuses to make to the servants. Oh, the nightmares, the nightmares I have gone through!"

What Vera said acounted for her worn, nervous look. She was no longer so deeply absorbed in spiritualism, I had heard, except that she believed that the place was haunted. There was a rattling of chains at night in the cellars, she said. Vera was now disposed to turn to the Roman Catholic Church. She attended mass frequently at a neighboring oratory.

Other guests began to arrive. Keetje came, very elegant.

"Welby was unable to come, my dear," she said to Vera, with whom she seemed to be on intimate terms. "He had an important meeting at the Carlton Club. Said he might turn up later, if he can get away."

"You have not murdered him yet, then?" said Julian.

"Not yet," said Keetje. "He's almost certain to get a peerage from the next Government, you see. One has to have patience. Oh, you mustn't suppose that the little scene at which you happened to be present was anything unusual. We are always tearing one another to pieces, Welby and I. I'm all black and blue with bruises."

With Keetje had come the Honorable Peggy Purcell. She was attired in the same masculine manner as when Julian had last seen her, and wore her eyeglass.

He enquired from her about Lady Katherine De Nivelle.

"Haven't you heard about poor Kattie?" said the Honorable Peg. "She was found dead in her room at Cavendish Square from cocaine

poisoning. Her thighs were pricked all over, it seems, with the hypo-
dermic needle, as though she had been bitten by fleas."

Mr. Humphrey Chatters, whom Julian had once met in Paris, also
came. He had come back to England, from Shanghai, since the war,
with a pile of money, and had bought a large place in Sussex. He was,
it seemed, continuing to indulge in his Chinese revels, forgetting that
England was not Shanghai. But was thinking, he said, of moving over
to the Riviera, as he had had some trouble with the police, who had
threatened to raise ridiculous questions about the age of consent.

"An extraordinary queer crowd," Julian remarked to me in an aside.
"Not at all the sort of people I should have expected Everard to go in
for."

"Friends of Vera, probably," I suggested.

She had just been called away. A servant had come to inform her
that Lord and Lady Sware would be arriving in a few minutes. A
telephone message had been sent up from the gate lodge. Vera rose in
a nervous flurry, throwing out her: "Excuse me" hurriedly without
looking back, while she ran up to the house. A rustle of excitement, of
servants hurrying, could be heard. To be honored with a week-end
visit from Lord Sware was almost like entertaining royalty. From the
lawn we heard presently, after the swish of cars on the gravel, the great
man's voice, a calm, highly-cultivated voice, an orator's voice which,
though not raised above ordinary conversational pitch, as he graciously
saluted his hosts, carried distinctly above the almost inaudible voices of
the women and Everard's nervous words of greeting.

An amused, sarcastic smile played on Keetje's lips and lit her eyes
while we sat in silence listening to all the hustle.

"He's one of the biggest brutes in all England," she said.

"Lady Bar looks very nervous," I remarked.

Keetje glanced at me, then at Julian, still with her mocking expression.

"Vera has a ghastly time of it," she said.

"So I gathered from what she told us just now," Julian said.

"Did she tell you everything?" said Keetje, drawing her chair closer
and lowering her voice. The Honorable Peg had strolled on with Mr.
Chatters. "Did she tell you that she takes Lord Bar up to London,

very secretly at night, to provide him with compensatory gratifications, at the Sybil, and elsewhere? The worst of it is that his cravings become more and more exacting. Vera has to go to great trouble to cater for them. Prostitutes have refused with horror to comply with the enormity of his caprices at any price, and Vera has had to induce society women to gratify them."

We could hardly bear to listen to the details which Keetje furnished, using English rather than Latin words.

"One cannot altogether wonder," Julian said. "Everard was always what is called highly sexed. Must be pretty rotten for the poor girl also, leading a nun's life."

"Oh, not such a nun either, though he is madly jealous," Keetje said with a laugh.

There was an evil taste in our mouths as we gathered with the others for dinner. Everard seemed morbidly excited. He regarded the presence of Lord Sware as the earnest of a place for himself in the next cabinet. We were presented to the great man as very dear college friends, Everard saying extravagant things of our services in the late war.

Lord Sware was as impressive as his reputation. He was large and tall, with a massive head curving evenly from brow to nape and set off by the thinness of his reddish hair. But his mouth and jaw gave to the lower part of his face an expression of brutality. It needed but a few touches to liken his countenance to a prizefighter's. The disagreeable impression was, however, largely neutralised by the easy, effortless exquisiteness of his urbanity, which was at times so overwhelming as to be positively insulting. By only a slight modulation, it could turn into a crushing snub. When, for example, he disapproved of a remark or reply, he would for a moment look blankly away or address some one else, immediately turning round again in apparent confusion, as though from a passing spell of absent-mindedness, and apologising profusely, saying:

"I *am* so sorry. Will you pardon me, I'm afraid I did not quite catch what you said."

Vera, whose efforts to entertain her distinguished guest were marred by manifest nervousness, thought it incumbent to talk politics. But, as

Lord Sware made it a rule never to speak of politics to, or before, women, considering that the subject lay entirely outside the capacities of their minds, replied with great courtesy by complimenting his hostess upon her published poetry, which he regretted he had not had time to peruse, but of which he had heard great praise from Lady Sware, who had a very sure taste for pure language and delicate sentiments. The conversation, which Lord Sware made it his duty to address to Lady Bar, was thus somewhat incongruously conducted on different topics by the two interlocutors. Vera hoped, she said, that there was no ground for the rumor that the Conservative leadership was about to be entrusted to a mere figure-head, a Mr. Baldwin, a Worcestershire iron and railway magnate. Lord Sware replied that he was curious to inspect the famous Clinton manuscripts, which included the chronicle of the Black Friars. Everard said that he would have them set out for inspection and would show them to Lord Sware on the morrow.

It was generally reported that Lord Sware was extremely brutal in his behavior towards women, and that he beat his wife. But there was nothing in his scrupulous courtesy to lend support to the gossip. Lady Sware was, Julian thought, no less impressive than her husband.

"You find only in the very purest English aristocracy that superb insolent and bored nonchalance," Julian remarked to me in an aside. "What a pure Norman type! Blonde and tall. After all, I must admit that blood will tell after generations of domination, idleness and wealth."

I was much amused by Julian's remark.

"Lady Sware," I informed him, "was a Miss Juff, of Evanston, Illinois. She is the divorced wife of Mr. Elmer C. Todd, a cotton millionaire. Her mother probably did her own scrubbing."

Julian joined in my amusement over his gaffe.

"Whenever I am tempted to admitting an exception to my considered conclusions, I find I am mistaken," he said.

Although Lord Sware endeavored to shed the charm of his personality over the dinner-party, he was not at his best in the presence of women, and being badly supported by the rest of the company, the result was dull and trivial. Chatters, who sat on Vera's left, kept speaking to her in a confidential undertone, ignoring Lord Sware's efforts to entertain her. Everard, who was eager to draw the ex-viceroy into brilliant political conversation, was compelled to devote his attention to Lady Sware, who wished to have his views on Lady Astor's influence on the destinies of the Empire.

Chatters, when the company had adjourned, with only a nominal observance of the decaying ritual of postprandial sexual segregation, gave a description of a prizefight between women at the French Club at Shanghai.

"The combatants are usually American creoles," he said, "and, as the challenge arises as a rule from genuine rivalry and jealousy, the women fight in grim earnest. It is far more exciting than a professional prizefight. The opponents wear heavy boxing gloves and are lightly attired in baggy trousers and a small jacket. But after a round or two, their garments are in shreds. Their persistance is wonderful. When one of the combatants appears to be entirely knocked out, she bounces up again and the pommelling starts again, livelier than ever. They will pound at one another for over an hour till there is not an unbruised spot on their bodies. The entertainment is in great favor with Shanghai society."

While Chatters, who behaved like a stark bounder, ignored the men and monopolised the women, plying them with questionable conversation, to the embarrassment of Lady Sware, Everard succeeded in drawing off Lord Sware, who was fond of a leather chair, a whiskey and a cigar. We joined them in the library, strolling up the stairs, while they went up in the lift.

Lord Sware stopped to caress with loving eye the battered fragments of Greek marble. He was a scholar, fond always of the fine things of classical tradition. The cultivated taste was linked with his brilliant 'varsity career—he had been president of the Union—and not unrelated to pride of caste in his Eton and All Souls upbringing.

"Let me see, which was your college at Oxford, Bar?" he asked Everard, turning round to him from the inspection of a noseless 'Psyche.'

"I'm Cambridge," Everard said.

Sware breathed with a very slight sniff, and changed the subject.

Miller, the butler, supervised the distribution of whiskey. Lord Sware drank Irish.

Everard launched at once upon the prospects of the next Conservative Government. He regretted the abstention of the indicated leader, glancing at Lord Sware, at a time when, if ever, a strong man was needed. Instead, we were offered a balderdash Baldwin. "Has any one ever heard of Baldwin?"

"But, my dear Bar, you are mistaken," Lord Sware said. "Baldwin is a strong man. No one can get a word out of him."

Confronting it with the presentment of stubborn dumbness, England has time after time defeated the world's intelligence, Julian commented sotto voce.

Everard deplored that England's position and prestige were jeopardised by weak and hesitating policies.

"We have compromised with Germany. We have engaged in a half-hearted war against the Bolsheviks, and have been beaten. We have fought a war by proxy against the Turks, and have been beaten."

Lord Sware was not easily drawn. He sat with wooden face, drinking whiskey.

"I grant you that we failed to take a stand with Sartip Riza Khan," he casually remarked. "Our treaty with Vossuq-ed-Dowleh has practically been scrapped."

Not being conversant with Eastern politics, on which Lord Sware was an authority, Everard was halted in the flow of his jeremiad while Lord Sware poured himself out another magnum. The nobleman had an unlimited capacity for whiskey, which never seemed to give rise to any symptom of intoxication, except perhaps a heightened glow of his florid complexion.

"We have surrendered in like manner at home," Everard pursued, "we have surrendered before the demobilisation riots, before the miners, we have surrendered over the dole, and now we are surrendering to Ireland."

Miller brought more bottles. The butler's condition was strange and his movements unsteady, his breathing shaken by suppressed eructations. As he strained at the cork, there was a double explosion, and his hand visibly shook as he filled the noble lord's glass. After he had retired and closed the door behind him, he was heard to hum:

> "Dirty old Robinson Crusoe,
> la-la la-la-la . . .
> la-la la-la-la . . .
> Because he was obliged to do so."

"I'm afraid your man is drunk," Lord Sware remarked sedately, gulping down another magnum. "Yes, we got diddled at Teheran."

"We got diddled at Versailles!" exclaimed Everard.

"The importance of our discomfiture there has been considerably exaggerated," said Lord Sware.

"Oh!" protested Everard, and was about to justify his surprise at the pronouncement, but turned to Julian. "What do you think, Bern?"

"To encourage the view that we are being fooled is in the best tradition of British diplomacy," said Julian.

Lord Sware raised an appreciative and approving brow and a glass of whiskey.

"You are in the diplomatic service?" he asked.

"Far from it," Julian said.

"But to return to Versailles . . .," Everard persisted.

"We are already a long way from Versailles," Julian said. "England is isolating France, slowly breaking up her scattered alliances, helping Germany to tear up the Versailles scrap of paper, to rearm, to put down liberalism and democracy, which offer at the present juncture too slippery a declivity towards Communism."

Lord Sware seemed for the first time in the evening to come to life as he leaned over with genial benevolence towards Julian.

"I now see that you are not in the foreign service," he said. "The first principle of foreign policy is not to talk about it."

"Bern has been to Russia," Everard said. *"Absit nomen!"*

"Ah! Then he understands," Lord Sware said. "Does Communism work?"

"Whether it does or not, does not matter," said Julian. "It is the one issue to which all the foreign policies, as likewise home policies, of every state in Europe are subordinate . . . as you doubtless know. Versailles, Berlin, or Teheran are but the weft and warp of the single web to which all politics are henceforth reduced. The British Empire itself will not weigh down the scale of British policy when the unnamed contemptible little issue is in the balance."

"The extirpation of Communism," Sware said, with swift seriousness. "Mr. Bern, you must join us, provided you will not lift the veil in public."

"I have no mind to espouse lost causes," Julian said.

"What do you mean?" asked Sware.

"Can Communism be extirpated?" Julian asked.

"It took us twenty-five years to put down the French Revolution," said Sware, with a complacent smile.

"My historical memory is then defective," Julian said. "I had not heard that England put down the French Revolution. I am surprised to hear it, seeing that at the present hour, she is still engaged in endeavoring to put down its much magnified avatar. Not a thousand British Empires can put down by force or cunning the light of liberated reason once it has flashed through the great pulsing heart of oppressed humanity. During a thousand years, the Mediæval Church, Roman and Catholic, gorged with the wealth and power of plundered and enslaved Europe sought to do it. It has failed, as you will fail, Lord Sware."

Sware's face grew purple-dark. As he was about to splutter something, Chatters entered the room attired in pyjamas.

"Come on, you fellows, and join us," he said cheerily. "We're having a pillow-fight. Lady Welby and your wife, Sware, are having a battle royal."

"Has everybody gone mad?" asked Lord Sware, bewildered.

In the drawing room Lady Sware and Keetje were hitting one another on the head with cushions, amid a blizzard of flurrying down. The Honorable Peggy was chasing Vera round the room, vaulting over the furniture. Julian and I slipped away quietly to our rooms.

Sawyer came up presently to enquire whether we needed anything. He was, like Miller, in a jocose state of inebriety.

"What the deuce is the matter, Sawyer?" I asked. "Has the whole place become bewitched? You're drunk."

"I'm afraid I am, sir," Sawyer replied unashamed. "It's that damned funny fellow, Lady Welby Penmore's chauffeur, an Irishman, who's let the devil loose in the servants' hall, sir. A funny son-of-a-bitch, sir, saving your presence, sir. Brought a lot of liquor from I dunno where. Sang songs and told us stories enough to make you split, he did. Mr. Miller and the housekeeper and the maids, all drank more than was good for them, till they 'ardly knew what they was doing, sir. All singing and dancing like mad."

"You ought to be ashamed of yourself," I said. "Go to bed and sleep off your disgraceful carouse."

"Yessir. They's all dead asleep, now, sir."

Julian and I tumbled into our beds, and, for my part, I was asleep as soon as my head touched the pillow.

Julian must have done the same, for it was from a sound sleep that he was awakened by sounds of some one moving about in the room. Vera's ghost-stories came first to his mind as he sat up, half-asleep, and reached for the switch. But before he could find it, the light was turned on, and he saw Keetje standing by his bed. "Confound the girl. Is she determined to rape me?" was his next thought after dismissing the ghost theory. But Keetje, who was fully dressed, manifested no amatory intentions.

"Get up and get dressed," she said. "The house is on fire."

Julian sprang out of bed, went to the open window and looked out, came back to the door and glanced up and down the passage. Everything was quiet.

"I don't see any sign of fire," he said.

"Can't you smell something burning?" Keetje asked.

Julian sniffed hard.

"Am damned if I can," he said.

"Well, never mind. I tell you the house is on fire. Wake up your friend and get dressed. I'm going to warn the others."

More to satisfy his curiosity as to what the practical joke might be than for any other reason, Julian came to tell me, and we threw on some clothes.

By the time we had more or less dressed, the house was in an uproar, and looking out once more, we saw smoke coming out from the ground-floor windows.

The fire broke out and spread with astounding rapidity. During the few seconds that we stood peering out from the window, tongues of flame shot out through the clouds of smoke that rose from below, and the whole ground floor seemed to be ablaze. We ran down the stairs. None too soon. In the hall, the wainscot was buckling from the heat of the adjoining rooms, which were crackling, blazing furnaces.

Everybody, visitors and servants, was rushing out. All gathered on the lawn in front of the main entrance. Lord Sware, in striped pyjamas and slippers, took charge with commanding energy. Was every one there? He told Miller, who had by that time sobered down, to check the servants. Every one seemed to be present, Keetje, Lady Sware, the Honorable Peggy, Chatters, Vera . . . Where was Lord Bar? Everard alone was missing. Had any one seen him? Yes, Chatters had seen him . . . on the second-floor landing, it was. Vera had seen him coming down to the hall. There seemed confusion in their reports. Everybody was in a state of confusion.

"Good God, Everard!" Vera cried.

The whole place was ablaze now, the flames creeping with a hissing sound to the upper stories. Red clouds of smoke were rolling out, as from the crater of a volcano, from the main entrance.

Sware was giving orders.

"Is there no hose?"

It was at the gardeners' cottages, some distance away.

"Get the fire-extinguishers out of the cars."

It was impossible and hopeless to attempt anything. The fire-brigade in the village had been summoned by telephone from the lodge. But there was not sufficient pressure, in any case, to use a hose to any purpose.

Standing in front of the entrance steps, Lord Sware was working vigorously a fire-extinguisher from one of the cars. Despite the tragedy of the situation, he looked ineffably comical, with his huge, hairy, gorilla-like chest showing through his open pyjama jacket, energetically and earnestly plying the futile squirt on the blazing conflagration.

Julian had found some towels in a car. He soaked one at a tap on the lawn and wrapped it round his face. I followed his example and we rushed up the steps in the blinding smoke. The hall, where the panelling and woodwork had gone up in flames like matchwood and burned itself out, was not at the moment blazing as fiercely as other parts of the house. We managed to gain a footing in it for a few moments. The stairs had collapsed and were smouldering. Through surging and drifting red clouds of smoke, we beheld a terrible sight. In the cage of the lift, which was hanging midway between the first and ground floor, was Everard, in black pyjamas, partly scorched and torn. Gesticulating like a madman, he was waving his arms and clutching at the metal bars of the cage. He spoke and shouted, but in the uproar his voice could not be heard. We caught only a glimpse of him for a few seconds. A moment later the upper part of the lift-well collapsed, and the cage crashed to the floor, completely buried under a mass of blazing beams. We had just time to rush out as the whole interior of the building came crashing down.

On the lawn the little group of people stood in the red glow of the conflagration, looking on. Rugs had been brought from the garage. With the rugs wrapped round them, they looked like a party of Red Indians. Sware, with his masterful red face, standing with a blanket draped about him, looked like a Sachem, with his squaws behind him. Chatters had curiously feminine pink crêpe pyjama trousers showing from under his dressing gown.

People had come from the village, on bicycles, on foot. There was a little crowd. The fire brigade had come too, with its engine, but there was nothing to be done. The whole house was now a blazing, crumbling ruin, only the outer shell and the chimneys left standing. It resembled the ruins of the Medieval Abbey.

Cars stood ready to take everybody away. Lord and Lady Sware got away first. Lord Sware was very cross. He forgot to say good-bye to Vera and the others. There were cars for the servants, and a local omnibus for those who had relatives in the neighborhood. Miller had reported that none was missing except Lady Welby Penmore's Irish chauffeur. Keetje got a lift in Chatters's car. Julian and I drove back to London with Vera, in her car.

Vera sat between Julian and myself, with a rug about her, whimpering and blowing her nose with a tiny wet lace handkerchief. She was not so collapsed as might have been expected. We spoke feeble words of comfort.

"It was I who killed Everard," she said suddenly.

"Nonsense. What do you mean?" said Julian.

She went on whimpering awhile, then said:

"When Keetje Penmore came, she found Everard standing at the door of my room. He had just come . . . and found Humphrey Chatters in my room. Everard was at the door, storming and raging. We dragged him down to the first-floor landing. But he struggled and fought like a madman. He seemed completely mad. The fire was already catching the stairs. We had to run. We got him to the lift, and ran."

Vera sobbed in silence. We arrived in London at dawn. Vera had decided to ask her friend Mrs. Jameson—formerly Sylvia Chantrey—to put her up for the moment. The car took us on to my rooms.

In the papers there were big headlines:

CLINTON ABBEY DESTROYED BY FIRE
EARL OF BAR THOUGHT TO HAVE PERISHED
PRICELESS ART TREASURES LOST
LORD SWARE LEADS FIGHT AGAINST FIRE

The article stated: "The cause of the disaster is completely unknown." A later paper had the following particulars:

The committee of enquiry over the disastrous fire at Clinton Abbey has arrived at the conclusion that the conflagration originated in the cellars. There is evidence of large quantities of petrol having been ignited. No facts have come to light showing in what manner the fire started. There is no evidence proving criminal arson, but the possibility is not excluded.

Completely carbonised and unrecognisable human remains have been found in the ruins, which are believed to be those of the Earl of Bar. An inquest has been opened which may throw light on the origin of the disaster.

The police are looking for an individual named Martin, or Michael, O'Shanaghan, a native of Ireland, who was in the employ of one of the guests on a visit to Clinton Abbey at the time the conflagration broke out.

Questioned by one of our reporters as to his view of the origin of the fire, Lord Sware, who was present at the time, said he had no information to offer on the subject. But he expressed the opinion that, should the disaster prove to have been the result of arson, it would probably be found that the hand of Moscow was not unconnected with the crime.

XIX

THE long-awaited opportunity came at last. I burst into Julian's lodging one morning in considerable excitement.

"Hooray, hooray, my boy!" I cried in exuberance. "We've got it at last. I told you it would come if only we waited. Now you see. The very thing, the very thing for which not you only, but all intelligent England has been waiting."

Briefly, my news was this. Landsmith, the most brilliant sub-editor on the *Survey,* had had a showdown with the chief editor and the proprietor. He had given them a piece of his mind as to their shuffling, colorless, timorous policies. Did they realize that we were living in a new world? In a great outburst, he had thrown up his post, although the editor and the proprietor, conscious of the prestige of his talent, were prepared to go more than half-way to conciliate him. A courageous fellow, Landsmith.

He had not decided to take the step without having provided fully for his retreat. Landsmith was about to found a new weekly. He had secured excellent financial backing. A well-known patron of advanced ideas, one of a family of bankers, commanding boundless resources, was shouldering whole-heartedly the enterprise. Already it was the talk of all the London intelligentsia, and the success of the venture was assured.

I had spoken to Landsmith about Julian. He already knew something of him, had noticed some articles of his and been impressed. He jumped at the suggestion, and asked me to bring Julian to lunch with him at Romano's.

Landsmith's opinion was heightened by the meeting. Of course Julian must join the staff of the *New World* and, as soon as he had learnt the ropes, he would, Landsmith hoped, consent to take charge as sub-editor. Landsmith was emphatic and determined.

"There's going to be no wishy-washy compromising this time, none of your milk-and-water pap," he said. "We are going to speak out, to call a spade a spade. I am counting on you, Bern. Please understand that you are to say absolutely what you please, without fear or favor. When I say absolutely, I mean ab-so-lute-ly. The *New World* is going to be an open forum. Whether I agree or not with all you say, does not matter. I have full confidence in your talent and judgment, and you shall have an entirely free hand. Let me have an article at the earliest possible. And make it hot. We are going to press on Thursday evening."

I was, I must confess, childishly elated. Julian, somewhat to my irritation, did not quite rise to the degree of enthusiasm which I had expected of him. He seemed nevertheless distinctly pleased. Shutting himself up for two days, he turned out an article which surpassed even my expectations. I was aglow with excitement, and kept running in every moment to discuss the triumphal entry of the *New World,* seasoned with Julian's stuff, into the intellectual firmament.

When I dropped in, the day before publication, at Julian's place, he handed me without comment and with an amused smile, a note he had just received from Landsmith. It was glowingly laudatory, but contained the following passage:

"Of course, I agree with every word you write; but in view of the public I have in mind, I feel that certain portions would ruin the appeal of the article. Please don't imagine that there is any question of cowardice in my advising that those portions should be deleted and a few verbal changes made."

I was furious, and exploded in words of indignation. Julian elaborately lit a cigar.

"I never expected anything else," he said. After puffing in silence a while, looking amused at my almost inarticulate fury, he lectured me meditatively. "My dear Laurie, like all Englishmen who breathe their native air—which slaves cannot breathe—you imperfectly understand England. What is unique about England is not its hide-bound tories, its reactionaries, but its liberated spirits, its advanced radicals, its revolutionaries. There are many countries immeasurably more reactionary, less free than England. But in all of them, even the most barbarian, such as Bulgaria, Hungary, Germany, are to be found minds able to think independently of the ambient tradition. In England it is not possible. The compact solidity of English tradition sets barriers so weathered and consolidated by age to the mind's expansion that no man, living within that invisible Chinese Wall, can transcend it. That is why English liberated thinkers are so funny. They are honest and sincere, for they are quite unaware of the moral dungeons of Englishness within which their minds are penned. I've been looking round, like Diogenes, for one man amongst them, for one wholly sound thinker in England. I have found none."

"What are you going to do about it?" I asked.

"Nothing," Julian replied. "That poor fish of a Landsmith is, after all, right. Since there exists no truly intelligent public in England, and not the slightest likelihood of there ever being any, as long as England is England, why write for one? Let him emasculate my poor words as he pleases. After being adapted to the limits of English thought, they will be worth just as little as anything that is being published or that is publishable in England."

As it happened, the circumstances of the time were rather favorable to the expression of Julian's comments upon them. Those were the years when England came as near as she ever did to being genuinely scared. The mounting figures of unemployment not only struck panic into the British soul, but rattled even the rulers of the country, who, as invariably happens, grossly exaggerated their own peril. The word "revolution" was being currently uttered in alarmed tones. It rose to the lips of the man in the street whenever a multitude of scared and miserable wretches marched through London, concealed from public view by a dense wall of escorting police, mounted and on foot, which surrounded them on all sides. (The old-time isolated figure of the policeman had given place to whole armies, moving in battle formation.)

Julian laughed at the typical naïveté of the notion that any revolution could originate in England. What he felt impelled to write was largely directed to showing the fantastic nature of such a fancy. He laid stress upon the unique stability of British institutions, the unparalelled loyalty and patriotism of all classes of the people, consistently molded through long ages by the tried efficiency of a mature national tradition, in which every modulation of thought was perfectly adapted to securing docility, and which not even the most rebellious spirits could shake off. The love of England was above party, that is to say, above intelligent thought, as it was above morality—England, right or wrong. The starving miners opened their seditious meetings with the singing of psalms, and their despair gave place to tears of emotion at the sight of a member of the royal family. Even though the nineteenth century, the age of England's supreme domination, had come to an end, England was not aware of it, and such were the enormous reserves of wealth of the oldest industrial and world-trading nation, that the staying-powers of the bull-dog breed could still weather many decades of adversity. What Julian had to say was thus, paradoxically, less disquieting than the alarmist hysterics of the conservative press, and tended to reassure, rather than to disturb, the natural unthinking optimism of his readers.

But those qualities were offset by one great fault which neutralised whatever virtues might have commended Julian's contributions. With unfailing instinct they were detected as being essentially anti-English in their inspiration. That is the unpardonable sin. The English are a self-criticising people, and modest self-depreciation is an ingredient of national complacency, so long as the amiable weaknesses to which it pleads guilty are viewed as the outcome of a too easy-going carelessness and good-nature, and are judged by the standards of English moralistic values. When those values themselves are detected as disguises of the fulsome collective egoism which, under the name of England, declares itself above moral law, to be defended by means fair or foul, "right or wrong," the bounds of British liberal broad-mindedness are transcended, and the pose of tolerant good-nature gives place to the rancor of implacable enmity.

Largely owing to the unpleasant flavor of Julian's articles and despite their careful editing, the *New World* soon attracted the attention of the law. Nothing in the articles themselves could, indeed, be discovered to bring them under any statutory charge. But other portions of the publication afforded opportunities to mark the public disapproval which its general tone called forth. Prosecutions for libel began to pour in. Once an article treating of the private life of a member of the royal family, with no implication of the divine and superhuman nature of the personage, led to seizure of the *New World* by the police and to a prosecution which threatened to land the printers, the editor, and several members of the staff in jail.

It must be said that Landsmith showed up nobly under those tribulations. They had the effect of maturing considerably his weaker outlook and of stiffening his editorial attitude. His financial backer, who had been prepared for such eventualities, handsomely paid up fines and legal expenses. To Julian's gratification, the editorial blue pencil became less ruthless, and both his "job" and his relations with his editor grew correspondingly more pleasant.

He relaxed the fierce unsociability of his habits so far as to consent to accompany me at times on my professional theatre rounds, after which we generally would adjourn for supper to the Criss-Cross Club, the popular resort, at the time, of the bright young people. Julian even allowed himself to be induced to acquire evening raiment. Keetje, who was now Lady Penmore of Penwood, Welby having come in for a peerage in the New Year's honors list, was a leader of the set. She stopped her dancing partner before our table one evening to tell Julian that Lady Irene Croom-Jones had been enquiring after him, and wanted very much to see him.

"You'll find her at the bar, upstairs," Keetje said.

"Croom-Jones?" Julian asked. "Know no such person."

"Shows a deplorable ignorance of social science on your part," said Keetje. "She was Lady Irene Sexborough. Married Captain Croom-Jones, of the Welsh Guards. Just back from her honeymoon."

Julian found Irene perched on a high stool, sipping cocktails in the company of some other women. She seemed little changed, but for the Eton crop, which made her look boyish. Irene's eyes greeted him with a casualness as facile as though they had met the day before.

"I would have rooted you out before," she said. "But I came back only this morning from the Lido. And what is Julian doing?"

"Libertà va cercando ch'è si cara,
come sa chi per lei vita rifiuta,"

Julian responded.

"Ah, your beloved Italy! You would scarcely know it now," Irene said, the casual levity of her manner sobering for an instant. "When we were in Florence we went one morning to the Carmine to have a look at the dear old frescoes of Masaccio. The workmen's quarter of San Frediano was being raided by the Fascisti. It was a Saint Bartholomew. The black-shirted bourgeois hooligans who are being

financed by your old friend, Count Osio, were throwing bombs into
the houses and massacring the unarmed workmen. The police kept
away, or looked on."

"That old rascal Count Osio and his friends must be in a pretty desperate way," Julian remarked.

"And so is the little king, who is negotiating with that ridiculous
mountebank, Mussolini, whom they have made brigand-chief of the
Fascisti, to hand over the country to him," Irene said. "But you must
come to the little rout I'm having next week," she went on, tossing
aside the transient gravity. "It's to be at Saxford House. A sort of
farewell party. You know the poor old barn is to be pulled down.
Sold to a company that's going to run up motor-car salesrooms and
a hotel on the site. Corky and I couldn't possibly live in it, of course.
We've got a tight little place in Tyte Street. I'll see you next week,
then. Only a few friends, you know. Bring along any one you care
to."

Julian got rather sentimental on the evening when we set out for
Saxford House.

"It almost makes one feel as though the limbo of the years between
were spanned," he remarked. "Makes one feel young again."

"Rot, man! You talk as though you were ninety," I protested, as I
sat patiently waiting while he finished adjusting his bow.

"It isn't the years, Laurie, with our generation. It's something
much more real than time's relativity. We've lived in two worlds. It
doesn't matter how old I am: I am pre-war." But he braced up wonderfully as we got into the taxi, and called out to the driver, "Saxford
House."

Having suffered complete dismantling and inevitable deterioration
while being used as a war-hospital and afterwards standing closed and
empty, the place had been temporarily redecorated—for its "last sacrament," as Lady Irene put it. The scheme of improvised internal reno-
vation had been carried out under the ingenious direction of Mrs.
Jameson—our old friend Sylvia.

The hall and monumental staircase had been transformed by wrap-
ping straw and dried African grass round the columns, and by the use
of raffia and bark-cloth mats so as to produce an effect suggestive of

an African Kraal. Captain Croom-Jones was an enthusiastic big-game hunter, and his numerous trophies, from Uganda and Tanganyika, supplemented by material hired from Rowland Ward's, of Piccadilly, were used effectively to enhance the artistic scheme. The walls were hung with skins of lions, zebras, and antelopes, and with mounted heads of animals, which snarled at one, as in a nightmare, from every corner. An enormous stuffed black gorilla stood on the main landing, at the entrance of the historic ballroom. The reproductions of classical statues which had once adorned the stately precincts were replaced by fetish figures in black wood, with short legs, protruding bellies, and staring mother-of-pearl eyes. There were huge elephant tusks, grinning witchdoctor masks from the Congo, Masaï and Zulu shields, and assagaïs. The walls of the great ballroom had been decorated by a follower of Picasso, with cubistic designs in orange and black, offering fantastic suggestions of scenes of battle, slave-raids, wholesale executions in Ashanti and Dahomey, initiation ceremonies by moonlight, and orgiastic yam-feasts. The blue room was converted into the likeness of a cave, one side of which was entirely occupied by the glass cocktail bar, surmounted by Voodoo emblems. Tables and chairs fashioned out of barrels were scattered about.

We had arrived rather early; it was barely midnight. Most of the company present were engaged in fortifying themselves with chain-lightning. Irene presented "Corky," her husband, a much-tanned young man with pleasant pucka sahib manner. She excused airily the informality of the occasion.

"I think you know . . .?" she said with a comprehensive sweep of her hand towards the company.

The Honorable Peggy, in masculine evening clothes and monocle, was paying little attentions to Nadia, who was in great request among the most influential members of the new aristocracy, such as Lady Male, her sister, Evelyn Nues, and Lady Pict-Oriel. Most of the habitués of the Criss-Cross were present, Lord Algy, Randy Coot, and Lord Stoney, wearing bangles on their wrists, Sir Sosoon Over and Mrs. Olatsee, Sir Mervyn and Lady Goof, Fred and Joan Ofterleg, and Baroness Capulet. Mrs. Cope-Higgins had to jog Julian's memory before he identified her with Claudine Cope. She had, since old Lady Cope's demise, disposed of her invalid husband in an expensive nursing home at Bordighera, and was having, she said, a ripping time. Lady Gluff, who was drinking Manhattans with Jerry Dushaw, introduced herself to Julian as a relative of Phoebe, whom she believed, with a wink, he had met during the war. Julian took the lady to be an elder sister or cousin of Phoebe's, but she turned out to be her grandmother. Keetje, gowned in gold-colored organdie, advanced towards him with a Bacardi in each hand, and setting the refreshments down on a barrel, entertained him with small talk. She had been presented by Lady Sware at the last Drawing Room, and did not conceal the gratification of her vanity. Vera had gone to Biarritz. Welby had taken up a vaudeville girl, and their home life had since become much more peaceful.

Things did not get thoroughly going until the arrival of the "Baby" party. Amid a hullabaloo of tin trumpets, whistles, rattles, pop-guns and other noise-producing devices, they made their triumphal entry into the state ballroom. Phoebe Battifol (née Gluff), Daphne Jude (née Tooley), and Felicia Cosmo-Smythe (née Kendrick), in short baby frocks, colored sashes, white socks and shoes, and diminutive, though conspicuous, frilled drawers, were wheeled in perambulators, waving rattles and sucking feeding-bottles charged with Baltimore eggnog. Other young women, garbed as more mature infants, nursed dolls and teddy bears. A bevy of young men in sailor suits and other boyish attire capered round on hobby horses, or dragged toy animals after them.

The din blended with the ragtime cacophony of the clanging and hooting jazz band. New arrivals poured in, and the floor soon became packed with couples violently jerking their hips against one another, under the epileptic dazzle of revolving colored lights, which particolored the dancers' faces purple and green, or blue and orange.

The Prince of Wales dropped in informally half-way through the evening. Miss Rita Dixie, an American cinema star, tried to teach him the latest steps from Alabama. Keetje danced three numbers with H.R.H., who seemed to be enjoying himself immensely.

Like every one else, Julian shuffled round clasping various corsetless torsos in the crush which limited the range of bodily movements.

"Could anything be more idiotic?" Pamela Porter, the niece of Canon Fuge, remarked, as she rubbed her belly against his.

"Is it more idiotic than a Church service, a meeting of the League of Nations, a battle, a trial by jury, or a Royal coronation?" Julian asked. "It is at least more innocuous and less portentous."

A fattish lady called out "Good evening!" as Julian went by, adding: "Are we on speaks?"

After an instant, Julian recognised Sylvia. Her face showed a slight tendency to drop into side-pockets, and the lustrous chestnut hue of her hair did not look quite natural beside her somewhat faded and veined complexion. But her eyes retained the velvety depth which he had known.

"Why of course," he said, sitting down beside her when he had disposed of his partner. It would be absurd to carry over bygones into another age. "Are you happy?"

"Don't be ridiculous!" Sylvia said. "If people were happy, do you suppose they would be doing this sort of thing?"

Sylvia was just back from New York, she said. No, not her first hop over by a long count. Had many friends there. Liked it and the people.

"A trifle naïve," Julian remarked.

"You who used to warn me against clichés! Every one is naïve—in different ways, that's all," Sylvia said. "The French stand agape at '*la niaiserie anglaise,*' but we find even the French naïve when they talk about '*la femme,*' or '*le sport.*' What price this for naïveté?"

One of the "babies" was being given a bath. Kicking violently in pretended protest, Daphne Jude was being placed, with her clothes on, into a tin tub half filled with champagne. Claudine Cope-Higgins, with an apron tied round her, was officiating, assisted by the "boys." After the baby had been emptied out with the bath, Pamela Porter came over, laughing, towards Sylvia.

"I'm all wet. Got a safety-pin about you?" she asked. Then, sitting down, "I'm not intruding, am I?"

"Not at all. We were talking about virtue," said Sylvia.

"How high-brow!" Pamela remarked.

"Had a most terrible attack of virtue when I was last staying at Newport," Sylvia said. "It broke out in the form of a boil in a most awkward place. Had amused myself falling in love with a young giant from Texas. Just as I had got him to the point of asking me down for a week-end at Atlantic City, I was compelled to be indignantly virtuous, as I found it almost impossible to sit down."

"Moral furunculosis," Julian diagnosed.

"Takes different forms on either side of the Anglo-Saxon pond," Sylvia went on. "Americans have sexual co-education, which tends to trivialise the mysteries of the universe. Produces amatory lignification in the women and ginger-pop effects in the men."

"Sylvia exaggerates so!" Pamela apologetically observed.

"All clever people do. They would else be debarred from making brilliant generalisations from the limited experience of a short life," Sylvia conceded.

"Have you got a safety-pin?" Pamela repeated.

"I have not," said Sylvia. "The Americans are, however, spared the fate of the Cities of the Plain."

The Honorable Peggy, who was dancing with Mrs. Cosmo-Smythe, smiled at Pamela.

"Whereas England . . . ?" Julian enquired.

"Is drifting towards sexual autarchy," Sylvia said. "What will you? The war, having brought out the finer qualities of the nation's womanhood, peace now leaves them short of two million men. Can you wonder if they are consumed by heavenly fire? Anyhow, they are no longer tongue-tied."

"You mean the gift of tongues has descended, with pentecostal fire, upon their souls?" Julian, falling into Sylvia's style, enquired.

"Ah, souls!" Sylvia retorted. "The councils of the Church have pronounced them to be manly prerogatives."

"I must really find a safety-pin," said Pamela. "My flimsies are coming down."

"You have a prophetic soul, Pam," Sylvia shot at her as Pamela darted off in the direction of the Honorable Peggy.

"Have you done corruscating?" Julian asked Sylvia.

Sylvia gave an elaborate sniff, and looked at him with challenging drollery. She repeated his first question, with mouthing ridicule: "And are you happy?"

He considered her for some time with steady eye, as she protracted the grimace, till she became slightly embarrassed.

"Yes," he replied, "having ceased to consider my happiness as important or to seek substitutes for it, as you, in the poverty of your cynicism, have to do."

Lord Jack came to ask Sylvia to dance.

Towards dawn, ham and eggs and sausages were served in the cave. Cave men and cave women crowded in with ready appetites.

"Here is a friend of yours," Irene said as Julian crushed past.

The woman with whom she was speaking turned round. It was Eleanor Astley. She looked fresh, with her firm virgin's complexion, her unchanging Greek-goddess figure. She had just looked in, she said, having been up all night at the House of Commons, reporting a debate on disarmament for the Temporary Mixed Commission of the League of Nations.

"How ghastly!" Julian said.

"I heard about you from Aunt Cecily," said Eleanor. "What you must have gone through. . . ."

"You are still with her?" Julian asked.

"No, I live in Paris, and her place is too small even to put me up. I have to go back tomorrow . . . I mean today."

"Where are you staying?"

"At the Carlton."

"I'll see you back," he said.

The promise of a beautiful morning gilded the pale sky. The stillness of the empty streets was broken only by the rattle of the milk carts. But in Grosvenor Square, Eleanor and Julian came up to the "Baby" party protracting their revelry in the open. The bright young people were holding a perambulator race round the Square, the boys escorting on scooters the baby carriages in which Phoebe and Daphne were sitting and shouting, to the accompaniment of the tin trumpets and rattles. Windows and doors were being opened, and old gentlemen in dressing-gowns were angrily protesting against the matutinal disturbance. A policeman came along, and with considerate and respectful manner, seeing that they were swells, advised the bright young people to move on. Claudine Cope-Higgins, presently driving up in a huge Hispano-Suiza, suggested a run up to Windsor. The perambulators and scooters were pitched over the Square railings, and after having refreshed themselves at a coffee-stall, most of the party crowded into the car.

Julian and Eleanor walked down Upper Brook Street towards the Park.

"So you're pottering round that grotesque 'League of Nations,' as you were with those 'Stop the War' cackling women?" Julian said.

"But it's not the same thing now. It isn't to stop the war, but to prevent another war breaking out," Eleanor said.

"Why?" asked Julian, with perverse irony.

Eleanor turned upon him pained questioning eyes. Even the simplicity of her candor was refreshing after idiocy and cynicism. He laughed gently at her.

"There, I won't tease you. I'll be serious," he said.

They sat down on a bench in the Park. A twitter of birds babbled in the trees clad in new spring foliage.

"In the first place," he said, "a league of bandits cannot prevent banditry. It is far more likely to promote it. Like all shams it is not merely grotesque, it is dangerous. It has been adopted by England as one more ignominious instrument of scheming and trickery to forward her own invariable ends under the invariable cloak of lofty moral ideals."

"But . . ." began Eleanor.

"Don't interrupt just yet. There are about a dozen fallacies in every current slogan; the reply needs must be longer than the slogan. Suppose for argument's sake that this sham council of war bandits could promote pacifism. Pacifism with a capital P is, in the present world situation, as grotesque, ignominious, and dangerous a sham as the Geneva farce. Is there nothing, then, in the deepening ignominy of the human world that cries out to heaven to be fought, fought tooth and nail? Why, then, dub such fighting deplorable?"

"Oh, it is. . . ."

"Not war, but the aims and motives of war. Unavowable motives—the pecuniary profit and advancement of bands of predatory exploiters who do not fight, the protection and prestige of their dependent tottering Governments, fearful of exposure and revolt, war of infamy disguised under the blatant demagogy of patriotism—*that* is the shame and horror. There is no shame in giving one's life for something which transcends it."

"It is unjust wars that must be prevented."

"Fallacy number three. All wars waged by unjust societies are unjust. That is not the question. Your League of Nations will not prevent the next European war, but the deadly fear of capitalist Governments will, quite sincerely, spare no means to postpone it, for the next war will not be a political, but a social war. If you and your pacifist friends do not perceive that inevitable fact, the Governments inspired by the interests of predatory profit do. They will, during the next decades, use their utmost endeavor to lay off the next inevitable war, because they know that it will not be like others, but will be the revolt of the servile millions."

"Oh! Every servile revolt has in the end been crushed," Eleanor said.

"Save in one instance."

"In one lucky exception."

"That one exception makes the world of difference. Every revolt of servile millions within the social state has been crushed as inevitably as you or I would be were we to throw bombs in the street. But the revolt which put an end to the last Armageddon has completely changed the position. It has created a revolted state and an army of tens of millions of fighters for liberation. The power of the new social state will not attack. But capitalist 'national' states, however sincerely they may avoid the issue, will, when sufficiently desperate and demented, seek to crush the new power with armies of workers who are no longer to be duped as easily as of yore by patriotic demagogy. A situation which transcends all precedents of politics and war. A situation of which the issue cannot for a moment be in doubt,"

"Alas that the cause of right and reason should have to borrow the weapons of evil—violence, bloodshed."

"It has taken several thousand years for right and reason to shake off the moral fraud which cripples them in the interest of those powers of evil, which have never measured violence and bloodshed, while holding before their dupes the moral ideals of meekness and peace. It is the fraud of Christianity, liberalism and reformism which, all three, having served their purpose, have passed over to the declared enemy."

The red hulks of early buses rumbled down Park Lane, loaded with shabby shop assistants carrying small pasteboard attaché cases. White-capped and blue-frocked servant girls were scrubbing steps and polishing door-knobs. The echoing double knocks of postmen travelled down

Hamilton Place. In the Park, flurries of sparrows swooped down with loud twitter in the wake of a mounted party of children wearing jodhpurs, and accompanied by a groom. A policeman went by, glancing at Eleanor and Julian, on the watch for any impropriety in a public place within the meaning of the act.

Julian's hand, passing behind Eleanor's shoulder, felt the rough wood of the bench.

"Ah, yes, here it is. One of the fellows carved his initials here one evening," he said.

"What are you talking about?" Eleanor asked.

"This was my bed for many nights," he said.

Eleanor started. "Oh, it is terrible. You. . . ."

"Oh, not so bad. I spent nights here that I would not exchange for the most luxurious slumbers of idiots. It is the mind's freedom and security that matter, not the body's."

"But you . . ." she glanced at him as though about to speak. Then she rose, silently.

"And I who have so much useless, useless money!" she said, as they walked down to the gates. He did not answer her.

It was too late now to walk back in evening clothes. They hailed a taxi.

When he got back to his room, Julian sat down to write. His contribution was due for press.

Landsmith asked him to lunch with him at Romano's on the following day.

"Look here," he said. "That last you sent in is positively great stuff. Sheer sedition, sacrilege, and all that, of course. But I don't care. I've printed it without changing a word. They can damn well do what they like about it. And I don't see that they can do anything. There's nothing actually indictable."

Julian thanked him.

"I say, I've got a scheme. Don't know whether it will come to anything, but I'm going to try it," Landsmith said. "I was speaking to an American fellow the other day. He suggested we get out an edition of the paper in New York. They've got, of course, all the same furious fanaticisms of menaced predatory interests over there as we have here.

But they haven't got the same compact calcified defence for their protection that dear old England has achieved, complete and perfect in every detail, with Public Schools, Sacred Royalty, Established Church, and all the rest of it. They haven't got age-old, venerable, complacent tradition. Thought and speech are in effect freer. If we had an American edition, it would come over here. Foreign publications don't so much matter, you know. The unpardonable sin about kicking the sacred things of English tradition is when it is done in England, within the sanctuary undefiled. When it's done in furrin' parts, or by benighted foreigners, or American bounders, who can't possibly understand, it doesn't matter so much. What can you expect? . . . and all that."

Landsmith asked Julian whether, in the event of the American project coming off, he would be willing to take charge. Julian said he was ready to do so.

The issue of the *New World* was seized by the police a few hours after publication. They alleged as the reason an article by Miss Ursula Dickleman which contained references to homosexuality.

Landsmith got terribly excited. He wanted to bring a test suit. He fussed round interviewing lawyers, members of Parliament, wanting to have questions asked in the House.

Julian regarded the whole thing with amusement.

"What the hell does it matter, Landsmith?" he broke out. "If the grotesque prudery of policemen were the sole instrument by which the English mind is throttled, it might be simple enough to fight it. But that is but a very small item in the perfected system which makes Englishmen. And do you suppose you can fight that perfected system by words, arguments?"

"But hang it all, one can't fight it with bombs, can one? One can't blow it up," Landsmith said.

"Quite unnecessary, my dear sir. England is blowing out her brains. She's so damned afraid that brains may imperil her pocket. But so will decerebration. As far as words are concerned, English peddlers of words, most of whose income is now derived from America, are already coming to regard the English public with considerable indifference. Let Scotland Yard, the Jixety Home Office, and the majesty of English legal periwigs clip English intelligence and literature. England will, after all, be the chief sufferer, as are in the end all licencers of thought."

"By the way, the American business is practically settled," Landsmith said. "Can you go over to New York in a few weeks?"

"With pleasure," Julian said.

Landsmith had insisted on dragging Julian round with him to attorneys, police courts, Parliament, the whole machine of democratic appeal from the moral ukase of a policeman, which proved to be as refractory to any inducement to start as a car-engine on a frosty morning. Julian had found it difficult to keep a straight face before the solemnity of wooden idiocy. He returned to his room feeling very tired and a good deal depressed.

He threw open the window wide. A mild breeze blew from down the river, with a tang of sea-salt. Over the murky, soot-soiled roofs and chimney-pots, there was a glimpse of the Towerbridge and the upper pool shining slimily in a shifting, cloud-veiled moonlight. The call of a steamer's siren blew in the distance. The propylæa of England's imperial highway to the seven seas! Great shredded clouds swept slowly across the murky skyscape, lit up by tawny reflections from the City and dockland.

Yes, he had once loved that England. The mellow grime, the sounds of that London had been enshrined in the wistfulness of the deepest feelings of his youth. With almost animal tenderness he could recall, in the rumbling, throbbing stillness of the night, the umbilical attachment of his younger self to those externals of his memories, of his awakening emotions. Julian breathed the salt air, harked to the distant sounds. He was bidding farewell to England.

He turned on the light, pinned a sheet of paper round it as a shade, and sat down by the open window to write.

Eleanor had written several times. He could read in her words the cry of her groping aloneness, not unlike his own. As well write to her as to the British public.

"...

..........., as though facing the Monster in the night, we two, alone, face to face. It spits upon me, contemptuous, its silent hate. It seeks to crush and bruise me. *A nous deux!* I fear thee not, O Monster. My contempt is deeper and more serene than thine. For I carry within me the germ of the future conscience of that race that shall judge thee, and shall live when thou shalt be dust and a memory accursed. Thy name shall be recalled as the foe of every flight to freedom, the instigator and abettor of every assassination of humanity and every harkening to the hideous and cruel past. As that monstrous England, insolent in the pride of impunity, shalt thou be remembered that clothed complacent crime in the still more fulsome loathsomeness of unmatched moral hypocrisy. Flash thy silent contempt upon me, spit out the subtlety of thy venom. I fear thee not, and with the liberated generations of the future I stand above thee, dust and dirt that thou art. The rising race of the new humanity, whose spirit flickers, be it ever so feebly, within mine, shall lay its heel upon thy ignoble ashes.

" . . . .

What can we do, you ask, we who dwell in the limbo between two worlds? Nothing, or almost nothing, except keep unflecked and unbowed the integrity of our thought. The single individual counts for very little. We have overrated his importance. Prepare, you say, teach, fight ignorance, make straighter the twists of crippled minds. We overrate, I think, the task to which we, intellectuals of the lost generation, naturally turn, and for whom the individual intellectual life that is in our foreground distorts the proportions of our human perspective. Not we shall shape it in its day of destiny, but the million masses in their sure strength. And they will not be urged against the foulness that weighs upon them and poisons them by our poor words, but by laws as irresistible as the process of the stars.

"We are the lost generation, not they who died in the ignominious shambles. Lost to blossoming life. For the life-force is of necessity diverted within us from the individual's achievement, from personal happiness, to the greater issue of the race, which includes the less. It is not in our power to deny that life urge, any more than it is in the power of the single life to deny the life-force. For us, of the lost generation, what we call happiness and peace lies in yielding to that greater urge, as, in other days, it lay in yielding to the narrower individual urge.

"We have to construct our world out of our thought, we intellectuals, and in the artificial process, we misunderstand, because it is so difficult to cast off all the false concepts with which our tradition and our words are saturated. The concept of Liberty, for instance. Liberty and social life are not compatible. So that the word means nothing, and is the plaything of any presumed definition. It arose as a cry against the intolerable tyranny of privilege and possession. Presently that tyranny used it to mean liberty of privilege and possession to tyrannise. I have heard intellectuals of distinction cry out, with all the forces of raving reaction, that the war dictatorship of the proletariat allows no liberty—no liberty to privilege and possession to tyrannise. Which 'democracy,' forsooth, nobly respects. Liberty of thought and speech has come, by parity of fraud, to mean liberty to seize upon every defenceless mind and mangle it with every weapon of mental murder into a mush of mendacity. There is but one liberty which is of vital worth: the liberty of the human mind to be unpoisoned with intentionally instilled lies, the liberty to think honestly. All others follow. Set me in chains and torture my body, so only my mind is inviolate, so only it has not been maimed in tenderest childhood with tyranny's fatal weapon of subtle falsehood. Man is naturally reasonable, else the faculty of adapting understanding to the reality of environing relations would not have been fashioned, step by step, throughout the æons of organic evolution. Reason was fashioned by natural evolution; lies have been fashioned by the interested tyranny of fearful privilege and possession. They are an artificial violence. Let that liberty of tyranny be forcibly destroyed, amid the howls and indignation of liberals, and man's natural reason is restored. Give me that undemocratic liberty and I shall call it happiness, peace, life, expanded to fuller blossoming than any privilege or possession can compass . . . .

. . . . "

All the pother, the shamelessly acidulous righteous comments of the press which had made capital out of the seizure of the *New World,* "that scurrilous rag," had, I must confess, unreasonably disturbed me. Such a chorus of malice unleashed as soon as a voice was fearlessly raised! I betook myself to Julian's eyrie in a detestable and dejected mood. Even the porter's "Fine morning, sir," grated on my irritable nerves, as I took the lift.

I found Julian also passably glum. My repetitious review of petty annoyances and my obvious comments sounded futile even to myself. It was a Sunday morning. The Church bells were insistent and raucous, like an idiot's laugh.

"Let's get out," I broke out after a miserable silence.

"Sunday *Wanderlust?* No, thank you," Julian said.

"Hang it! Let's get out for a real breath . . . right out of England. Let's go over to Paris."

"Right you are," Julian said, brightening up.

Less than two hours later we were driving over to Croydon, and taking our places in the winged monster which stood like a half-dismantled pantomime dragon on the sward. A fussy bushy-bearded Frenchman with a satchel from which he immediately pulled out papers, and two loud-spoken American women were our fellow-passengers. The sonorous chatter of the women was presently drowned in the roar of the bellowing engines. They roared louder and louder. . . . The thing jerked forward, bumped, shook as though the whole contraption were about to fly to pieces. The bumps grew softer and ceased, and trees and roofs rushed wildly underneath. The clock tower lurched to one side as though intoxicated. Suburbs with neatly laid rows of dolls' houses and tiny trams slipped by, and, like a map, the trim, tidy country, specked with clusters of desirable residences and genteel villas, and crawling toy-trains slid slowly below. The two American ladies took off their cloche hats, rested their heads back and closed their eyes; the Frenchman did not raise his from his papers. Trails of vapor swept underneath and licked round with tongues of mist, swallowing up the air-liner as it rose higher and higher for the crossing. It soared into an immense solitude, over a waving Sahara of white clouds, casting upon them the enlarged shadow of its wings. The massive clouds frayed, tore open, and glided back, and the white cliffs, with a miniature Dover, and a glittering ribbon of sea, blue as though it were the Mediterranean, glided from under the monster. Then, it was the French country, different, even from the height, less lush and trim, with long straight lines of roads and clusters of grey steep-roofed houses. Julian's lips moved, but I could not hear. He heaved a deep sigh and smiled. I understood.

The boulevards were a bellowing Babel of badge-bedecked Elks, Mohawks, Rotarians, Hurons, Morons, Knights of Columbus, American Legionaries, D. A. R.'s, Gold Star Mothers on a visit to the fields of battle and the Folies Bergères, screeching, and laughing from mouth to arse on the packed terrasse of the Café de la Paix. Vendors called *The New York Herald* and *Chicago Tribune;* hawked Wrigley's chewing-gum, peanuts, and pretzels. Guides proferred their services to show the ladies the night-life of Paris. A red-haired Montparnasse female expatriate offered banned literature, *Ulysses* and *Memoirs of a Masseuse.* Pseudo-Algerians offered pseudo-oriental rugs; peddlers produced jumping frogs and celluloid effigies of Josephine Baker attired in a girdle of bananas. Moving electric signs dithered out epileptically the last Wall Street quotations. A fat man in shirt-sleeves lit his cigar with a hundred-franc note. "The sky's the limit, boys!" Miss Ella Wapburn sat drinking Pernod with college girls from Toledo, Ohio, displaying Keyser stockings, and youths with permanent waves displaying Phi-Beta-Kappa keys. A brass band playing Dixieland escorted a delegation wearing enormous rosettes and bearing the Stars and Stripes, which was marching to the Arch of Triumph to revive the flame on the Unknown Soldier's grave.

Eleanor Astley, whom Julian had rung up from the hotel, met us with a friend, a Mrs. Wirth, at Weber's.

"Had to bring some one along with me," she apologised in an aside to Julian, "a woman can't go about alone in Paris. Nancy Wirth is a neighbor. Has lived, through war and all, some fifteen years in the Rue Jacob."

Mrs. Wirth was a husbandless brunette in the vague thirties, with understanding and experienced eyes, elegant, and shockingly well off, it seemed. She affected to be Parisian, though retaining the English manner and speaking no intelligible French.

"Oh, but Paris is occupied territory," she said. "It is becoming an annex of Broadway and Greenwich Village."

There were, in point of fact, some Frenchmen at a near table, conversing loudly—

"... *un bénéfice de quatre cent cinquante mille francs ... cent vingt-cinq ... payer le timbre de soixante-cinq sous ... une grosse affaire ...*" and some hard-faced Frenchwomen—

"... *dix sous meilleur marché qu'aux Grands Magasins ... alors je l'ai eu pour cent quatre-vingt dix ... onze francs soixante d'économie ... vingt sous ..."*

"Julian is going to America," Eleanor informed her friend.

"How superfluous!" said Mrs. Wirth. "But then everybody is going somewhere nowadays. I don't know why, but Eleanor and I find England intolerable. Such a lot of people do. They are always asking where one can live. Italy no longer is possible if one dislikes castor oil, Spain under Primo scarcely more so, and Germany never was. Maude Jennings and Fred told me they had discovered an island in the Ægean."

She suggested dining at the Pré Catalan and enjoying the mildness of the night in the Bois. Her car was roomy, she said, with a look of deep understanding. But Eleanor preferred a quieter place, and we compromised by driving to La Bonne Franquette.

The timbered front room was occupied by a French party—

"... *alors cent quarante-cinq francs ... soixante centimes ... cent vingt-cinq ... deux sous de plus ... cent sous ..."*

But under a pergola, at the back, were tartan-covered tables in the open. The fat, flustered wench, with sleeves rolled up, brought palatable Vouvray and hors d'œuvres while the chicken turned on the spit over the vine-branch fire.

The women got to talking of the exasperating obstacles placed by French shopkeepers in the way of acquiring their wares. And housekeeping was out of the question without a *gouvernante* to carry on the battle.

"When I was fixing up my place, I got near to committing suicide," Mrs. Wirth said.

"It's France which is committing suicide with her self-defeating avarice and her *petit commerce,* paring off the sous and losing millions. Quite out of the running in the capitalist contemporary race," I remarked.

"Poor slatternly, eighteenth-century France!" Julian exclaimed over his glass of golden wine.

"Eighteenth century exactly," approved Mrs. Wirth with an understanding smile. "France is 'period.' I always see the French in period clothes, in a period setting. It's amusing."

"It's a biological law," said Julian. "Every culture that has exercised any influence remains set and unimprovable at the period of its greatest influence."

"Then why on earth do you live in France?" I asked Mrs. Wirth.

"It's not cluttered up with cant, the categorical imperative of English cant, enforced coercively by snobbism. It's worth the discomfort of poor plumbing and the vexations of impossible catering and shopping."

"By the same biological law, England is irremediably arrested in the nineteenth century, the English age," Julian went on. "The French eighteenth century, which culminated in the revolution, though chronologically closer to the Middle Ages, was incomparably more alive than the foul Victorian nineteenth century. People don't so much belong to nations as to periods."

"What of the twentieth century?" Mrs. Wirth queried.

"According to Napoleon, it is to be either American or Moscovite," said Julian.

"What a prophecy!" pealed Mrs. Wirth. "I am a Communist, you know."

Ye Gods! Julian inwardly sighed.

Mrs. Wirth asked us all to her "at home" on the morrow.

"You will meet some most intelligent people," she assured.

There were a number of artists, most of whom did not paint, French poets who spoke American and Americans who spoke French, and several divorced wives of several famous American writers. The conversation soared scintillatingly on the themes of dissociated abstraction and postured morality. The latest masterpieces of Tristan Tzara were, we were informed, a totality. Every one was agreed that the future belonged to Dadaism. A dadaist poet consented to read his latest effusion—

the meat in
ou
sapient homo

she-bow-wow's a bother,
a bother, a bother,
she bow-wow and another
sheba wow, she bab oon,

> baboon, bare bum, boom.
> her big baboon brother
> she bow-wow,
> babu bow-wow backship,
> three pants full,
> bersheba wow
> lives in now allenby
> tic-toc ass by ow
> great and true nein
> she bow-wow to another
> she leaks in our alley,
> how why bashibother.
> she bow-wow is a bother
> a bother,
> a bo-o-o-o-ther.

The tea-party, petits fours, and Pipe-line cocktails petered on till the divorced wives had fixed their dates with the dadaist artists and drifted to their several destinations.

"So sorry I couldn't have a talk with you! Mr. Biskers was so intuitive, don't you think? O rewore, dear."

Mrs. Wirth opened the windows to let out the clouds of smoke and voted we go out, her apartment having become uninhabitable.

At the Moulin Rouge prohibitionist America thronged, fighting drunk, to the new riot of stage nudity. A western giant in evening clothes knocked down one of the red-coated attendants who had the insolence to demand a ticket. A multi-millionaire was led unconscious to his *baignoire*-box, tended by a deferential seraglio, and snored stertorously during the nude bridal procession.

Mrs. Wirth was in a perverse mood. She cruelly enjoyed Eleanor's uneasiness and, after waylaying us to a private show during the interval, proposed an exclusive club to which she had entry. Eleanor, who had an embarrassing lack of control over her blushes, resolutely demurred.

"Marjorie is a good soul," she said to Julian while Mrs. Wirth was ordering champagne, "but dreadful in some things. She once induced me to go with her to one of her friends' parties. I could not tell you. I did not dance, of course, but when the lights were turned out, some man . . . Always that gesture! It is disgusting."

"The Christian Church has during two thousand years endeavored to suppress that gesture," Julian remarked.

While Eleanor was getting her cloak, Mrs. Wirth said to Julian:

"Eleanor is such a nice girl. What a pity she is so distressingly prudish and puritanical. And she so liberated otherwise! I have tried my best to talk her out of it, but it's too deeply ingrained. It is a pity."

Eleanor wished to walk over the Ponts des Arts in the moonlight. While Julian saw her home, I, being clearly cast for the part of Boccaccio's friend, accompanied Mrs. Wirth to the place she wished to visit. Less would have been needed in the tension of the charged air, to make me lose my head, and I was no Saint Anthony. The women, belonging obviously to the richest circles, engaged under the seal of rigorous incognito in a greatly extended exercise of their customary occupation of exciting male rut. Marjorie Wirth reserved herself until we were back at her place. She was incredibly and eruditely lubricous, with the composure of an Englishwoman of refinement and breeding.

I did not know Paris well, never having been a tourist there, and wished to see one or two places of which I was as ignorant as a native Parisian. Marjorie Wirth was a pleasant and competent guide.

"*Ah ça non!*" Julian protested. "Much as I love you, Laurie, I draw the line at sightseeing. I'm not going to tramp round the dark and dusty galleries of the Louvre."

"Nobody asked you to," I said. "You can please yourself. . . ." Marjorie cast at Eleanor an understanding smile. "We're going to Père Lachaise."

"How cheery!" said Julian. "As a matter of fact, I've never been there myself," he inconsistently added. "If Eleanor and I are not *de trop*, we might accompany you on your ghoulish survey."

We hailed a taxi.

"*Père Lachaise? Ah, mais ce n'est pas possible, aujourd'hui. On ne passe pas,*" objected the rubicund-faced driver.

"*Passe pas?* What do you mean?"

"The demonstration, monsieur. I could take you only as far as the rue de la Roquette," the driver said.

When we got to the Place Voltaire, we found, in fact, all the approaches blocked by armed troops, mounted squadrons of the Republican Guard, and black masses of police.

Having paid off the taxi, we made our way through the cordons of police, who let us pass as innocuous English. In the rue de la Roquette, the demonstrators carrying the banners of their syndicates and associations, and wearing red rosettes or flowers, filled the roadway, between two lines of police. Crowds of onlookers stood on the sidewalk, at every window—men and women of the people, workers, small shopkeepers. They looked on respectfully in silence. There was scarcely a sound except the vague rustling shuffle and breath of the enormous mass of humanity. The street was black with people as far as the Place de la Bastille. The procession stood still, then advanced a few paces at a time. It grew denser and denser from the pressure of the advancing masses. The head of the procession was held up, somewhere ahead, higher up the street.

We went on, making our way through the crowds on the sidewalk. On the Boulevard de Menilmontant, before the main gates of the cemetery, the police were massed more densely. Mounted Republican guards barred the way on each side, their horses stood on the sidewalk of the boulevard and close up against the gates. Behind the mounted men could be seen the horizon blue of infantry troops on the boulevard. A line of "flics" stood across the entrance. Police inspectors and officials in heavily silver-braided kepis, in civilian clothes, were fussing about nervously. They were parleying with workers' officials wearing red brassards. There was a general covered with gold braid and decorations, a thin man with waxed white moustache and an imperial. The police officials parleyed, gesticulating and raising their voices, and stood consulting among themselves. They had not the right to prevent the procession from entering the cemetery, since legal permission had been obtained, but they wished the demonstrators to pass through the gates in single or double file between the police. They endeavored to raise difficulties, create obstruction, bring about some disorder that would afford a pretext to make arrests, to break up the demonstration. They looked nervously down the street, black with quiet, silent, orderly men. Still they came. Thousands and thousands. There were too many, too many. An underprefect spoke with the general. The general glanced over at the troops, the *poilus* in horizon blue, the successors of the men of Verdun, of the trenches. He looked back towards the procession. At the head of it were war veterans, *"mutilés de guerre."* He recognised the figure of a one-armed corporal, a famous hero of Fort Veaux. The general twisted his moustache.

The front ranks stood still while the officials parleyed. But they were obliged to move gradually, imperceptibly forward by the growing pressure from behind. The war veterans, armless, with disfigured faces, on wooden legs, on crutches, stood eventually face to face with the black cordon of policemen. There was nothing to do, the line of police broke, and the procession moved on through the gates.

We were swept along by the crowd. Inside the cemetery, there were more police and more troops, but they remained at some distance in the background, hidden in part by the bushes and the gravestones. Except when we reached the Wall, *le Mur des Fédérés,* the wall where the Commune had made its last stand against the Versailles troops. The police stood before the wall and round the emplacement. The inspectors, the prefect of police, the general, stood on a raised spot near by. The procession of workers marched in silence bare-headed. More and more arrived, thousands and thousands, filling the available space. More came and more. The police had to withdraw little by little farther and farther.

"Very sorry, comrade, but there's no room for you here," I heard a worker remark, smiling, to an *agent*.

The prefect and the officers of police fidgetted and scowled. But even though the police force was numerous, the unarmed workers were more numerous. It was impossible to stop the human torrent without shooting. The prefect looked at the general. The general twisted his moustache and raised his brows.

The space round the wall was full of workers, silent, calm. It was another France, this. They were another race, these French workers, large, good-natured, serious, another race from the wizened, bloated, French bourgeois, deformed outwardly to monkeylike, toadlike ugliness by corroding meanness, greed, vanity, fear, selfishness. Another France, another race. It was stupid, our assumed national classification—French, English. Racial distinctions of classes were deeper than those of fictitious national groups. This was the France which had made the revolution, the Commune.

On the site of the pits filled with the remains of the martyrs, the deputations, filing past in silence, deposited wreaths of flowers, red flowers—the color of life and liberty.

There were some speeches, calm, simple, direct. The martyrs of the Commune had not died in vain. The Commune was not dead. Twenty-four thousand men and women had been butchered here by the armed forces of infuriated bourgeois law and order, on the 28th May, 1871. Seventy thousand came to honor their memory today and to draw from it strength and undying hope. It was the inspiration of the martyrs who lay here that had called into being the first Social State.

A voice sang—

> Tout ça n'empêche pas
> Qu'la Commune n'est pas morte.

The huge crowd stood bare-headed. The police tried to look insolent, sheepishly conscious that they looked silly. The prefect and the general fidgetted nervously, pale with indignation. The workers stood calm, in oppressive silence for several minutes. Then slowly clenched fists were raised, and from thousands of throats rose, swelling, the strains of the *Internationale:*

> Debout les damnés de la terre,
> Debout les forçats de la faim.
> La raison tonne en son cratère . . .

> . . . .

> C'est la lutte finale, groupons nous et demain
> L'internationale sera le genre humain.

I had to get back to London. There was no need for Julian to do so. Landsmith had written that all arrangements were now satisfactorily completed. I would see to reserving his berth, I told Julian. The passport formalities had been already settled.

"But you will come back?" Eleanor asked.

They had driven out to Barbizon and were sitting on a hillock looking out over the forest.

"Yes," he said. "After all, it was here, in the heart of old Europe, that the light of sanity and reason was first kindled; and here the renewal will take place. It will be the battlefield. I shall not be long away from it."

Eleanor looked out in silence towards the trembling beech-leaves over which the sunbeams rippled. A waving breeze played with her hair.

A gust of deep bitterness crisped her brow and lips.

"Meanwhile it all goes on . . ." she said. "Oh, sometimes I despair utterly. I think at times that all hope may be but delusion . . . that the colossal folly, ignorance, malice and bestiality are irremediable . . . hopeless, hopeless. . . . And that there is nothing left but hate and contempt."

Julian remained silent a while.

"Faith does not rest on feeling, as it did in the old fraudulent mysticisms," he said, "but on understanding—on understanding that can pierce through appearances. It all goes on, you say. Yes, to the external eye. People rise in the morning to their daily tasks or their pleasures; they eat, work, make love, sleep. They have their petty problems, their narrow ambitions. The scene . . . the outward scene, looks much the same. It looked much the same a few days before ten million men went into the shambles of the war. Europe seems—to the external eye—to be still standing, much the same, after that blast and that shambles, does it not? But is it? In reality, not one building-stone of it, of the essential core and foundation of it, is left standing! Every one of its values, the animating sparks of meaning without which no building-stone and no life can stand—every one is fallen and lies level with the ground.

"Did you hear those imbeciles talking, the other day, of new starts in literature, in language, in art? New starts, because nothing is left of the immutable eternal standards. New starts, but in utter darkness, without an inkling of direction—because no new start is possible and no renewal till the world is renewed. New starts in the relation between man and woman, because no meaning is left in the old sacrifice of sex to the selfish stabilities of property, family, home, the sacrifice of woman as a conduit-pipe to that property and stability, and as a surrogate safety-valve for the suppression of the life-force in marital triviality.

"It all goes on. . . . But the Old World is devastated from its foundations. Its economics no less than its art and its morals. Its golden rules no less than its gold standards. And you say it still goes on! It goes on towards maniacal self-destruction. The fraud of democracy in a servile society—that, too, gone, the bottom fallen out of it. The mask thrown aside in raving, panic-stricken delirium. Simpler to sweep machine-guns over the servile millions, as is done at this very moment in Italy, Hungary, Germany, Spain. It all goes on, does it? Because as you walk the countryside or the streets, you do not see the men and women tortured in German, Italian, Spanish prisons—with the smiling approval of pretended 'democratic' countries—because you cannot read the despair and wrath in the hearts of the millions, you imagine it all goes on unchanged. Within ten years or so, Europe will be wholly in the hands of gangs of murderers in open war with humanity. But do you believe it can just go on?"

"It may go on long enough for us not to see the end," she said, still bitter in her inward protest.

"Possibly. Does every sower see the fruiting of the seed he scatters?"

Her eyes looked away, holding back welling tears.

"Meanwhile . . . meanwhile, we, the lost generation, are cheated . . . cheated of life, our one and only life." Her lips drew together tightly in a spasm of bitterness.

"All life finds its only achievement in giving itself up for the sake of future generations."

"Yes . . . yes, I know." Her face was aglow, her eyes moist and gleaming.

Then of a sudden she broke down. Dropping on her elbows among the lush helms of the seeding grasses, Eleanor buried her face in her hands.

In a choked voice she said: "I want a child."

She raised her head and looked out afar upon the sun-gilt woods.

"I want to think, even if it be but fancy, that a life issued out of mine shall see . . . see that for which I have foregone my own."

Julian was gentle with her and understanding.

He stayed on longer than he had intended, till there was only time to catch the boat at Cherbourg. Then the sailing was put off because of a strike among the dock-hands.

I came over from Southampton to see him off. There had been some rioting. The troops had been called out. Over the grey, turbid water, as the tender drew alongside, the gusts of the breeze brought over the distant strains of the *Internationale*.

At the last moment, after the second horn had blown, a telegram was brought to Julian. He read it as I was stepping off on the gangway:

HE LIVES WHO WILL SEE IT.